Stephanie Mohan

Jacqueline Winspear is the author of *An Incomplete Revenge*—a *New York Times* bestseller—and four other Maisie Dobbs novels. She has won numerous awards for her work, including the Agatha, Alex, and Macavity Awards for the first book in the series, *Maisie Dobbs*—which also received an Edgar® nomination for Best Novel. Originally from the United Kingdom, she now lives in California.

PRAISE FOR JACQUELINE WINSPEAR'S MAISIE DOBBS NOVELS

"A detective series to savor."

—*Time*

"Worth noting—and cheering about . . . In each book, Winspear has used a crime to widen our vision of what life was like in England in the years after the war." —*Chicago Tribune*

"Her books are less whodunits than why-dunits, more P. D. James than Agatha Christie. Although the plots center on solving murders, the crimes are rooted in the turmoil and enormous social changes created by the First World War." —*USA Today*

"Fans of Miss Marple and Precious Ramotswe are sure to embrace Maisie, a pitch-perfect blend of compassion and panache."

—*Booklist*

"If you haven't read the Maisie Dobbs stories, you are missing a treat." —*The Ledger Independent* (Kentucky)

"Maisie is immediately captivating. . . . Dobbs ponders the mysteries of life as well as the mysteries she is hired to solve. . . . Surprisingly eloquent, even moving." —*St. Paul Pioneer Press*

"Jacqueline Winspear's historical mysteries prove exactly what this subgenre can achieve, offering a prism of the past and a mirror of the future. . . . Fascinating." —*Sun-Sentinel* (Fort Lauderdale)

"An excellent series."

—*The Orange County Register*

AMONG THE MAD

A Maisie Dobbs Novel

JACQUELINE WINSPEAR

Picador

———

Henry Holt and Company
New York

www.picadorusa.com

Picador® is a U.S. registered trademark and is used by
Henry Holt and Company under license from Pan Books Limited.

For information on Picador Reading Group Guides, please contact Picador.
E-mail: readinggroupguides@picadorusa.com

ISBN 978-0-312-42925-6

First published in the United States by Henry Holt and Company.

20 19 18 17 16 15

Dedicated to my wonderful Godchildren:

Charlotte Sweet McEwan

Charlotte Pye

Greg Belpomme

Alexandra Jones

Keep True to the Dreams of thy Youth

Friedrich von Schiller

1759–1805

"But I don't want to go among mad people," Alice remarked.
"Oh, you can't help that," said the Cat. "We're all mad here.
I'm mad. You're mad."
"How do you know I'm mad?" said Alice.
"You must be," said the Cat, "or you wouldn't have come here."

—LEWIS CARROLL,
Alice's Adventures in Wonderland

A short time ago death was the cruel stranger, the visitor with
the flannel footsteps . . . today it is the mad dog in the house.
One eats, one drinks beside the dead, one sleeps in the midst of
the dying, one laughs and sings in the company of corpses.

—GEORGES DUHAMEL,
French doctor serving at Verdun in the Great War

AMONG THE MAD

ONE

Maisie Dobbs, Psychologist and Investigator, picked up her fountain pen to sign her name at the end of a final report that she and her assistant, Billy Beale, had worked late to complete the night before. Though the case was straightforward—a young man fraudulently using his uncle's honorable name to acquire all manner of goods and services, and an uncle keen to bring his nephew back on the straight and narrow without the police being notified—Maisie felt it was time for Billy to become more involved in the completion of a significant document and to take more of an active part in the final interview with a client. She knew how much Billy wanted to emigrate to Canada, to take his wife and family away from London's dark depression and the cloud of grief that still hung over them following the death of their daughter, Lizzie, almost a year earlier. To gain a decent job in a new country he would need to build more confidence in his work and himself, and seeing as she had already made inquiries on his behalf—without his knowledge—she knew greater dexterity with the written and spoken word would be an important factor in his success. Now the report was ready to be delivered before the Christmas holiday began.

"Eleven o'clock, Billy—just in time, eh?" Maisie placed the cap on her fountain pen and passed the report to her assistant, who slid it into an envelope and secured it with string. "As soon as this appointment is over, you should be on your way, so that you can spend the rest of the day with Doreen and the boys—it'll be nice to have Christmas Eve at home."

"That's good of you, Miss." Billy smiled, then went to the door where he took Maisie's coat and his own from the hook.

Maisie packed her document case before reaching under the desk to bring out a wooden orange crate. "You'll have to come back to the office first, though."

"What's all this, Miss?" Billy's face was flushed as he approached her desk.

"A Christmas box for each of the boys, and one for you and Doreen." She opened her desk drawer and drew out an envelope. "And this is for you. We had a bit of a rocky summer, but things picked up and we've done quite well—plus we'll be busy in the new year—so this is your bonus. It's all well earned, I must say."

Billy reddened. "Oh, that's very good of you, Miss. I'm much obliged. This'll cheer up Doreen."

Maisie smiled in return. She did not need to inquire about Billy's wife, knowing the depth of the woman's melancholy. There had been a time, at the end of the summer, when a few weeks spent hop-picking in Kent had put a bloom on the woman's cheeks, and she seemed to have filled out a little, looking less gaunt. But, in London again, the routine of caring for her boys and keeping up with the dressmaking and alterations she took in had not lifted her spirits in any way. She ached for the milky softness of her daughter's small body in her arms.

Maisie looked at the clock on the mantelpiece. "We'd better be off."

They donned coats and hats and wrapped up against the chill wind that whistled around corners and blew across Fitzroy Square as they made their way toward Charlotte Street. Dodging behind a horse and cart, they ran to the other side of the road as a motor car came along in the opposite direction. The street was busy, with people rushing this way and that, heads down against the wind, some with parcels under their arms, others simply hoping to get home early. In the distance, Maisie noticed a man—she could not tell whether he was young or old—sitting on the pavement, leaning up against the exterior wall of a shop. Even with some yards between them, she could see the grayness that enveloped him, the malaise, the drooping shoulders, one leg outstretched so passers-by had to skirt around him. His damp hair was slicked against his head and cheeks, his clothes were old, crumpled, and he watched people go by with a deep red-rimmed sadness in his eyes. One of them stopped to speak to a policeman, and turned back to point at the man. Though unsettled by his dark aura, Maisie reached into her bag for some change as they drew closer.

"Poor bloke—out in this, and at Christmas." Billy shook his head, and delved down into his coat pocket for a few coins.

"He looks too drained to find his way to a soup kitchen, or a shelter. Perhaps this will help." Maisie held her offering ready to give to the man.

They walked just a few steps and Maisie gasped, for it was as if she was at once moving in slow motion, as if she were in a dream where people spoke but she could not hear their words. She saw the man move, put his hand into the inside pocket of his threadbare greatcoat, and though she wanted to reach out to him, she was caught in a vacuum of muffled sound and constrained movement. She could see Billy frowning, his mouth moving, but could not make him understand what she had seen. Then the sensation, which had lasted but a second or two, lifted. Maisie looked at the man some twenty or so paces ahead of them, then at Billy again.

"Billy, go back, turn around and go back along the street, go back . . ."

"Miss, what's wrong? You all right? What do you mean, Miss?"

Pushing against his shoulder to move him away, Maisie felt as if she were negotiating her way through a mire. "Go back, Billy, go back . . ."

And because she was his employer, and because he had learned never to doubt her, Billy turned to retrace his steps in the direction of Fitzroy Square. Frowning, he looked back in time to see Maisie holding out her hand as she walked toward the man, in the way that a gentle person might try to bring calm to an enraged dog. Barely four minutes had passed since they walked past the horse and cart, and now here she was . . .

The explosion pushed up and outward into the Christmas Eve flurry, and in the seconds following there was silence. Just a crack in the wall of normal, everyday sound, then nothing. Billy, a soldier in the Great War, knew that sound, that hiatus. It was as if the earth itself had had the stuffing knocked out of it, had been throttled into a different day, a day when a bit of rain, a gust of wind and a few stray leaves had turned into a blood-soaked hell.

"Miss, Miss . . ." Billy picked himself up from the hard flagstones and staggered back to where he had last seen Maisie. The silence became a screaming chasm where police whistles screeched, smoke and dust filled the air, and blood was sprayed up against the crumbling brick and shards of glass that were once the front of a shop where a man begged for a few coins outside.

"Maisie Dobbs! Maisie . . . Miss . . ." Billy sobbed as he stumbled forward. "Miss!" he screamed again.

"Over 'ere, mate. Is this the one you're looking for?"

In the middle of the road a costermonger was kneeling over Maisie, cradling her head in one hand and brushing blood away from her face with the kerchief he'd taken from his neck. Billy ran to her side.

"Miss . . . Miss . . . "

"I'm no doctor, but I reckon she's a lucky one—lifted off her feet and brought down 'ere. Probably got a nasty crack on the back of 'er noddle though."

Maisie coughed, spitting dust-filled saliva from her mouth. "Oh, Billy . . . I thought I could stop him. I thought I would be in time. If only we'd been here earlier, if only—"

"Don't you worry, Miss. Let's make sure you're all right before we do anything else."

Maisie shook her head, began to sit up, and brushed her hair from her eyes and face. "I think I'm all right—I was just pulled right off the ground." She squinted and looked around at the melee. "Billy, we've got to help. I can help these people . . . " She tried to stand but fell backward again.

The costermonger and Billy assisted Maisie to her feet. "Steady, love, steady," said the man, who looked at Billy, frowning. "What's she mean? Tried to stop 'im? Did you know there was a nutter there about to top 'imself—and try to take the rest of us with 'im?"

Billy shook his head. "No, we didn't know. This is my employer. We were just walking to see a customer. Only . . . "

"Only what, mate? Only what? Look around you—it's bleedin' chaos, people've been 'urt, look at 'em. Did she know this was going to 'appen? Because if she did, then I'm going over to that copper there and—"

Billy put his arm around Maisie and began to negotiate his way around the rubble, away from the screams of those wounded when a man took his own life in a most terrible way. He looked back into his interrogator's eyes. "She didn't know until she saw the bloke. It was when she saw him that she knew." Maisie allowed herself to be led by Billy, who turned around to the costermonger one last time. "She just knows, you see. She *knows*." He fought back tears. "And thanks for helping her, mate." His voice cracked. "Thanks . . . for helping her."

"COME ON IN HERE, bring her in and she can sit down." The woman called from a shop just a few yards away.

"Thank you, thank you very much." Billy led Maisie into the shop and to a chair, then turned to the woman. "I'd better get back there, see if there's any more I can do."

The woman nodded. "Tell people they can come in here. I've got the kettle on. Dreadful, dreadful, what this world's come to."

Soon the shop had filled with people while ambulances took the more seriously wounded to hospital. And as she sat clutching a cup of tea in her hands, feeling the soothing heat grow cooler in her grasp, Maisie replayed the scene time and again in her mind. She and Billy crossed the road behind the horse and cart, then ran to the curb as a motor came along the street. They were talking, noticing people going by or dashing in and out of shops before early closing. Then she saw him, the man, his leg stretched out, as if he were lame. As she had many times before, she reached into her bag to offer money to someone who had so little. She felt the cold coins brush against her fingers, saw the policeman set off across the street, and looked up at the man again—the man whose black aura seemed to grow until it touched her, until she could no longer hear, could not move with her usual speed.

She sipped her now lukewarm tea. That was the point at which she knew. She knew that the man would take his life. But she thought he had a pistol, or even poison. She saw her own hand in front of her, reaching out as if to gentle his wounded mind, then there was nothing. Nothing except a sharp pain at the back of her head and a voice in the distance. *Maisie Dobbs . . . Miss*. A voice screaming in panic, a voice coming closer.

"MISS DOBBS?"

Maisie started and almost dropped her cup.

"I'm sorry—I didn't mean to make you jump—your assistant said you were here." Detective Inspector Richard Stratton looked down at Maisie, then around the room. The proprietress had brought out as many chairs as she could, and all were taken. Stratton knelt down. "I was on duty at the Yard when it happened, so I was summoned straightaway. By chance I saw Mr. Beale and he said you witnessed the man take his life." He paused, as if to judge her state of mind. "Are you up to answering some questions?" Stratton spoke with a softness not usually employed when in conversation with Maisie. Their interactions had at times been incendiary, to say the least.

Maisie nodded, aware that she had hardly said a word since the explosion. She cleared her throat. "Yes, of course, Inspector. I'm just a little unsettled—I came down with a bit of a wallop, knocked out for a few moments, I think."

"Oh, good, you found her, then." Stratton and Maisie looked toward the door as Billy Beale came back into the shop. "I've brought back your document case, Miss. All the papers are inside."

Maisie nodded. "Thank you, Billy." She looked up and saw concern etched on Billy's face, along with a certain resolve. Though it was more than thirteen years past, the war still fingered Billy's soul, and even though the pain from his wounds had eased, it had not left him in peace. Today's events would unsettle him, would be like pulling a dressing from a dried cut, rendering his memories fresh and raw.

"Look, my motor car's outside—let me take you both back to your office. We can talk there." Stratton stood up to allow Maisie to link her arm through his, and began to lead her to the door. "I know this is not the best time for you, but it's the best time for us—I'd like to talk to you as soon as we get to your premises, before you forget."

Maisie stopped and looked up at Stratton. "Forgetting has never been of concern to me, Inspector. It's the remembering that gives me pause."

A POLICE CORDON now secured the site of the explosion, and though there were no more searing screams ricocheting around her, onlookers had gathered and police moved in and out of shops, taking names, helping those caught in a disaster while out on Christmas Eve. Maisie did not want to look at the street again, but as she saw people on the edge of the tragedy talking, she imagined them going home to their families and saying, "You will never guess what I saw today," or "You've heard about that nutter with the bomb over on Charlotte Street, well . . . " And she wondered if she would ever walk down the street again and not feel her feet leave the ground.

DETECTIVE INSPECTOR RICHARD STRATTON and his assistant, Caldwell, pulled up chairs and were seated on the visiting side of Maisie's desk. Billy had just poured three cups of tea and filled one large enameled tin mug, into which he heaped extra sugar and stirred before setting it in front of his employer.

"All right, Miss?"

Maisie nodded, then clasped the tea as she had in the shop earlier, as if to wring every last drop of warmth from the mug.

"Better watch it, Miss, that's hot. Don't want to burn yourself."

"Yes, of course." Maisie placed the mug on a manila folder in front of her, and as she released her grip, Billy saw red welts on her hands where heat from the mug had scalded her and she had felt nothing.

"How does your head feel now?" Richard Stratton's brows furrowed as he leaned forward to place his cup and saucer on the desk, while keeping his eyes on Maisie. The two had met almost three years earlier, when Stratton was called in at the end of a case she had been working on. The policeman, a widower with a young son, had at one point entertained a romantic notion of the investigator, but his approach had been nipped in the bud by Maisie, who was not as adept in her personal life as she was in her professional domain. Now their relationship encompassed only work, though as an observer, it was clear to Billy that Richard Stratton had a particular regard for his employer, despite it being evident that she had brought him to the edge of exasperation at times—not least because her instincts were more finely honed than his own. Regardless, Stratton's respect for Maisie was reciprocated, and she trusted him.

Maisie reached with her hand to touch the back of her head, a couple of inches above her occipital bone. "There's a fair-sized bump . . . " She ran her fingers down to an indentation in her scalp, sustained while she was working as a nurse during the war. The scar was a constant reminder of the shelling that had not only wounded her but eventually taken the life of Simon Lynch, the doctor she had loved. "At least it didn't open my war wounds." She shook her head, realizing the irony of her words.

"Are you sure you're up for this?" Stratton inquired, his voice softer.

Caldwell rolled his eyes. "I think we need to get on with it, sir."

Stratton was about to speak, when Maisie stood up. "Yes, of course, Mr. Caldwell's right, we should get on."

Billy looked down at his notebook, the hint of a grin at the edges of his mouth. He knew there was no love lost between Maisie and Caldwell, and her use of "Mr." instead of "Detective Sergeant" demonstrated that she may have been knocked out, but she was not down.

"I'll start at the beginning . . . " Maisie began to pace back and forth, her eyes closed as she recounted the events of the morning, from the time she had placed the cap on her pen, to the point at which the explosion ripped the man's body apart, and wounded several passers-by.

"Then the bomb—"

"Mills Bomb," Billy corrected her, absently interrupting as he gazed at the floor watching her feet walk to the window and back again, the deliberate repetitive rhythm of her steps pushing recollections onto center stage in her mind's eye.

"Mills Bomb?" Stratton looked at Billy. Maisie stopped walking.

"What?" Billy looked up at each of them in turn.

"You said Mills Bomb. Are you sure it was a Mills Bomb?" Caldwell licked his pencil's sharp lead, ready to continue recording every word spoken.

"Look, mate, I was a sapper in the war—what do you mean, 'Are you sure?' If you go and fire off a round from half a dozen different rifles, I'll tell you which one's which. Of course I know a Mills Bomb—dodgy bloody things, saw a few mates pull out the pin and end up blowing themselves up with one of them. Mills Bomb—your basic hand grenade."

Stratton lifted his hand. "Caldwell, I think we can trust Mr. Beale here." He turned to Billy. "And it's not as if it would be difficult for a civilian to obtain such ordnance, I would imagine."

"You're right. There's your souvenir seekers going over to France and coming back with them—a quick walk across any of them French fields and you can fill a basket, I shouldn't wonder.

And people who want something bad enough always find a way, don't they?"

"And he hadn't always been a civilian." Maisie took her seat again. "Unless he'd had an accident in a factory, this man had been a soldier. I was close enough to judge his age—about thirty-five, thirty-six—and his left leg was in a brace, which is why people had to walk around him, because he couldn't fold it inward. And the right leg might have been amputated."

"If it wasn't then, it is now." Caldwell seemed to smirk as he noted Maisie's comment.

"If that's all, Inspector, I think I need to go home. I'm driving down to Kent this evening, and I think I should rest before I get behind the wheel."

Stratton stood up, followed by Caldwell, who looked at Maisie and was met with an icy gaze. "Of course, Miss Dobbs," said Stratton. "Look, I would like to discuss this further with you, get more impressions of the man. And of course we'll be conducting inquiries with other witnesses, though it seems that even though you were not the closest, you remember more about him."

"I will never forget, Inspector. The man was filled with despair and I would venture to say that he had nothing and no one to live for, and this is the time of year when people yearn for that belonging most."

Stratton cleared his throat. "Of course." He shook hands with both Maisie and Billy, wishing them the compliments of the season. Maisie extended her hand to Caldwell in turn, smiling as she said, "And a Merry Christmas to *you*, Mr. Caldwell."

MAISIE AND BILLY stood by the window and watched the two men step into the Invicta. The driver closed the passenger door behind them, then took his place and maneuvered the vehicle in the direction of Charlotte Street, whereupon the bell began to ring and the motor picked up speed toward the site of the explosion. Barely two hours had elapsed since Maisie saw a man activate a hand grenade inside his tattered and stained khaki greatcoat.

Turning to her assistant, she saw the old man inside the young. What age was he now? Probably just a little older than herself, say in his mid-thirties, perhaps thirty-seven? There were times when the Billy who worked for her was still a boy, a Cockney lad with reddish-blond hair half tamed, his smile ready to win the day. Then at other times, the weight of the world on his shoulders, his skin became gray, his hair lifeless, and his lameness—the legacy of a wartime wound—was rendered less manageable. Those were the times when she knew he walked the streets at night, when memories of the war flooded back, and when the suffering endured by his family bore down upon him. The events of today had opened his wounds, just as her own had been rekindled. And instead of the warmth and succor of his family, Billy would encounter only more reason to be concerned for his wife, for their children, and their future. And there was only so much Maisie could do to help them.

"Why don't you go home now, Billy." She reached into her purse and pulled out a note. "Buy Doreen some flowers on the way, and some sweets for the boys—it's Christmas Eve, and you have to look after one another."

"You don't need to do that, Miss—look at the bonus, that's more than enough."

"Call it danger money, then. Come on, take it and be on your way."

"And you'll be all right?"

"I'm much better now, so don't you worry about me. I'll be even better when I get on the road to Chelstone. My father will have a roaring fire in the grate, and we'll have a hearty stew for supper—that's the best doctoring I know."

"Right you are, Miss." Billy pulled on his overcoat, placed his flat cap on his head, and left with a wave and a "Merry Christmas!"

As soon as Maisie heard the front door slam shut when Billy walked out into the wintry afternoon, she made her way along the corridor to the lavatory, her hand held against the wall for support. She clutched her stomach as sickness rose up within her and knew that it was not only the pounding headache and seeing a man kill himself that haunted her, but the sensation that she had been watched. It was as if someone had touched her between her shoulder blades, had applied a cold pressure to her skin. And she could feel it still, as she walked back to the office, as if those icy fingertips were with her even as she moved.

Sitting down at her desk, she picked up the black telephone receiver and placed a telephone call to her father's house. She hoped he would answer, for Frankie Dobbs remained suspicious of the telephone she'd had installed in his cottage over two years ago. He would approach the telephone, look at it, and cock his head to one side as if unsure of the consequences of answering the call. Then he would lift the receiver after a few seconds had elapsed, hold it a good two inches from his ear and say, with as much authority as he could muster, "Chelstone three-five-double two—is that you, Maisie?" And of course, it was always Maisie, for no one else ever telephoned Frankie Dobbs.

"That you, Maisie?"

"Of course it is, Dad."

"Soon be on your way, I should imagine. I've a nice stew simmering, and the tree's up, ready for us to decorate."

"Dad, I'm sorry, I won't be driving down until tomorrow morning. I'll leave early and be with you for breakfast."

"What's the matter? Are you all right, love?"

She cleared her throat. "Bit of a sore throat. I reckon it's nothing, but it's given me a headache and there's a lot of sickness going round. I'm sure I'll be all right tomorrow."

"I'll miss you." No matter what he said, when it was into the telephone receiver, Frankie shouted, as if his words needed to reach London with only the amplification his voice could provide. Instead of a soft endearment, it sounded as if he had just given a brusque command.

"You too, Dad. See you tomorrow then."

MAISIE RESTED FOR a while longer, having dragged her chair in front of the gas fire and turned up the jets to quell her shivering. She placed another telephone call, to the client with whom she and Billy were due to meet this morning, then rested again, hoping the dizziness would subside so that she felt enough confidence in her balance to walk along to Tottenham Court Road and hail a taxicab. As she reached for her coat and hat, the bell above the door rang, indicating that a caller had come to the front entrance. She gathered her belongings, and was about to turn off the lights, when she realized that, in the aftermath of today's events, Billy had forgotten the box of gifts for his family. She turned off the fire, settled her document case on top of the gifts and switched off the lights. Then, balancing the box against her hip, she locked her office and walked with care down the stairs leading to the front door, which she pulled open.

"I thought you might still be here." Richard Stratton removed his hat as Maisie opened the door.

She turned to go back up to the office. "Oh, more questions so soon?"

He reached forward to take the box, and shook his head. "Oh, no, that's not it . . . well, I do have more questions, but that's not why I'm here. I thought you looked very unwell. You must be concussed—and you should never underestimate a concussion. I left Caldwell in Charlotte Street and came back. Come on, my driver will take you home, however, we're making a detour via the hospital on the way—to get that head of yours looked at."

Maisie nodded. "I think you've been trying to get my head looked at for some time, Inspector."

He held open the door of the Invicta for her to step inside the motor car. "At least you weren't too knocked out to quip, Miss Dobbs."

As they drove away, Maisie looked through the window behind her, her eyes scanning back and forth across the square, until her headache escalated and she turned to lean back in her seat.

"Forgotten something?"

"No, nothing. It's nothing."

Nothing except the feeling between her shoulder blades that had been with her since this morning. It was a sense that someone had seen her reach out to the doomed man, had seen their eyes meet just before he pulled the pin that would ignite the grenade. Now she felt as if that same someone was watching her still.

Stupid, stupid, stupid, foolish man. I should have known, should have sensed he was on the precipice. I never thought the idiot would take his own life. Fool. He should have waited. Had I not told him that we must bide our time? Had I not said, time and again, that we should temper our passion until we were heard, until what I knew gave us currency? Now the only one who knows is the sparrow. An ordinary gray little thing who comes each day for a crumb or two. He knows. He listens to me, waits for me to tell him my plans. And, oh, what plans I have. Then they will all listen. Then they'll know. I've called him Croucher. Little sparrow Croucher, always there, sing-song Croucher, never without a smile. I have a lot to tell him today.

The man closed his diary and set down his pencil. He always used pencil, sharpened with a keen blade each morning and evening, for the sound of a worn lead against paper, the surrounding wood touching the vellum, scraping back and forth for want of sharpening, set his teeth on edge, made him shudder. Sounds were like that. Sounds made their way into your body, crawled along inside your skin. Horses' hooves on wet cobblestones, cart wheels whining for want of oil, the crackle and snap as the newspaper boy folded the *Daily Sketch*. Thus he always wrote using a pencil with a long, sharp but soft lead, so he couldn't hear his words as they formed on the page.

TWO

Faced with advice to go home and rest, and knowing that it would be foolish to embark upon a long drive following a diagnosis of concussion, Maisie revised her plans and decided to travel on the train to Kent that very evening, given that trains would not run to Chelstone on Christmas Day. It would be a surprise for her father, who now did not expect her until Christmas morning. First, though, she wanted to ensure that Billy's boys received their gifts, so upon arrival back at her flat, she loaded the box into the MG and drove with care across London to Shoreditch. The city was wet, with an unyielding quality of gray light that made the words *Merry Christmas* seem hardly worth saying. In poorer parts of London, the soup kitchens had been busy, and rations had been distributed to those for whom the festive season was another reminder of what it was to want. Yet in some windows red candles burned a white-gold flame, as the occupants attempted to uplift spirits and reflect the season.

She pulled up outside Billy's house and was not surprised to see a Christmas tree lit with candles and paper chains framing the window. Silhouettes in the parlor suggested the family was gathered there to decorate the tree. As she walked to the door with the box of gifts, she heard a raised voice coming from the parlor, and wondered if she should not have come.

"Don't you touch those presents. They're for Lizzie. I bought them 'specially for a little girl, so don't you dare touch your sister's things."

A child began to cry. Maisie thought it was probably Bobby, the youngest son. She was about to turn away, when she heard Billy, the eldest boy, shout out to his father.

"Miss Dobbs' motor car's outside. Quick, let's have a look at it, Bobby!"

And before she could leave the box of gifts on the step and turn back to the MG, the front door opened.

"Aw, Miss, you shouldn't've gone to all that trouble, what with you not feeling well and all." Billy stood on the doorstep without a jacket, his shirt collar and tie removed and his sleeves rolled up.

"Is them for us?" Young Billy's eyes lit up when he saw the packages wrapped in Christmas paper.

"Yes, they're for you, Billy—and for your brother too! Merry Christmas!"

"Come on in, Miss, and have a cuppa with us before you go."

"Oh, no, you're all busy and—"

"Doreen and me won't hear of it, not after you bringing all this for the boys." Billy stood back to allow Maisie to come into the passageway, and then opened the door to the parlor. "Doreen, it's Miss Dobbs."

Maisie tried to hide her dismay when she saw Doreen Beale standing close to the Christmas tree, clutching a child's threadbare toy lamb to her heart. Her hair was drawn back, which accentuated sallow skin that had sunk into her face, and cheekbones that seemed to jut out from under her eyes. The cardigan she was wearing was soiled at the cuffs and her dress had some dried food on the front. Though Billy and his wife were working hard to put money by for passage to Canada, and what they hoped would be a new life, they were proud people, and Doreen was especially meticulous when it came to keeping the family's clothing clean and pressed, no matter how old it might be, or how many owners it might have had before.

"It's lovely to see you, Doreen." Maisie approached her and placed her hand on the woman's arm. "How are you keeping?"

She looked at Maisie's hand as if she could not quite fathom who this visitor might be, and how her arm had become thus burdened. Then, her eyes filling with tears, she beamed a smile filled with hope. "Have you brought a present for my little girl? She loves her dolls, you know, and her lamb. Did you bring her something?"

Maisie looked around at Billy, who set the box of gifts under the tree, and came to his wife, placed his arm around her and began to lead her to the kitchen.

"Let's go and put the kettle on for Miss Dobbs, eh, Doreen? Let's have a nice cup of tea, then we can all sit down and look at the tree."

"All right, Billy. I'll be better when I've had a cup of tea."

Billy returned to the parlor. Now that he was not wearing his jacket, as he did at all times in the office, Maisie realized that he too had lost weight.

"Sorry, Miss, she's having a bit of a turn. All the excitement of putting up the tree, I suppose. And—as you know—it's coming up to a year ago that we lost our little Lizzie. Apparently, it does this sort of thing, an anniversary."

Maisie wanted to ask questions, wanted to know how she might be able to help, but this was Christmas, and she knew Billy would want to settle his children and his wife, so the family might have a calm day tomorrow.

"I'd better be off, Billy. I've got to get down to Kent, and I'm taking the train—don't want to drive down, not with this bump on the back of my head."

"Oh, Miss, and you drove over here for us." He turned to his boys, who were silent and watching, and as Maisie could see, were fully aware of their mother's plight. "What do you say to Miss Dobbs?"

They echoed thanks, and Maisie said they could each sit in the driver's seat of the MG for a minute or two, then she had to leave. And as she drove away, Maisie looked back and saw Billy standing on the doorstep, one boy held to him, the other clutching his hand. The children waved and then the three turned and went inside the house.

December 26th, 1931

Christmas Day had passed with a mellow quietness, as Maisie and her father spent time by the fire, sometimes talking, sometimes reading, with her father's dog, a lurcher known as Jook, temporarily changing allegiance to sit at her feet. They shared a hearty festive meal of roast capon and all the trimmings, and enjoyed a short walk across fields whitened by ground frost, the length of the stroll dictated by Frankie's years and her lingering concussion, which, though subsiding, still caused some dizziness if she remained on her feet too long.

Maisie had planned a return to London early on the morning of December 27th, taking Boxing Day off to further recuperate and enjoy her father's company. She had arrived at Chelstone railway station late on Christmas Eve, and was collected at the station by the estate's chauffeur, who had been released to do so by her father's employer, Lady Rowan Compton, who was delighted to know that Maisie would be returning for the holiday. Lady

Rowan held a special affection for Maisie and had played a part in her rise from a lowly position on the household staff to the professional woman she was today. For his part, Frankie Dobbs had been relieved to have his daughter home on Christmas Eve, and felt all was well as they dressed the Christmas tree together and placed their gifts underneath, as they had done when Maisie was a child.

Now, waking on Boxing Day morning, Maisie reached for the small clock next to her bed. It was six o'clock. Her father was already downstairs pottering in his kitchen and talking to Jook as he prepared breakfast. For once, Maisie did not scramble out of bed to go to the kitchen, though she loved to share in the cozy warmth while sitting at the table in front of the black cast-iron stove that seemed to push out enough heat to drive a train. She had always enjoyed this time in the morning with her father, when the tea was strong in the pot, the hearth welcoming and the sizzle of bacon and eggs tempting her senses. But today she wanted only to listen to the morning sounds—a solitary bird outside singing despite winter's onslaught and the wind against the glass panes. She closed her eyes and must have fallen asleep again, for it was the shrill ring of the telephone that woke her. She heard her father complain, heard his steps along the red flagstones that led from the kitchen to the sitting room, and heard the telephone continue to ring while he considered who it might be.

Picking up the receiver and without first reciting his telephone number, Frankie shouted, "What do you want?" and then was quiet. Maisie sat up in bed, waiting.

"Well, she's not well, Inspector. Caught a bit of a throat and hasn't been feeling her usual self, you know." Silence again. "All right, all right, you wait here and I'll get her for you."

Maisie leapt from her bed and reached for her woolen dressing gown hanging on a hook behind the door. "I'm coming, Dad."

She ran downstairs and straight into the sitting room, where she smiled at her father as she took the receiver from his hand. "Yes, this is Maisie Dobbs."

"Miss Dobbs. Richard Stratton here. Sorry to bother you at home."

"How did you find me?" She paused. "Stupid question, Inspector. How can I help you—and on Boxing Day?"

"We have a situation of some urgency and importance on our hands. I would like you to come to the Yard as soon as you can."

"Well, I was planning to come back to London tomorrow on the train—I decided not to drive after all." She looked around to see whether her father was in earshot, then turned her back on the kitchen. "And thank you for not saying anything to my father about the incident on Christmas Eve. I can't have him worrying."

"Of course, I understood the situation. Now then, can you return today? I can have a motor car at your door by eight."

"That's certainly urgent."

"I wouldn't ask if it was not critical. We need to draw upon all resources, Miss Dobbs, and in this case, I believe you are a most valuable resource."

"I'll be ready at eight."

"Thank you. I will brief you on our return to London."

"Until then." Maisie frowned when she realized that Stratton would himself be coming to collect her. She set down the receiver and walked into her father's kitchen. Jook rose from her place alongside the stove and came to Maisie, nudging her hand with a welcoming wet nose.

"Dad, I'm sorry about this, but I've got to go back to London."

"I thought as much. You don't get these Scotland Yard blokes making telephone calls early on a Boxing Day morning for nothing." He paused, taking a frying pan from the stove and slipping two eggs and a rasher of bacon on a plate. "I've had mine, but you can't be shooting off up there without a good breakfast inside you, so get stuck into that. We can at least sit together for a while until you've to leave."

Maisie sat at the table and as she began to eat, her father filled two mugs with tea, set one in front of her and seated himself opposite his daughter.

"You know, I don't hanker after the Smoke at all." Frankie shook his head and shrugged. "I thought I would when I first came down to Chelstone, in the war. But aside from sometimes missing the market, you know, a bit of banter, the companionship of it all, I don't miss London. Not one bit. Last time I went up there to see you, it'd changed too much for my liking. I couldn't believe the racket. I mean, when I was boy, you had your noise, but not like now, not with all them motors and lorries and the horses and carts vying for a bit of road. And when you go into a shop, there's tills with bells, them adding and typewriting machines in the background when you're at the bank. Can't hear yourself think. And now it's full of people out of work. Then, of course, there's them who've got too much—mind you, that's always been the way. But it seems, oh, I dunno—a desperate sort of place to me."

Maisie stopped eating for a moment and regarded her father. It was at times like this that he surprised her most. He often began such proclamations with the words, "I'm an ordinary bloke, but . . . " And on such occasions, Maisie found him far from ordinary.

"Yes, it's a desperate place for a lot of people, Dad. And the irony of it is that it means, in many cases, someone like me stays in business."

Frankie nodded. "That's what worries me. And Detective Inspectors who know where to find you and ring early on a Boxing Day morning. Desperate, I would say."

Maisie changed the subject, though she knew Frankie was more than aware of her conversational maneuver. He would take her lead and speak of this and that, of minor goings-on at Chelstone Manor, anything except the fact that soon his beloved daughter would be collected by a senior Scotland Yard detective because something untoward had happened in what he considered to be a desperate sort of place.

"HERE'S THE SITUATION." Stratton turned to Maisie as the driver negotiated the narrow country lanes that led from Chelstone to Tonbridge and then on to the main London road. "A threat has been received by the Home Secretary and is now in the hands of Scotland Yard. I am one of three senior officers designated to deal with the situation. Seeing as the threat pertains to what amounts to murder, I was called in immediately."

"What sort of threat is it?"

"That's just it, it hasn't been spelled out, just the consequence. A letter was received at Westminster—you'll see it later—plain vellum, no postmark, no prints, no distinguishing marks at all, the handwriting could have come from anyone, though we have an expert looking at it, obviously."

"But there are demands."

"Yes. The man—or woman—is asking the government to act immediately to alleviate the suffering of all unemployed, starting with measures to assist those who have served their country in wartime. There's a bit of a rant about what they did for their country and now look at them, and there's a threat to the effect that, if no action is forthcoming within forty-eight hours—which will be up tomorrow morning—then he will demonstrate his power. We have to entertain the possibility that such a threat may be to the life of the Home Secretary, the Prime Minister, or another important person."

"And what about the possibility of a hoax, or some disenfranchised individual letting off steam?"

"As you know, Miss Dobbs, some of those disenfranchised people can be dangerous—take the Irish situation, the Fascists, the unions. There are a lot of holes in which this particular rodent might be concealing himself."

"Yes, of course." Maisie paused, looking out of the window as she considered Stratton's synopsis of the situation. She turned back to Stratton. "Look, I must ask you this, especially as I am now traveling back to London when I could have spent the day with my father—but what has this got to do with me? You have senior detectives working on the case—how can I help?"

"I can think of several different ways in which you can help, Miss Dobbs, and the talents that might render you a valuable member of the group. Certainly you are known at the Yard, and your contribution to the training of our women detectives has not gone unnoticed. But the fact is that your presence has been"—he slowed his speech, as if choosing his words with care—"*requested*, because whoever is behind the threats has mentioned you by name. 'If you doubt my sincerity, ask Maisie Dobbs.' That's what he said. So, whether you like it or not, you are part of this case. And unfortunately, the first thing you will have to do is submit to questioning."

Maisie shook her head. "So that's why you're accompanying me to Scotland Yard, to bring me in for questioning. I'm a suspect. I wish you had been honest at the outset."

"It's not quite like that, Miss Dobbs." Stratton took a deep breath. "On the one hand, we know who you are, we know your reputation. But at the same time we need to ensure that you are on our side before we go any further, especially as there's a suspicion that you may be implicated in some way." He paused. "And there's one more thing: Special Branch is taking care of this one."

"I should have guessed. And how are you connected to Special Branch?"

Stratton turned to look at Maisie directly. "Let's just say I'm moving in that direction. Detective Chief Superintendent Robert MacFarlane is leading the inquiry. And it's on the cards that I'll be reporting to him by Easter—leaving the Murder Squad and joining Special Branch—and that information is a bit hush-hush."

"Congratulations, Inspector Stratton." She wiped a hand across condensation inside the window and looked out at the frost-covered landscape for a moment. "Tell me more about MacFarlane—'Big Robbie' has a reputation that goes before him. Maurice Blanche has worked with him, and he came to talk to us when I was studying at the Department of Legal Medicine in Edinburgh." Maisie smiled and shrugged. "To tell you the truth, I liked him. I had a sense that you knew where you stood with MacFarlane—though I'll be honest, I thought he was a bit of a one with the ladies."

Stratton gave a half laugh. "Oh yes, and probably more so since his wife left him a couple of years ago. But there's no doubt, you know where you are with Robbie, all right. He's fair, speaks his mind, and gives his people the leeway they need to get the job done. Mind you, at the same time, he expects every ounce of you on the case."

"Well, I look forward to meeting him again. I wonder if he remembers me."

"Yes, he remembers you, Miss Dobbs. That's another reason why you were summoned at an unearthly hour on Boxing Day morning."

MAISIE'S FIRST VISIT to New Scotland Yard, on the Embankment, had taken place when she was working with Maurice Blanche as his assistant. She found the grand red-brick building intimidating, with its ornate chimneys, projecting gables and turrets at each corner. In the intervening years, she had come to take visits to "the Yard" in her stride. Today, though, she was escorted to the area of Scotland Yard occupied by Special Branch, and led into a sparsely decorated room, where she waited while Stratton left to inform others involved in the investigation that they had arrived. Soon she heard a voice booming down the corridor, but when Robert MacFarlane walked into the room with Stratton, the timbre was lower, with a soft Scottish burr belying his position, and the situation. Maisie rose from her chair and extended her hand in greeting.

"Miss Dobbs, thank you for coming." The Detective Chief Superintendent shook her hand, then nodded toward the chair. "Sit down, lass, sit down. I trust your father was not too upset by your sudden departure from the family hearth."

"He understands the nature of my work."

"Good, I'm glad one of us does." Taking his seat behind a wooden desk that seemed too small to accommodate his height—MacFarlane was well over six feet tall and, thought Maisie, had the frame of a docker. He was about fifty-five years of age, light of foot and precise in his movements. A track of baldness revealed a scar where a stray bullet had nicked him in the war—the fact that he had simply wiped blood away and sworn at the enemy for putting a hole in his tam o'shanter was the stuff of legend—and the cropped hair that flanked his shining pate was gunmetal gray and controlled with a whisper of oil.

"Stratton, bring in Darby, if you wouldn't mind."

Soon the four were seated: Maisie, MacFarlane, Stratton and Colm Darby, a man who had worked alongside MacFarlane since before the war and, when the policeman returned from France, joined him once more. Darby was probably a good five years older than his superior. Maisie knew him to be an expert in the analysis of personal markers left behind by the perpetrator of a crime. The nature of one's handwriting was an area in which he was said to have great insight. He had been with MacFarlane since the days when the main roles of the department encompassed intelligence and security to protect the country from extremist activity known as the "Irish problem." Now Special Branch had a broader role, and it seemed as if Colm Darby might never retire. MacFarlane introduced Maisie, then leaned forward so that his forearms rested on the desk.

"Miss Dobbs, I am dispensing with protocol here—because I can, and because I believe we have no time to lose." He sighed, looking directly into Maisie's eyes. "I know Maurice Blanche, I've worked with him in the past, and I remember you from Edinburgh—Blanche sent you there, I understand."

"Yes, that's correct, in preparation for my work with him, when I was his assistant."

MacFarlane looked down at an open manila folder, flipped over a page of notes, then closed the folder before resuming eye contact with Maisie. "Now, first of all, in your own words, describe the events of Christmas Eve."

Maisie drew breath and, as she had for Stratton before, described approaching the man on Charlotte Street, and witnessing him take his life with a Mills Bomb.

"Not a pretty sight, I'm sure."

"I've seen some ugly sights in my time, Chief Inspector."

"I bet you have, Miss Dobbs. And we don't, any of us, want to be seeing any more, though I imagine that might be a wee bit of a faint hope." MacFarlane cleared his throat. "Can you explain how a man who has made veiled threats that amount to a risk to our country's security might know the name of a little wee lassie like yourself?"

Maisie bristled, but checked herself, aware that the goading was deliberate, though she knew that, in the circumstances, she might have employed the same tactic herself. She leaned forward, mirroring MacFarlane's position. Darby looked at Stratton, and raised an eyebrow.

"Chief Inspector, to be perfectly honest with you, at this juncture I have no idea why I was mentioned in such a letter. However, your line of questioning regarding the tragedy I witnessed on Christmas Eve would indicate that you see a relationship between the two events, and I am inclined to veer in that initial direction myself." She turned to face Stratton and Darby, bringing them into the conversation. "I was the closest person to the victim to walk away without significant physical injury—and yes, I see him as a victim. So if—*if*—there was an associate of the dead man nearby, I would have been seen. If the two cases are linked, the person who wrote the letter could be that same individual, perhaps using my name as leverage to give some kind of weight to his endeavor. It might also be a means of subverting your attention, of course."

MacFarlane leaned back in his chair, as did Maisie in hers. The policeman smiled. "Just like bloody Blanche! I move, you move, I do this, you do the same thing. It's like being followed." He shook his head. "Look, Miss Dobbs, I know—*know*, mind—that you haven't anything to do with this tyke, but you might have had some brief contact with him, you might have seen him, or he might have an interest in you." He brushed his hand across his forehead. "I know this could be the work of a bit of a joker, but my nose tells me this boy is serious, that he means what he says. Now then, we can play a waiting game, see what happens next, or we can start looking. I favor action, which is why I've asked you here. You're involved in this whether you like it or not, Miss Dobbs, and I would rather have you under my nose working for me than anywhere else."

"I'm used to working alone, Chief Inspector."

"Well, for now you can get un-used to it. First of all, let me apprise you of the work of Special Branch. Even though I am sure you have some familiarity, if you are going to be reporting to me, then I want to start us off on the right foot. So, a little lesson, and I'll make it snappy. The Special Branch is, technically, part of the Criminal Investigation Department, but as you may have heard we like to go about our business in our own fashion. Suffice it to say that we only answer questions when the person asking has a lot of silver on the epaulettes, or around the peak of his cap. Our normal work is in connection with the protection of royalty, ministers and ex-ministers of the Crown, and foreign dignitaries. We also control aliens entering our country. We are responsible for investigation into acts of terrorism and anarchy, and to that end have a lot of people to keep an eye on. Before I go on, I should add—mainly because I can see a bit of a problem looming here—that on occasion we cross paths with Military Intelligence, Section Five, for obvious reasons. We try to get along, and they need us, mainly because we have powers of arrest. There, now I can take off my professoring hat and get down to business. Do you have any questions?"

"No, sir."

"Good. Back to the case in hand. Let's look at what we've brought together here in the way of information—facts. I want action and I want the man behind the letter brought in as a matter of urgency. And Miss Dobbs—whatever you're doing, I want you to report to Inspector Stratton here every single day."

Maisie nodded. "If that's the case, Chief Superintendent, before I see the letter, perhaps we can discuss my terms. The financial terms, that is."

"Not exactly music to the ears of a Scot, you know." The edges of MacFarlane's mouth twitched into a grin.

"That's why I didn't want to leave it any longer, Chief Superintendent."

* * *

"INSPECTOR DARBY, what do you think about the downstroke of the pencil, here, where the letter-writer makes his demands? It seems so thick, almost labored." Without touching the paper, Maisie used her forefinger to indicate her observation.

"Yes, I noticed that myself. Very deliberate, isn't it?"

"Like a child's hand—not in presentation, but in the execution, as if the person writing the letter were moving his hand slowly, so as not to lose control." She closed her eyes, her hand moving back and forth on the wooden desk to describe holding a pen. The three men looked at one another.

MacFarlane made an effort to control his voice, keeping it low while Maisie was thinking. "Stratton, I know you're not a tea-boy, but poke your head around that door and tell them that this isn't the desert and throats are parched in here." He turned back to Maisie, who opened her eyes and spoke again.

"I think he or she has trouble with dexterity and concentration. Don't you think so?" She turned to Darby.

Colm Darby nodded agreement. "I do—but what do you make of this?" He handed her a magnifying glass, then pointed to two places on the vellum. Stratton entered the room again and sat at the table alongside Maisie.

"It's been moistened—by saliva, I would say." She looked up, then down at the paper again. "Yes, that's saliva. The person who wrote this letter was so intent on the words that his mouth was open and spittle drooled onto the paper."

"So what does that tell us? That we have a dribbling person out there with perfect spelling?" MacFarlane was growing impatient.

The door opened again and a younger man in civilian clothes entered with four cups of tea on a wooden tray. He set the tray down on the table and left the room.

"It tells us that the person has trouble with muscular control, and that concentration is difficult. It tells us that the person is compromised in some way."

"That's if you're right."

"Yes, that's if Inspector Darby and I are right."

There was silence in the room. Stratton reached for two cups of tea, placing one in front of Maisie, who was beginning to feel the stirrings of a headache. She thanked Stratton and touched the bump on the back of her head.

"All right?"

"Yes, it's just reminding me, that's all."

MacFarlane reached for a cup of tea, as did Darby. "Well, that's bloody marvelous," said the Scotsman. "Thousands of—what did you say?—*compromised* people in London and we've got to find one of them. Needle in a bloody haystack." He scraped back his chair and began to pace the room.

"Do we have an identification on the dead man yet?" asked Maisie.

Stratton shook his head. "Proving very difficult, as you can imagine."

Maisie looked at each man in turn, then up at the clock above the door. MacFarlane followed her gaze. "Yes, it's time we got on with it. Miss Dobbs, a motor car will collect you from your office this afternoon at four, and we'll reconvene here to discuss progress—or, heaven forbid, lack thereof. In the meantime, I'll allow you to work in the way that you've said is best—alone. But be ready at four, otherwise you'll have someone from the Branch at your heels from dawn until dusk until we've closed this case. The forty-eight hours grace our letter-writer has allowed us will be up by six o'clock tomorrow morning or thereabouts. If we haven't got him, we'll soon find out if we have a practical joker on our hands.

And with a bit of luck, by then we'll have an identification on the other nutcase in Charlotte Street." He held out his hand. "We'll see you later, Miss Dobbs."

"Indeed, later."

"And don't forget—in all the work you do on this case, you're under the jurisdiction of Special Branch."

"I understand, Chief Superintendent."

MacFarlane nodded and took up the letter once more.

STRATTON WALKED MAISIE to a waiting Invicta police motor car.

"He may be a bit of a maverick, but he's very good."

"Yes, I know. Maurice has spoken about him in the past. And I expect the reason I am here is not only because my name was mentioned in that letter, but because he requested Maurice's help first."

"Blanche said to contact you, that you were his successor in every way. He told Big Robbie to trust your instincts."

"And does he?"

"He trusts Blanche, so yes, consider yourself trusted."

"I must be—his questioning was mild, to say the least."

As they reached the motor car, Maisie turned to Stratton and held out her hand. "I look forward to working with you again, Inspector."

"Ditto, Miss Dobbs. But we have to work fast."

"I know—I'm working already." She stepped into the Invicta. "I'll see you at four."

Hickory, dickory, dock. Tick tock, tick tock. Clocks and watches, clocks and watches, time in, time out. Here comes a chopper to chop off your head!

The pencil began to scrape, so the man shuffled to the kitchen, took a knife from a drawer and whittled a point to the lead, the chips of wood hitting a brown stain where the single cold tap dripped water day and night. He winced at the noise, tested the sharpness with the tip of his finger as if he were about to tune a string instrument, then shuffled back to the table again and proceeded to write.

They do not know, do not know which end is up, and that's always been the trouble with the brass. I remember, see. Oh, it was all very well, sending out those watches, so we all had the same time, down to the second, so that we all, thousands of us, went over the top at the same time, and . . .

Holding the pencil above the page the man gasped as memories pushed forward to become fast-moving pictures in his mind—the twisted grin of death on a uniformed corpse, the silent scream of a man he'd laughed with just moments past—and the relentless noise of battle reverberating from inside his skull into the solitude of his room, enveloping him in the fury of war. He dropped the pencil and pressed his hands to his eyes, hard, so that as his fingers touched the soft roundness he imagined that he could pluck the pictures from his head if he could stand the pain. And if he thought he would be left in peace.

In time the ghosts drew back to the place in his mind where they were quiet, spent, so he read back over his own words, picked up his pencil and began again.

So what's the point of getting the time right, if it's all you can get right? Time and consequence, time and consequence. Croucher knew about time and consequence. Poor Croucher. Very poor Croucher.

The man set down his pencil between the pages of the leather-bound book, then tied a string around the cover so the pencil would not be mislaid or clatter to the floor. He stood up and, taking small steps toward a cupboard, pulled out a large box containing a collection of empty demijohns, tubes and rubber piping. Another box held a series of bottles filled with liquids and tins of various sizes, each one labeled with care, in pencil. If Darby had brought his magnifying glass to the labels, he might have seen the paper discolored in spots here and there, where it had become soiled by saliva from the man's open mouth.

Setting the two boxes on the table, he began to attach tubing to a demijohn. Had an onlooker been observing the man, he might have been reminded of the tale of Dr. Jekyll and Mr. Hyde, and might have felt concern at the recollection. Having completed construction of what was to be something of an experiment, the man pulled at the string around his diary, opened the leather-bound book again and took up his pencil.

I was good at something, once. I was good at something, one thing, that could be of service. But they don't want to know now. I'll just have to show them. Toil and trouble, toil and trouble.

THREE

Maisie slotted her key into the lock and opened the outside door to the mansion in Fitzroy Square that housed her one-room office on the first floor. She closed the door behind her and walked upstairs with a certain weariness, but stopped to listen when she heard voices coming from the office. At first she was concerned, but then a child's squealing laughter echoed across the room, and a young voice said, "Chase us, Dad, chase me and Bobby." She wondered why Billy was at work—not only was Boxing Day a holiday, but they often only worked a half day on a Saturday, unless a significant assignment demanded their round-the-clock attention. And he had his children with him.

"Hello, Billy—and young Billy, and Bobby." Maisie smiled as she entered the office, taking off her hat and scarf, but keeping her coat on. "It's cold in here, Billy—why didn't you put on the gas fire? You don't want the boys catching cold."

Billy had been on the floor playing with his sons, but stood up, blushing, when Maisie came in. "You two play with your toys while

I'm talking to Miss Dobbs—and what do you say, again, for the presents she bought you?"

The two boys stood up side by side and in unison said, "Thank you, Miss Dobbs," with young Billy adding, "I really liked my fire engine!"

Maisie tousled the wheaten-hued hair of each boy in turn and told them they should play with their toys where the carpet gave way to wood. "Your fire engine will go faster there." She turned to Billy. "Come on, let's have a cup of tea and you can tell me what's going on—if you want to."

Over tea Billy explained that Doreen had become more withdrawn as the festive season approached, and though they had never been able to afford a big Christmas Day, as a rule they would try to put by enough money for a roast chicken, and a gift each for the boys. This year she had taken almost no interest at all, except for placing a small collection of toys for Lizzie under the tree, toys that Billy tried to remove so as not to upset the boys.

"She's just a shadow at times, Miss, a shadow. I thought over the summer she'd picked up a bit, that we were getting through it. I mean, I miss my little Lizzie too, but we've got two cracking boys here and they need their mum. I tell you, Miss, I come home of an evening and sometimes she's just sitting there, staring. The stove's gone down, she's got some dressmaking half done and I have to sort of get her going again, you know, help her to her feet, show her how to do this or that. There's days when you'd think she was right as rain, then it comes again. She's not eating much either, and I've always made sure there was food on the table. We might not live in clover—there's folk round our way making do in terrible conditions, rats from the river up and everywhere—but we always kept the house nice, kept the boys clean and going to school. Now it's like trying to stop someone falling down a big black hole."

"Oh, Billy, I am so sorry."

"So, I didn't think you'd be here until Monday, and we'd nowhere else to go, because I wanted to give Doreen a bit of a rest in peace and quiet, and—to tell you the truth—I wanted to get the boys out of the house, away from it all for a bit. The museums on Exhibition Road are closed today—and I wanted to take them to the Science Museum, you know, to that new children's gallery they've opened, with all the little machines for the kids to see how a steam train works and what happens down a mine, that sort of thing. But the office was here, so after we'd been for a walk to look in the shop windows, I brought them back for a bit of a play before we went home to Shoreditch."

"That's all right, Billy. You and the boys can stay here as long as you like today." Maisie paused. "Has Doreen seen a doctor? Or the nurse?"

"Well, she went when we first lost Lizzie, but it's hard to get her to go anywhere."

"But she might need a tonic, something to give her a bit of a lift. And she needs to be eating properly."

"I bought a tonic for her, and as for food, as I said, she's eating like a sparrow, and it's not as if Doreen ever carried weight." He put his hand to his forehead and rubbed it from side to side. "I tell you, Miss, it scares me sometimes, reminds me of me when I came back from the war—reminds me of men I saw in the hospital, you know, the ones you weren't supposed to see before they were sent off to another special hospital in the plain black ambulance. There's times she's got that look in her eyes, as if she were staring across an ocean." He paused again. "And every time she's like that now, I think about the bloke on Christmas Eve. That was just how he looked, out into the distance, as if there was no one else there."

"I think she needs to see the doctor again, Billy. She's suffering and she should see someone."

"I've got the bonus money. I thought I'd put it away for Canada, you know, to save for the passage, but I'll put it toward Doreen getting better."

"Do it soon, Billy."

"I will, Miss." Billy looked across the room to his boys, who were making motor noises as they pushed their toys back and forth. Then he brought his attention back to Maisie. "I didn't think you'd be here today, Miss—weren't you going to stay with your dad until tomorrow?"

"Yes, I was, but I was brought back by D.I. Stratton—and this is confidential, mind: Special Branch is involved."

Billy exhaled with a low whistle.

"I know—if they're on the job, it's serious. A threat has been received by the Home Secretary and my name is mentioned in the letter. In addition, it is likely that the threat has some connection to the man with the Mills Bomb who committed the crime of suicide on Christmas Eve."

"Can't get that out of my mind, Miss. At first I was a bit scared, I'll be honest with you. For a minute I thought I was back over there. But there's Doreen and the boys to think of, so I can't be letting myself slip now, can I?"

"No, you can't." Maisie paused, thinking of the time, two years before, when Billy's own slide into the abyss was caused by the lingering pain from his war wounds. "I've been seconded to work on the case with Special Branch," she went on, "so I'm going to have to depend upon you to keep our present customers happy. I'm to meet with Stratton each day, though you and I can start here in the mornings to go through work in hand."

"Right you are, Miss."

"But about the man in the street—we both believe he'd been a soldier, wounded in the legs, and it's likely he'd been shell-shocked to some degree."

"I would say so."

"So, who was he? The police don't seem able to get to the bottom of it, and I would like to have a name as soon as possible. If we know who he is, we can find out who he knows, then with luck we can find our way to the man who sent the threat."

"What will he do, the man?"

"I don't know—he wasn't specific. But he said he would wait forty-eight hours for his requests to be met, which means we now have only a very limited time to find a very angry or unhappy person in London who could be mentally ill."

"That doesn't narrow the field down much."

"I know. I sometimes wonder who's sane."

Their conversation was interrupted as a squabble broke out among the boys.

"Now then, now then, what's all this about?" Billy moved toward his sons and held each of them gently but firmly by the arm. "You're brothers, you're not supposed to fight—that's how wars start, with people fighting over the little things."

Blaming started as one boy pointed at the other, and vice versa, but Billy soon calmed the situation and the brothers made up, shaking hands like little men.

"We'd better be going, Miss. They'll be hungry by the time we get home."

Maisie helped Billy put the boys' coats on, winding scarves around their necks and slipping mittens onto little hands that would only too readily feel the cold. As she pulled a woolen hat down on young Billy's head, she saw his father take out a handkerchief and wipe Bobby's mouth.

Billy saw her watching him and shrugged. "I hope he gets over this soon. He's going on five now, you know, and this dribbling business started when we came home after the hop-picking. I reckon it's to do with his mum. She used to give them cuddles a lot, but now she don't. I've seen him run to her, but she just pushes him away, same with young Bill here." Billy spoke softly while the children claimed their toys. "I try to give him a cuddle, when I see it happen, but I'm not there when they come in from school. He sits there with his fingers in his mouth and before you know where you are, the front of his cardigan is all wet and matted."

Maisie was thoughtful. "The best thing for now is not to draw attention to it. Just keep him dry so that he doesn't get chapped in this weather. You're doing the right thing in trying to step in when Doreen can't, but it just points to the fact that she needs to see someone, as soon as possible."

Billy sighed. "We'll be off now. See you on Monday morning, Miss."

Maisie bid farewell to Billy and the boys, and walked to the window to watch them make their way across the square, each boy holding on to his father's hand as they skipped alongside him. Although she had been aware of time passing, and the letter-writer's deadline looming ever closer, she understood that Billy needed to talk about his wife and the threat her state of mind represented to the well-being of their family. Now Maisie knew she needed to think. She turned back into the room and pulled the armchair closer to the gas fire.

Sitting down, she gazed into the flaming jets, reflecting upon Bobby Beale and his distress as his mother receded into herself. She wanted to support the family as much as she could, but knew her efforts must be balanced with an employer-employee relationship with Billy, and must not compromise his pride. But she kept going back to the child and his physical response to emotional disappointment. Of course, one couldn't draw too many conclusions from a single serendipitous event, but she could not help but reflect upon the days following recuperation from her own war wounds. Once well enough, she had felt drawn to return to nursing, and

because of the wounds suffered by her sweetheart in the same incident, she decided to work in a secure hospital caring for men whose
minds were ravaged by war.

Now, still staring into the rasping white-hot gas jets, she saw
once more the twisted bodies, muscular responses not to physical
injury but to mental anguish. She saw the eyes rolled back or staring into the distance, the constant weeping, the uncontrolled
reflexes. There were men who cried, those who could not eat, those
who would cause themselves injury, as if to feel, physically, the
wounds that lay in their souls. And there were those who would sit
alongside a wall, banging their heads against the hard surface
again and again and again while saliva streamed from their open
mouths, as if to mirror the cavernous hell they looked into from the
time consciousness claimed them in the morning, until nightfall,
when a sedative would send them into oblivion.

Maisie came to her feet and walked across the room to a chest
of small drawers that resembled something one might find in a
pharmacy. She opened a drawer and flicked through the cards until
she found the one she wanted. Tapping it against her hand, she
walked back to the desk, picked up the telephone receiver and
dialed one of two numbers listed on the card. She continued looking at the card until her call was answered. Only someone close to
her would have heard her whispering, *Please be there, please be there,
please be there . . .*

Maisie started when the telephone was answered. "Yes, is Dr.
Anthony Lawrence on duty today, by any slight chance? Oh, good.
May I speak to him, please?"

Maisie waited while the doctor was summoned, running the
telephone cord through her fingers as the seconds ticked by.

"Lawrence here."

"Oh, Dr. Lawrence, I'm glad I've caught you, especially on
Boxing Day. I don't know if you remember me, my name is Maisie

Dobbs—I was a staff nurse on Oak ward at the Clifton Hospital in 1918, then sister on Ash, and—"

"You're the one who left to go back to Cambridge. Sustained a nasty head wound in France, if I remember correctly."

"Yes, that's right."

"What can I do for you, Miss Dobbs?"

"It's rather difficult to explain on the telephone, but it is urgent, and confidential—would you spare me about twenty minutes this afternoon, say about half past one?"

"I have to leave to keep an appointment at approximately two o'clock, so . . . well, all right, yes, but perhaps you could come along to my office a bit earlier—one o'clock?"

"Yes, thank you, Dr. Lawrence. I look forward to seeing you at one."

"And you, Miss Dobbs."

Maisie smiled as she replaced the telephone receiver in its cradle. There was something that Anthony Lawrence and Robert MacFarlane had in common—they were both honest, no-nonsense men dedicated to their respective professions. But with Lawrence, now considered an expert in the treatment of psychological trauma, she had observed his compassion when they had both worked at Clifton, had seen him square up against pension authorities who tried to label mind-wounded men as malingerers, and had seen him spend hours with one man simply to try to get him to speak his own name out loud. She didn't hold out hope for a breakthrough in the meeting, but if a conversation with Lawrence helped to crack into the frozen lock on this case, it would be more than worth the time.

ARRIVING AT THE Princess Victoria Hospital by half-past twelve, Maisie went first to the porters' office, whereupon her name was verified and a porter picked up a hefty bunch of keys attached to a bracelet-sized brass ring and instructed Maisie to follow him. The hospital where Lawrence now worked was much like other institutional buildings constructed in the heyday of Victoria's reign, with a certain flourish to the red-brick design signifying the industrial and commercial wealth of her Empire and a legacy for the people. The wooden banister was buffed to a shine, as was every brass fixture and fitting, and as they made their way toward the doctors' offices, a lavender fragrance wafted from just-polished floorboards. Maisie wondered if Sheila Kennedy, the hospital's almost legendary matron, was still in charge—certainly the level of order suggested that she remained at the helm. It was an order that belied the name accorded the hospital by the locals, who referred to it as "the Bin." First built as an asylum, it had been turned over to military cases of neurasthenia and other neuroses during the war, as had the Clifton Hospital. Although many of those wartime patients had been discharged over the years, some after just a few weeks of care, the hospital remained more or less full, with an increasing number of patients starting to be admitted in recent years whose mental anguish was rooted in an inability to deal with the ordinary and extraordinary in everyday life, rather than battles on foreign soil.

Where there might have been double doors that flapped open in hospitals for the physically infirm, the porter at the Princess Victoria Hospital unlocked each door and took care to secure it again as they passed through. Soon they reached the upward spiraling back staircase flanked by cream-painted walls with maroon and cream tiles at the base. The staircase opened onto a corridor with offices on both sides, each with a heavy oak door. In this part of the hospital there was not the same level of security, though the porter remained with Maisie at all times. He stopped at the door to Dr. Lawrence's office and knocked, only opening the door when a voice boomed, "Come!"

"A Miss Dobbs to see you, sir."

"Ah, yes, of course—oh, and I'll see Miss Dobbs out again later when I leave."

"Right you are, sir—but she will have to sign out."

"Not to worry, I'll ensure she stops at the office."

The porter stepped aside to allow Maisie into the room, then touched his forehead as if in salute and backed out into the corridor while closing the door as he went.

Maisie shook hands with Dr. Lawrence. His hair was combed to either side from the same center parting he favored as a younger man, though it was now gray, and not the coal black Maisie remembered when they both worked at the Clifton Hospital. His moustache seemed longer than it had once been, and Maisie noticed the ends were waxed, giving him something of a haughty appearance, though she could not recall such a character flaw. He wore round wire spectacles, and his skin bore the lines and folds of one who worked instead of slept over many nights, suggesting that worry and concern were elements he could never escape. His collar was tight around the neck, his tie pulled almost to his Adam's apple, and he was still wearing his white coat, which indicated that he had just finished his rounds.

"Please, take a seat, Miss Dobbs." He held out his hand toward a plain wooden chair.

"It was good of you to see me, Dr. Lawrence, especially at such short notice."

"Think nothing of it, glad to assist, if I can. You were a fine nurse, Miss Dobbs. I always thought you might enter medical school yourself—women seem to be turning their hands to everything nowadays, don't they? I suppose it's a case of 'needs must,' what with so many remaining spinsters, eh? Certainly we don't have so many nurses leaving to get married, because there's not enough men to go around!" He smiled briefly as he took his seat on the other side of the desk. Maisie noticed that his chair had two flat and worn cushions on the seat, probably brought from home in an attempt at creating more comfort. "And what have you been doing with yourself since you returned to Cambridge?"

As Maisie began to describe her life over the past twelve years, she took account of her surroundings. Lawrence's office was neat and tidy, with books shelved according to subject matter and a general sense of order. It was something that Maisie had liked about the doctor, that sense of order. He always counted instruments before and after procedures, always made legible notes immediately following each patient consultation, while thoughts were still fresh in his mind. But that was ten years ago. Now, as she spoke, she noticed he absently corrected the pile of papers and files on his desk, making sure that each was only so far from the edge, and never more than two inches apart. He reached forward and lined up his pens and pencils, then took a clean handkerchief from his pocket and wiped it back and forth across the wood.

" . . . so, when Dr. Blanche retired, I took over the business and set up on my own. I now have an office in Fitzroy Square."

"Hmm, impressive, Miss Dobbs, impressive." He looked up and returned the handkerchief to his pocket, pulled out a fob-watch from his waistcoat and checked the time before replacing the watch once more. "Mind you, we always hate to lose a good nurse." He cleared his throat. "So, what can I do for you—you said it was urgent."

"Yes, indeed—and confidential."

"Of course. As you know, we're used to keeping a confidence here, so do bear that in mind."

Maisie sighed. "The fact is, I do not have very specific questions, but I am anxious to make a dent in a very serious investigation. Suffice it to say that I am working on secondment to Scotland Yard on a sensitive case."

"Go on . . ."

"Did you read about the man who committed suicide on Charlotte Street on Christmas Eve?"

"Yes, of course—nasty, nasty business. It's a miracle he didn't take anyone with him, though according to the press, there were wounded."

"Thankfully, nothing too serious—though, as we both know, to witness such a thing scars the mind forever."

Lawrence ran his fingers along the sides of a pile of folders as he nodded. "Indeed. I take it the suicide is connected with your current work?"

"It is a distinct, but not confirmed possibility. I believe the man had been a soldier in the war. I was walking along Charlotte Street at the time, and was close enough to him to see that one leg was crippled in some way, perhaps an inability to bend at the knee, while the other leg was either amputated at the knee, or bent backward. I would say there had been an amputation. His remains would support such a conclusion. And though I was not able to speak to him—had I been any closer, I might not be here today—I observed movement of the head and hands that might suggest a shell-shock case."

"How can I help?"

"Dr. Lawrence, there are a considerable number of men who have remained locked away in institutions since the war and who are still suffering from war neurosis. And many more have been discharged in recent years, possibly to relatives, or to live in a hostel. Our man may have been one of them."

Lawrence sighed, rubbing his chin. "Miss Dobbs, the truth regarding this country's treatment of its shell-shocked soldiers is harrowing, and to someone like yourself—trying to discover the dead man's identity, for I imagine that must be of prime importance—it presents an obstacle of considerable proportions." He sighed again, picked up a pen and put it down, ensuring that the writing instruments remained parallel to one another. "There were approximately, say, seventy-five to eighty thousand men diagnosed with shell-shock during and immediately after the war. These were the cases that could be easily identified, corroborated and signed off to return to England or to receive treatment." He looked at Maisie with eyes the color of slate that reminded her of the sky on a bitterly cold day. "In my estimation—and I could be taken to task by the authorities for such comments, so please reflect upon this conversation with care—the numbers of shell-shocked men ran into the hundreds of thousands. And, arguably, there is no man"—he held Maisie's eyes with his own—"or woman, who returned from Flanders unscathed in the mind."

"I know."

"Yes, you do. However, I wonder if you know what pressures were brought to bear on doctors during and after the war?" He did not wait for an answer before continuing. "Not only were we pressed to declare a man fit for duty as soon as any physical wounds were healed, but in all but the most obvious cases—and here's my personal experience—our instructions, perhaps to send a man to a secure institution for additional care, were overruled by senior military staff who would label a man as a lazy item, or with low moral fiber. And off they would be sent, back onto the battlefield with their minds half destroyed." He shrugged. "Of course, there was another reason—pensions. If a man is physically wounded in battle, there is a small pension allowance. With increasing numbers of men suffering mentally from the effects of war, the government was becoming queasier and queasier about having to pay pensions it would never be able to afford—so those men were discharged at the earliest possible opportunity, because for many, there was no bleeding, no physical wound or scarring. Miss Dobbs, if you haven't realized it already, you must be aware that you are looking for a needle in a haystack. You could go through every record of every patient suffering from neurasthenia, war neurosis, melancholia and hysteria, and you will have touched only the tip of the iceberg."

"You are very frank, Dr. Lawrence."

"For every man on our wards who will never see the outside of an institution, there are five, six, seven out there"—he pointed at the window—"who are in a cell in their mind. They are trying to find work, trying to live from one day to the next. Some might have families or children, but they are ticking away inside, so that one day, when the baby wails in a certain way, the man will end up cowering in the corner or, worse, inflicting harm. And some take a deep breath every day, working, living, eating, breathing, holding all the components of life together in a vise-like grip so that no one will ever know they are broken as much as if their bodies had been crushed."

"I'm sorry if—"

Lawrence held up one hand. "Please, don't. You came to ask a question or two and you got more than you bargained for." He reached for a folder, taking care to pull it toward him without disturbing the rest of the pile. He tapped the top of the folder. "This is a collection of letters from the powers-that-be instructing me to decrease numbers of soldiers from the war still held here. They are to be sent out into the raw reality of London in the midst of winter, and with no prospects of work or any sort of support. Where will they go? Who will care for them? This is the sort of battle I have on my hands—now everyone wants to forget the war."

Maisie nodded. "Dr. Lawrence, you have been most kind to spare me so much of your time. However, I wonder if I can just ask one or two questions. Are there any behaviors common among men who are discharged? Do they remain close to the hospital? Do they go further afield?" She breathed deeply. "You see—and it's my turn to remind you of my need for confidentiality now—to give you more of an idea of the situation, there has been a threat received by a high-ranking government official. While others are working to see if the demands of the person who issued the threat could be met in some way that might placate him and give us time, my task is to try to find him. I have said the words *needle in a haystack* myself—I know from my war experience and my work at the Clifton how difficult that task might be. But I must continue, and in a short time follow any lead that presents itself to me. So, clutching at straws—if I take a gamble and assume the man who took his life on Christmas Eve was released from a secure institution at some point in the past couple of years, how might I find him?"

Lawrence replaced the folder and ran his fingers along the sides once more to align the pile. "You could start with the pensions people, but I can tell you now, that door is indubitably locked shut. I will try to gain permission for you to view the records held here of former patients. And I can give you an introduction to other secure hospitals. When people leave an institution—be it a hospital or prison—there is sometimes a need to retain a sort of relationship with that place. They might find digs with a view of the hospital chimneys, they might need to come back for outpatient examinations or medication. They might just want to know that the nest, even if it was the most dreadful place they had ever known, is still close. But that's just my opinion. My peers might suggest otherwise."

Maisie gathered up her gloves and scarf. "Thank you, Dr. Lawrence." She looked at the clock on the wall. "I had better be off now." She took a card from her black document case and put it on the desk in front of Lawrence, who had pushed back his chair. "Please send word as soon as you have permission for me to view the records. I hate to say this, but to gain informal access to the files would be so much better than having a warrant issued. I am sure

Matron would walk on hot coals rather than have that sort of thing going on in her hospital."

Lawrence laughed. "I will be in touch. Now then, I'd better escort you to the porters' office."

As they made their way down the staircase, Lawrence and Maisie spoke of times past, of improvements to the Clifton Hospital since she relinquished her nursing position, and of the doctor's children, who were now grown. He unlocked doors and locked them again as they passed through the lower corridors, and soon they had reached the entrance.

"Here we are." Lawrence stopped alongside the porters' office and knocked on the door. "Please let me know if I can be of any further assistance to you, Miss Dobbs."

Maisie shook his proffered hand, and turned to the porter who had just opened the door.

"Will you be back today, Dr. Lawrence?" The porter inquired, while holding the ledger for Maisie to sign out.

"Yes I will," replied the doctor. "See that Miss Dobbs doesn't have to wait too long for a taxi-cab, there's a good chap, Croucher."

"Right you are, Dr. Lawrence. I'll make sure she gets on her way." He turned to Maisie and smiled.

FOUR

The man opened his eyes and waited for a moment or two while sleep ebbed from his mind, in the way that the sea recedes from the shore, going back a little, then returning, going back, then returning. It was in the first few seconds of waking that he sometimes panicked and was paralyzed by fear, for there were times when he took to his bed, not because it was night and therefore time to rest, but because being awake—even in daytime—was more than he could bear. His body was always chilled, and though the room was dry enough, his clothes felt damp, and his toes were bitten with cold. He pulled the blanket up over his coat-clad body and closed his eyes, smacking his lips as if to soothe his jaw so that sleep would come again and he could be delivered from his waking nightmares, which always seemed worse than those inflicted upon him in slumber. There were times when he woke and held his breath, for he couldn't remember why he was steeped in melancholy, why his heart ached and his body hurt. Then the pictures began to play in his mind's eye again, and the sounds tormented him so that he would clutch his head as if to rip it from his shoulders. Those were the times when he would have welcomed death, if only to be cast free.

Once more he came to, rubbing his hand across his stubbled chin, and pressing his fingers to his tired, sunken eyes. He rolled over to bring the clock on the mantelpiece into focus. It was nearly time. The man sat up and, when he'd garnered strength enough, swung his legs over the side of the narrow, iron-framed bed, and stood, reaching for his stick. He wavered for a moment, as if he might fall back, then shuffled toward a wireless set on the table. He switched it on. First the pips, signifying the hour, then the news.

He listened, his head to one side, close to the wireless. Nothing. Nothing for him. There was no news indicating that he had been heard. No surprise announcements telling of handouts coming from Westminster, no word of special festive season meetings to discuss the plight of those who had given all for their country, no acknowledgment of the suffering of those who had nothing. His throat was dry in the way that thirst came after daytime sleep, so he limped toward the stove, lifted the kettle to see if there was sufficient water, and put it down on the gas-ring, which he ignited with a match. *It was to be expected,* he thought, as he stood back, considering, again, the substances he'd employed earlier, endeavoring to be as dexterous as he had been in the past, lest he make a mistake. Of course, he had cleaned his laboratory, such as it was, but you never could be too careful. There was a right way to do things, and in his work, he did things as they should be done. He stuck to the rules.

He waited for the kettle to come to the boil, then poured the scalding liquid into the mush of soggy leaves left in the pot from this morning's tea. With the weak but hot brew in hand, he sat at the table and pulled his diary toward him. He sipped the tea, put the chipped cup to one side, and opened the book to a clean page.

I am not heard. I am not taken seriously. I thought the Dobbs woman might believe me, if she were summoned. I saw the police go to her premises, so I know they have the letter.

He paused, then began writing again.

There was concern in her eyes when she walked toward Ian. Not pity, not disgust, and she did not cross to the other side of the road to escape the futility of him. She showed

He tapped the pencil on the table, then flinched at the sound.

She showed care. That is all I have asked for, these many years, that people are concerned, and that in their actions, they demonstrate care. It occurred to me that the woman did not wait for someone else to approach Ian. She did not ignore him. She walked toward him without looking in another direction. I noticed that. I have come to notice that people do not look at the Ians of this world, but instead turn their heads here and there.

The man paused and rubbed his hand across his chest, then took several breaths. Not deep breaths, because the air would scald his lungs with its coldness, which in turn would cause him to cough. And if he coughed, he might not stop and then the blood would come. He tempered the urge to gag, calmed his body, then began writing once more.

Oh, stupid boy. He should have listened to me, he would not have had to wait long, not now, not now when I have them almost where I want them. "Cry havoc and let slip the dogs of war." Yes, let them slip, poor unwanted beasts.

*   *   *

MAISIE PAID the taxi-cab driver and dashed across the square just as Stratton's Invicta pulled up outside her office.

"Blast!" She had wanted to be alone for a while to consider the meeting with Dr. Lawrence before having to go back to Scotland Yard and another encounter with MacFarlane.

"Ready?" said Stratton, as she approached the vehicle.

"Yes—and no. I would have liked more time before being called to report on my activities today."

"I agree, but let's face it, at least we know which side you're on."

Maisie rolled her eyes and shook her head. "I am really growing tired of this innuendo due to the fact that my name was mentioned in the letter. MacFarlane has questioned me and indicated his trust in me. I have told you all that I believe the threats should be taken seriously, so I would be obliged if you—and Colm Darby or anyone else who chooses to—would just cease baiting me. You know which side I'm on."

Stratton was taken aback by the strength of Maisie's response. "I apologize if I offended you, Miss Dobbs. My comment was meant to be taken lightly, given that we find ourselves in a troubling situation—I don't know about you, but I hardly made any headway today."

"I have had better days," Maisie conceded, sighing. "So I'm sorry if I was quick on the defensive. Mind you, I've chipped away at one avenue that might be promising—the possibility that the suicide was a soldier suffering from some level of traumatic neurosis."

Stratton shook his head. "I can't believe we've been unable to give a name to the dead man, unable to identify him. We've talked to the shopkeepers, residents—no one knows him, and he's not a regular."

"Known unto God." Maisie spoke the words softly, as she saw the man in her mind's eye again.

"I beg your pardon?"

"Oh, I'm sorry, Inspector. I said, 'Known unto God.' That's what it says on the new gravestones for unidentified soldiers buried in France, 'A Soldier of the Great War, Known unto God.'"

"Well, we'd better know something soon, or MacFarlane will be in high dudgeon."

"I can imagine."

"OH, FOR PITY'S SAKE! Anyone would think we'd all just come in off the beat. Two days and we still don't know that poor bugger's name." MacFarlane made no concessions to the fact that there was a woman in the room, and gave weight to his voice with a thump on the table with his right hand.

Maisie did not flinch, though Stratton moved on his chair in a way that revealed his discomfort. *He'd better get used to this if he wants to work with MacFarlane by spring,* thought Maisie.

"Miss Dobbs, perhaps you could enlighten me as to your activities this afternoon?"

"Of course, Detective Chief Superintendent MacFarlane."

MacFarlane raised an eyebrow as she came to her feet and pulled out a roll of wallpaper and several tacks from her document case. She unfurled the paper, held it to the wall and proceeded to pin the paper in place.

"If I wanted a decorator, I might have called one in, Miss Dobbs."

"Bear with me, please." She reached into her case and removed several thick wax crayons, keeping one and placing the others on the table, then turned her attention to the men. "My assistant and I use this as one of several means to follow developments in a case. It provides a map, if you will, of our progress, and no thought, idea or speculative hunch is ever considered too foolhardy or insignificant to record. We add to it as we proceed and it has proven useful in helping us to identify links, clues and opportunities that might not otherwise have been visible with the usual linear note-taking."

"We tend to prefer facts."

"This may sound contradictory," said Maisie, "but I do not think we have the time to entertain only firm facts—we have to broaden our canvas, in the short term at least."

MacFarlane acquiesced. "Continue broadening the canvas, Miss Dobbs."

Maisie paused, looking at each man in turn. If she was to work as part of a crew rather than alone, she would ensure that she was not only listened to, but heard. And she did not care to be under surveillance.

"Given our speculation that the Charlotte Street suicide was a soldier with rather serious wounds, I—"

"Serious?" queried MacFarlane. "He obviously walked to the place where he died. Can that be called serious?"

"Sir, as we believe, the man had an amputation and was also likely lame in his other leg, plus he might well have suffered exposure to chlorine or mustard gas. To say nothing of war trauma. I would say those wounds constitute 'serious.' I would add, further, that in becoming used to seeing those who have suffered in the war, we have also become somewhat immune to their plight. As we now know, contrary to the belief of military superiors, it takes more than fresh air and a week in the country to cure a man before we pack him off again into battle or, in this case, the skirmish of everyday society."

"Point taken. Go on, Miss Dobbs."

"Thank you." Maisie began writing on the strip of wallpaper. "So, I called on Dr. Anthony Lawrence, one of the country's leading experts in the care of those who remain sufficiently unstable as to warrant remaining in hospital care."

"Is that a nice way of saying 'locked up'?"

"Having been a nurse in a secure hospital and caring for men with shell-shock, I try to retain a level of respect, Detective Chief Superintendent. But yes, they are locked up. They require a degree of supervision that is not to be found in the home—if, of course, there is a home to go to. Now then, back to my meeting with Dr. Lawrence—I wanted to discover more about the habits of those who have been released. In short, I wanted to know if there was something about either the man in Charlotte Street or the letter-writer that would indicate they had been released from a hospital recently, and were perhaps feeling abandoned, at sea, so to speak. I confess, it was a stab in the dark, but I had to start somewhere."

"We're all stabbing in the dark." MacFarlane reached for a red wax crayon from the jar on the table and began to twirl it around in his fingers, as if it were a baton. "And your stab was as good as any. Did you come away with anything?"

Maisie shook her head. "Precious little, to tell you the truth. Dr. Lawrence made the point that the number of men so afflicted is far beyond official tallies. In addition, regression following release from hospital could happen at any time—one month, one year, five years."

"So what's your next move?"

"I'm not sure. However, I would appreciate it if I could report back to you in a less regimented fashion. Coming back here has deprived me of valuable time. My schedule is not prescriptive. Might I instead telephone Detective Inspector Stratton at a given time each day?"

MacFarlane looked at the other men. "Richard? Colm?"

Both nodded their accord.

"Right you are, Miss Dobbs."

Maisie thanked the men and returned to her seat. She had at least skirted the question of her next move, though she realized that MacFarlane might address the question again. In the meantime, she would do all she could to keep her next moves to herself. She might be one of a team, but she also knew she made greater headway when left to her own devices and following her own direction along the way.

Stratton was next. Taking up a wide black crayon he turned to the wallpaper. "I feel like a teacher at the blackboard."

"Don't tempt me." MacFarlane grinned, then waved his hand for Stratton to continue.

"Very straightforward—continued questioning of shop-keepers along Charlotte Street, working back to Oxford Street, though we were hampered by the shops not being open today, so we had to locate proprietors and so forth. We're hoping to retrace the dead man's movements. Of course, we have to entertain the possibility that these two events have no relationship one to the other, in which case, all we will find, eventually, is the deceased's name."

"Anything else?"

"We've located a woman who works at Bourne and Hollingsworth, who says she saw a man bearing the deceased's description alighting from the number thirty-six bus. She travels in from Camberwell and says she always sits in the same place close to the door and cannot remember him getting on the bus, so he must have got on anywhere from, say, Lewisham to Camberwell. We'll have men at bus stops along the number thirty-six route on Monday, at a time coinciding with the commuting habits of the woman. We'll question people along the way to see if anyone recalls seeing the man on Christmas Eve."

Maisie cleared her throat, then spoke directly to MacFarlane. "The man who made the threat is expecting a response first thing tomorrow morning. We seem to have forgotten that the threat stands. Will there be some announcement from the Home Office, perhaps on the wireless, by way of placating this person? Or are we waiting to see whether he is serious?"

"I'm sorry to say that, given our lack of headway, Miss Dobbs, we are presently in a wait-and-see situation."

"I don't think we'll be waiting long."

"Aye, I think you're right, as much as I hope you're wrong." He sighed, then motioned to Stratton. "See that Miss Dobbs is escorted home, Stratton. And settle upon a time to speak to each other tomorrow. I know it's a Sunday, but I can't see the PM making any offers as a result of the letter, so we'll still be on the case, come what may. The PM, by the way, has cut short the festive season with his family, and returned from Chequers." He turned to Maisie. "Do not rule out the possibility that we may have to convene here as a matter of urgency at any time over the next couple of days. In the meantime, you are on your own, but you are on our clock."

Maisie held out her hand to MacFarlane. "I'll be in touch, Detective Chief Superintendent."

STRATTON ESCORTED MAISIE home in the Invicta. When the vehicle pulled up yards from the main entrance to the block of flats in Pimlico, Maisie turned to Stratton.

"I can walk from here, Inspector."

"Are you sure?"

"The main door is just along this path, so if you wish, you can sit here to ensure I go in without being accosted."

"I'll do that." Stratton opened the door and stepped from the vehicle, then held out his hand to assist Maisie. "And let's not forget your luggage," he added, reaching back into the motor car.

"Thank you, Inspector." Maisie took the brown leather suitcase.

"May I suggest I telephone your office at Scotland Yard tomorrow—certainly it will not be before six o'clock in the evening."

"And at what time should I send out the cavalry, if I do not have word from you?"

"You'll hear by eight, Inspector—how does that sound?"

"Perfectly acceptable. May I ask what your next move will be?"

Maisie began to turn toward the modern building with glass doors leading to the flats within. "To be perfectly honest with you, I'm not sure yet. But I know it will involve as much speculation as detection."

"I'll be out with my men knocking on doors between Lewisham and Camberwell tomorrow—and I'll be in touch if there's news."

Maisie bid good-bye, waving from inside the small foyer before entering her flat. The radiators had been left on low, yet she could still see her breath condense in the air before her. She was tired and wanted nothing more than to go to bed, so without removing her coat, she took her suitcase into the bedroom and then went into the kitchen to put on the kettle for a hot water bottle.

Once settled under the covers, sleep did not come as she had hoped, and instead Maisie lay awake listening to the sounds of the night. Foghorns up and down the river, a motor car in the distance. It was a quiet night, a Boxing Day night. Soon the year would be done, soon it would be 1932. And as she edged her way into sleep, Maisie wondered if there would be any developments in the case, come morning. Another letter, perhaps? Or would the threat be revealed as a hoax, with no more said and her involvement with MacFarlane and Special Branch at an end? But as she shivered, despite the soothing hot water bottle held close, she had a distinct feeling that there would be more news on the morrow, and it would not be good.

December 27th, 1931

Billy was at his desk when Maisie arrived at the office the following morning. She was surprised to see him, and could not help but notice that he seemed even more drained than he had the day before.

"Billy, what are you doing here on a Sunday? You don't have to give up your Sunday just because I'm working on an urgent case."

"Well, I thought you might need a hand, and what with one thing and another . . ." He placed some papers in a folder, and shrugged.

Maisie thought it best not to press the point, and suspected that the situation at home might have deteriorated even more. She began talking about the case while removing her coat, hat and gloves.

"Billy, do you remember the coster who came to my aid in Charlotte Street on Christmas Eve?"

"I could recognize him in a crowd, if that's what you mean. Don't know the man's name—I was too worried about you, Miss, to tell you the truth. Mind you, I reckon I could find him, if that's what you want."

"Yes, that's exactly what I want. He may have seen the dead man before, know who he is, or at least have some nugget of information for us."

"Come to think of it, when I went back to find your document case, I don't recall seeing him again. Mind you, the police were moving people on, and he did say something about getting his horse out of there, that she was good and solid, but he didn't want to push it because even though she'd not bolted when the bomb went off, she was on her toes and a bit skittish."

"Do you think there will be anyone down at the market this morning? I know it's a Sunday, but there's sometimes someone around, a caretaker or watchman, someone who might know the man we're looking for." She sat down behind her desk.

"Tell you what, I'll nip down and have a look around. As you say, there might be a caretaker or someone like that. Could even be a copper on the beat who can put a name to the face, if you know what I mean."

Billy turned to gather his overcoat from the hook behind the door, continuing the conversation as he went. "I reckon I'll be back by twelve, then get on with that Barker case. Will you be here, Miss?"

"Probably not. I have a distinct feeling that I'll be talking to MacFarlane today—he's the Special Branch chappie I told you about. But in the meantime, I think I'm going to have to engage in speculation simply to get some names in the hat of people who might have sent the threatening letter."

"How will you do that?"

"By coming up with a template of the kind of person who would do such a thing—if they are serious. And we've assumed some link to the Charlotte Street suicide, as you know."

"Why is that, Miss? Why do you think they're connected?"

"That's a good question, Billy—and it comes down to me. The letter mentioned me by name, and the fact that it came hot on the heels of my being seen to approach a man who then killed himself in a very visible manner, as if to make some sort of point, has drawn the two together."

"Makes sense," Billy continued as he wound a scarf around his neck. "So what kind of person do you think he is?"

"That he has made a threat at all indicates a level of disengagement with everyday life. He's also drawn attention to the plight of old soldiers and wants to see something done about their situation. We know there are so many still suffering with their war wounds at a time when a job is hard to find for those sound in mind and body, but not everyone will be pressed to make a threat in such a way."

"You see that on the streets, Miss, men limping from one line to another waiting for work, but I reckon most people just moan to their mates, their missus, or they join one of them associations, you know, to try to get something changed."

"But this suffering has been going on for some years, yet this person has only just made his move. Of course, he could have been simmering for a long while, but at the same time I am going to stick my neck out and assume—at this stage, in any case—that the person we are seeking is a man who has either lost the support of a family or was released from an institution in the past two years. Frankly, if it's the former, it makes the job nigh on impossible, but if it's the latter, I might at least be able to get hold of some names."

"Still looking at a lot of people, though."

"I'll narrow it down to London—Dr. Lawrence gave me enough information to suggest that there is cause for a man to linger in the region of the hospital, unless he had a home to go to in another area." Maisie paused, slipping the cap of her fountain pen on and off as she considered her plan for the day. "The truth is, Billy, that if the man does carry out his threat, if there is an 'or else,' it might give us more information to work with. And I have avoided coming back to the fact that he mentioned me by name. Why? How does he know me?"

"Do you think he might be a danger to you, because if that's the case—"

Maisie looked at Billy, who stood in front of her desk as if wavering between leaving her alone and remaining with her. She leaned back in her chair.

"I didn't want to say anything, but on the day of the suicide, as we were leaving Charlotte Street with Detective Inspector Stratton, I had a distinct feeling that I was being watched."

Billy leaned forward. "And I didn't want to say anything either, Miss, but I kept looking back, something was making me shudder. I put it down to the noise, you know, reminding me of being back there, in the war, but it felt right strange, make no mistake."

"I have to entertain the possibility that we were followed back to the square, and that I may have been followed since. And there's something else."

"What's that, Miss?"

"People in this situation, people who make threats, or carry them out, have also been known to harbor a desire to be seen, to be apprehended. They want to be caught so that they can be heard. There's something about that attention."

"Not another one hiding in plain sight, Miss. We seem to get our share of those, don't we?"

"I don't know if he's in plain sight, but he may be closer than we think. In the meantime, I am going to prepare my template and then see if I can fill it with a few names."

"And I'll be off down to the market."

"Keep your eyes and ears sharp, won't you?"

MAISIE WORKED ON after Billy left. She had deliberately not asked about Doreen. If she inquired each day, it might give the impression that she was interfering in the family's domestic affairs. Even though she had come to know the Beales well and bore a great affection for them, on this occasion Billy's pride made it difficult to reach out a helping hand. It seemed to her that, in his manner, Billy seemed to think she had done enough for them already. Nonetheless, she worried about them, and particularly about Doreen's melancholia, which she realized was having an untoward effect on the children. Maisie knew only too well that the path of grief could not be scripted and was one taken alone, even if one grieved with family.

At half-past eleven the telephone rang, and before Maisie could give the number, Billy began speaking.

"Miss, I don't know if this is important, I mean, I don't think the police know about this, but it seemed a bit funny to me."

"What's that, Billy?"

"I was having a bit of a chat with this bloke I know who works down here at the market. Talk about having a stroke of luck—turns out he had a bit of a row with the wife and came over to the market for some peace and quiet, that's how I came to get talking to him. Anyway, his son works down at Battersea Dogs and Cats Home, a bit of a job on the side. Turns out that when he goes in to feed them this morning, in this one section six of the dogs were dead. He said he'd never seen anything like it—this stuff like beaten egg whites coming from their mouths, and their eyes popping out of their heads. They'd died gasping for air and choking on their own blood. Terrible sight it was for the poor young fella."

"What's happened since, do you know?"

"Apparently, they've got the vet in there today looking at the bodies, just in case it's a disease that spreads. But when he told me about it, you know what it put me in a mind of?"

Maisie felt her body shudder with cold. "I know what you're going to say, Billy—chlorine gas."

"I knew you'd know. You'd've seen it, eh? Chlorine gas."

"Stay right where you are—I'll pick you up at Covent Garden tube in twenty minutes. We'll go straight to Battersea and see if we can talk to anyone there. I want to find out how someone might get in after they're closed—and if they were open on Boxing Day. They might have been—there always seem to be more strays on the street at this time of year."

"If it is what we think it is, that'd be terrible, wouldn't it? I mean, not just for the dogs, but because it means that someone can do this sort of thing. It could be people next, couldn't it?"

"I know."

"Oh, and Miss—"

"Yes?"

"The coster—name of Bert Shorter. Got the name of the pub where he drinks, down the Old Kent Road."

"Good work. Now then—I'm on my way. See you at the tube, on the Long Acre side."

FIVE

"Miss Dobbs and Mr. Beale?" The smell of disinfectant and bleach wafted out of the room where surgical procedures were performed, as the veterinary surgeon closed the door behind him, still clutching a towel with which he continued to wipe his hands.

"Yes, thank you for seeing us, Mr. Hodges," said Maisie.

"I can't think why you might be interested in our six deceased dogs." He threw the towel into a basket at the side of the door.

Maisie stepped forward. "We heard that there were untoward symptoms prior to death, and—in confidence—given the nature of my work, I was interested, from a purely professional standpoint, you understand, as I explained to the administration clerk. The symptoms seem to mimic a condition I've seen before, so I was curious—"

"That's interesting, because they mimic something I've seen before. I was in the Royal Veterinary Corps during the war and one of the most terrible things I ever encountered was the effect of poisonous gas on both man and beast. In terms of canine sickness, I just can't imagine what disease or virus would mimic those markers for chlorine gas."

"Then that's what you're looking at—swollen lungs, fluid, the albumen-like saliva and severe blistering?"

"That's it."

"May I see a specimen, Mr. Hodges?"

"Well, it's not regular, but . . . " he faltered, rubbing his chin. "Oh, all right. I understand you've just made a nice contribution to our establishment here, so I should say it would be in order for you to come in."

"I'll stay here, Miss, if you don't mind."

"That's all right, Billy." Maisie turned to the veterinary surgeon. "Shall we?"

The spaniel-like mongrel of a dog lay on the cold metal operating table, its chest open to reveal the viscera. The head lay to one side and, crusted around blistered lips, a foamy substance had dribbled from the carcass to the table. The veterinary surgeon drew Maisie's attention to the lungs, pointing with a scalpel.

"I don't know how familiar you are with the physiology of the average canine, but the lungs here are swollen to about four times the normal size, an expansion due to the intense pressure of fluid building up as a response to inflammation and blistering. The dog was doing its damnedest to suck in air and stay alive. Now, see here"—he indicated where the incision extended to the base of the throat—"the blistering is closing off the windpipe."

"Just as it did with soldiers in the war." She looked up at Hodges. "I was a nurse in France, so I've seen my fair share of gas cases."

"Yes, of course, you would have." He set down the scalpel, pulled on a pair of rubber gloves, lifted the animal's head with one hand, and pulled out the tongue with the other. "And here's the blistering again—froth and pus-filled." With gentle respect he rested the head on the table once more, stroked an ear, then walked to a sink to remove the gloves and wash his hands, leaning forward and lathering the soap to cleanse every crevice in his skin. "I just wish I knew what had caused it. Never seen anything like it, not the usual sort of thing we come across here—and we have some poorly animals in this establishment. No, this is not your usual kettle of fish."

"I realize this question might elicit some concern, which is why I have taken care to ensure your confidentiality. Can you test to confirm exposure to gas?"

"To tell you the truth, in some ways, I don't need to—at the moment I'm trying to find some evidence to indicate it wasn't, because my first thought was, 'Bloody hell, they've been gassed!' Then I pulled myself together and began searching for another cause, because I can think of no good reason why anyone would want to gas a poor innocent creature, and how would they gain access?" Hodges sighed. "But the truth is that I *know* this has been caused by chlorine gas and, yes, though I can test to corroborate my suspicions, I am confident of the outcome."

Maisie nodded. "But you're right, you must confirm before you reach a conclusion."

"And who would do this? Who would take leave of his senses and punish an animal in this way—especially with a weapon of war—and a particularly nasty one at that. This is a place where abandoned dogs and cats are supposed to find shelter and, we hope, a good home, eventually." Hodges seemed thoughtful for a moment as he looked at the dog splayed out on the table. "The sad thing is that so many of our dogs are enlisted for military purposes. A good many served in the last war, you know, carrying messages, first-aid packs, patrolling, and generally keeping up morale. I'd love to get my hands on whoever's responsible."

Maisie looked up at the veterinary surgeon, the pained

expression revealed in the lines around his eyes, and touched him on the sleeve. "Don't worry, I'll do that for you. I'll find out who did this. It's best to do all you can not to let news of these deaths travel too far, and in the meantime continue with your tests. I hope you don't mind me asking if, just for now, you wouldn't mind making up an ailment that would result in similar symptoms."

"Of course, I can see your point. I should probably tell the police," said Hodges as he pulled a sheet across the spaniel's carcass.

"I'll inform them, Mr. Hodges. Although I generally work independently, I am currently seconded to Scotland Yard for a period of time." She reached into her pocket and pulled out a card. "Here's my card. You can reach me at this telephone number if you have any more observations you think might interest me, and if I am not there, you can send a postcard or telegram to my address. And please, remember that this must be held in tightest confidence."

Hodges regarded Maisie once more, tapping the card on the edge of the table. "If a man could do this to a dog, he might do this to a human being, mightn't he? Is that at the heart of your interest?"

"I should hope it doesn't come to that. Scotland Yard has some of its best detectives on this case, and no doubt you will be hearing from them in due course after I've made my report." Maisie turned to leave. "Keep this to yourself, Mr. Hodges. London can be a desperate sort of place at the best of times—we don't want to make it more so."

"Don't worry, I'll keep mum."

"SMELLY OLD GAFF, THAT," said Billy as they left the dogs' home.

"Well, they do a good job there, and they do their best."

"I must say, it's something I wonder about, you know, when there's so many people wanting for a good meal in this country and here they are, looking after dogs and cats."

They walked along the street toward Maisie's motor car, both wearing winter coats, hats and scarves to keep the cold wind at bay. "It may seem that way, I agree—" Maisie was about to go on, then checked herself. She wanted to say she believed that it was in the act of taking care of animals and showing respect for all life—especially when in need of support ourselves—that a certain dignity is sustained, a self-respect so often compromised in troubled times. But she knew it was not the time to voice such sentiments, especially to a man who walked through the slums of London to get to work each day, and who was himself so deeply troubled. She shrugged. "Well, I suppose it comes down to a belief that people who care for animals are more likely to be compassionate toward their fellow human beings. Something like that."

"Yeah, which doesn't say much for whoever killed them dogs, does it?"

"I'm not sure what it says, Billy."

"I mean, I know you've always said that inside the villain is a victim, but sometimes I find that hard to swallow, y'know?"

Maisie nodded. "I've only come across the truly evil on two occasions, while working for Dr. Blanche. And there's something in the person's eyes, as if they were born with it, as if it were a crippling disease and not something caused as a result of experience."

"You make me shiver, Miss."

"It should make us all shiver. I would venture to say that there is no overcoming that sort of ill character."

"But what about the rest, what about the others who do terrible things, how come they aren't evil, I mean, what caused them to be like that?"

Maisie shrugged and stopped for a moment. "It's different in each case, but if you go back to the root, I would venture to say it has to do with care. Those people don't feel cared for, don't feel enfranchised. In many cases they are simply invisible. But that's only my opinion, not the last word on the matter." She stamped her feet. "Come on, let's get going. It's freezing!"

Maisie dropped Billy at Covent Garden tube station once more. She instructed him to work on finding Bert Shorter, adding that she would see him at the office later. In the meantime, she planned to return to Fitzroy Square and place a telephone call to Stratton, and if he was not available, she would ask for MacFarlane. And she would telephone Maurice Blanche. Yes, she wanted to speak to Maurice now because she needed a door opened to a very locked establishment. She could think of no other place to discover how a civilian might procure chlorine gas or, indeed, garner the skills to handle such a substance, than the place she had heard much about but never been near: Mulberry Point, the military testing laboratories for chemical weaponry, close to the village of Little Mulberry in Berkshire.

"MAURICE?"

"Maisie—how lovely to hear from you. I am sorry you were not able to remain at Chelstone long enough to come and see me. Your father tells me that you were summoned by our friends at Scotland Yard early yesterday morning."

"Yes, that's right. Christmas seems weeks ago already. I'll come over to the Dower House next time, I promise."

"I will hold you to your word. Now then, I have a sense that you have not telephoned to speak of missing me during the festive season—what can I do for you?"

"Maurice, do you have any contacts at Mulberry Point?"

There was a moment's silence on the line.

"Their work is most secret, Maisie. And given the nature of that work, I am now concerned upon hearing of your need to speak to someone at the laboratories."

"It is urgent, Maurice. I am in pursuit of—and I think it's fair to say this—a most volatile person, and one who has access to some of the more chilling weaponry."

"Is there a threat to the general population?"

"Yes, in all honesty, I believe there is, though I cannot gauge the level of that threat."

Maisie knew that, if she were with Maurice, she would see him reaching for his pipe and tapping it on the chimney breast alongside his favorite wingback chair. He would place the pipe in his lap, then with his free hand lean toward the pipe stand again and lift his tobacco pouch. He continued to speak, even though, as she well knew, he was filling the bowl of his pipe, readying to light it as soon as the telephone call ended.

"Indeed. I see your dilemma. In that case, you should telephone the University of Oxford and speak to Professor John Gale. He's both a chemist and a physicist. He also has a relationship—yes, that's the best word to describe it—with Mulberry Point, and would keep counsel regarding your conversation. He was involved with the Special Brigades during the war." Maurice cleared his throat. "Following the first chlorine gas attacks by the Germans, the military virtually plundered the universities of engineers and physicists, effectively requisitioning brains and research to not only find an antidote, but to develop their own weapons. Britain was woefully behind the enemy in terms of research at the time. John—we are old friends—also has links to Imperial Chemical Industries. As you know, they were founded about five or six years ago, to some extent on the back of our experiences with the use of chemicals on the battlefield."

"Thank you, Maurice. May I use your name as an introduction to Professor Gale?"

"I will telephone him myself as soon as we are finished, so that he expects your call."

"Thank you, again."

"One more thing—do take care. If this man, whoever he is, has enough knowledge to use gas, he may go further. Take every precaution when close to suspects and wherever the man you are pursuing has left his mark. Keep your hands and arms covered, use a mask—as if you were back in the operating theater, Maisie."

"Not to worry, Maurice. I remember only too well the precautions we had to take. I'll be careful."

"MACFARLANE!" the voice was brusque, and Maisie imagined the Detective Chief Superintendent answering his telephone in haste while barking orders to a subordinate.

"This is Maisie Dobbs."

"Ah, Miss Dobbs." His tone softened. "What have you got for me?"

"I believe it's something important, Detective Chief Superintendent—and I couldn't reach Detective Inspector Stratton."

"Fire away."

Maisie described the lead via Billy's contact, and her visit to Battersea Dogs and Cats Home. She recounted the discussion with Dr. Hodges, and her own observations when confronted with the carcass of the deceased dog.

"And there's no other explanation for the dogs to have died in this way?"

"Dr. Hodges is testing now, but he is convinced it's either chlorine gas or something similar. He was in the Royal Veterinary Corps in France, so he knows what he's seeing. And I've seen it too, when I was a nurse, though obviously I am not au fait with the insides of a dog."

"Not 'au fait,' eh?"

Though Maisie shook her head at the hint of sarcasm, she sensed that it was spoken in jest, a gentle teasing, perhaps, to lessen the tension.

"And you've instructed Hodges not to speak of this to anyone."

"I asked him to think up a dog's disease that has similar symptoms."

"Good. Right then, I'll get down there straightaway. No army of blue, just me and a sergeant in the first instance. Can you come to the Yard at six-ish?"

Maisie looked at the clock on the mantelpiece. "Yes, though I have to place some telephone calls. I have the name of someone who can advise me further on the procurement of such chemicals. It might also help in identifying the type of person we're after."

"We're after a wicked bastard, Maisie."

Maisie was taken aback. Was he testing her with his language and his manner, trying to see whether she could be "one of the boys," able to work with Special Branch? More to the point, would he have been so blunt with Maurice, who demanded and received the utmost regard from Scotland Yard?

She sighed. If she countered to protect her opinion, she might be seen as thin-skinned—yet she could not let the retort go without comment. "You know, I am quite aware of the wickedness involved in the murder of innocents, but I think it's best if I reserve judgment on the perpetrator of this crime. If I jump to conclusions too soon, I might well blind myself to the right path when it's in front of me."

"Well said, but don't forget, we could be dealing with the Irish, the Fascists—I don't trust that Mosley and his band of merry men—or it could be Bolshevik union infiltrators pushing their luck. You name it, and we've got it here, and along with the gangs, there's not one in the clans of malcontents that wouldn't string up his own grandmother for their cause. I'll expect you at six." He ended the conversation without farewell, leaving Maisie looking at the telephone receiver.

"And good day to you too, Chief Superintendent," said Maisie to the receiver's continuous dial tone, as she reached forward, depressed the bar on the black telephone for several seconds to disconnect the line, then lifted her hand and began to dial the professor's telephone number at home, given to her by Maurice.

"Professor Gale? My name is Maisie Dobbs . . . Oh, he has? I am so sorry to have to disturb you on a Sunday, but I wondered if I might drive up to Oxford tomorrow to see you—could you spare me an hour of your time, perhaps? . . . Eleven? Yes, perfect. I'll see you then. Thank you, Professor."

Maisie did not want to discuss any aspect of her work with John Gale on an unsecured telephone line. She knew operators often eavesdropped on calls, flagging one another when a "good one" came on the line, to which they would all plug in and listen. She was sure Maurice had a secure line, with telephone calls to his number routed via a special government exchange. And the lines to Scotland Yard, especially to MacFarlane's office, would have been subject to the same level of security. But a telephone conversation with a professor at Oxford would not have been safe, and the last thing they needed was the mass confusion brought about by panic. She had already seen, in her career, the terror that can be wrought by an epidemic of fear.

MAISIE HEARD THE front door close with a thud, followed by Billy's uneven footfall on the stairs.

"Afternoon, Miss."

"Did you find Bert Shorter?"

"I found out where to find him, but he wasn't there. I hung around for a while, but he didn't turn up, so I thought I would come back here."

Maisie looked at Billy as he took off his coat and went to his desk, where he began going through files and his daily list. She chewed the inside of her lip for a moment, wondering whether to broach the subject of Doreen's health, then decided that now was as good a time as any.

"How's Doreen, Billy? Will she be seeing the doctor?"

Billy sighed, shaking his head. "I've got a confession, Miss." He leaned forward, rested his elbows on the desk in front of him, and could not meet Maisie's eyes as he spoke. "She first saw the doctor, you know, about how she was feeling and some of the things she was doing, a couple of months after we lost Lizzie. I saw that she was having trouble and I thought we should do something about it."

"Oh, Billy, and you've been struggling all this time?"

"Well, it wasn't too bad when we got away to Kent, but as I've told you, as soon as we got back here, it all came rushing back again. And I blame myself, I do."

"What do you mean?" Maisie pulled a chair across the floor so that she could sit in front of Billy's desk.

"Well, look at what she's had to put up with. First there's me hardly sleeping for years, getting up at night to go for a walk because if I closed my eyes I didn't like what I saw. Then because I was hurting—and you remember this—I took some of that white stuff to help me. I don't know what I was thinking, really I don't."

"You can't blame yourself. There are so many men, so many families struggling as you have."

"But then Lizzie died, and it tipped her—as I've told you already. So I broke into the Canada money to take her to the doctor, and now . . . " He pressed his lips together, as if he might himself break down.

"Now what? What's happened now?"

"I didn't want to say anything, because I didn't want to worry you."

"Billy—"

"They came for her early this morning, with the ambulance." He supported his head in his hands, and his voice cracked as he continued. "Things got bad last night. I thought I'd make a cup of hot milk for Doreen, to help her sleep." Billy breathed as if he had been running, and held his chest. "I had the saucepan on the stove, the milk was coming to the boil, so I turned around to ask her if she wanted a bit of sugar in the drink—and there she was with the carving knife in her hand, holding it over her wrist. I tell you, Miss, she was just about to slice into her vein, and I nigh on cut myself trying to stop her." He paused and pressed his lips together for some seconds, as if to stop himself breaking down in tears. "I banged on the wall to the neighbor, and yelled for them to run for the doctor. I didn't say what it was, mind, but they ain't stupid. They know. Anyway, the doctor came, took one look at what'd been going on and said he had no choice but to commit her, especially as there were children to consider. He gave her an injection of something to knock her out, and said that if she kept on trying to hurt herself, she might go for them too. So, she's been committed. They've taken her to Wychett Hill, out near Epsom. She's been taken to the bleedin' nuthouse."

"Oh, Billy, it must have been much worse at home than you've let on."

"It's been bad, Miss. And she's got a temper on her now, I can tell you."

"What about the children?"

"When we got home yesterday I sent them over to me mum's for the night, you know, to give Doreen a bit of a break. What with all the Christmas goings-on—you know how nippers can get. They're still there. And once she'd gone, the house was so quiet . . . and that's why I came over here to work. I'll go and get the boys from their nan's later." He sighed, shaking his head. "Part of me thinks she'll get the help she needs and be back with us in next to no time, and part of me wants to go down there, put my arms around her and bring her home now. But there again . . ."

"There again what?"

His voice cracked. "There's a bit of me that's just relieved. I won't have to worry about her. Won't have to wonder if the boys've been fed, or if they've been sent to bed with nothing inside them. And there's something else."

"What's that?"

"She's got to get well, because if she's not all right upstairs"—he tapped the side of his head—"we won't get into Canada."

Maisie sat back in her chair. "Oh dear, of course."

"You know, there's times I think we've copped more of a bad innings than we deserve, but then I look at what some other people have to look at in life. They've no work, they're still in pain with their war wounds, they haven't got pensions, and their kids are starving—and that's if they haven't lost one or two into the bargain."

Maisie stood up and paced to the window. "And they've sent her to Wychett Hill? Why wasn't she sent to the Clifton, where I used to work, or the Princess Victoria? The Clifton's closer, easier for you to visit—and it'd be much better for Doreen."

"The doctor said it was something to do with who could take her, and the seriousness of her condition." He shrugged. "I mean, I don't know the difference. They're all asylums, as far as I'm concerned."

Maisie began to explain. "No, not quite. Right at the outset, the Clifton was designed to have a more welcoming aspect than the old asylums. The wards are lighter, there are rooms where people can get together to play games or read. They have an outpatient wing, so I would imagine that, following initial treatment, if she were there, Doreen could be released with regular checkup visits. They are far more modern, nothing like the old-fashioned asylums. And it's also a teaching hospital, so there are many new methods employed, plus it's in Camberwell, so it's not stuck out in the country and hard to get to. The patients don't feel as if they're being isolated away from civilization, from everything they know."

"But she's in Wychett Hill now. I can't do anything about it." Billy shook his head. "I'm stuck, just as if me hands were tied behind me back. I just couldn't think straight. There was all this commotion, what with getting Doreen into the ambulance—I can't believe it's all happened, to tell you the truth."

"I know someone at the Clifton who might help." Maisie spoke as she walked over to the card file and pulled out a drawer. She began flicking through the cards. "In fact, I should see her soon anyway, about this case. Let me make a telephone call and see what I can do." She crossed the room to the telephone, and picked up the receiver. "And I'll be in touch with Maurice—perhaps he'll be able to pull a string or two."

"Miss, I feel awful, I mean, here I am again, in trouble and you're sorting it out."

"We all have trouble at times." Maisie held up a finger to indicate that her call was answered, and when Dr. Elsbeth Masters was not available, she asked the secretary to let her know that she would call later.

Maisie replaced the receiver and sat down again opposite Billy. "Look, you go on home now, spend some time with the boys this afternoon. You can see Bert Shorter tomorrow. We'll see if we can get Doreen into the Clifton. And then it won't be long before she's home, right as rain."

Billy brightened, and thanked Maisie once more. He gathered his coat and hat, and with a wave left the office.

As soon as she heard the front door close, Maisie put her hands to her face and rubbed her eyes, pinching the top of her nose to fight fatigue. The bump on the back of her head still throbbed yet she had much to accomplish before making her way to Scotland Yard and her next meeting with Special Branch. And more important than anything, now, was getting Doreen Beale out of an asylum with antiquated ways of dealing with its patients. Old ways that, under the guise of kindness, could kill, or drive an almost-sane person mad.

Time and tide, time and tide. They wait for no man. Now another letter to Mr. Home Secretary. And one to Mr. Prime Minister, Mr. This and Mr. That. Perhaps I'll send one to Mr. Robert Lewis MacFarlane, and even one to Miss Maisie Dobbs. Or perhaps not. Another rabbit down the hole, another mouse in the jar, another bird falling down. And will they listen now? Will they hear my voice—our voices? Voices, voices, voices. I am not one man, no, I am legion. And will they remember who we are, and what we are owed?

The man paused and held his head to one side, listening. He looked around to regard the silhouette negotiating the steps down to his door.

Here comes a candle to light you to bed, here comes . . . Croucher.

SIX

Maisie arrived at Special Branch headquarters at Scotland Yard and was shown directly to Robert MacFarlane's office. He was in the midst of a telephone conversation as she entered, but he waved her in and pointed to a chair. Maisie looked around the room while the call was completed, noticing that it was tidier than she might have imagined, with files and papers stacked in a neat pile, and a clean blotter on the desk. On the walls a series of framed photographs were evidence of a career in the police force, from a young policeman in uniform, to senior officer in an important department. In the middle of the gallery, a single photograph bore testimony to MacFarlane's war service, showing him in the uniform of a Scottish regiment.

"Beaumont Hamel, June the thirtieth, 1916."

Maisie turned to face MacFarlane. Having finished his call, he had leaned forward in his chair and was making a notation on a piece of paper before placing it in a folder and turning to look at the photograph.

"Just a day before the worst day of my life."

"Yes, I would imagine it was."

"And in all my years in the force, the people I would really like to bang to rights are the men who thought taking on the enemy along seventeen miles of the Somme Valley was a good idea."

Maisie nodded. "You're talking about men who cannot be touched, Superintendent."

"Och, aye, lass, I know. But it doesn't stop me thinking about it. I reckon there's more crooks over there in Westminster than there are lurking down the Mile End Road—but let that be between us, eh?"

"I didn't hear a thing."

"Stratton and Darby should be here in a minute or two. I thought we could have a little chat, a bit of a conversation, about the Battersea deaths. Never thought I'd be interested in dog murder."

"It could be just the beginning."

"Aye, of something pretty bloody nasty, if you ask me." He looked at her without moving for a second or two, then pressed his lips together before continuing. "Stratton's not sure anymore that this has to do with the fellow in Charlotte Street. He thinks it's a bit of a red herring."

"If you recall—" Having spoken, Maisie wondered if she had chosen her words wisely—after all, the Chief Superintendent gave the impression that there was nothing he would fail to recall. "The connection to Christmas Eve was drawn because my name was mentioned."

MacFarlane sighed, signaling a level of exasperation, not with Maisie, but with progress on the case. "Yes, and that might have thrown us off—have you thought of that?" He did not wait for an answer. "I'm very familiar with your work, Miss Dobbs, and with some of the more public cases you've been engaged with, and you might just as easily be known—very well known, in fact—to members of the underworld, or, given your social contacts, to the likes of Oswald Mosley's followers."

"I must point out that I am not at all acquainted with Mosley."

"Oh, but you know people who are—he was seen at the home of Mr. and Mrs. Partridge, for example, and was known to be spouting his 'come one, come all' rhetoric at a supper there, and I believe you were present on that occasion."

"I have known Mrs. Partridge since I was seventeen years of age. She worked tirelessly as an ambulance driver in the war, and I do not care to have her character besmirched because a certain man was under her roof. To set the record straight, yes, there was a supper. No, he was not invited, but came for drinks—prior to the guests sitting down—with people who wanted the Partridges to meet him. No, he did not stay. No, they didn't really care for him, because he hasn't been invited back. And finally, I was late because I was working, so by the time I arrived, Mosley had left, therefore we did not meet. I know him no better than you, Chief Superintendent."

"I might know Tom Mosley very well."

"If you know him as 'Tom' and not 'Oswald' then you probably do—so why do you suspect me of an alliance where there is none?"

MacFarlane shook his head. "I've never spoken to him in my puff, but I know where he is, whom he meets, what he does, who works for him. I know about his women. But you're right, I have no reason to suspect you are at all involved with his followers."

"Then why ask me?"

"Because I have to, because I don't know yet what I'm dealing with. We have a letter, you are mentioned in that letter, and when stated demands are not met—government works at its own pace, and hardly at all over Christmas—six dogs are murdered. And it comes to something when Special Branch gets into the stopping of wickedness to all creatures great and small—I'd rather leave that to the Royal Society for the Prevention of Cruelty to Animals. But the fact that chlorine gas was used to kill the beasts sends shivers up my spine, I can tell you. What, pray, is next?"

As if on cue, there was a sharp double rap at the door.

"Come!"

"Sir, message for you." The young detective, in civvies, passed a sheet of paper to MacFarlane, who read the note and frowned.

"I'll need my motor car, Bridges, and be quick about it." He stood up, and as he walked toward the coat-stand he turned to Maisie. "Hope you've not any plans for going to a ceilidh this evening, Miss Dobbs. We've got work to do."

"Another letter?"

"Yes, another letter. And with Colm Darby out with his contacts, and Stratton somewhere that doesn't happen to be here, you might as well join me."

"Where are we going?"

"Number Ten Downing Street."

"Oh, good lord!"

"No, I would say the Right Honorable Gentleman has never been that good, not with the mess this country's in, what with his shambles of a National Government."

Maisie took up her document case and wrapped her scarf around her neck, taking her gloves from her coat pocket as Mac-Farlane opened the door for her. "I am sure he speaks highly of you, too, Chief Superintendent."

A SINGLE LAMP illuminated the front door to Number Ten Downing Street as the police vehicle drew to a halt alongside the entrance. The uniformed driver and a plainclothes man alighted first, opening the passenger doors for MacFarlane and Maisie only after they had checked the street and nodded to the constable at the door, who had replaced the usual night watchman on Christmas Eve. By the time they reached the door, it was open and they were ushered inside.

"Detective Chief Superintendent MacFarlane and . . ." The private secretary looked at Maisie, then at MacFarlane.

"Miss Dobbs, Psychologist and Investigator, is working for me on this case. I asked her to join us."

"Very well. If you would come this way, the Prime Minister is already in the Cabinet Room with the Lord President of the Council, Mr. Baldwin, and the Minister for Pensions, Mr. Tryon. Gerald Urquhart from Military Intelligence Section Five is with us, as is the Commissioner of Police."

"Yes, I know—he summoned me."

"Good. Now then, here we are."

Though well used to meetings with important clients, Maisie felt her heart race and her hands begin to shake. But just before they were shown into the Cabinet Room, she closed her eyes for a mere three seconds and imagined her father's garden at Chelstone. Years before, when she was a girl, her mentor, Maurice Blanche, had taken her to his own teacher and friend, Basil Khan, who instructed Maisie in the stilling of the mind. It was with Khan's guidance that she learned that through the art of bringing calm to everyday thought one could delve deeper into levels of knowledge that were available only to those for whom true silence held no fear. And it was Khan who taught her that, in those situations where one became unbalanced in thought due to fear or exhaustion, one only had to bring a picture into the mind's eye of a place where one had known peace. So Maisie saw her father's garden, his embracing smile, and his arms opened wide to hold her. And she was calm.

Having barely noticed her surroundings while being escorted to the Cabinet Room, she was able to look around her self as introductions were made. Upon first taking office in 1924, Ramsay MacDonald had been appalled at what he deemed a distinct lack of both bookcases and works of art in the Prime Minister's Downing Street residence. Now shelves of books flanked the fireplace, as well as racks of maps, so that when world affairs were under discussion, the relevant map could be pulled out and referred to. On this occasion, all present were quite familiar with the geography of London.

Once again MacFarlane introduced Maisie, who held out her hand to each man present and took theirs in a firm grasp. She thought the Prime Minister quite resembled photographs she had seen in the newspapers and she could see how his physical appearance might inspire all manner of caricatures. His gray hair waved out from a left parting, and it seemed that the dour Scot eschewed hair oil. His small eyes were partially obscured by round spectacles, and there were deep furrows between his brows. His moustache was thick and broad, and he demonstrated an eccentricity in his choice of clothing—a wing collar with a black tie, a long jacket that would have been more appropriate in an Edwardian drawing room, and a pocket watch with a long fob. He clenched a barely lit pipe between his teeth. Despite this, she admired him, for it was no secret that Britain's first Labour Prime Minister was the illegitimate son of a maidservant, who as a young man had taken it upon himself to continue his education after leaving school at the age of twelve.

Ramsey MacDonald turned and took his customary seat at the table, in front of the fireplace. The secretary indicated the company to be seated.

"Now, I have received a letter today—as has Mr. Baldwin, as has Mr. Tryon, each of us sent identical letters—to the effect that London will know a terror never before unleashed if certain demands are not met." The secretary placed the letters on the table in front of Urquhart, MacFarlane, Robinson—the Police Commissioner—and Maisie Dobbs. Forgetting protocol, Maisie did not wait and was first to reach for the letter addressed to the Prime Minister. If MacFarlane brought her here, she meant to do her job.

MacFarlane looked at her and, though she could not be sure, she thought he might have winked. "What do you think, Miss Dobbs?"

Maisie cleared her throat and turned to the Prime Minister. "A letter-writer reveals much about himself in the manner of his script. That helps us to draw a picture of who he might be, where he might live, what his habits are. It helps us to narrow down the places where we might look. At first glance, the handwriting shows many of the markers noted by myself and Detective Inspector Darby when the first letter was received by the Home Secretary." Maisie looked at Robinson. "Sir, seeing as the three letters are identical in content, might it help if I read one aloud?"

He cleared his throat. "Yes, of course, please continue, Miss Dobbs." He glared at MacFarlane.

Maisie stood up so her words might carry without anyone straining to hear, and hoped that the shaking in her voice was not too obvious.

"You didn't listen, did you? You sat, fat, by your Christmas Day fires, with your turkey and plum pudding inside you, and you ignored my warning."

Maisie looked up for a second, to see how the writer's words were being received, then she cleared her throat and went on.

"And while you ate and drank, there were people without. There are people on the streets and among them are men who gave legs, arms and minds for you. And now look at you—you who thought I was nothing, a nobody. Will you do that now? Will you, The Rt. Honorable Prime Minister, do something about us all? Or you, Mr. Minister of Pensions? And Mr. Baldwin, how about you? Or will you scrap among yourselves for your

power? I think you know what I can do, the power I wield. Or is the life of mere animals not worth a measure of your time? I will not allow those to suffer who have suffered enough already, but you know what I want and what I can do. I can be hell itself, unless my demands are met. I want every man who served to receive a full pension he can live on—wounded or not. That's where we will begin, Honorable Gentlemen. That is where we will begin. I hope you can come to your senses before another day has passed."

Maisie placed the letter on the table, and sat down, smoothing her skirt as she took her place once more. She was relieved that she had chosen to wear her smart burgundy costume this morning, and not an older ensemble.

"Thank you, Miss Dobbs," said MacDonald. He looked at the Commissioner and Urquhart, then MacFarlane. "Gentlemen, your measure of the seriousness of this threat? Are the people of London at risk? When can I expect word that this man is behind bars, and what precautions will you be taking in the meantime?" He looked at his watch, then at his private secretary.

"Five minutes, Prime Minister."

The Commissioner cleared his throat. "I have been briefed by Detective Chief Superintendent MacFarlane that there is a medium risk, that you can expect word within twenty-four hours, and we will be increasing the number of men on the streets."

Maisie raised her eyebrows.

"Can I have a word?" Baldwin leaned forward. His manner was easier than that of the Prime Minister, with more resonance to his voice. "Thank you for the summation of your plans, Commissioner, but if I may address the Detective Chief Superintendent"—he looked straight at MacFarlane—"what is medium risk and is twenty-four hours attainable? We're used to looking over our shoulders, but will I need a neck brace?"

"Sir, 'medium risk' means we do not believe all of London will be flattened by midnight. However, we know already that this man has the means to cause some harm if he so chooses. Given what must be an amateur capability, damage—and let us be clear, we are talking about chemical weaponry—would be limited to about a quarter of a mile. And that's if it isn't a windy day when he takes it into his head to unleash his cocktails on a greater area than Battersea Dogs and Cats Home." MacFarlane coughed and cleared his throat, paused for a second, and looked at Baldwin, then the Prime Minister. "And to the matter of twenty-four hours, I would say that it is attainable. We are looking at the Irish, the Fascists, the possibility of a very disgruntled Bolshevik union man—or men. We're following recently released criminal elements, and of course we might have a lunatic on our hands."

Feeling a dryness at the back of her tongue, Maisie held her hand to her mouth and coughed. She wondered whether such intimidating circumstances always compromised a speaker's voice, because the visitors to the Prime Minister's residence were either clearing their throats or coughing every time they spoke. "If I might add a word—" She was aware of the men turning to look at her, and for a heartbeat it seemed as if the hands of time were turning through treacle, for their heads appeared to move so slowly and she could hear her own heartbeat throbbing in her ears. She took another deep breath. "As we've been speaking, I have had an opportunity to glance at the letters—and they obviously bear greater inspection—however, the manner in which the script has been executed suggests to me that this man is more desperate than he was two days ago. I suspect he is in some pain, and the penmanship suggests he is cold, very cold. Physical deprivation will enhance his emotions, so I would say that we are on something of a knife edge in terms of the threat."

The men looked at one another as MacDonald thanked Maisie for her summation of the situation, pushed back his chair, and addressed the group. "I expect a report in twenty-four hours. I want to know that London is safe, that my cabinet is at no risk of harm. Do what you have to do, Commissioner."

Along with the other visitors, Maisie stood up as the Prime Minister left the room, followed by Baldwin and Tryon.

"Gentlemen." The secretary stood by the door, his hand indicating the way, then he turned to lead the visitors from the building.

Maisie reached forward to gather the letters and was about to hand them to MacFarlane when Urquhart leaned over and attempted to grasp the collected papers.

"I'll take those, if you don't mind. Military Intelligence trumps the boys in blue."

"Oh, but I'm sure—"

"Hang on to those, Miss Dobbs, we don't want the Funnies getting above themselves, do we?" said MacFarlane.

"Now look here, Robbie—"

"I think we'd better catch up with the others. I for one do not want to be locked in here for the night. Now, why don't you take one letter, Mr. Urquhart, so that you can conduct your own tests." Maisie handed Urquhart the top letter, placing two in her document case as she walked at a brisk clip toward the front door, which was being opened by the private secretary. MacFarlane and Urquhart were behind her.

With a dull thump the door closed at their heels and the three stepped onto the pavement at the same time as Robinson, already seated in his motor car, wound down the rear passenger window.

"I'll see you at the Yard, MacFarlane. Soon as you're back." The window wound up again, and the driver pushed the vehicle into gear and drove away.

"Need a lift, Gerry?"

"Much obliged, Robbie."

The Superintendent's motor car drew alongside and Urquhart

opened the door, holding out his hand to steady Maisie as she stepped on the running board and into the vehicle. MacFarlane sat next to her, and Urquhart pulled down the extra passenger seat in front of them.

"I was surprised to see Miss Dobbs with you, Robbie—reckon that's why the boss wants to see you pronto?"

"I won't be answering that question, my man, especially in the presence of Miss Dobbs, who happens to be a most valuable member of my group."

"Not on the force though, is she?"

"That's enough, Gerry."

Maisie leaned forward to speak, thought better of it, and instead rested back on the seat. As MacFarlane had suggested, disagreements between Special Branch and Military Intelligence were sometimes unavoidable as they often tilled the same ground, and the last thing she wanted to do was to get in the middle. She wasn't sure why MacFarlane had taken her to Downing Street for what amounted to a "heads will roll" meeting. It was clear the government would never bow to a threat. But she had seen the handwriting, the stains on the paper, and she knew she would spend a restless night. There was work to be done, and she would need to be in Oxford in the morning.

December 28th, 1931

Maisie was surprised at having slept so well, given that she had arrived home late following what proved to be a heated meeting with Stratton, Darby and MacFarlane. The four had convened soon after the Chief Superintendent arrived back at Special Branch headquarters. She knew MacFarlane had been brought up short by his superiors, and was doubtless asked to explain why he had asked Maisie to accompany him to the meeting with the Prime Minister. It was a question she hoped to ask him herself, at an appropriate moment. What was clear was that the next twenty-four hours represented a race against the clock.

Twenty-past six in the morning. Time to leave London. The air was damp, with a smog so thick she was glad to be traveling by train. Taking the circle line to Paddington, she came up from the underground into the busy station, where a throng of passengers rushed back and forth, or lingered, clapping hands together to keep warm as they waited for departure announcements. Maisie bought her third-class ticket and walked toward the platform, clutching her document case with her left hand as she turned the clasp to secure her shoulder bag.

When she held out her ticket to the station guard, she glanced across and thought she saw Dr. Anthony Lawrence on the neighboring platform. She stopped to look again—after all, one gentleman waiting for a train can look much like another—but a train pulled in alongside the platform where the man was standing.

Maisie approached a guard. "Excuse me—"

"Hurry up, Miss, can't keep people waiting."

"I'm sorry—but could you tell me where that train is going?"

"The one just come in on platform six?"

"Yes."

The guard pulled out his watch. "That'll be the twenty minutes past to Penzance."

"Thank you."

As Maisie walked along the platform, the Oxford train chugged into the station, steam punching out sideways as the locomotive slowed to a stop at the buffers. She took a seat alongside the window, close to the heater, and settled in for her journey, soon so deep in thought that she held no awareness of the carriage filling, or of the guard's whistle and the lumbering side-to-side motion as the train pulled out of the station. She wondered where the doctor might be going on a working day. She knew the Penzance train stopped at stations in Berkshire and Wiltshire and then throughout the west of England on its way to Cornwall, and there were psychiatric hospitals in several places on the way, out in the country where men could be kept away from the noise and struggle of towns, cities and other conurbations. But really, even if it were Lawrence, it was nothing to do with her where he was going, was it?

THE PORTER AT St. Edmund Hall escorted Maisie along a corridor of the medieval college, knocking on the door to John Gale's rooms and announcing the visitor before allowing her to enter.

"Miss Dobbs. Right on time, that's what I like. Can't bear people who are late, completely befuddles my day, especially as I've a lecture in an hour. Now come along, take a seat by the fire."

John Gale was almost six feet tall and somewhat thin; his gown seemed to hang on his shoulders. His hair, silver gray and swept back, was longer than was fashionable and, Maisie thought, it might be likely that the business of getting a haircut was something that slipped his mind until the skin around his collar began to itch with chafing.

Maisie reached out to shake Gale's hand, then seated herself as instructed on a low slipper chair of red velvet set alongside a fireplace that could have benefited from a puff or two from the bellows. As if reading her mind, Gale knelt down in front of the fire and proceeded to blow on the smoldering embers to encourage a more active flame, then added more coal from the scuttle. He blew once or twice more, then came to his feet, taking the chair opposite her.

"There, that's better, soon have a roaring fire. I forget myself, you see—working on a paper for a meeting of physicists next week—and then I wonder why I'm cold. In any case, Maurice said you wanted to see me, that it had something to do with my work in the war."

"Yes, that's right. I'm interested in the gases used in the war. I was a nurse, so I know the effects of various gases—chlorine, chlorine and phosgene, and of course, mustard gas—but I want to understand how the government responded to the attacks in the first instance. I understand you worked at Mulberry Point, and wonder if you could enlighten me."

"Not sure I should be talking about this, to tell you the truth. Mind you, it was a long time ago when I worked there full-time."

"But there's still research in progress at Mulberry Point, isn't there?"

"Yes, of course. However, there's more organization at the laboratories now. In my day it was like a bit of a bun fight, to tell you the truth. We were scrambling to find antidotes, in the first instance, and . . . you know, perhaps I should start at the beginning."

"Yes, please."

At that moment there was a knock on the door and the porter entered bearing a tray with tea for two and a plate of biscuits. Gale thanked him, and Maisie offered to pour tea while he continued his story.

"The first attacks—with chlorine gas—were like a cosh on the back of the head to the military, took them completely unawares. They had to scramble, and scramble fast, to provide protection for the soldiers, and to find an antidote. The wounds from the gas were terrible, as you know; chlorine gas was just the beginning. Before you knew it, the military was crawling over every university in Britain, looking for the best and brightest physicists, chemists, biologists and engineers. They were effectively requisitioning people right, left and center."

"And you were one of them."

"Yes. I was still teaching because I have the most dreadful flat feet, so was passed over for military service. But not this time, not when it came to a different sort of part to play." Gale looked into the fire as he dipped a biscuit into his tea, biting off the end just as it was about to drop. "I was drafted to join a special group who were sent straight to France. We were with doctors examining patients, we collected skin samples, cultures and what have you, and some of us returned home to the laboratories as soon as possible. The army took many of the best students, and for those who were left, this was their research. It was all a bit hit and miss, to tell you the truth."

Maisie watched Gale as he spoke, his eyes now fixed on a coal that had just fallen from the grate and was rolling close to the edge of the fender. He did not reach for the tongs to pick up the still-hot coal, but kept staring at its ashen glow.

"I'd never seen anything like it. They'd taken over the casino in Le Touquet for the gas cases. It was hard to believe that the roulette wheels had been spinning just a year earlier, that men and women were laughing, playing blackjack and poker, placing their bets. Now all bets were off and the only thing you could hear was the wrenching sound of men screaming in pain as they died from their wounds, with gas-filled lungs, frothy and filled with a liquid that looked like the whites of eggs. Funny, I think the place was once called the Pleasure Pavilion, or something like that."

"What did you do? What was your job?"

Gale shook his head as if the movement would banish the memories, and turned back to Maisie. "Well, I'm no doctor, but along with other scientists, I was taking samples, as I said, and was questioning those who could speak. We were desperate to know what they saw, what they smelled, what were their first symptoms." He sighed and placed his cup and saucer on the tray. "It was the sort of thing that was never meant to happen. The Hague Declaration of 1899 clearly stipulated that poison gas was not to be used in a time of war, and there we were, groping in the dark for a solution, and the best advice we could come up with was to tell the men to hold urine-soaked cloths to the face when attacked by chlorine gas."

Maisie glanced at the clock, and asked another question. "Is that how you came to work at the War Department Experimental Ground at Mulberry Point?"

"Yes, that's it. The government bought three thousand or so acres of land, threw a fence around it and set us up in some huts. We had a gas chamber there, laboratories and various other facilities. And—between us—everyone who worked there, from the cleaning staff to the orderlies to the scientists and army personnel, we all became involved in the experiments. If you needed to run a test on a human being, you just called in one of the orderlies, or you tested on yourself. We had to get the job done, you see, there was no time to lose. And it may seem strange, but even with the daily tally of dead and missing in the papers, the press got wind of the fact that we'd used animals in our experiments and they kicked up a fuss. Not that we stopped, but you never knew how an antidote worked on a human being if you'd only ever used it on a dog, for example. Mind you, we wanted to test it on the dog before we moved on to the human, just in case."

"And you worked on weapons too?"

"Can't have one without the other."

Maisie was thoughtful. "Professor Gale, how easy would it be for an amateur to handle gas?"

"Depends on the substance—the risk increases with the effects of the gas and with the level of volatility. However, generally speaking, I would say it would be very, very difficult. And with something such as mustard gas, well, it would be lunacy even to think about it. Simply being close to the body of a man killed by the gas can have

you in suppurating blisters from stem to stern before you know it—
in fact, I am sure you would have had to take precautions against
such secondary wounds in the war."

"Yes, I remember." Maisie nodded. "I understand you still work
at the laboratories at Mulberry Point, and though I know your
work must be subject to high levels of security, I wonder if you can
tell me—and this has just occurred to me—how many people, do
you think, took on this kind of work during the war? Tens? Hundreds? And are there many still at Mulberry Point who were there
in 1918?"

"I'm still there on and off, for a start, and of course some of the
old team are still in situ. But they're like me—it's not my main job,
if you know what I mean. This is my work, I am an academic.
However, if in the course of my work I can come to the aid of my
country, so be it. And to your question, the military scoured the
universities, so you are talking about Oxford, Cambridge, Bristol,
Durham, Birmingham, London, Edinburgh, Glasgow—every
single seat of higher learning and research. Some students didn't
even know they were working for the war effort, but they were the
best and brightest. Some were literally conscripted right there and
then to join the Special Brigades, to spearhead our own chemical
attacks over in France and Belgium. But yes, there were a fair number, and, of course, they're all scattered now."

Maisie glanced at the clock again. "Professor Gale, I have taken
a good deal of your time, and I think you have a lecture in about
ten minutes."

Gale checked his fob-watch. "Oh dear, thank you for reminding
me. Yes, I must be off now. Time and tide wait for no man, eh?"

Maisie smiled and held out her hand. "Thank you so much for
helping me with my inquiries."

Gale frowned. "I'm not sure I understand why you are making
such inquiries—though I trust my old friend Maurice Blanche."

"And your trust is well placed. Good-bye, Professor Gale." Having shaken hands in farewell, Maisie pulled on her gloves, waited as Gale opened the door for her, and said thank you again as she left the room.

Croucher came to see me. Croucher brought apples. He said a bit of fruit would do me good. He brought soup, bread, some cold meat, a packet of Brook Bond, so I can make myself a fresh pot of tea. And matches. He sat and talked for a bit, made me chuckle. Croucher's like that, always was. Makes you have a bit of a laugh to yourself. The sparrow reminded me of Croucher, chirpy little fellow, wiry, quick about his business. Yes, Croucher looks after me. He went out for a sack of coal and made up my fire, kept me warm, for a bit. A bit of this, bit of that, bit of coal, only ever a little bit for a bit of a man. Yes, Croucher's kind. Now he's gone, though, and I've got to get on. Nothing's come from the wireless, so it looks as if I'll have to keep my word.

The man set down his pen in the middle of his journal, closed the book around it and secured them together with the string. Pushing the book aside, he cleared the table and shuffled across to the cupboard, where he opened the door and with both hands removed a large, empty aquarium. He placed it on the table, went back for the metal lid he'd fashioned to fit like a glove, snug and tight, then made his way toward the back of the flat. Stopping to cough, a phlegmy cough that caused him to thump his chest to clear congestion, he remained still for some seconds before opening a splintered door that led to the postage stamp of a back garden. Once outside he turned to the side and spat out the yellow, blood-threaded debris that had issued from his lungs, then walked in a deliberate manner along the path to a cage-like construction with mesh netting. Inside, birds had been captured, and as the man opened a door and reached in, the sparrows, blue-tits, robins, pigeons and starlings scattered and squawked. He winced at the sound, grabbed a butterfly net leaning against the side of the cage and an old sack, and one by one he removed the birds. Soon there was no furious chirruping, not even aggression between the more dominant birds and those they considered lesser, only their muffled movements as he carried the closed sack into the flat. With care he emptied the birds into the glass aquarium set up on the table, and secured his catch inside with a tight metal lid. He had to be careful, even more careful than last time. He couldn't afford a single mistake.

SEVEN

It was midafternoon by the time Maisie arrived back at her office in Fitzroy Square. Billy was already there, waiting for her.

"Any news, Billy?" asked Maisie, as she unwound her scarf and hung it over the top of her coat on the hook behind the door. She walked to her desk and took out the narrow wad of index cards she had used to take notes during the return journey from Oxford to London. "Have you managed to locate Bert Shorter?"

Billy's chair scraped against the wooden floor beyond the carpet as he came to his feet. He approached her desk, his notebook in hand. "Yes, I have, and it turns out Mr. Shorter had seen the man in Charlotte Street before, but usually down in Soho Square. He said the man sat in the park, never with his cap out, but people would usually walk by and press a few coppers in his hand. Shorter told me he stopped to talk to him once, and that he was wounded in the war. He'd lost a leg and the other one wasn't much good. He thought the man might have had a small pension, but not much of a life, as far as Bert could make out."

"Did he know his name?"

"That's the thing, he said he introduced himself to the man once, but didn't really catch his name in return—reckons it might have been Ian. He said he was in a pretty bad way with his lungs, and that every now and again he wouldn't be in his usual place for a month or so. Bert thought he might have been taken down to the coast, you know, like they do—I was taken once myself, when I got really bunged up in my chest."

"Then he must be known, must have a connection to a doctor or a hospital—perhaps he's an outpatient somewhere." Maisie rubbed her forehead. "I wonder if they would have missed him yet, if he's a regular patient?" She looked up at Billy. "Did Bert have any idea where he lived?"

"Remember, Bert was only surmising, so this is nothing definite, but he thought the man must've been local, perhaps living down in Soho—there's a lot of boardinghouses down there. He probably had a pension, but I bet it didn't amount to much. And it sounds like he couldn't work, even if he could've found a job."

"So, we've got a man who might be named Ian, who could be living in Soho, crippled by his war wounds. Anything else about him that Bert might have noticed?"

"He said he second-glanced him at first because he always had a book on him. Always reading."

"Did he see him with anyone, ever?"

Billy nodded, licked his finger and turned over the pages of his notebook. "Saw him with a man once. Small fellow, well dressed—but not in a toff way, more in a clean way, very correct, everything pressed. Bit like you might see a doorman at one of them hotels up near Hyde Park, when he's off duty and just leaving out the back door. The bloke was talking to him, ordinary, nothing strange, but went on his way when Bert came along with his horse and cart and Ian—or whatever his name is—waved at him."

"Let's recap again. We're talking about a man who *might* be called Ian, who could live in Soho—or anywhere between, say, Old Compton Street and Soho Square. 'Ian' suffered wounds to the legs and the respiratory system, and he liked to read. If he had a pension, it would not have been sufficient to cover the purchase of books, so he must have gone to a library. And if you remember, there was talk of him being on the number thirty-six bus from Lewisham. I think I might take a guess that that little piece of evidence has deflected us from narrowing down the search to find him and his place of domicile."

Maisie looked around at the clock. "Billy, I wonder how many lending libraries there are in Soho? Of course, Soho encompasses most of Charing Cross Road, so if we're on the right track, he might have a contact in one of the bookshops."

"I think I know where there are two lending libraries."

"Right, you go straight there. Describe 'Ian' and see if you come up with anything. I'll go to Charing Cross Road and visit each bookshop. I'll meet you in the caff on Tottenham Court Road—you know the one, where they never say 'I beg your pardon' before they pick up your cup and saucer to wipe the table—at about, oh, half-past five?"

Billy nodded. "Right you are, Miss."

STARTING AT THE TOP of Charing Cross Road, Maisie began to work her way down the street, going into each bookshop and engaging with the proprietor or assistant in a warm manner, before asking for a book recommended to her by her friend, Ian, who hadn't been well of late. In W. & G. Foyle, Ltd., Maisie consulted the most recent catalogues, and lingered for a few moments to peruse the Solar Radiation and Physical Culture catalogue, which featured a rowing machine for forty-nine shillings and sixpence, a sum that

Maisie thought amounted to highway robbery. She shrugged and moved on, inquiring in each department before leaving the shop.

She had continued on her way down Charing Cross Road, and was about to lose faith in her plan—the thought crossed her mind that she was acquiring an almost encyclopedic knowledge of the street's antiquarian book trade—when she opened the door of Tinsley and Sons, Booksellers. The shop was ill lit and somewhat cluttered, with an overflow of books stacked upon every available surface and each step of a cast-iron spiral staircase situated at the back of the shop. A man of about forty-five years of age was at the top of a ladder dusting the shelves.

"Just browsing, or can I help you with something in particular?"

"Browsing, thank you very much. I was advised to come here by a friend."

The man continued dusting, speaking as he went on with his task. "Always pleased when people recommend us. What's your friend's name?"

"Ian, he—"

"Ian?" The man stopped dusting and began to climb down from his somewhat precarious perch. "You know Ian? Wounded in the war—lost a leg and the other one's a bit gammy?"

Maisie nodded and cast her eyes down. "I'm here, in part, to remember him."

"Remember him? Is he all right? Haven't seen him since before Christmas, and he was a regular."

"He's dead, Mr.—"

"Tinsley. This is my shop." He pulled up a chair for Maisie and one for himself, close to the potbellied stove that held court in the middle of the floor. "What happened?"

"He took his own life, I'm afraid."

"Oh, what a shame, what a terrible thing." He shook his head. "Mind you, I can't say the news comes as a surprise, after all, he was in such pain. Not least in his mind, I think. And reading helped, took him away from his everyday life—as it does for so many."

"Yes, I think you're right." Maisie took off her gloves as the chill outside left her bones. "And he certainly loved your shop."

"Well, I did what I could for him. I knew he couldn't afford much and he was such a voracious reader. I would lend him books, in return for some cataloguing, that sort of thing." He leaned back to take a ledger from his desk. "Here, you can see how many books he read in November alone."

Maisie took the large, leather-bound book from Tinsley's hands and looked at the page indicated: Ian. She could barely read the last name, but thought it looked like Jennings. Flat 15a, Wellington Street, Kennington. A location close to the route of the number thirty-six bus as it made its way along Kennington Park Road.

"Was his surname Jennings?"

Tinsley took a pair of spectacles from a pocket in his knitted pullover. "I must admit, I never really looked at the name—in fact, I trusted him, so I didn't check the books. Let me see—yes, he was up to date. Brought back the last one in early December. And that's why I was a bit surprised at his absence, because I can't imagine him without a book, though I am sure he used libraries. I mean, look at this, he must have been reading one book every two days, something like that."

She ran her finger across the page. "Until December, when he only read two books."

"Yes, I've hardly seen him throughout the month, which is why I've been concerned. I thought I might go to his lodgings, but it seemed rather presumptuous to do so, and then of course, December can be so busy." He took back the ledger and placed it on the desk.

"Can you recall him saying anything after November that might have accounted for the absence?"

Tinsley removed his spectacles and returned them to his pocket. "I seem to remember him saying he'd met an old colleague again, and they'd sort of struck up a friendship."

"I've been away from London lately, so I've hardly seen Ian," said Maisie. "I wonder who the old colleague was?"

"He never mentioned the man's name, and I can't remember exactly what he said about him. I just thought Ian would come along again when he wanted a book, do some work for me, and we'd carry on as usual. He liked to discuss literature, and I was grateful for the company. It can get quiet sometimes."

At that moment the doorbell sounded the arrival of a customer, and the man stood up. Maisie thanked him and, before he could say more, left the shop and made her way toward Tottenham Court Road.

"MISS, I RECKON I've got it!" Billy was already at the café and waved as Maisie approached the table where he was seated.

She leaned forward and whispered, "Ian Jennings?"

"Flat 15a, Wellington Street, Kennington," added Billy. He stood up to go to the counter to buy two cups of tea. "And I thought I was being dead clever. Got all his particulars from the Boots library—bit of a regular, he was. Took out a book or two a week."

"And he read a book every two days or so from a shop on Charing Cross Road."

"Blimey, he must've been a clever one."

Maisie nodded. "He was—and I'm gasping for that cuppa, Billy."

* * *

SO AS NOT TO BE LATE, Maisie ran from the underground station to Special Branch headquarters at Scotland Yard, where she bumped into Stratton as she entered.

"Steady on there, people running in this place end up in the cells if they're not careful."

"Sorry—I'm a bit late and didn't want to incur MacFarlane's wrath."

"I doubt you'll do that, Miss Dobbs. Darby thinks that, as far as Robbie MacFarlane is concerned, you can do no wrong."

Maisie stopped. "What on earth do you mean?"

Stratton turned his wrist to consult his watch. "I, however, *can* do wrong—come on, we'll be late."

Together Maisie and Stratton made their way toward MacFarlane's office, only to find Colm Darby making notes on several sheets of paper.

"Darby." Stratton nodded as they entered the room.

"Stratton, Miss Dobbs. Any luck today?"

Maisie was about to speak when the door opened with a thud against the wall, and MacFarlane entered the room. His face reminded Maisie of a storm-laden sky, dark and brooding, while lines around his eyes spoke of the pressure to find a man who had proved that he could and would kill to be heard.

"Stratton! What have you got for me?"

"Sir, our narks within Mosley's party are coming up with precious little, I'm afraid, though we do have evidence to support the existence of an inner group who might be up to no good."

"Can you infiltrate further?"

"I understand money talks. Oh, and apparently there is some kind of recruiting meeting for those interested in the party, at a church hall in Kilburn this evening. This inner circle will be in attendance, and I understand they are a more militant strain."

"Hmm." MacFarlane took up a penknife set alongside a collection of pens and pencils on his desk, opened the blade, closed it again, then opened it once more. He snapped it shut, set it down, and looked at Darby. "Colm? Anything?"

"It's quiet, gov, to be sure. I've got my informers, but the IRA have had trouble regrouping lately. My only lead is a mere hairsbreadth of information to the effect that there's something of a move to recruit men who aren't all there upstairs, men who might have recently been discharged from an institution, for example. They offer them a sense of belonging, claim their loyalty, then set them off to do their dirty work. Apparently, the theory is that someone who's not dealing with the whole deck, if you know what I mean, can be easily directed, and won't have the same qualms about killing as a sane person."

Maisie cringed. The suggestion that the insane might be used to kill had not occurred to her.

"And as to union sympathizers," Darby continued, turning to Stratton, "again, there's a group within the Red Party of Britain, real Bolsheviks, who could up the ante. Mind you, they've never been known to keep quiet about who they are. In the meantime, I've got someone on it."

MacFarlane opened and closed the penknife again, and looked to Maisie for an account of her progress.

"And I know the identity of the Christmas Eve suicide. I discovered his name before coming over here." Maisie was aware of the attention of all three men as she spoke. "My assistant is paying a visit to his lodgings before going home this evening. If there is anything to report, he'll make a telephone call to this office. I would imagine we might hear from him soon."

MacFarlane looked up. "Name?"

"Ian Jennings. At least, that was the name given to a bookseller he befriended, and at a lending library in Soho—the man was an avid reader. According to the people who had made his acquaintance, he had lost one leg below the knee in the war, and the other leg was crippled with shrapnel wounds. Apparently, he also demonstrated symptoms associated with a gas poisoning." Maisie scraped back her chair, pulled a selection of colored wax crayons from her document case, and approached the case map, which was still pinned to the wall. MacFarlane leaned back in his chair to watch her make notations, linking various pieces of evidence with red lines and a question mark above a stick figure she named "the Gas-Man."

"Ian Jennings began spending time with a friend—he might have been an old colleague—in December. Could this man be our letter-writer? Or could the friend be associated with either Mosley's group, the Irish, or the unions?" She turned to Darby. "I agree with you—I think we can scale back any surveillance of the latter, though obviously we want to keep in touch with informers." Looking across at Stratton, she continued, "Jennings might have been recruited by the Fascists—certainly their rhetoric might resonate with a man living on the edge."

At that moment the telephone rang.

"MacFarlane!" The Superintendent bellowed, his usually tempered brogue unleashed on the operator. He held out the receiver to Maisie. "Your man."

Maisie reached for the telephone. "Billy?"

"Miss, I'm just leaving Kennington."

"Right you are. Did you find anything?"

"The landlord lives in the house—old gaff, it is, split into about six rooms that he lets out. Bit grim. You could hold a cup to the walls and have enough water for tea in a minute." He coughed.

"There's a right old pea-souper tonight, Miss." He coughed again and she heard him thump his chest. "Anyway, I talked to the landlord, slipped him a couple o' bob, and he led me upstairs to the room. Says that he was thinking of going in, but the rent's not due for a few days, and even though he hadn't seen Jennings since before Christmas, who was to say he wasn't coming and going? Mind you, I don't know how that poor man managed those stairs, even though he was only up one flight." Billy coughed once more. "So, he let me in and we both stood there, just staring, because the place looked like it had never been lived in. Neat as a pin, it was— apart from the mold, of course. But the bed had been stripped and the blankets folded, the furniture had all been wiped. You'd've thought that it was ready to be let out again—in fact, it probably is by now."

"And you didn't find one thing, one scrap of paper, old photographs, anything?"

"Not until I looked behind a chest of drawers. Found a pamphlet there, about that bloke, Mosley. Looked like it had fallen down the back, not hidden there on purpose."

"Yes, it would appear so, from your description. The tidiness in the room gives me pause, though."

"Very creepy, if you ask me."

Maisie sighed. "Right you are, Billy. You go home—and bring the pamphlet into the office tomorrow morning, please."

"Miss—"

"Yes?" Maisie looked around at the three men, who were waiting for her to complete the call.

"I telephoned Wychett Hill, before I made the call to you. Turns out Doreen is resting—that's what they said—following a 'procedure.'"

"What sort of procedure? Did they say?"

"Well, I asked, and of course it don't mean a thing to me. They said something about her being out for the count, and that she'd been on insulin."

"Insulin?" Maisie was aware of her raised voice, that the men were now all looking at her.

"Is that bad, Miss? I mean, she's never been a diabetic or anything, so I wondered . . . "

"No, don't worry. It was just me, a bit surprised, that's all—nothing for you to worry about. Look, I'll go back to the office—I should have a reply from the doctor I telephoned at the Clifton Hospital. I'll let you know tomorrow morning. Go home to your boys, Billy—is your mother with them?"

"Yes, Miss. Right then, see you tomorrow."

Maisie passed the telephone receiver to MacFarlane, who placed it back on the cradle.

"Everything all right?" inquired Stratton.

"Um, yes . . . well, no, not with our Mr. Jennings. Seems his premeditated suicide—or his departure, anyway—was thoroughly planned. His room looks as if no one ever lived there. I would bet that, if you sent in the boys to check for dabs, he'd have cleaned every surface and they'd come up with nothing. My assistant and the landlord made a thorough investigation of the small room, however, and they found one item of interest, which had slipped behind a chest of drawers—a pamphlet from Mosley's New Party."

"Hmm—I still think the suicide has been a red herring in this investigation," said MacFarlane. "But I don't trust that Mosley. He's been hobnobbing with the likes of the Italian, Mussolini, and there's talk that he's thinking of setting up a Fascist Party here. There's a recipe for terror, if ever I came across it. Look, here's what I want—you and Stratton, go along to this meeting of nutcase Fascists tonight. Dress well, but not too well, look well-to-do without flaunting it, if you know what I mean. Look, listen, and find out who's in this inner circle, and what they're doing. And there's something else I'd like you to look into, Miss Dobbs."

"Yes?"

"There's a little coven of women who seem to have taken it upon themselves to agitate for women's pensions."

"Yes, I know, sir. I've contributed to the cause. However, I take exception to the idea that they are a coven. Surely prejudice against women hasn't reached the point where we make accusations of witchcraft?"

"You've contributed to their cause?"

Maisie shrugged. "Why should an unwed woman not receive a pension, when she pays the same contributions as a married man?"

"It's not as if . . . "

"Not as if what?"

"Well, anyway, we've heard word that there are agitators among their number who aren't prepared to wait—just as you'll find in any group. There's always those who splinter off because they think if they show how strong they are, they'll get what they want. There are factory girls in there following their leader, and I'll bet some of them have the know-how to handle those gases."

"Sir, if I might make a bold statement, I think you're wrong, and we can't afford to have anyone following weak leads."

"And I think it's one for you, Miss Dobbs, being a woman. Apparently the girls are meeting tomorrow at lunchtime. Please wheedle your way in—here's the address." He handed a slip of paper to Maisie. "And in the meantime, Stratton, I want the Mosley group investigated. And the unions, Colm." He always referred to Colm by his Christian name, with due regard for their years worked together.

"But . . . " Maisie tried not to show her exasperation.

"You need to go to your office?"

"Yes."

"Stratton, divert to Fitzroy Square, then to her flat. Miss Dobbs, you'll have just enough time to assume some wealthy sort of character while Stratton waits. You'll be brought back to your flat later. All right?"

"All right, sir," echoed Stratton and Darby.

"Miss Dobbs?"

"Yes, that's all right, however, Superintendent, I—"

At that moment the meeting was interrupted by a single knock on the door. A detective sergeant entered the room, leaned toward MacFarlane and whispered in his ear. The Superintendent nodded and stood up as the messenger left the room. Reaching for his coat he turned to face Maisie, Stratton and Darby.

"I was due to bring the Commissioner up to date, per the Prime Minister's request, but the situation has just become more grave. A policeman in Hyde Park, close to Speakers' Corner, has reported finding some fifty or so birds, dead, on the path. I suspect this might be our man again, and if it is, then he has gone a step further. As you probably all know, chlorine gas did not kill birds in the war. But chlorine mixed with phosgene silenced birds across the Somme Valley. The situation is no longer medium risk, if you didn't know already. This man knows what he's doing. I expect another letter will be received soon. Now, get to work." He left the room.

STRATTON REMAINED in the Invicta while Maisie ran to her office, retrieving the post on the way. There was a card from Dr. Elsbeth Masters. She expressed pleasure at hearing from Maisie and suggested she visit her at the Clifton Hospital the following day, indicating she would be available after one o'clock. Maisie hoped that Doreen could deal with the indignities of Wychett Hill until her release was secured. There was a greater cause for her concern since the telephone conversation with Billy. Many of the old therapies and treatments for depression and mental imbalances in women had been less than humane. Maisie had been appalled observing some of the Faradism treatments—electric shock—as doctors tried to encourage traumatized patients to speak again or to lose the stammer that began when a young man saw his fellow soldiers blown up alongside him. But there were other kinds of shock, and insulin therapy had been used on women in mental institutions for many years. The patient was given excessive amounts of insulin so that the body began to break down under the pressure of toxic shock. It was thought that the shock would, in effect, startle the brain and lead to a resumption of normal behavior. In Maisie's estimation it was barbaric, and the thought of Doreen Beale enduring such terror made her doubly convinced that she must find a way to have her discharged into more tolerable care as soon as possible. She had pinned her hopes on Dr. Masters being able to provide a solution.

Until then, though, Maisie knew she had to endure the New Party meeting this evening. Later, while Stratton waited outside her flat in the Invicta, she dressed in a plain black skirt, her burgundy jacket, matching black hat with a burgundy ribbon, and black shoes. Dark clothes seemed to be the order of the day with Mosley's followers. Her hair had grown longer since the summer, and though it was still styled in a bob, it was less boyish, and in that regard, followed fashion, though Maisie was not generally interested in such distractions.

Although she was not convinced that this avenue of investigation represented good use of her time, she could not avoid the possibility that the man who committed suicide may have attended one of the meetings. After all, she was the one maintaining that a link between the dead man and the threats could lead them to the door of a man who had already made good on his warnings that he would kill.

Stratton opened the door of the motor car as Maisie emerged from the block of flats. "You think this is a complete waste of time, don't you, Miss Dobbs?" he said, as she reached the Invicta.

"I confess, I do. Even with the pamphlet found in Jennings' room, I think we're barking up the wrong tree, and we don't have much time to sniff out the right one. And, to be perfectly honest with you, I still wonder why I am involved at all."

"You are successful in your investigations, and you've been consulted by the Yard, particularly given your association with Maurice Blanche. I would have thought you would be delighted to be taken seriously by MacFarlane. He's a maverick, to be sure, and—if you want my opinion—I believe he's brought you in to shake things up, to challenge the way we do things, to inspire new ways of looking at a given problem."

"Then why does he appear to dismiss my ideas?"

"Because that's how he goes about his work, he likes us to keep asking questions. And I seem to remember you saying that a question has the most power before we rush to answer it, when it is still making us think, still testing us."

"Yes, of course, I've said that many a time, and especially when I've been called in to lecture your new detectives. Touché, again, Detective Inspector Stratton." Maisie wiped condensation from the inside of the window. "I think we're here."

The meeting place was a church hall constructed of gray granite. The entrance hall had a pitched roof, with carved eaves just visible through the smog. The front doors, shaped like those of the neighboring church, were open, and two men flanked the entrance. Another man sat behind a desk situated at the back of the meeting room. Stratton gave their names as Mr. and Mrs. Hutchinson, and as they walked in, Maisie automatically linked her arm through his. Stratton smiled down at her, and she blushed, hoping he had not seen her reaction to an unfamiliar feeling that touched her. It was not that she harbored feelings for Stratton, but rather that she was reminded of a sense of belonging, one that she had not felt for some time, not since she ended her relationship with Andrew Dene—and even then, there was always a sense of detachment. She wondered if the death, just a few months ago, of her beloved Simon had perhaps released her in some way.

"Let's take these seats before someone else claims them." Stratton pointed toward two available places at the end of a row of hard, straight-back wooden chairs. "If we're seated at the back, and on the end of the row, we can make a quick departure before the end, if we so wish."

"I take it you have other men here, should they be required?"

"Yes. They're ready if I give the signal to move on the leaders."

Maisie nodded, and began to read the pamphlet handed to her as they entered the room. Following a message of welcome, the pamphlet outlined the New Party's manifesto, much of it based upon a document known as the "Mosley Memorandum," which supported more power to the government and advocated a strong national policy to overcome the country's economic crisis. Though Mosley's party had not been as successful in the October general election as he might have hoped, the party was regrouping, and the wording of the pamphlet suggested a deeper engagement with the tenets of Fascism. Maisie closed the pamphlet. She had read enough.

As more people came into the church hall, Maisie looked around to survey the scene. Many of those attending the meeting were well turned out, and she thought they would be the target of requests for contributions. There were others, poorly dressed, with hollow cheeks and sunken eyes, people who wanted for a good meal and a warm room. She turned back and was just about to comment to Stratton on the broad spectrum of followers, when a scuffle broke out at the back of the room. Raised voices drew attention to the entrance, where several men had grabbed another man and were punching him to the ground.

"I've got as much right to be here as anyone else." The man's shouts attracted more attention, and Maisie was not the only one to witness two of Mosley's followers pushing him out.

Stratton looked at Maisie, and without words they agreed not to intercede. Instead they would continue to observe. First Maisie would keep an eye on the door, then, without attracting attention, Stratton would look around the room, all the time giving the impression that they were waiting for the meeting to begin.

"I think I know what they're doing," said Maisie.

Stratton nodded. "At first I thought they were getting rid of the rougher element, but they're not, are they?"

"No. If I'm not mistaken, they're not letting in any people who look as if they might be Jewish. It's appalling."

Stratton cleared his throat and nodded toward the front of the room. "Here we go."

A man walked up the steps to a small stage, where he talked about the New Party, and about their leader, Sir Oswald Mosley. Encouraging everyone to stand up, he then elevated his voice to introduce the politician Maisie had seen just once before, and whose manner had caused her to shiver. Oswald Mosley's eyes seemed as black as his hair, which was swept back close to his skull accentuating his high forehead. His moustache was narrow and clipped, and seemed as controlled as his manner of dress. He wore a well-tailored black suit, with a white shirt and black tie. Nothing was out of place.

Maisie closed her eyes as he began to speak and felt again the sense of foreboding as his words rallied those present to his cause.

Even though his manifesto reflected what so many wanted to hear, Maisie felt that she was witnessing a man whose ideas for the country might one day, if allowed, become not so much a government, but a regime. She looked at the assembled crowd, watched their eyes seem to catch fire with Mosley's rhetoric.

"We must build up our home markets, we must insulate ourselves from current world conditions and build a better Britain. You cannot build a higher civilization and a standard of life which can absorb the great force of modern production if you are subject to price fluctuations from the rest of the world which dislocate your industry at every turn, and to the sport of competition from virtually slave conditions in other countries."

His speech continued on apace, as he covered all aspects of life, from defense of the country and using military force only to protect Britain's shores, to the centralization of power, until he began to draw his oration to a close.

"What I fear much more than a sudden crisis is a long, slow, crumbling through the years until we sink to the level of a Spain, a gradual paralysis beneath which all the vigor and energy of this country will succumb . . . "

Another disturbance at the back of the hall claimed Maisie's attention, and as she turned, she saw a man beaten, his wife kneeling to his aid, and then both of them pulled out of the building. In her heart she knew that this was not the place where they would find a clue to the identity of a man who would kill to ensure his message was heard. But it was not a wasted evening, because she had seen evidence that there was indeed another man who would halt at nothing to achieve power. Such a man should be stopped at all costs.

Maisie nudged Stratton. "I think I've seen enough. Mosley is all but foaming at the mouth."

Stratton leaned down to whisper, "You're right. I don't think there's anything for us here. Too obvious. This man, or his

followers, would not resort to threats and quiet killing. They're per-
formers and they want to demonstrate power—despite their talk of
inclusion." He looked past Maisie. "Come on, let's go."

Maisie stepped out of the row, followed by Stratton, and
together they crept to the back of the room and opened the curtain
that formed a barrier between the entrance and the main hall.

"Leaving so soon?" A man stepped forward from alongside the
door.

"Yes, afraid so," said Stratton. "My wife is not feeling very well,
so we thought it best to leave. Pity, though, great chap, isn't he?"

The man looked at Maisie, who held her hand to her stomach,
then he stepped aside for them to pass.

"Perhaps we'll see you again, Mr. and Mrs. Hutchinson."

"Oh, I'm sure you will. Good night."

They left the meeting hall and walked down the road, Maisie's
hand resting on Stratton's arm. They did not speak until they were
sure Mosley's men on guard outside the church hall were out of
earshot.

"Do you think Mosley sanctioned what we just saw?" asked
Maisie.

Stratton shook his head. "I doubt he's given his blessing, but he
may be turning a blind eye—you know, 'what the eye doesn't see'
and all that."

"But that's approval by default. My guess is that his blind eye
will lead to more violence if those men are allowed to continue in
such a thuggish vein, then he'll be in trouble."

"I'm sure you're right." Stratton looked across the road as the
lights on the Invicta came on. "Ah, here's the motor car." He whistled
and four men emerged from the shadows as he stepped away from
Maisie to speak to them. "You know who to take in, don't you?"

"Yes, sir."

"Right. Don't wait until the end. Go now, softly-softly. Buckman and Smith are on the other side of the hall, and the van's around the corner. Take those thugs in one at a time and nail them for assault and battery—and that's just the start. Did you get the names of the victims?"

"Yes, sir."

"Good. I'll see you back at the Yard."

The first man nodded and opened the door of the motor car. Stratton took Maisie's hand as she stepped aboard, and sat down next to her, looking out of the back window as the Invicta drove away.

"Time to take you home, Miss Dobbs. You'll be seeing your protesting women tomorrow."

"Another bark up the wrong tree."

"Oh, I'm sure you're making your way up your own path on this one."

She smiled, but said nothing.

When they arrived outside the block of flats in Pimlico, Stratton alighted first and held out his hand to steady her as she stepped onto the pavement. She thought Stratton held on to her hand for one second too long, and drew back from him to take her keys from her bag.

"Good night, Inspector. I'll be in touch tomorrow."

"Good night, Miss Dobbs."

MAISIE WALKED TOWARD the glass front door, and when she turned saw that Stratton was still standing by the Invicta, watching until she was inside with the outer door locked once more. She waved one last time, and then stepped toward her flat, key in hand.

Later, as she sat cross-legged in front of the fireplace, a dressing gown covering her loose pajamas, she closed her eyes to meditate on her day, and to clear her mind for tomorrow. She now knew the identity of the man she had seen blow himself to pieces on Christmas Eve, but she knew nothing about him, except that he loved books and had been wounded and gassed in the war. He had met a friend, a neatly turned-out man, in Soho Square, and he had recently become reacquainted with someone who might have been an old colleague. Could there be two men, and were these men connected? And what of Ian Jennings? Who was he? Where had he come from, who knew him—who might have grieved for him?

Thoughts of grief brought back memories of Simon, of his passing, so recent and still so raw. Simon Lynch was the army doctor for whom she had burned a candle for so long, even though he was no more than a shell of the man who had stolen her heart. It was a strange death; after so many years he had simply slipped away. She felt as if she had been in mourning since the war, but only allowed to grieve for the past few months. Of course, there were the years when she did not see him, when she could not face the memories, or the terror of reflection upon the explosion that had wounded them both. She shook her head, as memories of France in wartime merged with Christmas Eve's tragedy and flooded her mind's eye.

Somewhere, most likely in London, a desperate man was planning another attack—of that she was sure. The dead creatures were just the beginning, until his demands were met or he was found. And as she knew too well, the latter was the only option, because the government would never act upon the petitions of someone considered a madman. She thought of her father, who held strong views on such subjects.

"You know, Maisie, that when you look at one of these politicians, you're looking at a thief, a liar and a murderer, that's the way I see it."

"Come on, Dad, that's not like you."

"No, I mean it. Look—they take our money, they lie through their teeth, and then they send our boys off to their deaths, don't they? And all the time, they're in clover, never a day's risk or a day wanting."

EIGHT

Maisie had been to Wychett Hill in the past, and as she turned the MG into the driveway, she looked at Billy in the passenger seat, and saw the tension in his jaw when he, too, looked up at the clock tower. She thought the years had tempered neither her memory of the asylum nor the reality of the building itself. Wychett Hill was a fine example of ornate Victorian construction that seemed both austere and ostentatious at the same time, like so many hospitals opened in the middle of the last century, including the Princess Victoria, the domain of Anthony Lawrence. But there was something even more foreboding about Wychett Hill, situated as it was on the North Downs in Surrey, where clouds congregated all too gray and all too ready to threaten with cold breezes and rain-filled air.

"Spooky sort of place, ain't it, Miss?"

"It gives me the shivers."

Billy turned to her as she negotiated the final sweep toward an area dedicated to the parking of motor vehicles. "I appreciate you bringing me here, Miss. It would have taken so long otherwise, what with the trains, then the walk from Tattenham Corner. I would never've been able to do it without leaving at the crack of dawn."

"I know. But don't worry about it—I'm concerned about Doreen's well-being too, you know."

"Yes, I know, Miss." Billy bit his lip and looked out of the window, then down to the base of an adjacent wall. "You're all right on this side, I reckon that'll do you."

Maisie braked and turned off the engine. "Look at that rain, it's really coming down now. Thank heavens for the humble umbrella, eh? Come on, we'd better run for it."

"You wait there, Miss." Billy turned up the collar of his raincoat, pulled his flat cap down deep on his forehead, grabbed the umbrella, and alighted from the vehicle. With the umbrella unfurled, he came to the driver's side and opened the door for Maisie, who was pulling a scarf around her neck, tucking it into the collar of her mackintosh.

"Thank you, Billy." Clasping her black document case in her left hand, she locked the MG and nodded to Billy. Together they ran to the main entrance, and were assaulted by the anticipated hospital smells of disinfectant and urine.

Maisie ran her hands across her shoulders to flick rain from her mackintosh, and stamped her feet. She looked around her and sighed. What had she ever done to deserve spending so much time in hospitals? But her choice of a professional life steeped in matters of life and death must of course include the place to which humans are tended in a time of sickness, whether that sickness was of the body or the mind, or both.

"That was a big sigh, Miss."

"Oh, I know, Billy. I was just wondering how many hospitals I will set foot in, in my life. Remember I've an appointment with Dr. Elsbeth Masters at the Clifton Hospital this afternoon." She shrugged. "Every one has its own mood, its own feel. Yet I could be put into a hospital blindfold and know where I was—there's the smell, the sounds, and if you touch the brick outside, or the plaster inside, there's always that same sensation. It's as if the suffering, the hope, the grief expended had seeped into the walls."

"And don't forget that reek of cabbage boiled until it's nothing but sopping wet shreds."

Maisie laughed. "You're right, the smell of overcooked vegetables." She looked around. "Now then, where do we go from here?"

"It's this way, Miss." Billy checked the time on his wristwatch and led the way up a staircase flanked by a cast-iron filigree banister, the top rail rough and cold to the touch.

In the distance Maisie heard a scream, then moaning. She heard footsteps moving back and forth, and echoes from the various wards ricocheting off the brick walls and sliding along the banister, so that it seemed as if the building itself had taken on a certain volatility, and a visitor might believe the staircase would begin to shake at any moment. Billy continued to lead the way to one of the women's wards, then stopped alongside locked double doors with frosted glass at eye level. He pulled a cord to the right of the door and soon a nurse came to let them in.

"Mr. Beale. I'm here to see Mrs. Doreen Beale."

The nurse nodded, looking Maisie up and down as she allowed her to pass.

"And this is a very good friend of ours, Miss Maisie Dobbs." Having introduced Maisie, Billy glanced back and forth along the row of beds. "Where's my wife?"

"Don't worry, Mr. Beale, she's in a recovery ward. She's as well as can be expected, but don't expect her to be able to speak."

Billy turned on the nurse, his mounting distress revealed by the swollen vein at his left temple. "What do you mean, 'don't expect her to speak'? What's the matter with her?"

Maisie set her hand on Billy's forearm and smiled at the nurse. "My friend is very concerned about his wife, as you can imagine. Perhaps you could describe her situation as we walk along to see her—has she been taken to a room on her own, by chance?"

The nurse relaxed her shoulders, and pursed her lips, frowning at Billy, but appeared more accommodating as she spoke to Maisie. "There was a little op, and she was, well, she was making a bit of a fuss afterward, so we had to put her on her own for a while so she wouldn't start the rest of them off."

Maisie glanced on either side of her as they walked along the ward. The "rest of them" seemed to be catatonic, with mouths open or staring into the distance. She suspected that peace and calm were achieved with various pills and medicines. The aroma of sour dairy suggested that some had been put on a milk diet, which Maisie thought had been discontinued a decade earlier. As they approached a third set of double doors, the nurse took a chain from her pocket and selected a key. She slotted the key in the lock, rattled the left door toward her and turned the key back and forth until she was able to unlock the door.

"Always sticks, that one."

Maisie nodded, but did not look at Billy. She felt his composure breaking again, realizing that his wife was now deeper in the bowels of asylum control, kept behind another set of locked doors.

"I understand that Mrs. Beale has undergone some kind of insulin therapy." Maisie volunteered the statement in a conversational manner.

"Yes, she had the second treatment yesterday."

"Do you know why?"

"The doctor thought it would get her mind on the rails again, give her the push she needs to overcome her melancholy."

"And there were difficulties?"

"Nothing out of the ordinary. She became a bit hysterical as she came out of it, so she's been sedated."

"I see. So, the insulin therapy is having no effect whatsoever, then?"

The nurse did not respond to Maisie's question.

They reached another door, and through the small observation window could see that this was the room where Doreen Beale was recovering. The nurse set the key in the lock and turned to Billy. "Now, she's not to be excited. She should remain calm—remember she's still not quite conscious."

She led the way into the room, where Doreen was lying on a cast-iron bed, her eyes wide open, her face contorted as she jerked her head back and forth on the pillow. Her wrists were secured to the bed on either side of her body, and her feet had been strapped to the bottom of the bed. Her slender wrists reminded Maisie of a sparrow's tiny bones, set against the dark leather biting into her skin. Doreen had lost so much weight it seemed as if the sheet and blanket were flush across the bed, with slight protrusions to indicate the position of her feet, knees and hips.

"Oh, my darlin' girl, my darlin' girl." Billy rushed to his wife's bedside and rested his hand on her damp brow, then leaned down to kiss her cheek.

Doreen stopped struggling and began to weep, tears falling across her face. "It's bad, Billy. It's bad here. Take me home, please, Billy. I want my boys, I want my Lizzie, take me home."

"We'll get you out of here, don't you worry. It won't be long now."

"Don't let them put them needles in me again, don't let them do it." Her breath came in short, rapid gasps, and her chest rose as she struggled for air.

A staff nurse entered and stepped across to the opposite side of the bed. "Now then, Mrs. Beale, you don't want any more injections, do you? Take a deep breath, come on, Mrs. Beale."

"I can look after my wife while I'm here, Nurse. Please leave us."

"Now, look here—"

Maisie moved toward the woman. "I can be of assistance while you are out of the room, Staff Nurse. I am sure Mrs. Beale will settle in a minute or two—and I was a nurse in a secure institution, so I understand the importance of summoning you if help is required."

Doreen calmed as she listened to the exchange, and the rhythm of her breathing slowed as Billy stroked her brow to settle her.

"Ten minutes, that's all you've got." The staff nurse shook her head and left the room.

"Who does she think she is—ten minutes, my eye!"

"Billy, you're not helping Doreen," Maisie whispered, as she came to the opposite side of the bed. She took a clean linen handkerchief from her pocket and wiped saliva from the sides of Doreen's mouth, then turned toward the side-table, where a pitcher and bowl had been placed, along with a square of clean white muslin. Maisie poured cold water into the ewer, then steeped the cloth into the water and squeezed out the excess. Shaking out the fabric, she folded it horizontally and smiled at Doreen. "Now if Billy will just lift his hand for a minute, let's cool you down a bit."

Doreen nodded, and looked at Billy, who was trying to release the straps that held her hands in place. And as Maisie wiped her face with soft strokes, then rinsed the cloth and swabbed her neck, she began to weep again.

"I want my boys, I want my little girl."

"Love, Lizzie's gone now, she's gone. That's why you've come here, so they can help you get over it."

Doreen began to gasp again, and Maisie shook her head at Billy. "Let's just keep her calm. If we can get her transferred to the

Clifton, Dr. Masters will know exactly how to approach her treatment. Let's just settle her so they'll release her from the straps and take her back to the women's ward."

"I don't want them doing this to her again."

Maisie continued to draw the cool cloth back and forth across Doreen's forehead, and soon her eyes were heavy, her breathing became more shallow and she began to fall asleep.

"Poor love, look at her, there's nothing of her. She looks barely more than a child herself." Tears welled in Billy's eyes.

"They'll work through a standard set of treatments, trying to find something that works," whispered Maisie. "I am sure she has had some kind of Faradism, and as for this insulin treatment—" She said no more, but gave silent thanks for the fact that removal of the ovaries, the fashionable treatment for melancholia in women some thirty years earlier, had long been abandoned.

"What do you think will help her, Miss?" Billy rested his hand on his wife's forehead once again, as Maisie ran the cloth down her arms and into her palms, removing the sticky sweat of fear from the exposed parts of her body.

Maisie did not speak for some seconds, instead stroking the cloth back and forth along the inside of Doreen's left arm, her eyes fixed on the thick leather strap and buckle that secured the sick woman to her bed. "Time is the great healer. I once knew a doctor who said that his real job was to keep the patient occupied while time and nature did their work. Doreen's grief has run so deep that it now colors every waking and sleeping moment. It has leached down into the fibers of her being, so there are physical as well as mental disturbances and consequences." She paused. "I do not want to preempt a doctor, however, I would imagine she will need a period of time in hospital, to stabilize her melancholia— the fatigue, anxiety, depression. She has doubtless suffered from the headaches and neuralgia that accompany her condition, so the doctors will want to get her on an even keel, alleviate her physical suffering to the point where they can address the deep-seated grief that has led to her malaise, her instability. She needs good nutrition, she needs to be calmed. And she needs to talk, but not to you or me or someone close to her. She needs to shed her sadness, like a snake sheds its skin, and that can be a troubling process, for a snake is at its most vulnerable at such a time."

"When you say, 'talking,' do you mean like Dr. Blanche did with me, when I went through my bad turn, a couple of years ago? And like you do with the people what come to you?"

"That's more or less what I mean." Maisie wondered how to express her frustrations without upsetting Billy. "The trouble is, it's always been those of a higher station in life than either you or I who could afford the sort of therapeutic process that Doreen needs. And progress must be accompanied by direction from a clinician such as Dr. Masters."

"Bleedin' typical, ain't it—about the toffs getting the best treatments, while the likes of us are packed away in nuthouses?"

"You could say that. Frankly, it stems from a belief that the lower classes—and that means both of us—do not think and feel in the same way as our *betters*. Times are changing, though."

"But not fast enough, eh?"

"No, not fast enough."

Billy and Maisie remained with Doreen until the staff nurse returned, and as she strode into the room, Maisie lifted a finger to her lips.

"Mrs. Beale is resting now," she whispered. "May we leave Mr. Beale alone with his wife for a moment?" She stood up and moved toward the nurse, taking her by the arm. "Perhaps you and I can have a word outside, while he says his good-bye."

The nurse frowned, but acquiesced, allowing Maisie to lead her from the room.

"She's a right nutter, that one," said the nurse, as Maisie closed the door without a sound.

"I beg to disagree with you, Staff Nurse. She is a woman who is wracked with grief, a woman who has buckled under the weight of losing a child. We now have to help her to her feet again, though that loss will always be with her."

"But thousands have lost, haven't they? They don't all end up inside, though, eh? Made of stronger stuff, that's what they are." The nurse tensed her jaw, and Maisie noticed the way she rubbed her hand back and forth across her abdomen as she spoke.

"Mrs. Beale's husband took her to the doctor, which is why she is here now."

"I don't know, I think she's had some mollycoddling, that's what it is. I mean, when I lost my—" The staff nurse paused, clutched her hands together, then released them to reach for the door handle. "It's time for him to go now. If she remains calm like this for the afternoon, then she'll be back on the main ward by evening."

Maisie looked on as Billy lingered with his wife a moment longer, then she reached forward and set her hand upon his shoulder.

"Better be off now."

Billy nodded, kissed Doreen on the cheek, and walked from the room without looking back.

"I do hope you can get her out of here, Miss. I'd discharge her, if I could."

"I know, Billy, I know. She won't be here for long."

And as they left the building, she thought of her father, and his words echoed once again: this was another desperate sort of place.

MAISIE DROPPED BILLY at Fitzroy Square and made her way directly to Camberwell and the Clifton Hospital. When Maisie was shown into her office, Dr. Elsbeth Masters looked up over her tortoiseshell spectacles, smiled broadly, and reached across the desk to shake her hand.

"Maisie Dobbs. I haven't seen you since you worked for dear Maurice—how is he?"

"In his mind, still very busy, but slowing down in his body—he's getting on now."

Masters held out her hand for Maisie to be seated, then sat down herself, moving a patient file to one side as she spoke. She leaned forward, hands clasped, as they exchanged pleasantries and caught up on Maisie's progression from Blanche's assistant to proprietress of her own business. When Maisie first came to work at the Clifton, it did not surprise her in the least to meet someone who knew Maurice. There always seemed to be someone, somewhere in her life, who was acquainted with her longtime mentor.

"Frankly, Maisie, I always hoped you would move into the clinical arena—we could do with more women doctors in the care of the mentally ill, you know, and things have moved on since my early days at the Royal Free. But I am sure your work is more than satisfying."

"Yes, it is—very much so."

"Now then, tell me what I can do for you."

"There are two reasons for my visit—the first is regarding the wife of my employee. I am close to the family and want to see an end to a difficult situation."

"Go on." Masters took off her spectacles and leaned forward as Maisie continued.

"Last year their young daughter died of diphtheria. They have two boys as well, but Lizzie was the apple of her mother's eye, and such a dear, dear child." Maisie bit her lip and paused. She felt quite ready to weep, an emotion that gripped her with such suddenness that she fought to stem the tears. "Since their loss the parents have struggled to come to terms with the fact that Lizzie is no longer there, but Doreen, my employee's wife, has taken a downward spiral. She had been under the care of a doctor for some months—the child died last February—when it was decided to section her and she was sent to Wychett Hill a couple of days ago with a diagnosis of melancholia and hysteria."

"Oh, dear . . . " Masters shook her head.

"They have already proceeded with insulin shock and changes of diet, and I can see—we visited her this morning—that she has been sedated with narcotics. When we arrived she had been strapped to a bed and left alone in a room. I think the treatment is rather harsh, and that she would do better closer to home and under your care, if it were possible to effect a transfer."

"I see." Masters tapped the desk with her long fingers, the backs of her hands embossed with a mesh of veins and dotted with liver spots. "Certainly, I believe we could make more progress with such a patient here. Let me make some inquiries—who was the admitting doctor, do you know?"

Maisie reached into her document case, brought out a sheet of paper and handed it to the doctor. "You'll find all the information you require here."

"Ah, as efficient as ever, Maisie." She took the page of notes and slipped it into a fresh file, which she then marked with Doreen Beale's name. "I take it I could telephone Mr. Beale at your office, if I need to reach him as a matter of urgency?"

"Yes, of course. However, we are out of the office a great deal, so if you do not receive an answer, please send a telegram or postcard."

"Right. Leave it with me. I'll see what I can do." She scraped back her chair as if to stand.

"Dr. Masters, there is one more thing, if you have a moment or two."

Masters looked at the wall-mounted clock. "Yes, of course. I've a few minutes." She smiled and leaned forward again, her hands once more resting on the desk.

"I know you were in France, during the war, and you were involved in the treatment of men with war neuroses of one kind or another."

"Well, *eventually* I was in France. At first, as you know, they told us women doctors that we should go back to our kitchens, but I joined one of the all-women medical units set up by Dr. Elsie Inglis—there was an indomitable woman for you—and was privileged to work with a truly dedicated and professional group of nurses and doctors. Before long my presence was requested by the boys at the top when shell-shock cases began coming through thick and fast, and I was able to work alongside men. And yes, it was my background in neurology and psychiatry that they were interested in."

"I am familiar with the different levels of war neuroses, Dr. Masters, the distinctions between neurasthenia, battle fatigue, soldier's heart and hysteria, but I am involved in a case at the moment that demands—I believe—a deeper understanding of the mind of a man who has seen battle at close quarters and is afflicted mentally and emotionally by that experience."

Masters tapped the desk again. "Remember, there were many cases of shell-shock recorded where the patient had been nowhere near a detonated shell, nowhere near the front line of battle. Simply anticipating a move up to the front could turn some men. Unfortunately, despite the best efforts of myself and others with specific training in dealing with injury to the mind of a man, the army doctors—and the brass, I might add—wanted clean-cut delineations between wounded and sick, between shell-shocked and malingering. Wounded and shell-shocked would be granted the 'W' armband—and the pension that went with it. Simply being an 'S' case—sick—meant you were turned around and sent back up the line at the earliest possible opportunity."

"I understand. I've also been speaking to Dr. Anthony Lawrence— do you remember, he was here for a while, then moved to the Princess Victoria? He has said much the same thing. Anyway, I simply wanted to get some sort of . . . " Maisie looked out of the window as she considered her words with care. "Some sort of reflection from you, as to what it was like to treat such an affliction."

Masters ran her hands through her short, bobbed gray-flecked hair. "That's an interesting question. I don't think anyone's ever put it like that." She sat back, then forward again, having considered the question. "I don't know whether you know this, but I was born and grew up in British East Africa. My father had a coffee farm—it's now run by my younger brother—so we had a very different childhood in comparison with our peers here. We were rather wild, if I may admit such a thing. We were both sent to school in England at age eleven, and although I returned briefly prior to commencing my studies at medical school, it is those early years that defined me, defined my sense of what I could do—I wasn't used to anyone telling me that a girl couldn't do this, or that. But here's something that struck me in France. It was the memory of something I'd seen as a child."

Elsbeth Masters pushed back her chair and walked to the window behind her, where she placed her hands on the bulbous radiator as if to cleave from it a warmth she had known at another time. She turned to Maisie and continued, now leaning back against the source of heat. "I remember going off one day with my friend, a young Masai boy, the son of one of our servants. No one seemed to mind us playing together, out and about for hours until sundown, following the men when they hunted. On this particular jaunt we saw a lion take down a gazelle—and I mean at close quarters. It quite took my breath away. It was as if something happened to the gazelle at the moment of capture, something awe-inspiringly terrible and wonderful at the same time—as if, in knowing the gazelle was to die a dreadful death, ripped apart by the jaws of the lion, the Creator had given the captive a reprieve by taking her soul before she was dead, so that no pain would be felt because the essence had gone already."

Maisie nodded, able to see the scene in her mind's eye, so charged was the doctor's description.

"And I saw the eyes of the gazelle again in France, and it struck me that perhaps a heartsick God had looked down and taken up a soul, leaving only the shell of a man." She shook her head as if to extinguish the recollection, and brought her attention back to her visitor. "I sometimes thought that, in my work, I was really trying to create the conditions whereby a soul might be persuaded to join a man's body once again, thus making him whole."

Maisie nodded.

"You're probably thinking, 'Physician, heal thyself.'"

"No, not at all, not at all." Maisie smiled. "I was just thinking back to the days when I worked as a nurse with shell-shocked men at this hospital—looking into their eyes and knowing that part of them was lost. Perhaps to return, perhaps not."

"Now, do you have any more questions for me?"

"Just a couple. Do you know Dr. Lawrence well?"

"Curious that you mention him again, because I hadn't heard from him in years, yet I received a letter from him this morning, wondering if we might meet." She shrugged. "I suspect he has a paper he'd like me to review before he reveals it to a wider peer group."

"How are you acquainted?"

"Funnily enough, it wasn't directly to do with our regular work with the insane, but years ago, in connection with patients who had suffered in gas attacks."

"I see."

"Yes. There was a team of boffins—you know, scientists, physicists, that sort of person—working in Berkshire on antidotes to gas. There was some *experimentation*, I think you would call it, and they were interested in having a degree of neurological and psychological assessment as part of their research."

"Did you work for them?"

"For a very short time. I wasn't sure if it was a command or request, to tell you the truth, but I didn't like what was going on. I looked into it, you see, and realized that they were—if you'll forgive the phrase—playing fast and loose with the health of anyone and everyone who worked there. Anyone or thing who breathed could be dragged in for an experiment or test. I could just imagine it: 'Just put down the teapot, Mrs. Smith—breathe through this mask and tell us how you feel.' "

"And Dr. Lawrence? Did he continue?"

"I believe he did, for a while."

Maisie nodded and looked at the clock. "Thank you so much for seeing me—and for anything you can do for Mrs. Beale. She is in a desperate situation."

"Yes, I understand. I'll take this along to admissions now—we could have her transferred within the next four or five days if all goes well."

Maisie stood up to leave, and as she held out her hand to Elsbeth Masters, the doctor stepped from behind her desk. It was only then that Maisie realized the woman was not wearing shoes, and stood before her with bare feet.

"Oh, don't take any notice of me. I just cannot abide wearing shoes to this day. I was barefoot until I was eleven and I try to reclaim that sense of freedom whenever I can. I think I would go quite mad if I couldn't take my shoes off several times a day."

Maisie said good-bye, and as she moved to leave, noticed a pair of polished brown leather shoes set on the floor just inside the door, each with a stocking folded and tucked inside.

NINE

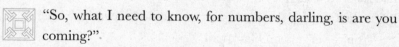"So, what I need to know, for numbers, darling, is are you coming?"

"Coming? Coming where?" Maisie frowned, taken aback when the telephone rang and she picked up the receiver to hear Priscilla's question, without so much as a "Hello, Maisie" by way of introduction.

"Old Year's Night—party, at our house. Everyone—and I do mean *everyone*—in London will be there. Do not let me down, Maisie, I have a very nice man for you to meet."

Priscilla was Maisie's dear friend from her early days at Girton College, and though they were as different as two young women could be—Priscilla's devil-may-care attitude toward work and play was intimidating to Maisie at first—they had been drawn to each other in the way that opposites attract. The loss of all three beloved brothers in the war, followed by the death of her parents, who succumbed to the flu epidemic, led Priscilla to escape to Biarritz on the west coast of France soon after the end of the war. It was here that she steeped herself in a raucous social life, and drank to anesthetize the pain of her losses. Then she met Douglas Partridge, who had been wounded in the war—his arm had been amputated and he required a cane to support his weight as he walked—and fell in love. She credited their marriage and family life with their three sons as having saved her from herself. Since returning to London for the sake of their sons' education, Maisie had noticed that Priscilla was not taking to life back in England.

"Oh, Pris, no—I don't think I could bear another one of your arranged meetings with so-called eligible men, who seem to me to be playing the field for all they're worth."

"But you will come to the party, won't you? Supper at half-past eight, then dancing before we see in the New Year—and let's all hope things get better this year. Now then, do not tell me you've had second thoughts. How long have we been friends? And this will be the first turn of the year we've been able to spend together."

"You're verging on blackmail, Priscilla."

"I know, look what you've driven me to—do say you'll be coming."

Maisie smiled and sighed. "Oh, all right, I'll come—in fact, it will be lovely. I could do with some lightness in my life."

"You could do with a lot of lightness, if you ask me. So, see you at half-past seven for drinks—opening salvo to the evening's festivities. And you never know, you may rub shoulders with the PM himself—not that we expect him to stay, being more of your dour sort."

Maisie thought she could hear the clink of ice against glass in the background. "I've already rubbed shoulders with him—and yes, he is a bit uninspiring."

"You've met the PM?"

Priscilla's voice was louder than was necessary, and now Maisie was sure that she was drinking, but she made no mention of the fact.

"I know what you're thinking, Pris—surprising in my line of work, eh?"

"Well, now that you come to mention it . . . but anyway, see you for the party. Wear something stunning. If you are not suitably clad, I will drag you to my dressing room to re-garb you. Remember it's a party, Maisie, not a wake!"

"I'm sure no one will be interested in what I wear—"

"Nonsense. Now, I must dash, so much to do. Bye for now, Maisie dear."

"Bye, Pris."

Priscilla's telephone call had come within moments of Maisie's return to her office in Fitzroy Square. Billy was out, and it was already late afternoon. She considered the worrisome possibility of Priscilla drinking so early in the day, before the pre-supper cocktail hour that had become so popular in the past few years, and could imagine her friend pouring a gin and tonic while saying, "Well, the sun must be over the yardarm somewhere in the Empire!" But she feared that in Priscilla's case, the distinction between a pleasant pre-prandial drink and being drunk was beginning to blur once again.

Maisie had intended to catch her breath and bring her notes up to date before going to the meeting in support of women's pensions. She couldn't think why MacFarlane insisted upon her going. She was aware that the interest of Special Branch in groups of women gathering together had started with the suffragettes long ago, based upon the threat they represented to the men who governed the country—yet she could no more imagine such a group involved with poison gas than she could imagine a woman taking over Ramsey MacDonald's job. But if such an investigation brought her ever closer to the real threat, then she had to go.

She set to work, checking the clock on the mantelpiece, for she would have to make her way to Scotland Yard following the meeting of women, but after spending some time making notations on her own case map pinned across the table by the window, Maisie sat back, her thoughts on the conversation with Elsbeth Masters.

She had always liked Masters. There seemed to be a wisdom about the woman, a way of carrying herself that suggested knowledge, capability and compassion, without the need to be strident, the latter being an unfortunate trait she had found in other women of a similar professional stature. More than anything, Maisie could not banish the picture of a dying gazelle from her mind, and kept seeing the fine-boned face, the luminous black eyes devoid of a spirit that had ascended as the lion's teeth clutched the animal by the back of the neck and brought it down. And she wondered: *Was that me?* Had her soul abandoned her as shell fire rained down on the casualty clearing station? In her youth, had she been unable to reclaim that essential part of her being? Might it account for her reticence, her lack of emotional mastery when faced with the possibility of a more intimate connection?

She stood up and stepped back from the desk to stand in front of the gas fire, first crouching down to turn up the jets. *Am I healing, now?* She had sensed a newness within her of late, as if spring itself were waiting behind winter's cold cloak. She had felt the need to bring color into her life, and music, for didn't song lift the spirit and provide a conduit for the soul's voice? And hadn't she read, somewhere, that in dancing we are seeking a connection with the Divine? Had she, simply by engaging in those endeavors that called to her, given her spirit permission to come home? She closed her eyes and thought of Simon, now gone, now nothing more than a memory and ashes wind-strewn across a field. Looking into the past was like looking into a long tunnel, and she knew the tragedy of his wounding and his passing no longer touched her with such an immediate rawness. It was more akin to an ache that came and went, like a breeze that lifts a lace curtain back from the window, then sets it down again. Now, it was as if those jagged and painful memories of him were clothing she no longer needed, that she had laundered, dried and placed in a sealed box in the attic. She might open that box on occasion and look inside, perhaps touch the fabric and hold it to her cheek, but she would never wear those clothes again, because they did not fit. She had changed. It was as if her tentative returning spirit had required nothing less of her.

Maisie looked at the clock once more. Perhaps the unrelenting grief she had worn like a heavy cloak had been akin to madness; after all, it had kept her incarcerated in a cell of wartime memories, and she had been her own jailer, the keys to her past jangling from her waist.

The telephone rang, causing Maisie to jump and put her hand on her heart. She reached for the receiver. "Fitzroy—"

"Miss Dobbs, MacFarlane here."

"Good afternoon, Chief Superintendent. I was just about to leave for the women's union meeting."

"I thought as much. Anyway, change of plan. There's a motor on its way to you now—it should be outside in about five minutes."

"Have there been developments?"

"Well, if you call finding out who's been messing around with poison gas and building a cache of Mills Bombs a 'development'— then we certainly have one."

"You have the culprit?"

"Culprits. Plural. Stratton is on his way. I'll see you when you get here." There was a click and then a single unbroken tone as MacFarlane hung up the receiver.

"And good-bye to you, Detective Chief Superintendent Mac-Farlane!" Maisie set the receiver down and went to the table, where she tidied the colored pencils and picked up her document case.

The door opened and Billy entered. "Afternoon, Miss. There's a big old Invicta just pulled up outside—that for you?"

"I'm afraid it is. I'm off to Scotland Yard."

Billy, placing his coat on the hook, took Maisie's mackintosh down and held it open for her. "Any progress?"

"Yes, they reckon they've caught the men behind the poison gas attacks."

"And you don't think they've got the right blokes—I can see it written all over your face."

"You're right, but I'm going to give them the benefit of the doubt." Maisie paused. "Look, come with me. I've managed to involve you, so you should be there. Get your coat on and let's go. I want to talk to you anyway, about my meeting with Elsbeth Masters."

Billy took down his coat and opened the door for Maisie. "Miss . . . I'm sorry to bother you, but . . . and I hope you don't mind me asking again, but—do you think we can get Doreen into the Clifton?"

Maisie reached out and placed her hand on his arm. "No firm 'yes' yet, but I believe we'll be in luck. And the sooner the better, after what we saw at Wychett Hill."

MACFARLANE, STRATTON and Colm Darby were together in the usual meeting room at Scotland Yard when Maisie arrived with Billy. After introducing her assistant to the policemen, they took their seats for a briefing from Robert MacFarlane.

"Acting on a tip-off, our men interrupted"—he looked at the group over the top of horn-rimmed spectacles, and winked—"*interrupted* a meeting of union troublemakers who had set themselves up in the cellar of a house in Finchley. Caught them red-handed with the wherewithal to make and activate incendiary devices at will. Though the laboratory chaps are still completing their investigation, we are given to believe these villains have constructed gas bombs ready to let loose across the city."

"How many men?" asked Maisie. She did not look up as she held her pencil ready to make notes on a clutch of index cards.

"Four. And one woman."

"And you say they are union sympathizers?"

"Yes. We found anti-government literature, along with details of likely targets, et cetera, et cetera."

"Have you details on the 'et ceteras,' Detective Chief Superintendent?" She turned to Colm Darby. "Inspector Darby, have you had the opportunity to view handwriting samples yet? And has there been some sort of psychological analysis?"

Stratton caught Maisie's eye and shook his head, as if to warn her against pressing MacFarlane too far. Maisie looked away, and back at MacFarlane, waiting for an answer.

"Miss Dobbs, I take it you doubt the integrity of our investigation."

"No, certainly not. You've acted upon credible intelligence and come up with proof of subversive activity that could compromise the well-being of the general public, possibly leading to loss of life on a frightening scale. No, I am not questioning the integrity of the actual investigation that has led to these people being brought in on suspicion of causing terror, but instead I'm wondering whether they are the people involved in the threats received by the Prime Minister, the Home Secretary and the Minister for Pensions, and if they are the ones responsible for the deaths of innocent animals. I am wondering if union sympathizers would not take another course of action—would it occur to them, for example, to show their intent in an initial attack on dogs and then birds? It doesn't seem to me to be the sort of thing a group of union activists might do. What do you think?"

MacFarlane shuffled his papers, set them down, then looked back at Maisie, supported by his knuckles as he leaned across the table. "I think I would like you to come down to a lineup of our little gang of subversive warriors and tell us if you have seen any of them before." He turned to Billy, who was following the conversation with an increasing degree of discomfort, and wondering whether his employer was pushing her luck. "And you too, Mr. Beale. You were also walking along Charlotte Street on Christmas Eve—you might recall a face or two."

Billy nodded. "Right you are, sir."

MacFarlane looked at Maisie. "See, even your man here thinks I'm right."

She inclined her head and stood up, ready to follow MacFarlane. "Then let's go down to view the suspects, shall we?"

The group was led by MacFarlane to a damp red-brick room without plaster on the walls, where four men and a solitary woman had been told to stand with their legs apart and their hands behind their backs.

"Let me introduce our motley crew here today," said MacFarlane. "First, Graham Tucker, thirty-four, union activist, small-time crook—though his mates here probably don't know about his previous, which includes pickpocketing and receiving stolen goods. Learned a thing or two about explosives in the war, courtesy of His Majesty's Army." He moved along the line. "Tommy Burgess. Thirty years of age. Mineworkers union and, again, a bit of previous behind him, including assault and robbery." He shook his head. "I think we're seeing something of a pattern here. Now to Miss Catherine Jones. Chemist, a university girl no less—and look where it's got her today."

Maisie suspected Catherine Jones was about to spit on MacFarlane's feet, but had thought better of it and instead looked at the ground. MacFarlane introduced the last two members of the gang, Wilfred Knight and Frederick Ovendale, both union men, both soldiers in the war.

"Right then, we've seen enough, I think we can resume our meeting now," said MacFarlane.

Maisie spoke in a low voice to MacFarlane: "I'd like to question Miss Jones, if I may?"

MacFarlane rolled his eyes. "Be my guest." He turned to a constable and a woman police auxiliary, and directed them to take Catherine Jones to an interview room, then held out his hand for Maisie to follow.

Maisie turned to her assistant. "Billy, perhaps you would be so kind as to return to the meeting room and take down my case map. I won't be long—about ten to fifteen minutes."

Billy nodded and looked at Stratton, who indicated that Billy should follow him.

When they entered the interview room, no more than twelve feet square with eggshell-finished walls and a small window that allowed only a narrow shaft of light in, Maisie held out her hand for the woman to be seated, then turned to the constable. "Perhaps you'd be so kind as to wait outside. I'll only need your Miss Hawkins here to witness the interview."

She kept her coat on, for it was cold in the room, and sat down opposite the woman.

"If you think I'm going to be the Judas here, you've got another think coming." Catherine Jones spat out the words and did not face Maisie, but sat with her legs to one side, so that she could look at the wall and not her interviewer.

"I'm not going to ask you to be disloyal to your friends, but I do want to establish the extent to which you have already used your skills and knowledge on behalf of the union agitators. You are an intelligent, well-educated woman, Miss Jones, yet you have risked everything by throwing in your lot with these men." Maisie paused, clasping her hands together on the table in front of her. "What led you to take such a gamble?"

The woman braced her shoulders as if to fight the urge to

respond, then breathed a sigh and slumped toward the table, her head resting on her forearms. The policewoman stepped forward, but Maisie held up her hand. Jones shook her head and looked up. "This is a bloody nightmare."

"Yes, it is. But it started somewhere, didn't it?"

The woman sat back. "I'd give my eyeteeth for a ciggie."

"Sorry, I don't smoke."

"No, I didn't think so. You're not the type, more's the pity."

"Tell me how you became mixed up in this, Catherine."

Jones shrugged. "I lost my job. Easy as that. Laid off with no money coming in. My parents are dead, my brother was wounded in the war and died in a hospital in Southampton—septicemia. I'm alone, so I need money to live. I'd joined the union, and became more involved in politics." She paused. "You probably have no idea what it's like, do you, not knowing where the next penny's coming from?"

Maisie wanted to respond, but held back, instead letting the vacuum of silence force the woman to continue.

"No, I thought not. You haven't a clue, not a bloody clue." Jones shook her head again. "Well, I might as well go on." Another sigh. "Looking for a place to go, I walked into the wrong crowd. As I said before—all as easy as that." She snapped her fingers into the space between her interrogator and herself. "Soon our band had broken away from the union, and we decided the only way to make our presence felt was ... was ... a show of strength." She sat in silence. "Not that we'd actually shown anyone anything, to tell you the truth. We were just getting going."

"So you had your cache of weaponry, but hadn't used it?"

"Not a bloody thing. To tell you the truth, I think we were all a bit scared. It soon became clear to me that Tommy Burgess had more interest in making plans to hold up banks than in making a point by showing the boys in Whitehall that the unions had something to say. I was on the verge of getting out of it, and I was sure that Wilf was an informer—bloody scab!"

"Do you know a man by the name of Ian Jennings?"

"Am I supposed to?"

"Answer the question, please, Catherine."

"Never met anyone by that name in my life."

"Could you make a bomb of poison gas?"

"Such as?"

"Chlorine. Chlorine and phosgene, or mustard gas."

"Old wartime favorites?"

"Yes."

"No, I couldn't. That takes more of an expert than I can lay claim to being. And I wouldn't. Saw what the gas did to my brother."

"But you were making bombs."

"Not like that, though. We might've created a stink, might have caused a few tears, or the police to run away from a march, but no, I'm not in the business of killing like that."

"But I understand Mills Bombs were found."

"They might have been found, Miss Dobbs. But I didn't know we had them. I was only involved in developing chemical concoctions to upset the police during our demonstrations. Not killing people."

Maisie nodded. "That will be all, thank you." She pushed back her chair to stand.

"Thought so. I tell you everything I know and I'm still not getting out of here."

"I'm sorry, Catherine. I have to be honest, I don't think I can get you out. At the very least, you are guilty of conspiring to cause an affray, and the men you were with were in possession of danger-ous weapons. But I will record our conversation. It may help when you come up before the judge. And try not to get in with the wrong crowd again—you are far too intelligent a woman to have done such a thing." She nodded to the policewoman and left the room, passing the constable as she departed. "You can escort Miss Jones back to her cell now."

Stratton was waiting for Maisie at the end of the corridor, and moved forward to walk in step with her as she alighted the staircase.

"What do you think?"

Maisie stopped, turning toward Stratton. "What do you think I think? They might have been planning subversive activity, they might have had a cache of weapons that they surely must answer for in a court of law, but they are not behind the threats we're investigating. I really don't know what's happening here, but—"

"MacFarlane is under pressure to produce suspects."

"I suppose next he'll round up the women unionists for even daring to ask for pensions."

"No, not quite, however—"

"Come on, Richard, you know he's wrong. Even he knows he's wrong." She continued on up the staircase, realizing she had just addressed Stratton by his Christian name. Her cheeks blazed.

"Stop, wait, please, Maisie."

"Yes?" She turned as he placed a hand on her arm.

"You and I do not have to discontinue the investigation."

"I know. I have no intention of stopping, even though I am sure my work here on this case has just come to an end, and even though it will be on my own time." Maisie did not try to hide her exasperation. "I just know there is someone out there, working alone—or with a close associate—who is on a knife edge. I just feel it. I have been trying to compose a picture in my mind's eye of the type of person we are looking for, and I do not see him reflected in any single member of that group we've just viewed. Catherine Jones may be a trained chemist, may be an intelligent woman, but there's something she does not have, something you would need to be able to kill dogs, birds—and eventually, a human being. She does not have the *suffering*. Even in the hard nuts who appear beyond any redemption, we see that terrible ache that took root and grew to take over a whole person. She had lost her parents, yes, her brother, yes, but she does not display a level of . . . " Maisie bit her lip, searching for words to describe an emotion she could feel but not give voice to. "Deep, deep melancholy, a darkness. She is not someone who truly has nothing to live for but to give up her life for others in a similar position." She turned to continue up the staircase. "And that makes the man we are looking for very, very dangerous indeed, for he has nothing to lose, not even his conscience. We should be thankful that he is choosing to increase the stakes slowly, but I fear his patience is wearing thin."

"I think you're right." Stratton kept pace with Maisie, who was now making her way toward the meeting room at a fair clip.

"Then tell Robbie MacFarlane."

"Tell Robbie MacFarlane what?" The Detective Superintendent's voice boomed from a room on the left as he walked into the corridor. "Tell Robbie MacFarlane what, Miss Dobbs?"

Maisie stood tall to answer MacFarlane. "Sir, I do not believe the people we have just seen are responsible for the threats sent to Downing Street."

MacFarlane placed a hand on Maisie's shoulder. "Well, Miss Dobbs, at this moment in time, it does not matter what you believe." He turned to Stratton. "I'll talk to you later. I just need a word with Miss Dobbs here." Bringing his attention back to Maisie, he cupped her elbow in his hand and steered her toward his office. "Sit down please, Miss Dobbs."

Maisie took a seat and placed her document case on the floor alongside her chair. She rested her hands in her lap and crossed her ankles, noticing that MacFarlane had followed each move.

"Now then, I know you think we've got the wrong people, and

perhaps you are right. I'm not going to dismiss your observations out of hand, but I will save you the time." He folded his arms and looked at his feet. Maisie noticed that the fabric of his jacket was taut across his shoulders, and thought he might have bought the jacket when he was a younger man and the intervening years were not accommodated easily by his clothing.

"Miss Dobbs, your services are no longer required by Special Branch. Your contributions have not been without merit, but now that we have suspects in custody, there would be unwanted speculation if we retained you for any longer than necessary, especially in these times of tight budgetary oversight. In short, the bean counters are watching me, so you had better be on your way."

"And you no longer have to keep an eye on me because my name was mentioned in a threatening letter sent to the Prime Minister's office?"

"We believe that to have been a shot in the dark, perhaps a device to throw us off the scent, so to speak. Plus, you have been mentioned in the newspapers before in one or two cases involving former soldiers." He laughed. "And I doubt you could make a bomb, Miss Dobbs."

"Yes, you're right—bombs and poison gas are hardly in my line." Maisie reached for her case and rose from the chair, holding out her hand. "Thank you for the opportunity to work with you, Detective Chief Superintendent MacFarlane. I am glad to have been of service." She cleared her throat. "I take it my account will be settled promptly."

"I will personally ensure you are not out of pocket."

"Thank you." She turned to leave, but MacFarlane reached out and placed his hand on her shoulder.

"I hope we meet again, Miss Dobbs."

"Yes, of course. I am sure our paths will cross." She pulled on her gloves. "Now then, I should be off."

Maisie made her way to the meeting room where Billy was in conversation with Stratton and Darby.

"Ready, Billy?"

"Yes, Miss." He held up a rolled-up length of paper. "I've taken the case map."

She turned to Stratton and Darby, holding out her hand to each in turn. "Gentlemen, it was a pleasure working with you. I wish you the best of luck."

As soon as they were outside, Maisie raised her hand to summon a taxi-cab.

"Pushing the boat out, aren't we, Miss?"

"I need to get back to the office, Billy, so we can get on with some real work."

A cab drew alongside and Billy opened the door for Maisie to take a seat before he instructed the driver and then clambered aboard. "I thought we were working, if you don't mind me saying so."

"As the Chief Superintendent said, Billy, I do not have the knowledge to make a bomb or some other sort of terrible weapon. But someone out there does and he's been letting us know that he has every intention of using that knowledge if his demands are not met—and we must assume they definitely will not be met." She looked out of the window at the already darkened skies of a winter's midafternoon, then turned back to Billy. "So, our job is to find the person who has that knowledge."

"There's a lot of people like that about, I mean, I could knock together an incendiary device if I had to."

Maisie shook her head. "But you are guided by goodness, Billy. Our man doesn't know what it is to feel that goodness anymore."

I feel as if I have been shouting at someone who is walking away from me, and who cannot hear. It has been like that since the war. And so, because I don't want to shout louder, I turn back, I don't bother. But now I have to bother. I can hear myself screaming inside my head. I can hear my voices, telling them how wrong they are, how wrong they have been. I can no longer plead in my prayers. Listen to me. Listen to me. Please, please, listen to me. But no one listens, because the man with his hand held out, the man who cannot walk as he once walked, or think as he once thought, has nothing that anyone wants to hear, not anymore. So now I have to shout. Only I no longer shout with words. There is no point. They only listen to me when I take action. Then they have to listen. So I shout with the doing, and it always comes back to what I do well.

TEN

The taxi-cab dropped Maisie and Billy at the junction of Warren Street and Fitzroy Street. As they walked around the corner into the square, a black motor car parked on the flagstones in front of the mansion that housed their office caught their attention. They both stopped walking and stood for a moment to observe the vehicle.

"It's not a police motor, but it is official," offered Maisie.

"Could be for someone else."

"It could." She paused. "But it isn't. Come on, let's see who it is."

They did not look into the motor car as they passed and made their way up the steps to the front door, but as Maisie took out her key, they heard a door open behind them and a voice call out.

"Miss Dobbs? And this must be Mr. Beale. Jolly good to have caught you."

They turned around, and Maisie slipped the key into her pocket.

"Gerald Urquhart. Remember me? Well, I just dropped by to have a little conversation, a little chin wag, as they say." With a lightness of foot, he came up the steps toward Maisie and held out his hand, though his voice was now low. His coppery brown hair was slicked back by oil that made it seem darker, and he wore a gray suit with white collar and black tie. His shoes were polished to a deep shine. "Military Intelligence, Section Five. It's a business matter. Let's go up to your office, shall we?" He nodded toward the door for Maisie and Billy to lead the way. "Just a few points to discuss. I'm sure you want to keep the Funnies up to date, eh? MacFarlane and his boys can be so cloak and dagger, can't they?"

Opening the door to her office, Maisie approached her desk, set her document case on the floor and her shoulder bag in a drawer. "Billy, pull up chairs for yourself and Mr. Urquhart, please." She sat down behind her desk and waited for the men to be seated. Behind Urquhart's back Billy caught Maisie's eye and raised his hand to his mouth as if holding a cup. Maisie shook her head. There would be no offer of tea for the man from Section Five.

"Miss Dobbs." Urquhart pulled at the trouser fabric close to his knees as he sat down. "I understand that our friend Robbie Mac-Farlane has dismissed you from the investigation regarding the source of those letters sent to the Prime Minister et al."

"Detective Chief Superintendent MacFarlane has a group in custody and believes them to be behind the threats. They are union activists, and one of the group studied chemistry at university, so has an understanding of combustible substances."

"I see. And you think he's wrong."

"I think it's worth continuing the search. I think it's worth leaving no stone unturned."

"Do you know why you've been dismissed?"

"I would have thought it's clear."

"Not at all." He crossed his legs, leaning back in a manner that Maisie interpreted as proprietorial. "No, you were dismissed because of Robbie's tendency toward maverick acts. Taking you to Number Ten was not one of his better strategic moves."

"I understood I was asked to accompany the Chief Superintendent because I was available and was working on the case. I believe he wanted to bring some immediacy to the meeting, to show that he was not thinking in the usual way, so to speak—that he was willing to consider intelligence beyond Special Branch."

"Or in other words, that he could do what he liked in his personal bailiwick."

Maisie did not respond. She wasn't about to agree with Urquhart, or disagree, though she could see his point.

"Moving to a more fruitful dialogue, I hope, I understand you have a—now, what would your old teacher Dr. Blanche say?" Urquhart put his finger to his chin in mock thought. Maisie said nothing, though she felt a welter of dislike for the man. She waited for him to continue.

"Oh, yes, he'd say that you had a *sense* of the author of the letters, wouldn't he? Good old Maurice."

Fighting the urge to stand—she didn't want to give the impression of needing height to have a voice with power behind it— Maisie responded with a certain coolness. "Dr. Blanche has been decorated for service to this country and, as you know, much of that service has been in intelligence, so I would prefer it if you referred to him with the respect his contribution to our nation's security deserves."

"I beg your pardon, however—"

"However," Maisie continued, aware that she may have sounded overprotective, "I do indeed have a sense of our letter-writer."

"And would you care to let me have a glimpse of your *sense*?"

Maisie rested her forearms on the desk. "Mr. Urquhart, your manner has done nothing to endear you to me, though I realize you did not come here in search of my friendship. If it weren't for the fact that I believe we have little time to find the letter-writer—who has proven already that he has the wherewithal to do the sort of damage to life that brings a chill to the bone—I would not be continuing this little *chin-wag*. But we have no time to lose. I will make no secret of the fact that I do not intend to wash my hands of this case, even though I really do need to concentrate on work that brings in an income."

"We'll pay for information."

"Yes, you will."

Urquhart took a deep breath and exhaled. "Miss Dobbs, tell me what you know of this man we're all after. We have our own specialists working on this case, but we . . . we feel that you may have a greater knowledge."

Maisie leaned back and looked across at Billy, who seemed to be on the edge of his seat as he followed the back-and-forth volley of words. She stood up and walked from the desk to the middle of the room, then walked back again. She continued pacing as she spoke. "The man we are looking for has most probably been released from a secure institution during the past two years, though there should be a margin for error—remember, this speculation is not an exact science." She paused to look out of the window, then began walking back and forth again. "In general, such a man would most probably have remained close to the institution in question, not making any significant moves to another region, unless there were family there to receive him, so I think we can expect him to have been previously in care in one of the London hospitals for the mentally ill, or a home specifically for soldiers with a psychiatric or emotional affliction. He is, I would say, poorly nourished, and has few, if any friends. He has some difficulty with physical adroitness and most probably suffers from night tremors and hallucinatory dreams. He is a haunted man."

"How can he handle chemicals with volatile properties if he has tremors and such like?" Urquhart was writing in a notebook, but paused and looked up at Maisie as he asked the question.

"Training. I would say that this man has some sort of training, perhaps as a chemist, an engineer, physicist. He might have been a doctor. He is an educated man—though I suspect he might come from lowly beginnings, and that there were other losses in his life. In my experience—and I am sure you are fully apprised of my professional experience—the men who suffered the most from the various war neuroses were those who had some difficulties in childhood, though that is by no means prescriptive."

She took her seat again, folding her arms as she faced Urquhart and looked into his eyes. "He's lonely, but at the same time is weary of company, has barely the will to communicate with others. He might have one friend, one person he trusts, but I am not sure. He feels disenfranchised. He may have tried to get work, but was turned away—we might even assume he has obvious wounds that are not attractive, scars and the like. He may be unable to control spittle when he talks. There are many manifestations of psychological wounds that are not pleasing to the eye, and those tics and so on are not something that people want to see, or want their customers to be exposed to. If you watch a man thus afflicted walk down the street, you will see the people coming toward him part as a river divides when it reaches an island. It becomes easier for him to go out after dark."

Urquhart was silent for several moments. "This means going through a lot of records. And what if he's moved in from somewhere else?"

Maisie sighed. "I didn't say this was a certain bet. It's a template, an idea rooted in my own understanding of the gamut of war neuroses, and also in the conversations I've had with experts at two hospitals."

"And they don't recognize the description you've given us?" Urquhart leaned back in his chair, resting his arm along the back of a vacant chair next to him.

"The description I've given you could probably match hundreds of men still held in asylums, but, to answer your question— no, they don't, not specifically, otherwise I am sure we would have the person in a cell by now."

"Do you think he might be part of one of these troublemaking organizations—the unions, the Fascists? Sounds like he would be drawn to them."

"I believe he is a solitary person, one who would not be welcomed into such company. But he might have tried to join, perhaps while looking for a suitable vehicle for his discomfort, his anger."

"So he might be in with one of these mobs of anarchists?"

"He could. Perhaps." She drew back from the desk and leaned into her chair. "His body might also be disfigured. A curvature of the spine, lameness, and it might come and go, so he may well be listed as having physical disability."

"Blimey, we'll be going through records from now to kingdom come!"

"Yes, you're right, it may take a while." Maisie picked up a pencil on the table and tapped it on her palm.

"And you've nothing else to add? Names?"

"No, no names for you. I am sure you have contacts at the psychiatric hospitals and you can have your men in there faster than I can visit all of them."

Billy cleared his throat. "I'll see you downstairs, then, Mr. Urquhart."

Urquhart stood up and extended his hand toward Maisie, who remained seated.

"I trust you'll contact me should you acquire knowledge that will help us."

"I have made the same promise to MacFarlane, so *I* must trust that he will inform you of all useful information that comes his way."

Urquhart walked to the door, where Billy was standing ready to escort him to his motor car. He turned to Maisie as he set his hat on his head. "You'll hear from Robbie MacFarlane again, I shouldn't wonder."

Before Maisie could respond, he left the room and was gone. Billy looked at Maisie and raised his eyebrows, then followed Urquhart down the stairs and returned as the motor pulled away.

"The cheek of it!" Maisie came to her feet.

"Bet you're glad he's gone, Miss."

"If he'd remained one second longer, I would have boxed his ears."

"He was a bit familiar, wasn't he? It's not on to talk about the Chief Superintendent like that."

"There's probably no love lost between Special Branch and Section Five."

"You gave him a lot of information, I thought."

Maisie reached for the telephone. "I can't, ethically, withhold information. We're under the gun, simply as people who live in London."

"You think it's that bad?"

Holding the telephone receiver in one hand, Maisie flicked through a series of index cards. "Yes, I do. We have to keep looking, even if we aren't being paid."

"Oh, I think there will be something for us."

Maisie rested the receiver back in its cradle. "What do you mean?"

"Well, I think Urquhart had a point. If you don't mind me saying so, I think the Chief Superintendent has taken a bit of a shine to you—I could see it myself. He won't see you go short."

"That's enough of that sort of speculation, Billy. Now then, where was I? Oh, yes . . . " She reached for the telephone once again, but it rang as her fingers touched the receiver.

"Fitzroy five—"

"Miss Dobbs?"

Maisie turned away from Billy. "Chief Superintendent. What can I do for you?"

"Our little Catherine the chemist says she wants to see you again. Could you come back to the Yard? I can have a motor car pick you up."

"No, that won't be necessary. I'll come straightaway by taxi-cab." She replaced the receiver and turned back to Billy, and spoke to him while keeping her head down as she leafed through papers on her desk.

"I have to go to Scotland Yard immediately, and I am not sure how long I'll be."

"What do you want me to do, Miss?"

She looked up, now with less of a blush to her complexion. "First job—review all current client work in progress, see where we are, and make sure we have something to report to our clients. We can't afford to lose business. Next—compile a list of every single psychiatric hospital or convalescent home in London. I'd like to know how we can get a roster of patients who've been discharged over the course of the past two years." She took a key from her shoulder bag and opened the bottom drawer of her desk. Taking out an envelope, she removed several pound notes and held them out to Billy. "You may need this to ease the flow of information."

"Right you are, Miss. Meet back here at the usual time?" He held out Maisie's blue woolen coat for her.

"Of course. See you later." She smiled as she left the room, but called back as she ran downstairs, "And, Billy, don't wait if I seem to be taking a long time. You should go home."

Billy walked to the window to watch Maisie run down the steps and toward Warren Street Station, then he turned to the bank of wooden drawers that held the collection of index cards. There was much to be accomplished before he saw his employer again.

AS MAISIE APPROACHED Scotland Yard, she counted four police vehicles screeching away from the curb, bells ringing as both motor and horse-drawn traffic pulled aside to let them pass.

"Oh, no . . . " she spoke the words aloud as she ran toward the main entrance, only to almost collide with MacFarlane, Stratton and Darby as they left the building.

"Excellent timing, Miss Dobbs." He pointed to an idling black motor car. "There's been another attack. We'll brief you on the way."

Maisie took a seat alongside the passenger window, while Mac-Farlane sat next to her and Stratton and Darby took the pull-down seats to face them.

"Has anyone been killed?" Maisie knew that this time the stakes would be ratcheted up a notch, that human life would be at risk.

"Yes. A junior minister with the Home Office, at his flat on Gower Street. They're cordoning off the street now and my instructions are not to touch the body. Sir Bernard Spilsbury and his cohorts have been called."

"Do we know the cause of death?"

"He was found by a housekeeper, and from the description— oh, merciful God help us . . . " MacFarlane closed his eyes and pressed his lips together as if in prayer. Both Stratton and Darby looked away, mirroring each other's unease.

"What has he used this time, Chief Superintendent?" Maisie thought she knew the answer, even before it was spoken.

"I can't fathom how he's done it, but from the description we've received, it has all the hallmarks of mustard gas."

Maisie felt the color drain from her cheeks, her hands become cold and damp, but she recovered quickly given the urgent circumstances. "Not only must we not touch the body, but people should be evacuated until we know the extent of possible exposure. And no one else should go into that building without protective clothing—gowns, gloves and masks."

"Don't worry—I'll get on to it as soon as we're there," said Stratton. "I'll have someone procure gowns and whatever else we need from the hospital."

MacFarlane was still deep in thought, talking as much to himself as to the group. "Could someone, an ordinary person, not only develop such a substance, but bring it to a private address and then kill another person with it?"

Maisie responded. "It would be a difficult task, but not insurmountable, especially for someone trained in the handling of volatile matter. Until we have a laboratory analysis we don't even know if it is mustard gas—it might be something completely new, or certain compounds might have been used to leave clues to tempt the olfactory system into thinking it is something known."

"But now he isn't even giving us the time he stated in his last letter—you've got forty-eight hours here, a day there, and it feels as if every day he's throwing out more proof that he can run rings around us. How does he do it? There must be a gang, a crew. One man could not pull off this sort of murder—that's what it is, murder."

"He may have no concept of time. The deadlines quoted in the threats are just what comes into his head." She turned to face Mac-Farlane. "You see, this man is just existing in his everyday life. He may not be aware of passing time except in the vacuum that is his world. There is only one point of control, and that is in this ability to work with chemicals."

"And it's not little Catherine Jones, is it, Miss Dobbs?"

"Not unless she can creep out of your cells in the middle of the morning."

"I apologize if . . . "

Maisie was aware of Stratton and Darby exchanging glances and directed her next question to ensure they were included. "Inspector Darby, do you agree with my speculation regarding our man?"

Darby looked at his hands. "Like you, I think he is at the edge. We may have only hours before he strikes again. However . . . however, he may now be exhausted. This outing may have worn him out, so he may lie low, may sleep fitfully for some hours, especially if—as you have suggested—he is poorly nourished. We may not hear from him for some time, but again, we may hear tomorrow."

The brakes screeched as the vehicle came to a halt outside the Georgian terraced house on Gower Street, close to Bedford Square, and MacFarlane barely waited for the motor car to stop before he swung the door open and stepped onto the street and toward the front door. "Get these people off the street, Constable."

Stratton remained aboard, ready to go straight to University College Hospital. Maisie spoke to him before joining MacFarlane. "Inspector Stratton, it's most important you ensure the house-keeper is kept in isolation at the hospital, and that everyone who has had contact with her is also quarantined. Talk to the doctors—they must know that they are likely dealing with a very dangerous substance. There may be no cause for concern and though I don't want to cause panic, my instinct tells me to be careful."

"I'll send the driver back with the gowns and gloves, and ensure the registrar is notified."

Maisie and Darby stepped from the motor car, which sped off along Gower Street with the bell ringing. They joined MacFarlane, who was speaking to a constable. He pointed to a gathering on the other side of the road.

"I want this road completely closed from Great Russell Street all the way down to the Euston Road, and I want all streets blocked from Tottenham Court Road across to Woburn Place. The only people on this thoroughfare should be in uniform."

"Not quite, Robbie." Gerald Urquhart slipped past another police constable and stood beside Maisie. "Nice to see you back in the fold, Miss Dobbs."

"Never mind the pleasantries, Gerry." MacFarlane turned to walk into the house.

"Wait!" Maisie reached for MacFarlane's sleeve. "Chief Superintendent, I cannot impress upon you the importance of delaying your investigation of the premises until suitable covering has been procured." She turned to the constable. "Is anyone in there?"

"The photographer went in some time ago, and another constable. Should have been out by now, I would have thought."

"Blast!" Maisie opened her document case and removed two linen masks. She handed one to Darby. "Come on, we'd better go in." She reached into her bag for a pair of rubber gloves, which she pulled onto her hands, then turned to MacFarlane and Urquhart. "I'm sorry, I don't carry supplies for an army, just myself. I think it would be best if you waited—I am sure the driver will be back soon. Is it all right if we continue, Chief Superintendent? I thought it best to give the mask to Inspector Darby, given his forensic knowledge."

In truth, Maisie did not want to enter the property without a witness and, given Urquhart's earlier veiled insinuation that MacFarlane may have designs on her, she did not want him to see her and the Chief Superintendent crossing the threshold together.

"Go ahead—I'll join you as soon as I can."

Maisie and Darby stepped inside the house, closing the door behind them. The hallway was typical of those found in terrace houses built from Georgian times onward. It was long and narrow, with a staircase ahead leading to the upper floors. A dado rail ran along the wall several feet up from the skirting board, with dark green paint below the wooden rail, and cream above. To the right, doors led to reception rooms, and if one continued along the passage past the staircase, there would be stairs down to the kitchen, and there would also be a means to enter a small walled garden, possibly through French doors at the back of the property.

Maisie's eyes began to water, and as she looked at Darby, he was pulling a handkerchief from his pocket to wipe his eyes.

"Nasty stuff, whatever it is."

Maisie nodded. "Hello! Anyone there?"

A groaning came from a room to the right of the hallway.

Maisie and Darby ran toward the room, where they found the photographer and the police constable slumped on the floor, and the body of the junior minister partially covered in a white sheet.

"We need to get them out of here, now—look, the back door. There's a small garden at the back." She looked around the room. "Cover your hands with something before you touch them." Darby opened doors until he found a lavatory, and grabbed a cloth towel hanging next to a hand basin. Together they dragged the two collapsed men out into the cold, diminishing daylight of a winter afternoon, now silent, given the lack of traffic noise from Gower Street.

"Close the door into the parlor, and if you can find a bowl or bucket, bring me cold water to bathe their skin—and bathe your hands and face too, anything exposed to air in the house."

Though she was in the garden, Maisie heard the front door slam in the distance.

"What the bloody hell's going on?" MacFarlane shouted as he entered the house with Urquhart at his heels, both wearing doctors' gowns, surgical masks and rubber gloves.

"Exposure to the substance the visitor employed to kill the junior minister," said Maisie as the men came out into the garden. "They'll be all right, but we have to get them down to the hospital—and quarantined, like the housekeeper."

"The PM should be informed," said Urquhart, his tone dictatorial.

"Sod the PM for just a minute, will you, Gerry? I swear, I will knock your block off one of these days, so I will."

"Now then, Robbie, I don't know who you think you are, but—"

"Don't you come the old 'I don't know who you think you are' with me, Mister Cambridge University. This is my murder, my case, and I'm in charge until the Commissioner decides otherwise. Right then, now we've got our matching frocks on, if you want to stay and observe, shut up and follow me."

Urquhart did not look at Maisie, who had exchanged glances with Darby and both had raised their eyebrows. She came to her feet and reached out for one of the white hospital gowns held by MacFarlane.

"Thank you, Chief Superintendent. I'll show you where the body is." Maisie led the way into the parlor, cautioning the men first. "Keep your masks on at all times, gentlemen, and do not under any circumstances touch the body with your bare hands."

"I think I've seen it all by now, lass, no need to warn me, though Gerry here might faint."

"Careful, Robbie." Urquhart's retort was bitter, his face still flushed with embarrassment.

The junior minister had been a man of approximately forty years of age, and was wearing a shirt, tie and woolen trousers when the attacker had struck. His jacket had been placed on the back of a chair and there was an open box with papers strewn across the table. The flesh of his face appeared to be melting across his cheekbones, and the skin at his neck was sunken, as if pulled in by the fight to breathe through what was left of his nose, and the frothing mass that had once been his mouth. With her gloves on, Maisie pressed against the back of the dead man's hands, only to see the skin concertina like the top of a custard when pulled away by a serving spoon. The veins broke open, and blood oozed in small clotted lumps.

"I would say that he invited the attacker into the house, brought him into the parlor." Maisie pointed to the table. "The victim reached for some papers—it's possible he was looking for something to write on—and when he turned around a substance was unleashed upon him with some sort of pneumatic spray, perhaps, to have accomplished such coverage. Pain was immediate, and he was blinded, falling backward. His tongue is doubtless little more than liquid where he opened his mouth to scream, and you will see his lungs have belched up froth as they have also liquefied. His hands took the brunt when a second dose was administered."

Urquhart began to cough, and left the room. He could be heard retching in the garden as policemen in white overalls, masks and gloves helped the photographer and constable to a waiting ambulance.

"Was it a gas, do you think?" MacFarlane spoke softly, then began to rub his forehead.

"We should all leave this room now," said Maisie. At that point, the police pathologist and two assistants arrived, each of them dressed as if to paint a room, rather than remove a body from the premises.

Within half an hour the house was evacuated of both the living and the dead, and with the hospital gowns removed for incineration, Maisie was on her way back to Scotland Yard with MacFarlane, Stratton and Darby.

"So, what do you think, Miss Dobbs?" Once again, MacFarlane singled out Maisie to answer a question.

"I think that, somewhere in London, there is a very clever man who has been marginalized by society. He may just have invented a new and very dangerous substance. At first blush, it could be taken for mustard gas, but I'm convinced it's something different—for a start, I don't like the look of this white powdery residue, but the laboratory people will no doubt get to the bottom of its chemical structure." She shook her head and looked around the room. "What we have to assume is that a man who has the ability to kill one person can use this same substance to kill many."

"And the way he's escalating his attacks, he could kill and maim a whole street—or the whole of London—tomorrow," added Stratton.

"Urquhart will have alerted the PM by now." MacFarlane looked out the window as he spoke.

"What does that mean for the investigation, sir?" asked Stratton.

"It means it becomes a three-ring circus. The Funnies, Special Branch, those boys at Mulberry Point, and not forgetting the mad professors. That's all I bloody well need—a cartload of boffins to deal with."

Maisie said nothing as she reflected upon that morning—was it just yesterday?—when she was about to board a train for Oxford, and saw Anthony Lawrence at Paddington Station, waiting for the Penzance train. A train that just happened to stop in Berkshire, close to the village of Little Mulberry.

ELEVEN

December 30th, 1931

Sometimes it seems there is only sleep. There is nothing to do, nowhere to go, and unless Croucher comes, there is no one to speak to, no human sound other than the voice in my head. Ian was another voice, but now he is gone. If only he had waited. If only he could have fought through Christmas, we might have brought them to their knees, these men who sit with their full bellies, by their warm fires, and wonder why we cannot work.

The man moved to the iron-framed bed and drew back a mildewed blanket, damp to the touch, the wool like wire to his fingertips. He curled under the threadbare cover and continued to write with a pencil.

I have taken a life. One more life. They should have believed me, after the dogs, after the birds. I told them. And now they know. I was discarded, not wanted, thrown aside. And soon someone, somewhere will remember. They will remember me and they will know, when little men with their little microscopes discover that what is in their little dish of flesh is something they haven't seen before. Then they will know what I have. Then our situation will change. There will be something more for us, men who are still waiting for their armistice.

As fatigue dragged on the man's eyelids and cold seeped through his skin, layer by layer, it seemed as if the very blood in his veins were slowing to bring him to the edge of death, a place where he would linger, in neither this world or the next, until his eyes opened once more, still encrusted with sleep.

MAISIE HAD ALLOWED Billy time off to visit Doreen at Wychett Hill, and was waiting for the clock on the mantelpiece to strike nine so that she could telephone Dr. Anthony Lawrence. She was now officially part of MacFarlane's team again for the duration of the case, and there was much work to be done.

Continuing with her notes, she was startled when a bell sounded, indicating that someone was at the front door. She walked to the window and looked down toward the door, but could see only the back of the visitor's coat as she waited for the door to open. Maisie glanced around the square, and was about to turn away when she saw a flash of blue in the distance—and the distinctive nose of a Bugatti parked on the far side of the square where it met Conway Street.

"Priscilla?" Maisie whispered to herself as she ran to the stairs and then downstairs.

"I thought you'd never get here!" Priscilla used her thumbnail to eject a cigarette onto the flagstones before stepping across the threshold when Maisie opened the door. She stopped briefly to kiss her on each cheek, then held out her hand. "You'd better lead the way, Maisie—show me up to your hive of industry."

"What are you doing here, Pris?" asked Maisie as they ascended the stairs. She drew Priscilla into her office, and pulled two chairs in front of the gas fire, turning up the jets for more warmth.

"So, this is where you beaver away day after day in the quest for justice, or whatever it is that you do here—you know, chasing criminals and the like."

"Would you like a cup of tea?"

"Do you have coffee, by any chance?"

"Sorry, Pris."

Priscilla waved a begloved hand. Always elegant, she was dressed in a pale gray costume, the jacket falling at thigh length with a narrow belt at the waist, and the straight, almost fitted skirt brushing her mid-calf. A black fur cape was draped around her shoulders, a match for black shoes and handbag, from which she took a packet of cigarettes.

"Do you mind?"

"Well, actually, I would rather you didn't. I'll be coughing all day." Maisie rubbed her arms, feeling cold despite heat from the fire. "Is everything all right, Priscilla?"

Priscilla's eyes welled with tears. "Oh, nothing, really. I just thought . . . look, perhaps we can nip out, somewhere where I can light up."

"You can wait for a bit. Come on, what's wrong?" Maisie looked at her friend of old, who even in her darkest hours had never been one to slouch, now slipping down in the chair and clutching her cape around her as if she yearned for comfort.

"Oh, Pris . . . " Maisie knelt at Priscilla's feet and enveloped her with her arms. "Tell me what's wrong."

"I—I just don't know what's got into me. Look at me—I have a lovely home, three simply smashing boys, a husband I adore, who adores me in return—and I am just flailing around like a woman drowning." Priscilla did not draw back, but allowed herself to be held, and seemed to be curling up like a child against her mother's chest, so that she was surrounded by her friend's warmth and strength. "I feel such a goose. I have felt this knot inside me getting tighter and tighter for days—and I am supposed to be looking forward to a party."

Maisie allowed silence to encroach upon Priscilla's weeping, and did not try to prevent the tears. Soon Priscilla sat back, but kept a firm grip on Maisie's hand.

"I don't know what I would do if you weren't here. All the time I was in Biarritz, I missed your company very much, you know." She pressed her lips together, then continued. "But I have felt so at sea here."

"You've had a huge change, Priscilla. Don't underestimate it. Life is very different here in London."

Priscilla nodded. "I just don't feel . . . I don't feel . . . as if I'm home."

Maisie nodded and, while allowing Priscilla to continue holding her hand, pulled a cushion from her chair and sat down at her feet.

Priscilla sniffed, drew a handkerchief from her bag and dabbed her eyes, then her nose. "I want to go back to Biarritz, only now, after that rather shaky start, the boys are thoroughly enjoying being in London, and Douglas is doing incredibly well indeed, so he's in no hurry to rush back." She sighed. "Oh, I don't know, I just can't seem to settle."

"You settled in Biarritz."

Priscilla nodded, and her eyes welled with tears once more. "What's wrong with me, Maisie? You know all about this sort of thing. What's wrong with me?"

Maisie leaned back in her chair. "I can only tell you what I believe ails you, Pris, though I may be wide of the mark."

"No, please, tell me. Tell me what you think is wrong with me. I mean, I am weeping from the time I say good-bye to my boys in the morning to the time they come home. And I bite my lip to maintain a cheerful face at social engagements." She dabbed her eyes again. "I feel so bloody selfish, Maisie. I mean, there are people starving in this country, men who can't work, people who dream of the advantages I have. And I'm a wilting mess."

"Priscilla, when I came to Biarritz last year, you talked to me about your life there. You were brutally honest with me, and you helped me to see how I hadn't stared down the dragon of my past—the dragon of all our pasts, men and women like us, who saw the war at first hand. I remember you telling me how you had come back from the brink, how you had built your life again, about your family and what they mean to you. You found a place where you could heal, a place that became your home. And that's what we are all looking for, isn't it? A home. We're looking for where we belong."

"But I belong with my family, and they're here."

"Yes, of course, but don't underestimate the wrench of leaving the place where you found life again, Priscilla."

"And I came back to the place where death stalked me." She looked down at her hand entwined in Maisie's. "I couldn't wait to get away from here, you know. England *was* my home. I didn't know it before the war, but my family was my cocoon. I was so happy, Maisie, so happy. I had my brothers, my mother and father, and life was just one big party, or so it seemed—then it was gone. Just like that." She snapped her fingers. "And I am so scared of losing it all again."

"You won't lose it, Priscilla."

"But I'm losing it already. My boys are growing, like little men. And I worry so." She paused. "Remember that summer before the war? None of us saw it coming, not really. I think of that summer all the time, think of my brothers, think of the past. And I am so scared it's all going to come crashing down again and I will lose them."

Maisie reached forward and clasped both Priscilla's hands in her own. "You know, none of us can guarantee the future. Your boys will be growing up wherever you are. They are as much at risk here as they were swimming in the Atlantic in Biarritz—you know that. You are torturing yourself with imaginings, Priscilla."

"What can I do? I sometimes think my head will explode with all these thoughts."

"Then counter them with action. Do something, get yourself out of that head of yours. It is no good lingering in the future, you have to drag yourself back to the present."

"How on earth . . . ?"

"Take your motor car into the country and find a place to ride—you used to love being out on a horse. Or do some voluntary work. I know you can't stand all that committee lark, but you never know, you might find a way to do some good. Worry about someone else's worries—there are plenty of them about, you know."

"You're right, it's terribly indulgent." Priscilla's smile was tight, a curve of red lips drawn up to show resolve.

"No, it's not indulgent. It's genuine, and what you feel comes from your love of your family—just don't let this emotion rob you of your time with them. I know your boys are growing fast, but remember that each day you are weaving a memory. Make sure you don't look back at these times through a veil of tears."

Priscilla nodded and reached for her handbag. "Look at the time. I've to be at Fortnum's this morning to meet Duncan's dowager aunt." She pulled on her black leather gloves. "She's a bit of an old misery, to tell you the truth, so I will take it as fair warning—be not like Gertrude!"

MAISIE SAW PRISCILLA to the door, waving to her until she reached the Bugatti, then returned to her first-floor office. She sat back in her chair alongside the fire, turning down the jets to save money, and thought about her dear friend Priscilla, who had countless advantages, or so it seemed. Yet with money, position, a happy family and a magnificent roof over her head, she still searched for some sort of anchor, some part of her soul that seemed to be missing. Even with such abundance, Priscilla did not feel safe.

With these thoughts on her mind, Maisie picked up her note-book and ran her finger down a list of names. She picked up the telephone receiver to place the call that was interrupted by Priscilla's arrival.

"May I speak to Dr. Anthony Lawrence, please?" She waited for a moment until a second voice responded to her request. "Not in, but you *expect* him tomorrow. I see. Yes. Do tell him that Miss Dobbs telephoned and would like an appointment at his earliest convenience." She paused again. "Yes, would you ask if he would be so kind as to telephone me at my office? Thank you." She gave the telephone number and set the receiver in the cradle once more.

It was not unusual for Dr. Lawrence to be unavailable, given his responsibility to the patients of more than one hospital, but the clerk who answered the telephone could not judge when he might return, which was unusual. Maisie was about to reach for the receiver again when the telephone rang.

"Fitzroy—"

"Miss Dobbs." MacFarlane's voice was low, as if he feared being overheard. "I'd like you to come to the Yard. Expect a motor car to be outside your office in the next ten minutes—a chariot to bear you here as usual."

"Have there been developments?"

"We can discuss the reasons when you get here—and not on this line."

"Right you are, Chief Superintendent."

Maisie replaced the receiver, consulted the clock on the mantelpiece once again, and lifted the receiver to dial an Oxford number. She cleared her throat, ready to speak.

"Yes, may I leave a message for Professor Gale?" She wove the telephone cord through her fingers. "Thank you. Tell him that Miss Dobbs telephoned, and I would like to speak to him at his earliest convenience." Once more she spelled her name and gave the office telephone number. Doubtless both calls would be returned while she was out of the office, and there would be more telephone calls on her part until she effected conversation with the men. That is, if she chose to wait that long.

As the police vehicle wove its way through the streets of London, Maisie wondered, not for the first time, why a man she did not know had mentioned her name in a letter. Had he known her after all? Could he have been a patient in the wards where she had nursed the casualties of war who were wounded in the mind? There were so many of them, men who had lingered, forgotten as time faded memory in the way that the sun took color from the back of an armchair set in front of a window. Had she known the man when she worked for Maurice? To each question she drew a blank. She had been familiar with the records of every man in her care, and there was no one with the knowledge to build a deadly weapon. For the most part these men had been bank clerks or carpenters; they had worked on the docks and in post offices; they had worked the land, the factories and the canals. And though the war might have rendered them a danger to themselves and others, there was not one who was as calculating as the man who had murdered the junior minister.

"WHAT DO YOU make of that, Miss Dobbs?" MacFarlane skimmed a manila file across his desk toward Maisie.

She leaned forward and took the file; then flipping open the cover, she began to read. The senior pathologist was Bernard Spilsbury, the famed forensic scientist. His notes were precise. The victim's death had taken place within three minutes of exposure to a substance with which the department was not familiar. Three minutes. She had only been sitting on the visiting side of MacFarlane's desk for about three minutes, and it felt like half an hour already. Three minutes in which one of the government's rising stars could feel himself dying, could feel his flesh being eaten by—what? The report concluded that the poison had been administered in a powder form, likely thrown into the man's face when he turned toward the murderer. A powder that had never been seen before.

"I see a sample of the powder has been sent for additional testing."

"Yes, to University College, the Department of Chemistry."

"Is a carbon copy of this available?"

MacFarlane held Maisie's gaze before pursing his lips and responding to her question. "You want to take the report to someone?"

She nodded. "Yes. And a sample of the powder."

MacFarlane shook his head. "You can sit here and take notes from the file, but you cannot have a sample. This stuff might be in powder form, rather than a gas, but we're not taking chances with even one speck of it in the air in London."

"I assure you I will take every care. I just want a small sample, a few grains."

"Who is he?"

"Professor John Gale. He's a professor at Oxford—a scientist—and he also works at Mulberry Point. He might be able to tell us if it has been used before, even in a laboratory setting."

"This will cost me my job, if it gets out."

"It won't."

He stood up, pushing his chair back against the wall. "I'll think about it. In the meantime, remember Catherine the chemist wanted a word with you. She's being transferred to Holloway to await trial."

Maisie nodded. "I'd better get on with it then."

CATHERINE JONES WAS sitting at the same table as before. She had made it clear that she would speak only if Maisie were left alone with her, though it was pointed out that a woman police auxiliary would remain in the room throughout the interview.

"You wanted to see me, Catherine?"

The woman nodded. She seemed frail, and betrayed her nervousness in the way she shook her head at the end of a sentence, as if this experience of incarceration could be dismissed as never having happened. She rubbed her upper arms in a self-embrace, and tapped the floor with one foot and then the other.

"What is it you have to tell me?"

She shrugged. "Don't know if you'll be interested."

"You've made it clear that you wanted to see me, so I am interested already."

The woman nodded, and rubbed her hands back and forth along her thighs. "I remembered someone. Someone who came to one of our meetings."

"A man?"

"Yes. Said he wanted to take action, that there were too many without work, that it was all very well the politicians wanting you for their armies when there's a war to win, but they didn't want to know about you and your problems once you were back."

"I'm sure there are many men and women who share those feelings."

She looked at Maisie—who did not flinch from her gaze. "You have no idea what it is like to be without work, what it's like for the men and women who walk from place to place each day in search of a job. Some haven't worked for years. *Years.* Year after year of walking and begging for a job every single day. Except the days when they don't have the will to walk anymore, when their insides are growling so much for want of food, it's as if the body is eating itself. Then there is only sleep. That's all you can do. Sleep until you wake and then walk again."

"I know, Catherine."

Catherine rubbed her arms again, and moved to sit sideways on her chair.

"Is there more you can tell me about the man? Do you remember his name?"

"I didn't think you were interested."

"Of course I am."

She sighed before continuing her story. "I remember him because he seemed, you know, a bit off."

"A bit off?"

"Not that he was soft in the head, not like some of them who come to the meetings." She paused. "He was bright. Very sharp. He talked about being over in France, in the war, about what he'd seen. It seemed as if every bone in his body shook when he talked about it. And he said he hadn't been able to get work, not since he'd lost his last job."

"Did he say where he worked?"

"He said he couldn't tell me, that it was a secret."

"What else did he say—and what else gave you cause to doubt him?"

"Oh, I didn't doubt him, Miss Dobbs. No, I didn't doubt him because we talked a few times about work, the sort of work I used to do but don't now because I don't have a job. This man knew what he was talking about. I would say he knew a lot more than me."

"Then what is it that you question?"

"Miss Dobbs, I do not know if you are aware of the leaps one has to take to become a university student, especially if one is a woman, and all the more so if one does not come from wealth."

Maisie allowed no emotion to show on her face, or in her manner. "I am aware of what is required to gain entrance, especially if one's field of study is in the sciences."

"And you know the cost?"

"Yes."

"Well, this man said, one day, that he was a foundling. 'I might have had a better chance in life, had I not been a foundling.' I thought it was a bit archaic, using the word 'foundling.' I thought he was gilding the lily, telling a lie about himself to spark interest. I mean, he could have been a boy from one of the Barnardo Homes, couldn't he? But how many of them go to a university to study?"

"Did you believe him, when you reflected on the conversation afterward?"

"I didn't know what to believe, to tell you the truth. He might have been a man with a gift for a tall story, and he certainly didn't seem all there."

"Did he have obvious wounds?"

"Sometimes he limped, then at other times he didn't, as if it came and went. And on those days when he was lame, there was no doubt that it was genuine. I had the feeling that he only came along for the company, and as I said, he only turned up to a few meetings."

"Were you afraid of the man?"

Catherine was silent for a moment, considering the question before she replied. "Funny you should ask that, because I *was* afraid of him. When you were talking to him it was as if you were in one of those rooms where the floors aren't level, you know, the sort you get in an old house, where the ground has settled and you could put a marble on the floor and it would start to move because there's a slope. You never felt as if you were on firm ground."

"Is that enough to point the finger at a man?"

"Probably not, Miss Dobbs. But he did tell me, the last time I saw him, that he could bring the city to its knees before the year was out."

"His name?"

"Oliver. Just Oliver. As in Twist, I would imagine."

TWELVE

Maisie checked her watch upon leaving Scotland Yard. It was now past noon. She had briefed MacFarlane on her conversation with Catherine Jones and thought he seemed skeptical at best.

"Oliver bloody Twist? A right joker, that one. If she thinks she can get out of—"

"I'm going to follow the lead anyway, Chief Superintendent. We have precious little to go on, so this may be just the breakthrough we need."

"Stratton's working on another tip-off, so I can't spare anyone to help you."

"That's all right, it's best that I work alone, or with my assistant."

"Telephone if you need anything."

"I will."

"And you can have that sample by tomorrow morning. I could be shot for this, Miss Dobbs."

"You won't be, Chief Superintendent. And thank you for your trust in me. I doubt if anything but a specialist laboratory will be able to shed light on the constituent properties of this particular compound—and I think I know just the person in just the right place to do the job."

Maisie asked the driver to take her directly to her flat in Pimlico. From there, she collected her MG, went to a petrol station to fill the tank, then drove to the asylum, where she hoped to find Anthony Lawrence. On the way, once again she tried to negotiate the web of clues left in the wake of a man who would kill to be heard.

Following the Embankment, she wove her way toward the City, then away from the river, and as she drove along the Gray's Inn Road, she remembered walking this very route just a couple of years before, on her way to Mecklenburg Square. And she remembered wondering about the rubble left behind following the demolition of a hospital built some two hundred years earlier, a place of great innovation in its day. It was not an institution where medicine was practiced, though it could be argued that it was a place where lives were saved. It was a place where unwanted children, some just hours old, were left to be cared for. Now it was closed, and with only part of the original building left standing, the site was languishing in the midst of the country's economic depression. Maisie felt a sensation across the back of her neck, as if the gossamer wings of a butterfly had touched her skin. She remembered the name: the Foundling Hospital. When first built, it provided respite for children who might otherwise have died on the streets, situated as it was amid fields and gardens. Now it was part of a growling metropolis where horses were giving way to motor cars, where trains belched their way across and underneath London, and trams clattered back and forth. If she remembered correctly, the Foundling Hospital had not closed entirely, but had moved out of London so the children would be where they were originally intended to be—in the country.

Foundling. It was a word used only by those of a certain

generation, a word that spoke of the time in which the hospital was first built, when the life of the poor was all but worthless, and new life was cast aside to die in the gutter. *Foundling*. An infant deserted at birth, a child abandoned, unwanted. Maisie turned the word around in her mind. Could the man who had the power to kill thousands have been an orphan? And if he were, how would he gain an education? How might someone of that order— Maisie checked herself. Though there was no witness to her thoughts, her cheeks burned with shame. She had been considered of a lower order herself, and but for good fortune and a serendipitous discovery by her employer, she herself might never have had the advantage of an education, or a profession. Other gifted children of working-class origins had been sponsored by her mentor, Maurice Blanche, but it was an unusual opportunity—and one for which she was eternally grateful. But to begin life as a foundling represented a more arduous ascent. And if a boy was able to make such a climb, he would be known and remembered. Unless, of course, he was something of a chameleon. Like herself.

MAISIE SLIPPED INTO a lower gear as she approached the Princess Victoria Hospital. She parked the MG outside and ran up the steps to the main entrance, where she pulled open the oak doors and stated her business with the porter.

"I'm afraid the doctor has only just arrived for his rounds. He was at the Queen Elizabeth all morning, and is very busy." The porter checked a list of staff, then verified the information again on a timetable of rounds that was hanging up on the wall behind the counter.

"Yes, I am sure he is, however, I wonder if you could tell me when I might see him."

The porter pulled a fob-watch from his waistcoat pocket and

frowned, then ran his finger along a row on the timetable with Lawrence's name at one end. "Well, I doubt it will be before two."

"May I wait?"

"Suit yourself, Madam, but as I said, you could be here for an hour or so."

"Right, Mr. . . . "

"Croucher."

"Right, Mr. Croucher, I'll just wait over there, if you don't mind. Perhaps you'd be so kind as to let me know when the doctor is available."

The man straightened his spine and looked at his watch again, then at the clock on the wall above the bench where Maisie was now seated. He pursed his lips and shrugged his shoulders. "Well, don't blame me if you're sitting there for a long time today."

Maisie took a notebook from her bag and smiled at the man. "Don't worry, I won't."

It struck her that the porter was as short in his manner as he was in stature. He was a stocky man, yet his movements were exact, and she observed—as she watched him across the counter—that he checked and rechecked every task, whether placing mail in departmental pigeonholes, or giving instructions to his fellow workers. He would say everything twice, verify an action twice, and then he would sweep his hands through his hair and back across his head. It was a lifetime habit, thought Maisie, looking at his receding hairline. And how old was this man? Probably about forty years of age, she thought.

She continued making notes, noticing that, as the turn of the hour approached, Croucher lifted the telephone and called to see if Dr. Lawrence had returned to his office. Half an hour later, a shrill single ring issued from the telephone and, after responding to the call, Croucher summoned Maisie to the counter, his finger crooked as he beckoned her to him.

"Dr. Lawrence is in his office now and can see you." He pulled a chain from his pocket at the end of which was a large ring and several keys of varying sizes. "I will have to accompany you, of course."

"Of course, I understand. I once worked with Dr. Lawrence, you know. Many years ago now, when I was a nurse."

The man's eyes opened wider at the news, though his only comment was, "You'll know how busy he is, then."

"THANK YOU, CROUCHER," said Anthony Lawrence, when Maisie arrived at his office. "I'll summon you when Miss Dobbs and I have finished talking." He turned to Maisie, holding his hand out toward the visitor's chair, and took a seat behind his desk. "I didn't expect to see you again so soon, Miss Dobbs."

"It's good of you to spare me some time, Dr. Lawrence."

"What can I do for you?"

"I understand that you once worked at Mulberry Point, the government's weapons testing laboratory, in Berkshire."

He shrugged, much in the way that Croucher had shrugged earlier. "It was quite some time ago now—just after the war. Not there long, short-term business."

"I understand that you were there to monitor the psychological effects of testing, and the effect of such work on the men who were employed at the laboratories."

"How do you know?"

"I met with Elsbeth Masters this week—on quite another matter, I might add—and she happened to mention that you had worked together there."

"I see. Yes, as I said, it was a long time ago."

"Dr. Lawrence, may I ask about your work at Mulberry Point?"

Lawrence slid his hands on either side of a pile of papers,

aligning them on the desk. He pushed them to one side, then pulled them to him, before pushing them away again.

"It was work to be held in the strictest confidence. I do not know what Dr. Masters thinks she's doing, telling all and sundry."

"I believe she felt confident in divulging the information."

Lawrence lined up a collection of pens and pencils and graduated them by size next to the files. Then he changed the order, and placed writing instruments of like color alongside one another. Maisie, now accustomed to this habit, watched each movement, waiting for his response.

"It's clear you know about the work that goes on at Mulberry Point, so I see little harm in allowing the following. The nature of experimentation at the laboratory is such that both physical and psychological responses to various substances had to be monitored. There is only so much testing that can be done on dogs, cats, birds and mice—and it seems the public are far more worried about the well-being of animals than they are human life—so various workers volunteered themselves for experimentation, in the interests of serving their country."

"That sounds rather dangerous."

"To a point, yes, it was."

"Were people always aware of the consequences?"

Lawrence began moving the items on his desk again. "Miss Dobbs, remind me why you are asking these questions?" He gave a half laugh. "I am finding it hard to reconcile the memory of an adept nursing sister with the woman who is questioning me now."

Maisie let the comment settle, and continued with her line of inquiry. "Was the testing with regard to weapons that might be used against our countrymen, or weapons that our scientists were developing?"

"Can't have one without the other." Maisie noticed that Lawrence's response was candid. He continued as if speaking to a child unable to grasp simple concepts. "You have to be one step ahead of the enemy, you know. As I said, my job concerned the mind's response to weapons that cannot be seen, the onslaught that can only be felt, experienced."

"I see."

"Is that all?" Lawrence shifted his chair, as if ready to leave the room.

"Yes, I think that's all—oh, no, one last thing." Maisie gathered her document case and stood up to face the doctor. "Did you ever get to know the men—or women, I suppose—who worked at Mulberry Point?"

He shook his head, and looked at his watch. "No, not my job to make acquaintances of my patients." He indicated the door. "Shall we? I expect Croucher is in the corridor somewhere—he'll show you out."

"So, you wouldn't have known a man called 'Oliver,' then?"

"Good heavens, no. No names, no pack drill, just numbers. In fact, I have never known an Oliver in my life—except Twist, that is!" He opened the door and shouted along the corridor for Croucher, who came at once when summoned.

IT WAS CLEAR to Maisie that both Anthony Lawrence and the porter, Mr. Croucher, had been glad to see the back of her. The former did not care for her questioning, and the latter appeared to object to anyone taking up space in the entrance hall, over which he seemed to reign supreme. She felt sure that Lawrence was holding something back. Or could his manner be put down to being a doctor, one who was not familiar with having his word questioned in any way, especially by a former ward sister? He would object to her inquiry as it suggested she doubted him, and in Maisie's experience, doctors saw their diagnosis as the last word, and their last word as law. One did not question the doctor's decision.

She glanced at the clock on the way out and walked to the MG at a brisk pace, then drove back to Fitzroy Square. She parked in Warren Street and walked across the square, in time to see Billy Beale opening the front door to enter.

"Hold the door, Billy!" Maisie ran the last few yards.

"Afternoon, Miss. Sorry I'm a bit late, but the train was delayed. According to the guard, there was a fair bit of ice on the line up from Epsom this morning, and it's slowed everything up all day."

"Not to worry. Come on, let's get a quick cup of tea and then get to work."

"Something come up?"

At the top of the stairs, Maisie unlocked the door to the office and, well used to their ritual, both she and Billy took off their coats and hung them behind the door before Maisie ignited the fire, and Billy put the kettle on. Having not stopped to eat, Maisie was hungry, but food would have to wait now as there was work to be done. Soon they were sitting at the table by the window with the case map spread out in front of them.

"Do you remember the Foundling Hospital?"

"Over toward Mecklenburg Square?"

"Yes. It closed—oh, I think in 1926 or '27, something like that. Can you remember where they placed the children? I don't think it was closed as in never to open again, but I seem to recall it was moved, out of London, to the country."

"I remember reading about that, Miss. I remember talking about it with Doreen, saying it was sad, you know, that little children aren't wanted, and have to live in them orphanages, growing up with—"

"But where did they go?"

"I could have sworn it was down Surrey way. Somewhere like that—Dorking? Reigate? Redhill? Come to think of it, I think it was Redhill."

"Find out for me—as soon as you can. I want the address, and I want the name of the principal, the headmaster, whatever they call the person in charge. Then I have to pay them a visit." She looked at her watch. "You have to get back to your boys soon, Billy, so I'll go alone."

"You'll never get down there at a decent hour today, Miss. Don't mind me saying so, but no one will see you."

Maisie gave a half laugh. "This is where I need a black motor with bells and a blue uniform. Or the words 'Detective Superintendent' in front of my name.' " She paused. "In fact . . . " She drew her chair back and stepped quickly to her desk, where she lifted the telephone receiver and placed a call to Scotland Yard.

"May I speak to Detective Chief Superintendent Robert Mac-Farlane, please?" She paused. "Well, is Detective Inspector Stratton there?" Another pause. "Detective Inspector Darby? All out. I see. In that case, as soon as Superintendent MacFarlane returns, please ask him to return my telephone call." Maisie gave her name and telephone number and replaced the receiver.

"Now what?"

"As soon as you have the information about the Foundling Hospital, Billy, I'll make an appointment and go tomorrow morning."

"What will you tell them?"

"Anything—whatever I have to say to gain an audience with someone who in turn has access to the records."

Billy nodded as he stood up and went to the wooden card file set against the wall alongside his desk. Maisie noticed his matte-gray skin and the lines around his eyes, which seemed even more pronounced than yesterday.

"Oh, Billy, I am sorry. I was so anxious to get to my desk that I forgot to ask about Doreen—and she has been on my mind so much. How is she?"

Billy bit his lip. "I want her out of there, Miss. I wish I could have just brought her home, but—I don't know what's right anymore. I don't know whether taking her out is worse than leaving her there, but at the same time, you should see her—I don't know what they're doing half the time. It seems to me they're keeping on with this business of trying to shock her mind into going back to what it was, as if they're trying to get a big enough jolt in her to come to terms with what happened to our Lizzie. She's holding on to it—with all her mind she won't let our little girl go. But she's gone, and I miss her just as much. There's the boys to think of, and our future, and the way things are going . . . "

"Come on, sit down, Billy." Maisie took Billy by the arm. "I'll telephone Dr. Masters again right now, to see if there's been any progress. I'll ask if she can bring any more urgency to getting Doreen transferred."

"I feel as if I'm giving up, Miss. Nothing seems to be going right for us, does it? Just when we think we might be on our way up the river, so help me a bleeding great wave comes and knocks the stuffing out of all of us. And the boys know it, it's taking its toll there, make no mistake." He sighed, taking in such a deep breath that it sounded as if it might be punctuated by a bronchial cough, but was not, for he continued talking. "Time was, I would look at all them poor sods walking for work, lining up for subsistence, and think, 'At least we ain't got that to put up with.' But now I don't. I don't feel better off anymore, because we've been playing with a rotten deck of cards, me and Doreen."

"It'll be all right, Billy, I promise. Look, you go and put the kettle on for a fresh cuppa, and I'll telephone Dr. Masters."

Billy nodded and set about collecting the tea tray, and when he left the room, Maisie picked up the telephone receiver. She had not wanted to place the call while he was in earshot, in case the news was other than they had hoped for.

"Dr. Masters?"

"Yes—oh dear, it's you, Maisie. I have been meaning to get in touch since yesterday, but I am clinging on to sanity myself. We always have more admissions at this time of year. Christmas and New Year, I am sure, sends everyone around the bend. Now then, you've called about Mrs. Doreen Beale—that's it, isn't it?"

"Yes. Do you have news for me?"

"Good news. We can admit her in the New Year, but we have to wait for the seasonal influx to be whittled down." Maisie could hear a shuffling of papers. "Right, here we are: we'll admit her on Monday, January the fourth. An ambulance has been arranged to bring her up from Wychett Hill—I have to complete some documents and then admissions will expedite matters."

"Oh, Dr. Masters, thank you."

"Not at all, not at all. Sounds like the poor woman was in a dreadful state, doesn't it?"

"Yes, and she has since suffered through more procedures."

"I'll assess her as soon as she arrives. We'll look after her, not to worry."

"Thank you, again, Dr. Masters."

"Yes, as soon as I heard your voice, I knew you were ringing to ask about either Mrs. Beale's transfer or the business of Anthony Lawrence."

"Is there something else you can tell me about Dr. Lawrence?"

Dr. Masters sounded distracted, as if other matters to hand were claiming her attention.

"Oh, yes, I'd just heard from him for the first time in years when you came to see me, hadn't I?"

"That's right."

"It wasn't about much, really. He is writing a book, about the effects of nerve agents and other such weaponry on the human psyche. Naturally, he wants to draw upon some of the work we did together years ago, so he sought permission to reuse material from several papers we co-authored at the time."

"I see. Was he worried that you might publish first?"

Masters laughed. "If he was, his mind is at rest now. I do not feel the need to leave any legacy other than my work with my patients. When I have given papers at meetings of my peers, it is to advance the work of us all. Oh dear, I really must rush in a minute or two. What was I saying? Oh yes, this field is changing all the time. In years to come, we will be laughed at and, though I hate to say this, I believe that any book hitherto written on this subject—and on the issue of what the public refers to as 'shell-shock'—is tainted by political interests."

"Even with someone as eminent as Dr. Lawrence? When I worked with him I thought he was one of the best at his job."

"And so he was—and still is. But when you have dedicated your life to your work, when you have more of that life behind you than in front of you, you start to think of ways in which your reputation can live on after you've gone."

"Yes, yes, I understand."

"Frankly, as soon as I'm gone, I'm gone, and that's all there is to it. In the meantime, I must now bring this conversation to an end, but if Mr. Beale is with you, may I have a quick word?"

Billy had just walked into the room, so Maisie held out the telephone receiver to him and mouthed the words *Doctor Masters*.

Setting down the tea tray, Billy took the receiver and listened to the news regarding his wife, and Maisie moved away toward the case map, which was now pinned to the table by the window. She looked at her assistant and believed she could see the lines diminishing from around his eyes. "I don't know how to thank you, Dr. Masters, really I don't." He rubbed his forehead to hide his tears as he spoke, then said good-bye and ended the telephone call.

"Almost there, Billy," said Maisie, as she heard the receiver returned to its cradle.

"Miss Dobbs, I thought she was going to be in that Wychett Hill place forever, I really did." He brought Maisie a cup of tea. "I don't know how to thank—"

"You don't have to thank me, Billy. But I do need the number for the Foundling Hospital, wherever it is in Surrey."

Ten minutes later, Maisie was calling a Dr. Rigby at the Foundling Hospital at its new location in Redhill. She would see him tomorrow morning, at nine.

AT MAISIE'S INSISTENCE, Billy left early to return home. Even though Doreen would be moved to a hospital according to her recommendation, where she believed the care to be more humane, it was still an asylum. She hoped her instinct had served her well, and that Doreen would make progress and begin her slow ascent from the depths of her instability to make a good recovery.

Maisie placed two manila folders, each containing a collection of papers, in her battered old leather document case; put on her navy blue woolen coat, her cloche and her gloves, and then pulled a pale blue cashmere wrap—a gift from Priscilla when she was in France—around her shoulders for additional warmth. She looked around the office, turned off the lights, locked the office behind her, and left the building.

A dirty ochre smog clung to her in the cold winter darkness as she walked to the MG, and the thick air seemed to lift up the click-clack of her shoes on flagstones, only to bring the echo back to her as if she were being followed. Once she would have been disconcerted by such a sound, would stop to listen, might even have called out, "Who's there?" Now she was more confident in her surroundings, she knew the streets, the shopkeepers, and if she were worried, she could run into the Prince of Wales public house—someone would help her if help were needed.

Reaching the MG, Maisie unlocked the door and placed her bags on the passenger seat before starting the motor. As she was about to take her seat, she saw a lame man come out of the swirling pea-souper smog, and with a shuffle and clump he moved past her. He did not wear a cap, and Maisie could not see the detail of him, but he moved with a deliberate slowness, as if his balance might fail him. There was a sour odor as he passed, a dank blight that the homeless carried with them, and she thought she might go after him and press a coin or two into his hand, for he was indubitably a man who had been to war, and it was the least she could do. But he had passed, the hard metal tip of his cane clattering against the pavement as he vanished into the noxious blend of smoke and fog.

I don't think I can stand another year of invisibility, another year of being one of the unseen. We make our way along the streets and are passed by as if we have no place, no value and worth. Ian could not bear such an existence anymore. He had only two friends, me and the man at the bookshop, who he thought did not even know his surname, even though he wrote it in a ledger each time he borrowed a book. Of course, he knew Croucher, and Croucher did what he could. And I know, now, that Ian was right. No one wants to see the broken, in body or in mind. We are better off kept out of sight in cold, sterile wards of efficient nurses, and doctors who only know you by the notes at the end of your bed. Or we are better off dead.

I thought some sign that I had been heard might follow my letters. I did not want to take life. I have seen too much death. But now it seems I have only one more opportunity to raise my voice. To be heard. The end of the year is almost upon me. There's only one thing left to do. St. Paul's, on Old Year's Night. For Auld Lang Syne, my dears. For old times' sake.

THIRTEEN

It was almost eight when Maisie arrived home. And even as she was looking forward to preparing a light supper, with perhaps a small glass of sherry to warm her from the inside out, she had a feeling that she would not be alone this evening.

"Miss Dobbs?" Robbie MacFarlane's voice reached her before his large frame emerged from the smog as she stepped from her motor car.

"Chief Superintendent?"

"I hope you don't mind me coming to see you at your home."

"Not at all—has something happened?" She squinted beyond him in the darkness, to see if a police vehicle awaited the detective. He was alone.

"No, no, not yet." He seemed unsure of his words, almost stuttering his response to her question. "You telephoned the Yard today and I wanted to make sure everything was in order."

"Yes. Look, would you care to come in? It's no good standing out here to talk, is it?"

"Thank you. I don't want to impose, but . . ."

"Come on." Maisie walked toward the main door of the building, opened the outer glass door leading to a foyer that on a clear summer's day would be bathed in light streaming through the windows, illuminating the center staircase. Once inside, she turned left toward the door to her ground-floor flat. "It's nothing grand, but it's home."

MacFarlane closed the door behind him and followed her along the hallway as she turned on the lights and walked into the drawing room. She ignited the fire, drew the blinds, and placed her document case and shoulder bag on the dining table before offering to take MacFarlane's overcoat and hat.

"I'll put them in the box room at the end of the passage—the main pipe for the heating runs up the wall there, so the room is always warm, whether I've turned up the radiator or not."

"Very nice flat, if I may say so, Miss Dobbs."

"Thank you. I'm happy here. Do take a seat."

MacFarlane sat down on one of the chairs close to the fire, and looked around the room. Above the mantelpiece was a watercolor painting of a woman on a beach, looking out to sea—a woman who resembled Maisie—and on the far wall behind the dining table was a simple woven tapestry. It was a blend of vibrant reds, golds, mauves, blues, yellows and greens and brought together wave after wave of color to depict a sunset across summer countryside.

"Interesting taste in art, Miss Dobbs."

"The watercolor was a gift, and the tapestry is one of my own—it's very simple, I'm not an expert at all."

"But you're an artist."

"Oh, no. Not me." Maisie paused. "Look, Detective Chief Superintendent, I must confess I have barely eaten a thing all day and I am famished. I have a hearty soup already prepared, some bread and cheese—would you care to join me?"

MacFarlane turned to face her, and the color rose in his cheeks. "Thank you, yes, I'm a bit peckish myself."

"Right then. There's a bottle of sherry in the sideboard, and some glasses, so do pour us both a glass—just a small one for me. And before you ask, there's nothing stronger—in fact, there's nothing else—so you won't find a single malt lurking away in the back."

"Sherry will be quite welcome."

Maisie stepped into the kitchen and leaned against the stove. What on earth was she thinking? Inviting the detective to stay for supper? What would he think? What would anyone think? A stockpot of soup, made the day before, sat on the top of the stove. She pulled it toward the larger burner and lit the gas-ring, then held the match close to the gas jets in the oven. She brought a wedge of cheese from the larder, along with a cottage loaf, placing the cheese on a wooden board and the bread in the oven. The bread was not in the first flush of youth, so she hoped a warming would soften it up. She brought knives and spoons from a drawer in the dresser, a tablecloth and cloth napkins from another drawer, and set the dining table for two.

"There you are, Miss Dobbs." MacFarlane held out a glass of sherry.

"Thank you, Chief Superintendent." She took the glass and held it up in a toast. "To the New Year."

"Aye, it's not long now. To 1932."

"Do take a seat in front of the fire. The soup will be ready soon—it's oxtail with carrots, potato and onion." Maisie returned to the kitchen, brought out two large soup plates, took a quick taste of the broth, and ladled the soup onto the plates. She set the hot bread on the wooden board alongside the cheese and took the board to the table. After she'd brought in the soup, she returned to the kitchen, opened the back door and lifted a porcelain butter dish from a covered pail, which also contained a half bottle of milk.

When he was summoned to the table, MacFarlane smiled and thanked Maisie again. "Miss Dobbs, this is kind of you."

Maisie nodded. "Dig in, Chief Superintendent, or it will get cold."

They had been eating in silence for some minutes when the detective set down his spoon. "It's been a long time since I had a home-cooked meal."

"Too busy?"

"For the most part."

Having sated her initial hunger, Maisie spoke again. "You wanted to know why I telephoned you today."

"Yes, indeed, that's why I came here." MacFarlane lifted his spoon and dipped it into his soup once more.

Maisie thought back to Billy's comments and wondered if there was more to the visit. Surely anxiety to see the case closed had led him to wonder why she had placed a call to him, which inspired him to wait for her at her flat—though he could have come to her office, instead. But the flat was more convenient to Scotland Yard, so it made sense that he would wait for her here.

"I don't know yet if my inquiry will carry weight, but I was not ready to dismiss Catherine's story today, about the man who had come to their meeting."

"I am sure there are dozens of nutters out there looking to join the agitators, Miss Dobbs. It's the need to belong to a group, isn't it? I've come across it before, and you've heard Colm Darby talk about it. Boys and men who'd never been in trouble, but they've been out on the edge somewhere, and they find family of sorts among men who would exploit them. One minute they are tired, lonely, misunderstood—some of them are misfits, in their way—and then they discover they are among people who give them a feeling of attachment. The next thing you know, they are up to their eyes in crime of some sort or another. The man described by Catherine Jones sounds the same—someone not quite right, someone who is shunned, so he tries to join this lot, only they don't take to him and he's on his own again. I'll concede there's a chance that he's our man, but it's also more than likely that the inventive Catherine is trying to ingratiate herself with us and thereby hoping to receive due consideration when it comes to sentencing. Seen it many times, I'm afraid."

"I'm looking into it anyway."

"Good." MacFarlane reached for the bread knife and sawed two thick wedges of crusty loaf, sliding one onto Maisie's plate with the knife.

"Thank you." She began to butter the bread, placed a sliver of cheese on top, and continued. "Apparently he referred to himself as a 'foundling.' The term is a bit old-fashioned, and was enough to pique my interest. I remembered the Foundling Hospital, the one built by Thomas Coram in the 1700s. It only moved out of London about four or five years ago, and now it's in Redhill. I'm going there tomorrow, to see if I can look at their records. There are a couple of members of staff who have been with the hospital for over thirty years." She paused. "And yes, I know it's a bit of a leap of faith, but if I assume that our man is, say, in his mid-thirties, I can perhaps isolate the years when he might have been there. And if his name really is Oliver, that gives me more to go on."

"And if you come up with nothing?" MacFarlane did not look up as he swept a scrap of crust around the edge of the bowl to soak up the last of the broth.

"I've asked Mr. Beale to compile a list of other orphanages—the Barnardo homes, for example." She watched as MacFarlane finished eating. "Would you like some more?"

He smiled. "That was a lovely bit of broth—and if there's more in the pot, I'll take it."

Maisie reached for his bowl and went to the kitchen, returning with a second helping, which she set in front of him. She continued outlining her plan. "I have been back to see one of the doctors I worked alongside years ago, when I was a nurse—I told you about him. He's an expert in the care of men who have suffered war neurosis, and he also has experience in working with men and women who have been exposed to weapons such as gas, nerve agents and so on—in wartime and in the laboratory."

"And what does he say?"

"Surprisingly little. He is writing a book at the moment, which might account for his reticence to speak. But he was most helpful at first, giving me vital information with which to outline a template of the kind of person we're looking for."

"Ah, yes, the template."

"I know you think I've wasted time."

"We've all wasted time, Miss Dobbs. When you don't know where you're going you run around in circles at first, whacking the bushes to see what vermin come out. Rather than a specific template, it's the scatter method of acquiring clues. Shake out every nasty piece of work you ever came across and see what sticks to the bugger."

The words echoed into the room, and then there was silence. Maisie looked at MacFarlane as he lifted his spoon again, and gauged the degree to which she should take him into her confidence, whether to share her belief that she would find a thread of possibility at the hospital tomorrow. There was a sense she had, an excitement that welled in her chest when she was close to the trickle of information that would lead to a stream, and the stream to a river. That sensation was with her now. She set down her spoon and leaned forward.

"Chief Superintendent."

MacFarlane had just lifted a spoonful of broth to his mouth and stopped when she spoke. "Yes, Miss Dobbs?"

"I think tomorrow's appointment will bear fruit."

"I know you do."

She nodded. "I believe I am close, very close."

"Aye, lass, you may be. But we all have to go on with the search, which is why Stratton is keeping an eye on the Fascists, and Colm Darby is still sniffing away at his Irish leads. We've seconded two of Dorothy Peto's women detectives to shadow our latter-day suffragettes, and we have infiltrated the unions. Our friend Urquhart tells me that there are German agents who have been trying to test their own nerve gases on our underground railway for months now—it's a wonder he told me anything, but this is no time for us all to take to our corners, much as we have to fight the urge to get into a huddle. And you have your orphans, and your doctors and your professors. We're all hoping for that little tap on the shoulder, aren't we? The wee bit of excitement when we know we've got something."

Maisie nodded.

MacFarlane's voice had taken on a softness she had not heard before. "So, you go on down your path, and you keep me well informed. And if you get that fish on the line, don't think you can land him yourself. I've seen your resolve, seen what you've accomplished—remember, it was my job to investigate *you*—but bringing in this man may take more than even you think." He finished the second bowl of soup, wiped his mouth with the table napkin, and leaned back. "Now, I don't want to outstay my welcome, Miss Dobbs. You've done me proud."

"I'm glad to have had the company, Chief Superintendent." Maisie stood up. "I'll get your coat and hat."

Having closed the main door behind Robbie MacFarlane and watched as he walked into the night, Maisie returned to the flat and locked the door. While attending to washing the plates, cutlery and utensils, she realized that she really was glad to have had the company. Though there was the occasional supper engagement, so often her evenings were spent alone, her staple diet being the large pan of soup she made at the beginning of the week. And later, as she donned her flannel pajamas and pulled a pillow from her bed to the floor, where she sat cross-legged to meditate before sleeping, she acknowledged that the Chief Superintendent gave no more weight to her inquiry than he had to the other leads being investigated by Special Branch and Military Intelligence. But he had made her feel as if she were accepted, part of his group. He let her know that she was not alone, that, in a way, she belonged.

December 31st, 1931

Maisie began her journey before seven in the morning. Despite being close to the river, and the mist that wafted in swirls around motor cars, horses and riverboats, the morning was crisp, and the ribbon of grass alongside the flats dusted with frost. The roads would doubtless be icy, so she expected the journey to take longer than usual.

Setting off, Maisie crossed the Albert Bridge and made her way toward the Brighton road, which would take her out of London, through Streatham and Coulsden, then down to Redhill. As was her habit, she used the journey to reflect upon the case in hand, and thought back again to the meeting with Anthony Lawrence. There was something changed about him, she thought. Was it a certain disillusionment with his work? At one time he had demonstrated the mark of an innovative thinker, but now, though he seemed no less dedicated to his role, there was something jaded about his demeanor. Perhaps writing the book was part of an endeavor to rekindle his former energy. She also remembered that, despite promises, he had never managed to effect access to the hospital's records so that she might peruse the lists of men discharged from care during the past several years. And she hadn't pressed him because they had discovered the name of the Christmas Eve suicide. She reminded herself that, though Christmas seemed as if it were months ago now, it was only a few days past, with the New Year almost at hand—not the best time to try to overcome the machinations of a hospital's administrative departments. And besides, she knew Urquhart's men were supposed to be doing just that, and hoped they would alert her if they found something of note.

She checked the hour on a church clock as she drove through Purley, and wondered if she might have time to go on to Oxford following the meeting with Dr. Rigby. She wanted to question John Gale further, but reminded herself that she would need to collect the substance sample from MacFarlane before setting off again.

The sun was poking through as she approached Merstham, where she stopped to check the address of the Foundling Hospital, before proceeding on to Redhill, the next town. Already busy by half-past eight in the morning, the High Street was flanked by two lines of shops and a large red-brick town hall, another testament to Victorian ostentation. Soon she was approaching the Foundling Hospital, now housed in a former convent, a building almost as dark and gothic as the Wychett Hill Asylum.

Dr. Rigby greeted Maisie with the efficiency she had observed before in those responsible for the institutionalized. He checked his watch upon greeting her and repositioned the monocle that made him seem older than his years, though he must have been past sixty. With his furrowed brow emphasizing his importance, she thought he resembled photographs she had seen of Rudyard Kipling, when the newspapers published photographs of the author and his wife visiting the battlefields of northern France in search of their only son's final resting place.

"Dr. Rigby, thank you for agreeing to see me."

"Quite, Miss Dobbs. I understand this is a police matter."

"Yes. I am currently seconded to Scotland Yard—I have a letter of introduction, if you would like to see it."

"If you don't mind, yes." He held out his hand to a chair, then waited until she was settled before taking his seat on the opposite side, next to a window overlooking the playground.

Maisie took an envelope from her document case and handed it to Rigby, who adjusted his monocle several times as he read.

"Detective Chief Superintendent . . . Special Branch." He raised his eyebrows, a move requiring another repositioning of the monocle, then handed the letter back to Maisie. "What can I do for you?"

"Sir, I'm looking for a man who might have been one of your children, perhaps some thirty-five years ago. I have little to go on, except that I suspect he would be in his mid-thirties at the present time."

"Do you have a name?"

"Oliver."

"May I ask what the man has done, why he is wanted by the police?"

"I am sorry, Dr. Rigby, I cannot divulge that information. However, the man I am looking for is—I think—an intelligent and academically accomplished man."

Rigby shook his head. "Then you won't find him among our boys." He leaned back, then forward, and clasped his hands together, circling his thumbs around each other as if part of his body had to continue moving at all times. "Right from the start, our boys here are groomed for military service, a fine place for a young man who has none of the advantages of a higher-born life."

He pointed to photographs on the wall, of young boys in military-style trousers and jackets, and girls in the uniform of domestic service. "Our girls are steered toward service, where they will have a roof over their heads and, with a strong moral compass instilled in them, will not repeat the folly of their mothers."

"And what if a child shows a particular academic inclination?"

Rigby pulled a collection of school exercise books toward him. "This is my marking for this morning. Have a look through the children's work."

Maisie took several of the books from the top and began to leaf through. The children's penmanship was perfect, the lines sharp, the curves exact. And though the number work did not demonstrate academic excellence, there was a level of workaday proficiency that would stand each child in good stead.

"When our children leave us, they leave with the ability to care for themselves. They can read and write, they understand the importance of personal hygiene and a strong individual discipline. In addition, they are exposed to the arts, to music and to a healthy level of recreation. But there are no academic miracles, no pauper-to-university stories to tell you."

"Thank you, Dr. Rigby." Maisie replaced the books on the top of the pile. "However, I wonder, might it be possible to look at your records for the years 1892 to the century's turn? Just in case I find something?"

Rigby shrugged. "As you wish. Of course, the records are packed away—we expect to move again in a few years, into new premises in Hertfordshire. The old convent here is but a stopgap. However, our records are catalogued. I'll have them brought to my office here."

Less than an hour later, Maisie closed the last ledger and placed it back into the box from which it came. She checked that she had replaced every folder, every book and piece of paper as it was found, and stood up, rubbing the small of her back. She had discovered nothing. Nothing among the Thomases, Fredericks, Arthurs, Alberts and Williams. Many of them had joined the army, and most of them were likely now dead. As instructed when Dr. Rigby left her to work in his office, she pulled a cord on the wall, and one of the school's secretaries came into the room.

"I'm finished now. Could you inform Dr. Rigby that I am ready to leave?"

Rigby returned, and began walking her to the front entrance. Maisie stopped to watch children playing a team game on an adjacent field.

"They are happy enough, Miss Dobbs."

"Yes, I can see that."

"They have fresh air, they have food, an education, and our staff here are as dedicated today as Sir Thomas Coram was when he founded the hospital." He walked down the steps, and turned to Maisie. "I must confess, I am not sorry that you are leaving empty-handed. It would be a sad day when the actions of one of our boys or girls attracted the attention of Scotland Yard in such a way. Of course, there are the wayward ones, but the fact that you are involved with Special Branch in a police investigation is gravely ominous."

Maisie nodded and smiled. "Thank you. I am grateful for your time and assistance."

She drove slowly along the graveled driveway, careful in case a child should run across chasing a ball. Pulling out through the gates and onto the road, she shook her head. She had been sure, absolutely convinced, that she would find the thread she was looking for today. And now she had nothing, and that nothing tugged at her all the way through Merstham, through Purley, Coulsden, Streatham, across London toward Lambeth and Scotland Yard. She would report to MacFarlane and watch his face as he observed her disappointment.

Robbie MacFarlane would know how she felt. She would telephone Billy to gather the list of orphanages, and in all likelihood MacFarlane would ask if another line of inquiry might be more fruitful. She parked the MG, entered Scotland Yard, and was taken to Special Branch headquarters by a police constable.

"There you are!" MacFarlane's voice echoed down the corridor when he heard Maisie talking to Colm Darby, who had also just arrived back at the Yard. "There's been a man on the telephone asking for a Miss Maisie Dobbs."

"Me?"

"Yes. Name of Rigby. Didn't want to talk to me, or to anyone else, but wanted Miss Dobbs, 'if you would be so kind'—*be so kind*, if you don't mind—as to place a telephone call to him." MacFarlane pointed to his office. "So you'd better get to it. And when you're done with that, I have something for you to take to Oxford."

Maisie stepped into MacFarlane's office and reached for the telephone while taking an index card from her document case. "Could you put me through to a number in Redhill? Yes. Thank you." She gave the number and waited.

"Rigby."

"Dr. Rigby."

"Ah, Miss Dobbs. I had a thought after you left. Strange— didn't put two and two together before. I tried to catch up with you, even sent a boy running after your motor car, but you'd gone."

"What is it? Do you recall a boy who fits the bill?"

"In a way, yes, I do, though he was not one of ours, strictly speaking."

"Go on."

"Sydney Oliver will probably go down as one of our most dedicated teachers. He spent every moment at the school, put his life into his work."

"How old is he?"

"Oh, Sydney and his wife—Amelia—are gone now. Amelia passed away some time ago now, and Sydney died a couple of years past." The line crackled.

"Hello!"

"Yes, still here. Anyway, to continue—no, it's not Sydney I thought you would be interested in, though he was an interesting study. Brilliant mathematician, but he devoted himself to our children rather than to life as an academic. Amelia was a house-mother of sorts and taught our girls the domestic arts. But it's their son I wanted to tell you about. Sydney and Amelia came to us before Stephen was born, having made a pact to dedicate their lives to helping unwanted children. So, he was, in fact, a late child, born while they worked at the Foundling Hospital."

"And how old would Stephen Oliver be now?"

"If I am right, he would be thirty-six years old. However, there's more I must tell you."

"Yes?"

"He was considered to be something of a genius, always excelling at school."

"Where was he educated?"

"That's the thing—Sydney and Amelia saw fit to send him to boarding school as soon as he was old enough. At six he went away to a prep school, in Eastbourne, I think. Then off to Kings College at Canterbury at eleven."

"You sound as if you found that odd."

"I confess, I did find it odd—and I am sorry, I was so busy thinking about the children here today that it didn't occur to me that you might be interested in Stephen." He paused and the line wheezed again. "You see, they had wanted a child very much—so I was always surprised that they sent him away at such a young age. There were perfectly good schools in London, and though I could see sending him at eleven or twelve, six seemed a bit much, and he was awfully upset. Here at the Foundling Hospital, we try to ensure our children are not unduly wounded by life in an institution, and Sydney was one of those who was almost soft on the children, and had a great deal of empathy for them. So you can imagine how it seemed, when they sent their own son away."

"I get the impression that, in your estimation, Sydney Oliver did not have that same empathy for Stephen."

"He held him to very high standards of accomplishment and behavior. They even had a tutor for him in the holidays, so he hardly saw the light of day. He went up to Oxford at seventeen, if I remember correctly. I confess, I lost track of him after that—it seems that when children reach a certain age, suddenly they're adults and before you know it, you find out that their parents are off to see the grandchildren. Only that wasn't the case with Stephen."

"He wasn't married?"

"No, it's not that. He was killed, in the war."

Maisie felt the excitement drain from her body. "Oh. I see."

"But he was quite brilliant, at the time considered to be on his way to greatness in his field. He was a scientist."

"You have been most helpful, Dr. Rigby. Is there anything more you can tell me?"

"No, I don't think so, but if you like, I'll look through his father's record of employment here, and if I come across any details that might be of interest, I will be in touch again."

"Thank you. And I'm sorry to have to remind you, but I must ask for your confidence in this matter."

"Of course. I am responsible for the lives of many children who come to me as foundlings. I am well used to secrets."

Maisie bid the man good-bye and replaced the telephone receiver.

"First you look excited, now you look as if a bomb has dropped," said MacFarlane as he reentered his office.

Maisie sighed, and without thinking, slumped into his chair. "I had my man, then he slipped through my fingers." She ran her hands through her hair. "And to make matters worse, I could barely hear Rigby when he was speaking."

"And how did he slip through your fingers?"

"He was killed, in the war."

"Are you sure?"

"I was just told as much." Maisie bit her lip and ran the telephone cord through her fingers.

MacFarlane smiled and narrowed his eyes. "But you don't quite believe it, do you?"

She shook her head. "You're right. I don't. I've worked on enough cases to doubt the official line regarding the dead and missing."

MacFarlane leaned across the desk toward Maisie, resting his weight on his knuckles. "Then keep chewing on that bone, Maisie Dobbs. My gut tells me you might be on to something. Now then, if you don't mind, you're sitting in the chair of the Detective Chief Superintendent."

Maisie apologized and stood up. She thanked MacFarlane and moved toward the door.

"And thank you, again, for that lovely drop of soup yesterday."

Stratton was passing the open door, so walked alongside as she left the office. "What soup?" he asked.

FOURTEEN

Before leaving Scotland Yard, Maisie was given a vial of the powder extracted from the clothing of the junior minister who had been killed by a suspicious substance. The pathologists had corked the vial and sealed it with wax, then wrapped it in cotton wool before placing it in a small tin resembling one that might have been used for tobacco, the lid also being sealed with wax. Maisie placed the tin in a plain brown paper bag and pushed it down into her document case. MacFarlane warned her to take care, though they had agreed that it was better she travel alone and without a police escort, in case her movements were being observed.

"It's completely against all protocol for handling this sort of thing," said Stratton, as he opened a door for Maisie on the way to her motor car. "This stuff should be under armed guard."

"And attract the attention of newspapermen, anarchists and—perhaps—the man who killed a junior minister of His Majesty's government?"

"I should come with you." Stratton seemed almost terse when he spoke.

Maisie stopped and faced him. "Look, don't worry. I shall drive straight to Oxford and go immediately to see Professor Gale. I know he will be in his rooms because I checked his teaching and tutorial hours last time I saw him, and doubtless Billy has contacted him by now, telling him to expect me."

"I wish you'd change your mind and let me come with you," offered Stratton.

Maisie shook her head, and they continued talking as they walked.

"We've got everyone out on this one," said Stratton, "but if I can see my way clear to looking into the Oliver lead, I'll get to it— if only to help put your mind at rest. Nothing like nosing after a suspect only to find he's dead."

They reached Maisie's MG, whereupon Maisie set her document case behind the passenger seat, and settled into the motor. She started the engine as Stratton added, "Do be careful, won't you?"

"I'll be all right. Now then, MacFarlane will be bellowing along the highways and byways of Scotland Yard for you, so you'd better get a move on back up to his lair."

THE GRAYNESS OF noontime held all the promise of a bitter, frostbitten night, one that she would rather spend at home in front of the fire with a book, and not at a party. Though her wrap was wound around her shoulders and up to her neck, and she wore gloves, she was still cold as she followed the A40 route out of London and on toward Oxford. The going was slow at first, but just as she was able to pick up speed on the outskirts of London, she became aware of a black motor car maintaining a certain distance behind the MG. It was close enough to keep her within sight, but not so close as to encourage a second look. At first she decided to pay little attention, but it became apparent—when she passed another vehicle, sped up or slowed down—that the motor car was following her. She took care to keep up with other traffic on the road, and accelerated when one vehicle pulled onto another road, or peeled off toward a shop. She began planning her exit from the MG when she reached Oxford—she wanted to be able to reach Professor Gale's office before she was approached by the occupants of the motor car, which she thought might be a Wolseley Straight Eight, a vehicle much faster than her own.

To her chagrin, the pack ahead soon dissipated, and now with no other cars immediately in front or behind, the Wolseley gained speed, pulled around her and braked, leaving just enough room for her to brake in turn without crashing into the rear. She locked the MG's doors and waited as a man emerged from the back of the jet-black vehicle. It was Urquhart. He strolled toward her without urgency and came alongside the MG, whereupon he leaned over so that his face seemed to fill the side window, and smiled. Maisie opened the door and turned sideways to look him in the eye.

"I'm in a bit of a hurry, Mr. Urquhart. Is there anything I can do for you?"

Urquhart smiled. "I am sure you can do better than that, Miss Dobbs. Indeed, I'm surprised you can be so calm, seeing as you're in possession of a volatile substance that could probably do us all a mischief." He brought his hand to his mouth and cleared his throat. "Now then, where do you think you're going with your precious cargo?"

"I am on my way to meet an eminent scientist who I am sure will be able to identify the constituent properties of the substance. It will not tell us who the junior minister's killer is, but it might point us in a given direction."

"Yes, I know all that."

Maisie gave no evidence of surprise, and simply looked ahead. "May I continue now?"

"No. Well, not in the direction you were going, Miss Dobbs."
Urquhart looked up as a vehicle slowed down and pulled around
them, the driver shaking his fist at the inconvenience. "First of all, if
you would be so kind as to open the passenger door, I'll be accompanying you." Maisie leaned across and unlocked the door.
Urquhart continued talking as soon as he was settled. "Bit cramped
in here, isn't it?"

"It suits me, thank you very much."

"No need to be like that. Now then, follow the Wolseley, if you
will. He'll pull over as soon as we find a suitable place for you to
park, then we'll continue on in a bit more comfort."

"And may I ask where we're going?"

"Mulberry Point. And do not be unduly concerned about your
appointment—Professor John Gale will be meeting us there."

Maisie said nothing as the journey continued, and as Urquhart
promised, they stopped only once, to leave the MG safely parked
next to a post office. After Maisie was settled in the saloon's back
seat, they sat in silence as the Wolseley's driver took the motor car
to top speed on its way past Reading to Little Mulberry. Maisie was
tired. The days since Christmas had been long and the visit to the
Foundling Hospital in Redhill already seemed more than just a few
hours ago. She listed back and forth, in and out of wakefulness,
and only when Urquhart spoke did she realize that she had given in
to sleep.

"We're here, Miss Dobbs."

"Yes, yes, good."

Urquhart looked around and smiled. "Look, Miss Dobbs, I
really don't know why you're worried about us. We're all on the
same side, you know—we just work in different ways. Big Robbie
does things his way and we do things our way. And no one gets anywhere when they're keeping secrets."

"Detective Chief Superintendent MacFarlane has said the same thing."

"Hmm, which is why you were on your way to Oxford with a valuable sample of heaven knows what and I wasn't kept in the picture."

Maisie bit her tongue, even though she thought of several suitable retorts.

A soldier emerged from a guardroom as the Wolseley drew alongside a barrier. He looked inside the vehicle as Urquhart pulled a wallet from his inside pocket and opened it to reveal his identification.

"Meeting Professor John Gale."

The soldier checked Urquhart's credentials, and read the letter provided by Urquhart, which was from Military Intelligence, Section Five.

"And is this Miss Dobbs, sir?"

"Yes."

The soldier peered across to the back seat. Maisie smiled, and though it was overcast, she thought the soldier blushed.

"Right you are, sir. Know your way?"

"Yes, Corporal. Thank you."

The motor continued on, and with the window still open, Maisie could smell the sharp freshness of countryside, of cold air across barren fields, and in the distance she heard the bleating of sheep.

"Here we are."

As soon as the Wolseley rumbled to a standstill, the driver came around and helped Maisie out of the vehicle.

"Follow me," instructed Urquhart, as he walked toward a series of low hut-like buildings that Maisie could see were well lit—and well guarded.

Urquhart led the way to the first building, where a soldier asked to see identification. When the uniformed man was satisfied that they were who they claimed to be, with a salute he allowed them to pass. A man in a pair of white overalls and a mask pulled down around his neck met them in the makeshift reception area. In the distance, coming from another low hut, Maisie could hear dogs barking.

"John's this way," said the man. "He's waiting for you in the lab, along with Christopher Anton and Walter Mason, both scientists under his guidance."

"Very good," said Urquhart.

They were shown into an anteroom adjacent to the laboratory, where they were joined by Professor John Gale.

"Miss Dobbs." He extended his hand to Maisie and smiled. "All very cloak and dagger, isn't it? Sorry about that." He turned to Urquhart, said the man's surname and nodded his head in acknowledgment, and then brought his attention back to Maisie. "Now then, Miss Dobbs, I understand you have something for me. My colleagues and I are anxious to start work."

Maisie reached into her document case and retrieved the brown paper bag. She held it out to Gale. "The vial is inside."

"Very good." He moved to leave, then turned back again. "Would you like to observe? You've worked in laboratories as a student, so you are well used to the environment. We have protective clothing available for you."

Anxious not to spend time in conversation with Urquhart, and anticipating that he would decline such an invitation—she was always surprised at how many men in his sort of position could not bear to be in a laboratory—Maisie nodded. "Yes, I would be most interested."

Urquhart shook his head. "I'll go for a cup of tea and a bite to eat until you've got something for me—and don't worry, I know the way to the canteen."

Maisie followed Gale along a corridor, which she realized was a connecting route between two huts. All the buildings were linked in this way, she suspected.

"Here you are. Put this pair of overalls on—there's a dressing room over there. Make sure the sleeves come right down to your wrists. You'll find masks, et cetera, in there." He pointed to a cupboard, then nodded toward another door. "We'll be in that laboratory."

Having taken the necessary precautions, Maisie joined the three scientists, and was introduced to the other two men in turn. She stood to one side and watched as the vial was removed and placed inside a glass tank that looked as if it had been designed to house goldfish. There were holes for the scientists to reach through, and soon all but a small amount of the powder was divided onto a series of glass slides, and secured with a clear substance. Maisie did not interrupt to ask questions; instead, she continued to watch as each man took two slides and went to work, first placing the slides under his microscope.

Gale called her to his side. "What we are looking for at the outset is the nature of the substance. Can we identify the constituent particles? How does it behave, and is there movement? Then, when we've each compiled a series of notes, we take samples into the experimentation room."

"Experimentation room?"

"Yes, my dear. Might not be something you want to watch—we expose animals to the substance and we see what happens. There's enough here, and remaining in the tank, to replicate something of the effect it had on the man who died—even though he was exposed to a greater dose."

Maisie nodded, but said nothing.

"You can talk to me while I'm working if you like, Miss Dobbs. In fact, I sometimes find that if I am having a conversation I discover more in what I am seeing. I think it has to do with letting the trained side of my brain do the work while the judgmental side of my brain is occupied with fielding questions." Looking into his microscope, he frowned. "Hmm, this is a sophisticated little stash of something, isn't it?"

Maisie cleared her throat. "Professor Gale, I wonder, did you ever know of a young man called Stephen Oliver?"

In the laboratory's bright lights, Maisie saw color drain from Gale's face. She wondered if he would tell the truth.

"Stephen Oliver?" He moved the slide he was handling to one side, and Maisie noticed his hands were shaking. "Well, yes, I certainly remember him. Very, very bright young man. One of those who came out to France—I told you about it, after the gas attacks and help was needed in identifying the substances and in developing antidotes. His work was invaluable."

"I have heard that he was killed."

Gale nodded, and set the slides in an enamel kidney-shaped bowl, along with the remaining powder, still in the vial.

"If I remember rightly, he was one of the first to take the work into the field. We'd asked for volunteers to go out and examine men who were gassed, so we could find out more about their symptoms closer to the time of the event, so to speak. In effect, we asked him to go into battle, because he was even issued a gun."

"And that's when he was killed?"

Gale pointed to the small bowl. "Sorry, Miss Dobbs, but I must move on—the sooner we know what we are dealing with, the sooner we can be prepared if it's used again, and on a greater number of people." He summoned his fellow scientists, who noted where the substance was moved to and from; then they left the laboratory and made their way in the direction of the barking. Maisie followed until they reached a series of huts where, from the sounds and smells that issued from them, animals were kept. They went into an adjacent laboratory. When a dog was brought in, Maisie decided that, strong as she was, Gale was right—it was probably better she did not watch. She left the room and waited in the corridor outside.

She could hear the men speaking to one another, and one of them speaking softly to the dog in a soothing manner. Then there was silence for some seconds, followed by a loud initial screech, then yelping. Maisie placed her hands over her ears and walked away, but soon the noise subsided. A bell rang outside, and as Maisie looked out of the window, into the gritty winter afternoon, she saw two men in overalls come to a side door and be given entry to the laboratory. They left moments later carrying the deceased animal between them, wrapped in sacking and a heavy rubber sheet.

Maisie was joined by John Gale, who led her along the corridor. "We expect to have more to report tomorrow morning. At this stage we have, we believe, identified the constituent properties of the powder, and we will replicate it and test it again here. Then we will work on an antidote. But it all takes time—frankly, it usually takes months. But we are used to responding to government requests with some speed, so we have to make assumptions that, as scientists, we might not usually leap to until we are much further along in our work. Sometimes we get a lucky hit. It's a bit like a game of darts. You'd like to be on firm footing, you'd like to stand and consider your shot, but if the other team is baying for you to go on, you just throw the dart and hope it hits the bull's-eye."

"Do you know anyone who has the knowledge to develop an agent such as this?"

Gale stopped in front of a sink, turned on the tap, and began to wash his hands, taking up a brush and scrubbing every crevice of skin. He looked up at Maisie. "We were just talking in the laboratory, and from what we have deduced thus far, the characteristics of this particular weapon—it is a weapon, no other word for it—required an innovator of some advanced ability. In fact, I would call him a genius."

"And there's a thin line between genius and insanity, isn't there?"

Gale nodded and dried his hands on a towel, which he threw into a laundry bin alongside the sink.

"Is that how you would have described Stephen Oliver?"

"He was brilliant, but—"

"Is that how you would have described him?"

He put his hands to his face and pulled them down toward his chin, then rubbed the skin along his jawline. Instead of resembling an absentminded academic, John Gale bore the look of a man shouldering a great weight. He folded his arms and looked down at the ground before speaking to Maisie again.

"Come along to my office, if you would, Miss Dobbs. We will have to go through a proper cleansing process first, though. When you go into the ladies' changing room you'll see a receptacle for your overalls, cap, gloves and mask, and there are instructions on the wall for you to follow. I will join you outside in the corridor. Hopefully that man Urquhart will still be occupied in the canteen."

Maisie followed the instructions to the letter, and when she emerged, Gale was waiting for her. He led the way to an office close to the first laboratory. Whereas his office at Oxford was colorful and cluttered, this office was spare, with few papers on the desk. A series of filing cabinets were each padlocked at the top, and Gale had taken out two keys to unlock the door to the office to gain entrance. He pulled up a chair for Maisie and flicked on an electric fire before taking his seat on the other side of his desk. He wasted no time in continuing the conversation.

"Stephen Oliver was an interesting study, even before the war. He was seventeen when he came up to Oxford. His academic record was about as unbeatable as I have ever seen in my days as a teacher and scientist. On the other hand, he lacked what one might term 'social skills,' though he was a compassionate person, I would say."

"In what way did he lack social skills?"

Gale shrugged. "There was this absolute finesse when working in the laboratory, and a fluency when delivering a paper or address-ing a group of students, or even when engaged in defending a posi-tion regarding his research. But if you asked him down to the pub for a drink, you would have thought he had never been out. He was uncomfortable around women. I would imagine that, as a boy, his teacher might have observed, 'This boy does not know how to play.'"

"So you had known him for some time?"

"Yes, he was one of my students. Later, he became involved in laboratory research and was already an accomplished scientist when the government effectively drafted us all in to deal with the crisis brought about by the enemy's use of chemical weaponry."

"Tell me about his death."

"That's where it gets . . . difficult."

"In what way?"

"Stephen lost his mind in the trenches. Even before he went up the line, he was probably not dealing with the situation as well as most."

"What do you mean?"

"The percussion affected a lot of people—even the noise in the distance, the constant ba-boom, the shells sounding as if they were coming ever closer. I tried to overrule his offer to go to the front, but—it was chaos, Miss Dobbs."

"Yes, I know." Maisie paused. "So, he came back from the trenches changed."

"War neurosis. Immediate repatriation to England, where he was placed in an asylum."

"Not a hospital for men with neurasthenia?"

"Strictly speaking, he wasn't in the army. As I said, it was chaos. He went into an asylum."

"What about his family?"

"Ah, yes. The family."

"What do you mean?"

"The family—his mother and father—were shocked when they saw him. There he was, a young man, constantly drooling from the mouth, not able to control many of the basic human functions. He was shaking, and was so very sensitive to sound."

Maisie nodded. "Yes, I understand. And did the parents try to have him moved? Was there a point at which he returned home?"

"No. In fact, his parents said that it was more than they could take on. By all accounts, they were committed to their work with orphaned children. Overcommitted, I would say."

Maisie leaned back in her chair, as the truth dawned upon her. "They told people their son had died—didn't they? It was the embarrassment, the possible humiliation of having their once brilliant son diminished."

"Yes." Gale looked up. "But he did get better, for a while."

"To what degree?"

"To the degree that he could take lodgings in Oxford, and continue with research at the university. In fact, the regimen seemed to help him—the order, the necessary discipline of the scientist, seemed to bring an element of control to every aspect of his demeanor. And communication with his parents remained severed, as far as I know."

"What happened to him?"

"A relapse. We brought him to work here." He held up his hand. "I know, I know, you may ask about the integrity of such a decision, but you have to realize, he was a brilliant man, a genius. We needed him. We were testing antidotes to every gas used by the Germans, and we were also involved in analyzing those we knew they'd developed but hadn't used. And we were working on our own weapons, everything from a biological agent to kill crops in Germany—the government thought we could starve the country to its knees—to gases and other nerve agents."

"And it was too much for him—he had a breakdown." Maisie offered the statement as speculation.

"Yes. In hindsight, it was to be expected. He was testing on dogs at the time, and the next thing we knew he had completely lost his mind again. Fortunately, one of our psychiatrists was here, and he took charge of the situation."

"And he took him into care, didn't he?"

Gale frowned. "How do you . . . you know, don't you?"

Maisie sighed, and stood up to pace back and forth. "Dr. Anthony Lawrence, wasn't it? He took charge of the situation by removing Stephen Oliver and taking him to one of the hospitals where he worked."

"Yes, that's it."

Maisie paced again, then stopped in front of the desk. "And if I am not mistaken, Stephen Oliver recovered again, didn't he?"

"Yes."

"And you needed him, so back he came once more. Until the next breakdown."

Gale nodded. "He's still locked away, poor man."

Maisie shook her head. "On the contrary, I suspect he was released between six months to two years ago."

Gale rested his head in his hands. "So it was Stephen, then. That dreadful substance we've just watched kill a dog is Stephen's work."

"I can't say for certain, but I believe it could be."

Without warning, and with no attempt at a knock, the door to Gale's office was flung open.

"Sorry to interrupt this little meeting of scientific minds, but I need *you*." Urquhart pointed at Maisie.

She held out her hand to Gale. "Thank you, Professor Gale," she said, and turned to follow Urquhart, but looked back as she reached the door. "You knew it might be him, even before we brought the vial to you today. Why didn't you say anything?"

"I—I didn't want to believe it. I knew he was unsettled, but I—you see so many people in my line of work, and so many of them are . . . are *eccentric*, and—he is a very brilliant man."

"And very dangerous." Maisie stepped into the corridor, as Urquhart, who had not heard the conversation between Maisie and Gale, stepped back into the office and informed the scientist that he would be in touch the following morning to check on "progress." The staff at Mulberry Point would be working around the clock.

"WHAT'S HAPPENED?" Maisie inquired as she was hurried toward the waiting Wolseley.

"To his credit—because he's never been one for playing the game with our department—Robbie has just been on the blower. His informers must have told him we were here, Miss Dobbs. Anyway, it transpires another letter has been received at the PM's office. And this time the trouble could be big."

"What did the man say?"

"That it will be a happier New Year for some, or something like that. Your boss man didn't elaborate."

"He's not my boss." Maisie climbed in the back of the motor car.

"Well, whatever he is, we're on our way to see him now. You can pick up your little roller skate of a motor and follow us to Scotland Yard."

The Wolseley set off again, and as they were cleared to leave the guard post, Maisie wondered if she should tell Urquhart that she thought she knew the identity of the letter-writer. She was about to tap him on the shoulder, but drew back. Something was stopping her from making such a claim. Even though it seemed most likely that Stephen Oliver was their man, it was as if a small voice within was urging her to wait, not to show her hand. She leaned back as the motor car accelerated once more, and wondered if the feeling was simply one of loyalty, that having worked with MacFarlane, she thought he should be the first to know of her discovery.

I always knew, always, that I would die alone. That there would be no caring relative, no wife, no mother, no love to say good-bye. So I will have to take some companions with me. For old time's sake. Tonight, I will go to my death as if to a party. I wonder whether that woman who tried to save Ian, that Maisie Dobbs, is going to a party? I'd seen her before, seen her walking along to the station, or crossing the square. I know what she does. I thought she would have found me by now. Not so clever, that clever woman. She always gives something to the people who hold out their hands. Pennies for the children, pennies for the beggars, pennies for madmen. Yes, I'd like to take her with me. She would be good company, perhaps. But not Croucher, even though he feels sorry for me. Even though I am pitied. Pity. "It's such a pity," said a woman passing me on the street. I never saw her again. Never saw my mother again, not after she thought she had a madman for a son. Not that it would have made much difference. She barely even knew me.

The pencil began to scratch, so the man took up his knife and whittled away slivers of wood until more lead was revealed. Then he licked the lead, and began to note a series of numbers and let-ters. John Gale, or another scientist, might have understood the notations. The man stuck out his tongue as he wrote, and onto the paper, alongside the numbers and letters, drops of spittle punctu-ated a new formula, one that he had been twisting and turning around in his mind for days.

FIFTEEN

 Maisie held the letter by the corner of the page, and brought it closer to the light to read.

"Written in pencil, again—and see here, there's the same evidence of moisture."

Colm Darby nodded, adding, "It's definitely the same man."

"Yes . . . " Maisie was thoughtful as she read.

I have no further use of this life, of this body, or of this mind. But before I go, before I decline the opportunity to step forward into another year of sidelong glances and piteous abuse, I will make my mark. You will be sorry, so sorry not to have listened to me. I wanted only to be heard, only to be heard on behalf of those who cannot speak, the men whom war has crippled and poverty has silenced. There will be no parties, no gathering of joyous anticipation for us, the forgotten. So I will stop the big party. For Auld Lang Syne.

"What are we supposed to do—police every drunken party in London on Old Year's Night?" MacFarlane paced in front of the gathering—Stratton, Darby, Urquhart and Maisie.

"We can stop the public affairs—the steps of St. Paul's Cathedral will be packed tonight, and I wouldn't mind betting that's our man's bull's-eye." Urquhart made his suggestion with a shrug.

"You could be right," said Stratton. "Public gathering at St. Paul's was supposed to be banned, and still hundreds come—but we can have mounted police on duty and turn people away." Stratton looked toward MacFarlane, as if putting a question to him.

"Turning away the inebriated on the eve of the New Year has never been a wholly successful venture." MacFarlane paused. "But it's a start." He clapped his hands together. "Right, then, I want all known venues of public gathering on December the thirty-first to be closed down. Turn the punters away and tell them to get on home."

"Gov, you'll have a riot or two on your hands," said Darby.

"Better that than have tomorrow morning's papers telling the world that a crowd of London revelers has been killed by a mystery substance—a nerve gas, if that's what he's going to use. At least we can explain a riot without causing wider public chaos."

"Robbie, I'm off back to HQ now," said Urquhart. "I've had men all over London for the past few days, and I want to know what I've got at my end. I'll be in touch."

"We'll be on each other's toes again, Gerry."

"I know—I'd rather it that way and not risk leaving a stone unturned."

"Aye, you're right. Be in touch."

Urquhart left the room, and as she heard the door click behind her, Maisie cleared her throat.

"I may have a lead on the letter-writer. I'm not one hundred percent sure, but I would be remiss if I did not bring this information to your attention for want of more corroboration."

"Go on, Miss Dobbs." MacFarlane turned toward Maisie, his attention followed by that of Stratton and Darby.

Describing the visit to Mulberry Point, Maisie recounted her conversation with John Gale. MacFarlane, who was standing in front of his desk, folded his arms and leaned back, causing a pile of papers to fall to one side. He made no move to set them straight, but attended to Maisie's words with a nod or a raised eyebrow. He waited until she had finished before she spoke.

"I would have warned you that Urquhart was on your tail, if I could have—but even though he gets under my skin, he has resources at his fingertips that I don't, and whether we like it or not, we do cross purposes at times, so we've got to try to work in tandem—and that means we pedal in different directions, most of the time. Now then . . . " He looked at the floor for a moment and rubbed his chin. "Miss Dobbs, I want you to go to your Anthony Lawrence and see what you can find out." He looked around at the clock. "Bloody hell, time flies. Not even six hours to go before Big Ben strikes twelve—and half of London gone home."

"I'll leave now." Maisie stood up ready to leave.

"Your man should be here. Beale. Where is he?"

Maisie shook her head. "I hope he's on his way home. I would prefer it if he were with his family on Old Year's Night."

"Going soft on the help?"

Maisie collected her hat and gloves, ignoring the comment. "I'll be in touch as soon as I have something to report—I want to catch Dr. Lawrence before he leaves for the evening."

She left Scotland Yard with haste, making her way with as much speed as she could in the direction of the hospital known as "the Bin."

MAISIE WAS PLEASED to find Mr. Croucher in the porters' office. Even though the man had never been particularly cordial to her, he was a familiar face.

"Oh, Mr. Croucher—is Dr. Lawrence here?"

"No, Madam. Dr. Lawrence has taken leave, won't be back for another two days."

"Oh, dear. Look, I need to see the record of one of his former patients. It's a matter of some urgency."

Croucher shook his head. "Can't do that without Dr. Lawrence."

"May I see Matron?"

He shook his head again. "Sorry, Madam, you'll have to come back after the new year now."

"This is a matter of life and death, Mr. Croucher—may I please see Mrs. Kennedy?"

"Madam, I've told you—" Croucher seemed to soften, as if reconsidering his obstructive stance. "Look, I'm sorry, it's Old Year's Night and Mrs. Kennedy isn't here anyway—it's late you know. Normally she'd be here all hours, but—"

Maisie could feel her stomach become tense. Time was ticking away toward midnight. "Mr. Croucher, I appeal to you to help me—do you know if there was a man here by the name of Oliver? Stephen Oliver? A former patient."

Croucher sighed, looked down at his ledger, and shook his head. "Don't mean a thing to me—never heard the name, and I see everyone in and everyone out, so I would know."

Maisie looked at him, his balding head, his sagging jowls. It seemed as if his job represented his only opportunity to assert himself.

"Thank you, Mr. Croucher. You have been most helpful."

Maisie turned to leave, but as she opened the main doors, she turned back to look through the glass at the porters' office. Across the counter, she could clearly see Croucher putting on his overcoat and hat. He seemed rushed, and it appeared he was giving another porter instructions for his absence—she could see him pointing to a timetable of sorts on the wall, stabbing it with his forefinger to make a point. She knew from the way he moved that his departure was the result of a sudden decision, he seemed flustered and was still calling out instructions as he opened the door that led from the office into the entrance hall. He walked quickly toward the door. Maisie stepped to one side, partially hidden by a bush so that she could not be seen in the shadows. Croucher was in a hurry. He came out into the cold air and pulled up his collar before making his way down the steps. Then he was gone, all but vanished into the thickening smog.

Maisie ran to the MG, started the engine, and drove along the road until she caught sight of Croucher again, lumbering toward a bus. He leaped on board just as it was about to pull away from the stop.

Keeping her distance, she followed the bus for some time, then waited when Croucher stepped off and caught another, which rumbled along the Marylebone Road. She was certain that Croucher would lead her to the man who had written the letters— the man who had taken innocent life, both animal and human. What kind of man was he? Someone who was abandoned, and had in turn abandoned life, to the extent that life was easy to take? She remembered conversations with Maurice, when they had talked about the nature of the killer, how some kept their secret close to them, like a seed planted deep in the soil, waiting for the perfect time to bloom—for the perfect time to be revealed. Some secrets could be hidden for years, while there were those who yearned for their secret, their crime—whether of passion or pre- meditation—to be discovered. Waiting for truth to come out. She had known case after case where the perpetrator instigated his own discovery—the stupid mistake, the blatant error, or the confession made to someone who might tell. Slipping through the MG's gears as the bus stopped again, she wondered if this killer wanted to be discovered, wanted to be noticed, to be acknowledged. He might want to be stopped before he killed again.

Once more Croucher stepped off the bus, walking a quarter of a mile to another stop. This was not an unusual journey—she knew that if Billy did not walk a good way to work to save money, he would be taking three buses instead of one. Now, watching Croucher from her parked motor car, the engine idling, Maisie wondered whether his pacing back and forth in front of the bus stop, his constant glancing up at the clock on a nearby church, was borne of nerves or the cold. She studied his movements with careful attention and noticed the nervousness to his gait. She recognized the fear. *He's on his way to warn him. To let him know we're on to him. He's going to see—Stephen Oliver?* She looked around for a telephone kiosk, and saw one illuminated just yards away from the MG. Leaving the motor running, she left the MG and stepped toward the kiosk. She opened the door, lifted the receiver, and dialed Scotland Yard, all the time keeping her eyes on Croucher as she asked to speak to MacFarlane.

"Yes!"

"It's Maisie Dobbs."

"Have you made any progress?"

"I'm calling from a telephone kiosk, on the Marylebone Road, going toward Euston Road. I've followed a man called Croucher— hospital porter. I think he's on his way to see our man."

"And what makes you think that?"

Maisie paused, wondering whether brutal honesty would stand her in good stead. "I can just feel it—is that good enough for you?"

"Makes a lot more bloody sense to me than all that scribbling across the walls. We'll find you. Don't take any chances." The telephone clicked.

Maisie returned to the MG in time to see another bus come

along, and Croucher jump on board. She pulled in behind the bus and followed it along Marylebone Road. She began going through the events of the past hour, since she first spoke to Croucher. Could his hasty departure from the hospital have simply been due to her detaining him with questions? Did he then have to run for a bus that he normally caught with some ease, given the time his working day ended? She wondered if she could be wrong in her conjecture, but shook her head. No, she knew where he was going.

Now she could barely see ahead of her in the thick pea-souper, and if it weren't for the bus and street lights casting their smudged shadows around and ahead of her, she might not have seen him jump off the rear platform of the bus and make his way along the Euston Road, then turn into Warren Street. At that moment, she felt an icy sensation at her neck, a feeling she knew came as a warning, tingling to attract her attention when all was not well, when something was not quite as it should be. It had alerted her on many an occasion, and now as it turned to a radiating pain, she wondered if the writer of the letters, if the madman himself, had been under her nose all the time.

She followed Croucher along Warren Street, and because the street was busy with people going in and out of the pubs—perhaps a little more raucous than usual on the last night of the year—she parked the MG where it could be seen by the police and then continued on foot, keeping Croucher in view. Where was MacFarlane? Was she being observed without her knowledge? Croucher continued on, and she wondered why he had not stepped off the bus earlier, when he'd had the opportunity, opposite Great Portland Street underground station. He could have simply walked across the road from there. Maisie allowed a distance to grow between Croucher and herself. It occurred to her that he might know he was being followed and was testing his theory by taking a circuitous route to his destination. With each step as she drew farther away from the more populated area around Warren Street, she knew she was on her own.

Turning again, this time into the top end of Cleveland Street, Croucher snaked back and forth across neighboring streets until he stopped at the top of a flight of steps leading down into a basement flat. She stepped back into the shadows when he stopped and looked behind him. Though she could only see him as a gray shape in the darkness, she was aware that it was only after he had scanned back and forth several times that he began his descent. She approached the house with care and took stock of the neighborhood.

It was said of the environs of Fitzroy Square—and they were not far from the square—that a peer could sit next to a plumber at supper, and neither would feel the worse for it. There were well-appointed houses adjacent to tenements, and clean properties neighboring slums. There were mansions where two people lived in comfort, and bed-sitting rooms where the landlord asked no questions, as long as the rent was paid. Some had only the soot-covered walls to look out upon, and others had compact walled gardens, where a riot of color fought against the grayness of buildings assaulted by smoke and damp. She could see that Croucher had come to visit someone who lived in a cold-water flat, cheap accommodation for a person on the bread line—an ugly place to live for someone who could not afford anything more, where the occupants vanished into the night, and were all but invisible during the day. It was a place where a sense of disenfranchisement could grow unchecked, where disappointment and despair were bedfellows, where a clammy damp kept the blood cold, and where warmth was sucked out, along with hope.

Peering over the iron railing, Maisie saw the pale light from an oil lamp grow, as if the occupant lived in the dark, but now, with a visitor, turned up the wick to illuminate the room. She moderated her breathing, placing the fingers of her right hand against her coat, just three fingers width below her waist, balancing herself so that she would breathe with ease, and move with dexterity. She looked around, just in case MacFarlane's men had discovered her whereabouts and help was on its way, but could wait no longer. She made her way down the steps and stood against the wall alongside the window.

The men's voices were low, almost indistinct. A few seconds passed, then there was movement toward the window, and she heard the voice of the man she knew to be the one for whom she searched. His words were thick, as if the man's gullet itself were mucus-filled. He cleared his throat and wheezed, coughing before he spoke again.

"I don't need you to protect me, Croucher. I am able to look after myself. You have shown kindness, in bringing me food."

"You've got to look after yourself, sir. You need better food, and I can't always get it."

"Don't worry. It will soon be all over, anyway."

"What do you mean, sir, what do you mean?" Croucher's voice escalated in tone, edged with a whine, as if he were a man facing the inevitable. Maisie frowned. The tone of the porter's response suggested he was trying to control the man in the flat, and was without power against his will.

"I mean, it's almost over. Midnight. Then they'll see."

"But you can't, please don't do it. I can't cover for you anymore. The Dobbs woman came back to see Lawrence this evening— didn't make an appointment first, just came to the hospital. I know she's after you, I know she'll find you. I've seen her type—she's a terrier."

Keep your mouth shut and leave. Leave now . . . Maisie whispered into the cold night, knowing Croucher was playing with fire. *Don't say another word, just leave.*

"I think you should just lie down, sir. Let me make you a nice broth, or a cup of tea—look, I've brought you some bits and pieces of food. Slim pickings today, but enough to keep you going."

Maisie flinched upon hearing something crash to the ground— a jar, perhaps, or a can and two or three items. Had the man swept Croucher's offerings from the table? She held her breath again as he raised his voice.

"I don't want your pity, and I don't want you telling me what to do."

The man slurped as he spoke.

It's him, I know—it is him! thought Maisie.

"But I'm only trying to help—"

A dull thud made Maisie flinch again. Had the man been pushed too far? Had he assaulted Croucher, perhaps with a sturdy walking stick, one with a steel tip, perhaps, or brass handle? She closed her eyes and imagined a cane brought against a head at a certain angle with weight behind it, and she knew that Croucher was down, and probably unconscious. He might even be dead.

She closed her eyes and in that moment asked for guidance, asked a God she had doubted on many an occasion to aid her, for she knew—knew in the gut—that when the man left the flat, it would be with the intent to kill and he would not kill just one person. In the distance she heard a clock chime. It was past eight o'clock. Crowds would be congregating on the steps of St. Paul's. People were already in the pubs—one only had to walk along to Charlotte Street to see that both rich and poor alike were merry-making. With barely a sound she stepped up into the street and looked both ways. Nothing. No sign of the men from Special Branch. She had hoped the police would find her distinctive MG and then conduct a sweep-search of the neighboring streets. If the man left his flat, she couldn't wait for them to arrive—she would have to stop him before he set foot on the street. At risk to her own life, she had to prevent him leaving.

THE MAN PULLED BACK his chair and watched blood ooze from Croucher's broken skull into a shallow puddle on the floor. He felt a coldness take over his body. It was not a chill that was the opposite of heat—he had, in any case, become used to the cold and damp, though sometimes it brought him down, took away his strength so that he could not emerge from his bed. No, this was another biting numbness. It was the thread of unfeeling that ran through his body as mercury runs in a line through a thermometer, the weight of the matter channeled along the tunnels of life, taking from him all sensitivity, all sense of horror, so that even when he regarded Croucher as his skin grew cold and his bones stiff, the man felt nothing. No shame, no sadness, no fear, no . . . nothing. If he had a soul, he could feel it no longer.

He looked down at Croucher as if observing an experiment, watched the blood coagulate and stop in a pool, then thicken, so that, if he pushed a finger against it, it would wrinkle. He had never struck a man before. It was not his way. But it did not matter. *What does anyone matter, after all?* He pulled the leather-bound notebook toward him, unfurled the string that bound the pages, and took out the pencil. He ran his thumb across the lead, and winced when he felt a sliver of wood against his skin. Limping to a drawer, he brought out a knife and a sharpening steel, and took his seat again in a way that suggested he was losing his balance. Sweeping the poker-like sharpening steel back and forth across the blade, his brow furrowed as he brought every ounce of his attention to the task at hand. Once more he tested the blade, and satisfied that it was now up to the job, he set down the steel and whittled the pencil again until the lead was sharp, with a good eighth of an inch free of the wood. He placed the knife on the table and began to write.

> *This is my last entry. I will write no more, for I will be gone. And no one will miss me. But I will not go alone, and perhaps, perhaps, perhaps, someone will take notice. I know my limitations, know the extent of what I can do, and if I could take the Prime Minister, or his self-serving cohorts, then I would. But I can't, so I must take who I can, and then those fools in Westminster will know what it is to be invisible. One of the forgotten, one of the lost.*

The pencil dragged across the page in a jagged line. The man closed the leather book, bound it with string, and placed it in a pocket inside his threadbare greatcoat.

THROUGH THE WINDOW, with barely any light to cast a shadow, Maisie Dobbs watched him turn up the wick and move to a cupboard. He removed a jar, and though she squinted, she could not tell whether it contained a viscous liquid or a thick powder. He collected matches and a vial. And as she watched, she knew she could not let him leave, could not let him go on his way. She could not let him kill again. She turned away from the window, took one step to the side, and knocked on the door.

SIXTEEN

"Who's there? Who's there at this time of night?"

"Mr. Oliver?"

"No one of that name here."

Maisie bit her lip and tried again. "Sir, I think you know who I am. My name is Maisie Dobbs. I believe you mentioned my name in a letter, delivered on Christmas Day."

Silence.

"Sir?"

"What do you want?"

Maisie cleared her throat. "I'd like to talk to you, if I may."

"What about?"

"Well . . . " She paused. "We could start with Ian Jennings. I believe you knew him, and so did Mr. Croucher. They were both friends of yours, weren't they?"

"*Weren't* they?" The man's eyes narrowed.

She realized her error—she had referred to Croucher in the past tense. *They were both friends of yours.* Now he knew, now the man knew she had seen him strike Croucher. She heard the rattle of a chain, then a key unlocking the door, and a bolt drawn back. The door opened.

Maisie showed no emotion when she saw the scarred face, the livid line that ran down from the man's forehead and across his eye until it reached his jaw. His back was curved as if he were a hunchback, and one foot was splayed to the side. His right shoulder was held higher than the other, and his hands were like fists in front of him as he stood before her. She imagined that he might once have been a tall man, perhaps six feet or more. Now, though, he was diminished by circumstance, and she could only speculate as to what might have happened to him. But she knew she had seen him before.

"I've seen you before, on Charlotte Street, I—"

Without warning, the man reached forward with one clawed hand and dragged Maisie into the room by the collar on her jacket. He slammed the door behind him.

"I have come to help you, sir, I—"

"Well, you're too bloody late!"

In the flickering shafts of light and dark caused by the oil lamp's wick burning down, Maisie fought the urge to steal a glance at the floor and the body of the man she had only seen as a taciturn hospital porter. Looking into the killer's dark, expressionless eyes, she knew an empathetic approach would gain her nothing. She had been surprised by his strength, and knew that there was no connection, now, between rational thought and his actions.

"Sir, I believe I understand why you've taken the lives of both men and animals, and I understand the . . . the great weight—"

"Oh, do me a favor, please!"

They stood facing each other, and Maisie wondered what words, what actions might placate a man for whom all accepted modes of human communication seemed to mean nothing. Even as he was facing her, his eyes rolled back in his head and saliva issued from his mouth.

"You have committed murder, and I believe you intend to murder again, only this time you plan to take the lives of many more innocent victims."

"Innocent? Innocent? Innocent of what? Innocent of being blind toward the plight of other people, when you can see with your own eyes what they have to put up with? That's a terrible thing, Miss Maisie Dobbs. I don't see innocence, I don't see innocence at all."

Maisie collected her thoughts again, hoping to play for time, hoping that soon the police would be searching street to street, door to door, for surely they would have found her motor car by now.

"I saw you. I saw you on the street and gave you what I could."

The man nodded. "Yes, and you tried to give something to Ian."

"It was you, then, the man who was watching me."

"Yes. It was me, I remembered you. Only I didn't know your name until I heard that bloke yelling at the top of his voice. 'Maisie Dobbs! Miss Maisie Dobbs!' But now you're working for them, aren't you? You're part of the merry-go-round. You don't know—none of your type know—what it is to be like us, to be alone, what it is to know that . . . no one knows you."

"Then how did you know Jennings? And Croucher?"

He looked at the floor. "Oh, yes, poor sparrow Croucher."

Maisie frowned, wondering what the man meant. She felt as if she were walking on ice that might crack at any moment. She felt as if her world could upturn in the time it took to take a breath. Still she did not look down at Croucher, though she could smell the death on him, could smell time sucking the warmth from his body, leaving it hardened and cold.

"I met Ian somewhere. I don't know where now. I can't remember, though it might have had something to do with Croucher, or . . . " The man seemed distracted, as if he had suffered a sudden fatigue. "I might have known him years ago. And he tried to help me, even though he needed the help." The man stared at the lamp, which was growing ever dimmer, and sighed. "They let him down, you know, the army pensions people. Called him up in front of three know-alls who said that he could do a job, what with his mind and the fact that he could get about." He drew his attention back to Maisie, his eyes rolling back as he tried to focus. He shook his head and spoke again. "But of course, poor Ian couldn't get a job—it's all a man with the parts still intact can do to get on, isn't it, Miss Dobbs?"

She nodded, anxious to appease him. "These are hard times."

"And Croucher, bless him."

"What do you mean?"

"He's one of those eternal helpers. Don't know what made him do it, but he saw me—I can't remember where he saw me, to tell you the truth—but he saw me, and he might have seen Ian, both of us holding out our hands in different places. And he tried to help." He shook his head from side to side, like a man trying to correct blurred vision. "Oh, yes, that's where I met Ian. I think Croucher brought him to me, to be my friend. I think he thought we had known each other, years ago."

"And were you friends, you and Ian Jennings?"

He shrugged. "He should have waited." He pointed to his head. "Not right up here, Jennings. I told him I had a plan, that I'd had enough of waiting, that I could bring this country to its knees. But he got lost in his mind, silly boy." He shrugged again. "Don't know why I always called him a boy. I don't even know if he was younger than me."

"And how old are you, sir?"

The man winced and clutched either side of his head. "I must be nigh on forty now, or thirty-eight, or——" He brought his attention back to Maisie. "I don't want to talk anymore. I've got to get on. In fact, I should do something about you. After all, I don't want you stopping me, don't want you——"

In the distance the ringing of a bell on a police vehicle could be heard, coming closer. Then another from the opposite direction. The man cocked his head this way and that, as if to try to ascertain where the sounds were coming from. Maisie took the opportunity to step back, but the man was quick, and lunged toward her, pulling the flank of his left arm around her throat as he held her from behind. Despite his disability, his strength overpowered her.

"Oh, no you don't. You've seen too much as it is."

"You can't leave here, sir. I know what you plan to do, I know where you're going with that jar." She wondered whether to play her trump card, and knew there was no time to take chances. She choked out her words, with the crook of his arm resting against her gullet. "The police know and so do the secret service. So you see, you don't stand a chance. Don't leave. I am sure——"

Maisie gagged and coughed, and with her hands tried to drag his arm away from her throat. She began to feel light-headed, with colored threads of light pulsating across her peripheral vision as she fought for air. With as much strength as she could muster, she pushed back, jabbing the man hard in the ribs with her elbow. She felt him lose his balance. His arm came free of her neck, and he fell against the table. The bells traveled closer; she could hear muffled voices in the distance, as if men were running to and fro, coming closer, then away again.

Gasping, Maisie turned to face the man she knew to be mad, a man whose thoughts were not tempered by the constraints that brought his behavior within limits considered "normal." As he used his strength to regain some semblance of balance, the jar rocked and fell to one side on the table, where it rolled back and forth. The man followed the jar with his eyes as if dazed, as if what he could see had no relation to the visions in his mind. Maisie lurched for the jar, and felt its weight in her hands, but when she looked back, it was into the eyes of a killer. He held out a knife toward her.

"Give that to me."

"Sir, this is a dangerous substance. The police will be here soon, and if you give yourself up, there will be leniency, you will be cared for, you will be—"

"Put away where I belong, eh? Put away where no one can see me and where I can't be a danger to myself. They always want you put away, until they need you again, until *your country needs you*." He mimicked the tone of wartime recruitment posters, and waved the knife in front of her, but she kept the jar clutched close to her body. "And they'll want what's up in here, won't they?" For the second time he pointed to the side of his head. "But I—"

The voices came closer, and when the man looked around to follow the sound, Maisie kicked out at him, as hard as she could. He fell backward, again, and braced his fall against the wall. Maisie staggered, feeling her feet slide in blood that had seeped from Croucher's broken skull. Still clutching the jar with one hand, she reached for the table to keep herself steady. Sweat poured from her brow as the man began to lumber forward again. Then he stopped and looked out the window, his face tilted upward to view the street. Footsteps running back and forth echoed on wet flagstones, but Maisie knew that even if she called out she would not be heard from inside the basement flat.

The man brought his attention back to her, as if he had just been woken from a deep sleep, his eyes moving slowly, reminding her of a patient after an operation, when the effects of ether were still evident, before full consciousness had been regained.

"It's over, isn't it?"

"Yes, it is," said Maisie, her voice soft. "It's over now."

"They won't take me, you know."

Maisie felt tears prickle against the corners of her eyes. She remembered Ian Jennings. She could see him in front of her, could see her hand held out to try to stop what she knew was about to happen, and she could feel, again, the knowing that came to her, that the man would take his own life.

She nodded. "Yes, I know."

"Do you think there's a heaven, Miss Dobbs?"

Maisie cleared her throat. "I think there's a better place than this."

The man shrugged, lifted the knife to his wrists, and, without a sound, sliced deeply into the flesh. And as he fell to the ground, the lifeblood pumping from his body, she began to weep. With one last ounce of energy, he held the knife steady with blade pointed upward, and rolled onto it so that his heart was pierced.

Maisie cried out and, still clutching the jar to her chest, moved around the body, opened the door and ran up into the street.

"MacFarlane! Are you there? MacFarlane!"

Two policemen came out of the layers of smog toward her, whistles blowing. Soon a black Invicta swung around the corner, and even before the driver had maneuvered to a halt, the back door opened and Robert MacFarlane was running to her side. He put his arms around her, and spoke with a softness, she realized later, that she had never heard before.

"It's all right, it's all right. We're here, we're all here, it's over now. It's all over."

Maisie allowed herself to be soothed, allowed herself to weep into MacFarlane's shoulder. Police cars swooped down the street, and soon MacFarlane had taken Maisie to the Invicta, and was barking orders to the men. Stratton and Darby arrived in minutes, and while Maisie leaned back into the firm leather upholstery, the scene of a murder and a suicide were secured, and the pathologist summoned.

The passenger door of the Invicta opened, and Maisie looked up, expecting it to be MacFarlane or Stratton. It was Urquhart.

"Nice work, Miss Dobbs. Two dead bodies and no one to question, and—oh, I think that's for me." He reached out toward the jar, but Maisie held firm.

"Mr. Urquhart. Two dead bodies, not two hundred. One murder—and I can recount the whole event to you now, if you like, or you can await my statement via Scotland Yard. I can also tell you about the suicide, which was going to happen anyway, because that's what the man had planned. Only he didn't take anyone with him—except Mr. Croucher."

Urquhart shook his head. "I'm sorry—you look like hell."

"That's how people look, when they have seen hell through another's eyes."

"May I?" He held out his hand toward the jar.

Maisie waited a moment, then handed it to him. "Be careful, Mr. Urquhart. I believe that within that jar is one half of another destructive agent—and if you go into the flat you'll find a vial, which I think is some sort of catalyst to render whatever you have there into a veritable killing machine."

"It will be going directly to Mulberry Point."

"I don't care where you take it, Mr. Urquhart, as long as it goes as far away from innocent human beings as possible."

"Thank you, Miss Dobbs. I know we haven't enjoyed the best working relationship, given that you're a civilian attached to Special Branch, but you've done a good job."

Maisie nodded and closed her eyes. "Shut the door as quietly as you can, if you don't mind."

MAISIE MADE HER statement and was questioned for over an hour at Scotland Yard, after which she joined MacFarlane, Stratton and Darby in MacFarlane's office. It was a quarter to twelve at night and it had been a long day for all concerned.

"We're going to have to be back here first thing in the morning—early."

"But—" Before he could say more, Stratton stopped speaking.

"Problem with that, Stratton?" MacFarlane looked up from notes taken during a search of the basement flat.

"No, sir. It was nothing." He stole a glance at Maisie, who knew Stratton had a son with whom he had doubtless promised to spend the first day of the New Year.

"Right then," MacFarlane continued. "Here's where we are." He looked at Maisie, then at the men. "Obviously our investigation will continue. For now, I can tell you all that there was nothing in the flat to identify the man who killed Mr. Edwin Croucher, a hospital porter residing in Catford. There were no letters, no bills, nothing."

"What about the landlord?" Maisie sat forward on her chair.

"According to the landlord, the man paid his rent in advance, from one week to the next, and was never late. He gave no name when he rented the flat, about eighteen months ago, and the landlord was happy to have the money, so no questions asked. The rent was always paid with coins—pennies, thrup'ny bits, ha'pennies, florins. He paid his rent with the fruits of his labors, sitting with his hand out on the streets of London."

"You mean there was not one single item in that flat that we could use to put a name to this man?" Darby frowned as he faced MacFarlane.

MacFarlane picked up a package wrapped in muslin and folded back flaps of cloth. "Nothing but this, the man's diary. The ramblings of a barely-there-at-all man."

"Have you read it, Chief Superintendent?" asked Maisie.

"I've had a quick gander."

"May I?" She reached out toward MacFarlane, and he placed the cloth-covered diary in her hands.

"Be careful, Miss Dobbs, that's got to go down to the lab boys."

"I understand. May I read it?"

"Well, you can, but before you do that, I thought you might all like to join me in a toast."

"Toast?" asked Darby.

"Colm, my old boy, we've been forgetting ourselves." MacFarlane stood up, opened a filing cabinet, and from the bottom drawer removed a bottle of malt whiskey and four tot glasses. He lined up the glasses on his desk and poured a full measure of the amber liquid into each glass. Keeping the bottle in his hand, he took a glass and clinked it hard enough against each glass in turn so that the members of his staff, including Maisie, had to be quick to grab their whiskey as it tilted toward them.

"A happy New Year to one and all. Slainte!" MacFarlane gulped his whiskey, then slammed the glass on the table to pour another, just as Big Ben began to chime the hour and the passing of the new year.

The men emulated their boss, drinking the toast back in one, while Maisie closed her eyes, tilted her head, and took but a single mouthful while trying not to cough.

"That's it, lass, get it down you, it cleans out the tubes—and it'll help you sleep tonight. Anyone for another?" He waved the bottle, then poured a second measure each for Stratton and Darby.

Maisie cleared her throat, which was burning. "I wonder, Chief Superintendent, may I use your telephone?"

"Stratton, show Miss Dobbs to the next office—give her a bit of privacy. If someone wants to place a telephone call when the New Year is still in swaddling clothes, you can bet it's personal."

"I can find my way next door. I won't be long."

Closing the door of the empty office behind her, Maisie went to the desk, lifted the telephone receiver, and placed a call to Priscilla's house. The telephone at the Holland Park mansion was answered by a housekeeper, and Maisie was asked to wait while Mrs. Partridge was summoned.

"I do hope you have an excellent excuse." Priscilla sounded terse, and—as Maisie expected—upset.

"Actually, Priscilla, I have an excellent excuse, only I can't tell you about it, not yet, not now."

Priscilla's tone softened. "You sound exhausted, Maisie."

"I am a bit. How are you? How's the party?"

"Lovely, as parties go. We're still at the champers, still dancing, still weaving our way into the New Year with all the glee we can muster."

Whether it was the whiskey or the events of the day, Maisie felt emotion well in her voice. "I've missed seeing you, Priscilla."

"Oh, darling, I've missed you too, my friend. Are you sure you can't come tonight? We're still going strong, and breakfast won't be served until half-past four to finish off the celebrations, then everyone can go home."

Hearing the eagerness in Priscilla's voice, Maisie was loath to upset her once more. "Pris, I—I'll see how I feel when I get back to the flat. But don't bank on it."

Maisie thought she heard Priscilla weep, and there was a pause before her friend spoke again.

"I suppose I'm being terribly selfish, aren't I? I just find the new year so trying. All that looking forward and saying, 'Happy New Year' and I'm standing here wondering what might happen before December the thirty-first rolls around again. I feel as if I'm under siege."

"Hush, Pris, hush. Go back to your party, shine that smile of yours at your guests, and though I can't promise, perhaps I'll get a second wind by the time I get home."

"Happy New Year, Maisie."

"You, too, Pris. You too."

MAISIE RETURNED TO MacFarlane's office, where the men continued to discuss the case. With one ear to the conversation, Maisie picked up the diary and began to read.

> *My name's not important anymore. I am not a person, not the person I was, and I can't remember who that person was anyway. I did what my country asked of me, I stepped forward to do my bit, and then, when I came home, they didn't want me anymore—well, except for my mind. No one wanted me, no one wanted to see me, or speak to me. They wanted me tucked away in a place where they wouldn't have to see me ever again. I am the man they sent to war, I am the man who went forward at their battle cry. And there are thousands of me, so many hundreds and thousands of me, all of us back here, but never to return home. Home doesn't even exist for us . . .*

"Well, you can't sit there and read all night." MacFarlane held out his hand for the dead man's diary, and instructed Stratton to escort Maisie to her MG, which had been brought to the Yard by a detective constable.

"Will you need me here tomorrow, Chief Superintendent?"

MacFarlane shook his head. "No, shouldn't think so." He looked at Maisie and smiled. "You've done a bloody good job, Miss Dobbs. We might not know that man's name, but we do know he was our letter-writer, and we do know he was our murderer. You brought him down before he killed in a way that doesn't even bear thinking of, ever. You should go home and rest."

Maisie shook hands with Colm Darby and with MacFarlane, who might have held her hand for a second longer than was necessary.

"It's been a long day, hasn't it?" said Stratton, as they made their way to Maisie's motor car.

"Yes, but we have our man."

"You were right to follow that lead, Miss Dobbs."

"And you were right to follow every other lead—MacFarlane could not limit his resources to just one possibility. He couldn't put all his eggs in one basket—and who knows when one of those groups might decide to up the ante and choose a more violent method of making a point, though I doubt whether the women fighting for equal pensions will resort to dynamite or chemical weaponry."

They reached the MG. "Well, happy New Year, Miss Dobbs— and a safe one. I daresay we will be in touch in due course. There's still much to do on this case. For a start, we'll be bringing in your Dr. Anthony Lawrence to identify the body tomorrow."

"Of course." She paused. "I'm sorry you'll be missing a day with your son though."

Stratton shrugged. "Name of the game, Miss Dobbs. I'll make it up to him."

Maisie smiled and as she took the driver's seat of her motor car, she looked up at Stratton. "Happy New Year, Inspector."

Stratton stood back as Maisie eased the MG out onto the road.

She drove home on all but empty streets, as the bells of London continued to peal, and those who could afford such levity raised another glass to 1932.

SETTLING BACK INTO a soothing hot bath, Maisie considered Priscilla's party and how much her friend had wanted her to be there. For her part, the last thing Maisie wanted was to see Priscilla with another drink in her hand to dull the fear in her heart. Even so, Priscilla was her dearest friend, and to Maisie, close associations always mattered. She sighed, closed her eyes, and thought about her day from beginning to end, and again saw Croucher running for his bus, and the final meeting with the man he had befriended, perhaps when he recognized his solitary condition. Men like Jennings and Oliver—she had assumed it was Oliver, though they had yet to find any letters or documents to confirm the killer's identity—were both incarcerated by their wounds, the latter being a man who had lost all semblance of rational thought, and in whose head the battle continued to rage, day after day. He had been an intelligent man, a man thought "brilliant" by his peers, and yet had taken up weapons to fight on behalf of those passed on the street and forgotten when war was done.

As the bathwater began to cool, Maisie's thoughts moved to Billy's wife, and it occurred to her that Doreen and Priscilla suffered from variations of the same affliction. But whereas Doreen was caught in the past's quicksand, trapped in a world where she ached for a daughter who was dead, Priscilla feared the future. She had fought the onslaught of grief in Biarritz, a place removed from the connections of her girlhood, where the only early memories were happy recollections of family holidays. Unlike England, Biarritz held no reminder of her parents' terror upon hearing of the loss of their sons, of her own sorrow when she received news that her brothers were dead. But now she had returned to the country from which her siblings left for war. Now she feared for her own sons, for the eldest, who would be on the cusp of manhood before the decade's end. And her fears were taking her back in time—a time when drink dulled the ache in her soul.

Priscilla had been safe in the world she controlled in Biarritz, as safe as a patient in a hospital. But now she was back in the thick of London society, and it was clear she was floundering. And she needed a friend.

Maisie stepped from the bath, toweled herself dry, then put on the black day dress that also served as suitable garb for a cocktail party. She had no gown to wear, but she was sure Priscilla wouldn't mind. Either that or Priscilla would drag her off to her dressing room to find something she considered more suitable. But that was all right, Maisie would allow her friend the indulgence of having all her guests in evening dress. After styling her hair, applying some kohl to her eyes, just the faintest dash of rouge to her cheeks, and red lipstick, she put on her black leather shoes with straps that buckled at the side, followed by her coat and hat. She pushed a handkerchief, some money and the lipstick into a black clutch bag, picked up her keys, and left the flat. It was a quarter to two in the morning when she set off for Holland Park.

"MAISIE, DARLING, I knew, just knew you would come!" Priscilla's eyes filled with tears as Maisie was led through the throng of guests who had spilled out into the entrance hall, and shown into the drawing room. Waving her cigarette holder in the air, Priscilla called out to her husband. "Douglas, Douglas, look who's here. It's Maisie."

As Douglas Partridge waded through the crowd toward them, taking a glass of champagne from a maid as he went, Priscilla turned to Maisie once again, linking her arm through Maisie's and looking into her eyes. "I know you must be terribly worn out, I can see it in your eyes, but . . . but . . ." She began to cry, pulling her arm away from Maisie so that she could squeeze the bridge of her nose to prevent the tears.

"Oh, Priscilla, don't weep. This is your party, your time to celebrate being here in London with your family. Come on, Pris, come on, look, here comes Douglas."

Douglas Partridge stood alongside his wife, rested his cane against his thigh, and put his arm around her. "Tears of happiness, aren't they, darling?" Keeping his arm around Priscilla's shoulder, he winked at Maisie and leaned forward to kiss her on each cheek. "We're so glad you could come. Priscilla's been looking forward to this evening for weeks. And it's a thumping good party, isn't it, love?" He looked into his wife's eyes, then kissed her on the nose. "Now, I am going to leave you with your dearest friend and see if I can find Raymond Grasslyn for a chat."

Priscilla took a deep breath to temper her emotions, and looked Maisie up and down, feigning bossiness. "Come on, five minutes in my dressing room. I want to see you in a gown. You're not in one of those Scotland Yard morgues now—it's a party!"

If it had been anyone but Priscilla, Maisie would have been offended, but on this occasion, she nodded and laughed. "Oh, all right, let's get it over with."

Fifteen minutes later, after Priscilla had pulled out four gowns for her to choose from, Maisie came downstairs to renew her entrance to the party wearing a gown of deep purple silk that reflected the color of her eyes. The boat neckline and hem were embellished with bands of sequins, as were the cuffs, which came to a point across the back of each hand. The dress was narrow to the hip, where a sequined seam sat above a fuller skirt that fell in soft folds to the floor. Maisie wore a pair of Priscilla's diamond teardrop earrings, and was relieved that she took the same size shoes as her friend, because she was now wearing a pair of black satin pumps with a low heel.

"Now then," said Priscilla. "Let's introduce you."

For the next hour, Maisie was introduced to guest after guest, always with Priscilla at her side, and always presented as "My dear friend Maisie," or "This is my bestest ever chum, Maisie Dobbs."

The dancing continued on, and though Maisie was weary, she took to the dance floor several times and found that as the music played, so her fatigue was beaten back. After thanking the gentleman who had asked for what she hoped might be her last dance, she went again in search of Priscilla, moving through the waves of people before reaching the bar. She always knew she would find Priscilla close to the bar.

"May I have a large glass of water, please? And some ice, if you have any left."

The waiter poured water from a crystal jug into a glass, which he passed to Maisie. She drank half the liquid and then turned to her left, where Priscilla had her back to her and was regaling one of the guests with stories of Biarritz. She tapped Priscilla on the shoulder.

"Oh, Maisie, are you having a lovely time?"

"Yes, I am—and I seem to be holding up against the onslaught of sleep."

"Good girl, not long now until breakfast is served. The spread is being set up in the morning room even as we speak."

"Pris, what's your New Year's resolution?" Maisie asked the question, drank the remaining water, and set her glass on the bar.

"That came out of the blue," said Priscilla.

"And what is it?"

Priscilla nodded to the waiter, who brought her another glass of champagne. "I don't know. I'll think about it tomorrow." She took a sip from her glass. "You look as if you are about to tell me what it should be."

"Come with me, Pris." Maisie took her friend's glass and placed it on another waiter's tray as he passed.

"Where are we going?"

"Upstairs."

"Upstairs?"

Maisie had stayed at the house before, so knew the geography of the Partridge home. She walked toward the large bedroom where Priscilla's three sons were sleeping and opened the door with care. A night-light was glowing on a table to one side of the room, and the two women looked in at the boys, asleep. The youngest, Tarquin, had thrown off his bedcovers and slept at the bottom of his bed, with one leg over the side. The eldest, Timothy, lay on his back, with one arm bent across his eyes. The middle son, Thomas, slept under the covers, the bump under the eiderdown making it seem as if an animal were in the midst of hibernation.

Priscilla began to weep again.

"They're all here," said Maisie. "And they're all safe. You can't keep them so forever, because one day they will be men, and I know they will be very fine men. But now they are safe, and they are well, and they are loved. You need do no more, or less, for them."

"But, I—"

Maisie closed the door without a sound. "But what you can do is not try to dull your fears with drink. You know, more than anyone, that it doesn't take away the pain of grief or fear, it only robs you of today."

Priscilla nodded. "I suppose I know what my resolution should be."

"Darling? Are you up there?" The voice of Douglas Partridge echoed on the stairs. "Ah, I might have known I'd find you here with 'Tante Maisie.' Come on, breakfast is about to be served and—believe it or not—even after that never-ending supper, every-one's famished."

"Just coming!" Priscilla turned to Maisie and took her hand. "Thank you, Maisie. Thank you for coming tonight. I know you were exhausted, but your being here means so much to me."

"I'm glad I came too," said Maisie. Then, louder, "You know, I am very, very hungry. Douglas is right—let's go down to breakfast."

SEVENTEEN

After a late start on New Year's Day, Maisie arrived just in time to join Frankie for a midday meal of rabbit stew and mashed potato. Father and daughter sat together at the kitchen table with the door of the cast-iron stove wide open, so the warmth of the blaze could be felt even as the sky outside was wreathed in the shimmering gray clouds that were known to herald a dusting of snow.

"I'll have to get Jook out soon, just in case that weather closes in."

Maisie pushed some potato onto her fork and looked out of the window. "I'll take her if you like, Dad. You stay here in the warm." She turned back to her father and continued eating.

"We'll go together, down to the meadow, across the field beyond, then double-back around through the woods to the front of the manor. I want to check on the horses, too. Drop in temperature like this can bring on a colic."

"And you'd better wrap up warm, Dad. You don't want to catch anything yourself."

As soon as they'd finished the meal, Maisie dressed in thick corduroy trousers more suited to a farm laborer, with a flannel shirt and a heavy pullover to keep the cold at bay. Woolen socks and heavy Wellington boots would keep the moisture and, hopefully, the cold from her feet, and she wore her old cloche to hold the warmth in her body—otherwise Frankie would remind her that heat escaped from the top of the head. Soon father and daughter were making their way across the field, with the lurcher at heel but ready to run in pursuit of a rabbit if given leave to do so. Maisie walked at a slower pace than she might if alone, for her father could not move as smartly as a younger man, and when they reached the bottom of the meadow, he stopped to catch his breath. Barely a sound dented the silence; on such a cold day not even birds sang. In the distance, they watched a fox steal across the top of a snow-dusted field, and all the while, the dog remained still, her head tilted up as she watched Frankie's eyes, her skin attuned to his every move.

Frankie turned his head at another sound, one that did not come from nature. "There's a motor car coming, just pulled up along by the Dower House."

"Is Lady Rowan expecting anyone today? Or Maurice, perhaps?"

"No plans for guests, as far as I know—and I always know who's coming and going."

Maisie looked back at the Groom's Cottage, and turned to her father. "We'll see who it is soon enough, when we come around the front. Ready then?"

"Right you are, love."

They began walking again, though Maisie wondered about

the crunching of tires on gravel, a sound that echoed in winter's stillness as the vehicle pulled into the estate. Motor cars were rare in the village still, and never seen on a Sunday or bank holiday. And because the Comptons did not entertain quite so much now, the arrival of guests was always known and expected, and the unexpected was unwelcome by the Comptons and their servants alike.

Leaves still crisp from an overnight frost crackled underfoot, disturbing the silence of a winter woodland. They crossed the stream where it narrowed, and Maisie held out her hand to help her father up the bank to join the path again. Now Jook was walking on in front, her head low, her nose to the ground as she loped along with such a light step that her paws left barely a print underfoot. Father and daughter climbed over a stile to begin the last lap of their walk, which would bring them out to the front of the estate, where they would continue along past the lawns until reaching the turning off to the Groom's Cottage, Frankie's home.

As they approached the narrow turning to the right, they could see smoke from the cottage's two chimneys lazily snaking upward, and the thought of easing back in armchairs on either side of a crackling fire caused them to walk a bit faster.

"I think I might sit down in that chair and go right off like a top, what with that lovely drop of stew inside me and a bit of fresh air. I can have a look at the horses later."

"You should, Dad. It'll do you good." Maisie was tired, and thought the idea of an afternoon's forty winks sounded like just the prescription she needed after the events of the past week and a late night behind her.

"Well, who's this then?" Frankie Dobbs stopped at the top of the lane leading to the cottage, and looked straight in front of him. His lurcher stood at his side and began to growl.

"Oh no, now what?" Maisie linked her arm through her father's. "They've no right to come here."

"That your Scotland Yard blokes then?"

Maisie nodded. "I could tell that black Invicta anywhere, Dad. Yes, it's them."

As Maisie and her father approached the cottage, Stratton and MacFarlane emerged from the motor car.

"Sorry to disturb you on New Year's Day, Miss Dobbs."

Maisie thought MacFarlane seemed less than contrite. "I trust you wouldn't have come to my father's home unless it were urgent."

"Yes, it is important," said Stratton, who held out his hand toward Maisie's father. "Mr. Dobbs, a pleasure. And I'm sorry we've had to come to your house today."

Frankie shook hands with both Stratton and MacFarlane, and stepped up to the front door. "You'd better come on in, instead of standing out here in the perishing cold."

Maisie made a pot of tea, which she served in front of the fire in the small sitting room. Frankie said he wanted to read the racing pages anyway and took his seat alongside the kitchen stove.

Maisie passed a cup of tea to MacFarlane. "What's happened?"

"Bit of a problem, I'm afraid. We brought in your man, Anthony Lawrence, to identify the body." MacFarlane took a gulp of the hot tea and winced as it went down. Then he set the cup on a small table next to his chair and folded his hands in his lap. "Anthony Lawrence says he's never seen this man in his life, and it's not Stephen Oliver, because Stephen Oliver is in a secure wing at the Princess Victoria Hospital, or should I say the loony bin."

"It's not Oliver?"

"No."

Maisie was silent. "But we know our man was the one who

wrote the letters, and was the same man who killed the dogs, birds and a junior minister—and who planned to kill again, most likely at St Paul's."

"Yes, that's right," said Stratton. "Our guest in the morgue is definitely the man we've been after. But we don't know who he is."

MacFarlane spoke again. "A couple of things came to light during the postmortem." He handed Maisie an envelope. "You will see he had areas of deep scarring to the legs, and upon closer examination there was a significant amount of shrapnel still embedded in his flesh. There was also that scar on his face and jaw. All of this indicates a man who served in the war—and given his age, it wasn't the Boer War. He was definitely British, we know that. Mind you, he might have gone overseas before the war, when thousands of boys went off to find their fortune, so he could have served with any army from the Canadians to the South Africans, Anzacs or the Doughboys. He could have been an airman, which I doubt, or on board ship, though evidence of his wounds would suggest a battlefield. But we should remember that men from the navy were pressed into the artillery and infantry, because that's where they were needed."

Maisie had been reading the contents of the envelope as MacFarlane spoke. Now she replaced the pages and pulled out the dead man's diary, which had also been placed in the envelope. She leafed through it, stopping at a page here and there, then closed the diary and returned it to the envelope, which she passed back to MacFarlane.

"You're very quiet about this, Miss Dobbs. What do you think? Who do you think this man might be?"

"I don't know, Chief Superintendent MacFarlane. My search led me to think it was Stephen Oliver, but there was an element of doubt—in fact, I think there's always an element of doubt. We know we have our man, and we're as sure as we can be that he acted alone, even though he had a friend, Ian Jennings—oh, and I wouldn't be too sure that Ian Jennings is the man's real name. Of course we were given to understand he received a pension, but we never saw any official forms with his name, did we?"

MacFarlane and Stratton looked at each other. Stratton cleared his throat. "What are you saying, Miss Dobbs?"

Maisie wondered how to couch her response, how to best present her sense of the situation. "I am saying it's a possibility you'll never discover the man's true identity. He might as well be John Smith. He destroyed or did not retain any identification and did not reveal his name in either his diary or to me when I was in his flat. If Croucher knew, it's too late, he took that information with him when he died, as did Ian Jennings."

"We've searched Croucher's rooms and there's nothing there, though it seems he was in the habit of trying to help out men who are homeless and who were soldiers in the war. We'll have more on him by tomorrow, in any case." MacFarlane sighed. "Well, at least we know there's a killer off the street and we're all safe, don't we?" He placed his hands on the arms of the chair, as if he was about to stand.

"I don't think we can be that complacent."

"What do you mean?" MacFarlane sat back again and looked at Maisie, then Stratton, and back at Maisie.

"Chief Superintendent, in our man we saw the symptoms of a disease. He was wounded in body and mind in the war—indeed, he was wounded in his soul. He came home to endure a great deal of pain and felt as if he had become invisible, as if he didn't exist—read that diary, it says as much. Now, according to Dr. Lawrence, there were about sixty, seventy, eighty thousand men who suffered some sort of war neuroses—shell-shock—to a greater or lesser degree. And if you listen to Lawrence for long enough, he'll tell you how that number has been massaged since 1915—first, to put the lid on a syndrome that few understood, and secondly to limit damage to the exchequer from a never-ending pensions liability. Lawrence says that some two hundred thousand men are alive today who were shell-shocked, and if you agree that anyone who served has sustained a psychological wound of some description, then you are looking at more than just a few time bombs."

"Are you saying that all these men are likely to go off and cook up nerve agents or get up to some other mischief?"

Maisie shook her head. "Of course not. Our man was clearly someone who knew his way around a laboratory, and who was capable and inventive enough to create those conditions in a small cold-water flat. He might be someone you can find on the basis of that skill alone, but don't count on it." Maisie considered her words with care. "Many of those men came back to loving families. When I was a nurse at the Clifton Hospital, you would see mothers and fathers who treated their sons with such care, such gentleness, as if they were children again. There were others who could not bring themselves to see a son so maimed, or you'd see a sweetheart, a young wife, perhaps, who could not bear to go unrecognized by her husband, who could not envisage sharing a home with a mate who was not the man she had taken into her heart. Many of those men were discharged from hospital care at the earliest opportunity, allowed to leave, told to find a job and settle down and live a normal life. But life will never be normal again, not when you've gazed into the jaws of death, not even when you have heard the cannonade in the distance. The screech of tires on the street or a motor car backfiring can send a man running for cover, can lead him to lose control of his physical movements, of his speech. And the people look away, don't they? We all know when someone isn't quite right, and for the most part, it's an element of our nature to want to be out of the way of people who aren't what we consider to be 'normal.'"

"So what are you saying, Miss Dobbs?"

"That there are others like our man. Most of them will never do what he has done, but others will be moved to do something. They might cut themselves off from those who love them, they might be cast out by relatives to live on the streets, or they could be alone, as alone as they have always been. They might take their own lives, because what is in their minds cannot be borne a second longer, or they could make their families' lives a misery, with jagged moods keeping everyone on tenterhooks as they try to placate the demon inside the man. They might have a short temper, followed by a time of regret, of extreme affection. They could be drinkers, or resort to narcotics to ease mental and physical anguish. Or they might just exist, until they die."

"But somewhere," said MacFarlane, "there's a man who is a time bomb, who wants to be seen and heard."

"Yes."

"And that man may sooner or later cause damage on a bigger scale."

"It's a possibility."

"And we'll never know who he is until it happens."

The three were silent for some moments, each alone with their thoughts.

MacFarlane slapped his knees and stood up. "Well, this will never get the eggs cooked. Come on, Stratton, we'd better get back to the Yard."

Maisie came to her feet. "You traveled all this way for such a short meeting?"

"We thought it best to come to see you personally with the news," said MacFarlane. "And we wanted to discuss the outcome with you—and not on the telephone."

Stratton shrugged. "And I think we've got a lot more to chew on now."

Maisie nodded. "I do have one more thought."

"And what might that be?" MacFarlane raised his eyebrows.

"Bring in Catherine Jones to identify the body, just to make sure. I know you've already heard from a very credible source, but I'd be interested to know whether the man in the morgue is the same man she saw and spoke to at one of the meetings, the one she told me about."

"I suppose it wouldn't hurt. I'll see what can be done. Thank you, Miss Dobbs."

"Thank you for coming, Chief Superintendent, Inspector Stratton. Let me see you out."

Frankie came to the sitting room upon hearing the door open and the company bid their farewells. Both Stratton and MacFarlane shook his hand again, and as they left, MacFarlane informed Maisie that they would be in contact if she was to be consulted again, though her presence at the inquest would be required.

As the black Invicta made its way toward Chelstone's main gate, Maisie watched the rear lights become smaller and smaller.

"Come on, love, let's sit by the fire now, eh?" Frankie was solicitous in his tone, setting his hand on Maisie's shoulder with a gentle touch, as if to apply greater pressure would hurt her.

"It's all right, Dad. Don't worry—I'm all right."

But Frankie remembered the early days of Maisie's recovery, after she came home from France in 1917. And still fresh in his mind was her breakdown during a return journey to France just fifteen months earlier. Even though she seemed more at peace now than at other times in recent years, he often found it best to move with care around his daughter, as a person might negotiate an unknown path in the dark.

EIGHTEEN

January 3rd, 1932

As sometimes happened following a visit to Kent, the city had a chill to it that went beyond a sense of the air outside. Though Maisie loved her flat in Pimlico, there was a warmth to her father's cottage, to being at Chelstone, that made her feel cocooned and safe. And she felt wanted. The flat was hers to do with as she wished, and to do exactly as she pleased within those walls, but sometimes she felt it still held within it the stark just-moved-in feeling that signaled the difference between a house and a home. Of course, it still was not fully furnished, and there were no ornaments displayed—a vase, perhaps, that a visitor might comment upon and the hostess would say, "Oh, that was a gift, let me tell you about it . . . " There were no stories attached to the flat—but how could there be, when she was always alone in her home. There were no family photographs, no small framed portraits on the mantelpiece over the fire in the sitting room as there were at her father's house. She thought the flat would be all the better for some photographs, not only to serve as reminders of those who were loved, or reflections of happy times spent in company, but to act as mirrors, where she might see the affection with which she was held by those dear to her. A mirror in which she could see her connections.

Maisie went to the kitchen to put the kettle on. She rarely kept much in the way of food in the flat, for fear that it might spoil during the long days of her work. The pot of soup made on a Sunday night would set her up for a few suppers at least, and sometimes she would bring home fish and chips, which she would eat from the newspaper, not seeing the point in setting the table just for one. And except for the times she joined Priscilla and her family for the evening meal, she was alone. Most of the time, though, she was not lonely, just on her own, an unmarried woman of independent means, even when the extent of the means—or lack thereof—sometimes gave her cause to remain awake at night. She knew the worries that came to the fore at night were the ones you had to pay attention to, for they blurred reasoned thought, sucked clarity from any consideration of one's situation, and could lead a mind around in circles, leaving one drained and ill-tempered. And if there was no one close with whom to discuss those concerns, they grew in importance in the imagination, whether they were rooted in good sense or not.

Having taken her cup of tea while sitting on the floor in front of the fire with a copy of *The Times* spread out in front of her, Maisie recognized that she was restless. Yet again, the case concerning the man who was not Stephen Oliver began invading her thoughts. To a point, she had accepted that he might never be identified. In fact, as it stood, chance favored such an incomplete conclusion. But she wasn't so sure, and could not draw back from a curiosity about the man's state of mind, and how he might have felt in the months leading up to the attack on the dogs. And more than anything, she wondered if one could take leave of one's senses, even if one had no previous occasions of mental incapacity, simply by being isolated from others. Is that what pushed the man over the edge of all measured thought? Were his thoughts so distilled, without the calibrating effect of a normal life led among others, that he ceased to recognize the distinction between right and wrong, between good and evil, or between having a voice and losing it? And if that were so, might an ordinary woman living alone with her memories, with her work, with the walls of her flat drawing in upon her, be at some risk of not seeing the world as it is?

She shook her head and stood up, pacing in front of the fireplace. Then, with barely a moment's thought, Maisie ran to the hallway, took her coat and hat from the stand, picked up her keys, and left the flat to walk to the telephone kiosk close to her home. She stepped inside, lifted the receiver, slipped coins into the slot, and dialed a number. As she waited for the connection, she wiped condensation from the panes of glass with the back of her begloved hand. She did not care to be in such a small space without being able to see outside, even if she could see only darkness.

"The Partridge Residence."

"May I speak with Mrs. Partridge?"

"One moment, please. May I say who's calling?"

Maisie gave her name, suspecting the housekeeper had almost added, "At this time of night."

"Maisie, darling, to what do I owe the pleasure?"

"Priscilla, I've just arrived back at the flat and was thinking about your party, and how little we've seen each other lately—and we didn't get *that* much time for a good talk at the party, did we? I wonder, are you at home tomorrow? Perhaps I could drop in for elevenses—will you be there?"

"Are you all right?"

"Yes, yes, fine . . . no, nothing wrong with me. Elevenses, then?"

Maisie thought she could hear Priscilla smiling. Priscilla was given to dramatic pauses in conversation, pauses that extended to her use of the telephone. Maisie had always maintained that a caller could hear the expression on her friend's face.

"Of course, that's splendid news—do come. I feel as if I've caught some of the crumbs falling off the table when you come to visit. You won't change your mind, will you?"

"Am I really that bad?"

"Well, you do get a bit carried away with that work of yours. But I'm glad you'll come—we might even pop out to the shops. January sales. Time for that?"

"Yes, I think I might have time. See you tomorrow, Priscilla."

Maisie set the receiver back on its cradle, pulled up her collar, and set off into the night again, this time with a warmth in her heart as she thought about seeing Priscilla the next day.

January 4th, 1932

"All right, Billy, so as I said, you should leave by eleven to go to the Clifton—didn't they say Doreen would be arriving there at twelve?"

"That's what they thought, yes." Billy paused, a frown creasing his forehead. "Look, Miss, are you sure? I mean, I've had a lot of time off lately, so I expect to see it docked from my wage packet."

Maisie shook her head. "We've had a good month, and the Scotland Yard bill will set us in good stead. It was a nice start to the year—financially, that is. And Doreen being at the Clifton will make it easy for evening visiting, won't it, though I am sure Dr. Masters has some advice about not overtaxing Doreen."

"I'm going to be talking to her about that today, Miss."

"Good, now—"

Maisie was interrupted by the telephone ringing.

"Fitzroy—"

"Miss Dobbs."

"Detective Chief Superintendent MacFarlane."

"We're having a bit of a tête-à-tête here today, what you might call a postmortem on the investigation in which your assistance proved to be invaluable. Would you care to join us at, oh, eleven o'clock?"

"I'm sorry, Chief Superintendent, but I have a previous engagement. Would two o'clock do?"

Billy looked across at his employer.

"We'll do it this afternoon, then. See you at two."

"Right you are, see you then."

Maisie rolled her eyes as she replaced the receiver. "That man was definitely being sarcastic. *'In which your assistance proved to be invaluable.'*" She recounted the conversation to Billy.

"Sounds like you put him in his place, Miss."

Maisie shrugged. "I've an important engagement this morning, and did not want to cancel it for MacFarlane or any other client. Not this time."

MAISIE SAT AT one end of the sofa in Priscilla's sitting room. Her friend had taken the other, so they resembled bookends, both with shoes kicked off and their legs folded to the side.

" . . . and before you arrived, the funny bit was when Tinker Osborne—do you know him? Bit of a lark, I must say, though if you read him in *Punch,* you would wonder why the government hasn't had him done away with—anyway, as I was saying, the funny thing was when he thought he could balance a bottle of champers on his nose. Normally that sort of thing just bores me rigid, but you should have seen him, tottering all over the place, especially as he came with that crashing bore Judith Burton, you know, the daughter of, oh, what is his name—yes, the architect, Otto Burton."

Maisie smiled, though she could not imagine finding Tinker Osborne in the slightest bit amusing.

"It was a good New Year, Priscilla."

"All in all, not a bad one. Of course, predictably, I glanced up at the staircase as the hour approached, only to see my three toads— in pajamas, mind—sitting on the stairs and watching everything through the banister. I nudged Douglas and he waved them down, so they joined us for the celebrations and even had a little tipple each—won't hurt them, a little drop of champers. No wonder they were asleep by the time you arrived."

Maisie nodded, watching Priscilla as she sipped the last of her coffee and set her cup and saucer on the side-table before glancing over toward the drinks cabinet.

"How are you feeling now? I've been worried about you since you came to my office."

"It comes and goes," said Priscilla, "but mostly it comes. I am not happy here, not as I was in Biarritz, and it's troubling, especially as I'm the only one in the family not to have settled, in one way or another."

"You were very busy in Biarritz, though, weren't you? You took the boys to the beach, you drove down into the town, saw friends, and even when you went to Paris a few times a year, you were among people you knew, and who knew you. You'd all, for the most part, gone down to Biarritz after the war to lick your wounds."

Priscilla was silent for a moment, running her hand up and down the arm of the sofa, as if she were stroking the back of a frightened animal. "Well, I'm a bit of a slug here, I must say. It's so . . . so . . . restricting. Or do I mean constricting? Perhaps a bit of both. And it's a bloody depressing place, if you ask me."

"I had a thought. Remember you had that grand plan of opening up the family house, where you grew up? Why don't you do it? Why don't you put your mind to setting up your home there, get out into the country and start enjoying yourselves and perhaps claim some of that freedom you had in Biarritz."

"But, Maisie, the boys are at school here and they love London, and Douglas . . ."

"It's not that far—what, an hour or two's drive out of London? You could go down on a Friday as soon as the boys are home from school, then come back on either a Sunday night or Monday morning. They can bring their friends and you can have the best of both worlds. And I bet you'll have all sorts of guests coming to see you." Maisie reached over and placed her hand on Priscilla's arm. "Do you remember what you said to me, when I was in France? *Face your dragons.* That house holds your memories, but think of the new memories you can build there."

Priscilla bit her lip and walked to the drinks cabinet. "I think you're right. I had all sorts of plans for the place when we first came back to England." She turned around and faced Maisie, changing the subject. "By the way, did I ever show you the photographs I took while you were with us last year? I found them the other day, as I was unpacking some boxes"—she picked up an envelope—"and I put them out to show you."

Priscilla passed each photo in turn to Maisie, reminding her of what had happened and when. "And this is you with Tarquin— look at that smile. Just like my brother, you know. He's definitely an Evernden through and through, no doubt about it."

"May I have this one?"

"Well, yes, of course. Would you like this photograph too? It's you and I in the garden, and here's one of you with all three toads. Tante Maisie is quite a hit with the boys!"

Maisie left Priscilla's Holland Park house after lunch, knowing that she had sown a seed of possibility in the mind of her dearest friend. And as she settled in the driver's seat of the MG, she sat for a while before setting off for Scotland Yard. She wanted to look through those photographs once again, photographs for which she would buy frames as soon as she could.

"RIGHT, GENTLEMEN—and lady." MacFarlane shuffled papers in a folder on his desk and took out the document he was searching for. Darby, Stratton and Maisie sat on the opposite side of the desk. He looked up at Maisie and smiled as he said *lady*. "Time for our little postmortem here." He cleared his throat. "You all know that our man has not been identified. Anthony Lawrence didn't know him, and—thanks to you, Miss Dobbs—we brought in Catherine the chemist. The poor lass began listing to starboard as soon as she saw the body, and though she wasn't sure at first, she said it wasn't him because the man who came to their meeting did not have a scar on his face."

Maisie shook her head.

"Anything to say, Miss Dobbs?"

"No, not really. It's a strange thing, though. Had I not spoken to Catherine, and had the word *foundling* not come up, I might not have found the killer."

"Oh, but you would have." MacFarlane tapped a pencil on the file in front of him. "You found our man because you were suspicious about Edwin Croucher. There was something about his manner that made you think twice, so you followed him. And that's good police work—listening to the gut while wearing out a bit of shoe leather."

"But I might not have been at the hospital had I not wanted to speak to Anthony Lawrence before he went home—and he'd gone already."

"Then it was luck. And I know your Dr. Maurice Blanche has a lot of time for a little bit of luck."

"Anything new from the pathologist?" asked Stratton.

MacFarlane flicked through more pages in front of him. "Interesting thing. Our man was lame, carried one hip higher than the other, and one shoulder similarly out of symmetry, giving the impression that he had suffered some serious wounds to the spine. Yes, there was scarring and shrapnel fragments still embedded in his legs, but the pathologist says that there was no physical reason why this man could not have walked upright, with perhaps the slightest limp."

"Shell-shock," said Maisie.

"Shell-shock?" Stratton turned to Maisie.

"Yes. Shell-shock. What you're describing is another sign of a deep wounding to the psyche, the outer manifestation of the scars in the mind." She paused, sighing before she continued. "When I was at the Clifton, I observed similarly afflicted men who, under the influence of hypnosis, shed their crippling disability and walked tall as if they were ready for the parade ground, only to shrivel again when taken out of the trance." She looked at each of the men in turn. "And before you say or think otherwise, these were men who were good soldiers, who had exemplary military records, men who had been repatriated after demonstrating some level of neurosis or hysteria that led to an inability to function as a soldier. They were not shirkers, but broken men."

MacFarlane, Stratton and Darby were silent for a moment, then Darby spoke. "What happens now, gov? Do we go on trying to identify him? What's going to happen to the body?"

"We're pretty sure he was working alone, so there's no urgency now to identify the body, however . . . " He looked at Maisie, then back at Darby and Stratton. "I've been thinking about what Miss Dobbs has said about this sort of person, and it's clear he may not be the last. So we will be doing a wee bit of what Miss Dobbs does very well—building a template of a type. In the meantime, the body will be released to Dr. Anthony Lawrence as soon as we've tied up our loose ends."

"Dr. Lawrence?" Maisie leaned forward.

"He made a special request, said the cadaver could be used for research purposes in the fields of"—he looked at a sheet of paper, then back at Maisie—"neurosurgery and psychiatry. They want to see what's in his brain. I would have thought you'd've understood that, Miss Dobbs. I'm sure you've cut up the odd cadaver yourself."

"Yes, of course, but—" Maisie did not continue, realizing that, of course, there was no family to receive the body. But she was still unsettled by the news.

"Anything else, Miss Dobbs?"

"What about Croucher?"

"Ah, yes, Croucher." MacFarlane shuffled the notes once again. "Another one living alone and with nothing in his rooms to indicate who our killer might have been, though he did not live as much a Spartan life as his two friends. There were other papers, other items that would identify him."

"But might there have been anything else there that would connect him to our man in some way? Something to indicate that he has known him for some time, perhaps?" asked Maisie.

"The only thing amiss with Edwin Croucher—aside from the fact that he was associating with a man bent on killing half of London on the steps of St. Paul's—was that he had a memory problem. Turns out he wrote down such things as when he had to be here or there, lists of what he needed for this or that. At work he tended to check, double-check, and then go back again for another look to make sure that something had been done. But there's nothing to be found in the rooms with either Ian Jennings' name, or our Mister No-name."

"That's strange."

"The pathologist says the nature of the man's forgetfulness was probably limited to certain tasks, the jobs that were before him each day. It would not affect his functioning as a member of society, though I can see why he lived alone. Imagine being married to someone who kept asking where they put something, or what was for dinner for the tenth time. There was a place for everything in his rooms, and those places were labeled."

"He was lucky to have a job, I suppose," said Stratton, as if to remind MacFarlane that he and Darby were in the room.

"And he's certainly not lucky now, eh?" quipped MacFarlane.

The men's laughter was nipped in the bud by Maisie, who had more questions. "Chief Superintendent, I wonder, would it be possible for me to speak to Catherine Jones? I'm still curious about the man she claims came along to the meeting of union activists—I'd like to ask her a question or two more, if that's all right."

MacFarlane shook his head. "Bit too late, I'm afraid, Miss Dobbs. Miss Jones has been released. The prosecutor went through everything we gave him and concluded that there wasn't enough evidence there to bring her to trial."

"Not enough evidence? I thought—"

MacFarlane shrugged, but did not look at Maisie directly, closing the folders as he answered her. "We always do our best, Miss Dobbs. We pull together as much as we can, then we send the whole case to the prosecutor. Her fellow anarchists will be sent down, but not Miss Jones. He's concluded that she was a person in the wrong place at the wrong time."

Maisie nodded her head as she replied, "I see. In the wrong place at the wrong time. Lucky Catherine."

"We can't win them all, Miss Dobbs."

Maisie began collecting her document case and shoulder bag. "Well, if that's all, Detective Chief Superintendent MacFarlane, I had better be off. As they say, time and tide wait for no man—or woman, come to that."

"Oh, but before you go, Miss Dobbs." MacFarlane stood up, as did Darby and Stratton. "I've decided to celebrate Burns' Night in

London with my immediate colleagues here at the Branch. I've bought tickets for a show at the Palladium for everyone, and there will be supper afterward upstairs at the Cuillins of Skye—it's a pub, just off Covent Garden. January twenty-fifth—I hope you will join us."

Maisie looked at MacFarlane, then at Stratton and Darby, as if to ask if they were going.

"You'll not be the only lassie there, Miss Dobbs," added Mac-Farlane.

"Perhaps I can let you know in a week or so, Chief Superintendent. And thank you for the invitation. Now, I should be on my way."

MacFarlane thanked Maisie again for her part in bringing the case to a close, and handed her an envelope with a check inside. She shook his hand and hoped she had made it clear by her demeanor that his occasional flirtatious manner had not borne fruit.

"I'm glad that's all over," said Stratton.

"Are you?" said Maisie.

"Of course I am. Can you imagine what it would be like if our man were still at large?"

Maisie opened her mouth to say more, but paused and instead commented on the invitation. "What's all this about Burns' Night? It's a bit unusual, isn't it, being treated to a night out by the Chief Superintendent?"

"I know. Darby says he's done it before, taking a whole gang out for the evening. Apparently he thinks it's good for morale, brings everyone together."

Maisie took out her keys as they reached the MG. "I think there's more to it than that, Inspector Stratton. I think he's a bit lonely. Didn't you say his wife left him?"

Stratton nodded. "A few years ago. It's a hard life, being married to a man who's married to his job. She was alone a lot, and as far as I know, took up with someone else and just up and left."

"And now he's the one who's alone. That's why everyone's invited to go out with him on Burns' Night." She inclined her head. "I really do have to rush now."

"Going anywhere interesting?"

"The Princess Victoria Hospital—only don't tell MacFarlane, will you?"

"Mum's the word," said Stratton as he brought a forefinger to his lips. "Do you think—"

"I'll let you know."

A PORTER INFORMED Maisie that she would have to wait to see Dr. Lawrence, and that he might not even be able to see her at all, given that he had been with his students for a good two hours this afternoon already and was late getting to his rounds.

"I'll wait," said Maisie, taking the same place as before on the bench seat facing the porters' office.

Over an hour passed before the porter came out of the office. "He's still on his rounds, Miss. Would you like a cup of tea while you're waiting?"

Maisie opened her mouth to answer, but was interrupted by Lawrence, who approached from the corridor behind her.

"Miss Dobbs! I wasn't expecting you today, so this is something of a surprise. What can I do for you?"

"May we go to your office, Dr. Lawrence? I would like our conversation to be in private."

"Yes, of course. One moment while I just use the telephone in the porters' office."

Lawrence stepped into the office, placed his telephone call, and joined her once again, leading her up the staircases and through locked doors that led to other locked doors before opening out into the floor that housed the staff offices.

"Here we are." Lawrence looked at his watch. "I'm a bit short on time, Miss Dobbs, so—"

"Oh, this won't take long, Dr. Lawrence. I just wondered if I might visit Stephen Oliver. I learned so much about him, you see, as part of my investigation, and feel rather sorry that he's here without visitors."

Lawrence began running his fingers back and forth along the files on his desk, setting them two inches from the right side and two inches from the top, so they were positioned much in same way that a stamp would be attached to an envelope. "Miss Dobbs, I cannot allow such a thing. After all, you are not a relative, and you must appreciate that Dr. Oliver is in a very delicate state."

"Yes, I suppose if one's seen as nothing more than a cadaver available for experimentation, he would be in a delicate state, wouldn't he?"

"Now you look here, Miss Dobbs—"

"The man who wrote the letters, who killed dogs, birds, a junior minister, and who planned to kill a legion of revelers on Old Year's Night was Stephen Oliver, wasn't he?"

"I categorically assure you—"

"Tell me what happened."

"Nothing happened, Stephen was a brilliant scientist—"

"I know how brilliant he was. I've heard it from two people already. And I know you do not have Stephen Oliver here at the hospital."

"And I assure you that we do, now if you don't mind—"

Maisie reached for the telephone receiver. "If *you* don't mind, I think I'd like to hear that from Sheila Kennedy. By the way, do you know how I am acquainted with Mrs. Kennedy? She was the Sister-in-Charge of the casualty clearing station where I was stationed in the war. I don't know if she'll remember me, but you never know." She dialed the operator.

Lawrence leaned forward and pressed down on the bar, cutting off the call. "No, don't."

Maisie replaced the receiver. "Are you going to tell me what's going on?"

Lawrence scraped back his chair, stood up and began to pace, then sat down again. "You should cease wondering about this case, Miss Dobbs, because you are out of your depth."

"I don't seem to be floundering, Dr. Lawrence, but if you are having trouble with the truth, then let me tell you what I think has happened here, and you can correct me if I'm wrong."

Lawrence clasped his hands together on the desk. "I have little time to indulge you, Miss Dobbs."

Maisie pressed her point. "Stephen Oliver was admitted to the Princess Victoria on at least two occasions since his initial release from an asylum, where he was committed during the war. I know that you witnessed at least one breakdown at Mulberry Point, and I know he was a very valuable person with regard to work undertaken at the government laboratories. And he was also a very interesting specimen, wasn't he? A man who had not only suffered shell-shock, but was so intent upon finding answers to the questions that dogged him in his work that he even became his own guinea pig."

"They all experimented on themselves, all of them. They don't call them mad professors for nothing."

"But the madness didn't stop there, did it? You increasingly saw Oliver as your own experiment. After all, time was marching on and you had a legacy to leave—a book about the psychological effects of chemical and biological testing on those exposed to contaminants. And every time he regained some semblance of normal functioning, you willingly went along with requests to send him back to Mulberry Point, because Stephen Oliver still had a razor-sharp mind when it came to his work—it was unfortunate that he just didn't have the emotional foundation for sustained experimentation, did he?"

Lawrence nodded, but was silent as he listened, his only movement being to pick up an item on his desk, look at it, then put it down again.

"Now, I haven't worked out the details yet, but at some juncture he was discharged. Was it an oversight at the pensions office? A young clerk perhaps, who added a name to the list of someone who should never have been added? Or was it that you had to release a certain number of patients to make economies, and because he could take care of himself, he was released? On the other hand, perhaps his release was part of your experiment—and then he managed to give you the slip."

Maisie bit her lip. Lawrence's manner was unsettling and she wondered if her speculation had been wide of the mark.

"Either way, you lost him, lost a valuable man who could only control himself physically and mentally for short periods of time while engaged in the same sort of work he was undertaking when he was first wounded—again, in his mind as much as his body—on the battlefield. That work was in the development of weapons that should never be given the light of day. And he could only immerse himself in such an endeavor for so long before the cannonade went off in his mind, or when he collapsed in a state of nervous exhaustion."

Maisie sat back and looked out the window, the view of falling snow obscured by iron bars. Iron bars, even in the offices of a doctor for whom she once had the utmost regard. She was about to speak when there was a knock at the door, and without being summoned the visitor walked into the office.

"Sorry, Lawrence, it took me a bit of a while to get here." Gerald Urquhart took off his hat and looked at Maisie. "A delight to see you again, Miss Dobbs. Now, I wonder what might bring you back to see Dr. Lawrence—after all, you're not on Special Branch time now, are you?"

Maisie looked at Urquhart, then Lawrence. "Is this what you meant by out of my depth?"

"Yes, it is."

"Oh, so Stephen Oliver was more than an experiment for you. He was an experiment for the Secret Service as well. Even though there was a risk to the general public, you knew he would continue with his work in whatever way he could." Maisie shook her head, her mind racing. "Or was he released deliberately, just to see who might come out of the woodwork and claim him, who might try to squeeze him dry before tossing him aside?" She looked at Urquhart again. "No wonder you were panicking when you lost him. You knew who you were looking for the moment that first letter was received, but you just couldn't find him, even with an array of intelligence resources at your fingertips." Drumming her fingertips on the desk, Maisie paused for thought before speaking again. "And I'll bet you didn't show your hand to MacFarlane until Catherine Jones was brought in—or perhaps you got to Jones first, and only later did the Commissioner step in and put an end to speculation by announcing the case closed."

"The case *is* closed, Miss Dobbs. It is only you who are showing continued interest in the man who tried to kill a significant number of innocent people."

"I think it's time for me to leave." Maisie stood up, collected her bags, and stepped toward the door, but before leaving she spoke directly to Anthony Lawrence. "I am sure you will write a very good book, but there will probably be something missing."

"What on earth do you mean?"

"Speak to Dr. Elsbeth Masters. Ask her what happens when a gazelle becomes a lion's prey."

Maisie left the office, but when she reached the first set of double doors she realized she was trapped without keys.

"Damn!"

"Rather a hasty exit, Miss Dobbs." Urquhart waved a set of keys as he approached. "I'll escort you out."

"I won't ask why you have a set of keys."

"No, better not."

They walked in silence down the stairs and through several more sets of locked doors before reaching the empty entrance hall.

"I'm sorry I can't tell you more, Miss Dobbs."

"Oh, I think I've got the gist of the matter." She looked over at the porters' office, then back at Urquhart. "I have a feeling that Edwin Croucher was once a porter or employed in a similar caretaker job at Mulberry Point, where as we know almost every member of staff became a subject in an experiment at some point or another. I suspect that's how he lost his short-term memory— possibly through overexposure to a nerve agent of some sort. But he never forgot Stephen Oliver. Perhaps Oliver had shown him a kindness, so that when he found out the scientist had been brought to the Princess Victoria, he applied for a job as a porter. Or it might have been just one of those serendipitous events in life. Am I getting warmer here, Mr. Urquhart?" Maisie raised a hand. "No, don't answer, but let me see if I can work this out. Lawrence didn't know about Croucher's previous employer, because people like him never see people they consider to be minions. He interviewed the scientists and those of a certain level working at the laboratories, but not the tea ladies or the other ancillary staff."

"An admirable imagination, Miss Dobbs."

"And I haven't finished yet. Croucher was a kind man, a man who gave the impression of being brusque, but really he was trying to keep his life in order, so that he could keep a job. But he always tried to help the men on the streets who had fought in the war—he had doubtless been a soldier himself. And then he met Jennings, saw that he was an educated man, and thought he and Stephen Oliver would be company for each other. Croucher must have wondered what he had done, when Oliver began planning his revenge on those he saw as perpetrators of want."

Urquhart nodded his head in a knowing way, so that even this movement smacked of sarcasm. "Considering you haven't had any formal training in intelligence gathering, Miss Dobbs, you do very well, don't you."

"But that's where you are wrong, Mr. Urquhart. I have had training from an expert in such matters. I just don't work for you."

"Well, you never know."

Maisie turned to leave, but Urquhart caught her arm.

"Miss Dobbs—before you go, please don't think of telling that wonderful story to anyone else, will you?"

Maisie shook off his hand and walked away.

MAISIE DROVE TOWARD Pimlico amid snow flurries and sleet. More than anything, she wanted to shut the door and wrap the walls of her flat around her. Outside, the world could do as it wished. She parked the MG and walked toward the main door, only to see MacFarlane's motor car waiting outside.

"Oh, not again!" Maisie uttered the words under her breath.

MacFarlane emerged from the vehicle. "Miss Dobbs, glad to have caught you."

"I don't have any soup, Chief Superintendent."

"And I'm going out to supper, so I'll pass on your kind invitation."

Maisie looked aside. "I'm sorry. That was unkind of me."

MacFarlane regarded her for a moment, then set his hand on her shoulder. "It's hard, but there are walls you can't hammer your way through."

"I know, I know. But aren't you angry, aren't you furious at what they've done, what they're doing, and how this *experiment* got out of hand? That a man . . . "

"I've learned over time to pick my battles, and to know when not to crush my knuckles pounding at doors that won't open. Urquhart had his job to do, Lawrence was doing his, and if you speak to your John Gale, he too knew about all or part of what was going on. When you get into the realms of the country's security, you find the right arm never, ever knows what the left arm is doing. We both have to get on with our work now, Miss Dobbs, and allow this case to be closed. All right?"

Maisie nodded. "All right. I know, I know. This is not the first time I've hit my own fist against that wall. And as they say, it's best to let it slip away, because time and tide wait for no man."

"I'm sorry, lass, you'll have to be a bit more succinct."

"They all said that, you know. It's one of those sayings that people pick up. I heard John Gale say it, then Stephen Oliver wrote it in his diary—and don't worry, I won't mention his name again. Anthony Lawrence repeated it too. It's a common phrase, but you find people tend to repeat that sort of thing when they live or work together. It only takes one to start the ball rolling."

MacFarlane laughed and shook his head. "That's something Blanche would have noticed. Anyway, talking of starting the ball rolling, I'll see you on the twenty-fifth, I hope."

"What's on at the Palladium?" Maisie called after him.

"Oh, you'll enjoy it. The show's been on the bill several times over the past few months now with that grand gang of funny men—you know, Flanagan and Allen, Jimmy Nervo, Teddy Knox, Charlie Naughton and Jimmy Gold. They call it Crazy Week."

NINETEEN

January 5th, 1932

Maisie wished it were closer to the week's end, so that she could pack her bags and drive down to Kent. She was fed up with London and was feeling a blend of frustration, anger and deep sadness every time she thought of Stephen Oliver and those like him, men who would only ever see life through a lens of instability. The war had been at the root of their distress, and for so many of those who came home—including Priscilla and herself—war dogged them still. And there was little or nothing she could do to help—unless she went back to nursing, but those times were behind her now. She had always felt that in her role as a psychologist and investigator, she had a part to play in the healing of those touched by crime and injustice. Maurice Blanche had instructed her in what he termed the "forensic science of the whole person," an inquiry that went beyond a dissection of the body and demanded engagement in a deeper investigation into the life of a person, who may be either the victim or the perpetrator of a crime.

Every time she thought of Stephen Oliver, she could not help but wonder how much of his distress could have been avoided, and how much was caused by men who were hungry for his knowledge, who would sap him until there was nothing left, until he was all but invisible.

But the fact remained that it was Tuesday and not the end of the week, so after sitting with Billy to go through other current cases, and to look at one or two inquiries regarding her services that had been received since the turn of the year, she knew it was time to begin the process she referred to as her "final accounting." This accounting did not require her to add or subtract rows of numbers, but rather to look back at a case and consider what had happened, person by person, event by event, and then to close the book so that work on new cases might begin with renewed energy. Indeed, it bore a resemblance to the passing of the old year, when one took stock of what had passed and started anew on New Year's Day, filled with determination and looking forward to what might come next.

Having given Anthony Lawrence due consideration, she realized that she could not let her previous regard for his work slide into the quicksand of recent experience. She had no knowledge of what had passed between Lawrence, Gale and the men of Military Intelligence, Section Five, but she knew that she could not burn her bridges. His actions had surely been directed by ambition and a professional curiosity, for even though he was a doctor, he was also a scientist, his area of expertise the geography of the human mind.

She took up her pen and began to write a letter to Lawrence. It was not a long communiqué, but spoke of her regard for his work, her appreciation for what he tried to accomplish with the men under his care, and how much she hoped his book would bring him the acclaim he deserved. She did not say that she thought he must have learned much from Stephen Oliver, and would continue to owe him a debt. Nor did she say that she thought his association with Urquhart ill-considered, as she suspected he may have had little choice. As her pen wavered toward the end of the letter, she wondered how she might refer to the previous day's heated exchanges without apology. She regretted neither her words nor her accusations, so puzzled over how she might phrase a sentence that would reflect her sadness that there had been such a level of discord, while also expressing that she felt betrayed by a level of subterfuge that undermined the words: First, do no harm. Tapping her pen on the desk, she wrote:

I am sure we will both reflect on the events of the past weeks with regret, and with concern that there might have been a more positive outcome. For my part, I believe there is much I can learn from what has come to pass. I remember you to be a man who cared deeply for his patients, and who always looked at what might have been done in this situation or that, and I believe the case of Stephen Oliver has given us both pause to reconsider how we could have conducted ourselves in our work in a different way, a way that might have been better for all concerned . . .

Maisie tapped her pen once again, then finished the letter with a note to the effect that she hoped that, when the body of Stephen Oliver had served its purpose, there could be a respectful disposal of the remains, and that she would like to pay her respects at that time. She asked Lawrence if he would be so kind as to inform her when a service of cremation or burial would take place.

With the envelope sealed, Maisie decided to walk to the post office to mail the letter herself. Having struggled to find the appropriate words, she thought it best to send the letter before she tore it open, ripped up the pages and started again. Halfway along Warren Street, she was drawn by the three golden spheres above the pawn shop and decided to drop in to see if there were any inexpensive frames for sale. Pawn shops had been doing brisk trade in recent months, with all manner of goods going up for sale at knockdown prices. She peered though the window, then opened the door and went in, the bell ringing to summon the proprietor.

"Miss Dobbs, keeping well?"

"Very well, Mr. Lombard, though it is a bit nippy out, isn't it?" She removed her gloves and unwound her scarf.

"Not going to get any better, if my rheumatism is anything to go by." He took out a handkerchief and rubbed his half-moon glasses. "Looking for anything in particular, or just looking?"

Maisie laughed. "I'm not your best customer, am I? All I ever do is poke around and never buy anything."

"No charge for looking."

"I'm actually after some smallish frames, for photographs."

The man shuffled around the counter to the front of the shop, and began moving an assortment of items displayed on a book-case—a pair of binoculars, a geometry set, a collection of gentle-man's brushes, a glove stretcher, a camera—before reaching for a trio of matching silver frames.

"Wait a minute." Maisie came to his side and pointed to the camera. "Is that easy to use?"

"Nearly new, that. Owner bought it in New York, then came back to London and went bankrupt, if you can believe it."

"Oh, I believe it." She reached for the camera and began study-ing it, turning it around with care.

"There's a handy little book that came with it, and rolls of film too. They're all up there in a box. It's called the Number Two C Autographic Camera, and it's got this thing that goes with it. They call it a rangefinder, helps you out when people are standing a bit of a way off." He looked up toward the top shelf and squinted over his half-moon glasses, then reached for a box. "See, it's made by the Eastman Company. Lovely piece of work, that."

"But do you think I could operate it?"

"Have a look at this book—looks simple enough to me."

Maisie studied the book, then opened the camera and pulled out the bellows. "How much?"

"Well, reckon that cost a pretty penny when it was first bought, you know. Let me have a look in the ledger."

Mr. Lombard stepped behind the counter and opened a thick ledger, running his finger down a list of entries. "What was the number on the ticket, Miss Dobbs?"

"Seven hundred and fifty-three."

"Here it is. Now let me see. Yes, I can let you have that for thirty bob."

"One pound ten?" She reached out to return the camera to its place. "I don't think I can run to that."

"What about a guinea?"

"Fifteen bob?"

"Phew, that's a bit of a difference, eh? A pound?"

"Seventeen and six if you add the frames."

"You'll see me poor, Miss Dobbs."

She smiled and looked around at the contents of the shop. "Oh no I won't, Mr. Lombard. Not with this little earner you've got here."

The pawnbroker laughed as Maisie pulled a one-pound note from her purse and set it on the counter. He packed up the camera along with six rolls of red and yellow film, and the small instruction book, then balanced the frames on top and gave Maisie her change. "You might be back for more frames then?"

"I'm sure I will. Good-bye, Mr. Lombard."

AS SOON AS SHE arrived back at the office, Maisie penned another letter, this time to John Gale. She did not need to see the professor again, but he was a friend of Maurice's and he had been as fair as he could in his dealings with her, so recognition of his time and expertise were warranted. She found his work unsettling, but she thanked him for his time, and his willingness to help her.

When she had finished with her letter writing and other tasks, she gathered her document case and shoulder bag and the box containing her new camera. Balancing the frames on top, she left the office and collected her MG, which was parked in Fitzroy Street. But she wasn't going back to her flat. Despite the fact she had drawn back from visiting Lawrence and Gale, there was one place she wanted to see again, to consider from afar, before returning home. She started the motor and began driving out of London on the Reading road.

She parked the MG on a hill overlooking Mulberry Point in the distance, close to a sign that informed anyone passing that entry beyond the barbed wire was forbidden, that the land was government property and that trespassers would not only be taken to court, but could be shot. The wind whipped around her as she stepped from the MG. Maisie counted ten or more huts clustered together in the shallow valley, and she noticed that, to the left of the compound, construction work was in progress. More building, more laboratories in which to invent and test the weapons of war. She remained for a while, considering Mulberry Point and wondering if spring itself might pause in such a locale. Did birds fly overhead as the grass grew tall? And could flowers bloom around a place where people's minds were on the business of killing? Where they worked toward the invention of a means of death less visible to the naked eye, with no sound, unless one counted the screams of the poor souls who were struck down.

January 6th, 1932

"How's Doreen settling in at the Clifton, Billy?" Maisie found that, increasingly, her first question of the morning was regarding Billy's family.

Billy set an enamel mug filled with hot tea on Maisie's desk, and picked up another for himself. He stood with his back to the fire as he replied. "Not so bad, Miss. They drugged her up a bit for the ambulance, so she's been a bit wobbly on her pins. I only saw her the once, but I'm going in on Saturday."

"With the boys?"

"No, Dr. Masters says it's best not to bring them yet, though Doreen might be up for it the following weekend."

"Has she spoken about treatment?"

"First of all she said they needed to stabilize her diet. None of this milk-only lark, and no procedures—well, at least until she's been there for a bit, then we'll have to see."

Maisie nodded. "I'm going in to see Dr. Masters today. Nothing to do with Doreen, though. I have to complete my final accounting, and wanted to see her so that I can get on with drawing my work on this case to a close."

"Wonder if she'll say anything about Doreen?" Billy turned to face Maisie.

"She won't tell me anything that she wouldn't tell you, Billy. Don't worry, your Doreen is in very good hands now."

"I know, I know, but . . . it was seeing her in that other place, the way they strapped her down, the things they did to her when she hadn't even been there for five minutes."

"But she's away from Wychett Hill now, so you have to get that particular institution out of your mind." Maisie sipped her tea. "How are the boys?"

"On the one hand they're missing their mother, but on the

other, I think they're scared of her coming home. My old mum has been a diamond, coming in to help out, so they've been used to things being calmer, if you know what I mean. But I worry about her, because even though it's not far for her to walk to ours, she's not getting any younger."

"Is Bobby still having trouble?"

"Not so much, not really. I did what you said, tried not to draw attention to it, just kept him nice and dry. Bit of a job, in this weather."

Maisie looked out of the window and saw snow falling again. "It doesn't help matters, does it?" She turned her attention back to Billy. "Don't worry, you're doing everything you can. It will be all right."

ELSBETH MASTERS WAS sitting sideways next to her desk, with her stockinged feet resting against the side of the radiator, when Maisie arrived at her office.

"Oh, come in, come in. Do excuse me, but I cannot stand this cold weather. It goes straight to my bones."

"I've felt like that since I was in France, in the war. A friend once asked me how I could be that cold and not be dead."

Masters laughed. "What can I do for you? Is this about Mrs. Beale?"

"No, I wanted to see you to thank you again for your time, not only in helping out the Beales, but in answering my questions when we last met."

Masters swiveled her chair to face Maisie, setting her feet on the floor. "And was it a case of all's well that ends well?"

Maisie nodded. "To the extent that it could be, in the circumstances."

The doctor pressed her lips together as if gauging whether to make further comment. "Lawrence was sailing close to the wind, wasn't he?"

The women looked at each other for a few seconds before Maisie replied. "You could say he was taking some chances with his research."

"Was anyone harmed?"

"Not as many as might have been."

"You managed to control damage, then."

"By the skin of my teeth, but that's between us."

Masters picked up a pencil and tapped it on the desk. "Not in my interests to tell tales out of school. As I told you before, I am in no hurry to create a legacy based upon publication to impress my peers. The sheer fact that I was accepted for medical training speaks as many volumes as I need to have to my name."

Maisie smiled. "I know. But your counsel helped enormously."

"Good." She sighed, "I still wish you'd chosen to move into clinical practice."

"I love my job."

"Your country needs you, you know."

"Oh, I doubt that very much."

"Anyway, it won't compromise my patient's health or compromise confidentiality to tell you that I believe Mrs. Beale will make a full recovery. It won't happen overnight, but it will come to pass. Our first steps will be toward getting her on an even keel, then we'll see what needs to be done to help her leave the past behind. In a month I expect she will be able to go home on Saturdays and Sundays, then we'll build it up from there. In about two weeks her boys can visit—only for a short time at first, mind. And all of that can change if she has a poor response to treatment."

"Have you told Mr. Beale all this?"

"Not yet."

"Please tell him soon. It will give him something to look forward to, something to imagine. He's rather lonely, I believe. His world revolves around his work and then his family, and he has such plans for the future."

"Canada?"

Maisie nodded.

"Not before a year has passed, I shouldn't think."

"I thought as much." Maisie stood up. "Anyway, I should be getting along now. I've appreciated making your acquaintance again, Dr. Masters."

"And you too, Sis— Miss Dobbs." Masters shook her head and smiled. "Old habits. Almost called you Sister Dobbs then. Time and tide, eh, they wait for no woman."

THE VISIT TO BATTERSEA was brief. Mr. Hodges was not on the premises, so Maisie penned a brief note, and then set off again, back to her flat, where she once again took out her camera and the instruction book. She had never used a camera before, let alone owned such a thing. Two copies of a magazine called *Kodakery* came with the camera, more evidence that the previous owner had serious intentions regarding photography as a hobby when bankruptcy changed his plans. And on the following weekend, Priscilla gave Maisie an opportunity to test her new purchase, when she issued an invitation to her family's country home—she was about to embark upon redecoration.

"The boys are coming and Douglas will join us on Saturday afternoon. I have made arrangements for various people to come in to look at what needs to be done—painting, some carpentry, brickwork repairs, that sort of thing—so that I can gather estimates. Elinor is coming too, so she'll keep the toads under control, and we can have some fun—do say you'll come."

"Yes, of course I'll come. I'll bring my new camera—I can't wait to use it."

Priscilla laughed and warned Maisie to keep the camera well away from the boys. "They break things, you know."

Maisie was still smiling when the telephone rang. It was Robbie MacFarlane.

"You said you'd let me know if you were coming to the Burns' night bash. What's the verdict?"

"Oh, I'm sorry. I've been very busy, so I—"

"It had better be a 'yes,' Miss Dobbs. Can't have this lot together without you, not after you worked with us on the letters case."

"Yes, yes, of course I'll come. The Palladium first, for Crazy Week."

"Aye, that's it. Then we'll all go on to the Cuillins of Skye from there."

January 6th – January 24th, 1932

With her final accounting complete and her notes up to date and filed away, Maisie was glad to turn her attention to challenges of helping several new clients who had come to her with problems requiring inquiry services. There was sufficient new work in hand to inspire what amounted to a rosy outlook regarding the fiscal health of her business.

Doreen Beale remained at the Clifton Hospital. Though her progress was slow, Billy reported that she was looking a bit better each time he saw her, which he took as a sign that life was looking up for the family.

At the same time, Maisie was spending more time with Priscilla, in particular a memorable sojourn at their country estate that was punctuated by deep conversation and much laughter. Indeed, despite the cloak of depression enveloping much of the country, for the first time in a long time, Maisie felt an optimism, a freedom that had been diminished by her wartime service, and that she had struggled to rediscover ever since.

January 25th, 1932

Stratton, Darby and Maisie were still laughing by the time they reached the upper dining rooms of the Cuillins of Skye, while Robbie MacFarlane was regaling one of the women detectives with the history of his family tartan.

"I think he's a bit crazy himself, only he doesn't restrict himself to a week of it," said Stratton.

Maisie shook her head. "No, he's all there. Doesn't miss a trick. But I've never heard of a night like this, not from the Yard."

"And I certainly haven't." Stratton reached for his glass of whiskey, which appeared to be the only beverage on offer.

MacFarlane cleared his throat as the hot cock-a-leekie soup was served. "I'll now say the traditional grace, and for you Sassenachs, this is known as the Selkirk Grace." He cleared his throat again. "Some hae meat and canna eat, and some wad eat that want it. But we hae meat, and we can eat, Sae let the Lord be thankit."

Courses followed speeches, and speeches followed more drinking. Maisie eventually bid farewell to MacFarlane, Stratton and Darby, and by the time she stepped into a taxi-cab it was the early hours of the morning. She arrived back at her flat, glad that she had made one glass of the amber liquid last several hours. As she opened the door into the hallway and switched on the light, she saw a plain brown envelope waiting for her—it had been pushed under her door. She picked it up, recognized the handwriting, and ran to the dining table, flicking on lights as she went. As luck would have it, she had discovered that one of the residents at the block of flats was a photographer, and to make extra money, he would develop film for friends and other associates. Maisie had taken a roll of film up to him as soon as she returned home from her weekend in the country with Priscilla and her family.

She spread out the photographs and began picking up each one in turn. The early prints revealed a lack of familiarity with the equipment, but later photographs demonstrated that she had become more adept at focusing the lens, at using the rangefinder. As she studied each successive image again, she smiled, and though the flat was chilly, she felt the residue of the evening's warmth rekindled. Unwilling to wait until she could buy more frames, she brought a small box of drawing pins from the kitchen and began to pin photographs to the wall, and soon they flanked the painting of a woman alone on a windswept beach. Then she looked at each photograph once more. There were the Partridge boys sitting on the MG's bonnet, and Priscilla and Maisie bearing the brunt of a snowball fight—she had passed the camera to Douglas and he was clearly a better photographer. There were photographs taken during walks, photographs taken of the boys in the garden. And as she looked at the prints, she felt as if the eyes that had looked into the lens were looking straight at her, and she knew she belonged.

Soon she would add more photographs. There would be Frankie and Jook, and Maurice. There would be photograph after photograph of the people she loved. But as was her way, Maisie could not help but think of Stephen Oliver again, and of Ian Jennings and those like them. She thought of the dispossessed who saw nothing but people moving to one side as they shuffled along the street, people who looked down as they passed so that they need not catch a glimpse of desperation lest it be a disease—something they might catch if they weren't careful. Maisie grieved for the two men, despite their crimes. She grieved for the men they could have been, men who were complete in body and soul. And she grieved for their innocent victims.

Again her attention came back to the prints, this time to a single photograph of herself. She leaned closer to the image and concentrated on her own eyes. And she smiled, for at last she knew she had reclaimed her soul.

ACKNOWLEDGMENTS

I would like to thank the following friends and colleagues who became, in effect, my "pit crew" as I wrote *Among the Mad*. Holly Rose—thank you for being my first and number one writing buddy and reader. To my cannot-be-named "Cheef Resurcher" (yes, the spelling is a joke between us), who has given me so much valuable information on the inner workings and history of Special Branch—thank you. To my parents, Joyce and Albert Winspear—as always, thanks for fielding those questions about the London you knew and loved in the best of times and the worst of times.

Once again, deepest thanks to the terrific team at Henry Holt, especially John Sterling, Maggie Richards, and Kelly Lignos.

I can never extend enough gratitude to Amy Rennert, agent extraordinaire, friend and mentor.

And to the Bluesman—my husband, John Morell—thanks for your unfailing support. It means the world to me.

THE MAPPING OF LOVE AND DEATH

PROLOGUE

Santa Ynez Valley, California, August 1914

Michael Clifton stood on a hill burnished gold in the summer sun and, hands on hips, closed his eyes. The landscape before him had been scored into his mind's eye, and an onlooker might have noticed his chin move as he traced the pitch and curve of the hills, the lines of the valley, places where water ran in winter, gullies where the ground underfoot might become soft, and rises where the rock would never yield to a pick. Michael could see only colored lines now, with swirls and circles close together where the peaks rose, and the broad sweeps of fine ink where foothills gave way to flat land. Yes, this was the place. He had wired his mother a month earlier, asking her to cosign a document releasing the funds held in trust for him from his maternal grandfather's will. Each of the Clifton offspring had received a tidy sum. His two sisters had set money aside for their own children and together had indulged in a little investing in land, while his older brother had rolled the bequest into an impressive property. Now it was his turn and, following the example set by his siblings, he had taken his father's advice to heart: "Land is where to put your money. And if it's good land, you'll get your money back time and time again." Edward Clifton would be pleased when he saw the maps, would slap him on the back. *Well done, son. Well done. Didn't I always say you had the nose? Didn't I, Martha? Didn't I, Teddy?* And his brother would shake his hand, perhaps add a friendly punch to the shoulder. *Good for you, little brother.* And there would be no rancor, no slight because he had acted alone, only familial joy because he had succeeded.

Soon, perhaps early next year, a sign bearing the Clifton name would be set above the new trail into the valley, and travelers passing on the old stage road would assume that the famous company founded some forty years ago by Edward Clifton—a young Englishman still in his teens who had disembarked from a ship at Ellis Island in search of his fortunes—was drilling for oil. But they would be wrong, for this Clifton was the youngest son, and this was his land, his oil.

Michael opened his eyes, gazed at the gold and green vista a few moments longer, and began packing away his equipment in a heavy canvas bag. One by one he took each piece and wrapped it carefully with linen and sackcloth: an octant, a graphometer, the surveyor's compass—a gift from his parents when he completed his studies—a waywiser, theodolite, and tripod. Using these tools attached him to the past, like a plumb line drawn across time connecting him to early mapmakers with that same curiosity. He'd always felt so young—the youngest son of a man who came to a young country as a boy. His roots were fresh, new, and in his love of the land—especially this very primitive land shaped by the power of nature—be felt those roots entrench into ancient soil.

He loaded the bag onto the back of a mule-drawn cart, the Mexican driver waiting patiently while he leapt up to sit on the floor and prepared to leave, his legs dangling down as he reached across for his stationery box. He opened the wooden box, checked that he had collected all his pens, sturdy German writing instruments each filled with a different colored ink. He liked the heft of the pens, the flow of ink, the narrow threads of color that issued from the pinlike point onto the heavy mapping paper. Michael Clifton might sometimes have been thought an impulsive young man anxious to make his mark, but he knew his business and he was nothing if not a diligent cartographer.

In Santa Ynez, Michael transferred his equipment and personal effects to a larger carriage for the journey into Santa Barbara. From there he could telegraph his father that he was on his way—but would save the good news for later, when he was home. He wanted to see the look on Edward Clifton's face when he told him of his discovery; he wanted to experience the joy and pride in person. For now he would check into the Arlington Hotel—the Clifton name alone meant a suite would be made available—bathe the dust from his skin, and then he would buy himself the biggest steak he could find in town. He might walk along the beach, smell that crisp Pacific air once more before boarding a California Pacific train bound for San Francisco tomorrow, and from there to the East Coast along the transcontinental railroad. Then before you knew it, he would be home. But he would return soon to this place. Yes, he would be back—and this new Clifton Corporation would be his.

It was the newsboy outside the hotel who caught his attention.

Read all about it. Read all about it. Britain goes to war! Kaiser to fight whole world. Read all about it.

Pulling a handful of coins from his pocket, Michael bought a newspaper and began reading as he made his way through the hotel foyer. He signed the guest register, only marginally aware of what he was writing, and where. He nodded upon receiving the key to his rooms, and continued reading as the bellhop struggled with his belongings. Once in the suite, he slumped down in a chair, looking up only to press a few cents into the bellhop's palm.

It had come as no surprise to his family that Michael Clifton would choose to become a cartographer. He had loved maps since childhood, drawn to the mystery of lands far away, fascinated by the names of places, and the promise he saw held within a map. "You always know where you are with a map," he had told his parents, while persuading them of his choice of profession. "And if you know where you are, why, you're more likely to be brave, to have an adventure, to search beyond where everyone else is looking. Think of what I could do for the company!" His father had laughed, seeing through the subtle entreaty. Yet Michael was right—it had been good for the company to have a man in the family business who could read the land. You knew where you were with family, and as Edward had told his children time and again, you knew where your money was when it was in land. But what Michael never even tried to explain was the sense of wonder that came with a map, for each one told a story and he, the surveyor and cartographer, was the storyteller, the translator, the guide to places a person might never otherwise see. He could tame a forest, prairie, or wilderness with a few strokes of his pen. And he had a knack for finding nature's buried treasures.

It had taken no time at all for Michael to make his decision. Before leaving his rooms he copied precise details from the maps and land documents into a small leather-bound notebook, carefully marking those places where drilling should begin. The fact that the valley held oil deposits was without question—William Orcutt, the surveyor for Union Oil, had the coast and much of the valley all but sewn up. Yet, to know exactly where to tap into the riches took an expert eye. Some said you had to touch the land to know, that a man who knew where to sink his shovel could hear oil rumbling in the earth.

His task complete, and with the series of maps rolled and placed in a leather tube along with the original title documents to the land—his land—he went directly to the Central Bank of California on State Street, where he left the leather tube in safe deposit, withdrew a portion of the funds held in his name at the bank, and then made his way to the railroad station where he purchased a ticket to Boston via San Francisco and New York. He left the office, then stopped short in the street before returning to the ticket counter, whereupon he informed the clerk that he had changed his mind, and would go only as far as New York. The clerk grumbled, but asked no questions as he made out the new ticket. From New York, Michael planned to sail to England as soon as he could secure a passage—and it was surprising the speed with which anything could be reserved, booked, obtained, and acquired when you were a Clifton.

It was only right that he go, because for his family, England was the old country. He'd read that other boys were going over, boys like him who had Limey blood in their veins. Of course, he suspected they probably wouldn't let him bear arms, being an American by birth, but he had a profession, and he was only too aware that in wartime armies needed to know where they were going, needed to know the lay of the land. He would wire his family and let them know of his decision just before he sailed. His father might argue, but he would also be proud that his son was going to fight for the country he'd left a lifetime ago. And his maps of the valley and the deed to his land would be safe until he returned; after all, according to reports the war in Europe would be over by Christmas. Thus, by the time a tall spruce tree was alive with baubles, tinsel, and lights in the window of the grand house on Boston's Beacon Hill, he'd be home.

CHAPTER 1

"Would you believe it, Billy—three years and we're still in business!" Maisie Dobbs turned away from the floor-to-ceiling window, where she had been watching gray, rain-filled clouds lumbering across an otherwise springlike sky. She smiled and sat down at the table where she and her assistant, Billy Beale, had been working.

Billy ran his fingers through blond hair threaded with gray at the temples. "And we've a few more clients on the books than we expected in January."

Maisie leaned back in her chair. "We've been lucky, there's no doubt about that. I just hope it continues throughout the year."

"Perhaps the Americans we're seeing this morning have a few friends over here who might need your services," said Billy. "I mean, that's how almost all the work comes in, isn't it? Through clients who were satisfied with what you did for them."

"Speaking of the Americans, I want to read that letter once

more before they arrive." Maisie stood up and walked across the room to her desk. "Apparently they're very good people, quite down to earth, but they'll be expecting me to be completely prepared for the appointment, especially with such a strong personal reference from Dr. Hayden."

She reached for a manila folder with the words, "Clifton, Edward and Martha" inscribed along one side, and took out a well-thumbed letter from Dr. Charles Hayden. Maisie had met the eminent American surgeon in the war when they were introduced by Simon Lynch, a Captain in the army medical corps. At the time, Dr. Hayden was a volunteer with a medical contingent from the Massachusetts General Hospital. They had corresponded since the war, and now he wrote in response to a letter from Maisie.

Please do not apologize for the delay in letting me know that Simon had passed away. Though my first concern is always for my patients, in my dealings with families of the sick and dying, I know the passage of grief is a difficult one to navigate, so please do not concern yourself that you should have written sooner. You have been in Pauline's and my thoughts so often over the years, especially given Simon's medical circumstances. As a doctor, I confess, I was amazed at the man's continued physical resilience, when there was no obvious function in his mind.

He continued with reminiscences of times spent with Simon, and followed with news of his family. Then the letter took a different tack.

Maisie, I hope you don't mind, but I have taken the liberty of referring a friend to you—he and his wife are more than willing to pay for your professional services, and they are in any case planning to sail for France in late March, then will travel on to England in April. I know they will be in touch and you will want to hear the story straight from the horse's mouth. But let me fill you in on what I know so that you might be prepared for what's in store.

I met the Cliftons though their son-in-law, Bradley Marchant. He's married to their eldest daughter, Meg, and is one of my colleagues here at the hospital. We went to their wedding at the family vacation home on Cape Cod, and I'm a godfather to their eldest. I don't know if you need all this detail, but I thought I should let you know anyway.

Edward Clifton is an Englishman by birth. He came over here when he was about eighteen, nineteen, something like that. He wasn't exactly penniless, but he knew how to work—and to make something of himself, he had to work hard. He turned his hand to anything he could, then started putting money into land— Bradley said that acquiring land was an obsession with Edward when he was younger. I guess it's something about coming from over there and starting again in a new country—he needed to own a part of it, stake his claim. From land he moved into building and founded a construction company, then he started invest-ing in stocks—and all tied to the land in some way. I'll cut to the chase here, and say that by the time he was thirty, Edward Clifton was very, very wealthy. Then he met Martha Stanbourne—she's from an important family, it's said their ancestors came to America on the Mayflower. The Stanbournes are what we call "Boston Brahmin" over here. They married—there's no doubt it was a love match—and had four children. There's Edward, Jr.—Teddy—then Margaret and Anna, and bringing up the rear, Michael. Couldn't have met a nicer family.

Maisie paused. When she had first read the letter, as soon as she saw the word "Michael" the thought had crossed her mind: *That's the one. It's Michael who has caused them pain,* for there was no doubt in her mind, even in reading a few paragraphs, that the Cliftons were in some emotional turmoil. Why else would they need her services?

In August 1914, Michael was out in California—he was a mapmaker, surveyor of some sort. Apparently he'd bought a tract of land with money left to him by Martha's father. It would have been a lot of money and, according to Bradley, there's still plenty held in trust. He was very excited about the purchase, and was due to come back to Boston—couldn't wait to see his parents to tell them all about it. Then I guess you could say he crossed paths with fate when he saw the news about war in Belgium. He changed his plans at the last minute and sailed for Europe. Edward will fill you in on the details, but Michael enlisted in England and was attached to a military cartography unit—no doubt if it wasn't for his profession he would have been sent packing back to Boston.

"Cuppa, Miss, before they get here?"

Maisie glanced at the clock. "Oh, yes please. They're bound to be shocked if they see me drinking out of my old army mug. Americans always expect to see the English sipping tea from fine bone china." She went back to the letter.

Michael was listed as missing in early 1916. Last year a farmer working the land (somewhere in the Somme Valley) put his plow into a gully, and when he and some other men were digging it out, the ground started to fall away and the bodies of several British soldiers were found. Michael was identified by his tags. By now you're probably wondering why the Cliftons need to see someone like you. Apparently the ground gave way to a dugout and a series of what you could only describe as rooms—so well made, the Brits might have been occupying an old German trench. It was there that the soldiers' belongings were found. They were members of a surveying team. Michael's journal was discovered along with other personal effects. Don't ask me how the Cliftons managed to get their hands on the journal. You know the soldiers weren't allowed to keep any sort of diary, so it's a wonder it wasn't retained by the authorities. It's now with Edward and Martha, along with a collection of letters. His wallet was tucked in his jacket pocket and apparently his surveying compass and other tools he'd taken with him were also returned to the family. Now, the reason they want to see you is this: The letters were from a woman, they think an English woman, and they want to find her. That's everything I know, but at least you'll be prepared when they arrive.

Please keep in touch, Maisie, Pauline sends her love—perhaps you girls will have a chance to meet one day.

It was signed with a flourish: *Charles.*

"There you are, Miss. Nice cuppa the old char."

"Lovely—thank you, Billy." Maisie pushed back her chair, leaving the letter open on the table as she looked out upon the square again. She cupped her hands around the chipped enamel mug. "I thought we were in for a warm spring, but look at that rain."

"Coming down cats and dogs, ain't it?" Billy sipped his tea and reached for the letter. "You know what I reckon happened to this here Michael Clifton?" Billy continued without waiting for an answer. "I reckon he heard about the war starting and came over all patriotic for the half of him that was British. That and the fact that something gets into lads when a war starts. Makes them get all mannish, as if they can't wait to get on with getting old. Look at me and my brother—and him buried over there."

Maisie nodded. "I know—though remember you and your brother were also pushed by public opinion. I remember Charles—Dr. Hayden—saying that in America in 1914 it was different. There were a lot of people who had just emigrated from Germany, so there was a significant allegiance to the kaiser at first. But thank heavens for the American doctors and nurses who volunteered when war broke out—they saved a great many lives."

"So, what do you think of this, Miss?" He held up the letter.

"Let's see what the Cliftons have to say—they'll be here in a minute. But I don't think it has anything to do with money. If they want to find that woman, it's because there's a link to Michael. The question is, what kind of link? It could be something as simple as wanting to speak to someone who knew their son at a time when he was at a great distance from them—it appears they were a close family. But my sense is that it's more than that." Maisie closed her eyes. "They want to unlock some door to the past, I would say. And they have reason to believe this woman holds the key."

The bell above the door began to ring.

"That must be them. Go on, Billy, go and let them in while I put these few things away."

AUTHOR INTERVIEW

This is your sixth novel to feature Maisie Dobbs, and the seventh is on the way. What is it like to develop a character over the course of multiple books, and how has Maisie changed over the years?

It's rather like getting to know a person over time. As much as I develop the characters, so the characters reveal themselves to me—it's a much more organic process, and very rewarding. In addition, I can follow characters as they grow and change, as they are impacted by events, over time—both personal and collective. There's something very satisfying in developing a relationship with the characters in this way.

Unlike other books in the series, this is a ticking-clock mystery, in which Maisie has only forty-eight hours to uncover a plot. What are the constraints of writing under this device, and how is it also freeing?

I think the "constraints" actually give the process a certain impulsion, an energy that is different than in a novel with no such parameters.

I wanted to see what it was like to write in this way, and I have to say it was really interesting—you have the heart of the story beating in your head all the time.

We often think of terrorism as a new form of violence, but people have used terror tactics throughout history. What drew you to write about a terrorist of the 1930s? Do you occasionally embed a comment about contemporary society in your books?

Coming from the British Isles, I am only too aware that terrorism is far from new—indeed, every year we celebrate overcoming a terrorist act, with Guy Fawkes Night, on November 5th. Everyone has bonfires and fireworks, which signify the Gunpowder Plot, when Guy "Guido" Fawkes tried to blow up the Houses of Parliament in 1605. Fawkes was actually an explosives expert in his day, and the plotters included a raft of wealthy and titled men.

In *Among the Mad* I wanted to try to get inside the head of someone who was so compromised in his mind that the only way he thought he could be heard was to commit a crime of terrorism. I wanted to see his side of the story, so to speak, as someone who was disenfranchised, left behind by society.

I don't ever deliberately embed comments about contemporary society in my work. The study of history is often like holding up a mirror to today—I don't have to do a thing, history and the turn of current events do it all for me.

Mental illness has a high profile today, and is treated with more empathy than in Maisie Dobbs's time. Talk about the specter of mental illness in Among the Mad, *and what it was like to render it in a different historical period.*

The essence of how madness is viewed in *Among the Mad* is that it can be painfully obvious, or it can be almost hidden. So, from the man who is suffering from mental trauma, to the doctor who is obsessive about his tidy room, and the woman whose grief is crippling her mind, you see that there are many faces of madness. Sometimes that madness will result in a person being institutionalized, and sometimes that madness is controlled, accommodated, so there is never a less-than-humane medical treatment.

In some ways it was probably easier to portray madness in a historical period, as there were such graphic examples of patient abuse. Experimentation was rife, and the treatment of women especially inhumane.

What was it like to write from two perspectives—that of Maisie and her nemesis? Is it like having multiple personalities?

The two personalities are very different, so no, it was not terribly hard—and it certainly wasn't like having two personalities. One of the questions I always ask when I put a character in a certain situation is, "How might this feel?" It's important to try to give a sense of the physical and emotional feelings that engulf a person in a time of stress—which for the mentally compromised person is much of the time.

Have you ever considered becoming a detective yourself?

Never. The idea of being a spy appeals to me, or an investigative reporter. That's the closest I could come to being a detective. And of course, with historical research, you are always a bit of a detective.

DISCUSSION QUESTIONS

1. Discuss the ways in which the Great War has affected Maisie Dobbs both personally and professionally, as psychologist and investigator. How do her experiences with soldiers and in combat palpably help her to solve the case at hand?

2. What are the differences and similarities between Stephen Oliver and Billy Beale's wife, Doreen? What distinguishes their psychological states?

3. Many of the characters in *Among the Mad* grapple with mental distress—Dr. Lawrence, Professor John Gale, Detective Chief Superintendent MacFarland, Dr. Elsbeth Masters—how do their individual psychological states bring dimension and suspense to the novel as a whole?

4. Under threat of mass terror, Stephen Oliver demands that the government immediately pay full pensions to all veterans—those who have sustained both physical and psychological injuries. At the same time, he writes in his diary "I just want to be heard." Is he an activist or a terrorist, and to what extent do you sympathize with him?

5. Though set in 1931, *Among the Mad* addresses many issues that are a part of our contemporary world—the political fallout of wars, terrorism, a struggling economy. How does Jacqueline Winspear's evocation of these troubles in another time shed light on turbulent days in the present?

6. Maisie Dobbs thrives in a career largely dominated by men. But what are some of the advantages she has over MacFarland and Urquart? In what ways does she successfully deflect their antagonism? Were you surprised to find social commentary on equality threaded through the mystery? Along those same lines, do you think that Maisie's intuitions as a detective are distinctly female, or are they coming from a different, higher place?

7. Stratton, Darby, and MacFarland immediately suspect Mosley's New Party and the student-union activists are responsible for the letters, while Maisie takes her time to investigate the real identity of Ian Jennings and to take a closer look at Ms. Catherine Jones. How are the two approaches different? Do the other detectives miss the forest for the trees by looking at groups instead of individual motivations?

8. Were you surprised by the brutality that Stephen Oliver faced at the hands of people who were charged with healing him? How is such corruption possible? Is it ever for the greater good?

9. Beyond acting as her loyal assistant, what role does Billy Beale really play in Maisie's life? Does she need him on an emotional as well as professional level?

10. Discuss Dr. Masters's story about the lion and the gazelle on page 136, and her rather spiritual understanding of shell shock. Do you agree with her, and if not, what metaphors would you select to illustrate that kind of suffering?

11. Would you describe Dr. Lawrence as a tragic character? How do you feel about Maisie's final gesture to reconcile with her at the end of the investigation?

The foundations of
modern political thought

VOLUME TWO: THE AGE OF REFORMATION

The foundations of
modern political thought

VOLUME TWO: THE AGE OF REFORMATION

QUENTIN SKINNER
PROFESSOR OF POLITICAL SCIENCE
UNIVERSITY OF CAMBRIDGE

CAMBRIDGE UNIVERSITY PRESS

CAMBRIDGE
LONDON   NEW YORK   NEW ROCHELLE
MELBOURNE   SYDNEY

Published by the Press Syndicate of the University of Cambridge
The Pitt Building, Trumpington Street, Cambridge CB2 1RP
32 East 57th Street, New York, NY 10022, USA
296 Beaconsfield Parade, Middle Park, Melbourne 3206, Australia

First published 1978
Reprinted 1979

Printed in the United States of America
Typeset by Western Printing Services Ltd, Avonmouth, England
Printed and bound by Vail-Ballou Press, Inc.,
Binghamton, New York

Library of Congress Cataloguing in Publication Data (Revised)

Skinner, Quentin

The foundations of modern political thought.

Bibliography: v. 1, p.
Includes index.
CONTENTS: vol. 1. The Renaissance. – vol. 2. The
age of Reformation.
1. Political science – History – Collected works.
I. Title.
JA81.S54   320.5'09'03   78–51676
ISBN 0 521 22284 2 (vol. 2) hard covers
ISBN 0 521 29435 5 (vol. 2) paperback

Contents

PART ONE

Absolutism and the Lutheran Reformation

I

The principles of Lutheranism

To begin the story of the Lutheran Reformation at the traditional starting-point is to begin in the middle. Luther's famous act of nailing up the Ninety-Five Theses on the door of the Castle Church at Wittenberg on the Eve of All Saints in 1517 (which may not even have happened)[1] merely marks the culmination of a long spiritual journey on which he had been travelling at least since his appointment over six years before to the chair of Theology in the University of Wittenberg. One of the main achievements of Lutheran scholarship in the past generation has been to trace the course of Luther's intellectual development during this forma-tive time. The basis for this reinterpretation has been provided by the rediscovery of the materials he used in giving his lectures on the Psalms in 1513–14, on the Epistle to the Romans in 1515–16, and on the Epistle to the Galatians in 1516–17. The outcome has been the suggestion that it would only be a 'slight exaggeration', as Rupp puts it, to claim that 'the whole of the later Luther' can already be discerned in the pages of these early lecture-notes (Rupp, 1951, p. 39). The implication is that it may be best to begin the story where Luther himself began: with the development of his new theology, which provided him with the framework for his subsequent attack not just on the Papacy's traffic in indulgences, but on the whole set of attitudes, social and political as well as religious, which had come to be associated with the teachings of the Catholic Church.

THE THEOLOGICAL PREMISES

The basis of Luther's new theology, and of the spiritual crisis which precipitated it, lay in his vision of the nature of man. Luther was obsessed by the idea of man's complete unworthiness. To a modern psychologist this may appear as evidence of a particularly severe crisis of identity, an 'integrity crisis' in which the sufferer comes to have a total mistrust in the value of his own existence (Erikson, 1958, p. 254). Luther's more

[1] For this allegation see Iserloh, 1968, esp. pp. 76–97.

conventional biographers, however, have been content to see this simply as a case of 'pitting one type of Catholicism against another, Augustinianism against Thomism' (Bainton, 1953a, p. 36). Luther's vision caused him to reject the optimistic view of man's capacity to intuit and follow the laws of God which the Thomists had characteristically emphasised, and led him back to the earlier and more pessimistic Augustinian emphasis on man's fallen nature.

This doctrine not only represented a break with Thomism, but an even sharper rejection of the elevated view of man's virtues and capacities which, as we have seen, the humanists had more recently popularised. Luther was thus prompted to mount a violent attack on the humanist ideal of a *philosophia pia*, and in particular on the 'heathen and publican' Erasmus, the most dangerous exponent of their arrogant creed. The occasion for this definitive breach with the humanists was provided by the publication of Erasmus's discourse *On the Freedom of the Will* in 1524. Erasmus had at first appeared as a cautious ally of the Reformation, applauding the Ninety-Five Theses and helping to ensure that Luther was not condemned unheard by the Imperial authorities (Rupp, 1953, pp. 264–7). He soon became more evasive, however, especially after Luther had been excommunicated. We find him writing to Wolsey in 1519 to deny that he had read Luther's works, and to Luther himself at the same time to urge him to proceed more cautiously (Allen, 1906–58, III, pp. 589–606). By 1521 he was insisting a trifle mendaciously that he had 'opposed the pamphlets of Luther more than any other man', and two years later he finally yielded to the demand – voiced by the Pope and Henry VIII amongst others – that he should compose an anti-Lutheran tract (Allen, 1906–58, IV, pp. 536–40). Luther's doctrine of man presented the obvious target for his humanist talents, and the outcome was the treatise *On the Freedom of the Will*, in which he not only opposed Luther's views with copious citations from the scriptures and Church Fathers, but also prefaced his discussion with the characteristically dismissive remark that he would 'prefer men to be persuaded not to waste their time and talents in labyrinths of this kind' (p. 41).

Luther clearly felt goaded as well as alarmed by this somewhat unexpected attack from such an influential quarter. He quickly produced an elaborate and exceptionally violent reply, in which he developed a comprehensive statement of his own theological position, and included a definitive presentation of his anti-humanist and ultra-Augustinian doctrine of man. This was published in 1525 as *The Bondage of the Will*. Gerrish has emphasised that it would be a mistake to characterise this assault on the idea of a *philosophia pia* as a completely 'irrationalist' one

(Gerrish, 1962, p. 25). Luther certainly never seeks to deny the value of natural reason, in the sense of man's reasoning powers, nor does he condemn the use of 'regenerate reason' when it is 'serving humbly in the household of faith' (Gerrish, 1962, pp. 25–6). He even makes a residual use of the concept of natural law, although he usually equates this source of moral knowledge simply with the promptings of a man's conscience (McNeill, 1941). He is implacably opposed, however, to Erasmus's central and typically humanist contention that it is open to a man to employ his powers of reasoning in order to understand how God wishes him to act. He repeatedly insists that in his context all man's reasoning powers are simply 'carnal' and 'absurd' (pp. 144, 224). We have all 'fallen from God and been deserted by God', so that we are all completely 'bound, wretched, captive, sick, and dead' (pp. 130, 175). This makes it ridiculous as well as sinful to suppose that we can ever hope 'to measure God by human reason' and in this way to penetrate the mysteries of His will (p. 172). The true situation, as Luther seeks to indicate in the title of his tract, is that our wills remain at all times in total bondage to sin. We are all so 'corrupt and averse from God' that we have no hope of ever being able to will 'things which please God or which God wills' (pp. 175–6). All our actions proceed from our 'averse and evil' natures, which are completely enslaved to Satan, and thus ensure that we can 'do nothing but averse and evil things' (pp. 98, 176). The result is that 'through the one transgression of the one man, Adam, we are all under sin and damnation', and are left with 'no capacity to do anything but sin and be damned' (p. 272).

This vision of man's bondage to sin commits Luther to a despairing analysis of the relationship between man and God. He is forced to acknowledge that since we cannot hope to fathom the nature and will of God, His commands are bound to appear entirely inscrutable. It is at this point that he most clearly reveals his debt to the Ockhamists: he insists that the commands of God must be obeyed not because they seem to us just but simply because they are God's commands (p. 181). This attack on the Thomist and humanist accounts of God as a rational lawgiver is then developed into the distinctively Lutheran doctrine of the twofold nature of God. There is the God who has chosen to reveal Himself in the Word, whose will can in consequence be 'preached, revealed, offered and worshipped' (p. 139). But there is also the hidden God, the *Deus Absconditus*,[1] whose 'immutable, eternal and infallible will' is incapable of being comprehended by men at all (pp. 37, 139). The will of the hidden God is omnipotent, ordaining everything that happens in the world. But it is also beyond our understanding, and can only be 'reverently

---

[1] The reference is to Isaiah, Chapter 45, verse 15.

adored, as by far the most awe-inspiring secret of the divine majesty'
(p. 139).

Luther is also forced to accept a second and even more despairing
implication of his doctrine of man. Since all our actions inexorably express
our fallen natures, there is nothing we can ever hope to do which will
justify us in the sight of God and so help us to be saved. This is really the
chief point at issue between Erasmus and Luther, and the main theme of
The Bondage of the Will (Boisset, 1962, pp. 38–9). The debate with Erasmus is not about the freedom of the will in the ordinary philosophical
sense. Luther is quite prepared to concede that men can freely 'eat, drink,
beget, rule', and even that they can freely perform good acts by following
'the righteousness of the civil and moral law' (p. 275). What he is concerned
to deny is Erasmus's definition of the freedom of the will in terms of 'a
power of the human will by which a man can apply himself to the things
which lead to eternal salvation' (p. 103). Luther insists on the contrary
that 'since men are flesh and have a taste for nothing but the flesh, it
follows that free choice avails for nothing but sinning', and that all men
are 'consigned to perdition by ungodly desire' (pp. 214, 226). The
despairing conclusion of *The Bondage of the Will* is thus that 'free choice
is nothing' and virtuous acts are of no value in relation to salvation (p. 241).

These conclusions suggest to Luther a further implication which, as he
goes on to tell us, at one time brought him 'to the very depth and abyss of
despair' (p. 190). He has conceded that man's impotence is such that he
can never hope to be saved by his own efforts. He has argued that God's
omnipotence is such that the hidden God who 'works all in all' must
already have a complete foreknowledge of all future as well as past events.
(Luther even takes sides at this point in the scholastic debate over the
nature of God's foreknowledge, affirming (p. 42) that 'God foreknows all
things, not contingently, but necessarily and immutably'.)[1] The implication of these claims, as he is forced to admit, is a doctrine of double
predestination – the contention that some men must already be predestined to be saved while others are predestined to be damned. And this
thunderbolt, as he calls it, seemed to open up an unbridgeable gulf
between God and man (p. 37). God appears terrifyingly inexorable: it is
entirely for Him to decide, and He must already have decided, which of
us is to be spared. And man is left completely helpless: it is possible that
we are all damned, and it is certain that no one can ever hope to change
his fate.

This conclusion at first induced in Luther a prolonged spiritual crisis.

---

[1] For a discussion of this debate, as conducted at the University of Louvain in the fifteenth
century, see Baudry, 1950, esp. pp. 27–46.

His affliction appears to have begun as early as 1505, when he suddenly abandoned his proposed career in law after a series of traumatic personal incidents and decided instead to enter the Augustinian monastery at Erfurt (Fife, 1957, p. 73). The crisis seems to have deepened in 1510, after he returned from a visit to Rome which seems to have left him, as Fife suggests, 'disillusioned and to some extent disheartened' about the state of the Church (Fife, 1957, p. 176). Luther himself gives an account of his spiritual condition during these years in the autobiography which he published in 1545 as a Preface to the Wittenberg edition of his Latin works (pp. 336–7). He tried the traditional monastic remedies of fasting and prayer, but these failed to bring him any solace. He turned to the study of Augustine, but this merely confirmed his sense of hopelessness. He found himself driven to the frightening blasphemy of cursing and hating God for providing men with a law which they are unable to keep, and then righteously damning them for failing to keep it. He speaks of coming to hate the very word 'righteousness' (*iustitia*), which he understood to refer to the justice of God in punishing sinful men, and he found himself unable even to look at those parts of the New Testament – especially the Epistles of St Paul – in which the concept of God's righteousness is assigned a central place (Boehmer, 1946, p. 110).

Then, after years of deepening anguish, Luther suddenly attained a tremendous new insight which brought him permanent relief. The moment evidently came to him while he was engaged in the mundane academic task of preparing a new lecture-course, working in the tower-room of the monastery at Wittenberg.[1] While reading over and paraphrasing the Psalms, he was struck by a completely new interpretation of the crucial phrase in Psalm 30, 'Deliver me in thy righteousness' – *in iustitia tua libera me* (Boehmer, 1946, p. 109). It suddenly occurred to him that the concept of the righteousness of God referred not to His punitive powers, but rather to His readiness to have mercy on sinful men, and in this way to justify them by delivering them from their unrighteousness. After this, as Luther himself reports in his autobiography, he felt that he had been 'altogether born again and had entered paradise itself through open gates' (p. 337).

Luther himself speaks of his 'tower-experience' (*Turmerlebnis*) both in his autobiography and in the *Table Talk* recorded by Conrad Cordatus (pp. 193–4). A number of commentators have recently sought to show

---

[1] But folklore tells a less polite story at this point, as W. H. Auden reminds us in the appropriate section of *About the House* (London, 1965, p. 117):

> Revelation came to
> Luther in a privy.

that the outcome, his ultra-Augustinian doctrine of justification, was in fact the product of a gradual evolution in his thought. But all the scholars who pioneered the study of Luther's intellectual development – in particular Vogelsang, Bornkamm and Boehmer – agreed in seeing this doctrine as the fruit of a sudden epiphany, which they all dated to some time in the year 1513. The dating will doubtless continue to be a subject of learned debate,[1] but the crucial significance of the episode in Luther's development is not in doubt: it suddenly enabled him to bridge the agonising gap between God's omnipotence and man's unrighteousness. It was at this point that he at last felt able, under the promptings of his spiritual adviser, Johann von Staupitz, to turn to the intensive study of St Paul's Epistles, and to compose his commentaries on Romans, Galatians and Hebrews. The outcome was the complete new theology in terms of which he then turned and rent the Papacy and the whole Catholic Church.

The core of Luther's theology is constituted by his doctrine of justification *sola fide*, 'by faith alone'. He continues to stress that no one can ever hope to be justified – that is, granted salvation – by virtue of his own works. But he now argues that it must be open to anyone to perceive God's *gratia* – the 'saving grace' which He must already have granted as a totally unmerited favour to those whom He has predestined to be saved. He is thus able to propose that the sole aim of the sinner must be to achieve *fiducia* – a totally passive faith in the righteousness of God and in the consequent possibility of being redeemed and justified by His merciful grace.

Once Luther attained this fundamental insight, all the other distinctive features of his theology gradually fell into place. He was able first of all to give a complete account of the concept of justification underlying his pivotal doctrine of faith. This was first fully stated in the sermons and disputations of 1518–20, and in particular in the sermon of 1519 entitled *Two Kinds of Righteousness* (Saarnivaara, 1951, pp. 9–18, 92–5). Here Luther moved decisively beyond the traditional patristic idea of justification as a gradual process of eradicating the believer's sins. He now sees it as an immediate consequence of *fides apprehensiva* – 'a grasping and appropriating faith' which enables the sinner suddenly to seize Christ's righteousness for himself, so that he becomes 'one with Christ, having the same righteousness as he' (p. 298; cf. Althaus, 1966, p. 230). The result is an intensely strong emphasis on the idea that the righteousness of the

---

[1] The evidence in favour of an evolutionary interpretation has been best presented by Saarnivaara, 1951, pp. 59–120. The original interpretation has been powerfully restated, however, in a reply to Saarnivaara by Bornkamm, 1961–2. The debate is well surveyed by Dickens, 1974, pp. 85–8, who inclines cautiously to Saarnivaara's side.

believer is never *domestica* – never achieved by himself, and still less deserved. It can only be *extranea* – an 'alien righteousness, instilled in us without our works by grace alone' (p. 299). The believer is at all times seen as *simul justus et peccator* – at once a sinner and justified. His sins are never abrogated, but his faith ensures that they cease to count against him.

Luther next proceeded to relate this account of faith and justification to the process by which the life of the sinner comes to be sanctified. This further theme also emerges clearly for the first time in the sermons of 1518–20 (Cranz, 1959, pp. 41–3). The Christian is now pictured as the simultaneous inhabitant of two realms – that of Christ and that of worldly things. The justification of the sinner comes first, and happens 'not piece-meal but all at once' (Cranz, 1959, p. 126). As Luther phrases it in his sermon on *Two Kinds of Righteousness*, the redeeming presence of Christ 'swallows up all sins in a moment' (p. 298). The process of sanctification then 'follows gradually' once the sinner has acquired his faith (Cranz, 1959, p. 126). The result is a distinction which is central to Luther's social and political thought, and also underlies Melanchthon's influential doctrine of 'adiaphora': the distinction between a primary and passive concept of justice which Christians are able to attain in the realm of Christ, and an active or civil justice which is not a part of salvation, but remains essential to the proper regulation of worldly affairs.

Luther's pivotal belief in God's redeeming grace next enabled him to resolve the cruel dilemma posed by the Old Testament, with its law which no one can hope to follow and its threat of damnation for those who fail to follow it. His answer, first explicitly stated in *The Freedom of a Christian* in 1520, takes the form of marking a sharp antithesis between the message of the Old and the New Testaments, an antithesis between God's impossible commands and his redeeming promises (p. 348). The purpose of the Old Testament is now said to be to 'teach man to know himself', in order that 'he may recognise his inability to do good and may despair of his own inability' – as Luther himself had so profoundly despaired (p. 348). This is 'the strange work of the law'. The contrasting purpose of the New Testament is to reassure us that although we may be unable to attain salvation 'by trying to fulfil all the works of the law', we may be able to attain it 'quickly and easily through faith' (p. 349). This is 'the proper work of the gospel'. The implication of this 'law–gospel dialectic', as McDonough has labelled it, is thus that it corresponds exactly to the individual's 'despair–faith' experience of sin and grace. And with Luther's contrast between these two positions, as McDonough adds, we return to 'the very heart and core of his basic convictions' (McDonough, 1963, pp. 1–3).

The relation between these doctrines serves in turn to illuminate a further characteristic feature of Luther's theology: his account of the significance of Christ. It is Christ who transmits to men their knowledge of God's redeeming grace. It is thus through Christ alone that we become emancipated from the impossible demands of the law and receive 'the good news' that we may be saved. This means that in spite of Luther's emphasis on the powers of the hidden God, there is nothing mystical about his outlook, in the sense of inviting us merely to contemplate God's remoteness and infinity. Luther is always at pains to present his theology as a *theologia crucis*, in which Christ's sacrifice remains the key to our salvation. Christ is 'the only preacher' and 'the only saviour', who not only lifts from us the burden of our moral worthlessness, but also serves as 'the source and the content of the faithful knowledge of God' (Siggins, 1970, pp. 79, 108).

Given this view of Luther's christology, it seems somewhat misleading to suggest – as Troeltsch has done in his classic account of Luther's social thought – that Luther found 'the objective revelation of the moral law' entirely in the Decalogue, and took this law to be 'simply confirmed and interpreted by Jesus and the Apostles' (Troeltsch, 1931, p. 504). This judgment certainly holds good for Calvin, who always laid a strong emphasis on the immediate moral relevance of the Old Testament. When applied to Luther, however, it appears to obscure the transforming role he assigned to Christ's sacrifice. For Luther, far more than for Calvin, Christ is perceived as coming not only to fulfil the law, but also to release the faithful from its demands by His redeeming merit and love. The consequence is that for Luther, though not for Calvin, it is always essential to understand the commands of the law in the light of the gospel, not the gospel in the light of the law (Watson, 1947, p. 153).

Finally, Luther's solfidianism – his doctrine of justification 'by faith alone' – leads him to enunciate the two main features of his heretical concept of the Church. He first of all devalues the significance of the Church as a visible institution. If the attainment of *fiducia* constitutes the sole means by which the Christian can hope to be saved, no place is left for the orthodox idea of the Church as an authority interposed and mediating between the individual believer and God (Pelikan, 1968). The true Church becomes nothing more than an invisible *congregatio fidelium*, a congregation of the faithful gathered together in God's name. This Luther saw as a sublimely simple concept, completely encapsulated in his claim that the Greek word *ecclesia*, which is habitually used in the New Testament to denote the primitive Church, should be translated simply as *Gemeine* or congregation (Dickens, 1974, p. 67). Despite his assurance, however, that 'a child of seven knows what the Church is', his apparently simple doctrine was widely misunderstood, especially by those who took him to be saying that he wished 'to build a church as Plato a city, which nowhere exists'.[1] In his mature theological writings he sought to counter these misconstructions by adding that while the Church is merely a *communio*, it is also a *republica*, and as such needs to have a visible embodiment in the world (Watson, 1947, pp. 169–70; Cranz, 1959, pp. 126–31). His treatise *On the Councils and the Church*, first issued in 1539, even includes an influential enumeration of the 'marks' or signs which are taken to be necessary (though never sufficient) for distinguishing a fellowship which genuinely constitutes 'a Christian holy people' from a mere group of papists or 'Antinomian devils' (Luther was thinking of the Anabaptists) who might claim to have received the divine light (p. 150). While introducing these later concessions, however, Luther continued to insist that the true Church has no real existence except in the hearts of its faithful members. His central conviction was always that the Church can simply be equated with *Gottes Volk*, 'the people of God living from the word of God' (Bornkamm, 1958, p. 148).

The other distinctive feature of Luther's concept of the Church is that, in stressing the idea of the *ecclesia* as nothing more than a *congregatio fidelium*, he also minimises the separate and sacramental character of the priesthood. The outcome is the doctrine of 'the priesthood of all believers' (Rupp, 1953, pp. 315–16). This concept and its social implications are most fully worked out in the famous *Address* of 1520 directed 'To the Christian Nobility of the German Nation'. Luther argues that if the Church is only *Gottes Volk*, it must be 'a piece of deceit and hypocrisy' to claim that 'Pope, bishop, priests and monks are called the spiritual estate, while princes, lords, artisans and farmers are called the temporal estate' (p. 127). Luther wishes to abolish all such false dichotomies, and to insist that 'all Christians are truly of the spiritual estate', since they belong to it not in virtue of their role or rank in society, but simply in virtue of their equal capacity for faith, which makes them all equally capable of being 'spiritual and a Christian people' (p. 127). He deploys this argument partly as a way of claiming that all believers, and not just the priestly class, have an equal duty and capacity to help their brethren and assume responsibility for their spiritual welfare. But his main concern is clearly to reiterate his belief in the ability of every faithful individual soul to relate without any intermediary to God. The result is that throughout his

---

[1] For these references, and for an account of Luther's response to these misunderstandings, see Spitz, 1953, esp. pp. 122ff.

ecclesiology, as in his theology as a whole, we are continually led back to the central figure of the individual Christian and his faith in God's redeeming grace.

THE POLITICAL IMPLICATIONS

Luther's theology carried with it two political implications of major importance, which together account for most of what is distinctive and influential about his social and political thought. First of all, he is clearly committed to repudiating the idea that the Church possesses jurisdictional powers, and thus has the authority to direct and regulate Christian life. It is of course the abuse of these alleged powers which Luther mainly denounces, and especially the traffic in indulgences, the subject of his original outburst in the Ninety-Five Theses. The sale of indulgences was a long-standing scandal (already satirised in Chaucer) which had been given a theological basis as early as the Bull *Unigenitas* in 1343.[1] This declared that the merit Christ had displayed in sacrificing himself was even greater than the amount needed to redeem the entire human race. It went on to proclaim that the Church has the power to dispense this extra merit by selling indulgences (that is, remissions of penance) to those who confess their sins. The doctrine was dangerously extended by Sixtus IV in 1476 with the claim that souls in purgatory could also be helped by the purchase of an indulgence on their behalf. It was a short step from this doctrine to the popular belief – cited by Luther in the twenty-first of his Ninety-Five Theses – that by offering an immediate cash-payment for an indulgence one might eventually curtail one's sufferings after death (p. 127). It will already be evident why this system was particularly liable to spark off Luther's protests. To Luther, the belief in the efficacy of indulgences was simply the most wicked perversion of a general doctrine which he had come to believe as a theologian to be wholly false: the doctrine that it is possible for the Church to enable a sinner to attain salvation by means of its authority and sacraments. As we have seen, he had reached the conclusion that if a sinner attains *fiducia*, he will be saved without the Church; if he does not, there is nothing the Church can do to help him. The Papacy's claim to remit the wages of sin thus appeared to Luther as nothing more than the most grotesque of all the Church's attempts to devalue these central truths. The point is fiercely made in the attack on the Papacy and its agents which takes up most of the *Address* to the Christian nobility. 'For payment of money they make

[1] I take the following details about the history of indulgences from Green, 1964, pp. 113–14, 119–20.

unrighteousness into righteousness, and they dissolve oaths, vows and agreements, thereby destroying and teaching us to destroy the faith and fealty which have been pledged. They assert that the Pope has authority to do this. It is the Devil who tells them to say these things. They sell us doctrine so satanic, and take money for it, that they are teaching us sin and leading us to hell' (p. 193).

The real focus of Luther's attack, however, was not so much on the Church's abuses of its powers, but rather on the Church's right to claim any such powers in Christian society at all. This first of all prompted him to repudiate all the institutions of the Church which were based on the assumption that the clergy constitute a separate class with special jurisdictions and privileges. This attack simply followed from his belief in the spiritual nature of the true Church, and in particular from the doctrine that, as the *Address* puts it, 'we are all consecrated priests through baptism' (p. 127). One outcome was a complete rejection of the canon law. Luther insists in the *Address* that the only reason why 'the Romanists' wish to maintain this separate legal system, which 'exempts them from the jurisdiction of the temporal Christian authority', is in order that 'they can be free to do evil' and remain unpunished (p. 131). One of his concluding proposals is thus that 'it would be a good thing if canon law were completely blotted out', since 'the greater part smacks of nothing but greed and pride' while the absolute authority of the Pope over the interpretation of its contents makes any serious study of it 'just a waste of time and a farce' (p. 202). Within six months of publishing the *Address* Luther had followed his own advice. He presided over a book-burning at Wittenberg in December 1520 at which he not only destroyed the Papal Bull *Exsurge Domine*, in which his excommunication had been pronounced, but also committed the *Decretals* and commentaries of the canonists to the flames at the same time (Fife, 1957, p. 581). This urge to reject the idea of a separate clerical estate also led him to attack the mendicant orders, and to repudiate the whole ideal of the monastic way of life. He broaches this theme in the *Address*, which includes the demand 'that the further building of mendicant houses should not be permitted' and that all existing convents and monasteries should be regulated 'in the same way they were regulated in the beginning, in the days of the Apostles' (pp. 172–4). But his main attack occurs in the major treatise of 1521 entitled *The Judgment of Martin Luther on Monastic Vows*. The monastic life is denounced both for violating 'evangelical freedom' and for assigning a misplaced value to works, and in this way being 'against the Christian faith' (pp. 295–6). The book ends with a defence of the sweeping assertion that 'monasticism is contrary to common sense and reason', in the course of which Luther ridicules the monastic ideal of celibacy and mounts a vigorous defence of clerical marriage (p. 337).

Luther's objections to the status and powers of the Church also led him to repudiate every claim by the ecclesiastical authorities to exercise any jurisdiction over temporal affairs. It is sometimes said that this involved him in defending 'the separate jurisdiction of the State as distinct from the Church' (Waring, 1910, p. 80). His central belief about the Church, however, was rather that, since it is nothing more than a *congregatio fidelium*, it cannot properly be said to possess any separate jurisdiction at all. It is true that his argument is easily misunderstood at this point, since he continues to speak of the Two Kingdoms (*Zwei Reiche*) through which God exercises His complete dominion over the world. The Christian is said to be a subject of both these 'regiments', and Luther even speaks of the government of the spiritual kingdom as 'the government of the right hand of God' (Cargill Thompson, 1969, pp. 169, 177–8). It is generally clear, however, that what he has in mind when discussing the rule of the spiritual kingdom is a purely inward form of government, 'a government of the soul', which has no connection with temporal affairs, and is entirely dedicated to helping the faithful to attain their salvation. This interpretation can readily be corroborated by considering the important tract of 1523, on *Temporal Authority: to what extent it should be obeyed*, one of the key documents of Luther's social and political thought. He bases his discussion on the distinction between the immediate justification and the later sanctification of the faithful sinner (p. 89). He agrees that all Christians live simultaneously in two kingdoms, that of Christ and that of the world. He then goes on to equate the first with the Church and the second with the realm of temporal authority. The Church is thus taken to be ruled entirely by Christ, whose powers are entirely spiritual, since there is by definition no need for true Christians to be coerced. The realm of temporal authority is equally claimed to be ordained by God, but is seen as wholly separate, since the sword is granted to secular rulers simply in order to ensure that civil peace is maintained amongst sinful men (p. 91). All coercive powers are thus treated as temporal by definition, while the powers of the Pope and bishops are said to consist of 'nothing more than the inculcating of God's word', and are thus 'not a matter of authority and power' in the worldly sense at all (p. 117). It follows that any claims by the Pope or the Church to exercise any worldly jurisdictions in virtue of their office must represent a usurpation of the rights of the temporal authorities.

Luther's theological premises not only committed him to attacking the jurisdictional powers of the Church, but also to filling the power-vacuum this created by mounting a corresponding defence of the secular authorities. He first of all sanctioned an unparalleled extension of the range of their powers. If the Church is nothing more than a *congregatio fidelium*, it follows that the secular authorities must have the sole right to exercise all coercive powers, including powers over the Church. This does not of course impinge on the true Church, since it consists of a purely spiritual realm, but it definitely places the visible Church under the control of the godly prince. This does not mean that the *rex* becomes a *sacerdos*, nor that he is granted any authority to issue declarations about the content of religion. His duty is simply to foster the preaching of the gospel and to uphold the true faith. But it does mean that Luther is prepared to envisage a system of independent national Churches, in which the prince is given the right to appoint and dismiss the officers, as well as to control and dispose of the Church's property. The point is emphatically made at the start of the *Address*, where Luther affirms that 'since the temporal power is ordained of God to punish the wicked and protect the good, it should be left free to perform its office in the whole body of Christendom without restriction and without respect to persons, whether it affects Pope, bishops, priests, nuns or anyone else' (p. 130). For Luther, this means that the tremendous theoretical battle waged throughout the Middle Ages by the protagonists of the *regnum* and the *sacerdotium* is suddenly brought to an end. The idea of the Pope and Emperor as parallel and universal powers disappears, and the independent jurisdictions of the *sacerdotium* are handed over to the secular authorities. As Figgis expresses it, Luther destroyed 'the metaphor of the two swords; henceforth there should be but one, wielded by a rightly advised and godly prince' (Figgis, 1960, p. 84).

Luther committed himself to an even more radical defence of the secular authorities when he turned to consider the basis of the powers they might rightfully claim to exercise. He is emphatic in declaring that all their enactments must be treated as a direct gift and expression of God's providence. This makes it strange to say, as Allen has done, that Luther never concerns himself 'with any question of the nature or derivation of authority' (Allen, 1957, p. 18). Luther could scarcely be more explicit in acknowledging that all political authority is derived from God. The text to which he constantly recurs, and which he regards as the most important passage in the whole Bible on the theme of political obligation, is the injunction of St Paul (at the start of Chapter 13 of the Epistle to the Romans) that we should submit ourselves to the highest powers, and treat the powers that be as ordained of God. Luther's influence helped to make this the most cited of all texts on the foundations of political life throughout the age of the Reformation, and it furnishes the basis for the whole of his own argument in the tract on *Temporal Authority*. He begins by demanding that 'we must provide a sound basis for the civil law', and his opening argument is that this must above all be sought in St Paul's command: 'Let every soul be subject to the governing authority, for there is no authority except from God' (p. 85).

This commitment in turn leads Luther's discussion of the power of princes in two different directions. He first of all stresses that the prince has a duty to use the powers God has given him in a godly way, and above all to 'command for truth'. The main exposition of this theme occupies the final section of the tract on *Temporal Authority*. The prince 'must really devote himself' to his subjects. He must not only foster and maintain true religion amongst them, but also 'protect and maintain them in peace and plenty' and 'take unto himself the needs of his subjects, dealing with them as though they were his own needs' (p. 120). He must never exceed his authority, and must in particular avoid any attempt 'to command or compel anyone by force to believe this or that', since the regulation of such a 'secret, spiritual, hidden matter' can never be said to lie within his competence (pp. 107–8). His main duties are simply 'to bring about external peace', to 'prevent evil deeds' and in general to ensure that 'external things' are 'ordered and governed on earth' in a decent and godly way (pp. 92, 110).

Luther does not in fact believe that the princes and nobles of his own day have been educated in such a way as to make them adequately aware of these duties. As he insists at the end of his *Address* to the nobility, very few of them have any sense of 'what an awful responsibility it is to sit in high places' (p. 215). In the *Address* he denounces the training offered in the universities, where godly students are exposed to the false moral and political principles of 'the blind heathen teacher Aristotle' (p. 200). And in the treatise on *Temporal Authority* he pours scorn on the fashionable humanist ideals of noble and princely conduct, ridiculing all 'the princely amusements – dancing, hunting, racing, gaming and similar worldly pleasures' (p. 120). The effect of all these pernicious influences is that 'a wise prince is a mighty rare bird' (p. 113). Luther repeatedly insists that in practice the leaders of political society are usually 'consummate fools' and 'the worst scoundrels on earth' (pp. 106, 113). He even despairingly concludes at one point that 'God almighty has made our rulers mad' (p. 83).

Luther makes it clear, moreover, that no respect or obedience is due to such worthless rulers when they attempt to involve their subjects in their ungodly and scandalous ways. He sets a firm boundary to the authority of princes by insisting, in a favourite phrase, that they are merely the 'masks' or *larvae* of God. If a ruler tears off the mask which identifies him as God's lieutenant, and commands his subjects to act in evil or ungodly ways, he must never be obeyed. The subject must follow his conscience, even if this means disobeying his prince. The point is underlined in the form of a catechism at the end of the tract on *Temporal Authority*. 'What if a prince is in the wrong? Are his people bound to follow him then too?' The answer is 'No, for it is no one's duty to do wrong' (p. 125). Luther is unwavering in his emphasis on this aspect of his theory of political obligation. He treats all claims to absolute power as a misunderstanding and perversion of the authority God has granted to princes (Carlson, 1946, p. 267). And he repeatedly appeals for the confirmation of this view-point to a passage in the book of Acts which unequivocally demands that 'We must obey God (who desires the right) rather than men'.[1] For Luther, no less than for the later reformers who continually reverted to the same text, this is always taken to establish a decisive limitation on the general duty of political obedience.

Luther is equally pulled in the opposite direction, however, by his over-riding emphasis on the Pauline doctrine that 'the powers that be are ordained of God'. Despite his stress on the idea that an ungodly ruler must never be obeyed, he is no less insistent that such a ruler must never be actively resisted. Since all powers are ordained, this would still be tanta-mount, even in the case of a tyrant, to resisting the will of God. This harsh contrast between the equal duties of disobedience and of non-resistance to tyranny is clearly brought out in the central section of the tract on *Temporal Authority*. If the prince commands you to do evil, you must refuse, saying that 'it is not fitting that Lucifer should sit at the side of God'. If the prince should then 'seize your property on account of this and punish such disobedience', you must passively submit and 'thank God that you are worthy to suffer for the sake of the divine word' (p. 112). Luther in no way mitigates his previous emphasis on the claim that such behaviour is tyranny, and that we must never 'sanction it, or lift a little finger to conform, or obey'. But he still insists that there is nothing further to be done, since tyranny 'is not to be resisted but endured' (p. 112).

In the early 1530s, when it seemed likely that the armed forces of the Empire might destroy the Lutheran Church, Luther suddenly and per-manently changed his mind over this crucial issue. Throughout the 1520s, however, he had a special motive for wishing to emphasise the doctrine of non-resistance as strongly as possible. He shared the common fear of the reformers that their demands for religious change might become associated with political radicalism and in consequence discredited. This

---

[1] See *Temporal Authority*, p. 125. The allusion is to Acts, Chapter 5, v. 29.

was the reason for the *Sincere Admonition* of 1522, which Luther addressed 'to all Christians', warning them 'to guard against insurrection and rebellion'. He optimistically predicted that, in spite of the wickedness of the Catholic Church, there would not in fact be any rebellion against it. But he also took the opportunity to remind his readers in a far more alarmed tone that 'God has forbidden insurrection' and to plead with those 'who read and rightly understand my teaching' to recognise that there is nothing in it which excuses or justifies any attempt to bring about political revolution (pp. 63, 65).

When the Peasants' Revolt broke out in Germany in 1524, Luther's fears that the radicals might distort his political teachings reached a peak of hysteria, and prompted him to react to the revolt with shocking brutality.[1] Before the serious fighting broke out, his initial response was to travel to Thuringia, one of the centres of unrest, and to publish there an eirenic *Admonition to Peace*. This merely urged the princes to attempt conciliation, and reminded the peasants that 'the fact that the rulers are wicked and unjust does not excuse disorder and rebellion' (p. 25). By May of 1525, however, the peasants had won major victories in Thuringia, and were pillaging throughout the south of Germany. Luther then responded with his famous outburst *Against the Robbing and Murdering Hordes of Peasants*. This brief but shattering tirade simply takes its stand squarely on St Paul's command that 'every person be subject to the governing authorities'. The peasants have totally ignored this command, and 'are now deliberately and violently breaking this oath of obedience'. This constitutes such a 'terrible and horrible sin' that all of them 'have abundantly merited death'. Since they have all attempted to resist the will and ordinance of God, we may safely conclude that all of them have already 'forfeited body and soul' (pp. 49–50).

It was not merely an immediate terror of rebellion which caused Luther to lay such an absolute emphasis on the duty of non-resistance, and it is impossible to excuse the tone of his tract against the peasants by treating it as a momentary aberration induced by an immediate political crisis. The stance he took up was a direct outcome of his key theological belief that the whole of the existing framework of social and political order is a direct reflection of God's will and providence. This appears most clearly in the major political tract he published in the year following the Peasants' Revolt on the question of *Whether Soldiers too can be Saved*. This begins by repeating all over again that the people must be prepared to 'suffer everything that can happen' rather than 'fight against your lord and

---

[1] For a survey of discussions about Luther's role, see Mackensen, 1964. For a full account of his activities, see Mackinnon, 1925–30, vol. 3, pp. 159–210.

tyrant' (pp. 112–13). Some of the reasons are practical: 'it is easy to change a government, but it is difficult to get one that is better, and the danger is that you will not' (p. 112). But the main reason is essentially theological: since the establishment of political rule lies 'in the will and hand of God', it follows that 'those who resist their rulers resist the ordinance of God, as St Paul teaches' (pp. 112, 126).

It might seem that such a stringent doctrine of non-resistance is bound to lead to one awkward consequence: it appears to make God the author of evil, since it commits us to saying that God ordains the rule of the madman and tyrant no less than that of the godly prince. Luther acknowledges and deals with this difficulty in the tract on whether soldiers can be saved. He propounds an extremely influential answer, derived from St Augustine, which is not merely compatible with his basic doctrine of non-resistance but actually contrives to enhance it. He simply insists that the reason why evil and tyrannical rulers are from time to time ordained by God is, as Job says, 'because of the people's sins'. It is 'blind and perverse' of the people to think that sheer power sustains the wicked ruler, and thus that 'the tyrant rules because he is such a scoundrel'. The truth is 'that he is ruling not because he is a scoundrel but because of the people's sin' (p. 109).

Luther's major political tracts may thus be said to embody two guiding principles, both of which were destined to exercise an immense historical influence. He treats the New Testament, and especially the injunctions of St Paul, as the final authority on all fundamental questions about the proper conduct of social and political life. And he claims that the political stance which is actually prescribed in the New Testament is one of complete Christian submission to the secular authorities, the range of whose powers he crucially extends, grounding them in such a way that their rule can never in any circumstances be legitimately resisted. The articulation of these principles involved no appeal to the scholastic concept of a universe ruled by law, and scarcely any appeal even to the concept of an intuited law of nature: Luther's final word is always based on the Word of God.

2

The forerunners of Lutheranism

Luther's new theology, and the social and political doctrines he derived from it, soon became officially accepted throughout a wide area of northern Europe. The earliest moves were made in Germany, where the Elector Frederick the Wise of Saxony effectively led the way when he granted protection to Luther after his excommunication in 1520 (Fife, 1957, pp. 586–91). Five years later, when Frederick was succeeded by his son the Elector John, Saxony became a Lutheran principality. The same year saw the acceptance of Lutheranism by Albert of Hohenzollern in the Duchy of Prussia, and in the following year the young Landgrave Philip of Hesse held a synod at Homberg at which he imposed a Lutheran Church ordinance throughout his territories. By 1528 the list of German princes who had left the Catholic Church included the Dukes of Brunswick and Schleswig, the Count of Mansfeld and the Margrave of Brandenburg-Ansbach; by 1534 they had been joined by the rulers of Nassau, Pomerania and Württemberg. Meanwhile a number of Imperial cities had become converted. By 1525 the Lutherans had gained control in Altenburg, Bremen, Erfurt, Gotha, Magdeburg and Nuremberg; by 1534 they had been joined by Augsburg, Frankfurt, Hanover, Strasbourg and Ulm.[1]

Scandinavia was the next region to adopt the new faith. The Reformation first took effective root in Denmark, after the Duke of Schleswig Holstein succeeded the exiled Christian II as King Frederick I in 1523. He mounted a successful attack on the Pope's right to confirm Danish bishops in the Herredag of 1526, and followed this up four years later by countenancing the Lutheran Forty-Three Articles prepared by Hans Tausen, 'the Danish Luther'. After a civil war and an interregnum in the early 1530s, the throne was finally won by the reforming King Christian III in 1536. He immediately removed the Catholic bishops, who had constituted the main resistance to his succession, and officially completed

---

[1] For these details see Dickens, 1966b, pp. 74–6, a brilliant synthesis to which I am much indebted.

the Reformation, which was then imposed on Denmark's dependencies, Iceland and Norway (Dunkley, 1948, pp. 45–6, 62). A parallel movement developed in Sweden after Gustav Vasa's success in the war of independence against Denmark in 1523. The first official moves were made at the Diet of Vasteras in 1527, when Lutheran preaching was freely permitted for the first time. The Reformation was finally completed at a further Diet in 1544, after a Catholic reaction in the south had been crushed (Roberts, 1968, p. 136).

The next areas to take up the new religion were Scotland and England. There seemed a chance of attaining an officially sponsored reformation in Scotland in the early 1540s, after the defeat at Solway Moss brought an increase of English influence. The Scots went on to ally with France, however, which instead brought them under the influence of the counter-reformation. The result was that they needed the further initiative of the radical Calvinists, and the revolution which they inspired in the late 1550s, before they finally accepted the Reformation. By contrast, the Reformation in England was a gradual and at most stages an official movement. It began with Henry VIII's breach with Rome in the early 1530s, and with the Parliamentary attack on the powers of the Church; it swung in a more doctrinal (and more Calvinist) direction under Edward VI between 1547 and the accession of Mary in 1553; and it was completed after Mary's death in 1558 with the successful implanting of that unique hybrid, the Anglican Church settlement.

The next question must clearly be to ask why Luther's message, and in particular its social and political implications, should have proved so powerfully attractive in so many different countries. There are doubtless many perspectives from which this question can be viewed, each of which may serve to suggest its own set of answers. To the historian of political ideas, however, the most important consideration must undoubtedly be the fact that Luther's political doctrines, and the theological premises on which they were based, were closely affiliated with – and partly derived from -- a number of deeply-rooted traditions of late medieval thought. As soon as Luther voiced his protest, the exponents of these traditions tended to become drawn into the wider movement of reform, strengthening it with their presence and helping to ensure that Luther's message was at first heard and analysed receptively, and in turn achieved an immediate and widespread influence.

THE INSUFFICIENCY OF MAN

It is evident in the first place that Luther's distinctive theology was to a considerable extent derived from two powerful currents of late medieval speculation about the relationship between man and God. As we have seen, Luther laid a special emphasis on the insufficiency of man's reason, on the correspondingly absolute nature of God's freedom, and on the consequent need for the sinner to place the whole of his trust in God's righteousness. These tenets echoed a number of doctrines already associated with the *devotio moderna*, a mystical movement developed by the Brethren of the Common Life in Germany and the Netherlands at the end of the fourteenth century. The movement was inaugurated by the saintly Gerard Groote (1340–84) with a campaign of preaching in which he stressed the need for a reformation of morals and defended the ideals of apostolic poverty and the communal life (Hyma, 1965, pp. 28–35). The central belief animating his teaching, which he may have derived from such earlier fourteenth-century mystics as Meister Eckhart (d. 1327) and his pupil Johannes Tauler (*c.* 1300–31), was that all the efforts men make to commend themselves to God are merely reflections of a sinful vanity, and thus that the aim of the faithful soul must be to remain passive in its acceptance of God's grace (Hyma, 1965, pp. 17–24). Groote's disciples went on to form themselves into monastic communities – the first being established at Windesheim in the Netherlands – in which they sought to train themselves, by teaching and mystical exercises, to cultivate this genuinely submissive relationship with God (Hyma, 1965, pp. 59–62). During the early fifteenth century these Brotherhoods began to spread into northern Germany – the first was formed at Munster in 1401 – and soon came to exercise an important influence. Their mysticism helped to stimulate a number of powerful writings, including the anonymous *German Theology* of *c.* 1400 and above all the *Imitation of Christ* by Thomas à Kempis (1380–1471) (Hyma, 1965, pp. 166–70). But their main influence derived from their Augustinian emphasis on man's fallen nature and his need to rediscover a personal faith in God's redeeming grace. This inspired a number of leading German theologians in the latter part of the fifteenth century, whose development of these themes has sometimes caused them to be labelled 'reformers before the Reformation'.[1] One of the most striking instances of this trend can be seen in the work of Johann Wessel Gansfort (*c.* 1419–89), who studied with the Brethren of the Com-

---

[1] The title of the influential study by Ullmann, 1855. Cf. also the account of the 'reminders' of Luther to be found in Wessel Gansfort in Ritter, 1971, esp. p. 32.

mon Life at Zwolle for seventeen years from 1432 until he moved in 1449 to the University of Cologne (Miller, 1917, I, 43–9). He gives a clear statement of his outlook in the open letter which he wrote in 1489 to Jacob Hoeck, who had attempted to defend the Papacy's practice of issuing plenary indulgences.[1] Gansfort replies that this is to misunderstand the nature of man's relationship with God. No human act, not even an act of the Pope's, can help a sinner to achieve merit. It is 'absurd and unbefitting' to believe that a mere 'human decree' can change 'the value of an act good in God's eyes' (p. 99). The only way in which it is possible to attain merit is through 'the infusion of grace' which God in his mercy may choose to bestow upon us (p. 110). This in turn means that all the efforts of the Papacy and the Church to help men attain their salvation are irrelevant, since 'the Pope cannot give grace to anyone', and 'cannot discern whether he himself or anyone else is in a state of grace' (p. 117). The only hope for the faithful sinner is to enter into a personal and trusting relationship with God, treating the scriptures and the Apostolic traditions as his 'only rule of faith' (p. 105).

The other powerful strand of late medieval thought which was mirrored in Luther's theology was the movement known as the *via moderna*, the last major school of medieval scholasticism. The *via moderna* originally evolved in the early fourteenth century as a conscious reaction against the *via antiqua* of the Thomists, with their characteristic contention that reason as well as faith has a role to play in the understanding of God's purposes, since nature is never contradicted but is merely 'perfected' by faith. The history of later medieval scholasticism can virtually be written in terms of the progressive loosening and eventual breaking of these alleged links. The process may be said to have begun with the work of Duns Scotus, but the most original and influential exponent of the *via moderna* was William of Ockham (*c*. 1285–1347), whose teachings were developed by a large number of distinguished followers in the course of the next century, including Robert Holcot, Gregory of Rimini, Pierre d'Ailly and Jean Gerson. One of their most distinctive doctrines was a radical, almost Humean critique of the extent to which the faculty of reason can be deployed to attain genuine knowledge. Very little space is left for reason in ethical debate: this is treated mainly as a matter of arguing about the commands and prohibitions of God. Nor is any significant role assigned to reason in theology: as Ockham himself insists, the dogmas of revealed religion, even the question of God's existence and attributes,

---

[1] My quotations are taken from the partial translation of the letter published in Oberman, 1966. See *sub* Gansfort, Wessel, *Letter in Reply to Hoeck*, in the bibliography of primary sources.

'cannot evidently be known' by reason and can be 'proved in theology only under the supposition of faith'.[1]

Ockham's attack on the *via antiqua* was revived at the end of the fifteenth century by a large number of disciples, two of whom went on to become theologians of considerable significance in their own right. One was John Mair (1467–1550), who began his long and brilliant teaching career at Paris in 1495, lecturing on the *Sentences* of Peter Lombard in an avowedly Ockhamist style. The other was Gabriel Biel (1410–95), the *Doctor profundissimus*. Biel turned away from the academic profession in mid-career in order to join the Brethren of the Common Life, but returned in 1484 to teach the doctrines of the *via moderna* at the new University of Tübingen, which he rapidly helped to make famous as a centre of nominalist scholarship (Oberman, 1963, pp. 14–16; Landeen, 1951, pp. 24–9; Burns, 1954, pp. 83–4).

Biel's influence was such that, a generation before Luther's name became known, two key issues were being discussed in the German universities in a spirit which, while Ockhamist in inspiration, appears in retrospect almost wholly Lutheran in character. One was the question of man's understanding of God. We already find this problem being debated in a remarkably Lutheran style in a work such as the treatise on *Eternal Predestination* written by Johann von Staupitz (1468–1524), who attended the University of Tübingen between 1497 and 1500, where he was taught by several of Gabriel Biel's immediate followers (Oberman, 1963, p. 19). Staupitz no longer conceives of God – in the manner of the Thomists – as the author of natural laws which it is possible for men to apprehend with their reason and employ in the conduct of their lives. God instead appears as an omnipotent and large inscrutable will, constantly but apparently arbitrarily at work in the world. We know that God is 'of infinite power and majesty', but 'His wisdom is unfathomable' and 'cannot be measured' (p. 177). If we attempt to appraise Him with our reason, He will inevitably 'transcend our every faculty' (p. 178). We can only hope to know Him 'through faith in Christ', for 'knowledge fails and scientific proof is out of the question' in relation to the understanding of His ways (p. 178).

The other key issue discussed in a similar style was the question of the relationship between merit and salvation (cf. Vignaux, 1934). Staupitz also raises this problem in his treatise on predestination, arguing that 'man's nature is incapable of knowing or wanting or doing good', and concluding that if anyone is saved, this must be 'due to grace and not to

---

[1] For these contentions see especially Ockham's *Quodlibeta* (disputations 'on all subjects') in *Philosophical Writings*, ed. Boehner, esp. pp. 100, 125.

nature' (pp. 182, 186). 'Let no one pride himself', he warns, 'that it is
because of his merits that he is enrolled among the faithful and let no one
claim for nature what properly belongs to grace' (p. 178). The same doctrine is even more strongly affirmed by Biel himself, who states it most
accessibly in his sermon on *The Circumcision of the Lord*. He insists that
'without grace it is absolutely impossible' for anyone 'to love God
meritoriously' and so to be saved (p. 170). But he adds that it is equally
impossible for 'a grace which would suffice unto salvation' to be 'acquired
through our works like other moral habits' (pp. 167–8). So he concludes that the attainment of grace, the key to salvation, must be
entirely 'a gift of God supernaturally infused into the soul' of the
helpless sinner, who can never hope to deserve or acquire it for himself
(p. 168).

It would obviously be an overstatement to imply that Luther's own
theology is simply a logical outcome of these earlier intellectual movements. Luther never shared the mystical belief that the faithful are
intended by God to engage in spiritual exercises in order to help them
find 'the paths which lead to a union with God'; his concept of *fiducia*
was even more passive than such a belief would presuppose (Post, 1968,
p. 314). Moreover, he rejected even the limited value which the exponents
of the *via moderna* continued to place on the idea of human freedom: he
far outstripped them in his despairing sense that it is absolutely impossible
for a man to act in such a way as to make himself worthy of being saved
(Vignaux, 1971, pp. 108–10). Nevertheless, Luther was unquestionably a
product of both these traditions of thought. As a student at the University
of Erfurt between 1501 and 1505 he received a formal training in the *via
moderna*, his teachers being Jodocus Trutvetter and Arnold von Usingen,
both of whom had in turn been pupils of Gabriel Biel (Oberman, 1963,
pp. 9, 17). During this period he must also have come into contact with
the faculty of theology, which had by this time become one of the leading
centres for the study of the *devotio moderna*, with Lurtz, Wartburg and
several other prominent Augustinians teaching there (Meier, 1955). Soon
after this, Luther turned to the systematic study of the *devotio moderna*
himself. It now seems doubtful if the traditional story that he received his
schooling in Magdeburg from the Brethren of the Common Life can be
credited, but he certainly lodged with them in 1496–7, and several of his
mentors were greatly influenced by their works (Post, 1968, pp. 628–30).
This applies above all to Staupitz, Luther's personal counsellor in the
Augustinian order and his predecessor in the Chair of Theology at
Wittenberg (Steinmetz, 1968, pp. 5, 10). Luther himself always regarded

Staupitz as one of the most formative influences on his intellectual development, and it was on Staupitz's advice that he undertook his intensive study of the German mystics (Saarnivaara, 1951, pp. 22–43, 53–8). Luther read and annotated Tauler's *Sermons* in 1516, and his first published work was an edition of the *German Theology*, which he produced in the same year, assuming it to be a summary of Tauler's works (Fife, 1957, pp. 219–20). He always recognised, moreover, that there were close affinities between the *devotio moderna* and his own religious thought. He declared in the *Preface* to his edition of the *German Theology* that 'no book except the Bible and St Augustine has come to my attention from which I have learnt more about God, Christ, man, and all things' (p. 75). And when he studied the letters of Wessel Gansfort in 1522, he felt moved to exclaim that 'if I had read this before, it could well have left the impression with my enemies that I copied everything from Wessel – so much are our two minds at one' (Oberman, 1966, p. 18).

The significance of these affinities and influences lies in the fact that, to anyone imbued with the tenets of the *via moderna* or the *devotio moderna*, there was much in Luther's message which was bound to appear both familiar and attractive. It is thus not surprising to find that some of the leading pioneers of the German Reformation began by receiving their training in one or other of these disciplines. Matthaus Zell (1477–1548) provides an important example of an early Lutheran leader who evidently owed his conversion as much to the influence of the *devotio moderna* as to the teachings of Luther himself (Chrisman, 1967, pp. 68, 73, 92). And there are many examples of Lutheran leaders who began as students and teachers of scholastic theology, and clearly found themselves attuned by this training to recognise and embrace the doctrines of the Reformation. This is true of Johannes Eberlin von Günzburg (*c.* 1470–1533), who began as a student of the *via moderna* at Basle and at first joined the Franciscans, the Order of which Ockham himself had been a member. He was converted in 1520 as soon as he read Luther's works, and went on to become one of the most prolific of the early Lutheran preachers and writers, publishing nearly twenty books on political as well as theological themes (Werner, 1905, pp. 9–11, 78–9). The same is true of Nicolas von Amsdorf (1483–1547), who began as a teacher of scholastic philosophy at Wittenberg, where he was employed to lecture, at the time of Luther's first outburst in 1517, on the logic of Aristotle and the Ockhamist commentaries of Gabriel Biel (Bergendoff, 1928, pp. 68–9). He found himself immediately attracted to the Lutheran cause, and later became one of the most radical of the early Lutheran ministers, both as a theologian and as a political theorist. Finally, the same line of development can be traced in

the career of Andreas Carlstadt (*c.* 1477–1541), Luther's original lieutenant at Wittenberg. He began as a teacher of Thomism, but shifted to a
strongly Augustinian position by 1518, and soon developed into such an
extreme mystic and iconoclast that he proved too radical even for the
Lutherans to tolerate (Sider, 1974, pp. 7, 17–19, 174–89).

THE CHURCH'S SHORTCOMINGS

Luther's attack on clerical abuses also echoed a number of attitudes
already prevalent in later medieval Europe. As we have seen, he focused
his main attention on the shortcomings of the Papacy, insisting on the
need to return to the authority of the scriptures and to re-establish a
simpler and less worldly form of apostolic Church. This line of attack
had already been pursued with no less vehemence by a growing band of
anti-clerical writers in the generation immediately preceding the Reformation. Much of the resulting literature of invective and abuse had been
produced by the most learned humanists of the age, but they had generally written a self-consciously demotic style, usually publishing in the
vernacular and often presenting their arguments in the form of plays and
satires in verse. The most influential contribution to this *genre* was
undoubtedly *The Ship of Fools* by Sebastian Brant (1458–1521), which
originally appeared in 1494 and went through six further editions within
Brant's lifetime (Zeydel, 1967, p. 90). Brant was a humanist by training
and a teacher at the University of Basle, who won the admiration of some
of the most outstanding scholars of his day. Reuchlin and Wimpfeling
were amongst his friends, while Erasmus actually composed a poem in
his honour, and described him to Wimpfeling as 'the incomparable Brant'
(Allen, 1906–58, II, p. 24). His *Ship of Fools* takes the form of a long
sequence of verses (the original contained a hundred and twelve) in which
all the evils of the age are ridiculed as nothing but follies. Many of Brant's
fiercest attacks are directed against the fools who rule the Church. There
are separate chapters denouncing the growing contempt for Holy Writ,
the universal vices of simony and nepotism, and the 'abuses of spirituality' perpetrated by the hordes of gluttonous monks and ignorant
priests. Above all, Brant bewails the irreligious tone of the age, the general
'ruin and decay of the faith of Christ' being brought about by the wealth
and worldliness of the Church (fos lxviii, clii, ccxii).

Brant's work was widely admired, and soon began to be imitated by a
number of humanist critics of the Church in France and England. Jean
Bouchet (1476–1557), whom we have already encountered as one of the
leading *Grands Rhétoriqueurs* at the Court of Louis XII, produced an

imitation of *The Ship of Fools* in 1500, in which the simony and immor-
ality of the Church's leaders were savagely satirised (Renaudet, 1953,
pp. 319–20). He went on to develop his attack in *A Lamentation on the
Church Militant* in 1512, in which the Pope was denounced for making
war on his own flock, while the avidity of the clergy and the dissolute lives
of the prelates were again held up to ridicule (Renaudet, 1953, p. 549;
Hamon, 1901, pp. 282–90). Bouchet's works in turn appear to have
inspired Pierre Gringore (*c.* 1485–1538), who published a morality-play
in 1512 entitled *The Folly of the Prince of Fools*, containing an even more
scurrilous attack on the Papacy and the Church. The Church is depicted
as 'Mother Fool', who confesses at her first entrance that 'men say I have
lost my wits in my old age' (p. 54). At first she appears imposingly in the
guise of 'Mother Church', but very soon her folly and hypocrisy become
clear. She is greedy for money, cynical about the value of 'good faith', and
anxious above all to ensure that she succeeds in 'keeping a hold over
temporal affairs by fair means or foul' (pp. 55, 57, 59). She spends her
time plotting and machinating with all the fools of the age, and ends by
making it obvious that her real ambition is to acquire worldly glory for
herself (p. 70).

The impact of this literature soon began to be felt in England. Alexander
Barclay (*c.* 1475–1552) published translations of both Gringore and Brant
between 1506 and 1509, while John Skelton (*c.* 1460–1529) managed to
assimilate all these influences, and went on to produce his famous series
of anti-clerical satires, using a verse-form which he virtually invented for
the purpose. The greatest of these is *Colin Clout*, which was probably
completed in 1522 (Heiserman, 1961, p. 193). This has usually been
regarded simply as an attack on Wolsey, but Heiserman has plausibly
argued that the Cardinal is intended to be seen merely as the most blatant
of the Church's spiritual failures, while the real targets are all the members
of the clerical estate as well as the general disorders of the age (Heiserman,
1961, pp. 196–8). Skelton begins by rudely reminding the clergy

> How they take no heed
> Their silly sheep to feed (p. 284).

He then goes on to reiterate all the familiar charges against the leaders of
the Church. He begins by stressing their ignorance, declaring that

> They have none instruction
> To make a true construction . . .
> Some can scantly read,
> And yet he will not dread
> For to keep a cure (p. 290).

Next he denounces them as corrupt and mercenary:

> Men say, for silver and gold
> Mitres are bought and sold . . .
> And no more you make
> Of simony, men say,
> But a child's play! (p. 291).

And finally, of course, he insists that all clerics are lecherous, and that all the money given by the pious laity for the saying of masses is 'spent among wanton lasses' (p. 295).

The most famous humanist satire in which there are clear signs of Brant's influence, and in which the device of treating the vices as follies is copied, is of course *The Praise of Folly* by Erasmus. This was first published in 1509, with a dedication to Sir Thomas More. (The Latin title, *Moriae Encomium*, includes a pun on More's name.) Folly mounts a rostrum and delivers a classical oration in her own defence. She first describes her powers, arguing that all warfare depends on folly, and that men 'drew together into civil society' out of folly and flattery (pp. 30, 34). She then goes on to enumerate her many admirers. These include all the leaders of the learned professions, in particular the lawyers (p. 76) as well as all the princes and their courtiers, by whom folly is 'worshipped sincerely and, as becomes gentlemen, frankly' (p. 93). But the greatest admirers of folly are the monks, the priests, the bishops and especially the Pope. 'Were wisdom to descend on them, how it would inconvenience them!' It would 'lose them all that wealth and honour, all those possessions, triumphal progresses, offices, dispensations, tributes and indulgences' (p. 98). And so the oration culminates in yet another sweeping attack on the corruptions and abuses of the Papacy and the entire Catholic Church.

One result of these affinities between Luther and the humanists was that, as soon as Luther made his initial attack on indulgences in 1517, a number of distinguished humanists found themselves strongly attracted towards his cause. This happened most obviously in Germany, in the case of such leading humanists as Crotus Rubianus (1480–1545), Willibald Pirckheimer (1470–1530) and Jacob Wimpfeling (1450–1528). Rubianus eventually repudiated the reformers, but he began by hailing Luther as 'the father of my country' and even dared, as rector of the University of Erfurt, to give Luther an official reception when he passed through on his way to the Diet of Worms in 1520 (Holborn, 1937, p. 124). Pirckheimer similarly ended up by disavowing the reformers, but his disgust at the corruption of the Church at first caused him to welcome Luther as 'a wonderful talent' and to defend him in print by writing a scandalous attack on Johann Eck, Luther's opponent at the Leipzig Disputations of 1518 (Spitz, 1963, pp. 177–9). A similar story can be told of Wimpfeling, who finally made his peace with the Papacy, but also began by welcoming Luther as an evident ally in his own campaigns against the abuses of the Church, and spoke of him at this time as someone who 'acts not only in his teaching but in his whole life like a Christian and evangelical man' (Spitz, 1963, pp. 53, 57–8).

A similar pattern of attraction and ultimate hesitation can be traced in France in the case of such leading humanists as Josse Clichtove (1472–1543) and his teacher Jacques Lefèvre d'Etaples (1461–1536). Lefèvre began to concern himself actively with the question of Church reform in 1521, when he was summoned by Guillaume Briçonnet, the recently appointed Bishop of Meaux, to help in the reorganisation of his diocese. Soon Lefèvre became the leading spirit amongst a group of devout humanists who began to meet at Meaux, and was visited there by a number of scholars (including Farel) whose concern with the reform of the Church eventually drove them into the Protestant camp. The Meaux group itself never became Lutheran: Briçonnet found little difficulty in defending his orthodoxy when he was arraigned before the Parlement of Paris in 1525 to answer a charge of heresy, and Clichtove always dissociated himself from the group, evidently in order to forestall any such charges. There is no doubt, however, that even Clichtove found himself (as Massaut delicately puts it) 'unable to resist a certain attraction for the theology of Wittenberg' (Massaut, 1968, II, p. 84). This derived in particular from his early doubts about indulgences and his lifelong concern with the need to reform the monasteries (Massaut, 1968, I, 433ff; II, 80ff). And it is clear in the case of Lefèvre d'Etaples that the same attraction was experienced with far greater strength. As early as 1512 he published an edition of St Paul's Epistles in which he argued that grace and faith represent the only means of attaining salvation. And later he went on to devote most of his scholarly energies – very much in the spirit of the reformers – to producing a vernacular version of the scriptures, publishing a French translation of the Psalms in 1524, followed by a translation of the entire Bible in 1530 (Daniel-Rops, 1961, pp. 368–72; cf. Rice, 1962).

The most important consequence, however, of these affinities between Luther's outlook and that of the humanists was that, as soon as he made his definitive breach with the Church, many prominent humanists felt impelled to follow him. This in turn helped to strengthen the intellectual foundations of the Reformation, and thereby played a key role in helping to foster its wider influence.

In Germany the leading example of such an immediate conversion is that of Philipp Melanchthon (1496–1540), the great-nephew of Reuchlin and the most prominent intellectual amongst Luther's early disciples. Melanchthon began by displaying a precocious and outstanding talent for the humanities. He learnt Greek under Rudolf Agricola at Heidelberg, and by the time he was twenty-two he had published a Greek grammar as well as an edition of Plutarch. He was appointed in 1518 to the Chair of Greek language and literature at Wittenberg, and it was there, under Luther's influence, that he abandoned the Catholic Church. Within a remarkably short time his status as an expositor of Lutheranism came to be second only to that of Luther himself, and it was Melanchthon, with the publication of his *Common Topics in Theology* in 1521, who provided the earliest systematic statement of the Lutheran faith (Manschreck, 1958, pp. 33, 40, 44).

Melanchthon was only the most prominent amongst a number of German humanists who entered the Lutheran Church by a similar path, and several of the others – such as Osiander and Capito – were of almost equal stature. Andreas Osiander (1498–1552) began as a typical humanist scholar, first studying the classics and later acting as a teacher of Hebrew. He then went to study at Wittenberg, and there he was immediately converted under Luther's influence. After this he moved to Nuremberg as a preacher in 1521, and soon achieved fame as one of the most eloquent expositors of the Lutheran faith (Strauss, 1966, p. 164). A similar story can be told of Wolfgang Capito (1478–1541). He also began as a student of Greek, working with Erasmus himself on his edition of the New Testament, and subsequently gained a reputation as one of the best Hebrew scholars in Germany (Chrisman, 1967, p. 88). He was at first hostile to Luther, and helped to prepare the case presented against him at the Diet of Worms. This evidently disturbed his conscience, however, and during the next year he decided to visit Wittenberg, where he too fell under Luther's influence and was converted. He thereupon resigned the position he held with the Archbishop of Mainz and moved to Strasbourg, where – like Osiander at Nuremberg – he soon went on to play a crucial role in the conversion of the city to the Lutheran faith (Chrisman, 1967 pp. 89–90).

The leaders of the Reformation in Scandinavia all followed a similar line of development. This can be seen most clearly in the careers of Olaus Petri (1493–1552) and his younger brother Laurentius (1499–1573), the two greatest propagandists of the reform movement in Sweden. Both

received a humanist education, and Olaus in particular became a competent Greek scholar – a talent he later put to work in the service of the
Reformation by helping to make the first translation of the New Testament into Swedish in 1526 (Bergendoff, 1928, pp. 102, 107). Both went
to study at Wittenberg in 1516, both were immediately converted, and
both returned to Sweden by the end of the 1520s, where they became the
outstanding spokesmen in favour of Gustav Vasa's breach with Rome
(Bergendoff, 1928, pp. 75–6). The same pattern can be discerned in the
case of Tausen and Pedersen, the intellectual leaders of the Reformation
in Denmark. Hans Tausen (1494–1561) provides a further example of a
humanist scholar who became converted to Lutheranism while studying
at Wittenberg (Dunkley, 1948, pp. 42–3). Christian Pedersen (c. 1480–
1554) provides yet another and even clearer case of the same influences
producing the same results. He began by following a humanist training
at Paris, where he published a scholarly edition of Saxo's Danish chronicles
and received the congratulations of Erasmus for his achievement. He then
went to study at Wittenberg, where he became converted to Lutheranism
in 1526. Thereafter – like Olaus Petri – he devoted his humanist talents
to the service of the Reformation, translating and publishing a number of
Luther's books in Denmark in 1531, and supplying the first Danish
translation of the Bible in 1550 (Dunkley, 1948, pp. 99–113).

The same pattern is even more clearly repeated amongst the earliest
leaders of the Reformation in England. The most famous instance is provided by the career of William Tyndale (c. 1495–1536). He began his
studies at Oxford, but found it full of 'the old barking curs, Duns's
disciples'. He accordingly transferred to Cambridge around 1516, where
he was able to begin his intensive study of Hebrew as well as of Latin
and Greek (Mozley, 1937, pp. 16–18). It was in the course of these studies
that he became converted to Lutheranism. He then went on to become the
most energetic as well as the greatest of the early Lutheran propagandists
in England. He produced the first systematic exposition of Lutheran
political ideas in English when he published *The Obedience of a Christian
Man* in 1528. And he engaged in the most famous literary duel of the
English Reformation when he replied to Sir Thomas More's denunciation
of the reformers in his *Answer to Sir Thomas More's Dialogue* in 1531.
As with Petri and Pedersen, however, Tyndale's most important contribution was made as a translator of the Bible. It was he who produced,
in 1525, the first printed version of the New Testament in English, and
he followed this in 1530 with a translation of the Pentateuch made directly
from the Hebrew texts (Mozley, 1937, pp. 51–2, 80–1).

Tyndale was only one amongst a considerable group of young Cambridge scholars who were attracted in a similar way from humanism to the Lutheran Church. The intellectual foundations of the English Reformation were in fact largely laid in Cambridge at this time. Some of the earliest discussions of the heresy took place at the White Horse tavern, which soon became known as 'little Germany' (Porter, 1958, pp. 45–9). And when the heresy eventually became accepted as official doctrine, all but one of the thirteen divines who met in 1549 to draw up the first Protestant Prayer Book for the Church of England were members of Cambridge University (Rupp, 1949, p. 19n.). One of the earliest converts in Cambridge was Thomas Bilney (d. 1531), who spoke of the Midas touch which transformed his humanist studies into a religious shape (Porter, 1958, pp. 41, 44). The example set by Bilney's saintliness rapidly led to the conversion of several other young scholars. The most important was Robert Barnes (1495–1540), who had returned to Cambridge from Louvain in 1521, totally absorbed in the new humanist learning, and with a special enthusiasm for the comedies of Terence and Plautus (Clebsch, 1964, pp. 43–4). He soon turned with equal enthusiasm to the doctrines of the Reformation, and went on to become one of the most radical and outspoken of the early English Lutherans. He travelled (like Tyndale) to Wittenberg to study with Luther himself, and published a series of important political as well as theological tracts during the 1530s, before being arrested in the conservative reaction at the end of Henry VIII's reign and burnt as a heretic in 1540. Barnes in turn appears to have played a decisive part in the conversion of Miles Coverdale (c. 1488–1569), who is characterised by his biographer as having made the same progress 'from Erasmus through Colet to Luther' (Mozley, 1953, pp. 2–3). Coverdale seems to have had a special admiration for Tyndale, and under his influence went on to produce the first complete English translation of the Bible ever to be published (Mozley, 1953, p. 3). Finally, the same line of development can also be traced in the career of Sir John Cheke (1514–57), unquestionably the greatest scholar amongst the English humanists of this period. Cheke began as a dazzlingly precocious teacher of Greek at Cambridge in the late 1530s, and was appointed the first Regius Professor of the subject in 1540, at the age of twenty-six (Jordan, 1968, p. 41). The date of his conversion is uncertain, but he was definitely a committed Lutheran by the end of the 1530s. After this he seems to have devoted some considerable energy to converting his pupils – and in this way he was able, by a quirk of history, to make a unique contribution to the eventual acceptance of the Reformation in England. He evidently had a hand in the conversion of Becon, Lever and possibly Ponet in the 1530s – already an achievement of some significance in relation to the later history of

Protestant political thought. But his unique opportunity came in 1544, when he was summoned to Court by Henry VIII and appointed tutor to the king's only son, the future King Edward VI (Jordan, 1968, pp. 41–2). Strype reports in his account of Cheke's career that the relationship between the prince and his tutor became a close one, and that even after Edward's accession in 1547 Cheke remained 'always at his elbow' in order 'to inform and teach him' (Strype, 1821, p. 22). Whatever Henry VIII's intentions may have been (and they have never been very satisfactorily explained) the outcome was that his heir grew up as a Protestant no less convinced than his teacher – a consequence which in turn had an incalculable but arguably a decisive effect in furthering the cause of the Reformation in England.

THE CHURCH'S POWERS: THE THEOLOGICAL DEBATE

If we turn finally from Luther's denunciations of Church abuses to his more fundamental attack on the very idea of the Church as a jurisdictional authority, we again find him echoing a number of arguments already prevalent in later medieval thought. As we have seen, Luther's concept of the Church as nothing more than a *congregatio fidelium* implied a strong dislike of the Papacy's role as a landlord and tax-gatherer, a distrust of its absolute powers over the Church, and a resentment of its capacity to act as an independent legal authority, operating its own code of canon law and cutting across the jurisdictions of the secular authorities with its own system of ecclesiastical courts. All these criticisms had already been voiced with mounting animosity throughout the later Middle Ages, both by the theological opponents of Papal monarchy, and by the numerous allies and spokesmen of the secular authorities themselves.

The theological attack was in part an heretical one, deriving from a long-standing tradition of evangelical opposition to the wealth and jurisdictions of the Church. In its most vocal form this opposition can be dated from the rise of the Lollard and Hussite movements at the end of the fourteenth century, both of which had centred on the demand for a simpler and more apostolic form of Christianity, and had called for the Church to act less as a jurisdictional and more as a purely pastoral authority. The Lollard movement originated in England with the campaign of preaching and writing initiated by John Wyclif (c. 1329–84) and a number of his clerical disciples at Oxford, including Aston, Repington and Hereford (McFarlane, 1972, p. 78). Their message appears to have been heard receptively in Scotland as well as England, and the movement soon began to attract a considerable degree of lay support. When the

Parliament met in 1395, a group of Lollard partisans even succeeded in presenting a manifesto to the Commons which included an attack on clerical corruption and on the subordination of the English Church to the dictates of Rome (MacFarlane, 1972, p. 132). The climax and conclusion of this popular phase of the movement came in 1414, with the dramatic but abortive attempt at a Lollard uprising led by Sir John Oldcastle (Thomson, 1965, pp. 5–19).

In the course of this campaign Wyclif produced a large body of heretical writings on the jurisdictions of the Papacy, including a vernacular tract of 1384 entitled *The Church and her Members*. This opens with an attack on the 'state and worldly goods' of the Pope, and denounces the entire clerical estate for acting as 'the most greedy purchasers on earth' (p. 347). Wyclif then goes on to repudiate the Pope's claim 'to bind and loose', insisting that he 'proves not his great power' in this respect, and that the arguments of the canonists 'fail shamefully here' (p. 355). He adds in more minatory tones that 'it is a great peril' for the Pope 'to feign such power', since none of his alleged jurisdictions are genuinely 'grounded in Christ' (pp. 356–7). The tract concludes by calling on 'the Pope with his cardinals and all priests' to give up their 'worldly glory' and powers, and to 'live in Christian poverty' as Christ himself taught by word and deed (p. 359).

In England the official response to these heretical demands was the enactment of a statute 'For the burning of heretics' in 1401, which established a legal framework for religious persecution for the first time (McFarlane, 1972, p. 135). In Scotland the response was even more alarmist, and included the founding of the University of St Andrews in 1413 with the express purpose of protecting orthodoxy, the passing of anti-Lollard legislation by the Parliament in 1425, and the execution of a number of Lollard sympathisers, the first victim being James Resby in 1407 (Duke, 1937, pp. 110–11, 115). Nevertheless, the Lollard movement not only survived throughout the fifteenth century,[1] but even succeeded in exporting its ideals to Europe, where they were enthusiastically adopted and developed by the Hussites in Bohemia. Jan Hus (*c.* 1369–1415) acknowledged that Wyclif's writings on the Church provided much of the inspiration for his own very similar denunciations of clerical corruption and the supremacy of the Pope (Spinka, 1941, pp. 6–9). And in spite of Hus's condemnation and execution by the Council of Constance in 1415, his followers quickly proved themselves far more successful than their Lollard progenitors both in crystallising their outlook into a definite programme and in organising themselves to fight for its acceptance. They first formulated their demands in the Articles of Prague in 1420, which

---

[1] On this point see Aston, 1964, and especially Thomson, 1965.

included an attack on the 'great worldly possessions' and the 'unlawful powers' of the Church (Heymann, 1955, p. 148). They then raised an army under the brilliant generalship of John Žižka and campaigned for nearly fifteen years to enforce their creed. The stand they took against the landowning and tax-gathering privileges of the Church proved so popular that they constantly managed to replace their losses, and eventually proved themselves to be unconquerable. At the Council of Basle in 1433 they finally succeeded in forcing the Pope and the Emperor to recognise the four articles of religious reform they had originally proposed – including the demand for a measure of redistribution of the Church's wealth (Heymann, 1959, p. 247). They were then able, under the long and determined leadership of John Rokycana between 1429 and 1471, to sustain this anti-papal and evangelical stance, and in this way to establish a semi-autonomous Czech national Church (Heymann, 1959, p. 243).

As well as this heretical strand of opposition to Papal power, there was a long tradition within the Church of resistance to the orthodox idea of the Papacy as an absolute monarchy. This first arose in the course of the twelfth century as a reaction against the increasing centralisation of Papal administration which had taken place in the wake of the Gregorian reforms.[1] This development prompted a number of canonists to wonder with some alarm what might happen if a pope with so much power should happen to fall into heresy or become incapable. The answer some of them began to propose – thus laying the foundations for the entire conciliar movement – was that the authority of the Papacy ought to be treated as inferior to the authority of a General Council of the Church. This suggestion was first fully developed as early as the 1190s by Huguccio, the Bishop of Pisa, in his commentary on the Decretals. He states his theory in the course of discussing the claim that the Pope is unanswerable to the Church 'unless detected in heresy' (*nisi deprehendatur a fide devius*).[2] He takes this to mean that the Church as a corporation must be 'above' the Pope at least in the sense that, if its welfare is at stake, the cardinals must possess the power to summon a General Council, which in turn must have the authority to sit in judgment on the Pope. Huguccio adds that there are two types of cases in which this must be legitimate (Tierney, 1955, pp. 58–65). He first endorses the received opinion that 'if the Pope

---

[1] Figgis's classic outline of conciliar political theory is thus at fault in assuming that the political ideas associated with the movement were only articulated in the later fourteenth century, and essentially consisted of applying to the Church a concept of popular sovereignty already developed in the secular sphere. For this assumption see Figgis, 1960, pp. 44–5 and for a critique see Oakley, 1969, pp. 369–72.

[2] Huguccio's Gloss on this proposition is printed in full as an Appendix to Tierney, 1955, pp. 248–50, the source from which my quotations are taken.

becomes a heretic', this is so harmful 'not only to himself but to the whole world' that 'he can be condemned by his subjects' (p. 248). He then adds the far more contentious – and highly influential – claim that if the Pope is 'a contumacious criminal' who persists 'in notorious crimes' which 'scandalise the Church', he can also be deposed for failing to fulfil the duties of his office (p. 249). For as Huguccio concludes – a flurry of rhetorical questions barely concealing the weakness of his argument – 'if a Pope scandalises the Church, is this not tantamount to heresy?'.

The next major campaign against Papal absolutism developed in the early fourteenth century as an aspect of the renewed conflict between the Papacy and the Empire. A dispute in the Electoral College in 1314 resulted in the elevation of two rival Holy Roman Emperors. One of the claimants was Louis IV of Bavaria, who succeeded in securing his position in Germany and went on to demand recognition from the Pope, John XXII. John responded in 1324 by excommunicating Louis, who riposted three years later by marching on Rome and having himself crowned as Emperor by Nicholas V, whom he installed as anti-Pope. The quarrel continued to reverberate throughout the following decade, in the course of which Louis called to his aid a considerable number of anti-Papal publicists. Amongst those whose support he managed to enlist were the two greatest political writers of the age, William of Ockham and Marsiglio of Padua, both of whom took refuge at Louis's court after being excommunicated by John XXII. The outcome was not merely a revival but an embattled development of all the arguments already advanced against the concept of Papal supremacy.

As we have already seen, Marsiglio's *Defender of Peace* embodied an unequivocal defence of conciliarism, as well as advancing two heretical claims which were rarely taken up by the later and more moderate opponents of the Papacy's *plenitudo potestatis*. One was the contention that the Pope is not in fact head of the Church by divine right, so that his claim to exercise a 'plenitude of power over any ruler, community, or individual person' is 'inappropriate and wrong', and 'goes outside, or rather against, the divine scriptures and human demonstrations' (p. 273). Marsiglio's other heresy – widely adopted in the course of the Reformation – was his insistence that all coercive power is secular by definition, and thus that the idea of the Pope as the wielder of 'any rulership or coercive judgment or jurisdiction' over 'any priest or non-priest' or any 'individual of whatever condition' is nothing but a 'vicious outrage', and one which is utterly destructive of the peace of the world (pp. 113, 344).

The political theories of Marsiglio and Ockham are often considered together, but there is no doubt, as several recent studies have emphasised, that Ockham was a more moderate and even conservative thinker.[1] He was not greatly concerned with the thesis of conciliarism, and his late treatise on *The Power of Emperors and Popes* even included a modified defence of Papal monarchy, arguing that 'the community of the faithful ought to be subject to a supreme head and judge', and that 'no one other than the Pope can be this head' (p. 25; cf. Brampton, 1927, p. ix). Nevertheless, he accepts in his *Dialogue* that 'if the Pope is a notorious heretic', then 'a general council can be summoned without the authority of the Pope' in order 'to judge and depose' him (pp. 399–400). And in addition to repeating this well-established tenet of conciliarism, he deploys two further arguments about the powers of the Pope which were both to be of great importance in the later attack on Papal monarchy.

He first argues that, although the Pope is undoubtedly head of the Church, his authority is not granted to him unconditionally, but only on the understanding that he exercises it for the benefit of the faithful. Ockham thus regards the Papacy not as an absolute but a constitutional monarchy (cf. McGrade, 1974, pp. 161–4). The point is firmly made in the *Brief Account of the Power of the Pope*, which he completed between 1339 and 1341 (Baudry, 1937, p. vii). There can be no question, he argues, of the Pope 'having such a plenitude of power' that 'he is able to do absolutely anything', as some of his supporters have maintained (p. 16). His supremacy 'is not given to him for himself', but 'only for the good of his subjects' (p. 22). And 'it follows from this', Ockham concludes, 'that the Pope does not have from Christ the type of plenitude of power' normally claimed for him, since 'he has authority from God only for preserving, not for destroying' the Church (p. 25).

Ockham's other subversive contention was that the spheres of spiritual and temporal jurisdiction must be kept sharply divided from each other (cf. McGrade, 1974, pp. 134–40). The implications of this commitment are worked out most clearly in his late treatise on *The Powers of Emperors and Popes*. He begins by emphasising that 'when Christ made Peter head of all believers', he 'prohibited him and the other Apostles from exercising any domination over kings and peoples' (p. 5). St Peter fully accepted this commission, moreover, for he in turn warned his successors that they 'should avoid any involvement in the occupations of daily life' (p. 7). These instructions are first of all taken to mean that 'the Papal principate instituted by Christ at no point includes any regular jurisdiction over temporal matters or secular business' (p. 7). So Ockham insists that 'if a Pope interferes in temporal affairs', he is merely 'putting his scythe into another

---

[1] See McGrade, 1974, esp. pp. 18–20, 28–43. See also Bayley, 1949, esp. pp. 199–201, Tierney, 1954, and Lagarde, 1963, esp. pp. 53–5, 86.

man's harvest' (p. 7). Christ's instructions are also taken to imply the more heretical claim – already emphasised by Marsiglio and later developed by Wyclif and Hus – that 'the Papal principate' is 'not a jurisdictional or despotic power at all' (p. 14). 'God has instituted principates of a dominating character in the world', but 'Christ told the Apostles that their principate was not of this nature' (pp. 15–16). So Ockham concludes that the Pope's so-called principate 'ought rather to be called a ministering power', a power established 'for the saving of souls and the guidance of the faithful', but not for any other and more political ends (p. 14).

The point at which these early attacks on the absolute powers of the Pope were most effectively developed was after the outbreak of the Great Schism in 1378. One of the main issues of concern during this period was the increasing corruption of the Papacy as a tax-gatherer and distributor of benefices. Jean Gerson (1363–1429), perhaps the most influential of all the conciliarists, wrote a *Tract on Simony* at this time, protesting at the Papacy's habit of 'extorting money from benefices under the title of first-fruits' (p. 167). He also wrote a tract entitled *Towards a Reformation of Simony*, in which he offered many proposals for curtailing the bestowal of ecclesiastical offices 'in such a disgraceful fashion and with such an appearance of avarice' (p. 180).[1] Similarly, Nicolaus of Cusa (1401–64) devoted several chapters of his major conciliarist treatise *On Universal Harmony* to discussing the urgent need for the Papacy to reform its corrupt practices. He criticises 'the mingling of spiritual with temporal business' by the leaders of the Church, and warns them, in an echo of St Peter's words, 'not to engage in any occupation of a mundane or business character' (pp. 265–6). Finally, he roundly condemns 'the pomp and blind avarice' of the Popes, and attacks their growing tendency to think of nothing other than the augmentation of their own possessions and revenues (p. 269; cf. Sigmund, 1963, pp. 183–5).

But the gravest scandal of this period was of course the Schism itself. After 1378 there were two different Popes, and after 1409 there were three, each demanding to be recognised as the sole rightful occupant of St Peter's throne (Flick, 1930, I, pp. 262, 271, 312). It soon became obvious that the only way to end the Schism would be to remove each of the rival claimants so that a new election could be made. It was no less obvious, however, that in order to secure this result it would be necessary to summon a General Council, and to insist on its capacity to sit in judgment on the head of the Church. So it came about that, in the name of healing the Schism, the cardinals officially accepted the doctrine of conciliarism: the Council of Constance duly met in 1414, proclaimed its

[1] On Gerson as a reformer, see Connolly, 1928, esp. pp. 90–112.

authority to be greater than that of the Pope, deposed two of the rival claimants to the Papacy, persuaded the third to abdicate, and elected Martin V in their place (Flick, 1930, I, pp. 312–13).

The first leading churchman to write in defence of this procedure for ending the Schism was Cardinal Francesco Zabarella (1360–1417), whose treatise *On the Schism* was completed in 1408.[1] But the most important expositions of conciliar theory were written in connection with the meetings of the Council of Constance between 1414 and 1418, and the Council of Basle between 1431 and 1437. Cardinal Pierre d'Ailly (1350–1420), one of the leading Ockhamists of the age, presented an important *Tract on the Authority of the Church* at Constance in 1416 (Roberts, 1935, p. 132). Jean Gerson, who had studied under d'Ailly at the Sorbonne, and who succeeded him as Chancellor of the University in 1395, read an even more radical essay *On Ecclesiastical Power* to the assembled Council in February 1417 (Morrall, 1960, p. 100). And Nicolaus of Cusa provided perhaps the most eloquent summary of conciliarist ideas in his treatise *On Universal Harmony*, which he completed in 1433 and submitted to the Council of Basle in the following year (Sigmund, 1963, pp. 35–6).

It is true that these writers are at first inclined to tread warily in applying a theory of popular sovereignty to the Church (Tierney, 1975, pp. 244–6). This element of caution is especially marked in d'Ailly and Zabarella, both of whom owed their cardinalates to John XXIII, perhaps the most dubious of the pretenders to the Papal throne. When d'Ailly in his *Tract on the Authority of the Church* raises the crucial question of 'whether the plenitude of power resides in the Roman pontiff alone', he appears unable to bring himself to give a definite answer (col. 949). At first he suggests that the plenitude lies 'separably' with the Pope, but 'inseparably' with the Church and 'representatively' with a duly assembled General Council (col. 950). But he then adds that 'properly speaking, the plenitude resides solely in the supreme Pontiff as the successor of St Peter' (col. 950). And he ends by conceding that 'the plenitude is only figuratively and in a certain sense equivocally to be found in the Universal Church and the General Council representing it' (col. 950; cf. Oakley, 1964, pp. 114–29).

When we come to Gerson's treatise *On Ecclesiastical Power*, however, we encounter an unhesitating and extremely influential statement of the claim that the Council unquestionably possesses supreme power over the Church – a claim which was subsequently worked out in greater detail by

---

[1] For Zabarella's conciliarism see the Appendix in Ullmann, 1948, pp. 191–231 and cf. Tierney, 1955, pp. 220–37.

John of Segovia and Nicolaus of Cusa at the Council of Basle (Black, 1970, pp. 34–44). Gerson begins in apparently concessive style by drawing a strong distinction between the Church and political society, contending that the Church differs in origin 'from all other powers' (p. 211). Whereas all other forms of authority are 'naturally established' and 'regulated according to natural or human laws', the Church is also 'the mystical body of Christ', with an authority which Christ 'supernaturally conferred by a special grant upon his Apostles, disciples and their legitimate successors' (p. 211). This means that in one sense – the sense in which the Pope is a descendant of the Church's mystical union with its founder – it must be 'conceded without a doubt' that the Pope 'holds a plenitude of power' and holds it 'immediately from God' (p. 226). Gerson then goes on to insist, however, that the Church as it now exists must also be viewed as a political society, a society in which the same criteria for legitimacy must be applied as in any ordinary *regnum* or *civitas*. He then argues – just as his master Ockham had already done – that 'notwithstanding any considerations' about the divine origins of ecclesiastical power, it becomes evident as soon as we adopt this perspective that 'the successors of St Peter have been and still are instituted mediately by men' for the benefit of the Church, and 'receive their office mediately by human ministry and allowance' (p. 226; cf. Morrall, 1960, p. 104).

This clears the way for Gerson's central argument. If the powers of the Pope are instituted 'mediately' by men on condition that 'he aims at the common good in his rule', then the Pope cannot possibly be 'greater than the body of the Church' – *maior universis* – as the canonists had characteristically affirmed.[1] Like Ockham, Gerson maintains that the Pope can only be a constitutional monarch, a minister or official of the Church whose authority remains contingent on his willingness to pursue the welfare of his subjects. So he insists that the power of the Church as a *universitas* or corporation remains 'greater than that of the Pope' – a conclusion which he then proceeds to underline in his highest rhetorical style. The Church is *maior* – 'greater than the Pope' – 'in amplitude and extension, greater through its infallible direction, greater as a reforming authority, both with respect to its head and members, greater in coercive power, greater in making all ultimate decisions in difficult matters of faith, and greater finally in its sheer size' (p. 240).

Gerson's vindication of the Papal *plenitudo potestatis* as a direct gift of God is thus rendered fully compatible with his claim that 'the ultimate

[1] See Gerson, pp. 226, 232, 247. The question Gerson initially asks (p. 222) is 'whether the authority of the Pope is greater than that of the Church (*maior quam ecclesia*) or the other way round'. Nicolaus of Cusa prefers to ask (p. 191) whether the Church is 'above the power of the Pope' (*supra potestatem Romanae pontifici*).

power over the Church lies in the Church itself', and in particular 'in the General Council which sufficiently and legitimately represents it' (p. 232). He considers that the *plenitudo* 'is only formally and materially lodged with the Pope', while 'the regulation and application of its use' remains the responsibility of the Council in its capacity as the Church's representative assembly (pp. 227–8, 232). He accordingly maintains that when the Church assigns the *plenitudo* to the Pope, it does so not in the form of an alienation of its powers to a ruler who thus becomes *legibus solutus*, but only in the form of a concession which assigns the Pope the use but not the ownership of his authority (p. 228). So he is able to conclude that, in spite of the absolutist appearance of ecclesiastical power, the highest authority in the Church *remanet in ecclesia* – 'remains at all times within the body of the Church' (p. 233).

Finally, this image of the Church as a limited monarchy operating through a representative assembly enables Gerson to draw the polemical conclusion in which he is chiefly interested. If the Pope is only a *rector* or *minister* who remains *minor universis*, it follows that it must be possible 'for a General Council to be summoned without a pope' and 'for a pope to be judged in certain cases by a General Council' (p. 229). Gerson insists, moreover, that heresy is not the only type of case in which it may be legitimate for a pope to be condemned. A General Council 'is also able to judge and depose a pope' if 'he is pertinacious in the destruction of the Church', and in this way fails to discharge the duties of the office which has been conditionally assigned to him (p. 233).

In the years immediately preceding the Reformation, this attack on Papal absolutism was restated in its most radical form by a number of avowed followers of d'Ailly and Gerson, several of whom were not afraid even to invoke the authority of Marsiglio of Padua. The background to this revival was provided by the conflict which, as we have seen, broke out between Pope Julius II and Louis XII of France over the dissolution of the League of Cambrai in 1510. After Louis's victory over the Venetians in the previous year, Julius attempted to repudiate the alliance which he had formed with the French in 1508. Louis promptly responded by appealing over the head of the Pope to a General Council of the Church. Allying himself with a considerable number of dissident cardinals, he summoned a Council to meet at Pisa in May 1511 and commanded the Pope to attend (La Brosse, 1965, pp. 58–9). At this point the Papacy appealed to Tommaso de Vio – later Cardinal Cajetan – to defend its cause against the conciliarism of the French, and he duly responded in October 1511 with his *Comparison between the Powers of the Pope and the*

Council, an energetic repudiation of the anti-papalist case (Oakley, 1965, p. 674). Not to be outdone, Louis XII immediately submitted the *Comparison* to the University of Paris, reminding the theologians that he was 'determined at all times to aid and defend' a General Council, and asking them to supply him with a written opinion on the book (Renaudet, 1953, p. 546). The outcome was the publication of several systematic works of scholastic political philosophy, in which the issue of the Council was treated as part of a more general account of the concept of the *regnum* and its proper relations with the Church. The first of these treatises to appear was the work of Jacques Almain (*c.* 1480–1515), who was asked by the Sorbonne to compose its official reply to the king, and responded in 1512 with an attack on Cajetan entitled *A Brief Account of the Power of the Church* (La Brosse, 1965, pp. 73, 75). It seems that Almain may have won this commission as the result of a disputation which he had conducted earlier in 1512 on *A Reconsideration of the Question of Natural, Civil and Ecclesiastical Power*, a work which later formed the conclusion to his *Exposition* of 'the views of William of Ockham concerning the power of the Pope'.[1] Almain's *Brief Account* proved sufficiently challenging to call forth an *Apology* from Cajetan in which he restated all the anti-conciliarist positions he had already maintained (La Brosse, 1965, pp. 77–8). This in turn provoked the other major contribution to the debate to be published in 1512, the treatise by Marc de Grandval entitled *The Best Form of Ecclesiastical and Civil Political Society* (Renaudet, 1953, p. 555 and note).

A few years later the same conciliarist doctrines were reiterated by John Mair, who had taught both Almain and Grandval at the Sorbonne. Mair was a Scotsman, originally a student at God's House (later Christ's College) Cambridge, who gained his Master's degree at Paris in 1495 and joined the Collège de Montaigu, then being reformed by Standonck. (Thus Erasmus was one of his contemporaries there.) As we have already seen, he then spent the most important part of his long and highly successful career teaching at the Sorbonne. The only time he left the University of Paris appears to have been between 1518 and 1526, when he returned to his native Scotland and taught first at the University of Glasgow and

---

[1] Almain's *Reconsideration* thus forms the final section of his *Exposition*. The *Exposition* first appeared in the posthumous collection of his *Brief Works* (*Opuscula*) edited by Vincent Doesmier (Paris, 1518), fos i–lxvii, with the *Reconsideration* at fos lxii–lxvii. The whole *Exposition* was first published separately at Paris in 1526. It was republished as an appendix to Jean Gerson, *Opera Omnia*, ed. Louis Ellies du Pin, 5 vols (Antwerp, 1706), Vol. 2, cols 1013–1120. Since this is the version from which I have taken my quotations, it is worth noting two peculiarities about it. One is that the *Exposition* appears under a different title, as *Concerning Lay and Ecclesiastical Power*, with the original title appearing as its sub-title (see col. 1013). The other is that the *Reconsideration* is presented as a separate tract (see cols 961–76).

then at St Andrews (Mackay, 1892, p. lxvii). Mair's teaching at Paris was initially based on the Collège de Navarre, which had numbered both d'Ailly and Gerson amongst its students over a century before, and thus had a well-established tradition of opposition to the idea of Papal absolutism (Launoy, 1682, pp. 97, 208). Mair not only acknowledged the influence of this background, but also saw himself as a follower of Ockham, whose political arguments he frequently invoked, in addition to presenting an influential interpretation of his nominalism. As a teacher Mair appears to have had an impact on a remarkable range of famous pupils, three of whom were later to develop his doctrines in unexpected ways: the Thomist Pierre Crockaert, the humanist George Buchanan, and the revolutionary John Knox, perhaps the most rabid of all the Pope's enemies (Renaudet, 1953, pp. 457, 591–3; Mackay, 1892, pp. lxvii, lxxii, cxxxvii; Burns, 1954, pp. 84–9, 93–4).

Mair's first published work of theology was *A Commentary on the Fourth Book of Lombard's Sentences*, which appeared in 1509 and was followed between 1510 and 1517 by similar commentaries on the other three books (Burns, 1954, p. 87). The commentary on the fourth book was reissued in 1512, and appeared in a new edition in 1516, again in 1519, and again in 1521. The first two versions scarcely referred to the problem of Papal authority, but the 1516 and later editions included a radical analysis of 'the status and power of the Church', and were advertised without undue modesty as 'the most useful questions' ever to have arisen out of the *Sentences*.[1] During these years Mair also supplied a more extensive account of his political views in his *Exposition of St Matthew's Gospel*, which he first published in 1518 and later incorporated in a revised form into his *Clear Expositions of the Four Gospels* in 1529. Here he again stated his theories about the proper government of the Church, setting them out in two sections of his commentary on St Matthew: in the first he defended 'the authority of a Council over the Pontiff', and in the second he mounted an attack on the alleged powers of the Pope in temporal affairs.[2]

[1] This discussion originally appeared as Distinction 24, Question 4 of Mair's *Most Useful Questions on the Fourth Book of Lombard's Sentences* (Paris, 1519), fo. ccxiii. This section was reprinted in the form of a separate tract, under the title *The Status and Power of the Church*, in Gerson, *Opera Omnia*, ed. du Pin, Vol. 2, cols. 1121–30. It is from this latter version that my quotations are taken. The 1516, 1519 and 1521 editions of *The Most Useful Questions* are virtually identical. (I owe this information to Professor J. H. Burns.) The page references which du Pin gives at cols 1121–2 show that he is following the 1519 edition. So this is the version I have used throughout.

[2] Both these discussions originally appeared in Mair's *Exposition of St Matthew's Gospel* (Paris, 1518), the first at fo lxviii, the second at fo lix. Both were reprinted in the form of separate tracts in du Pin's edition of Gerson, *Opera Omnia*, the first under the title *A Disputation about the Authority of the Church and Council over the Pope* (vol. 2, cols 1131–45)

Mair and Almain both begin by agreeing with Gerson that there is a basic difference between the Church and civil society, since the Church has arisen not as a result of human decision but rather as a direct gift of God (cf. Oakley, 1965, p. 677). They are no less strongly in agreement, however, that the organisation and justification of the two societies must be fundamentally the same. As Mair puts it in his discussion of *The Power of the Pope*, although 'the Church was instituted by Christ, it is even more concerned with the good of the community than the secular commonwealth' (col. 1151). The same point is echoed by Almain in the final section of his *Exposition* of Ockham's views on civil and ecclesiastical power. 'All sovereignty', as he declares in the title of his fourth chapter, 'lay as well as ecclesiastical, is instituted for the benefit not of the ruler but of the people', and needs in consequence to be judged on the same terms (col. 1107).

If the power of the Pope is established by the Church with the sole aim of protecting its own welfare, it is obvious according to Almain and Mair that the Pope cannot be said to possess an unchallengeable authority. Mair begins his *Disputation on the Authority of a Council* by citing the contrary opinion, 'commonly held by the Thomists', to the effect that the Papacy must be treated as an absolute monarchy (p. 175). He argues against this that 'the Roman Pontiff is our brother, and thus remains at all times subject to the reproof of the whole body of Christians who make up the Church' (p. 176). He is *maior singulis* in relation to the bishops, but *minor universis* in relation to the body of the faithful and to the General Council representing their interests. This is confirmed by the fact that 'the keys were not given to Peter except in the name of the Church', and by the further fact that it is possible to appeal from the Pope's authority to that of a Council, which must therefore be 'above the Roman Pontiff' (p. 178). The implication that the Pope's status is merely that of an elected official is even more clearly brought out by Almain at the end of his *Brief Account*. He begins by citing Cajetan's view that 'the power of electing a pope' lies 'with the Pontiff himself' (col. 998). He replies that the power in fact lies with God, but that insofar as it is a human power at all, 'it lies with the Church and not with the Pontiff' – a conclusion

the second under the title *The Power of the Pope in Temporal Affairs* (vol. 2, cols 1145–64). The first has also been translated by J. K. Cameron as *A Disputation on the Authority of a Council* in *Advocates of Reform*, ed. Spinka, pp. 175–84. In this translation it is erroneously stated (p. 175) that Mair first published this discussion in 1529. This mistake may be due to the fact that Mair reissued his commentary on St Matthew in his *Clear Expositions of the Four Gospels* in that year. But the 1529 version was in fact very different (and less radical) than the version of 1518. On this point see Ganoczy, 1968. In quoting from the first of these discussions I have used Cameron's translation. In quoting from the second I have made my own translation from du Pin's edition.

which is then elaborately defended by reference to the scriptures and the practice of the primitive Church (cols 999–1000).

If the status of the Pope within the Church is merely that of a *rector* or *minister*, it follows that the Papal plenitude of power can only have been granted as a matter of administrative convenience, and not in the form of an alienation of the Church's fundamental sovereignty. Mair draws this inference at the end of his *Disputation*, where he cites Gerson to help him provide this 'solution to Cajetan's arguments', concluding that 'the plenitude of power remains continually with the Church' (p. 183). Almain reiterates the same conclusion at the end of his *Reconsideration*. Here he simply asserts that 'the power of the Church, in character as well as in time, is in the Church itself rather than in the Pope', and promptly deduces three corollaries: 'the power of the Church remains greater in perfection and extent than that of the Supreme Pontiff'; 'the General Council of the Church is able to meet without the authority of the Pope'; and 'the General Council is able to exercise every act of ecclesiastical jurisdiction' (cols 971–4). The same points are more fully elaborated in chapters 6 and 7 of the *Brief Account*, in which Almain argues from many authorities that 'Christ transferred his power immediately to the Church' after which he again asserts that Cajetan is entirely mistaken in supposing that this power has at any point been alienated or granted away to the Pope (cols 995–8).

Finally, Mair and Almain both endorse with great emphasis the crucial polemical claim underlying the thesis of conciliarism: that it must be possible for a pope to be deposed and removed by a vote (even a bare majority vote) of a General Council of the Church. This is the chief theme of Mair's *Disputation*, and the same arguments recur in the last two chapters of Almain's *Brief Account*. Both begin by conceding that, as Mair puts it (p. 179) 'a bishop does not cease to hold office on account of heresy', and thus that (as Almain admits, citing Ockham as his authority) 'a pope who becomes a heretic is not *ipso facto* deposed' (col. 1005). A legal act is needed to remove a bishop or pope, and the problem is to discover who has the authority to perform it. Both insist that the authority lies with the General Council, which they agree with Gerson in treating as the sovereign representative assembly of the Church. They first present the traditional conciliarist argument that, as Almain remarks in Chapter 9 of his *Brief Account*, it is obvious 'in a case of heresy' that 'the nature of the supremacy of the General Council over the Pope' must be such that 'the Council may excommunicate and depose him' (cols 1005–6). They then add the further and more contentious claim – originally emphasised, as we have seen, by Huguccio – that there is a second case in which the

Church possesses the same right. Since the Pope is merely a *minister* chosen to govern in accordance with the laws of nature, it follows (as Almain argues in his final chapter) that the Church must have the authority to depose him 'not merely for heresy but for other notorious crimes', including 'negligent rule' (col. 1008). Mair ends his *Disputation* on the same note, stressing the parallels with political society and using them to meet the Thomist objection that 'since the Supreme Pontiff is from God', the Church cannot be said to have any power of deposition over him (p. 184).[1] This objection, Mair roundly concludes, 'is nonsense', for 'although the Roman Pontiff is from God, yet it is not true to say that God did not leave this power in the Church in the same way as this political power resides among the men of one kingdom' (p. 184).

After the outbreak of the Reformation, the leaders of the Lutheran movement were quick to associate themselves with these earlier strands of opposition to the absolutist pretensions of the Pope. Luther himself appealed to the authority of a Council at two vital moments in the early years of the Reformation. The first was in 1518, immediately after his return from the disputation with Johann Eck at Augsburg. Realising that his earlier appeals to the Pope were being studiously ignored, he proceeded to draw up a formal document in which he asked that his case be presented to a General Council of the Church (Fife, 1957, pp. 300–1). He renewed the same demand two years later, as soon as the Bull *Exsurge Domine*, announcing his excommunication, was published in Germany (Fife, 1957, p. 560). On this occasion he not only asked the city council of Wittenberg to support his move, but went on to publish his appeal in the form of a tract. This was printed as *The Appeal of Martin Luther to a Council* in November 1520, and went through eight editions within the next two months (Fife, 1957, p. 561). Luther begins his tract by denouncing the Pope for 'having treated his previous appeal with contempt' (p. 78). He reiterates his request for a Council to hear his case, and insists that such an assembly must be superior to the Pope, since 'the power of the Pontiff cannot be against or above' the authority of Scripture or the body of the Church (p. 79). So he calls on the Emperor, the electors and 'every Christian magistrate in Germany' to support him in his campaign against the Pope, whom he accuses of proceeding 'with iniquity and injustice, with tyranny and violence' (p. 79).

Luther and his disciples showed an even greater concern to stress their

---

[1] This is not the end of Mair's tract, but it is the end of his exposition of his own position, after which he turns to criticising Cajetan's case. It is also the end of the (substantially abridged) version of the tract translated by Cameron.

affinities with the Lollard and Hussite traditions of opposition to the powers of the Pope. Luther himself frequently emphasised the similarities between the Hussite heresy and his own attack on Papal tyranny. When he first received a copy of Hus's treatise *On the Church* at the end of 1519, he promptly wrote to Spalatin to assure him that 'its spirit and learnedness are wonderful' and to declare with amazement that 'I have taught and held all the teachings of John Hus, but thus far did not know it'.[1] And when Jerome Emser – whom Luther liked to call 'the Leipzig goat' – sought to trap him into admitting that he had defended a series of Hussite principles in the course of his disputation with Eck, Luther boldly responded in his tract of 1521 *Concerning the Answer of the Goat in Leipzig* by associating himself with the Bohemian heresy, and rejoicing in the fact that Hus 'is again coming to life and tormenting his murderers, the Pope and the popish set, more strongly now than when he was alive' (p. 134). A few years later Luther took the opportunity to acknowledge the Lollards in a similar way. When Johann Brismann sent him a Lollard *Commentary on the Apocalypse* in 1527, Luther immediately had it printed in Wittenberg and supplied a Preface addressed *To the Pious Reader* in which he warmly commended its violent denunciations of the Church's leadership (Aston, 1964, pp. 156–7). The great value of the book, Luther claims in his introductory remarks, lies in its clear recognition 'that the Papacy is to be interpreted as the reign of anti-Christ', and that 'the tyrannical fury of the Pope' is to be resisted in every way (p. 124).

A similar sense of continuity soon began to be emphasised by the leaders of the Reformation in England. The pioneer of this development was John Bale (1495–1563), a contemporary of Cranmer's at Jesus College, Cambridge who became converted in the early 1530s from a zealous Catholicism to an equally committed Lutheranism (Fairfield, 1976, pp. 33–5). Bale was active as a preacher amongst the north-country Lollards in the 1530s, but his major contribution to the English Reformation was made as an historian of the reform movement itself (Dickens, 1959a, pp. 140–2). He was one of the earliest writers to insist on the affinities between the English Protestants and their Lollard forerunners, and in this way helped to equip the Church of England with a new martyrology, an appropriate Church history, and a powerful image of its connections with an heroic evangelical past (Harris, 1940, pp. 13, 127; cf. Fairfield, 1976, pp. 121–30). Bale began this process in 1544 with *A Brief Chronicle*, in which he described 'the examination and death of the blessed martyr of Christ, Sir John Oldcastle', the leader of the attempted

---

[1] For Luther's discovery of Hus, see Fife, 1957, p. 471. For these comments to Spalatin, see Luther, *Letters*, Vol. 48, pp. 153, 155 and cf. Williams, 1962, pp. 216–17.

Lollard uprising of 1414. In his Preface Bale denounces Polydore Vergil for 'polluting our English chronicles most shamefully with his Romish lies', and calls for a history of the unsung heroes who have at all times stood out against 'that execrable anti-Christ of Rome' (pp. 6, 8). This leads him to consider the example of Oldcastle, whom he describes as making the discovery that 'the proud Romish Church' was dealing in 'superstitious sorceries' as soon as he 'thoroughly tasted' the true doctrines of Christ which John Wyclif had taught (p. 10). Bale makes it clear, moreover, that he intends his account of Oldcastle's martyrdom as a model for other histories of the same kind, and expresses the hope that 'some learned Englishman' may soon manage to 'set forth the English chronicles in their right shape' (p. 8).

Bale's hope was soon to be magnificently realised by his friend John Foxe (1516–87). Foxe was converted – like many others – while at Magdalen College, Oxford, and was obliged to go into exile at the accession of Mary in 1553 (Haller, 1963, pp. 55–6). He went to live in Basle, where he lodged in the same house as Bale, and where he completed and published a series of Latin *Commentaries on the Affairs of the Church* in 1554 (Haller, 1963, p. 56). These later formed the kernel of the massive and immensely influential account of the *Acts and Monuments* of the true English Church which Foxe went on to publish in 1563. Bale's influence on Foxe's so-called 'Book of Martyrs' is evident at several important points. Foxe evidently derives from Bale the idea of using the mystical numbers from the Book of Revelations in order to divide up his account of the true and false Churches (Levy, 1967, p. 99). And when he departs from this scheme in order to cover the Lollard movement in greater detail, the reason he gives is one which Bale had already foreshadowed. Foxe speaks of the fact that it has for a long time 'been received and thought of the common people' that the Protestant faith 'has sprung up and risen but of late', whereas it has in fact been flourishing 'for the space of these two hundred years, from the time of Wyclif' (III, p. 380). The image of Wyclif as the 'morning star' of the Reformation is thus definitively fixed, and Foxe goes on to provide an impressive history of Lollard influence, tracing it through Oldcastle's uprising, Hus's reformation, Žižka's revolution and the whole history of the true Church in the course of the fifteenth century (III, pp. 320–579).

The emphasis which the early Lutherans placed on their continuities with this historical background can be shown to have played a definite role in helping to further the cause of their own reform movement. For their propaganda helped to encourage most of the surviving Lollard and Hussite communities to link up with the wider movement of the

Reformation, a development which in turn helped to widen the basis of its support and in this way to increase its influence. In Germany, the Hussites began to coalesce with the Lutherans as early as 1519, when the Bohemian Brethren under the leadership of Luke of Prague (1458–1528) first established contact with some of Luther's followers (Thomson, 1953, p. 170). The Brethren were formally acknowledged by Luther himself in the following year as a legitimate part of the evangelical Reformation, and continued to propagate their doctrine of justification by faith and their policy of opposition to the powers of the Church over a wide area of Moravia and Bohemia (Heymann, 1970, p. 143; cf. Williams, 1962, pp. 213–15). The surviving Lollard communities in England soon began to make a similar contribution to the spread of the Lutheran Reformation. They appear to have gained in confidence in the decade following Luther's initial outburst of 1517, and readily joined forces with the new and more vocal movement of opposition to the powers of the Church.[1] It seems likely, for example, that a number of Lollard sympathisers amongst the London merchants – including Hilles and Petit – took part in the early 1520s in smuggling forbidden Lutheran books into England, and it is probable that Tyndale was supported by Lollard money while engaged in his translation of the New Testament (Rupp, 1949, p. 11). As Dickens has emphasised, it was largely on the basis of these syncretic foundations that the structure of English Protestant thought was successfully raised in the course of the next generation (Dickens, 1959a, p. 27; cf. Read, 1953, pp. 18–19).

THE CHURCH'S POWERS: THE LAY REVOLT

As well as being denounced by the theological critics we have now considered, the pretensions of the Papacy and the jurisdictions of the Church were also subjected to an increasing volume of criticism in the later Middle Ages by the laity and the secular governments of most countries in northern Europe. The privileges of the clerical estate had of course been challenged at many stages in the history of medieval Europe, but there is ample evidence that these protests rose to a new peak of intensity on the eve of the Reformation, especially in England and Germany. The German cities witnessed what Moeller has described as a series of 'explosions of hatred' against the Church during this period, especially in the years immediately after 1510 (Moeller, 1972, pp. 54–5). In Cologne, for

[1] Dickens, 1959a, p. 8 records that the Bishop of London felt the need to begin a series of anti-Lollard purges in 1527, as a result of which over two hundred heretics were forced to abjure various Lollard beliefs; cf. also Dickens, 1966a, p. 47.

example, there was a revolution against the ruling oligarchy in 1513, in the course of which the craft guilds took control of the city and set up a committee to consider how to reform its government. The outcome was a list of *Grievances and Demands* in which they constantly underlined their animosity towards the jurisdictions and privileges of the Church. They complain about the tax-exemptions of the clergy, and ask that the Church should be compelled 'to make a substantial loan to the city' (p. 140). They petition for the abolition of the Church's legal immunities, arguing that when a cleric commits a felony the law 'should punish the cleric as though he were a lay person' (p. 140). They denounce the way in which 'the monks hold on to their worldly goods' by the use of legal subterfuge (p. 142). And they summarise their demands by insisting that 'clerical persons should from now on bear the same civic burdens as burghers' (p. 141).

In England there were many signs of the same increasing hatred of the Church's jurisdictions amongst the laity on the eve of the Reformation. The most celebrated instance is provided by Hunne's case, a *cause célèbre* which came to the attention of the House of Commons in 1515. Richard Hunne, a London merchant of Lollard sympathies, had refused to pay a mortuary fee levied by his local priest, and on being sued for it had taken out a King's Bench action in 1513, directed against the authority of the Church courts. His staunchly anti-Papalist plea, which he derived from the statute of *praemunire*, was that since the Church courts merely sat by the authority of the Pope's legate, they had no jurisdiction over English subjects (Elton, 1960, p. 320). The Church responded to this impertinence by imprisoning Hunne on a dubious charge of heresy, and while awaiting trial in December 1514 he was found hanged in the bishop's gaol. It was almost certainly a case of murder at the hands of the ecclesiastical authorities, a fact which was widely rumoured at the time (Ogle, 1949, pp. 88–112). The suspicion was enough to cause an immediate uproar in London, which had to be pacified by the personal intervention of the King, and a further uproar in Parliament, which had to be hurriedly dissolved in order to forestall an all-out attack on the powers of the Church (Thomson, 1965, p. 169). Although the episode closed with a technical victory for the Bishop of London, who was able to ensure that Hunne's body was burnt as that of a heretic, no one failed to notice (as Pickthorn rather brutally puts it) that 'his ashes showed which way the wind blew' (Pickthorn, 1934, p. 114).

These mounting feelings of anti-clericalism found their chief outlet in a series of increasingly savage satires on the authority of the Pope. In Germany the most dramatic example of this trend was the so-called

Reuchlin affair, which straddled the years immediately before and after Luther's initial protest of 1517. The feud over Reuchlin's work originated in 1506, the year in which, as we have seen, he had published his pioneering work on *The Rudiments of Hebrew*. The book was denounced by Johann Pfefferkorn (1469–1524), a converted Jew who had gained a mandate from the Emperor in 1509, with the encouragement of the Dominicans at Cologne, in order to hunt out and confiscate Hebrew works. Reuchlin replied by contending that his Hebrew studies were essential for Biblical scholarship. The theologians appealed to the Pope, and a violent pamphlet war broke out (Holborn, 1938, p. 53). Reuchlin's own contribution was published early in 1514 as the *Letters of Famous Men*, and consisted of numerous messages of support he had received from the leaders of the learned world (Holborn, 1937, pp. 60–1). An apparent counterblast appeared at the end of the following year entitled *Letters of Obscure Men*. This took the form of a series of letters addressed to Ortus Gratius, the leader of the Cologne theologians, and purported to be an attack on the humanists. The intention was Swiftian, however, and the book was actually the work of Crotus Rubianus, who thus contrived a devastating satire on the churchmen's ludicrous ignorance.

The quarrel entered a new phase in 1517, when Rubianus's *Letters* were republished by Ulrich von Hutten, who added a new section containing sixty-two new items mainly written by himself. Much of this extra material was devoted to imitating and extending the original parody, but the tone of the additions was far more bitter, as well as more political, than in the earlier and more knockabout book (Dickens, 1974, p. 46). Von Hutten no longer confined himself to ridiculing the narrow and credulous outlook of the theologians in the approved humanist style. He clearly feared that Reuchlin's case would be decided against him by the Pope (which duly happened in 1520) and accordingly concentrated on questioning the underlying assumption that the Papacy had any right to regard itself as a final court of appeal in this or any other such case (Holborn, 1937, pp. 56, 112). The second section of the *Letters* thus includes a series of personal attacks on the Pope, and repeatedly accuses him of misusing his authority in siding with the theologians against the humanists (pp. 172, 201–2). As soon as Luther's diatribes against the Papacy began to appear, moreover, von Hutten's own writing took on an even bolder and more explicitly Lutheran tone. He started to collect and issue a series of earlier anti-Papal tracts, including, as we have seen, Valla's exposure of the Donation of Constantine. He also began work on his *Dialogue on the Roman Triad*, which he published early in 1520, characterising it himself as an attack 'of unexampled sharpness against

Rome' (Holborn, 1937, p. 114). He was now prepared to move far beyond the usual humanist preoccupation with clerical abuses, and in the course of the *Dialogue* he developed a sweeping condemnation of the powers and jurisdictions of the Church. He calls for a curtailment of ecclesiastical possessions, reviling 'the pomp of the prelates', 'the simony of the bishops' and 'the avarice of the Pope' (pp. 433, 443–5). He accuses the Papacy of 'extorting immense sums of money' from Germany, and demands that the payment of all contributions to Rome should cease (p. 429). He denounces the Curia's control over the Church in Germany, and proposes that it 'should be forbidden to elect bishops' or to fill any further German benefices (p. 436). And above all he repudiates the Papacy's temporal and political powers, crying out against 'the tyranny of Rome over Germany' and ending with a call to his fellow-countrymen to shake off the Italian yoke, 'the source of all the worst evils' in the world (pp. 467, 503–4).

A similar series of denunciations and satires appeared in England throughout the 1520s, the work of such pamphleteers as Jerome Barlowe and William Roy. This line of attack on the powers of the Church may be said to have reached a climax in 1529 with the publication of the anonymous *Supplication for the Beggars*. This was probably written by Simon Fish (d. 1531), a graduate of Oxford and a member of Gray's Inn. It is known to have been studied 'not with full disfavour' by Henry VIII, and it called forth a furious response from Sir Thomas More, *The Supplication of Souls* (Clebsch, 1964, p. 242). The tract is explosive but brief, and takes the form of an appeal addressed to the king by all the poor of the land. They spend much of their time complaining in a scurrilous fashion about the licentiousness of priests, who 'corrupt the whole generation of mankind in your realm' (p. 6). But they also complain in a more serious way about the excessive powers of the Church. They insist that the people are being kept in needless poverty by the fact that the clergy hold 'half the substance of the realm' (p. 4). And above all they remind the king that his own authority is constantly being undermined by the Church's legal and jurisdictional powers. The undesirable political consequences of this situation are tellingly spelled out. The bishops are 'stronger in your Parliament house than yourself'. The clergy as a whole are able to 'exempt themselves from obedience' by appealing to the authority of the Pope. And the ordinary people are continually harassed in the ecclesiastical courts – and even murdered, as in the case of 'that honest merchant, Richard Hunne' (pp. 4, 8, 12).

As well as this mounting wave of anti-clericalism, there was a more serious movement of legal and political theory on the eve of the Reformation which was similarly concerned with the need to curtail the jurisdictions of the Papacy and the Church. In Germany this was associated, as a number of scholars have emphasised, with a sharply increased 'consciousness of national solidarity'.[1] This found its clearest expression in a growing hatred of all forms of ultramontane interference in the running of secular affairs. One of the most strident proclamations of this new sense of outrage at the Papacy's influence over German politics can be found in the later writings of von Hutten, many of which are based on a Tacitean distinction between the sober, innocent and freedom-loving Germans on the one hand, and the worldly, corrupt and exploitative Italians on the other. The same sentiments were no less fiercely expressed by several other leading German humanists of this period, including Brant, Pirckheimer and especially Wimpfeling. In 1506 Wimpfeling published a life of Jean Gerson with a strong defence of his conciliarism, and two years later he issued an edition of Lupold of Bebenburg's fourteenth-century treatise against the powers of the Pope (Schmidt, 1879, II, pp. 1, 325, 336). Wimpfeling also reveals a deep strain of anti-clerical and anti-Italian feeling in his own major work, *The Apology for the Christian Republic* of 1506. The *Apology* is partly devoted to a familiar humanist recital of clerical abuses, especially simony and concubinage. But the main target is the underlying idea of a separate and privileged clerical estate, with the result that the institution of monasticism, the jurisdiction of the canon lawyers and the interference of the Papacy in German affairs are all subjected to vehement criticism (Schmidt, 1879, I, pp. 122–3).

The most extensive roots of this form of nationalist hostility are to be found in England, where the Roman code of law was never in force, and where the claims of the Papacy and the canon lawyers tended in consequence to conflict most radically with the demands of common law and the enactments of Parliament. The resulting feelings of xenophobia towards the canonists as well as the civilians can be traced as far back as Bracton's defence of custom in the thirteenth century, and were strongly reiterated two centuries later by Sir John Fortescue (*c.* 1394–*c.* 1476) in his *Praise of the Laws of England*. When the prince asks his chancellor at the start of their dialogue whether he ought perhaps to concentrate on studying the civil law, he is roundly informed that the whole of the Roman code is alien to the 'political' nature of the English constitution (p. 25). The civil law is then subjected to a number of detailed criticisms, while the contentions of the canonists, as well as the special rights and jurisdictions claimed by the Pope as head of the Church, are all pointedly

[1] See for example the discussions in Holborn, 1937, p. 15 and in Dickens 1974, pp. 40–2.

ignored. The prince is told to concentrate entirely on the study of English custom and statute, and to treat 'all human laws' as either 'customs or statutes' unless they are clearly laws of nature (p. 37). The customary laws are then commended on the grounds (later to be echoed by Sir Edward Coke and later still by Burke) that they are perfectly adapted to the peculiarities of the English situation, while the powers of Parliament are vindicated on the grounds that every Englishman is represented whenever a statute is enacted (pp. 39–41). The special sensitivity of these laws to English needs and conditions is then taken to show that they alone deserve to be recognised. The strong implication is that any attempt to defend any other type of jurisdiction must be condemned as an instance of foreign interference.

There are many signs that by the start of the sixteenth century these traditional feelings of hostility to the legal powers of the Church were coming to be held by an increasing number of Englishmen with an increasing degree of strength. One important indication of this trend is provided by the writings of Edmund Dudley (1462–1510), who is chiefly remembered for his notorious ministerial collaboration with Richard Empson under Henry VII, as a result of which both ministers were sacrificed to the wrath of Parliament at the start of the new reign. Dudley was a common lawyer by training, who had studied at Gray's Inn and first attracted the King's attention through his extensive legal knowledge (Brodie, 1948, pp. 2–3, 9–10). As we have already seen, it was while he was awaiting execution in 1510 that Dudley wrote his only abstract work of legal and political theory, *The Tree of Commonwealth*. This has sometimes been dismissed as a disappointingly conservative work, on the grounds that it consists of little more than 'a medieval allegory carried almost to the length of parody' (Morris, 1953, p. 15). It is true that Dudley's image of the commonwealth as 'a fair and mighty tree' is somewhat extravagantly elaborated (p. 31). The tree is said to have five roots, the chief of which is love of God, the other four being justice, fidelity, concord and peace (pp. 32–4). Each root is depicted as bearing its own appropriate fruit, with 'honourable dignity' growing out of justice, 'worldly prosperity' out of fidelity, 'tranquillity' out of concord and 'good example' out of peace (pp. 51–6). To treat this apparently bland typology, however, as nothing more than a repetition of medieval commonplaces is perhaps to miss the note of warning which is sounded three times when the question of the Church's relationship to this structure is raised. When Dudley first tells us that the chief root of the commonwealth is love of God, it occurs to him that 'you will say percase the bishops and they of the spirituality have special charge of this root' (p. 32). He immediately insists, however, that 'the prince is the ground out of which this root must chiefly grow' (p. 32). It is he who must ensure that the good discipline of the Church is maintained, that 'the danger of simony' is averted, and that 'the prelates and such other as have great cures' do not neglect them (p. 25). The second warning is sounded when Dudley demands that the root of concord should be 'fastened right well in the clergy of this realm' (p. 44). The king is told to take special care to ensure that this root does not become damaged or disturbed by the Church's efforts to enforce its special legal rights and privileges (p. 42). But the loudest note of hostility is struck when Dudley discusses the need for each root to bring forth its appropriate fruit. There is said to be a special danger that the clergy will 'covet or desire' the 'fruit of honourable dignity', which is intended for the temporal rulers of the commonwealth (p. 56). The king is particularly advised that any such worldly ambitions on the part of the Church's leadership must above all be curtailed. He must ensure 'that none of them be in any temporal offices', and he must insist that they 'show themselves true priests of Christ's Church' by confining themselves to 'preaching the word of God truly and plainly to the temporal subjects' (pp. 25, 42–3). So far from being conservative, Dudley's doctrine is virtually Marsiglian in character.

We find the same increasing hostility to the powers of the Church being displayed by the English common lawyers on the eve of the breach with Rome. The most remarkable instance of this development is provided by the work of Christopher St German (c. 1460–1540), a veteran lawyer who was already over seventy years old when the Henrician schism took place. St German appears to have practised in relative obscurity at the Inner Temple down to about the year 1511, after which he seems to have gone into retirement. He re-emerged in the course of the 1520s, however, and from then until his death in 1540 he produced a series of extremely influential and increasingly radical attacks on the jurisdictions of the Church (Hogrefe, 1937).

The political implications of St German's legal philosophy were first developed in the Latin *Dialogue* on the concept of law which he published in 1523. This takes the form of a discussion between a Doctor and a Student about the foundations of the law, and mainly consists of an exposition by the Doctor of the different gradations of law – the eternal law, the laws of nature, the laws of God – and the relationship between these and the laws of England (Chrimes, 1936, pp. 204–14). The outcome is to suggest, very much in the manner of Fortescue, that the customary laws of England must be regarded as supreme. As Chrimes remarks, the whole work in fact reads like a commentary on Fortescue's jurisprudence

(Chrimes, 1936, p. 204). The anti-clerical undertones of this position were given greater emphasis in 1531, when St German translated the *Dialogue* into English as *Doctor and Student* – in which form the work served as a standard textbook in English legal theory almost until the time of Blackstone. At this point St German added a second dialogue (already published separately in 1530) together with an important appendix of thirteen 'additions' in which 'the power of the Parliament concerning the spirituality and spiritual jurisdiction' was 'most specially considered' (sig. A, 1b).[1] It was during the following year, however, that St German launched his major campaign against the clerical estate – as a result of which he became involved in a fierce series of exchanges with Sir Thomas More (Pineas, 1968, pp. 192–213). The pamphlet-war opened with the publication of St German's *Treatise* 'concerning the division between the spirituality and the temporality' in 1532. More replied in his *Apology*, St German countered with a Dialogue 'betwixt two Englishmen' with the somewhat un-English names of Salem and Bizance, and More returned the fire with his *Debellacion of Salem and Bizance* (Baumer, 1937, pp. 632–5). By this time St German was prepared to question not just the right of the ecclesiastical courts to prosecute alleged heretics, but the whole fabric of the Church's legal powers. His basic appeal in the *Treatise* is to the supremacy of statute, and thus to the overriding right of the King in Parliament to remove any 'evil customs' being upheld by the ecclesiastical authorities (pp. 232–40). This in turn leads him to insist that in maintaining their parallel system of laws, the leaders of the Church 'have many times exceeded their authority' and have 'attempted many things against the law of the realm' (pp. 232–3). Finally, St German went on to complete his campaign in his *Answer to a Letter*, which appears to have been published in 1535 (Baumer, 1937, pp. 644, 649). Here he independently arrived at both the main conclusions which the government's propagandists were by this time advancing as part of the official campaign to legitimate Henry's breach with Rome. He insists that the Papacy has no right to exercise any jurisdictional powers in England, and thus that Henry's new degree of control over the Church ought to be regarded as the resumption of a set of rights which his predecessors must have chosen to delegate. As the *Answer* puts it, the king's claim to be 'supreme head' of 'the Church of England' does not involve arrogating to himself 'any new power' over his subjects 'that he had not before' (sig. A, 3a). St German is also prepared by this stage to define the king's headship of the

[1] See Baumer, 1937, p. 633. The 'new additions' were also issued in the form of a separate tract entitled *A Little Treatise Called the New Additions*, and it is from this version that my quotations are taken.

Church, and to argue that it must cover the entire *potestas jurisdictionis*, including even 'the power to declare and expound scripture' and thus to determine doctrine (sig. F, 6a; sig. G, 3a). The radical and indeed Marsiglian assumption underlying both these claims is that all coercive and jurisdictional power must be treated as secular by definition, and thus that it must be an act of usurpation for the church to claim any such capacities on its own behalf. St German's corresponding conclusion is thus that all such powers must be vested in the supremacy of the common law, and all legislative authority in the sovereignty of the King in Parliament.

Finally, the same feelings of hostility to the powers of the Church were increasingly voiced on the eve of the Reformation by the secular authorities themselves. They objected first of all to the traditional privileges and jurisdictions claimed by the clerical estate. This often went with an increasing temptation to cast a predatory eye over the vast estates which a large number of religious communities had by this time managed to accumulate. These attitudes are especially noticeable in those countries which were later most receptive to the Lutheran reformation. The Swedish, Rad, for example, began an anti-clerical campaign in 1491, ending a long period of quiet relations with the ecclesiastical authorities by questioning the fiscal privileges as well as the amount of landed wealth enjoyed by the Swedish Church (Roberts, 1968, p. 62). The English government initiated a similar campaign at much the same time. Although the reign of Henry VII was in general marked by a continuation of traditional and amicable relations with the Church, a number of official moves were made both to curtail the privileges of the clergy and to improve the crown's capacity to gather taxes from them. An Act of 1491 sought to reduce the tax-exemptions which a number of religious houses had managed to negotiate in the course of the wars of the roses (Chrimes, 1972, p. 243). And a further series of Acts passed in 1489, 1491 and 1496 – and extended by Henry VIII in 1512 – launched a war of attrition against the system known as 'benefit of clergy' – the system which enabled the clergy to secure immunity from prosecution in the ordinary courts in the case of many felonies (Chrimes, 1972, p. 243). But the most dramatic campaign against the clerical estate was mounted in the series of *Gravamina*, or 'grievances of the German nation', which began to be regularly drawn up in the second half of the fifteenth century by the Imperial Diets. The practice began in earnest as early as the Diet of Frankfurt in 1456, and was revived by the Emperor Maximilian on the eve of the Reformation (Dickens, 1974, pp. 7–8). The task of revising the list of charges was entrusted to Jacob Wimpfeling, who responded in 1515 with a list of Ten Articles attacking the privileges of the clergy as well as the powers of the Pope (Schmidt, 1879, I, 116–17). The climax of the tradition came after Luther's first protests, when the list of 1515 was expanded into over a hundred charges by the Diet of Worms in 1521. The historical irony needs no underlining: the same Diet which condemned Luther's heresy went on to produce the most spectacular *Statement of Grievances* against the Church. The authors of the *Statement* begin by complaining about 'benefit of clergy', arguing that the system is 'bound to encourage clerics to wicked acts, the more since ecclesiastical courts let them go scot-free, no matter what their offence' (p. 58). Next they claim that the clergy are 'undercutting secular authority', since they 'drag laymen into ecclesiastical courts' and 'take over what they wish' from the jurisdictions of the ordinary courts at the same time (p. 62). And above all they complain about the overweening wealth and power of the Church. Unless it is controlled, they contend, 'the secular estate will, in course of time, be altogether bought out by the Church' (p. 58).

The other and even more contentious point at which the secular authorities began to put increasing pressure on the Church was in connection with the supra-national jurisdictions traditionally exercised by the Pope. There was a growing sense of resentment at the Papacy's right to act as a tax-gatherer on its own behalf, and to control the award of benefices within each of the national Churches. One outcome was that in several countries the secular authorities managed to bargain with the Papacy and wring concessions from it on each of these vital points. This enabled them to preserve relatively friendly relations with the Church, while managing at the same time to insist on their status as 'imperial' rulers, exercising complete jurisdictional control within their own territories. The first kingdom to achieve such a resolution of these tensions was France. The Pragmatic Sanction of Bourges in 1438 not only adopted the thesis of conciliarism, but managed decisively to curtail the powers of the Papacy in France. The Pope's right to collect Annates was questioned, his right to make nominations to vacant sees by 'reserving' them was withdrawn, and his right to 'supplicate' in favour of a particular candidate for a benefice was in most cases transferred to the crown (Petit-Dutaillis, 1902, p. 268). Apart from the reintroduction of Annates, all these concessions were later confirmed by the Concordat of Bologna in 1516 (Lemonnier, 1903, p. 254). By this time a similar and even more sweeping set of Concordats had been arranged between the Papacy and the secular authorities in Spain. After a long quarrel with Ferdinand and Isabella, Sixtus IV finally conceded in 1482 that the right of 'supplication' should be transferred to the crown in the case of all major ecclesiastical appointments (Elliott, 1963, pp. 89–90). Four years later the crown gained a similar right of patronage and presentation throughout the whole of the conquered kingdom of Granada, and in 1508 the same concession was extended to cover the entire Church in the New World (Elliott, 1963, p. 90).

Where it proved possible to arrange such Concordats, the governments involved – as in France and Spain – tended to remain faithful to the Catholic Church throughout the Reformation. But where the disputes over Annates, appointments and appeals remained unresolved – as in England, Germany and Scandinavia – the pressures on the Papacy continued to build up. Even before Luther's protestations began to be heard outside Germany, it is clear that these pressures had already come almost to breaking-point.

In Denmark the danger-level was reached under Christian II, with his promulgation in 1521–2 of the Byretten Civil and Ecclesiastical Code. This proposed to end all Appeals to Rome, to remove the powers of the ecclesiastical courts in all cases involving property, and to establish a new royal court with ultimate authority to decide all ecclesiastical as well as civil causes (Dunkley, 1948, pp. 25–7). A similar crisis broke in Sweden at the same time. Gustav Vasa refused at his accession in 1523 to recognise the Pope's nomination to the bishopric of Skara, and it has even been argued that the severance of the Swedish Church from Rome ought to be dated from this point (Bergendoff, 1928, p. 10). By this time, similar pressures had begun to produce ominous signs of a breach between the *regnum* and the *sacerdotium* in England. The first cracks began to appear in connection with the Papacy's activities as a tax-gatherer. When the Pope sent his sub-collector Peter Gryphius to England in 1509, the government prevented him from acting for over a year (Pickthorn, 1934, p. 111). When a Papal subsidy was demanded six years later for an alleged crusade, this met with a point-blank refusal (Lunt, 1962, pp. 160–1). But the major government attack developed when Convocation attempted in 1515 to protest against the Act limiting benefit of clergy which had been passed in 1512. The Church's lawyers argued that since the legal head of the Church is not the King but the Pope, the King must have exceeded his authority in seeking to subject the clergy to the secular courts (Pickthorn, 1934, pp. 115–16). This in turn prompted the King and judges – in a portent of the ideological changes to come – to issue an uncompromising declaration of their superiority over any alleged jurisdictions of the Pope. They declared the whole of Convocation subject to a charge of *praemunire* for seeking to subordinate the King's authority to that of a foreign power, and the King went on to deliver a speech to Convocation in which he vehemently reasserted the 'imperial' rights of the English crown. The main argument he used – in direct defiance of canon law – was that 'kings of England in time past never had any superior but God', and he solemnly warned his bishops – in another portent of things to come – that 'we will maintain the rights of the crown in this matter' against any claims advanced by the Pope or the Church (Pickthorn, 1934, p. 117).

We must again turn to the *Gravamina* of the German nation, however, for the most dramatic evidence that, even before Luther's initial protest, a crisis had already been reached in the relations between the Papacy and the secular authorities. The lists of *Gravamina* had always focused on the extent of the Pope's powers in Germany, and when Wimpfeling redrew the charges on the eve of the Reformation he laid an overwhelming emphasis on this grievance against the Church. The popes 'fail to observe their predecessors' Bulls' and 'violate them with their dispensations' (Article I). They continually 'reject the elections to bishoprics made in Germany' and impose their own worthless candidates (Articles II and III). They reserve the best benefices for members of the Papal court, and take no care over the rest (Articles IV and V). And above all they make avaricious financial demands, 'continuing to exact Annates' and imposing more and more grasping taxes on the German people (Article VI).[1] When the representatives of the laity at the Diet of Worms came to draw up their definitive *Statement of Grievances* six years later, all these protests were reiterated. Again they complain that 'Rome awards German benefices to unqualified, unlearned and unfit persons', and that the 'taxes and tributes' paid by the German nation are 'almost daily raised in amount' by the Church (pp. 54–5). And above all they complain about the way in which Papal jurisdictions are used to infringe the rights of the secular authorities. The Church courts are continually claiming extra powers, so that 'secular cases are tried before ecclesiastical courts which are, needless to say, biased in opinions and judgment' (p. 53). And the greatest abuse of all – the first charge on the entire list – is that appeals are continually made to Rome 'in the first instance' over 'worldly concerns', a practice which can only be 'conducive to the curtailment of the competence of secular authorities' (p. 53).

Given this background of increasing hostility to the powers of the Church, it is not surprising to find that, as soon as the Reformation began to gather momentum, most of these lay critics found themselves increasingly attracted towards the Lutheran cause. This can be observed in the

[1] For this list of charges see Schmidt, 1879, I, pp. 116–17.

first place amongst a majority of the legal and humanist critics we have considered. Most of the leaders of the anti-clerical campaign in England, including Barlowe, Roy and Fish, turned to Lutheranism in the course of the 1520s (Clebsch, 1964, pp. 229–31). Fish seems to have gone on to become a dealer in censored Lutheran books and translations, for when Robert Necton was arraigned before Wolsey in 1528 to answer a charge of heresy, he confessed that he had been told 'Mr Fish had New Testaments to sell', and that he had bought several dozen copies of Tyndale's translation from him (Mozley, 1937, pp. 349–50). The same process can be observed amongst the leading anti-clerical writers in Germany. Wimpfeling eventually wavered, but von Hutten soon became an enthusiastic convert to the new faith. Although he began by dismissing the debate over indulgences as just another instance of monkish quarrelling, he was soon persuaded – by his hero Erasmus, ironically enough – to see the wider implications of Luther's protest, and by 1520 he had established contact with both Luther and Melanchthon and begun to correspond with them (Holborn, 1937, pp. 102, 122). Shortly after this he declared to Luther that 'I have been with you' and 'will stand by you, whatever comes' (Holborn, 1937, p. 125). And by the time of Luther's summons to Worms in the following year, von Hutten was writing to assure him that 'you need never doubt my constancy' (Holborn, 1937, pp. 157–60, 171).

But the point of major historical importance is of course that most of the secular rulers of northern Europe began to feel a similar attraction towards the Lutheran cause. Where they had been unable to gain satisfactory concordats with the Papacy, they began to flirt with Lutheran ideas, and in this way raised the pressure of their campaigns against the Church to breaking-point. This happened first of all in the course of their campaigns to improve their control over the fiscal privileges and landed wealth of the Church within their own territories. A sharply intensified pursuit of these aims provided the immediate background and (according to such authorities as Lortz) the main motive in every country for the official acceptance of the the Lutheran faith (Lortz, 1968, 1, pp. 158–64; cf. Grimm, 1948, p. 87). It is true that this process appears less clear-cut in Germany than elsewhere. This is partly because the acceptance of the Reformation in the German cities was unquestionably a more popular and less cynical process than this explanation assumes, but also because many of the German princes – even though their motives may have been wholly mercenary – proved incapable of realising the financial gains they clearly hoped to make out of their adoption of the Lutheran faith.[1] It is still evident, however, that even in Germany these ambitions often sup-

[1] On these points see Chrisman, 1967, and Moeller, 1972.

plied the dominant motive for the behaviour of the secular authorities. Albert of Hohenzollern's early defection to the Lutheran camp was accompanied by the secularisation of the lands of the Teutonic Knights, while Philip of Hesse's reformation of 1526 was accompanied by a seizure of monastic lands, out of which Philip's own gains have been assessed as 'very considerable' (Carsten, 1959, p. 161). And when we turn to the more unified national monarchies, we find the same ambitions being pursued in every case. In Sweden Gustav Vasa heralded his official acceptance of the Reformation in 1524 by transferring the receipt of tithes from the Church to the crown, and completed the process three years later by sequestering the entire property of the Church (Bergendoff, 1928, pp. 15, 40–1). In Denmark a similar campaign was initiated by Frederick I, who began to take over monastic lands as early as 1528. The process was completed under Christian III, who accompanied his removal of the bishops in 1536 with the abolition of all their temporal powers and the confiscation of their lands (Dunkley, 1948, pp. 55–9, 70–1). And in England a further campaign of the same character preceded the breach with Rome in the early 1530s. The schism was initiated with an attack on the payment of Annates, and immediately followed by the secularisation of all monastic lands, a move which appears to have been planned some considerable time in advance (Dickens, 1964, p. 197).

The same willingness on the part of the secular authorities to push their campaigns against the Church to breaking-point can be seen in the case of their long-standing attempts to curtail the supra-national jurisdictions of the Pope. The clearest instance is of course provided by Henry VIII's struggles with the Papacy over the question of his divorce.[1] When he succeeded to the throne in 1509 Henry had married Catherine of Aragon, the widow of his elder brother Prince Arthur. By 1525, however, a series of miscarriages had persuaded him that she would never succeed in providing him with a male heir. By 1527 he was eager in any case to marry Anne Boleyn (Scarisbrick, 1968, pp. 149–50). He accordingly petitioned the Pope, Clement VII, to grant him a divorce. The King undoubtedly had a case in canon law, but a combination of political circumstances in Rome after 1527 made it impossible to gain the Pope's consent (Scarisbrick, 1968, pp. 163–97). The king and his ministers thus found themselves committed to putting more and more pressure on the Church. First they insisted on a re-trial of the divorce case. Next they summoned a Parliament in 1529 and encouraged it to give free expression to its strongly anti-clerical feelings, simmering ever since Hunne's case. Finally

---

[1] The following details are mainly taken from Dickens, 1964, an account to which I am much indebted. See esp. pp. 151–6.

they indicted the whole clerical estate on a charge of *praemunire* and ordered them to buy the King's pardon by paying a vast fine (Lehmberg, 1970, pp. 109–13). None of these threatening gestures, however, showed any signs of cowing the Pope. The result was that, since the King remained determined to get his divorce, he increased his pressure on the Church to breaking-point in order to ensure that he duly got it.

These flirtations with Lutheran attitudes by the secular rulers of northern Europe in turn helped more than anything else to advance the cause of the Reformation and the Lutheran Church. It is of course doubt-ful whether the secular rulers themselves were genuinely interested in bringing about this result. Both the timing and the character of the reform movements they initiated suggest that they were largely uncon-cerned with the doctrines of the Reformation, except for their obvious value as ideological weapons in their struggles to control the wealth and power of the Church. Some rulers (notably Henry VIII) never showed any inclination to become Lutherans, while others who did become converted (such as Gustav Vasa) appear to have accepted the Lutheran faith purely as a means of furthering their own self-interested ends. The question of motivation, however, is not the crucial one. The main prob-lem for the secular authorities was to legitimate their campaigns against the powers of the Church. When they decided to repudiate the jurisdic-tions of the Papacy, this left them in quest of any arguments tending to show that the Church as a whole had no right to exercise any such juris-dictional powers. This in turn led them to make common cause with the Lutherans. Whatever their motives, the outcome was in each case the same: the spread of the Lutheran heresy proved to be the price of their breach with Rome. The same applies in the case of the campaigns they mounted to control the wealth of the Church. Their need to legitimate this move meant that they found themselves in quest of any arguments tending to show that the true Church is nothing but a *congregatio fidelium*, and thus that it has no title to possess extensive worldly goods. Again, this led them to ally with the Lutherans, and again, whatever their motives, the outcome was the same: the price of princely avarice proved to be the endorsement of a 'full and godly' reformation.

3

The spread of Lutheranism

Luther's enemies frequently compared the Reformation with the plague, seeing it as a bringer of spiritual death on a terrifying scale.[1] So far we have sought to explain why the disease proved so highly infectious over such a wide area of northern Europe. It remains to consider the stages by which the epidemic spread – the stages by which the social and political doctrines associated with the Reformation first of all succeeded in gaining such an extensive popular following, and subsequently came to be officially recognised by the secular rulers of Germany, England and Scandinavia.

THE EARLY PROPAGANDISTS

The first stage in the evolution of Lutheranism as a political ideology took the form of a propaganda campaign in which a number of Luther's closest disciples began to clarify and extend his relatively fragmentary insights by producing a series of more connected treatises on social and political life. Amongst the most influential contributors to this development were Osiander, Eberlin von Günzburg and of course Melanchthon. Osiander's most important observations on politics only appeared at the end of the 1520s, but Eberlin and Melanchthon were amongst the earliest Lutherans to discuss the political implications of the new faith. Eberlin wrote extensively on political themes, his most original contribution being a vernacular tract entitled *The Fifteen Confederates*, which first appeared in 1521. Melanchthon issued an important essay on the concept of 'worldly authority' in the same year, publishing it as the conclusion to his comprehensive survey of *Common Topics in Theology*.[2] Soon the impact

[1] The comparison is even made by a number of Luther's contemporaries – for example, John Mair – who had themselves been highly critical of the Church. As well as being a convinced opponent of Papal monarchy, Mair mounted a strong attack on indulgences in his *Clear Expositions of the Four Gospels* in 1529 (see fo lxxxiva). Nevertheless, his Preface to the *Clear Expositions* describes the Reformation as 'an infection' and attacks the Lutherans as 'a pestiferous sect' (see sig. Aa, 2a).

[2] My quotations are taken from the 1555 edition, which has some claims to be regarded as the definitive one. On this point see Manschreck, 1965, pp. xxiii–xxiv.

of these works and of Luther's own political writings began to be felt in England, especially amongst those converts who – like Tyndale and Barnes – had gone to study in Wittenberg during the early 1520s. Tyndale returned to complete his major treatise on *The Obedience of a Christian Man* in 1528, and in the following years Barnes produced a number of brief but significant political tracts, including an analysis of *What the Church is* and an essay on *Men's Constitutions*.[1]

Amongst these seminal attempts to amplify and propagate Luther's political ideas, the writings of Eberlin stand somewhat apart, being less homiletic and more speculative than the mainstream of early Reformation political thought.[2] His *Fifteen Confederates*, for example, takes the form of a Utopia in which the nobility and people of an imaginary commonwealth called Wolfaria are shown reforming their Church and imposing the institution of clerical marriage (cf. Bell, 1967). The political writings of Melanchthon, Tyndale and Barnes, however, can fittingly be considered together, since they all take up a similar range of questions, which they largely derive from Luther's own works, and generally analyse in a markedly similar style. They may thus be regarded as the most representative as well as influential of the pioneering contributions to Lutheran political thought.

The point of departure for all these writers is supplied by one os Luther's main theological premises: the claim that the whole world if providentially ordered, and that everything happening in it must be a reflection of God's will and purposes. Melanchthon begins his account of worldly authority with an apostrophe to the 'orders and works' which are 'decreed for the protection and maintenance of this life' (pp. 323–4). Tyndale begins *The Obedience of a Christian Man* in a similar style, praising the order which God has instituted throughout creation, and treating the obedience which is owed by subjects to their rulers as symmetrical with the obedience which God intends children to show to their parents, wives to their husbands and servants to their masters (pp. 168–73). All these writers then go on to derive from this premise the same funda-

[1] Barnes's analysis of the Church originally appeared in the Antwerp edition of his *Supplication*. In citing from this and from *Men's Constitutions* I am using the versions which appear in Tjernagel, 1963.

[2] It should be noted that none of the seminal works of Lutheran political theory were produced in Scandinavia, where the leaders of the Reformation generally confined themselves to the writing of devotional works. This is true of Tausen and Sadolin in Denmark, and even of Laurensson, except for the *Short Instruction* he published in 1533 on the nature of the Church and its relations with political society (cf. Dunkley, 1948, pp. 56, 115, 149). The same applies in Sweden, where even Olaus Petri devoted himself almost exclusively to theological questions, his chief vernacular works (apart from his translations) being his *Little Book Concerning the Sacraments* of 1528 and his Lutheran service manual of the following year (cf. Bergendoff, 1928, pp. 133–5, 169–77).

mental conclusion: that all existing political systems must be taken to form a part of God's providential design for the world. The whole of the first half of Melanchthon's discussion of worldly authority is devoted to this theme, and culminates in a citation of St Paul's claim that all the powers that be are 'ordained of God' (pp. 326–7). The same point is made at the beginning of Barnes's account of *Men's Constitutions* – with the same appeal to St Paul's authority – and is even more emphatically underlined at the start of *The Obedience of a Christian Man*. Tyndale begins his account of 'the obedience of subjects unto kings, princes and rulers' by citing St Paul's discussion in its entirety. He then goes on to offer an extensive gloss on it, declaring that God himself 'has given laws unto all nations, and in all lands has put kings, governors and rulers in His own stead, to rule the world through them' (p. 174). This is said to explain why rulers and judges 'are called gods in the scriptures'. The reason is that 'they are in God's room and execute the commandments of God' (p. 175).

The claim that God institutes the whole fabric of political life leads directly to the question these writers are chiefly concerned to analyse: the question of what political duties God has in consequence imposed on those He has ordained to be rulers and on those He has called to be subjects. The first strictly political issue they consider is thus the nature of the duties we owe to those whom God has placed over us. They all arrive with complete decisiveness at the same two conclusions. The first is that our rulers must be obeyed in all things – and not merely out of fear, but (as St Paul decrees) for conscience's sake. This is particularly stressed by Melanchthon, of whom it has been said that he 'dreads nothing so much as the charge of sedition' (Hildebrandt, 1946, p. 56). He insists, against the antinomianism of the radical reformers, that there is no reason why 'a member of Christ' should not 'use the authority of government' without any feeling 'that such works are against God' (p. 329). And he invokes St Paul in concluding 'that obedience is necessary, that disobedience hurts the conscience, and that God condemns it' (p. 334). The same point is made by Barnes and Tyndale at the start of their discussions of temporal power. As Barnes puts it in *Men's Constitutions*, 'we must be obedient to this power in all things that pertain to the ministration of this present life and of the commonwealth', and not only 'for avoiding punishment', but also 'for conscience's sake, for this is the will of God' (p. 81). The other conclusion they are equally at pains to establish is that it can never be justifiable in any circumstances for a subject to resist a ruler's commands. As Melanchthon declares, 'deliberate disobedience against the worldly authority, and against true or reasonable laws, is deadly sin, sin which God punishes with eternal damnation if we obstinately continue in it' (p. 333). Again both Barnes and Tyndale reiterate the same point. Barnes enunciates a simple rule in *Men's Constitutions* for a subject to follow if his ruler 'tyrannically makes any command contrary to right and law': you may 'only flee or else obey the thing that is commanded you' for 'in no case may you resist with sword and hand' (pp. 81–2). And Tyndale elaborates the same typically Lutheran theme. He begins by conceding that people 'for the most part' are 'ever ready to rise and to fight' (p. 165). He goes on to express his horror at this situation, citing St Paul's claim that to fight one's superiors is equivalent to resisting God, 'for they are in the room of God, and they that resist shall receive the damnation' (p. 175). These conclusions are then illustrated with a number of Biblical stories, all of which are taken to show that any resistance to lawful authority is always evil and never appropriate (pp. 175–8).

Next, these writers consider the complementary aspect of the same theme of political duty: the nature of the duties owed by the ruler to God and the people. The basic claim they advance is that, since all rulers are given by God to fulfil His own purposes, it follows that they have a duty to rule the people not as they themselves want, but rather as God wants. They must constantly remember, as Tyndale affirms, 'that the people are God's, and not their's', and that 'the law is God's, and not the king's' (pp. 202, 334). The true role of the king is that of 'a servant, to execute the laws of God, and not to rule after his own imagination' (p. 334). Tyndale is less concerned, however, with the duties of rulers than with their powers, and especially with the question of their powers over the Church. He thus confines himself to giving a general summary of their obligations in the 'rehearsal' which concludes *The Obedience of a Christian Man*. There he simply exhorts them 'to remember that they are heads and arms, to defend the body, to minister peace, health and wealth, and even to save the body; and that they have received their offices of God, to minister and to do service unto their brethren' (p. 334). If we turn to Melanchthon's account, however, we find a much more precise discussion of both the nature and range of the duties which are laid upon the 'godly prince'. First he gives an account of the limits which are placed on the prince's actions by his duty to enact only the laws of God. It is at this point that he develops his highly influential doctrine of 'adiaphora', or 'indifferent things' (Manschreck, 1957, pp. 176–81). This is based on a distinction between divine and human law. The laws of God are essential for salvation and must always be enforced. But there are many human laws which are not essential for salvation, and are in this sense 'indifferent'. It follows that God intends a number of activities neither to be prescribed

nor forbidden, and that 'an erroneous situation' will be created 'by enact-
ing them into laws' (p. 308). The same doctrine was soon taken up by
Barnes and several other Lutheran theorists in England. As Barnes
expresses it in his essay on the Church, the godly prince is limited in two
different ways. He needs of course to ensure that he never legislates
'directly against the word of God and the destruction of faith'. But he also
needs to ensure that he never attempts to 'command certain indifferent
things as if they must be done of necessity' (p. 90). Melanchthon's more
basic concern, however, in this section of his discussion is to analyse the
positive duties of the godly prince. He first argues that all rulers must
punish heresy and promote true religion. They are 'obliged to prohibit
all wrong doctrine, such as the errors of the Anabaptists, and to punish the
obstinate' (p. 337). They are also 'obliged to accept the holy gospel, to
believe, confess, and direct others to true divine service' (p. 336). The
other point he stresses is that all rulers must protect and never infringe
their subjects' property rights. It has been suggested that, in pointing in
this way to the purely social as well as religious aspects of good government, Melanchthon must have been attempting to widen the conception
of rulership which Luther had set out (Allen, 1957, p. 33). It is certainly
true that he lays a very strong emphasis on the idea that 'the goods of the
subjects are not to be appropriated by the master unless the common
necessity of the country requires this' (p. 338). He cites the 'frightful
example' of Naboth's vineyard, from which he derives the moral that a
subject's goods are 'part of the divine order in worldly government and
political society, just as judgment or punishment is. Therefore, the
princes should not destroy this order; they should know that they also
come under the commandment, "You shall not steal" ' (p. 338).

The great emphasis which all these early Lutherans place on the duties
of the godly prince points to a further and somewhat awkward question
which they are unable to evade: the question of what action, if any, should
be taken by the subjects of a ruler who fails to discharge his duties properly. Melanchthon offers a rather vague and timid version of Luther's doctrine at this point. He mentions the caveat that 'we should obey God
rather than men', but he mainly insists on the continuing duty of every
subject to 'be patient with reasonable rulers', even if 'mistakes and defects
occur' in their government (pp. 334, 340). Most of Luther's early disciples,
however, follow the more decisive lead which Luther himself had given
on this issue, and go on to offer two contrasting pieces of advice. The first
is that any ruler whose orders offend against the conscience of his truly
religious subjects must always be disobeyed. This simply follows, as
Barnes points out in his essay on the Church, from the fact that it is 'more

right to obey God than man' (p. 86). The implication of this injunction, as Tyndale indicates in the conclusion of his *Christian Man*, is that if we receive a 'command to do evil, we must then disobey, and say "We are otherwise commanded of God" ' (p. 332). Their other piece of advice is that, even in this situation, no subject must ever offer actively to resist. As Barnes goes on to insist, they must 'let the king exercise his tyranny. Under no circumstances shall they withstand him with violence, but suffer patiently all the tyranny that he imposes on them in their bodies and their property' (pp. 84–5). The same harsh lesson is equally under-lined in Tyndale's account. Although we are told to remind our rulers, when they command us to do wrong, that we are otherwise commanded of God, we are told at the same time that we must in no circumstances 'rise against them'. Tyndale imagines the protest we may be inclined to make: ' "They will kill us then", sayest thou.' But his answer is that we are still bound to submit: 'Therefore, I say, is a Christian called to suffer even the bitter death for his hope's sake, and because he will do no evil' (p. 332).

Sir Thomas More, in his *Dialogue* of 1529 against Tyndale, fixed on this insistence that an evil command must never be obeyed, and went on to declare that Tyndale in 'his holy book of disobedience' was arguing in favour of treason and rebellion (p. 273). The charge is manifestly unfair, unless More had in mind the consequences which might follow from very widespread civil disobedience. Tyndale in fact lays an unusually strong emphasis on the absolute Lutheran distinction between disobedience and resistance. He regards all 'heads and governors' as 'the gift of God, whether they be good or bad' (p. 194). And he goes on to infer that 'evil rulers' are simply 'a sign that God is angry and wroth with us' (p. 195). He is thus committed to repeating the harsh conclusion which Luther himself had already reached – the conclusion that it may be *particularly* wrong to resist tyrannical rulers. They are sent to plague us 'because that when they were good, we would not receive that goodness of the hand of God' (p. 194). If we resist them, we are really trying to evade a just punishment deliberately imposed by God. We are thereby laying our-selves open to the danger that in 'seeking to set ourselves at liberty' we may only succeed in angering God still further, with the result that we may find ourselves cast into a 'more evil bondage' than ever before (p. 196).

The political writings of the early Lutherans were in many cases confined exclusively to the themes we have now discussed. This applies, for example, to Melanchthon's account in his *Common Topics*. His sole concern is with the question of political duty, and especially with the duties of the godly prince. A number of Luther's disciples, however, went on to consider a second basic premise of his theology, and to derive from it a further set of political conclusions. The point of departure in this case was Luther's concept of the Church. Melanchthon is curiously reticent on this issue, even though he includes a chapter on the Church in his *Common Topics*, and begins by defining it in a characteristically Lutheran fashion as nothing more than a 'gathered company' (p. 226). But if we turn to the early Lutherans in England, we find that – perhaps because of the political situation there – they often showed a special interest in submitting the concept of the Church to a more detailed analysis. As we have seen, part of Robert Barnes's *Supplication* is devoted to considering 'what the Church is and who be thereof'. He begins by pointing out that 'the word *ecclesia*' is 'often used for the whole congregation', but he argues that two different sorts of congregation need to be distinguished. One is simply 'the whole multitude of the people'. This cannot be equated with the true Church, since it includes all the reprobate as well as the saved. The other is the congregation of the faithful who 'believe that Christ has washed them from their sins'. It is this type of congregation, and nothing else, which makes up 'the Church of God' (pp. 37, 39). This means that 'the very true Church' is 'invisible from carnal eyes', because it consists of nothing more than 'the congregation of faithful men wherever they are in the world', and 'neither the Pope nor yet his cardinals are more this Church or of this Church than the poorest man on earth' (pp. 40–1).

Tyndale provided this argument with powerful support in his translation of the New Testament. He invariably renders *ecclesia* as 'congregation' rather than as 'church', while *presbyteros* is at first translated as 'senior' and in later versions as 'elder', but never as 'priest' (Mozley, 1937, pp. 90–3). More denounced these 'Lutheran' renderings in his *Dialogue*, asserting that the attempt to find heretical errors in Tyndale's translation was like attempting 'to find water in the sea' (p. 207). Tyndale begins his *Answer* of 1531, however, by mounting an able defence of his work against these charges of deliberate mistranslation, a defence which modern scholars have largely upheld (Mozley, 1937, p. 97). He reiterates his claim that *presbyteros* should be rendered as 'elder', while conceding that 'senior' is 'no very good English' (p. 16). And he insists that *ecclesia* must be taken to refer to 'the whole multitude of all them that receive the name of Christ to believe in him', adding that this is acknowledged even by More's 'darling Erasmus', who frequently translates '*ecclesia* into *congregation*' (pp. 12, 16; cf. also p. 226).

This treatment of the Church simply as a congregation presided over by its elders carried with it a crucial political implication which Luther himself had already underlined. Since the Church is on this account a purely spiritual body, and since the exercise of power is essentially a temporal matter, it follows that the Church cannot properly be regarded as a jurisdictional authority at all. This implication is rigorously drawn by Barnes in his tract on the nature of the Church. 'It has nothing to do with the external justice and righteousness of the world, and, therefore, it has no power by right and law to make any statutes to order the world, but only to preach faithfully and truly and to minister the word of God' (p. 89). This implies in turn that the Church's officers cannot claim any right to exempt themselves from the ordinary laws. This further point is especially stressed by Tyndale, as a corollary of his basic contention that everyone has a duty to obey his ruler in all things. 'No person, neither any degree, may be exempt from this ordinance of God: neither can the profession of monks and friars, or any thing that the Pope or bishops can lay for themselves, except them from the sword of the Emperor or kings, if they break the laws. For it is written, "Let every soul submit himself unto the authority of the higher powers." Here is no man except; but all souls must obey' (p. 178).

Tyndale finally goes on to consider two further implications of this argument, both of which involved him in a strong defence of the secular authorities, and help to explain why Henry VIII is said to have found *The Obedience of a Christian Man* 'a book for me and all kings to read' when Anne Boleyn rather cunningly brought it to his attention in 1529 (Mozley, 1937, p. 143). He first insists that all existing jurisdictions claimed by the Pope and the Catholic Church must be illegal and even damnable usurpations of authority. The argument is broached in a section entitled 'Against the Pope's false power', and takes the form of an attack on the views of John Fisher, the Bishop of Rochester, who was soon to become a martyr to the old religion along with Sir Thomas More. Fisher had delivered a famous sermon in 1521, defending the jurisdictions of the Pope against Luther's attacks (Surtz, 1967, pp. 302–7). Tyndale denounces it as 'stark mad with pure malice', and insists that the powers it claims for the Papacy amount to an illegal attempt to withdraw the Church 'from all obedience to princes' and to rob 'all realms, not of God's word only, but also of all wealth and prosperity' (pp. 191, 221). The 'rehearsal' with which Tyndale concludes his treatise returns fiercely to the same attack on 'the wickedness of the spirituality, the falsehead of the bishops, and juggling of the Pope' (p. 336). By this stage Tyndale claims to have proved that the Church's demands for 'so great authority and so great liberties' are not merely divisive but are also condemned 'by all the laws of God'.

He thus ends by threatening that since 'no king has power to grant them such liberty', the secular authorities will be 'as well damned for their giving' the Church such powers as the Church will be 'for their false purchasing' of them (p. 333).

Finally, Tyndale draws the conclusion that all these ecclesiastical jurisdictions and liberties ought immediately to be abolished and taken over by the secular authorities. This is the theme of the section entitled 'Anti-Christ'. The present political situation in all Christian countries is that 'the Emperor and kings are nothing nowadays but even hangmen unto the Pope and bishops' (p. 242). But the proper situation, as specified by 'God's ordinance in every land', is that there should be 'one king, one law' (p. 240). It follows that the secular authorities ought to rid themselves of the 'wily tyranny' currently being imposed on them by the prelates, to 'take away from them their lands which they have gotten with their false prayers', and to 'rule their realms themselves, with the help of laymen that are sage, wise, learned and expert' (pp. 206, 240, 335). Tyndale's final word thus brings him very close to the call soon to be heard amongst the protagonists of the Reformation all over Europe: the call for 'a godly prince' to enact 'a full and godly reformation'.

THE DEFECTION OF THE RADICALS

The political theories of the early Lutherans played a vital role in helping to legitimate the emerging absolutist monarchies of northern Europe. By arguing that the Church is nothing more than a *congregatio fidelium*, they automatically assigned the exercise of all coercive authority to kings and magistrates, and in this way crucially extended the range of their powers. This in turn led them to reject one of the traditional limitations on the authority of secular rulers: they explicitly denied the orthodox Catholic claim that a tyrant may be judged and deposed by the authority of the Church. Secondly, they introduced a new note of passivity into the discussion of political obligation. By insisting that all the powers that be must be treated as a direct gift of God's providence, they committed themselves to saying that even tyrants rule by divine right, and that even when they do manifest wrong it must still be blasphemous to oppose them. They thus withdrew the other traditional limitation on the authority of secular rulers: they rejected any suggestion that the law of nature may be used as a touchstone for condemning or even questioning the behaviour of our superiors. Thus it came about that when Abednego Seller produced his *History of Passive Obedience* at the end of the seventeenth century, he was able to trace the theories of absolutism and non-resistance back to 'the infancy of the happy Reformation', and to point out that 'the most eminent of the reformed divines beyond sea' as well as 'the martyr Tyndale' and all his English followers had been amongst the first to argue that any ruler must be absolutely unaccountable to his subjects, since 'a king is accountable to God only for his faults' and 'has no peer upon earth, being greater than all men, and inferior to God alone'.[1]

It would be misleading, however, to give the impression that the political theories associated with the spread of the Reformation were exclusively of such a deeply conservative character. First of all, it would be a mistake to suppose – although it has often been argued – that Luther and his immediate followers 'never allowed the right of overt resistance', and at all times preached that 'there is no justification in any case whatsoever' for active opposition to our rulers and magistrates.[2] There is no doubt that if we concentrate on the early years of the Reformation, we find a doctrine of absolute non-resistance being vehemently defended by all the leaders of the Lutheran Church. If we turn, however, to the period after 1530, we encounter a complete *volte face*: we find Luther, Melanchthon, Osiander and many of their most prominent followers suddenly changing their minds, and arguing instead that any ruler who becomes a tyrant may be lawfully and forcibly opposed. As we shall later seek to show, this more subversive strand of Lutheranism – though never dominant – subsequently came to exercise a powerful influence: it helped to inspire the radical theories of the later Calvinists, and in this way made a crucial contribution to the formation of the revolutionary political ideologies which emerged in the latter half of the sixteenth century.[3]

The other and more familiar element of radicalism which developed in the early years of the Reformation was largely the outcome of a reaction against the original and unmitigated conservatism of the Lutheran leadership. A number of the earliest and most ardent converts to the cause of reform, especially in Switzerland and Germany, began to insist on the need to bring about religious and political change without any of the

[1] The three basic contentions advanced by the early Lutherans – that all rulers are divinely ordained, accountable only to God, and able to command absolute non-resistance – are together treated by Figgis as definitive of the ideology of 'the divine right of kings'. See Figgis, 1914, pp. 5–6. For Seller's remarks quoted above see his *History*, sig. A 2b, and pp. 20, 126.
[2] For these judgments see respectively Figgis, 1960, pp. 74–5, 86, and Allen, 1957, pp. 8, 29. The fact that Luther changed his mind over this issue is noted by Mesnard, 1936, p. 228. The fact that the change of opinion was permanent is emphasised by Carlyle, 1936, pp. 280–3. Despite the availability of these judgments, however, most textbooks on the Reformation continue to insist that the 'doctrine of obedience' to constituted authority 'characterises all political thought of the period, Catholic as well as reformed'. For this claim see Elton, 1963, p. 63 and cf. the similar claims in Strohl, 1930, p. 126, Walzer, 1966, p. 23, etc.
[3] For a fuller discussion of the emergence of this strand of Lutheran radicalism, see below pp. 199–206.

'tarrying for the magistrate' demanded by Luther, Melanchthon and their more moderate followers. They resented the dependence of the Lutherans on the secular authorities, and soon felt driven to break away from the mainstream of their movement. The consequence was the emergence of a large number of independent and increasingly activist sects which have come to be known collectively as 'the radical Reformation'.[1]

The main source of these divisions has traditionally been traced to the quarrels which arose in Wittenberg in 1521-2 between the Lutherans and the followers of Carlstadt, including the group whom Luther scornfully named the Zwickau prophets. Luther himself had withdrawn at this period to the Wartburg, under the protection of the Elector Frederick, in order to complete his German translation of Erasmus's New Testament (Friedenthal, 1970, pp. 304-5). It was at this point that the Reformation in Wittenberg fell under the leadership of Carlstadt, who not only persuaded his congregation at the Christmas festival in 1521 to celebrate the first genuinely Protestant communion, but also encouraged Zwilling and his followers to engage shortly afterwards in acts of mass iconoclasm (Williams, 1962, pp. 40-2). This brought Luther hastening back in March 1522 to preach his famous series of sermons against his own lieutenant, who promptly fled the city (Friedenthal, 1970, pp. 321-8). Carlstadt's radical message was by no means lost, however, for it was immediately taken up at Zwickau under the alarming leadership of Nicholas Storch and Thomas Müntzer. They had visited Wittenberg during Carlstadt's ascendancy, and returned to Zwickau in 1522 (where Müntzer had become pastor) in order to preach against infant baptism and in favour of iconoclasm (Williams, 1962, p. 46). Müntzer published an explicitly anti-Lutheran *Protestation* in 1524, in which these characteristic doctrines of the radical Reformation were violently asserted (Williams, 1962, p. 52). Soon after this he delivered his famous *Sermon before the Princes*, in which he sought to persuade the Elector Frederick's brother to impose these radical doctrines by force (Stayer, 1972, p. 82). After failing in this objective, Müntzer decided to join the peasant uprising at Mulhausen in the hope of leading the revolution himself, and soon came to a sad end. He was captured after the peasant forces surrendered at the end of 1524, and in spite of a last-minute recantation he was immediately executed on the orders of Philip of Hesse (Williams, 1962, pp. 76-8).

It has recently been suggested that this traditional account of the sources and emergence of the Anabaptist movement – propagated by such German scholars as Boehmer and Holl – relies too heavily on the hostile analysis originally published by Bullinger in 1560, in which the different

[1] See Williams, 1962, an account to which I am greatly indebted.

strands of Anabaptism were scarcely distinguished, and the whole blame
for their later excesses was laid on the Zwickau prophets (Bender, 1953,
pp. 13–14). It now tends to be argued that the main source of Anabaptism
lay in Zwingli's Zurich rather than Luther's Wittenberg, and that the
activist and eventually revolutionary political theory of Müntzer and his
followers, so far from being the hallmark of Anabaptism, was merely an
unfortunate aberration in a generally pacifist movement (Oyer, 1964,
pp. 155–6). It is possible that this revisionist account underestimates the
extent of the contacts which seem to have been established at an early
stage between the Zurich and the Zwickau groups (Clasen, 1972, pp. 7–8).
But there is no doubt that a separate movement with a very different social
and political theory did develop at the same time in Zurich, and that it is
from the appearance of this group that the major schism within the
Lutheran movement needs to be traced.

The emergence of these radical evangelists in Zurich has been represented by Fritz Blanke as a five-act drama, beginning in 1523 with the
conversion of their leader Conrad Grebel (1498–1526) from Biblical
humanism to a fundamentalist outlook, a move which led him to denounce
Zwingli for failing to conduct the Reformation in Zurich precisely along
the lines indicated in the Old Testament (Blanke, 1961, pp. 8–11). This
was followed by an abortive attempt to persuade Zwingli to abandon his
alliance with the existing temporal authorities in order to clear the way for
a more thorough-going reformation. The third and climacteric act came
in 1524, when Grebel and his main associates, Felix Mantz and Balthasar
Hubmaier, began to turn away from Zwingli, to hold their own separate
meetings, and to establish contact by letter with Carlstadt, Müntzer and
the Zwickau prophets (Blanke, 1961, pp. 13–17). The fourth act consisted
of a renewed attempt to persuade Zwingli and the Zurich town-council
to endorse the new theology which the radicals had by this time fully
worked out. Grebel and Mantz engaged in two public debates with
Zwingli at the end of 1524, in which they sought to convert him to their
new and central contention that infant baptism is not a necessary condition of a child's salvation, and correspondingly that only adults who are
true believers ought to be baptised. This merely resulted in the imposition of a ban on their conventicles, which in turn precipitated the final
act of the drama. Grebel held a meeting on the day the ban came into
force, in the course of which he rebaptised one of the priests present,
Georg Blaurock (Blanke, 1961, p. 20). The special significance of this
gesture, as Zwingli immediately recognised, was that it added to Grebel's
distinctive theology the visible sign that he was inaugurating a new Church.
As soon as the movement acquired this symbolic identity, it began to

spread very rapidly – one line of advance moving northwards up the Rhine towards Strasbourg, while the other moved eastwards along the Danube and centred on Augsburg (Clasen, 1972, pp. 17–20).

There were two contrasting ways in which the leaders of these Anabaptist sects began to attack and repudiate the social and political assumptions of Luther, Zwingli and the other leaders of the 'magisterial' Reformation. Some of them were undoubtedly genuine political revolutionaries. The most dramatic instance of this outlook can be found in Müntzer's *Sermon before the Princes* of 1524. His theme (p. 64) is that 'a new Daniel must arise' to instruct the rulers of the world in their duties, since they are currently allowing themselves to be misled by 'the false clerics and vicious reprobates' amongst the Lutherans, and above all by Luther himself, who is brutally dismissed as 'Brother Fattened Swine and Brother Soft Life' (pp. 61, 65). The Lutherans are first attacked on theological grounds, in particular for rejecting direct revelation and arguing 'that God no longer reveals His divine mysteries to His beloved friends by means of valid visions or His audible word' (p. 54). Müntzer's main and most violent attack, however, is concentrated on their political theories, and especially on their passive attitude towards the secular authorities. They are accused of leading their rulers 'into the most shameful conceptions against all established truth' (p. 65). They preach that the princes are 'able to maintain nothing other than a civil unity', thus failing altogether to instruct them in their most important duty, which is to 'hazard all for the sake of the gospel' by mounting a crusade 'to wipe out the godless' and impose a full and godly reformation (pp. 65, 67, 68). This vision of the princes as fighters for the truth is corroborated by a reinterpretation – or rather a deliberate misreading – of the crucial passage at the start of Chapter 13 of St Paul's Epistle to the Romans, which Müntzer treats in such a way that the apostolic doctrine of obedience is turned into a demand for a holy war. By reversing the sequence of the opening verses, Müntzer contrives to suggest that St Paul is in fact attacking 'the wicked who hinder the gospel' and is calling on all godly rulers to 'get them out of the way and eliminate them' (p. 65). This in turn leads Müntzer to issue his final threat – that unless the princes agree to impose the gospel by force, 'the sword will be taken from them' by the sovereign and righteous people (p. 68).

The main group of Anabaptists under the leadership of Grebel and Mantz felt driven by quite different considerations to reject the political outlook associated with the leaders of the magisterial reformation. They were anarchists rather than revolutionaries. While they attacked the alliance between the leading reformers and the secular authorities no less vehemently, this was not because they felt that the godly should assume political power themselves, but rather because of their belief that they ought to ignore it altogether, withdrawing from all political involvement in the name of attaining their ideal of a truly Christian life (Hillerbrand, 1958, esp. pp. 89–91).

The clearest profession of this pacifist creed is to be found in the so-called *Schleitheim Confession of Faith*, which was drawn up in 1527 after a series of discussions held at the border town of Schleitheim by a number of Swiss and German Anabaptist groups who had met to clarify the doctrines on which they were all agreed (Clasen, 1972, pp. 43, 49). Their basic assumption was that although 'the sword is ordained of God', it is ordained 'outside the perfection of Christ' (p. 133). The secular authorities form no part of the regenerate world: they merely exist because of the unfortunate necessity for sinful men to be coerced. This leads to the conclusion that, even if the apparatus of secular power may be needed to keep the peace amongst the unregenerate, they themselves have no need of it, since they have all been released from their sins by the illumination of the Holy Spirit, and have thereby become an elect community within the unregenerate world. It was thus entirely logical for them to insist on what they unceremoniously called 'a separation from the abomination' (p. 131). They saw God as admonishing them 'to withdraw from Babylon and the earthly Egypt' so that 'we shall not have fellowship with them' and 'may not be partakers of the pain and suffering which the lord will bring upon them' (p. 132). The outcome was a political creed which was wholly anti-political: they refused to bear arms or to make use of any 'unchristian, devilish weapons of force'; they declared that 'it is not appropriate for a Christian to serve as a magistrate', and accordingly refused to use the lawcourts or to 'pass judgment between brother and brother'; and they declined to pay war-taxes, to recognise existing laws of property or to take any part in civic or political affairs (pp. 133, 134–5; cf. Clasen, 1972, pp. 174–5).

These groups were thus led to reject with equal force the attempts of the Zwickau prophets to dominate the secular authorities, and the tendency of Luther and Zwingli to submit passively to their ordinances. As soon as Grebel and his followers learnt the tenor of Müntzer's *Sermon before the Princes*, they sent a letter in which they charged him with a dangerous misunderstanding of the gospel, and attempted to persuade him to adopt their own pacifist stance. 'If thou art willing to defend war', Grebel wrote,[1] 'then I admonish thee by the common salvation of us all

---

[1] My quotations are taken from the translation published in *Spiritual and Anabaptist Writers*, ed. Williams. For the full reference see *sub* Grebel, Conrad in the bibliography of primary sources.

that thou wilt cease therefrom' (p. 84). 'The gospel and its adherents are not to be protected by the sword, nor are they thus to protect themselves', since 'true Christian believers are sheep among wolves, sheep for the slaughter' (p. 80). Müntzer's militancy is thus denounced for the orthodox Lutheran reason that all true Christians must accept and not resist their fate: 'they must be baptised in anguish, tribulation, persecution, suffering and death' (p. 80). This does not mean, however, that Grebel feels any greater sympathy for Luther's own political attitudes. He writes with the greatest contempt of Luther's attempts to ingratiate himself with the princes, 'to whom he has tied his gospel' (p. 83). He also insists that all the other 'slothful scholars and doctors of Wittenberg' have failed even more ignominiously to recognise what he conceives to be the central truth about political life: that all true Christians who wish 'to hold to and rule by the word alone must sever all connections with the unregenerate rulers of an unregenerate world' (pp. 78, 80). The result is that if we look for a positive political theory in the pronouncements of Grebel, Mantz or Hubmaier, all we eventually find is a pious hope: that once all men have received the illumination of the Holy Spirit, the government of people will be replaced by the rule of love.

It would be a mistake to suppose that the Anabaptist challenge ever succeeded, even in Germany, in drawing off any very substantial volume of support from the main body of the magisterial Reformation. It has recently been computed that, if we exclude the later Hutterite groups, the total number of Anabaptist converts during the whole century after their emergence in the 1520s probably amounted to little more than eleven thousand souls (Clasen, 1972, p. 26). However, the political impact of the radical sects was out of all proportion to their size. First of all, it was largely in response to their antinomianism that the more orthodox leaders of the Reformation felt goaded into strengthening their ties with the secular authorities. As early as 1520 Carlstadt was preaching against Luther's worldliness and 'loveless faith', while Müntzer devoted a special tract to inveighing against 'the spiritless soft-living flesh in Wittenberg' (Williams, 1962, pp. 40, 76). This soon drove Luther and Zwingli to lash back, calling on the sword as well as the pen. It was Luther who ensured that Carlstadt was expelled from Electoral Saxony in 1524, and who solemnly warned Duke John against Müntzer's influence (Edwards, 1975, pp. 36–48). It was Zwingli who persuaded the civil authorities in Zurich to imprison Grebel and Mantz in 1525, and to torture Hubmaier until he recanted (Williams, 1962, pp. 121, 125, 141). It also seems to have been due to Zwingli's influence that the Zurich authorities agreed in 1526 to impose a penalty of death by drowning on anyone who attended an

Anabaptist service, and went on to carry out this sentence against Mantz in the following year (Williams, 1962, pp. 144–5). During the same period the leaders of the magisterial Reformation began to issue a series of increasingly vitriolic denunciations of the rapidly proliferating Anabaptist sects. Luther published his *Letter in Opposition to the Fanatic Spirit* in response to a plea from Bucer in 1524. Its brevity allowed him no space for argument, and he gave himself up entirely to invective, attacking 'the rebellious and murderous spirits' of Müntzer and his followers, and accusing Carlstadt with his 'storming and fanaticism' of pouring out 'smoke and mist to obscure altogether the sun and light of the gospel' (pp. 67, 69). Even the diplomatic Melanchthon soon began to adopt the same violent tones, first in his tract of 1528 *Against the Anabaptists* and then in a letter of 1530 to Friedrich Myconius, who had been disturbed by the fact that six Anabaptists had recently been executed on Lutheran territory. Melanchthon disposes of all such scruples with the assurance that the Anabaptists are 'angels of the devil' and must be 'treated with the utmost severity, no matter how blameless they might appear' (Oyer, 1964, pp. 126, 155).

The Anabaptists had an even more dramatic impact when they started to put their revolutionary social and political theories into practice. Every government in Europe in the early sixteenth century felt strongly sensitive to the possibility that, once they heeded the call for religious reform, this might in turn unleash a demand for social revolution. These fears must have seemed amply confirmed when the Anabaptist groups founded in Strasbourg by Melchior Hoffmann (*c.* 1495–1543) began to run out of control in the early 1530s. Hoffmann first arrived in Strasbourg in 1528, after a disputation with Amsdorf had revealed an unbridgeable gulf between his views and those of the orthodox leaders of Lutheranism (Williams, 1962, p. 261). He was initially treated with caution by Bucer and Capito, but his preaching and writing on his successive visits soon proved so violently inflammatory that they eventually succeeded in 1533 in getting him sentenced to life-imprisonment (Kreider, 1955, p. 109). This had little effect, however, in quenching the ardour of his growing bands of 'Melchiorite' followers, who began to spread the Anabaptist word throughout the Netherlands and the area of the lower Rhineland. Their message was taken up with particular fervour in the Imperial city of Münster, where the Lutheran leadership was ousted and the Anabaptists took control under Jan Matthys and John Beukels of Leyden (Stayer, 1972, pp. 227–34). There followed a notorious episode which contrived more than any other incident to associate the Reformation with the cause of revolution, and in this way to alienate moderate men of all persuasions.

Matthys and Beukels began to recruit soldiers to fight for their new Jerusalem early in 1534, but their plans were cut short when the Prince Bishop sealed them off by laying siege to the city. Matthys at first assumed command, and proceeded to establish a regime which included the sharing of goods. This was partly a response to the siege conditions, but it must still have seemed a desperately revolutionary move. Soon afterwards he was killed in a sortie from the city, after which John of Leyden took over the leadership and proclaimed another new regime, in which the sharing of wives was added to the sharing of property, and John had himself crowned 'king of righteousness over all' (Williams, 1962, p. 373). His kingdom was short-lived, for the town was betrayed and taken in June 1534, the inhabitants were slaughtered to a man, John himself was executed and the remnants of his followers were easily dispersed (Williams, 1962, pp. 380–1). But in spite of the brevity of the episode, the spectres of communism and revolution had been terrifyingly raised, and remained throughout the century to haunt the moderate reformers and give pause to all those who felt sympathetic to their cause.

THE ROLE OF THE SECULAR AUTHORITIES

The next formative stage in the evolution of Lutheran political theory was reached when the secular authorities in many of the German cities, followed soon afterwards by the rulers of Denmark, Sweden and England, all chose to adopt and propagate one crucial feature of the Lutheran political creed. The doctrine which was officially taken up in this way was the Lutheran view of the Church. By a series of simple moves – strikingly similar in each country – the Lutheran assumption that the Church must be regarded as nothing more than a *congregatio fidelium* ceased to be treated as a heresy, and came to be accepted as the basis of a new and official view of the proper relationship between ecclesiastical and political power.

This outline implies that the imposition of this new orthodoxy was largely the product of a series of official initiatives. In general this was the case, except that in a number of German cities the populace adopted the doctrines of the Reformation and imposed them upon their rulers rather than the other way round (Moeller, 1972, pp. 60–1). This can be seen most clearly in such Baltic cities as Rostock and Straslund, and in a number of Imperial cities in the south, the best example being Strasbourg (Dickens, 1974, pp. 146–60). The Reformation in Strasbourg may be dated from 1521, when Matthäus Zell preached a series of sermons on the gospels in the Cathedral, attended by huge crowds, in which he defended

Luther's doctrines and read out passages from his works (Chrisman, 1967, p. 100). By 1523 both Martin Bucer and Wolfgang Capito had been attracted to the city, and by the end of the following year there were evangelical preachers in five of the main Churches (Chrisman, 1967, pp. 108–9, 116–17). The City Council at first tried to stem the tide, and dismissed both Zell and Capito from their benefices (Chrisman, 1967, pp. 112–13). By 1524, however, the Reformation had become entrenched as a popular movement, and five of the nine parishes had drawn up petitions to the Council demanding the appointment of Lutheran preachers. The councillors, as Chrisman remarks, 'had neither plan nor systematic programme' in the face of this revolution, but were anxious above all to retain their political control, which was beginning to be shaken by the collision between the old and new faiths. The outcome was that they found themselves committed to endorsing the Reformation as the price of political stability. They thereupon arrogated to themselves the right of appointment to benefices, reinstated the evangelical preachers, and turned the Reformation into an official movement, quickly bringing about the conversion of the whole city (Dickens, 1974, pp. 151–2).

It is easy, however, to exaggerate the contrast between the development of the Reformation as a popular movement in Germany, and its imposition elsewhere 'from above' (Moeller, 1972, pp. 60–1). The existence of an initial popular reform-movement is not always evident in the *Reichstädte*, or free Imperial cities. Sometimes there was no reform-movement at all – fourteen of these cities were still refusing even at the end of the sixteenth century to tolerate a Protestant congregation within their walls (Moeller, 1972, pp. 41, 61). And sometimes it is clear that the adoption of the new religion was largely the outcome of official policies – this appears to apply, for example, in the case of both Magdeburg and Nuremberg (Moeller, 1972, p. 61). When we turn, moreover, to the two thousand or so *Landstädte*, the cities directly under the control of a local prince, there are few signs of the more populist pattern being repeated. As Moeller emphasises, the situation in these cases was that 'the Reformation could only develop if the territorial lord permitted it', with the result that the first moves had to come from the secular rulers themselves (Moeller, 1972, p. 68).

The first move towards the acceptance of the Reformation in a majority of German cities thus tended to be no different from the first step taken in Denmark, Sweden and England. It consisted of giving government protection to a number of leading Lutherans who had previously been harassed or silenced, and encouraging them to publicise their views. A clear example of this process in Germany can be seen in the case of Nuremberg, where Osiander was given an official appointment as a preacher at an early stage, and where the town-council, as Strauss puts it, led the Lutherans 'quickly and directly to victory' over the established Church (Strauss, 1966, p. 61). The first signs of a similar step being taken outside Germany are to be found in Denmark. Christian II invited Carlstadt to Copenhagen in 1521, and at the same time appointed a Lutheran chaplain, Martin Reinhard, who converted several members of the court, including the Queen herself (Dunkley, 1948, pp. 23–4). The same process was continued by Frederick I after his accession in 1523. He allowed a press to be set up in Kiel to publish a vernacular Bible, and in 1526 he issued a letter of protection to Hans Tausen to enable him to continue preaching the Lutheran faith (Dunkley, 1948, pp. 54, 114). During the following year he refused a request by the Herrdag to withdraw this protection, and in 1529 he went on to appoint Tausen as preacher in one of the main churches in Copenhagen (Dunkley, 1948, pp. 50, 57). The same kind of official steps began to be taken soon afterwards in Sweden. Gustav Vasa appointed Olaus Petri in 1524 as preacher at the Church of St Nicholas in Stockholm, and thereby placed 'the most influential pulpit in Sweden', as Roberts calls it, at the disposal of an enthusiastic Lutheran (Roberts, 1968, p. 69). During the same year the King refused a request from Brask, the conservative Bishop of Linköping, that the sale and reading of Lutheran books should be banned, and two years later he ordered the closure of the press which Brask had set up to publish anti-Lutheran tracts (Bergendoff, 1928, pp. 11, 23, 27). Finally, a similar series of steps began to be taken soon afterwards in England. An attempt was made in 1531 to persuade Tyndale to return from the continent and 'to win him over to the king's cause', and a successful effort was made soon afterwards to recruit both Barnes and Coverdale into the service of the government (Mozley, 1937, p. 187). Coverdale was officially employed by Cromwell as a translator in 1537, while Barnes was appointed as a royal chaplain in 1535 and used as a negotiator with the continental Lutherans, first when the princes of the Schmalkaldic league were approached in 1535, and again when the Cleves marriage was being discussed four years later (Tjernagel, 1965, pp. 143–4). By this time several of the most radical Lutheran preachers had gained preferment in the Church, the most important example being Hugh Latimer. He had been under suspicion of heresy throughout the 1520s and had been prohibited from preaching in 1525 by the Bishop of Ely (Chester, 1954, pp. 25–6). By 1530, however, he was preaching before the court, by 1534 he was appointed to preach weekly before the King, and in 1535 he was consecrated by Cranmer as Bishop of Worcester (Chester, 1954, pp. 53–5, 100–4).

The next and most crucial step which was officially taken in all these countries was the convening of a national assembly, which the government used in each case to proclaim a definitive repudiation of the separate legal and jurisdictional powers hitherto exercised within their territories by the Papacy and the Catholic Church. These changes were in each case legitimated by way of appealing to an essentially Lutheran conception of the Church as a purely spiritual body, the sole duty of which was to preach the word of God without laying claim to any other powers.

The first ruler outside Germany to make this crucial move was Frederick I of Denmark. He summoned a meeting of the Rigsdag at Odense in 1527, and defeated an attempt by the bishops to defend the traditional jurisdictions of the Church by allowing full rein to the anti-clerical feelings of the nobility (Grimm, 1954, p. 238). The same step was taken in Sweden at almost the same time. The Rigsdag which met at Vasteras in 1527 produced an Ordinance in which the right to make ecclesiastical appointments was transferred to the crown, the legal immunities of the clergy were withdrawn, and the independent powers of the ecclesiastical courts were abolished. By a Latin rescript added to the Ordinance, the duty to pay Annates to Rome was also rescinded and the right of the Papacy to confirm ecclesiastical appointments was finally repudiated (Bergendoff, 1928, p. 37). Finally, a similar campaign was mounted in England during the early 1530s. When the Reformation Parliament first met in 1529, there were spontaneous demonstrations by the Commons (who remembered Richard Hunne) against the 'great polling and extreme exactions' practised by the clergy, as well as against the whole system of 'Ordinaries' or ecclesiastical courts (Lehmberg, 1970, pp. 81–2). When Thomas Cromwell gained control of the government these denunciations were turned into official policy. The decisive moves were made during the session of 1532. Cromwell began by reviving an anti-clerical manifesto which he had probably drafted himself on behalf of the Commons in 1529, and which had been known at that time as the Supplication of the Commons against the Ordinaries (Elton, 1951, pp. 517, 520). This was now given the status of an official remonstrance, and presented by the King to Convocation with a request that they should formally consider its complaints. The first outcome was a spirited *Answer* in which the leaders of the Church defended their traditional jurisdictional powers. This was evidently composed by Stephen Gardiner, the newly-appointed Bishop of Winchester and the leading canon lawyer in the English Church (Lehmberg, 1970, p. 150 and note). When the King himself denounced the *Answer* in an address to the Commons, however, Convocation suddenly gave way and responded in May 1532 with the epoch-making 'Submission of the Clergy', in which they abandoned their claims to act as an independent law-making authority (Lehmberg, 1970, pp. 151–2). It is true that this remarkable surrender was endorsed by a mere rump of Convocation, and that the views of the whole House appear never to have been canvassed (Kelly, 1965, pp. 116–17). The submission was none the less eagerly seized on by the government, and was later confirmed by the Act for the Submission of the Clergy in 1534. The decision to confirm the Submission by registering it as an Act served in itself to symbolise the triumph of Statute over canon law, while the contents of the Act made it abundantly clear that the Church's status as a separate *regnum* was finally at an end (Dickens, 1964, p. 472). The right of Convocation to sit without a royal writ of summons was withdrawn. The members of Convocation were also required to renounce their authority to create any further Canons of law, and to submit all existing Canons to a commission appointed by the King in order to ensure that none of them were 'contrarient or repugnant' to 'the customs, laws and statutes of this realm' (Lehmberg, 1970, pp. 149–50). Finally, the clergy were made to confess that (in the words of the Act) all the ordinances 'which heretofore have been enacted' by Convocation have been 'much prejudicial to the king's prerogative royal and repugnant to the laws and statutes of this realm' (Elton, 1960, p. 339).

This does not mean, of course, that the demarcation dispute between the *regnum* and *sacerdotium* finally came to an end in all these countries at this exact point. It might be argued, at least in the case of England, that since the bishops continue to sit in the House of Lords to this day, the issue is still a live one. The problem certainly revived in England in a threatening form at the end of the sixteenth century, not only because of the hostility of the Puritans, but also because of the stance taken up by Downame and the other anti-Calvinists, who began to argue the 'Arminian' case that since the bishops hold their offices *iure divino*, they must to some extent remain independent of the secular authorities (Tyacke, 1973). Nevertheless, it was during the revolution of the 1530s that the theoretical basis was laid for the virtually disestablishmentarian policy which was officially advocated nearly two centuries later by the ruling whig oligarchy, and endorsed at that time by such ecclesiastical exponents of Lockean liberalism as Benjamin Hoadly – who was even prepared to indicate his approval of the government's decision at the start of the eighteenth century to end the calling of Convocation altogether (Sykes, 1934, pp. 310–14, 350).

The final step taken by the government in each of these countries consisted of drawing the corollary of these campaigns against the independent powers of the Church. This took the form in each case of proclaiming the King instead of the Pope to be head of the Church, and effecting a transfer to the crown of all the jurisdictional powers which the Church had previously exercised.

This step was taken in Denmark and Sweden only after an interval of some years. It was taken in England almost immediately, however, largely due to the legislative genius of Thomas Cromwell, whose preambles to the major statutes passed during the Henrician schism provide one of the most incisive accounts of the political theory which accompanied and legitimated this stage of the Reformation. It was with the passing in 1533 of the Act in Restraint of Appeals to Rome that the transfer of the Church's jurisdictions to the crown was decisively signalled.[1] Cromwell's famous preamble to the Act, the best statement of his own political creed, takes it for granted that the Church is in no way a separate *regnum* within the body politic, but is nothing more than a body of believers. It is simply 'that part of the said body politic called the spirituality, now being usually called the English Church' (Elton, 1960, p. 344). It is said to follow from this Marsiglian premise that the powers of the crown must in consequence extend in an unbroken line, taking in all spiritual as well as temporal affairs. This is affirmed at the beginning of the preamble in the form of the contention that 'this realm of England is an empire', and is thus 'governed by one supreme head' who wields 'plenary, whole and entire power'. The King's Imperial rights are said to be such that he is able 'to render and yield justice and final determination to all manner of folk', lay as well as spiritual, and to serve as the final judge 'in all causes', whether temporal or spiritual in character (Elton, 1960, p. 344).

The heretical assumption underlying these claims is of course that the King is head of the Church. Henry VIII first tried to wring this acknowledgement out of Convocation in 1531, at the time when the clergy had been indicted for *praemunire* and were seeking the royal pardon (Lehmberg, 1970, pp. 109–13). By a proclamation which Archbishop Warham read out to the bemused Convocation in February 1531, the King simply informed them that he was entitled to be regarded as the 'sole protector and supreme head of the Church and clergy in England'.[2] The spokesmen for Convocation contrived to remind the King in their reply that this was only true 'as far as is allowed by the law of God'.[3] But in spite of this

---

[1] On the special importance of this statute, and on Cromwell's role in its drafting (including an analysis of the detailed revisions he made to the eight surviving drafts), see the reconstruction in Elton, 1949.

[2] See Elton, 1960, pp. 330–1. Lehmberg, 1970, p. 112 renders the claim as 'sole protector and supreme head of the Anglican Church and clergy', but this is of course an anachronism and hence a somewhat misleading translation.

[3] '*Quantum per legem Dei licet.*' Lehmberg, 1970, p. 114 mistranslates this as 'as far as the word of God allows', implying that the Scriptures are being invoked, and thereby giving a 'Lutheran' interpretation to the disclaimer which the Convocation would have been certain at this stage to repudiate.

reminder, the headship was in effect presupposed in the legislation of the next two years, and in particular in the Act of 1534 confirming the succession upon Elizabeth, the daughter of Anne Boleyn. To accept the validity of this line of succession was to recognise the divorce which the new Archbishop of Canterbury, Thomas Cranmer, had granted the King in the previous year. But to recognise the divorce was to concede that (as the preamble to the Act of Succession maintained) the jurisdictions claimed by 'the Bishop of Rome' were 'contrary to the great and inviolable grants of jurisdictions given by God immediately to emperors, kings and princes' (Elton, 1960, p. 7). And to acquiesce in the claim that *all* such jurisdictions are 'immediately' given by God to the king was to repudiate the independent powers traditionally claimed by the Papacy and the Church, and in this way to reject the whole Catholic vision of the proper relations between the *regnum* and the *sacerdotium*. The ideological claim implied in the Act of Succession was thus of an epoch-making character, as More and Fisher correctly recognised. And there is no doubt that the government fully intended to make it. This was first made clear in an oath attached to the Act itself, which turned a refusal to acknowledge the headship into a treasonable offence. The same point was then reiterated even more clearly in the Act of Supremacy in the following year, which simply proclaimed (not altogether truthfully) that everyone admitted the right of the King to be styled 'the supreme head of the Church of England' (Elton, 1960, p. 355).

This final step of proclaiming the royal headship of the Church, and in this way vindicating the 'imperial' rights of the secular authorities, was taken soon afterwards both in Denmark and Sweden. In Denmark the campaign was completed with the meeting of the Rigsdag at the end of the civil war in 1536. It was explicitly asserted, in the Recess published at the end of the session, that the sole functions of the Church are 'to preach the word of God and to instruct the people in the Christian faith' (Dunkley, 1948, p. 75). The way was thus cleared for the proclamation, issued in the King's electoral charter at the same time, that there would now be 'a concentration of all civil and ecclesiastical power in the hands of the king and Council' (Dunkley, 1948, pp. 74–5). Finally, the same moves were made in Sweden three years later, after the appointment of Conrad von Pyhy as the King's Secretary. Here the campaign was even more swift and decisive. The Church Council was summoned to meet under Pyhy's presidency in 1539, and when he failed to persuade the Archbishop, Laurentius Petri, of the implications of the injunction 'preachers shall ye be, and not lords', the Council was simply dissolved (Roberts, 1968, pp. 114, 116). The King then proclaimed himself 'out of the plenitude of our royal power' to be the head and 'supreme defender' of the Church, which he then went on to reorganise in a wholly Lutheran style, assuming control of all appointments as well as taking over all its powers and wealth (Martin, 1906, p. 456; Roberts, 1968, pp. 116, 119).

It is arguable that the ideological importance of these assertions of 'imperial' rights against the Church has been much underestimated by a number of recent political historians. They have tended, especially in discussing the Henrician schism in England, to concentrate on the undoubted fact that by the end of the fifteenth century the crown had already attained a considerable degree of *de facto* control over the powers nominally exercised by the Papacy within the English Church. This has made it easy to picture the Henrician Reformation as nothing more than 'the fruit of the medieval regality'. The invocation of the king's 'imperial' powers by Thomas Cromwell is thus dismissed as 'impeccably medieval', while the whole campaign of the 1530s is treated as nothing more than the completion of an 'inexorable development towards a national Church' which had already made it 'an integral part of the State' by the beginning of the sixteenth century (Harris, 1963, pp. 11, 16–17).

It is of course true that, in emphasising the 'imperial' rights of the crown, Cromwell was reiterating 'the language of the Middle Ages' (Harris, 1963, p. 12). As we have seen, the contention that every ruler is *sibi princeps*, that every *rex* has the powers of an *imperator* within his own *regnum*, had been deployed as early as the middle of the fourteenth century by Bartolus and his pupils as a means of defending the autonomous jurisdictions of the secular powers. We still need to ask, however, about the different uses to which these concepts were put at different times. When the idea of the king as *imperator in regno suo* was cited in the Middle Ages – as it was, for example, in England in 1393 and again in 1399 – it was generally invoked in the course of a demarcation dispute with the Papacy over the crown's control of the Church. It was simply used, that is, to question the extent of the Papacy's right to interfere. When it was invoked by Cromwell, however, in the preamble to the Act of Appeals in 1533, it was used to claim that no such demarcation ought to be made. It was used, that is, not to legitimate an attempt to curtail the Papacy's jurisdictions, but rather to legitimate a denial that the Papacy possessed any such jurisdictions at all.

It thus seems quite proper to emphasise – as Elton in particular has done – that Cromwell's political creed was a revolutionary one, and that the application he gave to the traditional concept of the crown's 'imperial' powers constituted a radically new departure (Elton, 1956, p. 88). This is not to deny that every attempt was made at the time to minimise the novelty of the position being taken up. Cromwell twice baulked at the King's attempts to have the Act of Appeals phrased in such a way that the novelty of its ideological claims should be made explicit, and he sought to reassure the readers of the preamble that its arguments had already been 'manifestly declared and expressed' in 'divers sundry old authentic histories and chronicles' (Elton, 1960, p. 344). To accept these arguments at face-value, however, is to be deceived by Tudor propaganda, in just the way that Cromwell doubtless intended. Although the Act employs 'the language of the Middle Ages', there are two vital points at which the use of the language is revolutionary. First, the idea that the English Church is merely a limb of the 'Catholic' (that is, universal) Church based on Rome is definitively discarded: the Church in England begins to mutate into the Church of England. And secondly, a distinctively modern concept of political obligation begins to emerge: it was at this point, but not before, that it became possible for the secular authorities to legitimate the claim that they should be regarded as the sole jurisdictional power within their own territories, and thus that they should be recognised as the sole appropriate object of a subject's political allegiance.

THE ENFORCEMENT OF THE REFORMATION

The last and most decisive stage in the evolution of Lutheranism as a political ideology was reached when the secular authorities who had begun by dabbling in the heresy went on to demand the acceptance of their new Church settlements by their subjects. This appears to have been achieved without much additional effort in Denmark and in the Lutheran areas of Germany. As we have seen, the Reformation in Germany was to a considerable extent a popularly-generated movement, so that the need for a separate campaign of enforcement scarcely arose. The Reformation in Denmark was largely enforced 'from above', but since it was imposed at the end of a long civil war it seems to have been accepted rapidly and with relief. If we turn to Sweden and England, however, we find that before these governments succeeded in imposing the new orthodoxies, two further steps had to be taken: one was that the most recalcitrant opponents of the new settlements had to be silenced; the other was that the vast bulk of the population, often restive and ill-informed about the changes, had to be persuaded to accept and endorse them.

The imposition of the royal supremacy in Sweden was opposed by some of the King's leading advisers, the main doubts being raised in 1539 by the Chancellor, Lars Andraea, and by several leading churchmen, including Olaus Petri. An even more dangerous challenge developed two years later, when a rebellion under Nils Danke broke out in the remote southern province of Småland. Both forms of protest were rigorously suppressed by the government. The scruples voiced by Andraea and Petri caused them to be arraigned early in 1540 before a tribunal of senators and condemned to death on a charge of high treason – though their sentences were subsequently commuted to a fine and imprisonment (Martin, 1906, pp. 459–60). The uprising in Småland proved more difficult to control, but by 1543 the troops mustered by Danke had been defeated in battle, Danke and his family had been executed, and many hundreds of the peasants involved had been deported to Finland (Roberts, 1968, p. 136).

A similar pattern of protest and repression marked this stage of the Reformation in England. Elton has recently insisted that it would be a mistake to think of this as a 'ruthless persecution' (Elton, 1972, p. 399). There is no doubt some room for argument as to what constitutes true ruthlessness, but it is a striking fact that, whereas the ringleaders of the opposition in Sweden were mainly imprisoned or deported, in England they generally forfeited their lives. The government – as in Sweden – had to contend with two distinct forms of disaffection. There was a popular uprising led by Robert Aske – generally known as the Pilgrimage of Grace – which developed in the more remote northern areas, especially in parts of Yorkshire. This looked threatening during the winter of 1536, but was quickly and efficiently contained at the start of the following year. Some doubts about the royal supremacy were also raised within the government, and even within the circle of the King's own family. The opposition from Henry's own kinsmen stemmed from the family of Sir Richard Pole, while the opposition in the government centred on the figure of the Lord Chancellor, Sir Thomas More, whose scruples were shared by several leading churchmen, notably Stephen Gardiner of Winchester[1] and John Fisher of Rochester.

The stance taken up by More and Fisher constitutes a famous and heroic episode, which is also of considerable importance for the theoretical issues it raised. But it is probable that the opposition of the Pole family seemed more alarming to the government. It not only included the possibility of a Yorkist threat to the throne,[2] but also led to the publi-

---

[1] As we have seen, Gardiner had already attempted to defy the Government in leading the counter-attack by Convocation on the changes proposed by his hated enemy, Cromwell. Gardiner managed, evidently after a considerable internal struggle, to make his peace with the Cromwellian government in the 1530s. He survived, however, to lead the Catholic reaction at the end of Henry's reign, to dispose of Cromwell, and to become the leader of the Catholic revival under Mary. See below, pp. 93–4.

[2] This was doubtless a fantasy, but its basis in fact was that the widow of Sir Richard Pole was not only a Plantagenet, since she was a daughter of the Duke of Clarence, but was also inexorably opposed to the King's marriage with Anne Boleyn through loyalty to Catherine

cation, by Reginald Pole, of the most important theoretical exposition of the orthodox case against the King's assumption of the headship of the Church. Although Pole served as a patron to several radical humanists, including Thomas Starkey and Richard Morison, he remained unswervingly loyal to the Church, and survived to be appointed, at the start of Mary's reign, the last Roman Catholic Archbishop of Canterbury (Schenk, 1950, p. 144). His attack on the royal supremacy originally took the form of a personal letter to Henry VIII in 1536, in reply to a set of questions about the powers of the Pope which the King had put to him through Thomas Starkey two years before (Schenk, 1950, pp. 62–5, 67). This was published in 1539 in the form of a Latin tract entitled *A Defence of Ecclesiastical Unity*. The work is in four 'books'. The last is a prayer for Henry VIII to mend his ways. This is preceded by a long personal attack on the King as 'head of the Church of Satan' (p. 229) which Starkey characterised as 'frantic', and which even Pole's advisers felt to be too bitter to have any beneficial effect (Schenk, 1950, p. 72). The first two Books, however, consist of a learned defence of the claim that it must be 'totally impossible for the King to be head of the Church' (p. 205). The argument is mainly conducted in the form of a reply to a defence of the royal supremacy which Richard Sampson had published in 1535. Book I attacks his position by deploying one of the main tenets of scholastic political thought. The king cannot be head of the Church, it is argued, since the Church is a gift of God, whereas the *regnum* is merely a creation of the citizens themselves, who 'spontaneously submit' to an authority which they establish to meet their own needs (pp. 91, 93). Book II corroborates this distinction by attacking Sampson's suggestion that the Pope is merely the Bishop of Rome (p. 116). Pole is able to cite an overwhelming number of authorities for the claim, which he constantly reiterates, that since the keys of the Church were originally given by Christ to St Peter, they must still be in the care of St Peter's successor, the Pope (pp. 138–9, 145–8).

It proved impossible for the English government to capture or silence Pole, though Cromwell is said to have remarked that he would make him 'eat his own heart' for writing the *Defence*, while the King demanded that he should be 'by some means trussed up and conveyed' back to England to answer for his views (Schenk, 1950, pp. 79, 88). Such threats proved vain, for as soon as Pole had his first quarrel with the King over the divorce in 1532, he prudently contrived to get permission to visit Italy,

of Aragon, whose daughter Mary she had helped to educate in the 1520s. As well as this family link with the Kingmaker himself, the Poles were further related to Henry VIII, since Sir Richard Pole had been a cousin of the King's father.

and there he continued to live in relative safety (Schenk, 1950, p. 29). But
Pole was lucky, as he acknowledged himself. Both More and Fisher, for
expressing much the same doubts, found themselves imprisoned in the
Tower in 1534, and both were executed for treason in the middle of the
following year (Reynolds, 1955, pp. 281, 286). Soon afterwards, a number
of Pole's relations were victimised for their alleged expressions of sympathy for the position he had taken up. His brother Geoffrey was arrested
in 1538 and forced to implicate the rest of his family on charges of treason.
This led to the arrest of his other brother, his cousin and his mother, and
by 1541 all but one had been executed (Schenk, 1950, pp. 82–4).

The opposition of Pole, Fisher and More has generally been characterised as that of 'conservatives'.[1] Elton has added that in More's case the
essence of his conservatism lay in his insistence on holding fast to a 'conception of a universal Christian law to which man-made law must conform'
at a time when Thomas Cromwell was deliberately emancipating the
authority of statute from any such constraints (Elton, 1955, p. 167). It is
arguable, however, that this is to misunderstand the theoretical basis of
More's and Fisher's intransigence. They appear to have resisted not so
much because they saw in Cromwell's legislative programme anything so
improbable as an attempt to place the powers of statute on a wholly
positivist base, but simply because they saw that it entailed removing the
independent rights and privileges traditionally exercised by the English
Church.

The claim that this formed the basis of More's and Fisher's protests
seems to be confirmed by considering the nature of the questions over
which they found themselves reaching a sticking-point. The issue over
which More resigned as Lord Chancellor was the Submission of the
Clergy in 1532 (Chambers, 1935, p. 241). The issue over which he and
Fisher were both condemned was their refusal to sign the oath attached
to the Succession Act in 1534 (Chambers, 1935, p. 287). The dilemma
raised by both these pieces of legislation was that they contravened the
traditional status of the Church as a *regnum* co-ordinate with rather than
subordinate to the secular authorities. More was of course prepared to
concede the right of the King in Parliament to be obeyed in all temporal
affairs. He was even willing to acknowledge Elizabeth as heir to the throne,
as the Act of Succession required, even though he was of course bound to
regard her as illegitimate (Chambers, 1935, p. 291). He clearly saw, however, that to recognise the Submission of 1532 was to jeopardise the
Church's jurisdictional rights, and to swear the oath of 1534 was to presuppose the King's right to dispense with the authority of the Pope. The

---

[1] For this judgment see, for example, Baumer, 1940, p. 63 and Elton, 1960, p. 231.

sticking-point for More and Fisher was thus that, in their religious and political outlook, they treated the independence of the Church as inviolable: the essence of their conservatism was simply that they were Catholics in the fullest sense.

The official campaigns to impose the Reformation in Europe seem in general to have come to an end at this point, with the repudiation of Rome, the assumption of all ecclesiatical powers by the secular authorities, and the forcible suppression of any opposition to the new settlements. The imposition of the Henrician Reformation in England, however, included one further development which is of special significance for the historian of political thought. This consisted of an attempt to secure the acceptance of the Church settlement not merely by repression, but also by an official campaign of political propaganda, the first ever to be mounted in England with the help of the printing-press.

The engineering of this campaign was mainly the achievement of Thomas Cromwell, during whose ministry nearly fifty books were published in defence of the Henrician schism, most of them being issued by Berthelet, the King's printer (Baumer, 1940, pp. 211–24).[1] It would of course be an overstatement to see all these works as a direct product of the government's initiative (Elton, 1972, pp. 171–2). But there is no doubt that a planned and orchestrated campaign of propaganda was financed by Cromwell and his agents, and it has even been argued that if we examine the nature of Cromwell's relationship with the propagandists he employed, we are bound to conclude that he often suggested as well as publicised their arguments (Elton, 1973, pp. 38, 52).

It is possible to distinguish two aspects, or rather two successive phases, of Cromwell's campaign. His first move was to induce a number of leading canon lawyers to write in defence of the new settlement, and in particular to defend the legality of the royal supremacy in the Church. This was a considerable coup in itself, for it was canon law – with its emphasis on the Papacy's separate jurisdictional powers – which seemed to offer the opponents of the government their most powerful theoretical support. As a result, the sincerity of the writers Cromwell employed has often been questioned (e.g., Hughes, 1950–4, I, 342). It is true that Dickens has recently sought to argue that they must genuinely have accepted 'the whole royalist position' and 'really believed' what they wrote (Dickens, 1964, p. 243). But it seems likely that in some cases they were looking above all for rapid preferment in the Church. This applies

[1] The best and most up-to-date discussions of Cromwell's campaign are contained in Elton, 1972 and in Elton, 1973. My own analysis is greatly indebted to both these valuable accounts.

especially to Edward Foxe (*c.* 1496–1538) and Richard Sampson (d. 1554), both of whom were given bishoprics as soon as their defences of the schism were produced. Foxe, who had been the king's almoner, was appointed to the see of Hereford in 1535 for his services; Sampson, who had been dean of the Chapel Royal, was granted the see of Chichester in the following year (Elton, 1972, p. 182). Some of them, moreover, appear to have written under considerable duress. This applies in particular to Stephen Gardiner (1483–1555), whose support the government was especially anxious to secure in view of his reputation as a canonist. The King himself spoke of his suspicions about Gardiner's 'coloured doubleness', and it was rumoured that he only produced his defence of the settlement after being threatened with imprisonment and even death if he refused (Muller, 1926, p. 65; Smith, 1953, p. 184).

If we treat consistency as a criterion of sincerity, it is hard to resist the conclusion that the government had good grounds for doubting the good faith of at least some of these churchmen. Sampson later backed Gardiner against Cromwell, supported the Catholic reaction at the end of the reign and survived to do homage to Mary in 1553 (Smith, 1953, pp. 142, 216). Gardiner went on to become one of the leading figures in the so-called Marian reaction in the mid-1550s. He was appointed Lord Chancellor in 1553, immediately re-enacted the anti-heresy statute of 1401, and in the following year began his notorious persecution of the English Protestants (Muller, 1926, pp. 218, 266). During the 1530s, however, Sampson, Foxe and Gardiner all published important tracts in defence of the divorce and royal supremacy. The first to be issued, and the most cautious in tone, was Sampson's *Oration* of 1534, concerned (in the words of its subtitle) 'to teach everyone that they must be obedient to the will of the King'. This was followed later in the same year by Foxe's 'short treatise' on *The True Difference between the Regal Power and the Ecclesiastical Power*. This may have been written before Sampson's book, although it contains a more sweeping attack on the authority of the Pope. Finally, Gardiner produced the most important and radical of these tracts, *The Oration of True Obedience*, which was first published in 1535.

The main aim of these treatises, as Gardiner affirms, is simply to vindicate the King's right to be 'divorced from unlawful marriage' and to declare himself 'in earth the supreme head of the Church of England' (pp. 87, 91). But the need to argue in favour of these conclusions involved them in expressing a view of temporal and spiritual authority which was markedly Lutheran in tone. (Gardiner even appears to allude at several points to Tyndale's *Obedience of a Christian Man*.)[1] They all begin by

[1] This is suggested by Janelle, 1930, p. liv.

stressing that the only proper source for an understanding of political authority is the scriptures. Gardiner immediately goes on to point out that in the Old Testament God declares that 'princes reign by his authority', and in the New Testament St Paul adds that 'whosoever resists power resists the ordinance of God' (p. 89). Foxe provides an even more emphatic discussion of the same theme, presenting it as the conclusion rather than the introduction to his book. He first cites a large amount of Old Testament history, which is said to prove that 'God did give with His own mouth kings to be rulers of His people' (fo 56). He then passes on to St Paul's Epistle to the Romans, the favourite text of all the Lutheran reformers, and asks the reader 'to tarry awhile and diligently to ponder and discuss this place (fo 68). The outcome, he argues, will be a recognition that St Paul is making three crucial points: he 'bids all men to be obedient'; he 'excepts no man at all'; and he promises damnation to any man who disobeyes his ruler in any respect (fos 68–9). All these writers then go on to argue that, once this view of temporal power is thoroughly understood, the King's decision to proclaim himself Head of the Church presents no difficulties. He is merely removing what Gardiner calls 'the false pretended power of the Bishop of Rome', and thereby ensuring that 'the power pertaining to a prince by God's law' is 'more clearly expressed with a more fit term' (p. 93). The result is that they all vest the headship of the Church in the figure of the King himself. Whereas the common lawyers (such as St German) were beginning to argue that the supremacy must be held by the King in Parliament, the canonists seem to envisage a purely personal headship, and never discuss the role of Parliament in ecclesiastical affairs at all (Baumer, 1940, p. 58).

They recognise, however, that one major objection is bound to be levelled against this account of temporal authority. As Gardiner expresses it, everyone will agree 'that obedience is due', but they will still want to ask 'how far the limits of requiring obedience extend' (p. 99). The next issue this leads them to consider, again in a markedly Lutheran spirit, is the question of the relationship between the secular authorities and the Church. Here they all take their stand squarely on the claim that, as Foxe insists, the Church is nothing more than 'the multitude of faithful people' (fo 10). Foxe reiterates this definition throughout the opening section of his book, in which he presents his main attack on the jurisdictions of the Pope. The same point is no less decisively made by Gardiner, who insists that the Church 'is nothing else but the congregation of men and women of the clergy and of the laity united in Christ's profession' (p. 95). This commitment then allows them to revert once more to the question of the royal supremacy, and to argue that it must be absurd to deny that the

King is head of the Church. Gardiner presents the grounds for this conclusion with particular neatness. No one denies, he says, that the King 'is
head of the realm'. And everyone agrees that what is 'comprehended' in
'the word "realm" ' is 'all subjects of the king's dominions'. But he
already claims to have shown that 'the Church of England' merely refers
to 'the same sorts of people at this day that are comprised in this word
realm, of whom the king is called the head' (p. 93). It follows that it must
be 'absurd and foolish' to suggest that the King may be 'head of the
realm but not of the Church', for these are one and the same thing under
different 'terming of words' (pp. 93, 97).

A complete repudiation of Papal authority is clearly implicit in these
accounts of spiritual and temporal power. The next obvious move is to
turn this into an explicit attack. With Gardiner this is the way the argument is organised, but in Foxe's and Sampson's treatises this provides
them with their opening theme. Foxe begins with a particularly elaborate
attack on the idea of Papal supremacy, pointing out that it has engendered
'false traditions' and especially that it has no scriptural basis, and thus no
authority by the law of God' (fos 6, 21). Gardiner goes on to analyse the
way in which the mistaken belief in Papal supremacy has grown up. He
insists that 'the supremacy of the Church of Rome in times past' was
solely a matter of its pre-eminence 'in the office of preaching God's
word' and 'advancing the cure and charge of Christ's name' (p. 151). He
thus regards it as a complete confusion to suppose 'that God ordained the
Bishop of Rome to be the chief as touching any absolute worldly power'
(p. 155).

If the jurisdictions claimed by the Papacy have all been 'usurped', it
follows that the relationship between canon and common law must have
been misunderstood. This is the final point which all these writers make.
The canonists had traditionally distinguished, in discussing the powers of
the Church, between the *potestas ordinis* and the *potestas jurisdictionis*. The
apologists for the Henrician Reformation all continue to accept the
validity of this distinction. They are generally content, moreover, to concede that the *potestas ordinis* – the power to confer grace by consecration
and the sacraments – can only be exercised by an ordained member of the
Church.[1] But when they turn to the *potestas jurisdictionis*, they all go on
to suggest a crucial redefinition of terms. The canonists had usually
divided this aspect of the Church's powers into the *jurisdictio poli*, concerned essentially with the power to help men attain salvation, and the
jurisdictio fori, which included all the legislative, judicial and coercive

---

[1] Foxe is perhaps an exception. See fo 85, where he appears to grant the king the right not
merely to appoint but to consecrate bishops.

functions of the Church. Foxe in particular traces the growth of the *jurisdictio fori* as a distinct 'papistical power', and illustrates the process by which the early canons of the Church eventually became accepted as laws, and so began to encroach upon the temporal powers of the medieval Empire (fos 36–41). All these writers then go on to redefine the terms used to describe these powers, using the terminology of the canon law against the orthodox canonists themselves. This process can be illustrated most readily from Gardiner's account. He offers his reinterpretation of the *potestas jurisdictionis* immediately after his defence of the King's supremacy in the Church. He concedes that his account will probably make 'some men startle', since it runs counter to the usual legal distinction 'between the governments of a prince and of the Church: that is, that the prince should govern in temporal matters and the Church in spiritual' (p. 103). He insists, however, that such a belief in two separate and parallel jurisdictions is 'a blind distinction and full of darkness' (p. 105). He admits that there must be a distinct sphere of spiritual *activity*, since 'God has committed the office of teaching and the ministry of the sacraments' to a particular group of men, as part of his 'sundry distribution of gifts' (p. 103). But he denies that this creates any distinct sphere of spiritual *jurisdiction*. You cannot say of a Christian prince that it is 'not for him to know any further' (p. 105). The fact is that 'God has put princes in trust' in order 'that they should not only rule the people but rule them rightly, not in any one part alone but in all particularly' (p. 113). This means that the prince has a special duty 'to take charge not only of human matters, but much more of divine matters' (p. 117). Gardiner thus concludes by advising the godly prince to 'take care also of holy or spiritual matters' in the manner of the Old Testament kings, and to recognise that 'the administration of divine matters' is a part of 'the discipline of his regal office' (p. 109).

The reinterpretation which all these writers propose is thus that all jurisdictional authority is secular by definition: as they express it, the Church possesses authority but not dominion. This makes it potentially misleading to speak of them as accepting and crystallising 'the doctrine of the two swords' (Hughes, 1965, p. 235). It is true that they sometimes continue to use this terminology, but they generally make it clear that they are referring only to the Church's right to retain the *jurisdictio poli*. As Gardiner puts it, the sword which the ministers exercise should be wielded only in 'preaching and excommunicating', and never in any jurisdictions outside the Church itself (p. 107). The Church cannot lay claim to any further powers, for this would be to infringe the authority of the King to 'meddle with the one half of the people' and would thus be to force him 'to be negligent almost in all things' (p. 107). The implication is that the distinction between the *potestas ordinis* and the *potestas juris-dictionis* becomes equivalent to the distinction between spiritual and temporal authority: the concept of spiritual jurisdiction simply lapses (Baumer, 1940, p. 67).

Although these writings clearly contributed a strong theoretical prop to the royal supremacy, Cromwell seems to have been quick to recognise that it would not be appropriate to confine his propaganda campaign exclusively to works of this character. These were all technical treatises which were published in Latin, and could hardly be expected to persuade or reassure very many people outside the ranks of the clergy and the learned world. Soon after they appeared, moreover, the political situation altered in two important respects, both of which needed to be accommodated. The first was that Pope Paul III finally agreed in 1536 to summon a General Council to consider the question of the reform of the Catholic Church. This was a potentially embarrassing development for such theorists as Sampson, Foxe and Gardiner. They had all repudiated the authority of the Pope, but had tended to endorse the moderate conciliarist thesis that, as Foxe explained, 'truth and justice' might still be expected from a 'Holy Council' of the Church (fos 10, 24). The other political development was that, as we have seen, the year 1536 saw the start of a reaction in England to the government's policies: at the theoretical level, Pole contributed his attack on the King; at the practical level, the Pilgrimage of Grace revealed the depths of popular doubts about the new settlement.

Cromwell responded to these new developments in two ways. He first of all showed himself willing to adopt an even more explicitly Lutheran standpoint by making use of the Bible as a weapon of political propaganda. As we have seen, Tyndale had already demonstrated that the authority of the New Testament could be invoked to support the claim that the true Church is solely concerned to preach and convert, and that its leaders have an absolute duty, no less than ordinary citizens, not to resist any commands of the secular authorities. Cromwell proceeded to encourage this highly congenial outlook by patronising the production of printed Bibles in English for the first time – a move which has caused some of his biographers to insist that he must have been concerned to advance the cause of the Reformation for genuinely religious rather than merely for tactical or political reasons (Dickens, 1959b, pp. 122–3). When Coverdale's first translation was published in 1536, with its New Testament based largely on Tyndale's version – *ecclesia* being rendered as 'congregation' and *presbyteros* as 'elder' throughout – Cromwell took the opportunity to prescribe in his Ecclesiastical Injunctions of the same year that a copy of the Old and New Testaments in English as well as in Latin should be placed in every parish church (Mozley, 1953, pp. 71, 86, 105). When John Rogers published the so-called 'Matthew Bible' in 1537, incorporating a series of marginal glosses largely derived from Luther's own translations, Cromwell gained the King's permission to allow the book to be freely sold (Bruce, 1970, pp. 64–5). Finally, Cromwell commissioned a new translation of the entire Bible from Coverdale in 1538, partly paying for it out of his own pocket, and soliciting from Cranmer a Preface to the second edition of 1540 which was virtually Lutheran in tone.[1]

Cromwell's main effort, however, was devoted to mounting a more popular propaganda campaign in favour of the breach with Rome. One device he used was to patronise the nascent secular drama for political purposes. The leading contributor to this aspect of the campaign was John Bale, who composed over twenty plays during the 1530s, many of them violently anti-Papal in tone. The earliest seems to have been *A Comedy Concerning Three Laws*, probably completed in 1532 and first published in 1538 (Harris, 1940, p. 71). This has been characterised as the first Protestant morality-play in English, and includes a scurrilous attack on the Papacy and the monastic life (Harris, 1940, p. 85). The figure of Sodomy appears as a monk, while the Papacy is portrayed as Covetousness, demanding to be worshipped in defiance of the laws of God (pp. 23, 42–3), Bale followed this with *A Tragedy of John, King of England*, drafted in 1538, in which the King is represented as a good ruler who is foiled by the perfidy of his own Archbishop – who appears as the figure of Sedition – and by the machinations of the Pope – who is represented as Usurped Power (pp. 218–20; cf. Fairfield, 1976, p. 55).

The propaganda value of Bale's plays was not lost on Cromwell, who seems to have taken some trouble to protect him and even to ensure that his works were performed (Harris, 1940, pp. 26–8, 100–2). But Cromwell's main concern in this later phase of his campaign was naturally to commission some further political tracts designed to legitimate the repudiation of the Pope's supremacy. This prompted him first of all to take an interest in the use of history for propaganda purposes. The idea of employing history for ideological ends had already commended itself to a number of English reformers, notably William Tyndale (Pineas, 1962a). But the

---

[1] See Mozley, 1953, pp. 201, 207, 218, and cf. Yost, 1970, who emphasises that Richard Taverner similarly went out of his way to introduce Lutheran elements into the translations he was commissioned to make in the 1530s.

earliest attempt to re-write the English chronicles in such a way as to legitimate the breach with Rome appears to have been made by Robert Barnes in the 1534 version of his *Supplication*. This is thought to have been commissioned by Cromwell, and was dedicated to the King (Pineas, 1964, p. 55). It includes an historical account of the growth of Papal power in which Barnes seeks to show that the Church and the clerical estate have increasingly become a subversive political force in every realm (sig. C2b–Sig. D1a). The same themes were quickly exploited by a number of anonymous contributors to the Government's cause,[1] and were later taken up more seriously by the indefatigable John Bale. His first contribution to this *genre* was his *Image of Both Churches*, a verse-by-verse exposition of the Book of Revelations, originally published in 1541, in which the Pope is cast in the role of anti-Christ, and the mystical numbers are taken to point to the various dates at which the Papacy made its direct inroads on the rights of the secular authorities (pp. 311–43). This was followed by a highly scurrilous tract entitled *The Acts of English Votaries* which Bale published in 1546. Part of his aim in this work – as in some of his earlier plays – was to undermine the veneration of saints. He accordingly devotes a great deal of space to recounting the disreputable amatory exploits allegedly performed by men who were subsequently canonised by the Catholic Church (fos 17b–24b; 32b–39b, etc.). But his main purpose was to supply an historical justification for the Henrician schism. He attempts to prove that a genuinely apostolic version of Christianity existed in England from the earliest times, and that Augustine's celebrated mission, so far from establishing the English Church, merely began the long process of its corruption by decadent Romish practices (Pineas, 1962b, pp. 223, 226). This is taken to establish that the powers of the Papacy merely constitute a latter-day usurpation, and that the breach with Rome must be seen as a contribution to recovering the pristine purity of the English Church (fos 25b–31b).

The backbone of Cromwell's popular propaganda campaign, however, was provided by a second and more significant group of political tracts, all of which he seems to have commissioned himself. These were mainly produced by a group of radical humanists, a group which included Richard Morison, William Marshall and Richard Taverner, as well as the more significant figure of Thomas Starkey, whom we have already encountered as the author of the *Dialogue* between Pole and Lupset, one of the major treatises of humanist political thought to be produced in sixteenth-century England. These writers were ideally suited to furthering the government's cause, and probably believed in what they wrote

[1] For examples, see Baumer, 1940, pp. 43–4; Levy, 1967, pp. 96–8.

rather more sincerely than their learned predecessors. They were all humanists by training, who had already become hostile to the Church and sympathetic to Lutheranism, although none of them (except Morison) had yet become Lutherans themselves (Bonini, 1973, p. 218). They were also suited on personal grounds to act as propagandists for the government. Some had already seen public service under Wolsey, and all of them, as Zeeveld remarks, were still 'hoping for a political career through their studies' (Zeeveld, 1948, p. 244). The result was that they displayed an active willingness to help in Cromwell's campaign. Some scholars have spoken of their recruitment by the government, but the fact is that they all approached Cromwell themselves in order to volunteer their services (McConica, 1965; cf. Elton, 1973, pp. 47, 56).

The first to make contact with the minister appears to have been Marshall, who offered himself to Cromwell in 1533 as a translator of books 'for the defacing of the Pope of Rome' (McConica, 1965, p. 136). He was commissioned as a result to produce the first English translation of Marsiglio's *Defender of Peace*, and evidently received a loan of £12 from Cromwell to cover his costs (Baumer, 1940, p. 44 note). The translation appeared in 1535, with the inconvenient passages on the popular origins of political authority judiciously omitted, and a Preface added by the translator in which he asserted that the book not only provides the means 'utterly to confute' the arguments of 'the Papistical sort', but also demonstrates that the Popes have at all times been 'proud and presumptuous usurpers' as well as 'murderers, traitors, rebellers contrary to their allegiance' (fos 1a–1b; cf. Stout, 1974, p. 309).

It is possible that Starkey was also in contact with Cromwell in 1533, for he seems to have sent the minister a favourable legal opinion on the royal divorce at that time (Elton, 1973, p. 74 note). Zeeveld argues that this brought him to Cromwell's attention, and that he found himself encouraged to desert the Pole circle at Padua and return to England (Zeeveld, 1948, p. 142). Elton suggests, however, that it must have been Starkey who 'realised that his time had come', since he returned to England on his own initiative at the end of 1534 and introduced himself as a virtual stranger to Cromwell early in the following year (Elton, 1973, pp. 47–8). If this is so, then his hopes were rewarded with remarkable alacrity, for within two months of his arrival he received a summons to Court. He was first appointed as a royal chaplain and employed to correspond with Pole in the hope of changing his mind about the divorce, but he soon moved on to engage in more wide-ranging political discussions with Cromwell himself (Elton, 1973, p. 49). Cromwell appears to have prompted him in the course of these meetings to draft a defence of the Reformation settlement, and may even have had a hand in revising the manuscript which Starkey produced (Elton, 1973, pp. 50–1). The outcome was Starkey's important tract, *An Exhortation to the People*, 'instructing them to unity and obedience', which was presented to the King at the end of 1535 and first published in the following year (Zeeveld, 1948, pp. 128, 149).

It may well have been Starkey's success which encouraged Morison to follow him in deserting Pole at Padua in order to return home (Zeeveld, 1948, pp. 157, 165). We first find him writing to Cromwell from Italy in October 1534, and he seems to have been taken into government service at some point in the following year, with the evident intention that he should remain abroad and report on foreign reactions to the progress of the English schism (Elton, 1973, pp. 56–7). He asked to be recalled early in 1536, however, and after a rather long pause he was duly sent enough money to pay his passage back to England.[1] The details of his initial reception by the government are shadowy, but he soon became the most prolific and violent of the pamphleteers employed by Cromwell to write in favour of the breach with Rome. He began by revising a long history of the schism, including an attack on More and Fisher, which he had probably started in Italy early in 1536, and which he eventually published in 1537 as *Apomaxis Calumniarum*.[2] He then moved on to publish a sequence of tracts denouncing the sinfulness of those who were trying to resist the new regime. He began in a leisured, humanist style with his *Remedy for Sedition*, but after Pole's defection and the Pilgrimage of Grace he responded with a greatly increased sense of urgency in his *Lamentation* in which he showed 'what ruin and destruction comes of seditious rebellion' (Elton, 1972, pp. 200–1). This hasty pamphlet was followed in 1539 by two important works in which the treasons of the northern rebels and his former patron Pole were both fitted into a general framework for viewing the whole breach with Rome. The first to be published was *An Invective against the great and detestable vice, Treason*, which went through two editions in the course of the year (Elton, 1972, p. 202). This was followed soon afterwards by *An Exhortation to stir all Englishmen to the defence of their country*, in which Morison presented the final version of his patriotic and highly influential vision of the reformation settlement.

The political doctrines stated by Starkey and Morison (and later restated by Bekinsau in his Latin tract of 1546 on *The Supreme and Absolute Power of the King*) are to some extent the same as in the earlier and

---

[1] Elton, 1973, p. 58. This corrects the account given in Zeeveld, 1948, pp. 94–5, 158.

[2] The story of this manuscript is complicated. For the full details, see Elton, 1972, pp. 190–1 and note.

more technical treatises of Sampson, Foxe and Gardiner. Morison in *Apomaxis Calumniarum* even cites the authority of Foxe and Gardiner at several points (e.g., sig. X, 1a). It is true that the arguments of the later pamphleteers are presented in a rather different style. They almost always write in English rather than Latin, they generally avoid any discussion of the niceties of canon law, and they are much more prone to engage in personal attacks on the probity and scholarship of their enemies.[1] But there is still the same basic concern to vindicate the divorce and the royal supremacy, and the same appeal to the Lutheran concept of the Church in order to support their analysis of the relationship between spiritual and temporal power.

Where these writers chiefly differ from the earlier propagandists is in going on to appeal to a further and even more explicitly Lutheran argument, which they use to place the whole Henrician Reformation in a new and more reassuring perspective. This is the doctrine of 'adiaphora', or 'things indifferent' for salvation. As we have seen, this was originally developed by Melanchthon and imported into England by Barnes. It was now taken over in particular by Starkey, who argues in his *Exhortation* that the entire statutory programme of the Henrician Reformation ought to be treated as a thing indifferent for salvation (fos 41a, 43b). This enables him to insist that everyone must now submit to the changes, since they have been found to be 'for the time convenient to a certain policy' and are based on the consent of 'common counsel' – that is, on the law-making authority of the King in Parliament (fo 82a; cf. Zeeveld, 1948, p. 152). But this also enables him to add the more reassuring claim that no one need feel any 'scruple of conscience' about making such a submission, since such obedience cannot in any way compromise one's hope of being saved (fo 69a). It is true, as Starkey recognises, that this involves him in a difficulty: he is committed to pointing to an authority capable of distinguishing faultlessly between things indifferent and things necessary for salvation. He is content, however, to leave this question to be settled by 'the authority of the prince and the common counsel of the realm', from whom, as he soothingly suggests, we may expect 'some remedies will shortly be provided' (fo 74a; cf. Zeeveld, 1948, p. 155). There is no reason to fear that they will fail to draw the necessary distinctions or be tempted to legislate in a manner 'which justly may appear contrary to the grounds of scripture'. We have a complete guarantee against this danger in the fact that the King himself 'by his clear judgment' always 'sees what is best' for the country and unerringly follows it (fo 83a).

---

[1] These usually seem unfair, although Elton has recently urged us to accept at face value the attack mounted by Morison on Sir Thomas More; see Elton, 1972, p. 192.

This remarkably sanguine view of the legislative process serves to explain a second difference between the outlook of Starkey and Morison and that of the earlier Henrician propagandists. As we have seen, Sampson, Foxe and Gardiner had all tended to envisage the royal supremacy as having an essentially personal character. But the common lawyers had already begun to insist that the supremacy must be vested in the King in Parliament, on the grounds that this authority (as St German had already maintained) 'represents the whole Catholic Church of England' (cf. Baumer, 1940, p. 59). It is this latter interpretation which Starkey and Morison adopt, stressing the powers of statute and decisively rejecting any hieratic interpretation of the King's headship. Starkey in particular reiterates again and again that 'the common counsel' of the King in Parliament must always be consulted in any attempt to legislate about ecclesiastical affairs, since it constitutes the 'sentence of common authority' (e.g., fo 82a). For Starkey, as Zeeveld puts it, 'the voice of Parliament had become the voice of God' (Zeeveld, 1948, p. 155).

It seems something of an overstatement to say (as Zeeveld has done) that this adaptation of Melanchthon's concept of 'indifferent things' became 'through Starkey, the direct ideological forebear of the Anglican polity' (Zeeveld, 1948, p. 129). The doctrine had already been put into currency some time before Starkey wrote, in particular in the writings of Frith and Barnes. There is no doubt, however, that Starkey was able to make a fruitful use of the concept at a crucial moment, as a means of steering a *via media* between the position of the radical Lutherans and the traditional Catholics. The Lutherans, with their doctrine of *sola scriptura*, are accused of 'an arrogant blindness' in attempting 'under the pretence of liberty' to 'destroy all Christian policy' and to 'bring all to manifest ruin and utter confusion' with their continual disputes about the proper interpretation of the Bible (fos 18a, 25a; cf. Zeeveld, 1948, pp. 153–4). The traditional Catholics, with their extravagant reverence for masses, ceremonies and the Papal supremacy, are in turn accused of 'a superstitious blindness' in failing to see that these are all things indifferent, over which it is absurd that supposedly learned men should 'run to their death' – an evident allusion to the stand taken by Fisher and More (fos 18a–b, 22a, 43b; cf. Zeeveld, 1948, p. 154). Starkey thus feels able to call on both sides to 'keep the mean' and agree on a compromise, the Catholics by giving up 'false and vain superstition', the Lutherans by giving up 'proud and arrogant opinion' (fo 88a). This is the only way, he concludes, to ensure 'good order' and 'charitable unity', which as a good humanist he prizes above all (fos 14a, 32a).

There are two other significant differences between these writers and the earlier Henrician propagandists, both of which may be explained in terms of the changing political circumstances in which they wrote. The first is that the later writers are obliged to make a determined effort to deal with the new problems posed by the summoning of the General Council of the Church. Starkey inserted a long discussion of this issue – evidently at the last moment – into the Preface to his *Exhortation*. He concedes, in line with moderate Protestant opinion, that the idea of a Council is 'not to be rejected', since the idea 'was of wise men and politic brought in' and may be of value in the attempt 'to conserve the political unity' (fo 9a). But he is now prepared to argue that the powers of General Councils must be purely advisory, not executive, and thus that they have no authority 'among the people in any country, till they be confirmed by princely power and common council' (fo 9a). He adds that in any case 'it is great superstition and plain folly' to think that the decisions of a Council form a part of divine law, since the status of General Councils is that they are themselves 'things indifferent' (fo 9a). He thus takes up a position very similar to the one later adopted by Hooker in the *Laws of Ecclesiastical Polity*, and very much less concessive than the one Foxe and Gardiner had permitted themselves in discussing the same point. He already wishes to say, as Hooker was later to put it, that although Councils have a certain 'force', we must remember that 'the just authority of civil courts and Parliaments is not therefore to be abolished', and that the authority of a Council can only extend to dealing with questions which are not 'matters of necessity' (I, pp. 252–3).

Starkey's views about the status of Councils again proved very useful, and were soon reiterated and developed in an anonymous *Treatise concerning General Councils, the Bishop of Rome and the Clergy* which Berthelet published in 1538. The traditional appeal which Foxe and Gardiner had made to the thesis of conciliarism is now dropped in favour of Starkey's more radical approach. The King is said to have divine authority to rule the Church as well as the commonwealth, which gives him power both to summon a Council of the Church and to adopt or reject any Decretals it formulates (Sawada, 1961, p. 198). The outcome, as in Starkey, is that the question of the king's authority over Councils is simply treated as part of the general defence of the rights of the *regnum* against the alleged jurisdictions of the *sacerdotium* (Sawada, 1961, p. 204).

Finally, these writers go on to place a new and timely emphasis on the dangers of disorder and rebellion, which they denounce in increasingly hysterical terms. This applies especially to Morison, who was not only writing after the defection of Pole and the Pilgrimage of Grace, but must also have been mindful of the fact that Clement VII's excommunication of

Henry VIII, which had been suspended between 1535 and 1538, had been reimposed in the latter year, with the result that the King's subjects had again been proclaimed by the Pope to be freed from any oaths of allegiance (Baumer, 1940, p. 88). Morison's basic answer to these problems consists of reiterating an essentially Lutheran account of the absolute need for non-resistance in all circumstances. As the *Exhortation* repeatedly insists, the King is sole ruler 'by the will and ordinance of God'. He alone is 'God's minister, into whose charge God has committed this realm' (sig. C, 2b). The crucial implication appears in the *Invective*, supported with copious Biblical citations: no one, for any reason, must ever 'think to pull down a prince whom God has chosen to rule over his people' (sig. A, 5b).

The most notable feature of Morison's account is that he invests these Lutheran commonplaces with a special force by embedding them in a patriotic – and highly influential – interpretation of the meaning of the whole schism with Rome. He first argues, both in the *Invective* and the *Exhortation*, that since God intends the King to be our sole ruler, the powers claimed by the Papacy must be contrary to the will of God. It follows that the King and the whole nation must be engaged in a patriotic as well as a religious act in seeking to repudiate them. This enables Morison to denounce the Catholics – and particularly his former patron Pole – with a chauvinistic as well as a religious ferocity. 'The pestiferous Pole' is characterised in the *Exhortation* as 'a traitor against his country' as well as against the laws of God, while all the 'papists' are equally accused of treasonously attempting to rupture the political unity which God has ordained in every Christian commonwealth (sig. A, 8b; sig. B, 2a–b). The same attack is repeated in the *Invective*, which simply equates being a 'papist' with being unable to 'bear the king such a heart as a true subject owes his sovereign lord' (sig. F, 3b). This in turn enables Morison to equate the acceptance of the Henrician Reformation with the cause of patriotism. The repudiation of the Papacy is simply treated as the outlawing of a foreign power, and the *Exhortation* culminates in a plea to the people to stand by their King in defending his rightful authority against any attempts by his enemies to resume the jurisdictions which they have for so long usurped (sig. D, 2b–3a).

The fact that Henry VIII is claimed (not altogether accurately) to have led the way amongst the princes of Europe in rejecting the powers of the Pope finally suggests to Morison a further and even more stridently patriotic theme. The *Exhortation* argues that the King must have been specially chosen to perform this godly task. He is 'the wind ordained and sent by God to toss the wicked tyrant of Rome and to blow him out of all Christian regions' (sig. D, 8a). This means that to uphold the cause of the

Bishop of Rome is not only to ignore a great honour which God has bestowed on the English nation, but is thereby to reject one's calling as an Englishman. The cause of the Reformation is thus equated with the true destiny of the nation. 'See you not to what honour God has called our nation? May we not rejoice that God has chosen our King to work so noble a feat?' It is on this strongly rhetorical note that the *Exhortation* ends (sig. D, 8b).

With this culmination of the government's propaganda campaign, the most characteristic features of Anglican political theory can already be discerned. The same contention that 'with us the name of a Church imports only a society of men' later formed the starting-point for Hooker's classic analysis of the relationship between the Church and the common-wealth in his *Laws of Ecclesiastical Polity* (III, p. 329). And in Hooker's account, no less than in the writings of the Henrician propagandists, we find the same inferences being drawn. He treats it as 'a gross error' to suppose 'that the royal power ought to serve for the good of the body and not of the soul' (III, p. 363). And he concludes that the King must in consequence be acknowledged to have authority 'to command and judge' in all ecclesiastical as well as temporal causes, and must be treated as the sole head of the commonwealth (III, pp. 408ff).

As well as adumbrating this Anglican preoccupation with the idea that – as Hooker expresses it – 'the Church and the commonwealth' are 'one society', the Henrician propagandists may also be said to have established much of the tone of later Anglican political thought (III, 329). On the one hand, many of them already write in a self-consciously eirenic style. This note of carefully modulated reassurance is already audible in Starkey's *Exhortation*, recurs in the account of 'things indifferent' in Cranmer's Forty-Two articles, and reaches its culmination in Hooker's *Laws*, with its calming insistence that there are many things 'free in their nature and indifferent' which God 'permits with approbation either to be done or left undone' (I, p. 296). On the other hand, the Henrician propagandists also begin to strike a loudly contrasting note of apocalyptic nationalism. This can already be heard in Bale's martyrology, increases in volume with Morison's appeal to the elect nation, and comes to a climax in the writings of John Foxe, at which point – as Haller remarks – 'the saga of the chosen people of the Old Testament' begins to be identified in the popular mind with 'the elect people of England' (Haller, 1963, p. 240). It was this image of the English commonwealth to which Bishop Aylmer appealed at the start of Elizabeth's reign when he proclaimed that God is English (Haller, 1963, p. 245). And it was the same image to which Milton reverted in 1641 when he spoke of God revealing himself first to his Englishmen, and sought to rally his fellow-countrymen in the peroration of his treatise *Of Reformation* with his vision of their 'great and warlike nation' pressing confidently onwards 'with high and happy emulation' towards the day when God will 'judge the several nations of the world' and distribute 'national honours and rewards to religious and just commonwealths' (p. 616).

Further Reading

(1) *Ockham and the Conciliarists.* For the origins of conciliarism see Tierney, 1955. For a classic outline of the movement see Figgis, 1960, Chs 1 and 2. McGrade, 1974, gives an excellent account of Ockham's political theory, prefaced by a survey of other interpretations. For a fuller but more idiosyncratic analysis, see Lagarde, 1963. On the political theories of individual conciliarists, the most useful introductions are as follows: on Zabarella, Ullmann, 1948; on d'Ailly, Oakley, 1964; on Gerson, Morrall, 1960; on Nicholas of Cusa, Sigmund, 1963; on Almain, La Brosse, 1965; on Mair, Oakley, 1962 and 1965.

(2) *Luther.* The fullest biography is by Fife, 1957, carrying the story down to the Diet of Worms. For the background to Luther's protest see Dickens, 1974, an admirable introduction. Boehmer, 1946 (supplemented by Rupp, 1951 and 1953) gives a classic account of the development of Luther's theology. But this interpretation has been challenged by Saarnivaara, 1951. For an outline of Luther's theology see Althaus, 1966, and for a briefer analysis see Watson, 1947. Cranz, 1959, discusses the evolution of Luther's views on law and society, while Wolin, 1961, includes a fine account of the political element in Luther's thought. For a more general sketch of Luther's 'world of thought', see Bornkamm, 1958. Some important articles on special topics: on the 'godly prince', Spitz, 1953; on the 'two kingdoms', Cargill Thompson, 1969; on the development of Lutheran theories of political resistance, Baron, 1937 and Benert, 1973.

(3) *The Radical Reformation.* The origins of Anabaptism are discussed in Bender, 1953 and in Blanke, 1961. Dickens, 1966b, provides an excellent outline of the movement, while Williams, 1962 contains the fullest general survey. For a social history of the Anabaptists see Clasen, 1972, and for their views on politics, particularly political violence, see Stayer, 1972. On their relations with the 'evangelical' reformers see Oyer, 1964 and Edwards, 1975.

PART TWO

Constitutionalism and the
Counter Reformation

4

The background of constitutionalism

'Had there been no Luther there could never have been a Louis XIV' (Figgis, 1960, p. 81). Figgis's epigram has been criticised as unhistorical, but there is no doubt that the main influence of Lutheran political theory in early modern Europe lay in the direction of encouraging and legitimating the emergence of unified and absolutist monarchies. Luther's doctrines proved so useful for this purpose that his most distinctive political arguments were eventually echoed even by the leading Catholic protagonists of the divine right of kings. When Bossuet, for example, came to address his major political work to Louis XIV's heir in 1679, he based his entire discussion on the typically Lutheran assumption that all political principles must be derived from the pages of the Bible, entitling his treatise *Politics Taken from the Words of Holy Writ*. Moreover, in analysing the concepts of political authority and obligation, he laid a very strong emphasis on both the doctrines which we have already seen to be most characteristic of early Lutheran political thought. When he considers 'the nature of royal authority' in Book IV, he maintains that the power of the king must extend to judging all causes, ecclesiastical as well as temporal, and that his power itself must be absolute, since 'there is no one to whom the king is accountable' (pp. 92–4). And when he turns in Book VI to deduce the nature of 'the duties which subjects owe to their princes', he takes his stand squarely on the Pauline doctrine of passive obedience which the reformers had so often invoked. He first cites St Paul's command that 'every soul must be subject to the highest powers, for all power is of God' (p. 192). And he concludes that any subject who resists the commands even of a wicked king 'is sure to receive damnation', since 'any resistance to authority is resistance to the ordinance of God' (p. 192).[1]

However, the sixteenth century not only witnessed the beginnings of

[1] The same use of Lutheran political arguments to uphold the cause of absolutism can also be observed in a large number of German political theorists of the seventeenth century, including such writers as Reinking, Horn, Graswinckel, and Muller. For these and other examples see Gierke, 1939, esp. pp. 85–6.

absolutist ideology, but also the emergence of its greatest theoretical rival, the theory that all political authority inheres in the body of the people, and thus that – as Filmer put it in *Patriarcha* – all rulers must be 'subject to the censures and deprivations of their subjects' (p. 54). The next question we need to consider is how it came about that this 'new, plausible and dangerous opinion', as Filmer called it (p. 53), was able to develop so dramatically during this period, so that the aspiring absolutist governments of early modern Europe were eventually challenged – initially in Scotland, then in Holland, then in France and finally in England – by the first wave of successful political revolutions of modern times.

There are two main components to the answer, the first of which will be examined in the present chapter, the other in the one that follows. The first is that a considerable body of radical political ideas had already been built up in the course of the later Middle Ages, and had reached a new peak of development at the start of the sixteenth century. There was thus a large arsenal of ideological weapons available to be exploited by the revolutionaries of late sixteenth-century Europe. The other important point is that all the most influential works of systematic political theory which were produced in Catholic Europe in the course of the sixteenth century were fundamentally of a constitutionalist character. As Filmer shrewdly observed, a number of leading Jesuit theorists of the counter-reformation showed themselves scarcely less willing than the most 'zealous favourers of the Geneva discipline' to defend the cause of popular sovereignty (p. 53).

THE CONCILIARIST TRADITION

Perhaps the most significant strand of radical political theory in the later Middle Ages arose out of the conciliar movement. It is true that when Huguccio and his followers originally articulated the thesis of conciliarism at the end of the twelfth century, they were content to present it as a relatively *ad hoc* series of arguments about the need for the Church to protect itself against the possibility of Papal heresy or misrule. But when the theory came to be restated and developed by Gerson and his followers at the time of the Great Schism, the idea of the Church as a constitutional monarchy was deduced from a more general analysis of political societies – a genus of which the Church was now taken to be a species (Figgis, 1960, p. 56). This in turn meant that, in defending the authority of General Councils over the Church, Gerson in particular committed himself to enunciating a theory about the origins and location of legitimate political power within the secular commonwealth. And in the course of setting out this argument, he made two major and deeply influential contributions to the evolution of a radical and constitutionalist view of the sovereign State.

Gerson's point of departure is the contention that all political societies must by definition be 'perfect'. Commenting on this essentially Aristotelian category at the end of his treatise *On Ecclesiastical Power*, he begins by laying it down that there are two main classes of political society, 'one of which is normally called ecclesiastical, the other secular' (p. 247). In describing each of these as 'perfect', Gerson's intention, as he tells us, is 'to distinguish them from household communities which are not self-sufficient' (p. 247). A *communitas perfecta* is thus defined as an independent, autonomous corporation, possessing the fullest authority to regulate its own affairs without external interference.

It is this characterisation of secular political societies as 'perfect' which leads Gerson to make his first radical contribution to the theory of the State. For it leads him to argue that any secular government must be independent of any other form of jurisdiction, including the alleged jurisdictions of the Church. As we have seen, William of Ockham had already insisted on making precisely the same sharp distinction between the spheres of ecclesiastical and secular authority. Largely due to Gerson's influence, Ockham's argument now entered the mainstream of late scholastic political theory, and began to exercise its corrosive effects on the traditional hierocratic theory of Papal supremacy *in temporalibus* – the theory which Boniface VIII had most recently and most unequivocally upheld. Gerson does not of course deny that the Church is capable of wielding 'coercive temporal power' (p. 216). He agrees that its legal representatives must have the capacity to punish heresy and uphold the true doctrines of the Church, and argues that this must include 'not merely the power to excommunicate', but also the ability to impose 'temporal punishment and censure' in the form of 'fines or imprisonment' (pp. 216, 218). He is quite certain, however, that the Church's 'plenitude of power' extends no further than the wielding of this 'spiritual sword' (p. 218). He is eloquently silent about the question of whether the Pope may be said to have the authority to intervene indirectly in secular affairs – an authority consistently defended by the Thomists, but already dismissed by William of Ockham in his *Eight Questions on the Power of the Pope* as having 'no validity in the ordinary course of events' (p. 203). And he is absolutely explicit in denying the claim advanced by Boniface VIII – whom he cites and criticises by name – to the effect that the Papacy enjoys a plenitude of power 'to bind and loose' in worldly as well as in spiritual affairs (p. 238). On this vital issue, according to Gerson, it is necessary to steer a middle course between two opposing errors, one of which 'detracts from' the position of the Church, while the other 'unduly adulates it' (p. 236). The 'error of detraction' consists of the belief that 'ecclesiastics have no capacity for temporal jurisdiction, even if princes wish to confer it upon them', since they have a duty 'not to implicate themselves in worldly affairs' and have no title even to the possession of worldly goods (p. 236). But the 'error of adulation' is no less serious, and consists of the belief that the Church 'has been given all power in heaven and earth', and thus that 'no temporal or ecclesiastical, no Imperial or regal power can be held unless it is held from the Pope' (p. 237). For Gerson, the truth must be sought between the two extremes, a contention which leads him to conclude that the spheres of secular and ecclesiastical jurisdiction must be kept virtually separate.

Gerson's theory is even more radical in its account of the location of legitimate political power. As we have seen, he maintains that, in the case of the Church, the highest governing authority lies with the General Council as the representative assembly of the faithful, and that the Pope's apparent plenitude of power is in effect conceded to him as a matter of administrative convenience. But he also lays it down that the legal characteristics of the Church must be symmetrical with those of any other 'perfect' society. So it follows, for Gerson, that the highest law-making authority within a secular commonwealth must analogously be lodged at all times within a representative assembly of all its citizens.

It is true that Gerson treats the origins of the Church and the origins of secular commonwealths in a deliberately contrasting style. He regards the Church as a divine gift immediately bestowed by Christ, but he later goes on to maintain – in a strongly anti-Thomist and anti-Aristotelian style – that all secular societies have arisen 'as a result of sin' (p. 246). Adam was originally granted 'complete dominion over the fowls of the air and the fish of the sea', but this was a purely paternal rather than a political form of authority, since there was no need for any coercive power in a sinless world (p. 246). After the Fall, however, men found it hard to protect themselves from the consequences of their own and other people's sinful behaviour, and eventually decided to limit their natural but precarious liberties in the name of assuring themselves a greater degree of 'tranquillity and peace' (p. 247). The outcome was the gradual establishment of secular commonwealths, which arose 'by a purely natural process', developing out of man's efforts to use his God-given reason in order to improve his natural lot (p. 246; cf. p. 228).

When Gerson turns, however, to consider the location of legitimate power within such commonwealths, he offers an analysis which closely parallels his earlier account of the Church. This is presented at the end of his treatise *On Ecclesiastical Power*, when he broadens his focus in order 'to speak about the concept of politics', and 'to describe the nature of the community established for the perfecting of this end' (p. 247). As his earlier discussion of ecclesiastical authority makes clear, he believes that three claims can be made about the location of authority within any *societas perfecta*. The first and central one is that no ruler can be *maior* or greater in power than the community over which he rules. The two crucial corollaries are first that the ultimate power over any *societas perfecta* must remain at all times within the body of the community itself, and secondly that the status of any ruler in relation to such a community must in consequence be that of a *minister* or *rector* rather than that of an absolute sovereign. Gerson now goes on to relate these claims to secular political societies by way of developing a 'subjective' theory of rights.[1] He equates the possession of a right or *ius* over anything with the power or *potestas* to dispose of it freely (p. 242). He has already laid it down, however, that no ruler, not even the Pope, may be said to have the power to treat a commonwealth or the goods of its members as his own property (p. 236). So it follows that no ruler may be said to have any rights over a commonwealth: he has duties as a *minister* or trustee of other people's rights, but no rights of ownership himself. This in turn leads Gerson to make his final and most strongly constitutionalist point. He insists that any community in which the ruler is 'above the law' or enjoys absolute rights over the goods of his subjects is *ex hypothesi* not a genuinely 'political' society at all. And he concludes that any ruler worthy of the name must always rule 'for the good of the republic' and 'according to the law'. He is not 'above' the community, but a part of it: he is bound by its laws and limited by an absolute obligation 'to aim at the common good in his rule' (p. 247).

When John Mair and his pupils at the Sorbonne revived Gerson's thesis of conciliarism at the start of the sixteenth century, they also revived and restated his accompanying theory about the location of political power within the secular commonwealth. They first of all argued, with even greater assurance, that the spheres of secular and ecclesiastical jurisdiction must be treated as wholly distinct from each other. Mair makes the point briefly in *The Power of the Pope*, insisting that 'kings are in no way subject to the Roman pontiff in temporal affairs' (col. 1150). Almain presents a more extensive statement of the case in his *Exposition* of

---

[1] For the claim that the 'subjective' analysis of a right in terms of a liberty to act originates with Ockham, see Villey, 1964. For a very fine discussion of the evolution of the 'subjective' conception, and for an account of Gerson's key role in its development, see Tuck, 1977.

Ockham's theory concerning lay and ecclesiastical power. He goes far beyond Ockham's own position, virtually endorsing the heretical claim originally advanced by Marsiglio of Padua – whose authority he explicitly invokes – to the effect that all coercive power is secular by definition, and thus that the Church has no role to play in political society at all (cols 1038–40). In Chapter VI he raises the question of whether both lay and ecclesiastical power can be held by the same person, and in Chapter VII he considers whether a spiritual ruler can legitimately annex temporal dominion. He emphatically repudiates both suggestions, his argument in each case being that the spheres of lay and ecclesiastical authority must be kept completely separate (cols 1028–32; cf. Oakley, 1962, p. 14).

When Mair and his pupils turn to consider the origins and legal character of secular commonwealths, they develop an equally radical and influential version of Gerson's ideas. They begin by repeating the patristic and anti-Aristotelian account which Gerson had given of the formation of political societies – a story which Gerson may well have derived in turn from Ockham's very similar analysis in his *Brief Account of the Power of the Pope* (pp. 85–7). The clearest restatement of this position is given by Mair in the 1519 edition of his *Questions* arising out of the fourth Book of Lombard's *Sentences*. He agrees with Gerson that Adam enjoyed a paternal but not a political form of dominion, since there was no need for coercive authority in a sinless world (fo ciib). So he accepts the patristic view that the need for secular commonwealths originally arose in consequence of the Fall. Wandering and congregating in different parts of the world, men found it expedient for their own protection 'to constitute heads for themselves' and so to set up 'kingly forms of government' (fo ciia). The origins of political societies are thus traced to two complementary developments: the fact that God gave men the capacity to form such communities in order to remedy their sins; and the fact that men duly made use of these rational powers in order 'to introduce kings' by 'an act of consent on the part of the people' as a way of improving their own welfare and security (fo ciia).

When the so-called 'Sorbonnists' move on to consider the location of legitimate power within such commonwealths, they again reiterate and amplify the claims which Gerson had already advanced. They first of all agree that no ruler whom the people freely consent to establish over themselves can possibly be *maior* or greater in authority than the people themselves. Almain in particular presents an influential argument at this point in criticism of the Thomist allegation that any ruler must be 'above' the community over which he rules. Aquinas had pointed out in analysing the concept of injustice in his *Summary of Theology* that although 'private persons' have no conceivable authority to 'execute malefactors', it is obvious that 'the killing of malefactors' is 'legitimate' when it is done by 'rulers who exercise public authority' (p. 27). This tended to suggest that, even if political societies may be said to originate (as Aquinas elsewhere conceded) in an act of consent on the part of the people, the act of establishing the commonwealth must involve them in creating a power over themselves greater than any power which they originally possessed. Aquinas explicitly draws this inference elsewhere in his *Summary*, notably in his discussion of the concept of human law. Any head or sovereign, he declares, must be 'exempt from law with respect to its coercive power', and must in this way be 'above' and 'greater than' the whole body of the people, who are powerless to 'pass sentence condemning him' if he breaks the law or ignores it (p. 135). Undaunted by this orthodoxy, Almain responded by developing a theory which was later characterised by John Locke – who also accepted it – as the 'very strange doctrine' that each individual in his pre-political state must be pictured as the 'executioner of the law of nature', with the right to wield the sword of justice on his own behalf (p. 290). Almain presents this argument at the start of his *Reconsideration*, where he analyses the difference between natural and political rule. He treats it as obvious that 'no one can give what he does not possess', and goes on to use this principle in order to argue that 'the right of the sword' which a community grants to its ruler in the act of forming a political society must be a right originally possessed by the community itself (col. 964). It does not come into being with the installation of a prince as the Thomists had implied. It is 'merely conceded' (*concessum est*) by the people to their ruler in order that it may be more safely exercised for the common protection of all (cols 963–4). Almain reiterates both these contentions at the start of his *Brief Account of the Power of the Church*, where he again discusses the formation of political societies. Once more he insists on the principle that 'no one can give what he does not possess' (col. 978). And once more he affirms that the rights which a prince enjoys under positive law must originally have been possessed by the community under the law of nature, and must at some determinate point have been 'committed (*commissa*) to some certain persons by means of the right reason God has granted to men' (col. 978).

The Sorbonnists next go on to deduce both the corollaries about the location of sovereignty within political society which Gerson had already emphasised. Far more decisively than any of their predecessors, they insist that political authority is not merely derived from but inheres in the body of the people. So they conclude that the people only delegate and never alienate their ultimate power to their rulers, and thus that the status of a ruler can never be that of an absolute sovereign, but only that of a minister or official of the commonwealth. Almain summarises both these key contentions at the start of his *Reconsideration*, in which he paraphrases the central sections of his *Exposition* of Ockham's views about the proper relations between the *regnum* and the Church. Having laid it down that 'civil dominion' was originally a gift granted by God to man after the Fall, he proceeds to derive five corollaries. The third and main one is that the highest political power must remain within the body of the community at all times, and thus that the status of the prince in relation to the *regnum* can never be higher than 'that of an official' (*ministeriale*) (col. 964). Almain concedes in his fifth corollary that 'since it is not possible for the whole community to meet together regularly', it is appropriate that they should 'delegate (*delegare*) their jurisdiction to some certain person or persons who are able to meet together readily' (col. 965). But he still insists that these persons can never be more than delegates, since 'the power which the community has over its prince' – as the fourth corollary asserts – 'is one which it is impossible for it to renounce' (col. 964). Finally, the reason for laying such a strong emphasis on the inalienable character of the rights of the community is brought out in the second corollary. If a society grants away its original and absolute powers, it potentially grants away its capacity to preserve itself. And no community can possibly do this, Almain concludes, 'any more than an individual can abdicate his power to preserve his life' (col. 964).

It is possible that Almain originally learnt these doctrines from Mair's lectures on the fourth Book of Lombard's *Sentences*. If we can judge, however, from the printed versions of Mair's *Questions* arising out of the fourth Book, it seems that Mair may only have arrived at his most radical conclusions at a relatively late stage. He first states them at Distinction 15, question 10, in the course of discussing the place of natural and positive laws in political life. This section does not appear in the original versions printed in 1509 and 1512, but in the 1516 and later editions Mair enunciates both the key elements of a radical theory of *Imperium*, as well as mounting a brisk attack on Accursius and a number of other Glossators for having failed to grasp the nature of the jural relationships which obtain between rulers and commonwealths. He first insists that although a ruler may well be regarded as 'the chief member of the whole body', the fact remains that 'kings are instituted for the good of the people, not the opposite', and thus that 'the whole people must be above the king'.[1] He

---

[1] Mair's phrase is *supra regem*. See the 1519 edition, fos ciib–ciiia. The whole discussion reappears in the final edition of 1521 at fo lxxv. See also Mair's *History*, p. 213, where he maintains that 'a free people confers authority upon its first king, and his power is dependent on the whole people'.

immediately goes on to add that the original rights of the people 'are at no point yielded up' when they consent to the formation of a commonwealth. The right of the sword 'remains at all times the property of the free populace' (*apud populum liberum*), who merely delegate to their prince the authority to exercise it on their behalf (fo ciia).

Mair later corroborates these conclusions by taking up and developing the 'subjective' view of rights which Gerson had already evolved. The clearest statement of Mair's concept of a right appears in the 1519 edition of his *Questions* arising out of Lombard's *Sentences*, where he intimates that to say of someone that he has a right to something is equivalent to saying that he has 'a free power' to dispose of it: thus a man may be said (in Mair's own example) to have the right to his own books, because he is at liberty to do what he likes with them (fos ciib–ciiia). The main application of this concept to the discussion of political power occurs in Mair's *History of Greater Britain*, a work which he completed after his return to Scotland in 1518 and first published at Paris in 1521 (Burns, 1954, pp. 89–90). Mair continues even in the course of his narrative to write in an argumentative, scholastic style, often deploying the historical information in such a way as to underline his more general political claims. One of the issues he raises is the extent of the power a king may be said to have over his own kingdom. He first considers this question in relation to John of England, and later in connection with the claims of Robert the Bruce to the Scottish throne. In both cases he applies his concept of a right to set stringent limits to the power of kings. He lays it down that, since anyone who is 'king of a free people' merely has the status of a minister, he cannot possibly have the power to dispose of his kingdom in any way 'against the will of that people' (p. 158). But to say that a king has no such power is, for Mair, tantamount to saying that he has no genuine rights over his kingdom at all. For to have a right is precisely to have the kind of 'unconditional possession' and liberty of disposal which a man may be said to have – in Mair's own example – in relation to his own coat (p. 216). So he concludes that if a ruler of France, England or any other free people 'were to part with his rights in respect to his kingdom to the Turk, or any other not rightful heir of the same', the grant would be 'worthless', for the king of a free people possesses no right to make such a grant (p. 158). A king is merely a 'public person', who rightfully 'presides over his kingdom' only so long as he upholds 'the greater advantage of the same' (p. 220). He can never be said to have 'that full and fair possession' of his kingdom 'which a private owner has of his own estate' (p. 219).

Finally, Mair and Almain both go on to state – with far greater confidence than Ockham or even Gerson – the most subversive implication of this radical theory of *Imperium*: the implication that any ruler who fails to govern properly may rightfully be deposed by his own subjects. Almain insists at the start of his *Brief Account* that any community must possess 'such a power over its prince by the manner of its constitution that it is able to remove him if he rules not for the benefit but for the destruction of the polity' (col. 978). He regards this as obvious, as he has already indicated, 'since otherwise there would not be sufficient power in the community to preserve itself' (cols 978–9). Mair endorses the same conclusion in the 1519 version of his *Questions*, treating it as a straightforward corollary of applying his 'subjective' theory of rights to the political realm. Since any ruler is in effect an official, 'who cannot have the same free power over his kingdom as I have over my books', it follows that 'the whole people must be above the king and in some cases can depose him' (fos ciib–ciiia). And again Mair uses his *History* to illustrate and underline the same general argument. He considers the case of Robert the Bruce and his rivals for the crown of Scotland, and defends the proposition that 'Robert Bruce alone and his heirs had and have an indisputable claim to the kingdom' (p. 213). One reason he takes to be decisive is that Robert's rival John Baliol, in 'departing from his just rights, and relinquishing his whole claim to Edward of England, showed himself thereby unfit to reign, and was justly deprived of his right, and of the right inhering in his children, by those in whom the decision alone vested, namely the rest of the kingdom' (p. 213).

This leaves one vital practical question over which Almain and Mair are both curiously indecisive: who may be said to have the authority to depose a ruler who has overstepped his powers or betrayed his trust? (cf. Oakley, 1962, p. 18). Sometimes they appear to uphold the dramatically populist claim – classically defended much later by John Locke – that this authority must remain at all times with the whole body of the people. Almain implies at several points that 'the entire community' may remove their ruler if they find him 'pernicious' to their interests.[1] And Mair suggests at one moment in his *History* that 'a people (*populus*) may deprive their king and his posterity of all authority, when the king's worthlessness calls for such a course, just as at first it had the power to appoint him king' (p. 214). It is generally clear, however, at least in Mair's case, that he bases his answer on reverting to the parallels between the secular commonwealth and the Church. In the Church, as all the conciliarists had agreed, the supreme authority to judge and depose a heretical or incapable Pope must lie with the General Council acting as the representative assembly of the faithful. Similarly, Mair generally seems to assume that the power to

---

[1] See for example Almain, *Reconsideration*, col. 964 and *Brief Account*, col. 977.

remove a tyrannical king must be lodged with a representative assembly of the three Estates. The point is made most clearly in the *History*, in the course of the chapter on whether John Baliol was 'justly deprived of his right' as putative ruler of Scotland (p. 213). At the outset of his analysis Mair suggests that it chiefly belongs to an assembly of 'prelates and nobles' to 'decide as to any ambiguity that may emerge in regard to a king' (p. 215). And by the end of the chapter he is prepared to insist much more firmly that 'kings are not to be deposed' unless there has been 'a solemn consideration of the matter by the three estates', so that a 'ripe judgment' can be reached 'wherein no element of passion shall intrude' (p. 219).

THE LEGAL TRADITION

When John Maxwell published *The Sacred and Royal Prerogative of Christian Kings* in 1644, the first question he raised was whether kings are 'independent from the body of the people' (p. 6). He noted that the Jesuits and Puritans both tend to argue in favour of their public accountability. But the Puritans are more radical than the Jesuits, for while the latter generally concede that the people alienate their sovereignty in transferring it to their king, 'our rabbies' (as he dubs the Puritans) maintain that although 'the people communicate this sovereignty to the king by trust', yet 'they deprive not themselves of this sovereignty', since they grant it 'only communicatively' (pp. 7–8). So the question arises as to where this further and especially dangerous doctrine first arose. Maxwell mentions that the orthodox Jesuits trace it back to John Knox, but he argues (correctly) that this is a mistake (p. 12). The true answer, he declares, is that the English 'rabbies' have 'borrowed their first main tenet of the Sorbonnists' (p. 12). It was William of Ockham, and especially Jacques Almain, who first asserted that kings hold their power 'only communicatively' from the people, and that the people never alienate but only delegate their ultimate sovereignty (pp. 12, 14–15).

Maxwell's insistence on treating Ockham and the conciliarists as the originators of radical constitutionalism has been widely echoed in modern scholarship: Figgis speaks of the line running 'from Gerson to Grotius'; Laski declares that 'the road from Constance to 1688 is a direct one'; and Oakley cites and endorses both these judgments.[1] There is a danger, however, that in laying so much emphasis on the constitutional implications of the conciliar movement, we may tend to overlook a further

---

[1] See Figgis, 1960, esp. p. 63; Laski, 1936, p. 638; Oakley, 1962, pp. 4–5 and Oakley, 1964, pp. 211–32, for a discussion of Maxwell and other seventeenth-century divine-right theorists who adopted the same point of view.

and even more influential source of radical political ideas – the Roman law.

It may appear paradoxical to treat the Roman law as one of the major sources of modern constitutionalism. For there is no doubt that the authority of the Digest was constantly invoked by aspiring absolutist rulers in order to legitimate the extent of their dominion over their subjects. They were particularly fond of citing the maxim that any prince must be regarded as *legibus solutus*, 'free from the operation of the laws', as well as the maxim that whatever pleases the prince 'has the force of law' (11, pp. 225–7). Due to the constant repetition of these propositions by the defenders of absolutism, it eventually became a commonplace – restated in much modern scholarship – to associate the Roman law with the extinction of political rights, and the cause of constitutionalism with the jurists' enemies. There is of course some truth in these connections, but they overlook the fact that the civil and canon codes of law were also invoked with no less assurance by some of the most radical opponents of absolutism in early modern Europe.

One way in which the authority of Roman law was used to uphold a constitutionalist position was through the adaptation of a number of private-law arguments about the justifiability of violence. While the jurists normally construed all acts of violence as injuries, they also discussed a number of special cases in which they were prepared to allow this fundamental axiom of the law to be set aside. It is of course true that none of these exceptions were intended to have any bearing on public or constitutional law. But the authority of the law-books was so immense that all such concessions were eagerly seized upon and adapted by those who were anxious to justify acts of political as well as private violence.

The main section of the canon law to be exploited in this way was the Decretal dealing with the problem of unjust judges. One of the most influential discussions of this issue was furnished by Nicolaus de Tudeschis (1386–1445), a pupil of Zabarella's who became Archbishop of Palermo (and in consequence is usually known as Panormitanus), and who gained the reputation of being one of the greatest canonists of the later Middle Ages. Tudeschis's account of unjust judges appears in his *Commentary on the Second Part of the First Book of the Decretals*, the relevant title being the eighth chapter (*Si Quando*) of the rubric *On the Office of Judges* (fo 75a). The question at issue is 'Whether it is legitimate to resist a judge who is proceeding unjustly' (fo 78b). Tudeschis begins by conceding that the original Decretal answers in the negative, insisting that judges 'are not to be resisted with violence', and adding that the only recourse for the injured party is 'to entreat his judge with prayers to alter his judgment' (fo 78b). He maintains, however, that 'against this and against the text' we ought to set the opinion of Pope Innocent IV, who argued in his commentary on the Decretals that 'if a judge proceeds unjustly in a case not committed to his jurisdiction', then 'he can in fact be resisted with violence' (fo 78b). Tudeschis admits that Innocent lays it down that 'if a judge proceeds unjustly in a case which has duly been committed to his jurisdiction', then 'he may not be resisted with violence unless there has been a previous appeal' (fo 78b). But against this he cites 'another notable dictum of Innocent IV' to the effect that 'if a judge does any injury to anyone', then 'he may be resisted violently and with impunity' (*impune potest violenter resisti*) (fo 78b). When Tudeschis turns, moreover, to give his own opinion on the problem, he strongly endorses the most radical point of view. In his Additions to the text he alludes to various authorities who maintain that, even when there has been no appeal, an unjust judge 'may be resisted with violence' (fo 78b). And he adds that this appears to him to license two conclusions. One is that 'if a judge proceeds unjustly' and the injury involved is 'notorious', then the plaintiff may resist immediately, although 'if the injury is not notorious he ought first to lodge an appeal' (fo 79a). The other is that, even in the case of a lesser injury, 'we must always remember Innocent's dictum to the effect that it becomes possible to resist with violence as soon as an appeal has been made' (fo 79a).

As well as this discussion of the justifiability of resistance in the canon law, there were several passages in the civil code in which the deliberate infliction of injury or even death were treated as legitimate. There were two main types of case in which the compilers of the Digest had allowed that the normal prohibition which the positive law places on all acts of violence might be overridden by the dictates of the laws of nature. The first related to certain cases of adultery. It was regarded as legitimate for a father to kill a man found in adultery with his daughter (and to kill his daughter at the same time), and it was similarly accepted that a husband might lawfully kill a man found in adultery with his wife (xi, pp. 41–2). The other range of cases arose in connection with the right of self-defence. The assumption underlying the treatment of this issue in the Digest is that *vim vi repellere licet* – that it is always justifiable to repel unjust force with force.[1] This is first of all taken to apply in any case where sudden 'violence and injury' is offered to one's person. In such circumstances it is always lawful to resist, for 'whatever anyone does for the protection of his body is considered to have been done legally' (ii, pp. 209–10). The same

---

[1] See especially the Digest, XLIII, XVI, 27 (vol. 9, p. 311): 'one can repel force with force; for this right is conferred by the Law of Nature'.

consideration is also held to apply in any case where a thief offers violence in the course of perpetrating a robbery. If I respond by killing him 'I shall be free from liability', since 'natural reason permits a man to protect himself from danger' (III, p. 324). And even if it is only my property rather than my life which is at stake, it may still be lawful for me to kill the man as long as I give fair warning (III, p. 324).

Although it is obvious that none of these cases was intended to have any direct bearing on the political realm, this was not enough to deter a number of radical theologians from appealing to these various justifications of private violence in order to legitimate acts of political resistance to tyrannical kings. This development can be observed most clearly in the case of the civil-law maxim that it must always be lawful to repel unjust force with force. We already find William of Ockham applying this private-law theory of resistance in the form of a political argument in his *Eight Questions on the Power of the Pope* in the early 1340s. Ockham raises the issue in his second Question, in the course of discussing the problem of whether the Pope is judge of the Emperor or the Emperor of the Pope (p. 85). He points to the obvious inconvenience of treating each as the potential superior of the other, and goes on to argue – employing a favourite distinction – that the answer lies in distinguishing between superiority 'in the ordinary course of events' (*regulariter*) and superiority 'in exceptional circumstances' (*casualiter*) (p. 86). He then exemplifies the nature of the distinction he has in mind by considering the relationship between a king and his kingdom. 'The king is superior to his whole kingdom in the ordinary course of events', but 'in exceptional circumstances he may be inferior to the kingdom' (p. 86). This is proved by the fact that 'in cases of dire necessity' it is lawful for the people 'to depose their king and keep him in custody'. And this in turn is said to be justified by the fact that 'the law of nature, as the first book of the Digest says, makes it lawful to repel force with force' (*vim vi repellere licet*) (p. 86).

As with many of Ockham's most radical suggestions, this doctrine was later taken up by Jean Gerson, and in turn passed from his writings into the mainstream of radical scholastic political thought. In his treatise *On the Unity of the Church* Gerson claims that 'many cases may arise' in which 'it would be permissible' for the members of the Church 'to withdraw obedience' from the Pope, just as 'it would be permissible to resist force with force' (p. 146). And in his pamphlet entitled *Ten Highly Useful Considerations for Princes and Governors* he includes a more extensive adaptation of the same private-law argument to the public sphere. He begins his seventh 'consideration' by declaring that 'it is a mistake to claim that kings are free from any obligations towards their subjects', since 'they owe them justice and protection by divine law and the laws of nature'. And he goes on to warn that 'if they fail in this, if they act unjustly towards their subjects, and if they continue in their evil behaviour, then it is time to apply that law of nature which prescribes that we may repel force with force' (*vim vi repellere*) (col. 624).

As well as being manipulated by the theologians, the authority of Roman law was sometimes put to radical use by the professional jurists themselves. One potentially subversive opinion which a considerable number of civil lawyers endorsed was the claim that the concept of *merum Imperium* – perhaps the key concept in Roman public law – ought to be interpreted in a constitutional sense. The term *merum Imperium* was invariably used in Justinian's Code in order to describe the highest forms of public power, in particular the power to command armies and to make laws (Gilmore, 1941, p. 20). The Code appeared to assign this form of authority to the Emperor alone, but a number of commentators sought to argue that the same range of jurisdictions, including the *ius gladii* or right of the sword, could also be exercised by 'inferior magistrates'. The issue was classically debated at the end of the twelfth century by the jurists Azo and Lothair – a dispute which Bodin conveniently summarises as an introduction to his own discussion of *Imperium* in the *Six Books of a Commonweal*. Lothair had declared that *Imperium* – which Bodin simply equates with 'the power of the sword' – could never be wielded by 'inferior magistrates', while Azo had wagered a horse that this was not the case. The Emperor was called upon to adjudicate, and (perhaps not surprisingly) he awarded Lothair the prize. However, the feudal realities of the Holy Roman Empire were such that, as Bodin relates, 'almost all the rest of the famous lawyers' took Azo's side, claiming that local princes and other magistrates have the right no less than the Emperor to wield the sword of justice. Hence it became a favourite joke to say that, although Lothair had carried off the horse (*equum tulerat*), Azo had nevertheless been in the right (*aequum tulerat*) (p. 327).

There were two ways in which Azo's interpretation helped to underpin a constitutionalist attitude towards the legal structure of the Holy Roman Empire. First of all, it tended to support the feudal and particularist view of the Imperial constitution – the view which eventually triumphed in 1648. According to this account, each Emperor at his election could be said to have signed a contract with the electors and other 'inferior magistrates' of the Empire, swearing to uphold the good of the Empire as a whole and to protect the 'liberties' of his subjects. This was taken to establish that the Emperor is not *legibus solutus*, but is bound by the terms of his coronation oath, and depends for the continuation of his authority on the proper discharge of his duties. And this in turn was held to license the radically constitutionalist conclusion that, since the electors and other princes of the Empire are bearers of the *ius gladii* no less than the Emperor himself, it must be lawful for them to use the sword against the Emperor if he should fail to observe the terms of his original oath (Benert, 1973, pp. 18–20). This theory was actually put into practice in 1400, when the Imperial Electors pronounced the deposition of the Emperor Wenzel, and notified his subjects that they were no longer bound by their oaths of allegiance. The Electors argued that the Emperor had sworn to maintain the unity of the Empire and the peace of the Church; that he had failed to keep these promises; and that it fell to them in consequence to remove him from office, acting as a court and executing judgment upon him for the violation of his contract (Carlyle, 1936, pp. 182–3).

The idea of the electors and other 'inferior magistrates' as wielders of *Imperium* also tended to support a second, less particularist but no less radical view of the Emperor's standing. According to this analysis the Empire constituted a *universitas*, an organic unity in which each member has a duty not merely under positive but also under natural law to maintain the integrity of the whole. This was taken to include the possibility that the electors might wield the *ius gladii* against the Emperor in the name of the Empire if they judged that his conduct was undermining the norms of justice which, it was claimed, he had promised in his coronation oath to uphold.[1] This theory was taken up by a number of theologians as well as jurists: it was gestured at by Aquinas in his *Summary of Theology*, and influentially put into currency by William of Ockham in his *Eight Questions on the Power of the Pope*. Ockham presents the argument in the course of discussing the views of 'those who say that the Pope can depose the Emperor' (p. 203). He insists that the Pope has no such authority 'in the ordinary course of events', a conclusion which prompts him to consider who may rightfully be said to have the authority to depose an Emperor 'if he deserves to be deposed' (p. 203). The answer, he suggests, depends on recognising that the Empire constitutes a 'mystical body' in which each 'member' has a natural duty to protect the well-being of the whole (p. 204). 'Just as in a natural body, when one limb becomes defective, the rest make up the deficiency if they are able', so in a *universitas* 'when one part becomes defective, the other parts, if they have the natural power, ought to make up the deficiency' (p. 204). This in turn suggests to Ockham that if the head of the Empire becomes a tyrant, he

[1] For a full analysis of this view of the Imperial constitution, see the excellent article by Benert, 1973 esp. pp. 21–32.

may rightfully be removed 'by those who represent the peoples subject to the Roman *Imperium*', and in particular 'by the elector-princes', who may be compared to the chief 'limbs' or 'members' of the body of the Empire (pp. 203–4).

The radical implications of Ockham's position were not of course spelled out by the Imperial authorities themselves, but his basic concept of a mystical body whose members all have an equal duty to preserve the whole was reiterated soon afterwards in the *Golden Bull* which Charles IV promulgated in 1356 as a new constitution for the Empire (Jarrett, 1935, pp. 171–2). The exordium speaks of the prince-electors as the 'members' of the Empire and the 'columns' which maintain its fabric in place (p. 221). The section on the election of Emperors repeats that 'each and all of the elector-princes' must be considered as 'the nearer members of the Empire' (p. 230). And the next section includes an elaborate development of both these metaphors. 'The venerable and illustrious prince-electors' are 'the chief columns' of the Empire, who 'sustain the holy edifice by the vigilant piety of their circumspect prudence'. And they are also the chief members of its mystical body, whose 'concordant will' is essential if 'Imperial honour' as well as Imperial unity are to be preserved (p. 231).

These anti-absolutist accounts of Imperial authority were brought to a new peak of development at the start of the sixteenth century. This happened largely as a result of the changes introduced into the study of the law by the later *quattrocento* humanists. As we have seen, the humanists began to take a new interest in the history of law, and thus in the study of local and customary forms of legal right. This made them far more attuned than their Bartolist predecessors to the investigation of feudal relationships, which they now began to analyse intensively for the first time. One outcome was a new understanding of the feudal system of obligations and rights which had underpinned the workings of the Holy Roman Empire throughout much of the Middle Ages. Perhaps the most distinguished exemplar of this trend was Ulrich Zasius, whom we have already encountered as one of the leading humanist jurists of the first half of the sixteenth century. When Zasius examines the constitution of the Empire in his treatise on *The Custom of Fiefs*, he makes it clear that he sees the Emperor not as an absolute ruler 'above' the Empire, but rather as the apex of a feudal pyramid. He points out that 'a king within his kingdom has more rights than the Emperor within the Empire', since 'a king is able to transmit his kingdom to his lawful heirs', whereas 'no one is able to succeed to the Empire unless he is elected to it' (col. 225). And he later insists, in his section on 'what a vassal can ask of a lord, and a lord of a vassal', that when a vassal admits a particular person to be his lord –

as the prince-electors admit the Emperor – the resulting obligations are essentially feudal and 'reciprocal in character' (cols 270, 278).

The implications of this analysis for the legal position of the Emperor are spelled out most clearly by Zasius in his *Judgments*, in the course of giving his opinion on a case where the Emperor Maximilian had 'overturned and set aside' a court decision 'out of the plenitude of his absolute power' (col. 409). This leads Zasius to consider the key question of whether the Emperor may properly be said to possess such a degree of power that he stands above the positive law and is capable of annulling it at will (col. 411). His answer takes the form of contending that the Emperor's legal authority is in fact limited in two ways. First he insists that 'the laws have been unsatisfactorily interpreted' by those who allege that 'the Roman Emperor has a kind of absolute power' (*quasi absoluta potestas*) which extends to overturning the legal rights of his individual subjects (col. 412). The Emperor's powers 'are very great indeed', but 'they only extend to maintaining the safety of his subjects and upholding the cause of justice' (col. 412). The Emperor has in effect contracted to perform these duties, so that 'if his power is to be legitimate, it must be reasonable and just', and cannot possibly extend to 'taking away or injuring the rights of anyone at all' (cols 411, 412). His second and even more restrictive claim is that the Emperor is not merely 'bound by his contracts' to remain within the sphere of natural justice, but is also limited by the constitution of the Empire itself (cols 411, 415). He recalls that 'some years ago' the Emperor Maximilian 'together with the leading citizens and princes' of the Empire 'promulgated a constitution' in which the Emperor bound himself not to 'rescind or interfere with' the decisions of his own courts (col. 415). For Zasius this is absolutely decisive: 'since the Emperor promised to uphold this ordinance', and 'since he is also bound by any contracts he makes', it follows that 'it cannot be lawful for him to proceed' in any way contrary to the positive laws (col. 413).

It remains to consider a further and even more influential way in which the authority of Roman law was used by a number of professional jurists in order to uphold a radical political stance. It was sometimes argued that, when a free people makes a grant of *Imperium* to a ruler, the terms of the *Lex Regia* in which they announce their grant must be taken to include the stipulation that they are merely delegating rather than willing away their own original sovereignty. As we have seen, this form of legal argument was originally developed by Bartolus and his pupils as part of their campaign to legitimate the claims of the northern Italian cities to legal independence from the Empire. They first insisted that any city which legislates on its own behalf must be *sibi princeps*, 'a *princeps* unto itself', and must in consequence be free from the *Imperium* of the Empire. Having thus opened up the question of who may be said to possess *Imperium* in such cities, they went on to answer that the only possible bearers of such authority must be the citizens themselves. Bartolus puts the point quite unequivocally in his commentary on the Digest. He admits that the people generally grant away the actual exercise of their sovereignty to an elected ruler or body of magistrates. But he affirms that any 'right of judgment' held by these officials 'is only delegated to them (*concessum est*) by the sovereign body of the populace' (p. 670). The government cannot 'make any statutes contrary to those agreed by the whole people', nor can it initiate any legislation without first gaining 'the authority of the people' in 'their ruling council', which remains at all times the ultimate locus of sovereignty (p. 670).

As in the case of the study of feudal law, this populist way of interpreting the *Lex Regia* received a new emphasis through the development of humanist jurisprudence at the end of the fifteenth century. As an aspect of their characteristic interest in the evolution of Roman law, a number of humanist jurists began to examine the exact circumstances in which the grant of *Imperium* was originally made by the Senate and People of Rome to the Emperor Augustus at the start of the principate. One outcome was that a number of the most distinguished pioneers of legal humanism came to the conclusion that the grant of sovereignty embodied in the original *Lex Regia* ought to be interpreted in a constitutionalist sense.

One leading jurist who employed these humanist techniques in order to underpin an essentially Bartolist theory of popular sovereignty was Andrea Alciato, whom we have already encountered as the first scholar to export the new methods of legal humanism from Italy to France (Carlyle, 1936, pp. 298–301). But the clearest instance of this syncretic approach can be found in the series of dialogues entitled *The Sovereignty of the Roman Patriciate* which Mario Salamonio completed in 1514 (d'Addio, 1954, pp. 3, 15). As we have already seen, the second half of Salamonio's book is given over to a detailed discussion of the specific problems which had arisen in Italy as a result of the French invasion of 1494. But this is prefaced by a completely general discussion in which, as the figure of the Philosopher begins by observing, the aim is to elucidate 'the arduous and subtle problems' surrounding the character of the *Imperium* which a free people may be said to assign to their prince at the inception of his rule (fo 5a).[1]

---

[1] It would thus be a mistake to think of the humanist jurists as turning completely away from an abstract, Bartolist concern with the principles of law and their relationship to the law of nature in order to focus instead on the study of positive law and its historical development. Characteristically the jurists who used humanist techniques – such as Salamonio and Alciato –

Although Salamonio begins with the natural freedom of the people, he is not interested in analysing this concept in the hypothetical or quasi-historical fashion of the theologians or the later 'social contract' theorists[1]. His reason for insisting that 'God has created all men free and equal' and that 'no man is naturally in subjection to any other' is simply to bring out the fact that all *Imperium* should have 'a basis in covenants' (fos 21a, 28b–29a). The two leading speakers in the early dialogues – the Philosopher and the Jurist – readily agree that any legitimate political society must originate in a free decision on the part of the citizens to contract with a ruler, to draw up a *Lex Regia*, and in this way to establish *Imperium* over themselves. They only start to disagree when they turn to consider the nature of the *Imperium* which a *Lex Regia* may be said to inaugurate. The Jurist begins confidently enough by asserting that after a prince has been installed in power 'there is absolutely no right of controlling him', since 'the *Lex Regia* assigns him absolute authority' (fos 5b, 8b). The Philosopher refuses to believe that he has heard correctly, and when the Jurist innocently remarks that he seems surprised, the Philosopher answers that he is 'totally stupefied' (fo 6a). The second dialogue is then devoted to vindicating the Philosopher's sense of amazement. Beginning in what he likes to think of as 'a Socratic style', he eventually bullies the expostulating Jurist, as well as the almost silent figures of the Theologian and the Historian, into accepting his own Bartolist account of the people's inalienable right to rule.

There is something of an irony embodied in this way of presenting the argument. One might well conclude from Salamonio's account that the most radical analysts of *Imperium* were the philosophers, that the jurists were all defenders of absolutism, and that the theologians had almost nothing to contribute to the debate. It is difficult, however, to think of many philosophers who would have been prepared to endorse the account of *Imperium* which Salamonio's Philosopher provides – except of course Marsiglio of Padua, whom Salamonio may well have had in mind. On the other hand, the views advanced by the Philosopher would have been fully acceptable to a number of jurists, including Bartolus and his pupils, as well as to the radical theologians we have already discussed, whose main arguments about *Imperium* the Philosopher virtually repeats. First of all,

nevertheless retained strong Bartolist allegiances. For the element of traditionalism in Alciato, see Viard, 1926, pp. 139–64, and for the continuing links between humanist jurisprudence and philosophy see Kelley, 1976.

[1] This point seems to me misunderstood in d'Addio, 1954, whose main thesis is that Salamonio's writings occupy a central place in the history of 'the idea of the social contract' (see d'Addio, 1954, esp. pp. 111–15 and 119ff.). This view has since been endorsed by Gough, 1957, who speaks (p. 48) of Salamonio presenting the theory for the first time in a form which is 'fully fledged, and ready to enter the modern world'.

he agrees that the people never alienate but only delegate their sovereignty in the act of setting up a government. This can be proved, he claims, by considering the way in which 'the Senate and the people of Rome' originally consented to the establishment of the principate (fo 8b). The *Lex Regia* which they promulgated 'was made by the will of the people' in such a way that they not only 'bound their prince to obey its terms', but made the principate itself 'answerable to the people' (fos 8b–9a). Later the Philosopher generalises this claim, arguing that a free people can never give up its ultimate sovereignty, and that 'anything a ruler does must always be seen to be done by the consent and authority of the entire populace' (fo 15b). After the figure of the Theologian, emerging from a long silence, has assured the Jurist that 'this view cannot possibly be denied', the Philosopher feels free to proceed directly to his other major point (fo 9b). He insists that, since any prince must be 'constituted by the authority of a *Lex Regia*', it follows that his status can never be that of a sovereign who is *maior universis*, but only that of an elected official who acts as 'a *minister* of the commonwealth' (fos 11b, 17a, 21a). At first the Jurist refuses to countenance such a possibility, but he changes his mind when the Philosopher persuades him that there is a direct analogy between rulers and other magistrates. They readily agree that a magistrate must be 'above each individual citizen in authority' (*maior singulis*), but 'inferior to the populace as a whole' (*inferior universo populo*) (fo 13a). This makes him 'a mere *minister* of the people' and means that 'whatever is done by a magistrate is in fact done by the authority of the people' (fos 13a–b). The Philosopher then argues that a prince 'is really no more than a sort of perpetual magistrate', who is simply mandated to hold his authority 'with the consent of the whole people' (fos 13b, 15b). But it is obvious, he adds, that 'anyone to whom a mandate is assigned must be a mere *minister* of the mandating authority'. So it follows, he triumphantly concludes, 'that a prince can only be a *minister* of the commonwealth', and that the people 'as the creator of the prince must be greater than the prince whom they create' (fos 12b, 17a, 21a).

Finally, Salamonio summarises his argument in the form of the claim – which he stresses far more than the theologians – that 'no prince can possibly be said to be *legibus solutus*' (fo 5b). As the Philosopher insists, any ruler is under a perpetual obligation, arising out of his acceptance of the *Lex Regia*, to govern 'in a just and honest fashion according to the laws of nature and the customs of the country concerned' (fos 7a, 27b). Again the Jurist begins by professing his astonishment at such a limitation on the power of princes, and assures the Philosopher that he must be 'either joking or deranged' (fo 27b). But again he is finally brought to accept that any lawful ruler must be the servant rather than the master of the laws, and that it must even be possible for a law propounded by a prince 'to be abrogated in the name of justice' by the sovereign people if they subsequently discover it is not 'conducive to stability and common welfare' (fo 27b).

5

The revival of Thomism

One of John Mair's pupils at the Collège de Montaigu in the opening years of the sixteenth century was Pierre Crockaert (*c.* 1450–1514), who had come from Brussels at a relatively late age to study at the University of Paris. Crockaert began as a student and teacher of the *via moderna*, but in 1503 he seems to have suffered a revulsion from his training: he abandoned the study of Ockham, turned instead to Thomism, entered the Dominican Order and joined the Collège de Saint-Jacques, famous for its associations with Aquinas and Albert the Great (Renaudet, 1953, pp. 404, 464). In 1509 he began to lecture on Aquinas's *Summary of Theology* instead of the traditional *Sentences* of Peter Lombard, and in 1512 he published a commentary on the last part of the *Summary* in collaboration with his pupil Francisco de Vitoria (Renaudet, 1953, pp. 469, 594). Crockaert died in 1514, but his influence as a teacher, and in consequence the popularity of the *via antiqua* at Paris, continued to increase. His College financed the publication of further commentaries on Aquinas in 1514, while Crockaert's own Thomist teachings were carried on by a number of brilliant pupils, including Fabrius and Meygret as well as Vitoria (Renaudet, 1953, p. 659).

Out of these small beginnings at the University of Paris arose the great sixteenth-century revival of Thomism, a revival of crucial importance for the development of the modern natural-law theory of the State. Perhaps the central figure in this story is Francisco de Vitoria (*c.* 1485–1546), who entered the Dominican Order – the Order of which Aquinas himself had been a member – in 1504, and was sent two years later to pursue his studies at the Collège de Saint-Jacques in Paris.[1] There he remained for

---

[1] See Getino, 1930, pp. 19–20. There is considerable uncertainty over Vitoria's date of birth. Getino, 1930, the standard biography, suggests a date 'no earlier than 1483 and no later than 1486' (p. 14). But some commentators (e.g., Mesnard, 1936, p. 455) suggest a date as early as 1480, while others (e.g., Fernández-Santamaria, 1977, p. 63) suggest a date as late as 'around the year 1492'.

nearly eighteen years, first as a student of the *via antiqua* under Crockaert, and later as a lecturer on Aquinas's *Summary of Theology* (Getino, 1930, pp. 28–33). In 1523 he returned to his native Spain, and three years later he was elected to the Prime Chair of Theology at Salamanca, a position he continued to occupy until his death in 1546 (Hamilton, 1963, pp. 172, 176). Vitoria published nothing, so that his views are only known directly from a series of manuscript *relectiones* which happen to have survived.[1] But he clearly had an immense impact as a teacher, and by the time of his death nearly thirty of his former students held professorships in Spanish universities (Hamilton, 1963, p. 175). The long list of his famous pupils includes several prominent jurists, including Diego de Covarrubias (1512–77), as well as a number of leading Dominican theologians and political philosophers, the outstanding examples being Melchior Cano (1509–60), Fernando Vazquez (1509–66) and Domingo de Soto (1494–1560) (Wilenius, 1963, p. 15).

Domingo de Soto was amongst the earliest as well as the most important of Vitoria's numerous disciples. He became a convert to Vitoria's interpretation of Thomism while studying at the University of Paris, and followed Vitoria back to Salamanca in 1526 (Hamilton, 1963, pp. 176–7). In 1531 he took over some of Vitoria's lectures when the latter fell ill, and in 1532 he was elected to the Vespers Professorship of Theology (Hamilton, 1963, p. 177). De Soto continued to lecture at Salamanca for the next thirteen years, but in 1545 he resigned his Chair in order to obey a summons from the Emperor Charles V to attend the General Council of the Church which Paul III had originally attempted to convene nearly ten years before, and which eventually began to meet at Trent in December 1545 to consider the reform of the Church. De Soto went on to play a prominent part in the early years of the Council, acting both as Imperial theologian and as a representative of the Dominicans (Jedin, 1957–61, I, 513; II, 93). He then returned to Spain, regained his former position at Salamanca in 1551, and continued thereafter to hold it until his death in 1560. It was during this second period of his active teaching career that he completed his major work of legal and political philosophy, the *Ten Books on Justice and Law*. This was first published in six parts between 1553 and 1557, and went through twenty-seven further editions before the end of the century (Hamilton, 1963, pp. 177–80, 190).

During the second half of the sixteenth century the doctrines pro-

---

[1] A *relectio*, or 're-reading' was a summary of a lecture-course, normally delivered once a year in the form of an oration before the whole Faculty. For these and other biographical details, see Baumel, 1936, pp. 24–69.

pounded by the Dominicans began to be taken up by their greatest rivals, the Jesuits, who went on to propagate them with unparalleled energy in Italy and France as well as in Spain. The leading political writers amongst the Italian Jesuits of this period were Antonio Possevino (1534–1611) and Cardinal Robert Bellarmine (1542–1611), whose sequence of *Controversies*, first published between 1581 and 1592, constitutes the most learned and comprehensive of the numerous Jesuit attacks on the political as well as theological assumptions associated with the Lutheran faith. A similar set of doctrines began to be developed at the same time by a large number of Jesuit writers in Spain. By the end of the 1540s the Jesuits had managed to establish eight of their own Colleges in Spanish universities, including one at Alcalá, one at Salamanca, and one at Burgos (Kidd, 1933, p. 30). Thus began the process by which they succeeded in wresting the intellectual control of the Spanish universities out of the hands of the Dominicans. The new Jesuit Colleges soon began to produce an impressive stream of theologians and political philosophers, including Alfonso Salmerón (1515–85), Pedro de Ribadeneyra (1527–1611), Francisco de Toledo (1532–96), Gregorio de Valencia (1549–1603) and Gabriel Vazquez (1549–1604).[1] But the two greatest figures amongst the Spanish Jesuit philosophers of this period were Luis de Molina (1535–1600) and Francisco Suárez (1548–1617). Both began their studies – as did Francisco de Toledo and Gregorio de Valencia – at the University of Salamanca. Molina entered the Society of Jesus in 1553, but since it was not yet fully incorporated in Spain he moved to Portugal in order to gain a teaching post. He became Arts Professor at Evora, transferring to the Chair of Theology in 1568 (Fichter, 1940, p. 203). It was out of the course of lectures he delivered there between 1577 and 1582 that he compiled his *Six Books on Justice and Law*, first published between 1593 and 1600. Suárez was something of a rival of Molina's, and both were contenders for the Chair of Theology at Coimbra in 1593, a contest which Suárez won (Fichter, 1940, p. 204). Suárez was famous (like his hero Aquinas) for the slow start he made in his philosophical studies, and later for the enormous erudition he poured into the thirty large volumes of his published works (Fichter, 1940, pp. 47–60). It was while he was at Coimbra, after returning from the Jesuit College in Rome, that he found himself particularly encouraged to write on legal and political philosophy. Prompted by the university rector, he began to lecture on the concept of law, a series which he first delivered in 1596. The course was eventually published in 1612 as the massive treatise on *The Laws and God the Law-*

---

[1] For biographical and bibliographical details on all these writers, see Backer, 1853–61.

giver.[1] By this time he had also been encouraged by Caraffa, the Papal nuncio in Madrid, to compose a refutation of the *Apology* in which King James I had sought to defend the English oath of allegiance against the attacks mounted on it by Bellarmine and the Pope himself. Suárez's characteristically lengthy consideration of the question was also published in 1612, appearing as *A Defence of the Catholic and Apostolic Faith*. These two works not only represent his own major contribution to legal and political thought, but also provide the clearest summary of the remarkably homogeneous outlook which had been developed by the whole school of Thomist political philosophers in the course of the sixteenth century (cf. Daniel-Rops, 1962, p. 342).

One phrase which is constantly used by all the writers of this school may be taken to summarise the underlying polemical thrust of their political works. One of their main concerns, they often claim, is to refute 'all the heretics of this present age'. The heretics with whom they are chiefly concerned are of course the Lutherans, and it is one of their basic aims to repudiate not merely the Lutheran concept of the Church, but the whole vision of political life associated with the evangelical Reformation.[2]

Turning first to the Lutheran view of the Church, the Thomists recognise a special need to be able to confront and demolish two major Lutheran heresies: the doctrine of *sola scriptura*, with its accompanying dismissal of Catholic tradition; and the key contention that the true Church is nothing more than a *congregatio fidelium*, with its consequent rejection of all ecclesiastical hierarchies and its denial of the law-making powers of the Pope. Vitoria's *relectio* on *The Power of the Church* is largely directed against 'the exceptionally imprudent words of Luther' and the other 'incredibly arrogant heretics' who ignore the traditions of the Church, who argue that 'all Christians are equally priests', and who insist that 'the power of the Church resides in everyone, containing no gradations or ecclesiastical orders at all' (p. 129). The same heresies are subsequently singled out by all the Thomist champions of the Tridentine Papacy in the latter half of the sixteenth century. They concentrate in particular on the fact that, as Bellarmine puts it in his treatise *Concerning Councils*, 'the

---

[1] All subsequent citations from Suárez refer to this work, except where it is specifically indicated that they refer to the *Defence*.

[2] For its emphasis on the extent to which the Thomists of the sixteenth century were writing in conscious opposition to the Lutherans, I am indebted to the pioneering discussion of these writers contained in Gierke, 1934; cf. also Gierke, 1939. I am also much indebted to the excellent survey of the Spanish contribution to the revival of Thomism contained in Hamilton, 1963. I regret that Fernández-Santamaria, 1977, which concentrates on Vitoria's political theory, appeared too late for me to take full account of its findings.

Lutherans have made the Church invisible' (II, pp. 317, 344). De Soto points out that this is an old mistake, which was 'first taught by the Waldensians, later by Wyclif and later by the Lutherans' (fo 18a). Molina prefers to trace the heresy back to Marsiglio of Padua, but he confirms that Luther is simply 'teaching the same mistakes' (p. 1866). And Suárez agrees with Molina that 'this has been an old error', that 'Marsiglio was without doubt the principal author of it', and that it has by now become a matter of urgency to root it out, since 'Luther, followed by Melanchthon' has succeeded in deceiving so many people into holding the same false beliefs (I, p. 297).

In developing their theory of secular political society, the Thomists were equally concerned to repudiate a number of Lutheran heresies. As we have seen, the Lutheran vision of man's relationship with God had undermined any attempt to base the conduct of politics on the foundations of natural law. The reformers had contended that men with their fallen natures cannot hope to apprehend the will of the *Deus Absconditus* and in this way produce a reflection of God's justice in the arrangement of their lives. They had thus concluded that the powers that be must have been directly ordained by God and granted to men precisely in order to remedy these moral deficiencies. It was this doctrine which, as the Thomists recognised, it was particularly important for them to be able to reject. The desire to overturn this heresy provided one of the main motives for the debates about justification and the rejection of 'twofold justice' at the Council of Trent (Philips, 1971, pp. 351–8). As Jedin observes, the theologians at the Council 'took up the problem Luther had set them' (Jedin, 1957–61, II, p. 167). They accepted the need to be able to show, in the words of the *Decree concerning Justification*, that while men are doubtless full of moral weakness and are 'servants of sin', the Lutherans must nevertheless be in error in denying men any element of 'indwelling grace' (pp. 30, 33–5). The same attack on what de Soto called 'Luther's pestiferous doctrine' concerning man's inherent lack of justice was then reiterated by all the Jesuit theorists in the latter part of the sixteenth century (fo 244a). Bellarmine acknowledges in his treatise *Concerning Justification* that the main heresy which needs to be resisted is the widespread and dangerous belief (which he cites from Luther's discussion of Galatians) that 'faith alone justifies' and that 'there cannot be any inherent justice in the soul of man' (VI, pp. 172, 178). And Suárez similarly recognises, at the start of his account of man's subjection to law, that the error which needs above all to be extirpated is 'the blasphemous suggestion of Luther' that 'it is impossible even for a just man to follow the law of God' (I, p. 65).

As de Soto and Suárez both indicate, the significance of Luther's denial that man possesses any inherent justice is that it forms 'the root and basis of all the other heresies' which the Lutherans had gone on to propagate about the principles of political life.[1] There were two such heresies which the Thomists clearly felt a special need to attack. The first was the Lutheran doctrine of the godly prince. It is true that this is never discussed (or even mentioned) by Vitoria, perhaps because his own views about the origins of political authority are curiously similar. Vitoria tends to argue (though he is not completely consistent at this point) that our rulers are directly ordained and assigned to us by 'a providential power' which he generally equates with the will of God. He was strongly criticised for this assumption, however, by several of the Jesuit theorists, all of whom are emphatic in rejecting any suggestion that dominion must be founded in grace. Bellarmine argues in his treatise on *The Members of the Church* that in advancing this claim 'the heretics of the present age' have merely revived another completely discredited position, one which was 'originally asserted by Wyclif and Hus'. He concedes, however, that the mistake is still a dangerous one, and thus that it is correspondingly important to be able to argue against the underlying assumption that political society arises directly out of 'the justice and grace of God' in such a way that the godliness of the ruler is made a condition of his rulership (III, p. 14). Suárez agrees in tracing the same heretical line of descent, and in emphasising the need to expose 'the erroneous belief' that 'the power to make laws depends on the faith or morals of the prince', a view which leads to the subversive conclusion – 'which the heretics maintain' – that 'the civil power cannot remain in the hands of ungodly rulers' (I, pp. 190, 327).

The other and closely related heresy which the Thomists feel a special need to oppose is the Lutheran contention that the commands of an ungodly prince cannot be binding in conscience, and must never be obeyed. Vitoria emphasises in his *relectio* on *Civil Power* that certain 'seditious individuals' are claiming that 'evangelical liberty constitutes an impediment to kingly power' (p. 186). De Soto (fo 247b) goes on to identify these individuals as the Lutherans, and all the later Jesuit writers agree that this further heresy must be uprooted. Molina notes that 'one of the things the Lutherans nowadays are most prone to assert' is that secular rulers can be disobeyed in good conscience (pp. 1870, 1876). Suárez repeats the same observation, and treats it as one of the most shocking of the 'errors of the heretics' that they believe 'it is possible to answer in the negative the question of whether a civil magistrate can oblige his subjects in conscience to obey his laws' (I, p. 325).

[1] See de Soto, fo 247a; Suárez, I, p. 67.

As well as denouncing the errors of the Lutherans, the Thomists recognised a scarcely less urgent need to correct a number of heresies being propagated by the humanists. They first of all turned their attention to the dangerous views about the Church which Erasmus and a number of other Christian humanists had espoused. The need to oppose their outlook, and in particular to submit the works of Erasmus himself to a detailed critical scrutiny, was first fully recognised in the course of a conference of theologians held at Valladolid in 1527, at which Vitoria and his associates withdrew their earlier sympathy for the programme of Christian humanism, and proceeded to attack a sequence of nineteen heresies which Diego López de Zuñiga had allegedly discovered in Erasmus's published works (Bataillon, 1937, pp. 264, 266). The campaign against Erasmus was later intensified at the Council of Trent, and culminated in 1559 with the publication of the first official Index of Prohibited Books. Erasmus was at this point placed in the highest category of offenders against the teachings of the Church, the entire corpus of his writings being wholly condemned (Putnam, 1906–7, I, p. 197).

It is important to emphasise how quickly and decisively Vitoria and de Soto hardened in their opposition to Erasmus, since their own outlook has sometimes been characterised, perhaps misleadingly, as an attempt to combine scholasticism with Christian humanism.[1] The Dominicans and their allies in fact recognised that there were two features of the Erasmian programme which it was essential for them to repudiate if orthodoxy were to be preserved. One was Erasmus's 'Lutheran' tendency to demand that a new and purified translation of the Bible should be made freely available, and his corresponding denunciations of the accuracy and hence the authority of the existing Latin Vulgate translations. His other error lay in his ideal of religious education – his quasi-Lutheran suggestion that the laity should be taught by means of a catechism of faith (a *methodus*), and that the clergy should be further educated by means of compulsory Bible studies (Jedin, 1957–61, II, 99). Both these proposals were cited with considerable hostility at the Valladolid Conference and at the Council of Trent. By this time it had come to be recognised that the influence of Erasmus's 'manifest lying', as Bellarmine roundly called it, would have to be countered by an authoritative restatement of the orthodox view about the place of the Bible, and more generally of religious instruction, in the teachings of the Church.[2]

The most dangerous of the humanists, however, were those whom the

---

[1] See for example Mesnard, 1936, p. 455; Hamilton, 1963, p. 174. See also (putting the point more generally) Dickens, 1968, p. 171.

[2] See Jedin, 1957–61, II, pp. 56–7, 267–8. For Bellarmine's judgment see his treatise on *The Word of God*, I, pp. 109f., 138f.

Thomists perceived as having affinities with the Lutherans in their views about political society. The attempt to confront these further heresies involved them in attacking two separate strands of humanist political thought, each of which they treated as heretical in a somewhat similar way. They were anxious first of all to respond to the claims which Juan Ginés de Sepúlveda and his followers had begun to make about the legitimacy of the Spanish conquests in the New World. Sepúlveda (1490–1573), who had studied the humanities at Bologna as well as receiving a theological training, became the leading champion of the Spanish colonists, his basic concern being to vindicate their legal and moral right to carry on their policy of enslaving the local Indian inhabitants (Fernández-Santamaría, 1977, pp. 163–9). The essence of his argument was that since the Indians possessed no knowledge of the Christian faith, they could not possibly be said to be living a life of genuine 'political liberty and human dignity' (Hanke, 1949, p. 132). Their status, he argued, was to be identified with the Aristotelian category of 'slaves by nature',[1] while their way of life was to be regarded as one of 'natural rudeness and inferiority' (Hanke, 1959, p. 44). He was thus led to conclude that it was proper to treat the Spanish conquests as an instance of a just war against infidels, and to enslave the conquered local inhabitants as an aid to converting them.

Sepúlveda presented this argument in person at the Council of Trent and, more notoriously, at a special conference convened by Charles V at Valladolid in 1550 to consider the justice of the Spanish conquests in the New World (Hanke, 1974, p. 67). His thesis was somewhat difficult for the orthodox Jesuit and Dominican theorists to oppose, since it was based on an appeal to the *Politics* of Aristotle, an authority which they naturally held in the highest reverence. Nevertheless, they clearly regarded it as essential to repudiate Sepúlveda's way of defending the ethics of Empire. They evidently felt some concern about the heretical overtones of the argument, especially its reliance on the quasi-Lutheran contention that any genuine political society must always be founded in godliness. And they were no less genuinely opposed, on purely humanitarian grounds, to the shocking human consequences which had already followed from the fact that the argument was in practice becoming almost universally accepted (Parry, 1940, pp. 57–69).

The other group of humanists whom the counter-reformation theorists felt an even stronger desire to answer were the defenders of *ragione di*

---

[1] It is true, as Quirk has stressed, that it may not be altogether fair to Sepúlveda's case to translate his phrase *natura servus* as 'slaves by nature'. He may only have intended to argue that it was appropriate to treat the Indians in the same way that serf-labourers were treated at this period in Spain. See Quirk, 1954, pp. 358–64.

stato, especially Machiavelli and his atheistic disciples. The early Jesuit theorists clearly recognised the pivotal point at which the political theories of Luther and Machiavelli may be said to converge: both of them were equally concerned, for their own very different reasons, to reject the idea of the law of nature as an appropriate moral basis for political life. It is in consequence in the works of the early Jesuits that we first encounter the familiar coupling of Luther and Machiavelli as the two founding fathers of the impious modern State.[1] Ribadeneyra's vernacular treatise on *Religion and the Virtues of the Christian Prince*, first published in Madrid in 1595, not only begins by linking the names of these two great heretics of the age, but goes on to argue that even the dangers of Lutheranism are 'not so great as those which the doctrines of Machiavelli' have brought. This is why it is vital, he goes on, to demonstrate how 'false and pernicious' is the assumption which he takes to be fundamental to Machiavelli's political thought, the assumption that the prince's basic value must simply be 'the conservation of his state', and that 'for this end he is to use every means, good or bad, just or unjust, that can assist him' (p. 250). Possevino cites the same doctrine in his bitterly hostile *Judgment* on the writings of Machiavelli, and agrees that in urging princes 'to imitate the lion and the fox' Machiavelli reveals 'the most pernicious possible misunderstanding' of the proper moral framework of political life (pp. 131–2). Finally, Suárez reiterates all the same claims, devoting a special chapter to presenting them in *The Laws and God the Lawgiver*. He refers his readers to Ribadeneyra's 'prudent, excellent and erudite' attack on the whole idea of *ragione di stato*, and indicates in very similar terms the nature of the task which now confronts the Christian political philosopher in consequence of Machiavelli's alarming influence. 'The doctrine which Machiavelli has above all tried to put to our secular rulers' is that the question of whether or not they should behave justly 'depends on which course of action will be most useful to the temporal commonwealth'. The influence of this impiety makes it essential to be able to show that this is not merely a 'pernicious' doctrine, but one which constitutes 'a totally false and erroneous view' of political life (1, pp. 197–8).

---

[1] The first Jesuit writers to mention this linkage were Possevino and Ribadeneyra, in the works cited above. During the ensuing generation a number of similar attacks on Machiavelli appeared in Spain by such writers as Márquez (1612), Jesús-María (1613), Bravo (1616), and Homen (1629). The *genre* may be said to culminate with Claudio Clemente's *Machiavellianism Decapitated*, which appeared in Latin in 1628 and in Spanish in 1637. For Clemente see Bleznick, 1958, p. 543. For the other writers mentioned, see Fernández de la Mora, 1949, pp. 424–5n., 427n. For the coupling of Luther and Machiavelli by modern commentators, see for example Figgis, 1960, pp. 71ff., and MacIntyre, 1966, pp. 121ff.

THE THEORY OF THE CHURCH

Confronted on all sides by 'the heretics of the age', the Dominican and Jesuit theorists reached back to the doctrines of the *via antiqua*, using them as a basis for developing a new, systematic and self-consciously orthodox view of the Church and its proper relationship with the secular commonwealth. Turning first to repudiate the prevailing errors about the Church, they argued that a proper understanding of the holy scriptures serves to reveal that two central truths need to be grasped about its character. The first is that the Church is unquestionably a visible and jurisdictional institution, the structure and traditions of which are derived directly from the inspiration of the Holy Ghost. The strongest defence of this contention is contained in the official *Decree concerning the canonical Scriptures* promulgated by the Council of Trent in 1546. The scriptures reveal, it is argued, that the Church was founded as a visible institution by Christ himself, and embodies a set of traditions relating 'to faith and to morals' which – 'the Holy Ghost dictating' – have been received from Christ and the Apostles, have been 'preserved in the Catholic Church in unbroken succession', and have in this way 'come down to us, transmitted as it were from hand to hand' (p. 17). It is said to follow that the Apostolic traditions, no less than the scriptures, must be regarded as a source of revelation, and that no one can in consequence be said to live a fully Christian life who chooses to live it outside the confines of the visible Catholic Church (Jedin, 1957–61, II, 58, 73–4).

These official doctrines were later endorsed by all the Jesuit champions of the Tridentine Papacy in the latter part of the sixteenth century. Bellarmine concludes his treatise *Concerning Councils* with a lengthy defence of the assertion that 'the Church must be visible', arguing that the 'marks' of the true Church include its antiquity, its uninterrupted life, its world-wide extent, its apostolic succession of bishops, its unity under the Pope and its agreed body of Catholic doctrines (II, pp. 345, 370–86). Suárez later summarises and develops the same argument, adding an extensive list of references to the various Biblical passages from which, it is claimed, these conclusions can be derived. Both Suárez and Bellarmine lay a special emphasis on the significance of Christ's affirmation to Peter, 'To you I give the keys.' This is taken to leave no doubt that the Catholic Church, as a visible institution with the power 'to bind and loose' in Christian life, was originally established by, and thus derives its authority from, the commandments of Christ himself.[1]

The other central truth which a proper reading of the scriptures is said

[1] See Bellarmine *Concerning Councils* II. 370–86. Suárez, I, pp. 289–90.

to reveal is that the Church constitutes a hierarchical and law-making authority directly under the control of the Pope. It is true that Vitoria, writing before the hardening of lines which followed the Council of Trent, appears much less of a Papalist than the later Jesuit theorists (Jedin, 1957–61, I, 42, 287). He even commits himself in his *relectio* on *The Power of the Pope* to the virtually conciliarist doctrine that it may sometimes be possible 'to convoke a Council of the Church contrary to the will of the Pope', and that if such a Council 'declares anything to be a matter of faith' this decision 'cannot be altered by the Pope' (II, pp. 227, 277). These conclusions are later repudiated by the Jesuit theorists, however, and in particular by Suárez, who remonstrates with Vitoria for having failed to recognise that 'it is sufficiently proved by long tradition and the observation of General Councils that they always require the confirmation of a Pope' (I, p. 320). The two positive conclusions reached by Suárez and the other Jesuit theorists reflect a much more conscious attempt to echo the absolutist ambitions of the Papacy, which had by then gained a definitive ascendancy in the Church as a result of the Council of Trent. They all insist on the traditional claim that the visible Church is unquestionably an independent legislative authority, operating its own code of canon law in parallel with, and never in subjection to, the civil laws of the commonwealth. As Suárez expresses it, there is 'a directive and coercive power' embodied in the Church which is essential in order 'to direct men by the law' to their attainment of 'their supernatural ends' (I, pp. 299, 300). And they all hold very strongly to the far more contentious claim that the supreme power to legislate in the Church remains at all times with the Pope. This is said to be clearly evident from the scriptures, especially from Christ's promise 'On this rock shall I build' and from his injunction 'Feed my sheep', both of which are constantly cited and glossed by the Jesuit theorists. Bellarmine quotes them in his treatise on *The Supreme Pontiff* as proof of the fact that 'the power of the keys' was not only granted to Peter directly by Christ, but that the same plenitude of power must in consequence have descended to the Pope with undiminished force as 'a complete power over the whole Church' (I, pp. 495, 503). Molina refers to all the same passages, and agrees that what they establish is that 'no one at all in the Church is exempt from the jurisdiction of the Pope' (p. 1435). And Suárez again supplies the fullest summary of the doctrine, as well as the Biblical texts on which it is based, concluding that 'it is clearly evident from the scriptures' and 'from the traditions of the Church' that 'the Pope has immediately received from Christ, and from the strength of his position, the power to legislate for the entire Church' (I, p. 307).

Having arrived at these conclusions, the Thomists proceed to turn them against their enemies, thus responding to the manifold errors about the Church being propagated by 'all the heretics of the age'.[1] Their main concern is of course to answer the Lutherans. They are now able in the first place to repudiate the Lutheran doctrine of *sola scriptura*. This was officially dismissed as a result of the debates about the role of the Church's traditions which occupied the third session of the Council of Trent. The outcome was the contention that, since it can be satisfactorily proved from the scriptures that the Church's traditions supply a source of revelation, the Lutheran contention that the scriptures are self-sufficient must be automatically discredited (Jedin, 1957–61, II, 52–98). The same argument was later reiterated by the Jesuit champions of the Tridentine Church, and especially by Bellarmine in his treatise on *The Word of God*. The fundamental mistake, he claims, which the Lutherans have been making in trying to establish that 'everything necessary for faith and behaviour is contained in the scriptures' is that of failing to recognise that 'as well as the written word of God we require the unwritten word, that is, the divine and apostolic traditions' (I, p. 197). Since the scriptures are often 'ambiguous and perplexing', there are 'many places in which we shall be unable to reach certainty' if we refuse to supplement them 'by accepting the traditions of the Church' (I, pp. 203–4).

The other Lutheran doctrine which the Thomists repudiate is the idea that the true Church consists of nothing more than a *congregatio fidelium*. This assumption, they argue, is not only based on devaluing the authority of tradition, but is even more obviously founded on ignoring all the scriptural evidence which shows that the Church as a body needs at all times to be guided by the Pope as its head. We already find this seductive and crucial metaphor being invoked against the Lutherans in Vitoria's *relectio* on *The Power of the Church*. Vitoria's essential contention is that since it is clear from the scriptures that the Church no less than the secular commonwealth takes the form of a visible and jurisdictional body, the Lutheran conception of an invisible community must embody an absurdity. For 'if we listen to Luther, it seems that the feet can say to the head "You are not necessary to us" ' (p. 132). The same image of the Church as a body which can only have a single head is emphasised by the champions of the papacy at the Council of Trent, and is turned polemically against the Lutherans by several of the later Jesuit theorists, notably by

---

[1] In speaking of the Thomists turning their arguments against their enemies – both here and in my discussion of their views on political society – I am of course reconstructing what I take to be the logic of their arguments rather than following their actual organisation. The Thomists in practice tend to present their own views and criticise those of their opponents at the same time.

Bellarmine in his treatise *Concerning Councils*. 'When Luther claims that the Church is nothing but the faithful people of Christ', what he forgets is that 'the true Church, of which the scriptures speak' is no less 'a visible and palpable assembly of people than the people of Rome, the kingdom of France or the republic of Venice'. And since it is no less 'a living and visible body with living members', it is no less in need of being guided and directed by 'a single head and shepherd of the entire Church' (II, pp. 317–18).

The counter-reformation theorists are also able to refute the various heretics whom they took to be in sympathy with the Lutherans, and especially the Erasmian humanists. First they denounce the humanist attack on the authority of the Vulgate, and the corresponding demand for a new and purified official translation of the Bible. The reason for thinking that this ought not to be countenanced, they now contend, is that such a demand involves a devaluation of the Church's traditions, which have sanctified the existing translations through 'long and varied use' (Jedin, 1957–61, II, p. 92). The logical outcome of this response, embodied in the *Decree concerning the edition and use of the sacred Books* issued by the Council of Trent in 1546, was the demand that 'the old Latin vulgate translation which, in use for so many hundred years, has been approved by the Church', should now be 'held as authoritative' to such a degree that no one should 'dare or presume under any pretext whatsoever to reject it' (p. 18).

Finally, the counter-reformation theorists respond to the underlying and heretical ambition of the humanists to reform the Church's traditional system of clerical instruction by concentrating on individual catechising and the study of the Bible. A number of *spirituali*, led by Cardinal Pole at the Council of Trent, still nourished the fading hope that if the Church were to accept these reforms, it might yet prove possible to establish some form of reunion with the Protestants and so avert a final schism (Fenlon, 1972, p. 124). It was argued by the Dominicans, however, and especially by de Soto in his crucial speeches at the fourth session of the Council, that these proposals not only embodied a heretical individualism – almost a doctrine of *sola scriptura* – but in consequence failed to give due weight to the traditional teaching methods of the Church, and especially the techniques of scholasticism, which de Soto regarded as 'indispensable for theological controversy' (Jedin, 1957–61, II, p. 118). The outcome was a decisive victory for scholasticism over humanism. The immediate consequence was that Pole and his ecumenical sympathisers withdrew from the Council of Trent (Fenlon, 1972, pp. 169–73). The long-term significance of the decision was that, in rejecting the programme of the humanists no less firmly than that of the Lutherans, the Tridentine Church made a deliberate and, as it proved, a final decision to close off any prospects of a reunion with the proliferating Protestant sects. By reasserting the traditional theory of the Church with such intransigence, they also ensured that its universal acceptance was finally brought to an end.

THE THEORY OF POLITICAL SOCIETY

As well as responding to the manifold errors being propagated about the nature of the Church, the Thomists developed an equally systematic theory of political society in conscious opposition to 'all the heretics of the age'. They deliberately turned away from the form of scholasticism developed by Ockham and his disciples, perceiving it to be too closely linked – especially in its sceptical analysis of man's reasoning powers – to the heresies of the Lutherans. They reverted instead to the fundamental assumption of the *via antiqua*, contending that man has the capacity to use his reason in order to supply the moral foundations of political life. It was on the basis of this rejection of the *via moderna* that the orthodox counter-reformation theory of political society was raised.

The fundamental move which the Thomists made in discussing the concept of political society was to revert to Aquinas's vision of a universe ruled by a hierarchy of laws. First in order they place the eternal law or *lex aeterna* by which God himself acts. Next comes the divine law or *lex divina* which God reveals directly to men in the scriptures, and on which the Church is founded. Next comes the law of nature or *lex naturalis* (sometimes called the *ius naturale*) which God 'implants' in men in order that they should be able to understand his designs and intentions for the world. And finally comes the positive human law, variously described as the *lex humana*, *lex civilis* or *ius positivum*, which men ordain and enact for themselves in order to govern the commonwealths they set up.

The essence of the natural-law theory which the Thomists develop may in consequence be expressed in terms of the relationships they go on to trace between the divine will, the law of nature and the positive human laws enacted by each individual commonwealth. The account they give of these relationships may in turn be summarised in the form of two propositions which they all endorse. The first connects the idea of positive human law with the law of nature. They all insist that if the positive laws which men create for themselves are to embody the character and authority of genuine laws, they must be compatible at all times with the theorems of natural justice supplied by the law of nature. Thus the law of nature provides a moral framework within which all human laws must operate; conversely, the aim of these human laws is simply to give force in the world (*in foro externo*) to a higher law which every man already knows in his conscience (*in foro interno*). These contentions are strongly supported by all the Dominican theorists. As de Soto puts the point, 'every human law must derive from the law of nature' if it is not to forfeit its legal character (fos 17b, 18a). And they are later reiterated by all the Jesuit theorists. As Suárez concludes, 'a law not characterised by this justice or righteousness is not a law, has no binding force and must never be obeyed' (p. 39).

The other proposition which they all endorse connects the law of nature with the will of God and thus with the divine and eternal laws. The law of nature is said to possess a dual essence. It embodies the quality of law both because it is *intellectus* (it is intrinsically just and reasonable) and because it is *voluntas* (it is the will of God). They thus take up a middle Thomist position between the early realists on the one hand, for whom the law of nature was lawful simply because it was just, and the later nominalists on the other, for whom it was lawful simply because it expressed the will of God. Suárez mentions Gregory of Rimini as one of the main exponents of the earlier realist point of view. The difficulty he finds with this argument is that it appears to make the law of nature unalterable even by God himself. The more recent nominalist position he associates principally with Ockham and his disciples, especially Almain and Mair. The problem he finds with this alternative is that it seems to abandon any hope of trying to grasp the law of nature not just as an arbitrary fiat (*lex praescriptiva*) but also as a set of self-evidently just rules. Suárez's main conclusion, and that of the other Jesuits he quotes, is that both these extremes must be avoided if the law of nature is to be treated both as a genuine law (which means it must be the product of a law-maker's will) and also as the basis of justice in political society (which means it must specify what is intrinsically right) (I, pp. 96–104).

It is true that some of the earlier Dominican theorists, perhaps in their anxiety to emancipate themselves from the *via moderna*, tend to fall away from this middle position, and to incline rather strongly towards the realist conclusion that the law of nature is simply a dictate of right reason. De Soto, for example, is criticised by Suárez for having virtually reverted to the mistaken belief that 'law is simply an act of the intellect' (I, p. 17). If we turn to the later Jesuit theorists, however, we find them all emphatic in their refusal to distinguish between God's will and intellect in discussing His role as a maker of laws.[1] Molina provides an intensely assertive and repetitious account of the need for the concept of law to include the element of *voluntas* as well as *intellectus*, a conclusion which he claims, not surprisingly, to have 'copiously demonstrated' (pp. 1676, 1701, etc.). Suárez reiterates the same doctrine with no less emphasis, ending his historiographical survey of the various positions which have been taken up on the issue by repeating that 'a middle course should be adopted', one which enables us to acknowledge that while the law of nature is certainly 'indicative' in virtue of being inherently just, it is also 'imperative' in virtue of embodying the will of God (1, pp. 100–4).

The adoption of this middle position in turn enabled these writers to arrive at two crucial and contrasting doctrines about the relationship between the law of nature and the divine laws contained in the scriptures. They first of all stress their connections. Since the law of nature is also the will of God, the commands and prohibitions of the divine positive laws in the Bible cannot differ from, but must rather be contained within, the dictates of the law of nature. (Hobbes was later to pounce rather cunningly on this point.) They concede of course that a fundamental distinction must be drawn between the laws of the Old and New Testaments. As Vitoria puts it in his *relectio* on *The Power of the Church*, the coming of Christ has brought 'an entirely new power', and thus 'an end to the spiritual power which existed in the Old Testament' (p. 54). They still insist, however, on making two connections between the law of nature and the law of God. The first is that even though Christ's coming releases us from the bondage of the Old Law (at what precise moment became a subject of learned dispute) this does not mean, as the Lutherans claim, that we are thereby released from the bondage of law itself. As de Soto explains, the laws of the New Testament are merely intended 'to impress more potently upon us' the dictates of the law of nature, which have already been 'inscribed in our hearts' by God, but which we are nevertheless prone, because of our fallen natures, to neglect unless we are continually reminded of what they command (fo 61a). The other connection is that even under this new dispensation the injunctions of the Old Testament still retain their character as laws. Since the Mosaic Code is known to represent the will of God, it cannot differ from, though it may be less inclusive than, the dictates of the law of nature. It follows, as Molina and Suárez especially emphasise, that any genuine code of law we may now seek to establish will have to include within it all the commands and

---

[1] It has even been argued that Descartes's conflation of God's will and His intellect is derived from his study of Suárez's discussion of this point. See Cronin, 1966, p. 151.

prohibitions which were originally made known by God in the Decalogue (Molina, p. 1690; Suárez, I, pp. 104–5).

The other and contrasting claim they make is that, since the law of nature is also right reason, we do not need to have any knowledge of revelation or divine positive law in order to be able to grasp and follow its essential principles. The law of nature is in short made known to men simply as men. This contention is presented by all these writers in the form of an appeal, with only minor variations, to the same cluster of metaphors. According to de Soto, we must picture the law of nature as something 'imprinted' (*impressa*) on our minds, so that it 'exists as a habit in us' (fo 9b). According to Molina, we must imagine the law of nature as 'nothing other than a natural intellectual faculty' which has been 'planted within us' (*indita nobis*) (p. 1681). And according to Suárez, we must think of it as being directly 'written in our minds' (*scriptam in mentibus*) by the hand of God himself (II, p. 645). It was on the basis of these images that our knowledge of the principles of natural justice was said to be wholly independent of any knowledge of revelation or the scriptures. The opposing view was definitively disposed of by Laínez and Salmerón in the course of their attack on the notion of 'twofold justice' at the Council of Trent (Pas, 1954, pp. 32–3, 51). Laínez in particular made a deep impression, according to Jedin, with his elaborate speech in defence of the Thomist thesis that 'we already possess the justice of Christ in our own innate sense of justice' (Jedin, 1957–61, II, p. 256; Pas, 1954, p. 38). The same argument was later reiterated by all the Jesuit theorists. Molina is admittedly much less certain about this issue than the rest, but even he concludes that since 'we know the principles and the conclusions concerning moral matters naturally', there is no reason in general to doubt that 'we are capable of reaching conclusions about moral matters simply by the light of our intelligence' (pp. 1701, 1702). Suárez is much firmer in his insistence that 'it should not be possible for anyone to neglect' the law of nature, since 'all men from the beginning of creation have in fact been subject to it' (I, p. 65). And Bellarmine in his treatise on *The Members of the Church* even anticipates the formula which Grotius was later to make famous in discussing the same theme: 'even if *per impossibile* man were not God's creation', he would still be able to interpret the law of nature, since 'he would still be a rational creature' (III, p. 18).

Despite their essentially Thomist allegiances, however, these writers are also responsible for engineering an important simplification, and in this sense an alteration, in the traditional Thomist analysis of the law of nature. Aquinas had sharply distinguished in his discussion of law in the *Summary of Theology* between the local laws of particular societies (the

ordinary *lex positiva*) and the laws which all nations are found to possess
(the so-called *ius gentium*). He had gone on to suggest that whereas the
law of nature may be said to supply the moral basis for the positive laws
of individual commonwealths, the same moral underpinning may instead
be supplied, in the case of those laws which are common to all societies,
by the concept of the *ius gentium* or law of nations (p. 115). He had thus
tended to imply that the concept of the law of nations must be analogous
to, but also separate from, the concept of the law of nature, and that it
must also be separate from, in the sense of being more fundamental than,
the ordinary positive laws. The special position which was thus carved
out and assigned to the law of nations was that of explaining how it is
possible for those institutions which are found to exist in all known
societies (such as buying and selling, and the holding of private property)
are capable of being established and conducted in accordance with the
principles of right reason and natural justice (pp. 115–17).

This method of distinguishing between the *lex naturalis*, the *ius gentium*
and the *lex positiva* was at first accepted by the sixteenth-century Thomists, and a version of it can be found, for example, in Vitoria's discussion
of Aquinas's own account of the law of nature and nations.[1] It tended to
breed confusions, however, especially about the proper line of demarcation between these two types of law, and these difficulties were compounded rather than resolved by the various attempts which were then
made to distinguish between 'primary' and 'secondary' laws of nature. It
was obvious that a simplification was desirable, and that only one of two
basic moves was possible.[2] One was to argue that the law of nations really
formed part of the law of nature. This was the traditional thesis of the
civil lawyers, based on the opening pages of the Digest, and a number of
Spanish jurists – such as Covarrubias – now began to restate the argument
with renewed emphasis. The alternative was to suggest that the law of
nations ought on the contrary to be regarded as an aspect of positive
human law, and simply treated as a collection of widely-held judgments,
not as a series of deductions from (or instances of) right reason itself.
This possibility seems to have occurred to Vitoria, who alludes to it –
somewhat inconsistently – at various points in his political works. A
similar suggestion is developed more boldly by de Soto, though still in a
rather incoherent style.[3] By the time we come to Molina and Suárez,

---

[1] This is not included in the Madrid edition of Vitoria's *Relectiones*. It can be found, however,
printed in an English translation as Appendix E of Scott, 1934, pp. cxi–cxiv.

[2] It is arguable that they are confused in Gierke's account. See Gierke, 1934, pp. 38–9. But it is
of course true that the writers involved were often confused themselves.

[3] For an excellent account of these confusions, with page references to de Soto's own discussion, see Hamilton, 1963, pp. 16f.

however, we find the same argument being mounted with much greater confidence, and soon after this the theory was classically restated by Grotius in *The Law of War and Peace*. Suárez even attempts, somewhat disingenuously, to show that what St Thomas himself must really have been trying to say was what Suárez himself believes, namely that the law of nations 'differs in an absolute sense from natural law', and 'is straightforwardly a case of human positive law' (I, p. 153; cf. Wilenius, 1963, pp. 63–5).

This conclusion generated an awkward difficulty, however, in connection with the concept of private property. The right to hold property had always been treated in the Thomist theory of political society as part of the law of nature – an assumption which Vitoria still seems to endorse. But once it was conceded that the law of nations simply represents an aspect of positive human law, it appeared to follow that the institution of private property must initially have been established by an authority no higher than that of the laws which men construct for themselves after the formation of individual commonwealths. And this conclusion carried with it a somewhat radical and inconvenient implication: it appeared to follow that the rights of property-holders may in principle be altered or even abolished without involving any direct affront to the principles of natural justice.

It was precisely this implication which the Anabaptists had already begun to explore, and which the Levellers in the English revolution a century later were to turn into one of the main foundations for their most radical political arguments. For obvious reasons, however, the more orthodox exponents of the natural-law theory of political society were anxious to avoid this implication at all costs. The best line of escape from their dilemma – later adopted and presented in its definitive form by John Locke – was obviously to invoke the interpretation of the law of nature offered by the jurists rather than the theologians, and to argue directly that the right to hold property must be a right of nature, and not a mere privilege derived from positive law. Since they had already closed off this possiblity, however, the Thomists found themselves obliged instead to revert to a distinction which Aquinas had originally drawn between the 'positive' and the 'negative' injunctions of the law of nature – between what Suárez called its 'preceptive' as opposed to its merely 'permissive' aspects (I, p. 129). This enabled them to suggest that while the communal as opposed to the private holding of property may in a sense be an injunction of the law of nature, it is only a negative injunction which serves the function of reminding us that (as Suárez puts it) 'all property would be held in common by the force of this law if it had not happened that men decided to introduce a different system' (1, p. 129). This allowed them to argue that the law of nature can be used to sanction either the continuation or the abolition of communal ownership. They were thus able to reach the convenient conclusion – later adopted by Grotius – that the question of whether there ought to be a division of property is one which it must have been left for men to decide for themselves, but in such a way that the decision to institute a division is not a mere aspect of positive law, since it 'comes under the law of nature negatively speaking', as Suárez affirms, no less than if a decision had been made to maintain the primitive condition of communal ownership (1, p. 130).

Once it was accepted that the law of nations represents an aspect of positive human law, it was a short step to the further and extremely influential suggestion that, since this form of law is known within each political society (*intra se*), it ought to be capable of being formulated into a special code of law for the regulation of the relations between different societies (*inter se*) (Barcia Trelles, 1933, pp. 458–62). This suggestion is already implicit in the account which Vitoria gives of the law of nations in his *relectio* on *Civil Power*. He describes the law of nations as a set of precepts 'created by the authority of the whole world' which serve to ensure that there are 'just and convenient rules for everyone in it', and which have the force 'not merely of pacts or agreements between men, but of genuine laws' (p. 207). This has often caused Vitoria to be hailed as the 'creator' of the modern concept of international law (e.g., Scott, 1934, p. 98). It is true that this is probably to conceptualise his discussion – which in any case is far from completely coherent – in terms he would not have recognised himself. But there is no doubt that by the end of the sixteenth century, due to the progressive refinement of the underlying idea that the law of nations is simply an aspect of positive human law, the later Jesuit theorists were able to bequeath to Grotius and his successors a recognisable analysis of international law as a special code of positive law founded on the principles of natural justice (Barcia Trelles, 1933, pp. 391–6, 415–21).

In stressing the inherent capacity of all men to apprehend the law of nature, the main polemical aim of the Thomists was to repudiate the heretical suggestion that the establishment of political society is directly ordained by God. They wished on the contrary to be able to claim that all secular commonwealths must originally have been set up by their own citizens as a means of fulfilling their purely mundane ends. It is obvious, however, that in order to arrive at this conclusion it is not enough to vindicate man's ability to use the law inscribed in his heart as a basis for constructing a system of positive laws. For it is clearly the necessity and not merely the possibility of creating a commonwealth which needs to be demonstrated if there is to be any prospect of showing that it is actually a mistake to picture political society as a gift of God rather than an invention of man himself.

The Thomists were clearly aware of this difficulty, which they sought to overcome by way of considering the nature of the situation in which men may be said to find themselves 'simply in the nature of things'. Their aim was to establish that this condition would not be a political one, and thus to infer that, since no commonwealth has a natural existence, they must all have been deliberately brought into being – as it were at some later stage – by some form of concerted action on the part of their own citizens.

This is in effect to deduce the necessity and in consequence the lineaments of political society from an imagined 'state of nature'. It is true that these theorists rarely make use of this canonical phrase from the so-called 'social contract' analysis of the formation of the State. Suárez invariably prefers to speak of deriving man's power to make laws and set up a commonwealth from an examination of what may be said 'to exist immediately in the very nature of things'.[1] There is no doubt, however, that these writers possess the concept of the state of nature even when they do not possess the phrase, and that they already recognise the heuristic value of employing it as a device for elucidating the relationship between the positive laws and the theorems of natural justice. It would be a mistake, moreover, to suggest (as some commentators have done) that the phrase itself is never used by any of these theorists (Copleston, 1953, p. 348). Molina, for example, refers at several points to the condition of mankind '*in statu naturae*', and he imagines the '*status naturae*' as that situation in which all men may be said to have found themselves after the Fall and before the inauguration of political societies (e.g., pp. 1688, 1689; cf. Romeyer, 1949, pp. 40–2).

The basic assertion which the Thomists make about this original or natural condition is that it must be pictured as a state of freedom, equality and independence. The first objection Vitoria mentions, in discussing the possibility of political subjection in his *relectio* on *Civil Power*, is the fundamental fact that 'man has been created free' (p. 183). De Soto repeats the same assertion that 'all men are born free by nature' (fo 102b). And Suárez agrees that the main difficulty in explaining the origins of

---

[1] The original reads: *immediate existat in natura rei*. Suárez repeatedly cites the phrase in his discussion in Book III on the power to make laws. The above phrase comes from the chapter-heading to Book III, Ch. 11 (vol. I, p. 164).

legitimate political authority derives from 'the fact that in the nature of things all men are born free' (I, p. 165). The quality of this natural liberty, Vitoria goes on to add, is such that 'before men congregated together' in commonwealths, 'no one man was the superior of all the others' (p. 182). De Soto again agrees that, even though the capacities of men may differ widely, this can never be held to derogate from the fact that their natural liberty gives them all an equality and independence of status (fos 102b–103a). And Suárez accepts the same conclusion that 'no one man can ever be said in the nature of things to possess any power greater than the power of anyone else' (I, p. 164). These conclusions are then corroborated, especially in the later Jesuit theorists, by reference to the fact that no one is constrained in the nature of things by the power of any positive human laws. As Molina remarks, the *status naturae* includes no right of dominion (p. 1869). And as Suárez emphasises, 'since all men are in the nature of things born free, it follows that no one person has political jurisdiction over any other, just as no one person can be said to have dominion over anyone else' (I, p. 165).

A number of these writers go on to corroborate this basic commitment by mounting an explicit attack on the thesis of patriarchalism. They already recognise – in the manner of Locke, Sydney and the other opponents of patriarchalism a century later – the need to counter this view of political authority, and to demonstrate that (as de Soto puts it) 'paternal right and dominion' must be wholly distinct from 'just political dominion' (fos 70a–b). Suárez supplies the fullest discussion of the point. The thesis he considers – which he associates with Chrysostom – is that 'since all men have been formed and procreated from Adam alone, the case for an original subordination to a single ruler seems to be established' (I, p. 165). He answers by reviving an argument which the Ockhamists as well as the Thomists had often employed, and which we have already encountered in such followers of Ockham as Almain and Mair. He maintains that 'Adam must originally have possessed domestic but not political power'. He agrees that it is compatible with the natural freedom of mankind that 'Adam may at the beginning of creation have possessed a primacy and thus a form of dominion over all men', since 'he had powers over his wife as well as the power of a father over his children as long as they were not independent of him.' He denies, however, that this makes it possible 'to claim that Adam in the nature of things possessed any political supremacy', since 'it is not in fact the right of the progenitor, simply by the force of natural law, that he should be regarded in addition as a king over his own posterity' (I, p. 165).

Nevertheless, there are two important points at which these writers circumscribe their commitment to the idea of man's natural condition as one of complete freedom and independence. They insist first of all that in describing this condition as one in which there would be no positive laws, they are by no means implying that it would be a state of pure lawlessness. They maintain on the contrary that the state of nature would be governed at all times by a genuine law. This is simply treated as a corollary of the fact that, as Molina stresses, the law of nature is equally available and known to all men in every condition in which they find themselves (p. 1689). Suárez develops the same argument at greater length in the course of discussing 'whether the law of nature constitutes a single whole' (I, p. 107). He declares that this law is known to all mankind as 'a single law at all times and in every state of human nature' (I, p. 109). 'It derives not from any particular state in which human nature is found, but rather from the essence of that nature itself' (I, p. 109). This means it must be impossible for any man in any condition 'to be in any way ignorant of its primary principles'. It follows that even before the establishment of political society, the dictates of this law must have been fully present 'in the hearts of men' (I, p. 109).

The other limitation they emphasise is that, in speaking of man's natural condition as one of freedom and independence, they are not suggesting that it would ever be a solitary or a purely individual state. They specifically attack the stoic belief – which Cicero had defended and a large number of humanists had more recently espoused – that men began as solitary wanderers before the formation of civil societies. They insist instead on the typically Thomist axiom that, as Vitoria puts it in his *relectio* on *Civil Power*, 'it is in fact essential to man that he should never live alone' (p. 177). Bellarmine refers specifically in his treatise on *The Members of the Church* to those who speak of 'a time when men wandered about in the manner of wild animals', and asserts with great force that 'it is quite impossible that there could ever have been such a time' (III, p. 10). The same claim is reiterated by Suárez, who also reveals most clearly why these writers feel so concerned to repudiate any suggestion that man's natural condition should be seen as a solitary and pre-social state. This would be to imply that 'any power over a whole community of men assembled together must be derived from men as individuals', whereas Suárez is anxious to insist that 'while it is true that this power does exist in men, it does not exist in them as individuals, nor does it exist in any one particular man' (I, pp. 165–6).

All the Thomists give the same reason for dismissing the suggestion that man in his original condition must have lived a life of individual solitude: they insist that this embodies a mistaken view of human nature, since they take it to be inherent in man's nature to live a social and communal life. The pattern is set by Vitoria, who argues in his *relectio* on *Civil Power* that it would be impossible to learn or even subsist in solitude, and thus concludes that it must be essential for men 'to live at all times together in societies' (p. 177). The later Thomists all reiterate the same claims, generally summarising them in the form of the Aristotelian contention that man is by nature a social animal. De Soto points out that even though men may be created free, they are endowed with a powerful instinct to congregate, so that they are in fact always to be found living together in a communal life (fo 108b). Bellarmine follows Vitoria in contrasting the animals 'who are able to be self-sufficient' with man 'who is by nature an animal in need of society'.[1] And Suárez agrees that 'since man is by nature a social animal', the idea of a community – not of course a political one, but some form of 'domestic' association – is 'to the greatest possible extent natural to man, and is as it were the fundamental situation' (I, p. 161).

The Thomists may be said to emphasise three features of the natural condition of mankind: it would involve a natural community; it would be governed by the law of nature; and it would be based on acknowledging the natural freedom, equality and independence of all its members. This serves to remove the problem which, as we have seen, they had in effect raised for themselves when outlining their theory about the origins of political society: by stressing that man's natural condition is social but not political, they are able to explain how it comes about that men not only have the ability but also face the necessity to create their own commonwealths. But this account tended at the same time to raise a further difficulty which the Ockhamists – with their insistence that political societies arise in consequence of sin – had scarcely needed to confront: if men naturally find themselves in the enviable position of living a life of liberty under a true law, it is not clear why they should ever have agreed to the formation of political societies, and thus to the curtailment of their natural liberties by the bonds of positive law. As John Locke was later to put the point in his *Second Treatise*, 'if man in the state of nature be so free, as has been said; if he be absolute lord of his own person and possessions, equal to the greatest, and subject to nobody, why will he part with his freedom? Why will he give up this empire and subject himself to the dominion and control of any other power?' (p. 368).

As the most sophisticated Thomists recognised, there are really two distinct though closely related issues which this question raises. One is a

---

[1] See Bellarmine, *The Members of the Church*, III, pp. 6, 9; cf. Vitoria, *Civil Power*, pp. 175–6.

straightforward problem about motivation. If all men are 'by their nature free and subject to no one', as Suárez begins by admitting in his analysis of human laws, and are nevertheless to be found everywhere in subjection to positive laws, there must have been some general and compelling reason which prompted them to give up (or caused them to forfeit) their natural liberties (I, p. 161). The other problem is less obvious, though Suárez in particular is clearly aware of it. It might be characterised as a question about what serves to legitimate the act of inaugurating a commonwealth. The most famous statement of this dilemma is offered by Rousseau at the beginning of *The Social Contract*. Man is born free, but everywhere he is in chains. The problem is not so much to explain how this change comes about, but rather to explain what is capable of rendering it legitimate.[1] The same problem is no less clearly stated by Suárez at the beginning of his discussion of man's power to create the positive laws of the commonwealth. If man 'is by his nature free and subject to no one', we need to be able to explain 'how it can come about, if we simply consider what exists in the nature of things, that some men can claim to rule over others, and to place them under a genuine obligation by means of laws which they enact themselves' (I, p. 161).

It would certainly be an overinterpretation to imply that these questions are answered or even recognised by the early Dominican theorists. By the time we come to the later Jesuit writers, however, it would be no exaggeration to say that a method for dealing with both these remaining difficulties had been fully worked out, a method which in turn helped to lay the foundations for the so-called 'social contract' theories of the seventeenth century. It consists of giving an account of the sort of lives we might be imagined to live if we made no attempt, as John Locke was later to put it, 'to get ourselves out of a condition of mere nature'.[2]

The answer which Molina and especially Suárez suggests is that, had we continued to live in our natural and pre-political communities, without submitting ourselves to the rule of positive law, we should soon have found our lives gravely impaired by increasing injustice and uncertainty. This follows from a sombre Augustinian perception about the nature of man which they introduce at this point in their argument, and which

[1] 'L'homme est né libre, et partout il est dans les fers . . . Comment ce changement s'est-il fait? Je l'ignore. Qu'est-ce qui peut le rendre légitime? Je crois pouvoir résoudre cette question' (p. 351).

[2] The structure of Suárez's theory seems in particular to be very similar to the structure which Dunn, 1969, finds in Locke: the concept of the state of nature seems to serve two functions, first to inform us of the condition into which we have been placed in the world by God, and secondly to imagine the form of life which would ensue if we attempted to live our lives in such unmediated communities. See Dunn, 1969, esp. pp. 96–119. I have found Dunn's suggested distinctions of great value in seeking to interpret the analogous structure of Suárez's thought.

considerably modifies the optimistic analysis of human rationality and morality to which they are basically committed by their Thomist allegiances. They continue to insist on the capacity of all men at all times to apprehend and follow the dictates of the law of nature. But they now go on to emphasise the implications of the fact that all men at the same time are inescapably fallen creatures (see Romeyer, 1949, pp. 43–5). Despite the fact that the dictates of morality have been 'written in our hearts', as Molina affirms, 'it is nevertheless easy, especially in view of our loss of innocence, to ignore many aspects of morality and to be uncertain of many others' (p. 1705). The consequence, as Suárez expresses it in his account of 'the necessity of laws', is that 'peace and justice can never be maintained without convenient laws', since 'ordinary individual men find it difficult to understand what is necessary for the common good, and hardly ever make any attempt to pursue it themselves' (I, p. 13).

This vision of man's propensity to selfishness, combined with the weakness of his moral will, leads to the emphatic conclusion that, if we continued to live our lives in the natural communities in which God has placed us, we should never flourish and scarcely manage to survive. Suárez gives the fullest and gloomiest picture of the conditions which would result. Life would be primitive, for many of 'the offices and arts necessary for human life' would be lacking, and we should be 'without any means of gaining a knowledge of all the things we would need to understand'. Life would be inharmonious, for 'families would become divided amongst themselves' in such a way that 'peace could scarcely be preserved amongst men'. And life would almost certainly be short, for without a power to impose the dictates of the law of nature, 'no injuries could be properly averted or avenged'. The result, 'for lack of any power to govern such a community', would thus be no better than a state of 'total confusion' (I, p. 162).

As Molina and Suárez go on to argue, we can now see what prompts men to give up their natural liberty in favour of the bonds of positive law: the decision is clearly motivated by calculations of oblique self-interest. We come to recognise that unless we introduce some regulatory machinery into our lives to ensure that the dictates of the laws of nature are properly observed, we cannot hope to lead a decent or secure form of life at all. As Suárez puts it, our natural condition is one in which 'each private individual will be concerned only with his own private advantage, which will often be opposed to the common good'. This makes it 'preferable' to exchange this condition for a more structured one 'simply from the point of view of our welfare'. We recognise 'the further necessity' of agreeing to establish a commonwealth, and are moved 'to create some public authority whose duty it is to maintain and promote the common good' (I, p. 162).

Suárez later confirms this analysis by way of considering the rather different explanation offered by Vitoria. Vitoria was opposed to the suggestion that such a perfect institution as political society could possibly be built on such unworthy foundations as our mutual calculations of self-interest. Discussing the issue in his *relectio* on *Civil Power*, he accepts that the reason why it is essential to establish commonwealths is that 'no society can continue to maintain itself without some force and power to govern and provide for it', since 'if all men remained equal, and no one was ever made subject to any power, each individual would simply pursue his own will and pleasure in completely diverse directions', with the result that 'society would necessarily be torn in pieces' (p. 179). But he thinks that the resulting need to formalise our natural communities must have been directly supplied for us by 'a providential force' and specifically by the will of God himself, 'by whom all power is ordained' (pp. 172, 179). So he insists that it must be a mistake 'to suppose that the origins of republics and commonwealths can be treated as human inventions' (p. 179). When Suárez addresses himself to this analysis, however, he remonstrates with Vitoria both for his evident confusions[1] and for his apparent acceptance of the heretical assumption that 'the power to create a commonwealth is immediately given by God as the author of nature' (I, p. 166). This is to treat God as both the material and the efficient cause of political society, whereas the truth is that 'God does not grant this power as a special act or gift distinct from creation' (I, p. 167). He merely grants men the power to create their commonwealths for themselves, by placing them in such a situation and endowing them with such capacities that this act of creation is rendered both necessary and possible (I, p. 167).

The Thomists also use their account of man's natural condition in order to answer the question later classically posed by Rousseau: the question of how it is possible for the change from a situation of natural liberty to the constraints of political society to be legitimately made. The answer they suggest is that, since we would come to recognise the impossibility of maintaining justice in a natural community, we would find it rational to give our free consent to the establishment of a commonwealth, agreeing mutually to limit our liberties in the name of attaining, by this oblique means, a greater degree of freedom and security for our lives, liberties and estates. It is thus through the medium of consent, according to all these

---

[1] Which are compounded by the fact that Vitoria later goes on to speak of the king 'being constituted by the commonwealth', p. 191. For full analysis of Suárez's debate with Vitoria at this point, see Jarlot, 1949, pp. 79–83.

writers, that the transition to political society is capable of being rendered a legitimate change. The point is authoritatively made by Vitoria, who speaks in his *relectio* on *Civil Power* of the indispensable need for consent (*consensus*) in any case in which the people 'mandate their powers to someone for the good of the commonwealth' (p. 192). De Soto repeats the same claim, emphasising 'the necessity that the populace should consent' (*consentiat*) before 'any ruler can be instituted' (fos 108a–b). And the same conclusion is later reiterated by all the Jesuit theorists. Molina refers to the need for the power of any ruler to be 'in line with both the will and approbation' (*arbitrio ac beneplacito*) of the people (p. 1869). And Suárez gives a more polemical summary of the same argument. He reverts at this point to his criticism of Vitoria for failing to recognise that while 'political power undoubtedly arises out of the law of nature', its establishment 'must still be the product of human choice' (1, p. 168). He concedes that men have a powerful and almost irresistible motive for setting up political societies, but he denies that 'they are absolutely compelled into this course of action by the force of the law of nature' (1, p. 168). A choice is still involved, which the community must decide and consent to make. For 'the power to set up the commonwealth reposes in the nature of things immediately in the community', from which 'it follows that in order for it to be justly bestowed upon any individual person, such as a supreme prince, it is essential that it should be granted to him by the consent of the community' (*ex consensu communitatis*) (1, p. 169).

The concept of consent is thus invoked by all these writers in order to explain how it is possible for a free individual to become the subject of a legitimate commonwealth. It is worth underlining this point, since it has often been misleadingly claimed that what these writers are arguing is that 'the ultimate test of the juridical validity of any system of government is the consent of the governed' (Fichter, 1940, p. 307). As we have seen, however, they all assume that the question of whether an established system of government is juridically valid is not a question about consent, but simply a question about whether the government's enactments are congruent with the law of nature. It is in fact asserted quite explicitly by several of these writers that the consent of the governed need not be formally sought on every occasion as a condition of the legitimacy of the government's actions. Vitoria, for example, is quite clear that a ruler is not necessarily bound by the *Lex Regia* to follow any specific set of constitutional procedures, while Molina and Suárez both assume that it is only in a certain range of cases (notably taxation) that it is essential for the consent of the people's representatives to be secured before a law can be legitimately enforced. The idea of consent is in short not used to establish the legitimacy of what happens in political society; it is solely used to explain how a legitimate political society is brought into existence.[1]

The idea that any legitimate polity must originate in an act of consent was of course a scholastic commonplace, one which the followers of Ockham no less than Aquinas had always emphasised. There is no doubt, however, that the analysis of the concept was carried to a new peak of development by the sixteenth-century Thomists, and in particular by Suárez, whose discussion in *The Laws and God the Lawgiver* may be said to have supplied the guidelines for the handling of the same theme by some of the leading constitutionalist writers of the seventeenth century. The first point on which Suárez lays a special emphasis is that the act of consenting constitutes the sole means by which a legitimate commonwealth can be set up. 'The holding of civil power in any way, if it is to be rightful and legitimate, must result either from a direct or an indirect grant from the community, and cannot otherwise be justly held at all' (1, p. 169). Suárez is not of course so naïve as to suggest that this is the only means by which every commonwealth which claims legitimacy has in fact been founded. He concedes that 'Empires and kingdoms have often been set up and even usurped through tyranny and force' (1, p. 164). He also admits the concept of prescription, the idea that one might be said to acquire a duty 'to accept a particular ruler in course of time', even though he may initially have attained his position 'by unjust force' (1, p. 169). Neither of these apparent shifts, however, really alters Suárez's basic stance. When he considers the undoubted fact that many commonwealths have been founded in conquests, he takes up a completely intransigent position – one which was later adopted by Locke, and is far more radical than that of Grotius or Hobbes. He simply replies that 'if a kingdom comes into being purely by unjust means, the ruler cannot be said to possess any genuine legislative authority' (1, p. 169). Nor does he contradict this commitment when he concedes the possibility of a prescriptive right to rule. For he argues that the only reason why the concept of prescription is allowable is that it collapses into the concept of consent. To say that a people 'admits' a power founded in force is the same as saying that 'the power can be traced back to an act of transmission and donation on the part of the people' (1, p. 169). It follows that 'this mode of

---

[1] For the suggestion that the (sole) reason why the natural law theorists appeal to the concept of consent is as a means of explaining how it is possible for a free individual to become the subject of a legitimate polity, see the discussion of consent in Locke's political theory in Dunn, 1967. Dunn does not of course discuss the sixteenth-century expositions of the same body of doctrines, but his analysis serves to shed a great deal of light on their assumptions as well as on those of Locke, and I am greatly indebted to his analysis in the account I have given above.

acquiring power may after all be said to include, in a certain sense, the consent of the commonwealth' (I, p. 169; cf. Wright, 1932, pp. 38–9).

Suárez reveals the force of this contention when he uses it to repudiate two political attitudes which had traditionally been widely held in Catholic Europe. One was the thesis of the canonists – a thesis shared, as he observes, by a number of jurists – to the effect that 'political power is divinely conferred upon one particular prince, and ought always to continue in one particular person by a process of hereditary succession' (I, p. 164). He replies that this conclusion is based on forgetting that 'it is essential that the first possessor should have derived his supreme power immediately from the commonwealth, so that his successors, less directly but still fundamentally, must still derive their authority from the same source' (I, p. 169). The implication is that 'a right of succession cannot in fact be the basic source of a king's power' (I, p. 169). The other view he considers is that of the Imperialists, with their characteristic allegation that 'there is one particular prince with temporal dominion throughout the whole of the world' (I, p. 170). His response is simply that this belief constitutes 'a moral impossibility'. One of the conditions for the existence of such a power would have to be the fact that 'it was received from the hands of men'. The truth is, however, that 'it has simply never happened that men have even consented to confer such a power or to institute such a single head over themselves'. It follows that even if a universal Empire existed, it could never be legitimate (I, p. 170).

The other important feature of Suárez's discussion is his clear recognition of the fact that there is a certain peculiarity about the idea of political authority being brought into existence by a general act of consent performed by men in a state of nature. As Gierke originally emphasised, the problematic feature of this analysis can be expressed as follows. If the natural condition of mankind includes no positive laws, and is thus a condition in which each individual is independent of any formal legal ties, how is it possible for men to perform such complex, apparently unified and obviously legal acts as consenting to the establishment of a sovereign, transferring their authority into his hands and contracting to acknowledge the legitimacy of his laws? If the situation in which we are to imagine these events taking place genuinely lacks any legal bonds, how can it include the performance of such legal acts?

One of the points emphasised by Gierke in his discussion of this issue was that these questions were never answered or even raised by the medieval writers on the natural law theory of political society (Gierke, 1900, pp. 67–73). It would be fair to add, moreover, that they were still somewhat hazily perceived, and sometimes not perceived at all, by a number of their most distinguished seventeenth-century successors. Hobbes skirts round the issue in the typical manner of the nominalists, while Locke's analysis at this point appears evasive and somewhat confused. There is no doubt, however, that the problem was clearly perceived by Suárez, who presents his answer in the form of a strongly holistic theory about the capacity of the people to perceive themselves as a *universitas*, and thus to engage univocally in the performance of corporate legal acts (cf. Mesnard, 1936, pp. 627–8).

Suárez takes as his point of departure the fact that the crucial characteristics of men in the state of nature are possessed by them all in common: they are all 'by nature free', all 'possess the use of their reason' and all 'have power over their own faculties' (1, p. 167). It follows that there must be two distinct ways in which it is possible to conceive of men in this state. Since they all possess these characteristics as individuals, we may think of them as 'simply forming a kind of aggregation without any particular order amongst them' (1, p. 165). Suárez concedes that if they are considered in this way, it is impossible to regard them as 'the authors and bestowers of the powers which are established over their communities', since 'such a capacity can scarcely be said to exist in them as individuals, or even in what we might call the rough collection or aggregate of men' (1, p. 166). But since the same moral characteristics are also possessed by all men in common, it is equally possible to think of the state of nature not as a community of individuals, but rather as 'a single mystical body' in which all the members recognise the same obligations, follow the same rules, and are thus 'capable of being regarded, from the moral point of view, as a single unified whole' (1, p. 165). It is Suárez's essential contention that once we think of men in their natural condition in this alternative way, there is no difficulty about conceiving of them as having the power to act with a single unified will to set up the legitimate authority of a commonwealth. For the fact that they constitute a single mystical body implies that they must possess a single unified will – what Suárez calls 'a special will or common volition existing in a single body of people' (1, p. 166). And the fact that the community may in this sense be said to possess a general will in turn implies that its members must be able, as Suárez concludes, 'to gather together by common consent (*communi consensu*) into a single political body through a single bond of society and for the purpose of helping each other mutually to attain for all of them a single political end' (1, p. 165).

As we have seen, a similar adaptation of the Roman law theory of corporations had already been made by Ockham and his disciples, and in particular by Gerson in his theory of the Church. But this holistic way of thinking about the legal personality of the *populus* had scarcely been explored by Aquinas or his immediate followers (Gierke, 1900, p. 68). Suárez's invocation of the concept of a *universitas* may thus be said to represent a considerable advance on the accounts offered by the earlier Dominican theorists of the process by which a legitimate commonwealth can be brought into being. Vitoria had ignored the difficulties in his *relectio* on *Civil Power*, briskly asserting that 'it is enough, in order to do anything legitimately, that the majority should agree on the decision to be taken.' When the people 'decide to mandate their power to some particular individual', one must not think that 'the dissent of one or a few' should be held to matter, since 'if the consent of all were needed, there would not be enough care for the good of the commonwealth, since unanimity is rarely if ever achieved by a multitude' (p. 192). De Soto similarly argues that 'when a king or Emperor is instituted', all that is necessary is that 'the greater part of the people should consent to the choice' (fo 108b). Suárez by contrast clearly recognises that, if the people are to be assigned the power to act legally and definitively in a situation which is not in fact bound by positive laws, it is essential that they should be viewed not simply as a 'multitude', in Vitoria's somewhat dismissive characterisation, but rather as a body possessing a corporate legal personality and a single voice to express their common purposes.

THE REPLY TO THE HERETICS

Having presented their account of the nature and origins of legitimate political societies, the Thomists were finally able – as in the case of their theory of the Church – to turn their arguments against their enemies, and to respond to the various errors about the concept of secular authority being propagated by 'all the heretics of the age'. As we have seen, the main enemies they were concerned to answer were again the Lutherans. They were now in a position to produce a reply to the fundamental Lutheran contention that man is unable, due to his fallen nature, to understand the will of God and so to live his life according to a genuine law. The error involved in this belief, they now point out, is that of failing to recognise that all men at all times are in fact equally capable of consulting and following the law which is 'inscribed in their hearts'. The point is made with particular force by the later Jesuit theorists, in the wake of the rejection of 'two-fold justice' at the Council of Trent. Bellarmine emphasises in his treatise *Concerning Justification* that the mistake made by 'all the heretics of the present time', when they argue that 'all our acts are the product of our fallen natures', is simply that of failing to acknowledge that the scriptures, the Fathers and our natural reason all concur in assuring us that we possess 'an inherent justice' which enables us to apprehend the laws of God and employ them in the conduct of our lives (IV, pp. 319, 323, 349). The same points are later reiterated by Suárez. 'The fundamental error of the heretics', he insists, is that of failing to see that 'we are truly and intrinsically justified through an inherent justice given by Christ', and thus that we are 'subject to a true law at all times' (I, p. 67).

These writers all agree, moreover, that this idea of 'imputed justice' constitutes what Bellarmine calls 'the seed of all the heresies of the present time', or what Suárez, varying the metaphor, prefers to call 'the root of every other heresy'.[1] 'Once this is plucked out', as Suárez goes on, the two major errors in the Lutheran theory of political society can easily be uprooted at the same time. The first is the Lutheran contention that the godliness of a ruler must be regarded as a condition of his rulership. The error underlying this doctrine, as Bellarmine declares in *The Members of the Church*, is that of failing to concede that political society is not a God-given but simply a man-made thing, and thus that 'the foundation of dominion is not in grace but in nature' (III, p. 14). Suárez goes on to develop the same argument. It is obviously a mistake to think that 'political power presupposes either faith or any other supernatural gift in the prince possessing it', since 'the power is created in a purely natural way without ever being directed to supernatural ends'. It is merely established by men for their own purposes according to the law of nature, so that 'it is not in the least required that, in order to be able to exercise this power, the ruler should be faithful' or even that he should be baptised (I, p. 191).

The other and even more dangerous conclusion which the Lutherans had reached was that the commands of an ungodly ruler can never be binding in the court of conscience. Vitoria and de Soto set the pattern in responding to this heresy when they insist that we are in fact obliged *in foro interno* to obey all genuine positive laws.[2] This conclusion is then turned polemically against the Lutherans by several of the later Jesuit theorists. Bellarmine supplies a full account of the orthodox answer when he discusses the concept of political power in his treatise on *The Members of the Church*. His fundamental contention is that 'a just civil law is always a conclusion or an outcome of the divine moral law' (III, p. 18). Suárez makes the same cardinal assumption when he discusses the obligatory force of human laws in Book III of *The Laws and God the Lawgiver*. 'It is

[1] See Bellarmine, *Concerning Justification*, vol. VI, p. 153 and Suárez, I, p. 67.
[2] See Vitoria, *Civil Power*, pp. 195-9; de Soto, *Ten Books on Justice and Law*, fos 17b-19b.

not possible', he insists, 'for anything to be a precept of the civil law which is not a precept of the law of nature' (I, p. 237). This means, they both maintain, that in claiming the right in certain circumstances to disobey the commands of a legitimate ruler, the heretics are in effect claiming that it is possible to set aside the law of nature. For as Bellarmine puts it, 'the rationale of divine and human laws is the same' (III, p. 18). They had already laid it down, however, that the law of nature is not merely a dictate of right reason, but is also an expression of the will of God, since 'all forms of law' (as Bellarmine reminds us) 'in fact participate in the eternal law of God' (III, p. 18). But this in turn means, as Bellarmine goes on, that 'anyone who sets aside either the natural, the positive, the divine or the human law must in every case be sinning against the eternal law of God' (III, p. 18). The Lutheran position is thus revealed not merely as mistaken, but as blasphemous in the highest degree. The true doctrine, as Bellarmine begins his chapter by stressing, is that 'the civil law no less obliges in conscience' and is 'no less firm and stable' than the divine law itself (III, p. 17).

As well as responding to the heresies of the Lutherans, the counter-reformation theorists also direct their arguments against their various humanist enemies. They are able first of all to supply an answer to Sepúlveda's notorious suggestion that infidels are incapable of maintaining a genuine political society, and thus that it is legitimate for the Indians of the New World to be conquered and enslaved (Jarlot, 1949, pp. 71–2). The error underlying this belief, they now insist, is the same as the fundamental error of the Lutherans. Sepúlveda and his followers are failing to recognise that, since it is open to all men to apprehend the law of nature, it must equally be open to any group of men to establish a political society, without benefit of revelation, simply by consulting and following their instincts about the rules of natural justice.

It is true that while this answer is energetically defended by the Dominicans, it is not taken over with the same assurance by the later Jesuit writers. Molina, for example, is much less certain than his predecessors about the self-evidence of the law of nature, and is correspondingly closer to Sepúlveda in his views about the status and capacities of the Indians. If we turn to Bellarmine or Suárez, however, we find that while they have less to say about this topic than the earlier Dominican theorists, they are still prepared to offer a fairly emphatic endorsement of their general humanitarian claims. 'All men are equally made in the image of God with a mind and reason', as Bellarmine puts it in *The Members of the Church*, so that 'the infidels, who possess this nature' must 'without doubt be able to have true dominion' (III, p. 14). The same point is reiterated by Suárez. 'The law of nature is written in one particular way in the minds and in the hearts even of the infidels' (II, p. 645). There is thus no reason to doubt that genuine forms of political authority 'existed in the world before the coming of Christ, and are now exercised by many infidel and unbaptised peoples' (I, p. 191).

The earliest and most extensive development of this insight – a development which issued in the first unequivocal defence of the Indians against their conquerors – was provided by Vitoria in a remarkable pair of *relectiones* which he delivered as public lectures at some time in the 1530s, and which evidently caused a considerable sensation at the time (Scott, 1934, pp. 84–6). His first lecture (a long essay in three parts) is most directly concerned with – and is entitled – *The Recently Discovered Indies* (The second takes up the question of the law of war in relation to the conquests.) Vitoria moves straight to the crucial question of 'Whether the barbarians were true lords in relation to private and public affairs', and whether they were maintaining a genuine political society with 'true princes and rulers' and 'true ownership of private possessions' before the coming of the *Conquistadores* (p. 292). He immediately goes on to point out that the only way of returning a negative answer to these questions would be to embrace an old heresy – one which he associates particularly with Wyclif and Hus – and to argue that true dominion must always be founded in grace (p. 294). Vitoria of course rejects this as a fundamental mistake about the law of nature. So he concludes his first section by arguing that 'there can be no doubt that the Indians possessed true dominion both in public and private affairs', and that 'there is no case at all for despoiling either their rulers or their subjects of their property on the grounds that they had no genuine dominion over it' (p. 309). This conclusion is corroborated in two later sections of the same *relectio*, in which Vitoria considers two 'illegitimate titles' used by the Spanish crown in the attempt to justify its conquests in the New World. One is the refusal of the barbarians to recognise the fact that the Spanish have been granted all rights and jurisdictions over these areas by the Pope. This is very sharply dismissed. 'Even if the barbarians refuse to recognise the power of the Pope in this matter, this can scarcely constitute a reason for making war on them and seizing their goods, because the fact is that the Pope possesses no such power' (p. 330). The other is the suggested right of the Spaniards to make war on the barbarians on the grounds that they ought to be forcibly converted. Vitoria simply reverts at this point to the pivotal Thomist claim that there is an equal capacity in all men, whether or not they are Christian, to establish their own political societies. He is thus led to the decisive conclusion that 'even if the Christian faith has been announced to the barbarians with complete and sufficient arguments, and they have still refused to receive it, this still does not supply a reason for making war on them and despoiling them of their goods' (p. 345).

Nearly twenty years later, Vitoria's fellow-Dominican Bartolomé de las Casas (1474–1566) went on to produce a famous application of these arguments when he was chosen to defend the cause of the Indians against Sepúlveda at the Valladolid debate in 1550. Las Casas had first visited the New World in 1502, where he began by following the brutal way of life lived by the colonists. But in 1514 he experienced a sudden revulsion against the treatment being meted out to the Indians, and after retiring for a time into his Order he went back to America in order to fight on their behalf, only returning finally to Spain in 1547 (Hanke, 1949, pp. 54–71). It was thus on the basis of an extensive as well as compassionate understanding of the local situation that he offered to defend against Sepúlveda the proposition that the Indians 'fulfilled every one of Aristotle's requirements for the good life', and thus that the Spanish system of conquest and enslavement could never be justified (Hanke, 1959, p. 54).

It is not clear how sympathetically Las Casas's arguments were received at the Valladolid debate. It is true that de Soto was one of the judges, and that he was well-known, as befitted a pupil of Vitoria's, for his strongly anti-imperialist views. Las Casas had already appealed to him to use his influence to stop the progress of the conquests, and he had himself complained to the Council of the Indies about the treatment of the Indians 'as though they were brute animals'.[1] But it is also true that the judges at Valladolid never managed to return a collective verdict, and it seems all too probable, had they done so, that the growing financial interests of the Spanish crown in the New World might have inclined a majority towards Sepúlveda's side. Nevertheless, the testimony which Las Casas provided in his treatise *In Defence of the Indians* still constitutes an impressive and a mainly persuasive document, in spite of the fact that, in his anxiety to vindicate every aspect of Indian life, he goes so far as to include a long defence of cannibalism and human sacrifice (pp. 185–254). The essence of his argument is based on repeating Vitoria's central contention that all men, except perhaps a very few barbarians, are equally endowed by God with the same reasoning capacities (p. 38). He thus insists at the outset that Sepúlveda is fundamentally mistaken in supposing that the Indians are barbarians in the strict sense that God 'has willed them to lack reason' (p. 28). Las Casas concedes that they are of course barbarians in the sense

---

[1] See Bataillon, 1954, pp. 366–87; Hanke, 1959, p. 27. But Losada, 1970, p. 287, thinks that de Soto may have abstained in the judges' final vote.

that they are not Christians, but he maintains that this has in no way inhibited them from forming a genuine political society with 'sufficient natural knowledge and ability to rule and govern itself' (p. 38). He concludes that, since they have constructed society without benefit of revelation, there can be no question of using their lack of Christian understanding as an excuse for enslaving them. He agrees that it is of course lawful 'to instruct them in the word of God' in the hope that they may be 'lovingly drawn to accept the best way of life' (pp. 39, 40). But he still affirms, very much in the manner of Vitoria, that even if they refuse to be guided in this way, this provides no reason for proceeding in the way the Spanish have in fact proceeded – acting 'like a ferocious executioner', trying 'to press them into slavery' and exploiting them for their own 'ease and pleasures', all of which he takes to be contrary to the true spirit of Christianity (p. 40).

Finally, the counter-reformation theorists are able to respond to the more insidious and dangerous threat which, as we have seen, they had found in Machiavelli's writings, and especially in his suggestion that, in considering whether or not to act justly, the prince ought to settle the question by adopting whatever course of action seems most likely 'to maintain his state'. The error underlying this impious advice is said to be the same, once again, as the fundamental error of the Lutherans. As Possevino loftily puts it in his *Judgment*, Machiavelli is failing to recognise, no less than the other leading heretics of the age, that 'the minds of wise men are imbued with a divine and natural light sent from God', a light which enables us to see that we have a duty as well as a capacity 'to be sure of acting only with the greatest probity' (p. 129). Ribadeneyra makes the same point in his anti-Machiavellian treatise on *Religion and the Virtues*. When we are asked, he declares, to 'take as our rules what authors like Machiavelli write', we are being asked at the same time to 'leave the road straight and plain which natural reason itself uncovers for us, God teaches us, the most blessed son manifested to us' (p. 252). And Suárez reiterates the same argument in the special chapter which he devotes to Machiavelli in *The Laws and God the Lawgiver*. Machiavelli is blind to the crucial fact that 'the civil law must only be constructed out of honest materials', and must be 'limited by the claims of justice', never simply by the claims of political expediency (i, p. 197).

As several of these writers perceive, however, it was no longer very realistic to respond to the growing threat of 'Machiavellism' by simply reiterating their basic belief that, as Suárez repeatedly puts it in his attack on Machiavelli, the dictates of natural justice 'form the only possible materials for true civil law', so that 'there must be nothing in the law which directly overturns equity or natural justice' (I, p. 198). To rest content with this response, as Ribadeneyra in particular seems to recognise, is to ignore the implications of the fact that two rival political moralities were by now confronting each other in every commonwealth of late sixteenth-century Europe. One was the natural-law theory, which Ribadeneyra takes to be 'supported on God himself and on the means that he with his paternal providence reveals to the princes'. The other was the theory of 'Machiavelli and the *politiques*' (*los politicos*), with its impious exhortation to our rulers to imitate both the lion and the fox (p. 253). As Ribadeneyra begins by conceding, the difficulty is that between these 'two political ways of thinking' there is virtually no common ground, since the truth of the one entails the falsity of the other, and each is claimed by its exponents to provide the only correct analysis of the moral standards to be applied in political life. The implication for the defenders of the natural-law theory was clear: if they were to succeed in answering the Machiavellians, they would need to move beyond the repetition of their own assumptions; they would need to bridge the gulf between the two moralities, and attempt as it were to defeat the Machiavellians with their own weapons.

It is arguable that the Jesuits writing at the end of the sixteenth century – notably Possevino and Ribadeneyra, followed by Mariana and Suárez – constitute the first group of political theorists who clearly grasped the epoch-making challenge of Machiavelli's political thought, especially the fact that he had introduced a new political morality in conscious opposition to the tenets of Catholic Christianity.[1] The significance of this awareness was that it led them to offer a second argument against Machiavelli, an argument which was clearly designed to refute his manipulative account of political morality in its own terms. As we have seen, the earlier humanist attacks on Machiavelli had always insisted on the principle that the fundamental aim of the prince must be to uphold the dictates of justice at all times. The Jesuits, by contrast, are willing to concede that a prince may often be obliged to treat 'the maintenance of his state' and 'the safety of his kingdom' as overriding political values. But they argue that, even if we grant these ends, it would still be a mistake to suppose that Machiavelli has supplied us with a correct analysis of the best means of attaining them. This line of attack appears to originate with Ribadeneyra, who insists that the doctrine of *ragione di stato* is 'insane' as well as impious, since the most prudent course of action to

---

[1] One reason it is worth stressing this point is that none of these writers is discussed or even mentioned in Meinecke's classic analysis of the early debates about 'Machiavellism'; cf. Meinecke, 1957, pp. 49–89.

follow, in order to maintain one's state, will always be to keep God 'pleased and propitious' by 'keeping His holy law' and 'obeying His mandates' (p. 253). Machiavelli's image of the hypocrite prince is thus rejected on pragmatic as well as moral grounds. It is no less 'pernicious for the conservation of his state than it is abhorrent to God' (p. 277). The same allegation is enthusiastically endorsed by Mariana in his account of *The King and the Education of the King*, first published in 1599, which includes a special chapter entitled 'Mendacity' (p. 229). Mariana insists that 'the principles of good government depend especially on good faith and truth', which must always be upheld (p. 231). He imagines the objection that 'the interests of the commonwealth demand that the prince practise deceit and prevarication' (p. 231). But his immediate response is that 'in the first place, there is no practical use' in adopting such Machiavellian tactics, since 'there is much more harm than advantage' to be gained from them (p. 232).[1] Finally, the same pragmatic considerations are repeated by Suárez, who concludes his attack on Machiavelli with the assurance that 'the doctrine of these *politiques* (*politici*) is not in fact of any value for the maintenance of a temporal republic or kingdom', simply because 'honesty is in fact of greater power in maintaining peace and political felicity' than anything else (1, p. 198).

---

[1] Bleznick, 1958, in discussing Mariana's attack on the Machiavellians – an attack which he believes to be tempered by certain 'Machiavellian' elements in Mariana's own outlook – fails to mention this aspect of Mariana's discussion, and in this way perhaps overestimates Mariana's sympathy for Machiavelli's doctrines.

6

The limits of constitutionalism

THE RADICAL PERSPECTIVE

The Thomist philosophers of the counter-reformation have often been portrayed as the main founders of modern constitutionalist and even democratic thought. Suárez has been hailed as 'the first modern democrat', Bellarmine has been praised for revealing 'the true sources of democracy', and the Jesuits as a whole have been credited with 'inventing' the concept of the social contract and exploring for the first time its implications for the theory of justice.[1] There is of course an element of truth in these claims. By drawing on their Thomist heritage, the counter-reformation theorists not only arrived at a number of radically populist conclusions, but also served as the main channel through which the contractarian approach to the discussion of political obligation came to exercise its decisive influence in the course of the following century. If we glance forward, for example, to John Locke's *Two Treatises of Government*, we find him reiterating a number of the most central assumptions of the Jesuit and Dominican writers. He agrees with their analysis of the *ius naturale*, declaring that reason 'is that law' and that the same law must also be treated as 'the will of God' (pp. 289, 376). He agrees with their sense of the pivotal role which ought to be assigned to the *ius naturale* in any legitimate political society, describing it as 'an eternal rule to all men' and insisting that all the enactments of our legislators must be 'conformable' to its demands.[2] And when he turns to consider how it is possible for a political society based on this law to be brought into existence, he endorses both the main arguments which the Jesuits and Dominicans had already advanced. He offers a classic restatement of their suggestion that, in order 'to understand political power right, and derive it from its

---

[1] For these claims see respectively Fichter, 1940, p. 306; Rager, 1926, p. 129; Jarlot, 1949, p. 98; Figgis, 1960, pp. 201–3.

[2] For the claim that Locke founds the legitimacy of political society upon the law of nature, construed both as reason and the will of God, see the brilliant analysis in Dunn, 1969, esp. pp. 87–95 and 187–202.

'original', we must ask 'what state all men are naturally in' and recognise that this state would be one 'of perfect freedom' (p. 287). And he accepts that 'the only way whereby anyone divests himself' of this natural freedom, and 'puts on the bonds of civil society' is through the mechanism of consent, by 'agreeing with other men to join and unite into a community' (pp. 348–9).

As well as arriving at these conclusions by way of developing their Thomist heritage, a number of counter-reformation theorists, especially in the latter part of the sixteenth century, began to take over several of the key features of the theory of *Imperium* originally outlined by Ockham and his disciples. This syncretic approach can be observed first of all in relation to their theory of the Church. As we have seen, the Ockhamists had mounted a strong attack on the belief – endorsed by a number of earlier Thomists – that the Pope may be said to enjoy certain direct powers to control political affairs. They had countered this assertion with the claim that ecclesiastical and temporal government ought to be envisaged as virtually separate. It was this radical and secularised outlook, rather than the arguments of the earlier Thomists, which now began to be wholeheartedly adopted by the Jesuits and Dominicans. Vitoria led the way in his *relectio* on *The Power of the Church*, maintaining that 'the temporal commonwealth is perfect and complete in itself, and is therefore not subject to anything outside itself, otherwise it would not be complete' (p. 67). The spheres of ecclesiastical and secular authority are thus held to be virtually distinct, since 'even if there were no spiritual power at all, there would still be an order in the temporal commonwealth' (p. 71). The same argument is later repeated by most of the Jesuits in the same emphatic tones. Even Bellarmine, whom Hobbes was later to single out in *Leviathan* as an uncompromising defender of Papal authority, nevertheless concedes in his treatise on *The Supreme Pontiff* that 'ecclesiastical and political power are simply two distinct kinds of power' (p. 155). And Suárez agrees that the two types of authority must be absolutely distinguished, since 'civil power is ordained simply to rule political life', and is thus 'of no different a character than the power to be found in the governments of heathen princes' (I, pp. 195–6).

All these writers proceed, moreover, to derive the corollary that the Papacy cannot possibly be said to possess any direct coercive power over secular commonwealths. Vitoria puts the point with remarkable force in his *relectio* on *The Power of the Church*. To say that 'the Pope possesses direct temporal authority and jurisdiction in the whole world' is not only 'indubitably and manifestly false', but is 'merely offered as a piece of flattery and adulation of the Pope' (p. 64). The truth is that 'temporal power does not in the least depend on the Pope', and that 'civil authority is in no way directly subject' to his control (pp. 65, 66). The same arguments are again presented, and the same corollaries drawn, by the later Jesuit theorists. Bellarmine simply refers us to Vitoria's authority at this point in his treatise on *The Supreme Pontiff*, confirming his conclusion that 'there is no case for saying that by divine authority the Pope possesses any direct temporal jurisdictions at all' (pp. 146, 148). Similarly, Suárez insists that although a number of Papal decrees – notably those of Boniface VIII – may appear to contradict this conclusion, it is clear 'in spite of what they say' that Vitoria is unquestionably correct to maintain that 'the Pope has no direct temporal jurisdictions over the whole world' (p. 176).

This willingness to endorse the more radical outlook originally associated with the exponents of the *via moderna* can also be observed in relation to the theory of political society which the Thomists began to evolve in the latter part of the sixteenth century. One notable innovation was that they took over the 'subjective' view of rights which had originated with Ockham and his followers, and had been restated by Almain and Mair at the start of the sixteenth century.[1] It is true that the Dominican theorists at first showed themselves highly suspicious of this move. If we turn, for example, to de Soto's analysis of the concept of *ius* at the beginning of Book III of his *Ten Books on Justice and Law*, we still find him maintaining very emphatically that 'justice is to be defined in terms of *ius*', and that *ius* is to be understood simply 'as the object of justice' and not as a subjective notion at all (fo 67b). By the time we come to Suárez's discussion in *The Laws and God the Lawgiver*, however, we find him offering a complete endorsement of the subjective view which Mair in particular had already developed a century earlier – though without, of course, citing Mair's authority or that of his Ockhamist predecessors. Suárez's main discussion of the issue is presented near the beginning of his opening Book, in a chapter entitled 'The Meaning of *Ius*' (I, p. 5). He begins by observing that '*ius* is frequently taken to be interchangeable with law', but he argues that 'it is in fact essential to discriminate between the two terms' (I, p. 5). The reason is that *ius* does not refer merely to 'that which is right' – as de Soto and the earlier Thomists had supposed (I, p. 6). The concept can also be used to denote 'a certain moral capacity which everyone possesses' – a capacity in effect to justify engaging in certain kinds of normative action (I, p. 6). So to speak of *ius* is not merely to speak of 'rightness' but also of 'rights' in the sense of 'having a right in relation to a certain thing' (I, p. 7).

---

[1] For discussions about the emergence of the 'subjective' concept, I am greatly indebted to James Tully and Richard Tuck; cf. also Tuck, 1977, Chs I and II, and Tully, 1977.

Far from admitting that this is simply to repeat the analysis which his great opponent John Mair had already proposed, Suárez seeks to show that this way of thinking about the concept of *ius* is implicit in the civil law, and is explicitly invoked at several points in the Old Testament. When he turns to provide us with examples, however, his discussion becomes very reminiscent of the analysis we have already encountered in Mair's *Questions* and in his *History*. Like Mair, Suárez argues that in speaking of 'having a right to something', what we must fundamentally have in mind is the idea of 'having a certain power' over it. And like Mair, he gives as his main instance the case of 'an owner, who may in this sense be said to have a right over his possessions' (I, p. 6).

Suárez's acceptance of this definition is of great importance in relation to his political theory, for he also follows Mair and Almain in applying this subjective view of rights as a way of answering what he calls 'the great question' of whether the subjects of a tyrannical ruler may be said to have a right to resist his rule. Suárez presents his main discussion of this problem in the course of his attack on James I's oath of allegiance, the chief topic of his massive *Defence of the Catholic and Apostolic Faith*. He eventually turns to examine the question at the end of the final Book, in the course of considering whether the people of England are in fact obliged by the oath of allegiance promulgated by their heretical king. As in the discussion which Almain had mounted in his *Reconsideration*, Suárez answers the question by way of developing the analogy between the rights of individuals and of communities. Just as in the case of an individual person, Suárez affirms, 'the right to preserve one's life is the greatest right of all' so in the case of a commonwealth, 'where the king is actually attacking it with the aim of unjustly destroying it and killing the citizens', there must be an analogous right of self-defence, which 'makes it lawful for the community to resist its prince, and even to kill him, if it has no other means of preserving itself' (II, p. 287).

Suárez first deploys this doctrine in order to set careful limits to the possibility of legitimate resistance. He insists that if the ruler is not in fact 'engaged in an aggressive war designed to destroy the commonwealth and to kill large numbers of citizens', but is 'merely injuring the commonwealth in other and lesser ways', then 'in that case there is no place for a defence of the community either by force or by treachery directed against the life of the king'. When the life of the community 'is not actually being threatened' it must suffer in silence (II, p. 287). However, he is quite emphatic that, if the community as a whole is in jeopardy, then its right to preserve its life against unlawful destruction unquestionably makes it legitimate to resist. This highly radical application of the subjective theory is first suggested by Suárez at an earlier point in his *Defence*, in the course of presenting his objections to James I's account of his own sovereignty (I, p. 189). Suárez declares that even though a community 'may have transferred its power to its king' in the way King James alleges, it nevertheless 'reserves the right to preserve itself' (*ius suum conservare*). It follows that 'if the king converts his just power into tyranny' in such a way that his rule becomes 'manifestly pernicious to the entire commonwealth', then it must be lawful 'for the community to make use of its natural power to defend itself' (I, p. 190). The same conclusions are later reiterated in the chapter on whether the people of England are obliged to accept the new oaths of allegiance. Again Suárez cautions that 'the power of deposing a king' can only be wielded 'as a method of self-defence when it becomes vital for the commonwealth to preserve itself' against imminent destruction (I, p. 290). But again he argues that, if the life of the community is genuinely at stake, 'then in virtue of their natural right' (*ex vi iuris naturalis*) it does become lawful for the people to resist. The reason is that – as Hobbes was later to express it in *Leviathan* – the right of self-preservation is one which 'can by no covenant be relinquished' (p. 272). This in turn means that, as Suárez concludes, 'it must always be understood to be exempted from the original contract by which the community transfers its power to its king' (II, p. 290).

Finally, Suárez raises the grave practical problem which arises out of this application of his theory of rights: the problem of where the right to resist and depose a tyrannical prince may be said to be located within a given community. As we have seen, Mair and Almain had failed to express themselves decisively on this point, sometimes appearing to incline to the dramatically populist answer that the right must inhere at all times within the whole body of the people. Suárez, however, leaves no doubt that the right can only be exercised once the most careful deliberations have been made by an appropriate representative assembly 'of the whole commonwealth' (II, p. 290). Only after such an authority has taken 'public and communal advice', has established that the proposed course of action is acceptable to the various cities within the kingdom, and has consulted its leading citizens, can an act of deposition finally and legally be performed (II, p. 290).

THE ABSOLUTIST PERSPECTIVE

Although there are many radical elements in the political outlook of the counter-reformation theorists, and although these undoubtedly contributed to the later development of constitutionalist thought, it still seems a considerable overstatement to think of these writers as the chief originators of a modern 'democratic' view of politics. To interpret their writings in this way is to overlook the fact that, while they were prepared to adopt various features of a radical and secularised theory of *Imperium*, they were no less concerned to counteract what they took to be the excessively populist concept of sovereignty which the followers of Bartolus as well as of Ockham had begun to articulate.

This aspect of their outlook can be clearly observed in their account of the Church and its proper relationship with political society. One of their concerns was of course to repudiate Marsiglio of Padua's heretical suggestion that all coercive power must be secular by definition, and thus that the Church cannot be regarded as a jurisdictional authority at all. Vitoria begins his analysis of the relationship between spiritual and temporal power in his *relectio* on *The Power of the Church* with a sharp attack on 'those who exempt secular rulers from the jurisdiction of the Church to such an extent that almost nothing in the way of ecclesiastical power is left, and even spiritual causes are referred to the civil courts and decided there' (pp. 61–2). His own view, reiterated by all the later counter-reformation theorists, is that since 'secular princes are ignorant of the relationship between spiritual and temporal matters, they cannot be entrusted with the consideration of spiritual causes'. It follows that, at least in this area, the temporal sphere must remain subject to the spiritual, and that 'the Pope must be able to do anything necessary for the conservation and administration of spiritual affairs' (pp. 61–2).

As well as emphasising this orthodox view of the Church as a *regnum*, the counter-reformation theorists introduced one crucial reservation into their argument about the parallel jurisdictions of the Church and the secular commonwealth. Ockham and his disciples had tended to imply that, in denying the Papacy any direct power to intervene in temporal affairs, they were vindicating the right of any secular ruler to regard himself as virtually autonomous within his own sphere. By contrast, the Thomists continued to insist on the almost hierocratic claim that, even though the Pope may not have any direct power to control temporal affairs, he must nevertheless be admitted to have indirect powers of an extremely extensive character.

It is true that not all the Thomists defended this theory with great conviction. Bellarmine, for example, raises certain doubts about it in his treatise on *The Supreme Pontiff*, as well as repudiating very firmly the suggestion – previously advanced by Vitoria – that no clear dividing line can be drawn between direct and indirect power. He emphasises that 'Christ, while living as a man on earth, neither accepted nor wished for any temporal dominion', and he concludes that since the Pope is Christ's vicar on earth, the extent of his power must be limited in a similar way (p. 148). It is clear, however, that Bellarmine's analysis was viewed by th Papacy itself as unduly concessive: although *The Supreme Pontiff* was condemned by the Sorbonne (and later by Bossuet) as excessively ultra-montane, it was treated by Pope Sixtus V as heretical, and was actually placed on the Index of Prohibited Books (Brodrick, 1928, I, pp. 270–6). If we turn, by contrast, to the writings of Vitoria or Suárez, we find the theory of indirect Papal power being presented in a far more forceful and inclusive style. Vitoria insists in his *relectio* on *The Power of the Church* that the authority which the Pope holds 'indirectly' (*mediante*) 'over all princes' as 'a means of attaining the spiritual ends of the Church' is 'a form of temporal power in the highest degree' (pp. 76–7). He even adds that we must not assume that 'this temporal power can only be exercised indirectly', since 'the Pope can also exercise temporal power directly' if a vital spiritual issue is at stake (p. 77). Suárez presents the same doctrine of 'indirect' power in his *Defence of the Catholic and Apostolic Faith* – supporting it so fulsomely that he has sometimes been credited with inventing the argument (e.g. Wilenius, 1963, p. 113). He treats the question of the Pope's right to act *mediante* as 'the very heart and principal issue in the controversy' about James I's oath of allegiance (I, p. 281). He answers that the Pope is in fact licensed 'to exercise coercive power over temporal princes' in two distinct ways (I, p. 281). The first, which 'even Marsiglio of Padua is not so rash as to deny' is that 'the Pope is able to coerce princes and kings, especially heretical ones, with the ecclesiastical penalties of excommunication and even interdict' (I, p. 283). The other is that 'the power of the Pope also extends to the coercing of kings with temporal punishments and even deprivation of their kingdoms' (I, p. 286). This latter conclusion – the climax of his attack on James I – is based on his view of the Pope as a shepherd who has been given the divine injunction 'Feed thy sheep' (I, p. 286). This means, Suárez claims, that 'it falls to the Pope not only to correct wandering sheep and bring them back to the fold, but also to chase away wolves and defend his flock against its enemies' (I, p. 286). This suggests, by analogy, that 'it falls to the Pope to defend the subjects of an heretical prince and to liberate them from any manifest danger' to the safety of their souls (I, p. 286). It follows from this, Suárez concludes, that the Pope must be able to wield his indirect temporal power in such a way as to 'remove a prince, deprive him of his dominion in order to prevent him from harming his subjects, and absolve his subjects from their oaths of allegiance' (I, pp. 286–7).

The same urge to set limits to the excessive radicalism of existing constitutional theories can be observed even more clearly in the Thomist analysis of political society. As we have seen, Bartolus and his pupils, as well as a number of Ockham's followers, had argued that all the powers committed to a ruler at the inauguration of a legitimate polity must originally have been held by the people themselves. They had thus concluded that, in the act of establishing a commonwealth, the citizens never assign their ruler any powers greater than they themselves possess: they merely transfer their existing rights to be exercised on their behalf, and in this way ensure that their ruler remains *minor universis*, his legal status being that of a mere *rector* or *minister* of the community. The Thomists, by contrast, develop a view of the legal status of rulers which deliberately contradicts this analysis at every point.

This intention can be observed most clearly in the account Suárez gives of the community's power to make laws, the theme of the third Book of *The Laws and God the Lawgiver*. He begins by laying it down in Chapter 11 that 'multitudes of men can be thought of in two different ways'. We can think of them as 'gathered together by common consent in a single political body' for 'the attainment of a given political end'. But we can also think of a multitude 'simply as an aggregate of people' who 'do not in any sense constitute a political body, and accordingly stand in no need of a single ruler or head' (1, p. 165). Once this distinction is drawn, Suárez is able to state his first major conclusion: as long as we think of men simply as an aggregate, and not as members of a political society, it must be a mistake 'to speak of the power of making laws as inhering in them at all'. They 'do not formally or properly possess' any such power, 'but only possess, so to speak, the potentiality for it' (1, p. 165; cf. Costello, 1974, pp. 45–6).

In his next chapter Suárez corroborates this account by arguing that, as soon as a community consents to the establishment of a genuine political society, the act of setting up a ruler involves its members in creating at the same time a new kind of power over themselves – the power of *Imperium*, the power of the ruler to make laws and wield the sword of justice. He begins by repeating that this is a power 'which does not directly appear in human nature, since it does not appear at all until men congregate together in a "perfect" society and become politically united' (1, p. 167). He then argues that 'the moment at which this political body is constituted' is also the moment at which this new power 'comes instantly to reside in it by the force of natural reason' (1, p. 167). This account in turn allows Suárez to draw his second major conclusion: 'that a political body of men, by the very process of being brought into existence, not only comes to have power to govern itself, but in consequence comes to have power over its members as well, and hence a special kind of dominion over them' (1, p. 167).

Having reaffirmed this traditional Thomist distinction between natural and political communities, Suárez is finally able to turn his argument against those who had sought to insist on the radically populist claim that the status of a ruler in relation to the society over which he rules can never be that he is *maior universis*, but only that he is *maior singulis* (cf. Costello, 1974, pp. 64–5). At this point Suárez merely reiterates a conclusion which all the counter-reformation theorists had already emphasised. Vitoria had already argued in his *relectio* on *Civil Power* that, since 'many powers are lacking' in a natural community, notably the judicial power 'to kill a man', it follows that after this form of authority has been assigned to a ruler at the inauguration of a commonwealth, 'the ruler must stand above the entire community as well as above each individual member of it' (p. 193). And de Soto had already agreed that 'since a prince is head of the whole body of the commonwealth', he 'must in consequence be greater than all its members considered together' (*maior universis*), as well as 'greater than all its individual citizens' (*maior singulis*) (fo 106a). Suárez alludes to these earlier arguments in Chapter IV of Book III – in the course of drawing 'corollaries' from his previous two chapters – and proceeds to emphasise their underlying assumptions about the power of rulers in relation to the communities over which they rule (1, pp. 168–9). The chief corollary he draws is that 'when a community transfers its power to a prince', he 'is then able to make use of this power as its proper owner', and must in consequence be treated as 'above' and 'greater than' the whole body of the people (1, p. 171).

As well as developing a more radical view about the status of rulers, many of the followers of Bartolus as well as of Ockham had gone on to uphold a correspondingly radical theory about the powers which a community may be said to possess over its ruler after the formation of a commonwealth. They had argued, as we have seen, that the people never alienate their original sovereignty, but only delegate it to be exercised on their own behalf; they had concluded that the community must in consequence be able at all times to bind its ruler to obey the positive laws. Again it is clear that one of the major concerns of the counter-reformation theorists, in developing their own views about community power, was to counteract what they took to be the highly subversive implications of this concept of popular sovereignty.[1]

---

[1] It is true that this further intention has perhaps been somewhat obscured in several recent discussions, perhaps due to the influence of Figgis's classic analysis of the Jesuit theorists in *From Gerson to Grotius*. Figgis maintains that according to the Jesuits the power of a com-

The fullest statement of the Thomist counterattack is again provided by Suárez, who takes up the issue in Book III, Chapter IV of *The Laws and God the Lawgiver*, in the course of stating the corollaries of his argument about the power to make laws (1, p. 171). He begins by acknowledging that according to some authorities 'all those who exercise human legislative powers' merely 'have the status of delegates' (1, p. 171). Amongst the theologians who accept this interpretation he particularly singles out Panormitanus, who speaks at one point in his commentary on the Decretals of the people of Pisa 'deputing' their sovereignty to be exercised on their behalf (1, p. 171). But the most influential proponent of this argument, as Suárez correctly recognises, is Bartolus of Saxoferrato. Citing Bartolus's commentary on the Digest, Suárez points out that according to this analysis it is possible for a community 'to retain essential power itself' and 'merely to delegate this power to its prince', who 'may not in turn sub-delegate the power assigned to him', since he is not its ultimate possessor, but 'only holds it as a delegate' in order to wield it 'according to the will of the community' (1, p. 171).

Having propounded the Bartolist thesis, Suárez responds without hesitation that 'if this analysis is understood to refer to the Emperor, or to kings or other princes, then it constitutes a false doctrine' (1, p. 171). The reason is that in all these cases 'the power of the community is transferred absolutely' to its ruler (*simpliciter translata est*), so that 'it can never be said to be held in a merely delegated form' (1, p. 171). It follows that we can never speak of the community's action 'in transferring the power of the commonwealth to the prince' as an act of delegation which leaves the community itself in ultimate control. On the contrary, we are bound to agree that 'such a transfer is not an act of delegation but rather a kind of alienation' (*non est delegatio sed quasi alienatio*), as a result of which the ruler 'is granted absolute power, to be used by himself or his agents in whatever manner he may think fit' (1, p. 171).

Finally, this entails for Suárez the further corollary that no ruler can ever be said to be bound by the laws of the community over which he rules. This implication is finally spelled out in the concluding chapter of Book III, which is entitled 'Whether a legislator is obliged to obey his own laws' (1, p. 288). Suárez first cites what he describes as 'the common view' of the civil lawyers to the effect that 'since the prince has no superior', it follows that 'there is no one by whom he can be compelled', even though one might wish to say that 'he ought in conscience to follow

munity over its ruler can be expressed by saying that 'he is its delegate' – a highly misleading contention which has been repeated by a number of more recent commentators. See Figgis, 1960, p. 201 and cf. Fichter, 1940, p. 306; Hamilton, 1963, pp. 160, 162.

the laws which he promulgates' (1, p. 289). He then offers to defend the proposition that 'the common view is also the correct one' (1, p. 296). He approvingly mentions Aquinas's dictum to the effect that 'the positive laws can hardly bind the prince', since 'the prince has no superior' and it makes no sense to speak of him 'binding himself' (1, p. 292). And although he agrees with the jurists that the prince has a moral duty to obey whatever laws he makes, he ends by endorsing very strongly their basic contention that, should he fail to do so, there is no action which can be taken, since there is no one by whom the prince can be lawfully coerced or judged (1, p. 295). For Suárez, no less than for Aquinas, there is no escaping the fact that ultimately 'the prince must be *legibus solutus*, free from the coercive power of the positive laws' (1, p. 296).

This counter-attack on the Bartolist theory of *Imperium* was destined to be of considerable ideological as well as intellectual significance. According to Suárez, the act performed by a free people in constituting a ruler must be interpreted – in the manner later discussed by Grotius and especially Hobbes – as an act not merely of transferring but also of abrogating their original sovereignty. At an ideological level, the importance of this claim was that it served to accommodate the natural-law theory of the State, with its emphasis on the original freedom of the people, to the political climate of late sixteenth-century Europe, with its growing emphasis on the absolute powers of the prince. At an intellectual level, the no less important result was the establishment of a vocabulary of concepts and an accompanying pattern of political argument which Grotius, Hobbes, Pufendorf and their successors all adopted and developed in building up the classic version of the natural-law theory of the State in the course of the following century.

Further Reading

(1) *Vitoria*. The standard biography is by Getino, 1930. Mesnard, 1936, includes a useful outline of Vitoria's political thought. The key concepts are valuably discussed in Hamilton, 1963, and there is a good general survey in Fernández-Santamaria, 1977, with a full bibliography. On Vitoria's theory of international law, see Scott, 1934. On his theory of Empire, see Hanke, 1949 and 1974, and for a more detailed account see Baumel, 1936.

(2) *Suárez*. Copleston, 1953, contains an outline of Suárez's general philosophy. For surveys of his political thought, see Mesnard, 1936, Book VI, Ch. 3 and Hamilton, 1963. For a fuller account see Wilenius, 1963. There is also a good deal of relevant material in Costello, 1974 and in Gierke, 1934, the classic study of natural-law theories of the State. Two illuminating articles: Romeyer, 1949, discusses Suárez's view of the state of nature, and Jarlot, 1949, his theory of absolutism.

PART THREE

Calvinism and the theory of revolution

7

The duty to resist

In 1554 John Knox sought an interview with Heinrich Bullinger, Zwingli's successor at Zurich, in order to put some deeply troubling questions to him about the limits of political obligation. One of Knox's questions was 'Whether obedience is to be rendered to a magistrate who enforces idolatry and condemns true religion' (p. 223).[1] Bullinger was clearly much alarmed by the implications of the enquiry, and answered that it was 'very difficult to pronounce' on such a topic, that he would need to have 'an accurate knowledge of the circumstances' before he could offer any advice at all, and that even then 'it would be very foolish' to try to say 'anything specific upon the subject' (p. 225). Bullinger's sense of panic is not surprising, but nor is Knox's sense of urgency. For Knox was asking the question against a background of growing fears about the whole future of the Protestant faith. After years of vacillation and compromise, the Catholic rulers of northern Europe had turned with violence against the reformers, and by the time of Knox's agonised enquiries they were engaged on a policy of reimposing religious unity by force.

The first country to experience this dramatic *volte face* was Germany. Abandoning any further attempts to negotiate with the princes of the Schmalkaldic League, Charles V moved his armies down the Rhine in 1543 and began to make plans for a holy war against the heretics. First he signed a secret anti-Lutheran pact with Francis I, securing his compliance or at least neutrality; next he gained a promise of money and arms from Pope Paul III; and finally he succeeded in detaching the Protestant Duke Maurice of Saxony from his co-religionists by offering him John Frederick of Saxony's lands in return for supporting the Imperial crusade (Elton, 1963, pp. 242–8). These preparations panicked the Schmalkaldic League into mobilising in July 1546, a move which brought them swift and total defeat. Charles won a crushing victory over their combined forces at

[1] For Knox's visit, see Burns, 1955, pp. 90–1, and Ridley, 1968, pp. 178–9. For Knox's questions and Bullinger's answers see *sub* Knox, *Certain Questions* in the bibliography of primary sources.

Mühlberg in April 1547: John Frederick of Saxony was captured, and within a week Philip of Hesse, enticed to the Imperial court by a trick, was also placed under arrest. Charles then summoned a Diet to meet at Augsburg in 1548, in the course of which he promulgated an 'Interim' outlawing the Lutheran Church throughout the Empire. Luther himself had died in 1546, but a number of the other leaders of the German Reformation – including Bucer and Dryander – were immediately forced to flee to England. After nearly thirty years of temporising and conciliation, it seemed that the Lutheran movement might be about to be stamped out (Elton, 1963, pp. 248–50).

Less than five years later, the progress of the Reformation in England was brought to an even more sudden halt. At Henry VIII's death in 1547 the Protestants had effectively come to power: a number of avowed reformers became bishops, including Hooper, Ridley and Ponet, while the Protector Somerset sought advice about ecclesiastical reform from Calvin himself (Elton, 1955, p. 210; Walzer, 1965, p. 62). When Mary succeeded her brother in 1553, however, there was a sudden and devastating change. The first session of Parliament reversed all the Church legislation of the previous reign. Cranmer was arrested on a charge of high treason, and Reginald Pole returned from twenty years' exile to take his place as Archbishop of Canterbury (Schenk, 1950, pp. 128–30). Over two thousand beneficed clergy were dispossessed in 1554, and in the following year Stephen Gardiner, as Lord Chancellor, authorised the start of the persecutions which were later to win his sovereign the title of 'Bloody Mary' amongst generations of Protestants (Loades, 1970, pp. 138–66). Many leading reformers managed to escape to Switzerland, but over three hundred were arrested and burnt, including Hooper, Latimer, Ridley and Cranmer himself (Loades, 1970, p. 232). As in Germany, it seemed that the Catholic Church might be about to obliterate its enemies by force.

By this time a similar crisis had struck the Reformation in Scotland. During the 1540s, as a result of the ascendancy of the English after their victory at Solway Moss, the Scots had nearly achieved a 'full and godly' Reformation with the blessing of their government. Cardinal Beaton, the Catholic Archbishop, had been removed from office and imprisoned in 1543; the Scottish Parliament had voted to permit the circulation of vernacular Bibles in the same year; and a number of Lutheran preachers, including Rough, Wishart and Williams, had begun to attract massive popular followings (Donaldson, 1960, pp. 30–1). After 1547, however, the aggressive behaviour of the Protector Somerset drove Scotland to ally with France, in consequence of which the Catholic Church regained its former ascendancy. In 1547 a French naval force cornered many leading Protestants at St Andrews, laid siege to the city and carried off its more intransigent defenders – including John Knox – to serve as galley slaves (Ridley, 1968, pp. 59–65). In 1548 the young Queen of Scots was betrothed to the Dauphin, after which she left Scotland to be brought up as a good Catholic in France. In 1554 the regent Arran, suspected of Protestant sympathies, was deposed and replaced by the Catholic Queen Mother, Mary of Guise. And in the following year, as in England, the persecutions began, culminating in a trial of the leading Protestant preachers in 1558 (Brown, 1902, pp. 48–9).

During the same period the Protestant communities in France suffered an even more crushing series of reverses. At first the reformers had entertained some hopes of converting the French court to their cause. Francis I had flirted with the new heresies, while his sister Marguerite d'Angoulême had become deeply involved with the Biblical humanists at Meaux, as well as serving as a patron to some of the earliest French Calvinists (Salmon, 1975, pp. 85–6). By the end of the 1530s, however, the king's attitude seems to have hardened. In 1540 he promulgated the Edict of Fontainebleau, calling on his Parlements to seek out and execute all manner of heretics, a policy which was duly pursued with increasing ferocity in the closing years of his reign (Lecler, 1960, II, pp. 24–6). When Henry II succeeded in 1547, the persecutions were further intensified. In the year of his accession he instituted the *Chambre Ardente*, a special court for the trial of heretics, which secured over five hundred convictions within its first three years (Léonard, 1965–7, II, p. 110). And in 1557 he proclaimed in the Edict of Compiègne that the sole punishment for heresy would hereafter be death (Lecler, 1960, II, p. 29). Finally, when Henry II died in 1559 the control of the government fell into the hands of the militantly Catholic Guises, who became regents for the young King, Francis II. They promptly instituted a new wave of persecutions which were so savage that within two years they succeeded in pushing the country into the maelstrom of religious war (Neale, 1943, pp. 46, 57).

THE DEVELOPMENT OF LUTHERAN RADICALISM

Confronted with this sudden and deepening threat to their very existence, how did the Lutheran and Calvinist communities react? If we turn first to consider the Calvinist response, we find that at the outset of the crisis their leaders were almost wholly unprepared to defend their Church with either the pen or the sword. They remained firmly committed to a theory of passive political obedience, a theory very similar to the one originally developed by the Lutherans in the course of the 1520s. This applies particularly to Calvin himself. At the time when the first religious war against the Protestants broke out in Germany in 1546, the only major pronouncement on politics which Calvin had produced was the chapter on Civil Government at the end of his *Institutes of the Christian Religion*, first published ten years before. This barely offered any support to the idea of actively resisting a ruler who might be seeking – in Knox's phrase – to enforce idolatry or condemn true religion. It consisted of an almost completely uncompromising statement of the need to obey, and in no circumstances to resist, all duly constituted authorities.

It is true that Calvin's doctrine of non-resistance is not a wholly unyielding one, and it seems a slight exaggeration to suggest, as Chenevière has done, that his position allows 'no rights at all against the magistrate' (Chenevière, 1937, p. 325). Calvin is at all times a master of equivocation, and while his basic commitment is unquestionably to a theory of non-resistance, he does introduce a number of exceptions into his argument. First he makes two concessions which were commonly allowed even by the most committed exponents of passive obedience. One is that, as he expresses it in his closing paragraph, 'in that obedience which we have shown to be due the authority of rulers, we are always to make this exception, indeed, to observe it as primary, that such obedience is never to lead us away from obedience to him, to whose will the desire of all kings ought to be subject' (p. 1520). The other concession, inserted into every edition of the *Institutes* after 1539, is that if the people 'implore the lord's help', God may sometimes respond by raising up 'open avengers from among his servants', arming them 'with his command to punish the wicked government and deliver his people, oppressed in unjust ways, from miserable calamity' (p. 1517). As well as these fairly orthodox concessions, Calvin also permitted two further and much less usual exceptions to his general rule of obedience. He first canvasses the possibility of popular magistrates resisting in the name of the people. It is sometimes claimed that this dramatic and strategically-placed suggestion was only added in later editions of the *Institutes*,[1] but in fact the whole discussion is already present in the original version of 1536, and reappears unaltered in every subsequent edition of the book. And finally, there is no doubt that, in the definitive Latin edition of the *Institutes* in 1559, Calvin begins to change his mind. This never prompts him to state a clear and unequivocal theory of revolution, but it certainly results in a tendency, as Filmer shrewdly observes in *Patriarcha*, for Calvin to 'look asquint' at the possibility of justifying active resistance to lawful magistrates (p. 54).

[1] See for example Morris, 1953, p. 156; Kingdon, 1955, p. 95.

When due weight has been given to all these exceptions, however, the fact remains that, until the closing years of his life, Calvin's political stance, no less than Luther's in his early works, remained firmly anchored to the Pauline doctrine of absolute non-resistance. It is important in this connection to recall that the chapter on Civil Government in the *Institutes* was first published within two years of the radical social experiments which had been conducted by the Anabaptists and commended in such documents as the *Schleitheim Confession of Faith*. Calvin begins his chapter (p. 1485) by denouncing these 'insane and barbarous men' who 'furiously strive to overturn this divinely established order' of government, and much of his ensuing discussion takes the form of a running battle against the assumptions of the Anabaptists, including their denial of magistracy, their pacifism and their rejection of due processes of law.[1] To counter what he calls the 'outrageous barbarity' of these 'fanatics', Calvin turns first to defend the necessity and godliness of 'the office of the magistrate' (pp. 1488, 1489). He begins by underlining the fact that 'it has not come about by human perversity that the authority over all things on earth is in the hands of kings and other rulers' (p. 1489). He cites St Paul's celebrated formula in the Epistle to the Romans, insisting that all power 'is an ordinance of God, and that there are no powers except those ordained by God', since all princes are 'ministers of God' and are 'wholly God's representatives' (pp. 1489, 1490). This means that Calvin is relatively uninterested in questions about the best form of government. He concedes in Aristotelian vein that 'a system compounded of aristocracy and democracy far excels all others', but he soon reverts to stressing what he takes to be the far more important point that 'although there is a variety of forms' of magistracy, 'there is no difference in this respect, that we must regard all of them as ordained of God' (pp. 1492, 1493).

After analysing the concept of law, which takes up the middle of his chapter, Calvin turns to discuss the implications of his views about the office of the magistrate. The first implication, and 'the first duty of subjects towards their magistrates' is that they ought 'to think most honourably of their office' (p. 1509). The next is that they ought not only to be obedient, but also to avoid any gratuitous political activity, taking care not to 'intrude in public affairs, or pointlessly invade the magistrate's office' (pp. 1510, 1511). But the main implication is that the commands of the magistrate must never be resisted. Calvin is absolutely emphatic on this crucial point. 'Let no man deceive himself here. For since the magistrate cannot be resisted without God being resisted at the same time, even

---

[1] See respectively pp. 1490–1; 1499–1500; 1505–8. It has been suggested that Calvin is actually alluding at various points to the *Schleitheim Confession*; cf. pp. 1487n. and 1492n.

though it seems that an unarmed magistrate can be despised with impunity, still God is armed to avenge mightily this contempt towards Himself' (p. 1511).

Calvin concedes, however, that he has been concentrating up to this point on the case of a magistrate 'who truly is what he is called, that is, a father of his country' (p. 1511). This leaves open the question of whether a similar duty of non-resistance is owed to those who wilfully neglect or deny the duties of their office. But the answer in this case is no less unequivocal than before. 'We are not only subject to the authority of princes who perform their office towards us uprightly and faithfully as they ought, but also to the authority of all who, by whatever means, have got control of affairs, even though they perform not a whit of the princes' office' (p. 1512). Calvin admits that this hard doctrine 'does not so easily settle in men's minds', but this only prompts him to repeat it with greater emphasis (p. 1513). Even 'a very wicked man utterly unworthy of all honour' must be 'held in the same reverence and esteem by his subjects' as 'they would hold the best of kings if he were given to them' (p. 1513). The reason is that 'they who rule unjustly and incompetently' have been raised up by God 'to punish the wickedness of the people' (p. 1512). This means that even tyrants are deliberately ordained by God to fulfil his designs, and are no less 'endowed with that holy majesty with which he has invested lawful power' (p. 1512). This in turn means that even if 'we are cruelly tormented by a savage prince', or 'vexed for piety's sake by one who is impious and sacrilegious', the same hard lesson still applies: we are 'not allowed to resist', but must turn the other cheek, recognising that 'no command has been given' to us except 'to obey and suffer' (pp. 1514, 1516, 1518).

By contrast with the Calvinists, the Lutherans found little difficulty in defending the idea of active resistance to their lawful overlord when they decided to declare war on Charles V in 1546. They had already built up a considerable stock of radical arguments about the justifiability of political violence when they had first contemplated the possibility of resisting the Emperor some sixteen years before. This earlier crisis had arisen out of Charles V's manoeuvrings at the Diet of Speyer in 1529. Despite his preoccupations with Francis I and with the Turkish advance in the course of the 1520s, Charles had never given up his intention, originally announced at the Diet of Worms in 1521, of pushing the Lutherans by force back into the unity of the Catholic Church. In 1529 it seemed that his opportunity had at last arrived. The threat of an invasion by Francis I was neutralised: Charles inflicted a decisive defeat on the French in June,

as a result of which they signed the Peace of Cambrai in the following
month (Brandi, 1939, p. 279). And the threat of an invasion from the east
was suddenly removed: the Turks failed in their assault on Vienna, and
soon began to withdraw their armies back into Hungary (Grimm, 1954,
p. 198). It was against this background of growing military and diplomatic success that Charles convened the Imperial Diet to meet at Speyer,
and demanded that all the concessions previously made to the Lutherans
should now be withdrawn. The Lutherans replied with a formal protest
(hence the name Protestant) which was presented in the name of six
princes and fourteen cities, the moving spirits being John of Saxony,
George of Brandenburg-Ansbach and the young Philip of Hesse, who
emerged at this point as by far the most militant of the Lutheran princes.
But the Catholic majority remained unmoved by the protest, and proceeded to draw up a resolution of the Diet in which they agreed to insist
that the Edict of Worms outlawing the Lutheran heresy should be
imposed forthwith, if necessary by force (Brandi, 1939, pp. 297–303).

It was at this moment that the leaders of the Lutheran Reformation first
squarely confronted the problem of active resistance. They had never
doubted the lawfulness of resisting if they were attacked by another prince,
but the far graver question which now arose was whether it was lawful in
the same way to form a defensive alliance to resist the Emperor himself,
if he were now to attack them as the leader of the Catholic majority. The
initiative at this dangerous moment was taken by Philip of Hesse, who
appears to have debated the issues with a number of sympathetic legal
experts. The outcome was an ingenious restatement of the feudal and
particularist theory of the Imperial constitution – the theory in terms of
which, as we have seen, the Electors had already resisted and removed the
Emperor Wenzel in 1400. As interpreted by the Hessian jurists, this view
of the constitution enabled them to perform two vital ideological tasks: it
legitimated the idea of armed resistance to the Emperor, but it managed at
the same time to uphold the fundamental Lutheran assumption that all
the powers that be are ordained of God. Philip himself outlined the theory
in two letters of December 1529 addressed to his more conservative
co-religionists, the Elector of Saxony and the Margrave of Brandenburg-
Ansbach.[1] He begins his letter to the Margrave by conceding that 'the
powers that be are ordained of God', but he proceeds to modify this
orthodox assumption in two crucial respects. He first of all maintains that
St Paul must have intended to refer to all territorial sovereigns, so that his
doctrine must be taken to apply to all jurisdictional powers within a given

[1] For these letters see Schubert, 1909, esp. pp. 287–9 and cf. Luther, *Letters*, ed. Krodel,
vol. 49, pp. 254–5.

kingdom or Empire. The venerable dispute between Azo and Lothair is thus revived and applied at this point to vindicate the right not merely of the electors, but of all the territorial princes, to regard themselves as powers ordained of God, wielding the *ius gladii* on their own behalf. Philip's other crucial modification of the apostolic doctrine is that all these powers are said to be ordained to perform a particular office, a stipulation which is taken to include the duty of observing a number of legal obligations towards each other, as well as ensuring the well-being and salvation of their own immediate subjects. Once these modifications are introduced, the idea that it may be lawful to resist the Emperor readily follows. It is evident that any wielder of *Imperium* must have the legal right to defend himself against any violations of the treaties he may have concluded with another sovereign power. But it is now asserted that the Emperor and the princes stand in just such a legal relationship with each other, and not in a relationship of ruler and ruled. The conclusion is thus that if the Emperor oversteps the bounds of his office by persecuting the gospel or offering violence to any of the princes, he must be in breach of the obligations imposed on him at his election, and can thus be lawfully opposed.[1]

Nothing at first came of Philip's militant move. One reason was that it still seemed to most of the Lutheran leaders worth waiting upon events, especially after the Emperor agreed to summon a new Diet to meet at Augsburg in 1530, promising to appear in person and give 'a charitable hearing' to the Lutheran case (Brandi, 1939, pp. 303–16). But the main reason was that the leading Lutheran theologians still found themselves completely unable to overcome their scruples about the idea of forcible resistance (Baron, 1937, pp. 416, 423). When the Elector John of Saxony consulted Luther about the letter he had received from Philip of Hesse, he received an unyieldingly conservative response.[2] Luther explicitly repudiates the Landgrave's suggestion that the Emperor is no more than 'a sovereign of equal standing' with the princes, insisting on the contrary that 'the Emperor, of course, is the lord and governmental superior of these sovereigns' (pp. 258, 259). He goes on to reiterate the orthodox and wholly passive conclusion that 'even if it were the Emperor's intention to proceed against the gospel with force', it would still be impossible 'with a good conscience' to 'bring troops into the battlefield' (p. 257). The Elector appealed to Luther again early in 1530 about the same question, but again he found him adamant in his stance. 'It is in no way proper for

---

[1] See Schubert, 1909, pp. 288, 289 and cf. Luther, *Letters*, ed. Krodel, vol. 49, pp. 254–5.
[2] All references, both here and below, to the correspondence between Luther, Brück, Philip of Hesse and John of Saxony are taken from Luther, *Letters*, ed. Krodel, in *Works*, vol. 49.

anyone who wants to be a Christian to stand up against the authority of his government, regardless of whether that government acts rightly or wrongly', for even if 'his Imperial Majesty acts unjustly and operates contrary to his duty and oath, this does not nullify the authority of the Imperial government, nor does it nullify the necessity of obedience' (p. 257).

The situation began to look far more threatening for the Lutherans, however, after the meeting of the Diet in 1530. The Augsburg Confession which Melanchthon had drawn up in the hope of reaching a compromise with the Catholic princes was finally rejected in August, when Charles V ordered a *Refutation* to be read aloud to the assembled Diet, and thereafter refused to engage in any further argument (Reu, 1930, pp. 124–7). By the end of the following month the Catholic majority had agreed to a resolution demanding that all Lutherans should return to the unity of the Church by the following Easter, and that all Lutheran preaching should in the meantime be suspended (Reu, 1930, p. 133). The Diet concluded with an agreement by the Catholic princes to form a league for the defence of the Empire, a move which deliberately posed a direct military threat to the Protestants. It is true that, due to the re-emergence of the Turkish threat in 1531, together with the revival of the dangerous alliance between the Pope and the French in 1532, the impetus of this attack was not in fact sustained. Nevertheless, the situation at the end of 1530 looked extremely alarming, and prompted Philip of Hesse to revive his idea of a defensive alliance, thereby reviving the underlying question of whether the Emperor could ever be lawfully opposed. Knowing Luther's influence on John of Saxony, Philip wrote to Luther in October 1530, outlining his constitutional theory of resistance and trying to persuade him to overcome his doubts about the idea of a Protestant League (pp. 433–4). He also wrote at the same time directly to John of Saxony, as well as to his Chancellor Gregory Brück (*c.* 1483–1547), urging them to accept his scheme for a Protestant alliance, and asking them to accept his underlying claim that it was in fact possible for armed resistance to the Emperor to be justified (p. 430).

This time John of Saxony clearly felt a far more urgent sense of crisis, and decided to consult with Brück and his other jurists about the possibility of endorsing Philip's conclusions. The outcome was that, at the end of October 1530, Brück and his staff presented the Elector with a brief in which the idea of 'violent resistance' to the Emperor was finally and unequivocally justified. While Brück was now prepared to accept the implications of Philip's federal interpretation of the Imperial constitution, however, he made no use of such constitutional arguments himself. He

preferred to rest his case entirely on an adaptation of the private-law doctrine that in certain circumstances the use of violence need not constitute
an injury. As we have seen, there were several points in the civil and canon
law where it was treated as justifiable to repel unjust force with force. The
doctrine which Brück chose to invoke was the canonist claim that it may
sometimes be legitimate to resist an unjust judge. It is of course true that
those canonists – such as Panormitanus – who had strongly defended this
possibility had exclusively been concerned with the question of legal
rather than political violence. But it was only necessary to insist that the
status of the Emperor was in effect that of a judge for Panormitanus's
arguments to apply directly to the case. This is accordingly the move
which Brück proceeds to make. His brief is entitled *Whether it is lawful to
resist a judge who is proceeding unlawfully.* He first gives his answer in
general terms, with copious citations from the canon law – perhaps chosen
with an eye to condemning the Imperialists out of the mouths of impeccably Catholic writers whose authority they would find it hard to repudiate. There are said to be three types of case in which 'it is possible for a
judge to be resisted with violence'. The first is 'where there has been an
appeal'. The second is 'where the judge proceeds outside his lawful jurisdiction' and the resulting injury is 'notorious' and 'irreparable'. The third
is 'where the judge proceeds according to his jurisdiction, but unjustly,
and where the charge is irreparable' (pp. 63–5). The first of these situations happens to be important to Brück's case, but the main weight is laid
on the other two possibilities, both of which are treated in terms of the
lawfulness of defending oneself against unjust force. Both cases are
treated, that is, as situations in which, either by the suspension or the
inherent limitations of the judge's authority, 'he is no longer acting as a
judge in the relevant matter but merely as a private person' (*non est
iudex . . . sed privatus*), so that it becomes lawful to resist him in the same
way that one would resist and defend oneself against any other private
person offering one unjust violence (p. 66). Brück next proceeds to the
facts of the present case. The Emperor is seeking to impose his judgment
in matters of faith. But even if this were within his competence, 'his jurisdiction has been suspended', since 'the princes and the cities are appealing not merely to the Emperor but to a General Council of the Church'
(p. 65). The fact is, however, that 'in matters of faith the Emperor has
absolutely no jurisdiction at all', since 'he is not a judge in such affairs'
(pp. 65–6). These propositions are then taken to license the conclusion
that resistance is unquestionably justified in the present circumstances.
'The injustice of the Emperor' is said to be 'notorious and indeed far
worse than notorious' (p. 66). But it has already been laid down that 'it is

lawful to resist a judge' in such circumstances, even if the case falls within his jurisdiction, provided that 'he is proceeding unjustly, or else there has been an appeal from his judgment' (p. 66). This is said to establish that 'it must *a fortiori* be lawful to resist' when – as in the present case – the judge in question 'is no longer a judge at all', but merely has the status of 'a private citizen' who is inflicting 'notorious injuries' (p. 66).

By the end of 1530, Luther and the other leaders of the German Reformation thus found themselves confronted with two distinct theories alleging the lawfulness of opposing the Emperor – the constitutionalist theory of the Hessians, and the private-law theory of the Saxon jurists. They also found themselves urged on all sides to reconsider their scruples about the idea of forcible resistance. The outcome was that, at the end of October 1530, the leading Lutheran theologians – Melanchthon, Jonas and Spalatin as well as Luther himself – all suddenly capitulated. Although they made no reference to the arguments put to the Elector of Saxony by Philip of Hesse, they now pronounced themselves willing to endorse the theory of resistance outlined by Brück in his most recent brief.

There had been one or two earlier hints that the theologians might be prepared to change direction in this way. Johann Bugenhagen (1485–1558) had tentatively suggested, in a letter which he sent to the Elector of Saxony in September 1529, that if the Emperor were to exceed the bounds of his office and to act 'like a Turk and murderer', then it might be argued that he was 'no longer a lord' or a genuine magistrate (Scheible, 1969, pp. 25–9). Luther had begun to wobble in a similar direction as early as August 1530, when he suggested in a letter to Brück that one might distinguish between genuine acts of the Emperor and the acts of 'tyrants' who may attempt to 'use the name of his Imperial Majesty' (p. 398). It remains essentially correct, however, to say that the first formal acceptance of the idea of forcible resistance by orthodox Lutherans can be precisely dated to the end of October 1530. As soon as John of Saxony received Brück's brief, he asked for a conference between the jurists and the theologians to discuss its arguments. As a result of this debate, which was held at the Palace of Torgau between the 25th and the 28th of October, Luther issued a formal capitulation, written in his own hand and signed by Melanchthon, Jonas and Spalatin as well as by himself.[1] They accept that the question of lawful resistance 'has been settled by these doctors of law' and that 'we certainly are in those situations in which . . . one may

[1] These details are owed to Hortleder, 1645, II, p. 82. He misdates the document, however, to 1531. For the correct details see Luther, *Works*, vol. 47, ed. Sherman, p. 8 note, and for the document signed by Luther and the other theologians see Luther, *Works*, vol. 49, ed. Krodel, pp. 432–3.

resist the governing authority'. They explain away the fact that 'until now we have taught absolutely not to resist the governing authority' by 'the fact that we did not know that the governing authority's law itself grants the right of armed resistance'. So they conclude that since they have 'always diligently taught that this law must be obeyed', it follows that 'in this instance it is necessary to fight back, even if the Emperor himself attacks us'.

It has often been argued that, in spite of this capitulation, we should not treat too seriously the suggestion that Luther and his followers genuinely changed their minds at this point on such a fundamental issue as the theory of non-resistance. Mesnard remarks that he 'does not consider the position taken up by Luther in 1530 as spontaneous', since 'its acceptance by Luther was literally extorted from him' under the pressure of the immediate political crisis (Mesnard, 1936, p. 228). Baron similarly claims that Luther acted 'unwillingly and under compulsion' and emphasises that his response really took the form of a concession that the theologians were not competent to judge the issues, rather than being a positive endorsement of the position the jurists had taken up (Baron, 1937, p. 422).

There is no doubt that the theologians had good reason to feel suspicious of the thesis advanced by Brück and his staff. They must have been greatly embarrassed by the elaborate invocations of canon law, and they appear to have been alarmed by the radical implications of Brück's willingness to make use of private-law arguments. By resting his case on the proposition that a ruler who exceeds the bounds of his office automatically reduces himself to the status of a felonious private citizen, Brück had in effect sought to vindicate the lawfulness of political resistance on the grounds that it is always legitimate for an individual to repel unjust force – that no one is obliged to turn the other cheek. By alluding in this way to the position of the individual under private law, however, he appeared to be implying that it might be lawful for private citizens, and thus for the whole body of the people, to engage in acts of political violence, an implication which the Lutherans were of course anxious to avoid at all costs. The dangers were explicitly spelled out by Martin Bucer (1491–1551) in his *Explication* of St Matthew's Gospel, which he first published in 1527, and republished with suitable additions at the time of the 1530 crisis. While he was concerned to vindicate the lawfulness of resistance, he was no less concerned to repudiate any suggestion that 'even a private individual may lawfully repel with force the force of a prince or magistrate' (*vim vi . . . repellere*). This led him, both in his *Explication* and in his later *Commentaries on the Book of Judges*, to mount a direct attack on the private-law theory of resistance. He insists that 'to say those who are oppressed in our own day by tyranny would be acting lawfully if they repelled it with force themselves' (*si vi eam a se repellant*) would simply be to introduce a calamitous confusion between 'the office of private individuals' and 'the office of public powers', and in consequence to obscure the crucial fact that 'it is never lawful for private individuals to repel any force with force, but only those who have been granted the sword' by the ordination of God himself.[1]

It still seems misleading, however, to argue that the adoption of a radical political stance by the leaders of the Lutheran reformation at the time of the Torgau conference represented nothing more than a temporary aberration in a moment of crisis. This is to overlook two important contributions to the development of the theory of resistance which were made by a number of leading Lutheran theologians both at the time of the 1530 crisis and throughout the rest of the decade.

The first was that, even after the immediate crisis had passed, the Lutherans not only continued to endorse the private-law theory of resistance, but even began to revise and develop it. This is true in the first place of Luther himself. When Lazarus Spengler wrote to accuse him in February 1531 of 'recanting his former opinion that resistance to the Emperor was wrong', Luther replied by reiterating his acceptance of the private-law argument. He admits that the jurists 'did not satisfy me' when they merely 'alleged the maxim that force might be repelled with force'. But he goes on to stress that they also 'pointed out that it was a positive Imperial law that "in cases of notorious injustice the government might be resisted by force"'. His defence is thus that he was merely accepting what 'the law commands' when he accepted that, 'if the Emperor *had* thus limited himself', then it must of course be legitimate to 'resist him by force' (Smith, 1911, p. 217). Shortly after this, moreover, Luther published his *Warning to his Dear German People*, in which he offered a much less conditional endorsement of the same private-law argument. The tract first appeared in April 1531 and went through five editions within the year.[2] The warning Luther issued was that the Catholics might still be thinking of starting a war. He argues that, if this happens, they cannot be regarded any longer as lawful magistrates. They will be acting with unjust force, since 'their plans are built exclusively on force and their cause relies on the power of the fist' (p. 12). But this means that they are the real rebels, since they are nothing but 'assassins and traitors', refusing to 'submit to government and law', and are thus 'much closer to the name and quality which is termed rebellion' than those whom they accuse of being

---

[1] See Bucer, *Explication*, fo 55a and cf. Bucer, *Commentaries*, p. 488.
[2] For these details see Luther, *Works*, vol. 47, ed. Sherman, pp. 6, 9.

in rebellion against their supposed authority (pp. 16, 20). Once this characterisation is established, the crucial conclusion readily follows. Luther announces that 'if war breaks out', he 'will not reprove' those who decide to resist these 'murderers and bloodthirsty papists'. He will 'accept their action and let it pass as self-defence', since it will not in fact amount to an instance of rebellion against a lawful magistrate, but only an instance of repelling unjust force with force (p. 19). Finally, the same sense that a magistrate who exceeds the bounds of his office automatically reduces himself to the status of a felonious private citizen continued to recur more informally in Luther's *Table Talk* throughout the 1530s. When he was asked in February 1539, for example, whether it would be legitimate to resist the Emperor on behalf of the gospel, he replied by citing the civil-law doctrine that it is always lawful to kill in self-defence. 'The Emperor is head of the body of the political realm', and as such is 'a private man to whom political power is granted for the defence of the realm'. The implication is that if he fails to perform the duties for the sake of which he has been constituted a public person, it is lawful to resist him in the same way that we are permitted to resist any other private individual who offers us unjust violence.[1]

If we turn from Luther to Melanchthon, moreover, we find an even more elaborate presentation of the same arguments in favour of lawful resistance. It is true that in Melanchthon's case this development appears to have taken place more slowly, for as late as 1532, in his *Commentaries on the Epistle of St Paul to the Romans*, we still find him insisting that all magistrates are 'gifts and ordinances of God', and emphasising that St Paul 'offers a simple and straightforward precept to the effect that the magistrate must be obeyed by everyone' (pp. 710, 711). The earliest work in which he reveals a definite change of front is the Latin tract on *The Office of the Prince*, which first appeared in 1539 and was subsequently included in the 1540 and later editions of *The Epitome of Moral Philosophy*, a treatise which Melanchthon had originally published in 1538.[2] This begins by stressing that 'the magistrate is guardian of the first and second tables of the laws', and goes on to ask what should be done if, instead of upholding these laws, he ignores them and chooses instead to persecute the true Church (pp. 87, 105). The answer, as in the civil law, is said to depend on whether the injuries which are thus committed are of an 'atrocious and notorious' character (p. 105). 'If the injury is not a notorious one, the jurists rightly insist that such magistrates must be tolerated'.

---

[1] For this discussion see Luther, *Colloquies*, ed. Bindseil, I, pp. 363–4.
[2] For these details, see Melanchthon, *Opera Omnia*, ed. Bretschneider, vol. 16, pp. 19–20 and 85 note. My citations are taken from the *Epitome*.

And even if the injury is atrocious, we must remember that 'no private individual ought ever . . . to resist the *Imperium*, for, as Romans 13 says, anyone who resists the magistrate resists the ordinance of God' (p. 106). This by no means implies, however, that no redress at all is available. Melanchthon turns at this point to consider the position of the individual under private law, pointing out that 'it is conceded as lawful' in the Digest for a private citizen 'even to kill a consul' in certain circumstances, for instance if he discovers him in bed with his daughter or wife (p. 105). This is then treated as strictly parallel with the case of tyrannical rule. If the magistrate 'plagues his subjects with atrocious and notorious injuries, it is lawful for them to defend themselves, in a manner pertaining to the commonwealth, just as they would in a case of private danger' (p. 105).

Melanchthon goes on to repeat and develop this doctrine three years later in the second edition of his *Prolegomena to Cicero's Treatise on Moral Obligation*, a work which he had originally published in 1530.[1] A new section was added to this edition dealing with the office of the magistrate, in which Melanchthon analysed the relationship of the ruler to the Church and the laws. This emphasises even more firmly that the position of the ordinary citizen under private law supplies a justification for resisting a magistrate who exceeds the authority of his office. It is true that the more clearly Melanchthon states this doctrine, the more he tends to uncover the dangerous confusion which had already caused Bucer to reject the private law theory outright. On the one hand, Melanchthon is anxious to insist that 'the dictum that it is permissible to repel force with force' must always 'be understood to refer to powers which have been ordained'. So he continues to insist that 'it is never permissible' for private individuals 'to engage in acts of sedition' on their own behalf against any legally constituted authorities (pp. 573–4). But on the other hand, his reliance on private-law arguments tends to leave the impression that the power of lawful resistance may in fact be a property of each individual citizen, as in the case – which is again cited – of 'a consul taken in adultery, who may justly be killed by the woman's father' (p. 574). While Melanchthon's account remains equivocal over the question of who may lawfully resist, however, there is no similar equivocation about the grounds of lawful resistance. The discussion opens with an extensive account of 'the natural instinct of self-preservation implanted by God' in beasts as well as men, through which 'they are moved to the repulsion of unjust violence' (p. 573). This 'natural knowledge' is said to be 'the testimony which God has given us for discriminating between justice and injustice' (p. 573). This means that 'in any case of manifest injury which is both atrocious and notorious',

[1] For these details see Melanchthon, *Opera Omnia*, ed. Bretschneider, vol. 16, pp. 529–32.

it is clear that 'nature allows force to be repelled with force' (*vim vi repellere natura concedit*) (pp. 573, 574). His conclusion is thus that 'if the magistrate fails in his office or falls into acting criminally', then 'it must be lawful to repel this unjust force' with 'whatever help one is able to call upon, or indeed with one's own hands' (p. 573).

The other reason for insisting that the reaction of the Lutheran theologians to the crisis of 1529–30 amounted to much more than a mere capitulation to Brück's arguments is that a number of leading Lutherans, clearly suspicious of Brück's appeal to canon law, turned instead to develop the other theory of resistance thrown up by the crisis – the constitutional theory which the Hessian jurists had originally put forward in 1529, but which Brück and the Saxon jurists had never taken up.[1] So far from merely capitulating to the private-law argument, this meant that the Lutherans were actually able to supplement it, and in such a way as to avoid the alarming implication that it might be legitimate for individual citizens to resist their ordained magistrates.

The first prominent Lutheran theologian to adopt the constitutional theory of resistance appears to have been Andreas Osiander. He was probably the author of a letter written late in 1529 with the intention of persuading the City of Nuremberg to join the defensive alliance against the Emperor being proposed at that point by Philip of Hesse.[2] He begins by conceding that a major obstacle to forming such a League seems to be constituted by St Paul's account of the duty of obedience in Chapter 13 of his Epistle to the Romans (p. 83). He goes on to circumvent this apparent difficulty, however, by making the same moves which the Hessian jurists had made in presenting their constitutional theory of resistance to the Margrave George of Brandenburg. He first maintains that St Paul can only have intended to refer to such powers as execute their office properly, and not to sinful magistrates (pp. 83–4). He then argues that the powers described by St Paul as 'ordained of God' must be taken to include not just 'superior' rulers but 'inferior' magistrates as well, including territorial princes and a range of other local authorities (p. 84). This in turn provides him with a constitutional theory of lawful resistance. If a superior magistrate should fail to perform the duties for the sake of which he has been ordained – and which he may even have sworn to per-

---

[1] The best analysis of this theory, which holds that 'inferior magistrates' may legitimately resist tyrannical superiors, is contained in Benert, 1967, an excellent account to which I am very greatly indebted.

[2] See *sub* Osiander in the bibliography of primary sources. Baron accepts Osiander's authorship, following the ascription argued by G. Ludewig. See Baron, 1937, p. 421n. This *Brief* and the one following it are both printed in Hortleder and assigned by him to 1531. See Hortleder, 1645, II, pp. 83, 85. I have followed Baron, however, in treating them both as arising out of the debates following the Diet of Speyer in 1529.

form, as the Emperor swears in his election Capitularies – he may lawfully be resisted by his inferior magistrates, who are 'no less ordained of God' to ensure that the paramount need for good and godly government is unswervingly upheld (p. 85).

The main development of this theory, however, was owed to Martin Bucer, who presented it first in his *Explications of the Four Gospels*, and later in his *Commentaries on the Book of Judges*.[1] The relevant portion of the *Explications* first appeared in 1527, without including any reference to the justification of armed resistance. The passage in which Bucer outlines the constitutional theory was first added to the edition of 1530, evidently under the pressure of the immediate political circumstances. The same ideas were then largely repeated in the *Commentaries*, which were first published posthumously in 1554 (Eells, 1931, pp. 65, 69). Bucer begins his account in the *Explications* conventionally enough, stressing that 'in the case of private men' the injunction 'do not resist evil' is absolute, so that 'whatever harm is done to them, they must never offer any resistance' (fo 54a). But he then argues that the situation is altogether different in the case of public authorities. While he continues to accept that 'the powers that be are ordained of God', he takes up a radical position in the traditional legal debate about who should properly be counted as 'powers', and thus as holders of the *ius gladii* or power of the sword. He sides in effect with Azo against Lothair, translates the argument into the vocabulary of Lutheran theology, and so maintains that 'in order for human affairs to be ordered to the best effect', God has in no case 'transferred all power to a single man' within a given kingdom or Empire (fo 54b). He cites the model of the Davidic kingdom, both at this point and in the *Commentaries*, to confirm the fact that God 'always disperses power to many people', and specifically to a set of inferior magistrates (*magistratus inferiores*) as well as to one superior power (*potestas superior*), all of whom are said to be holders of *merum imperium* and thus capable of wielding the *ius gladii* on their own behalf.[2] His conclusion is thus that all these authorities taken together 'are indeed the powers (St Paul did not say power) which have been ordained of God' (fo 54b). Bucer's next move is to lay an equally strong emphasis on the claim that all these powers have been ordained for a particular purpose, and to discharge a specific set of duties. He insists that the prime duty of 'the Christian prince and magistrate' is to 'study

[1] Bucer's influential defence of the claim that 'inferior magistrates' have a duty to resist tyrannical princes has been overlooked in a good deal of modern scholarship, but it was well known to the Protestant radicals of the later sixteenth and seventeenth centuries. John Milton, for example, quotes Bucer's statement of the theory in his *Tenure of Kings and Magistrates*, p. 247.

[2] See Bucer, *Explications*, fos 54a–b and cf. Bucer, *Commentaries*, p. 488.

to live and rule according to the will of God in all things' (fo 54b). So he concludes that all such magistrates are constituted to rule not merely as they themselves may wish, but 'in order to preserve the people of God from evil and to defend their safety and goods' (fo 55a). Having emphasised these two claims, Bucer's conclusion in favour of forcible resistance readily follows. The only difference between his position and that of the Hessian jurists is that, whereas they had mainly been concerned with the Emperor's legal obligations, Bucer is more anxious to insist on his paramount duty to uphold the true (that is, the Lutheran) faith. He first maintains that, if all governmental authorities are basically ordained to ensure that the law of God is upheld, it follows that the obligation of inferior magistrates 'to defer to their superiors in all things' must be limited by a higher obligation 'not to allow anything against God' (fo 54a). He then argues that if the superior powers should happen to 'withdraw from their office' and to fall into ungodly or tyrannical rule, this in turn makes it 'impious' for those inferior powers who have equally 'accepted the godly task of defending the innocent' to 'leave the people to the lusts of such a godless tyrant' (fo 54a). The inferior magistrates in such a situation have no further duty to remain obedient to their superiors. They actually have a positive duty, 'which must not be neglected' to ensure that 'if a superior power falls to extortion or causes any other kind of external injury', they 'must attempt to remove him by force of arms' (fo 54b).

THE LUTHERAN INFLUENCE ON CALVINISM

It has often been argued that, in responding to the crisis of Protestantism in the middle of the sixteenth century, the Calvinists were much better equipped than the Lutherans to develop a radical theory of political resistance. The Calvinists, it tends to be argued, were able to draw on the 'firm basis in radical aspiration and organisation' which arose out of the 'revolutionary potential' of Calvin's own political thought. But the Lutherans found themselves unable to establish a similar 'basis for resistance', since Luther's own influence was always exerted in the direction of insisting that it can never be legitimate to rebel against any lawfully constituted authority.[1] We have now seen, however, that it was Calvin, not Luther, who faced the crisis armed with little more than a theory of passive obedience; and that it was Luther, not Calvin, who first introduced the concept of active resistance into the political theory of the 'magisterial' Reformation. We next need to note that, in so far as the

[1] For these claims see respectively Walzer, 1966, pp. x, 64 (and cf. p. 188); Allen, 1957, p. 29; Hudson, 1942, p. 185.

Calvinists succeeded in developing a theory of revolution in the course of the 1550s, this was not because they exhibited a more creative response to the crisis than the Lutherans, as has often been implied; it was rather because they took over and reiterated the arguments in favour of forcible resistance which the Lutherans had already developed in the 1530s, and had subsequently revived in order to legitimate the war against the Emperor fought by the Schmalkaldic League after 1546.

The main argument in favour of forcible resistance which the Lutherans chose to revive in the middle years of the century was the constitutional theory allowing for opposition by 'inferior magistrates'. Bucer's *Explications of the Four Gospels* was reissued in 1553, while his *Commentaries on the Book of Judges*, in which he espoused the same theory, was first published in 1554. But the most important restatement of the constitutional theory was presented in a *Confession* which the pastors of Magdeburg printed in Latin and German in April 1550. The background to this remarkable tract is supplied by the decision of the city of Magdeburg, one of the first Lutheran communities to join the Schmalkaldic League in 1531, to uphold its militant traditions by refusing to yield to the Imperial forces after the Protestant defeat at Mühlberg in 1547 (Grimm, 1954, pp. 257–8). The city was promptly placed under the Ban of the Empire, and its property was promised to Maurice of Saxony in return for his agreeing to reduce it by force. The siege began in earnest in 1550, at which point the inhabitants began to issue a torrent of pamphlets in justification of their armed resistance. The most important of these was the *Confession*, which was evidently written by Luther's close friend Nicolas von Amsdorf, whose name appears at the end of the text, followed by the names of eight other leading Lutheran ministers. The Latin and German versions were both published, according to their title-pages, on the 13th April, 1550, each bearing the full and resounding title of *The Confession and Apology of the Pastors and other Ministers of the Church at Magdeburg*.

Since it is commonly argued that 'up to the year 1550 the Lutherans and Calvinists alike preached with rather singular consistency a doctrine of non-resistance', it tends correspondingly to be maintained that the *Confession* represents 'the first formal enunciation' by orthodox Protestants of 'a theory of rightful forcible resistance'.[1] But the main argument of the *Confession* is in fact a repetition of the constitutional theory of resistance originally stated by the Hessian jurists in 1529 and restated by Bucer,

[1] For these claims see respectively Allen, 1957, pp. 103, 104; Hudson, 1942, p. 126; cf. also Oakley, 1964, p. 227.

Osiander and other Lutheran writers soon afterwards. The theory itself is outlined with impressive concision on the opening page of the *Confession*, in the form of 'a syllogism containing the argument of the book'. The major premise boldly asserts that 'whenever a superior magistrate persecutes his subjects, then, by the law of nature, by divine law and by the true religion and worship of God, the inferior magistrate ought by God's mandate to resist him'. The minor points out that 'the persecution which is already being imposed on us by our superiors is in fact concerned with the oppression of our true religion, the true worship of God, etc.'. The conclusion is thus that '*ergo* our magistrates ought to resist this oppression by the mandate given by God' (sig. A, 1b).

This is not the only argument in favour of resistance developed in the course of the book, but it would seem from this exordium that the authors of the *Confession* regarded it as the chief foundation of their case.[1] This is borne out by the way in which the rest of the book is organised. Part one is devoted to the 'confession' cited in the title – the confession being one of faith in Luther's doctrines of God, creation, law, justification, the sacraments and the Church. Part two then offers the promised 'apology' for Magdeburg's armed resistance. This includes two arguments derived from the civil law, but the section begins and ends with an emphatic repetition of the constitutional theory of resistance. It is first argued, very much in the spirit of Bucer's account, that 'it would have been absurd' if God had ordained only one magistrate in every kingdom and 'allowed him to determine everything by his own will'. The fact is that 'God has communicated this honour to all legitimate magistrates, and not simply to one grade or to one particular man' (sig. G, 4b). This multiplicity of powers, moreover, is ordained in every case to fulfil a particular set of duties. 'The work of the pious magistrate' is that 'he can and ought, by the ordination and mandate of God, to serve the kingdom of God by setting up and maintaining the true ministry, sacrament and word', and by seeking 'to defend the whole Church against any unjust persecution' (sig. G, 1a). The powers that be are thus said to be ordained 'for the defence and honouring of the good but not of evil things' (sig. G, 4b). It is then claimed that 'these reasons are absolutely decisive in proving the necessity of a defence by inferior magistrates against a superior who is engaged in the persecution of the faith', and that the same reasons are 'sufficient to assure the consciences of all pious and good men' about the lawfulness of armed resistance (sig. H, 1a).

---

[1] This means I demur at the suggestion, in C. G. Shoenberger's otherwise excellent dissertation on the *Confession*, that it 'belongs more securely in the natural-law tradition' of resistance tracts. See Shoenberger, 1972, p. 171.

Once this theory about the duty of inferior magistrates had been reiterated by the Lutherans, the main radical move made by the Calvinists in the face of the mid-century crisis simply consisted of taking over and repeating the same constitutional arguments, with the *Confession* evidently acting as an important direct channel of influence. It is true that we need to exercise a certain caution in speaking about the direct impact of the *Confession*. Some very large claims have been made about its alleged influence on the development of Calvinist radicalism. Kingdon has suggested, for example, that there is 'one thread' running through all the later Calvinist theories of resistance, which can be traced back in each case to 'the example of the City of Magdeburg' (Kingdon, 1955, p. 94 and 1958, pp. 227–8). It is clear, however, that some of the earliest Calvinist revolutionaries took their statements of the constitutional theory of resistance directly from the debates of the 1530s, rather than relying on the *Confession* as an intermediate source. This is evident, for example, in the case of Pierre Viret (1511–71), the leader of the Calvinist community in Lausanne, who was a close friend of Martin Bucer's, and is said to have learnt his ideas about the lawfulness of resistance directly from Bucer's *Explication* of St Matthew's Gospel in 1530 (Linder, 1964, p. 139 n.). Viret's *Remonstrances to the Faithful* first appeared in 1547, three years before the publication of the *Confession*, and already contains the suggestion that inferior magistrates are powers ordained by God with a duty to protect the people even against their supreme rulers should they happen to fall into tyranny or ungodliness (Linder, 1964, p. 138).

It would be equally misleading, however, to dismiss the direct influence to the *Confession*, as Caprariis perhaps tends to do when he implies, in discussing Beza's first statement of the constitutional theory of resistance, that his arguments were simply derived from the position adopted by Calvin in the *Institutes* (Caprariis, 1959, p. 16 n.). This is to overlook the fact that Beza's tract, which was published in 1554 and entitled *The Punishment of Heretics by the Civil Magistrate*, includes a direct reference to 'the remarkable example we have seen in our time of the City of Magdeburg on the Elbe' (p. 133). Beza is only one of several writers, moreover, who refer specifically to the example of Magdeburg at this time. Johann Sleiden (1506–56), the official historian of the Schmalkaldic League, makes much of the fact that 'the ministers of the Church' at Magdeburg 'set forth a writing' in 'the month of April' 1550, in which they declared 'how it is lawful for the inferior magistrate to defend himself against the superior compelling him to forsake the truth' (fo 345b). This paraphrase of the *Confession* appeared in Sleiden's account of *The State of Religion and Commonwealth* in 1555, a work which John Daus translated into English as early as 1560. Four years after this, according to John Knox's account in his *History of the Reformation in Scotland*, when Knox himself was debating with Lethington at the General assembly in Edinburgh, he 'presented unto the Secretary the Apology of Magdeburg; and willed him to read the names of the ministers who had subscribed the defence of the town to be a most just defence' (II, pp. 129–30). Finally, Kingdon has plausibly claimed to see a further allusion to the *Confession* in a letter of February 1566 from Du Hames to Count Louis of Nassau, the younger brother of the Prince of Orange.[1] Du Hames outlines the crisis in the Netherlands, which had suddenly become acute in the previous October, when Philip II had demanded the enforcement of the new Tridentine decrees against heresy, and had thus succeeded in alienating the local nobility. Du Hames pleads with Louis to 'hasten to assist us with your advice' and asks him to 'send us a certain tract which you have promised us about the causes which allow the inferior magistrates to take up arms when a superior is acting neglectfully or tyrannically' (p. 37).

The important point, however, is not of course the alleged influence of one particular tract, but rather the fact that the basic argument in favour of resistance advanced by the Calvinists at this time was largely a repetition of the Lutheran constitutional theory we have already analysed. It is true that a rough distinction needs to be drawn between the arguments used by Calvin's disciples on the continent of Europe and the rather different and more radical arguments used by the revolutionary Calvinists in Scotland and England at the same time. This distinction reflects the fact that the position of the Calvinists in South Germany and Switzerland during this period was a much more equivocal one. The chief aim of their propaganda was the promotion of their religion in France, an ambition which required them to move with some circumspection, since they were still hoping to avoid any violent confrontation with the Catholic government. By contrast, the position of the Calvinists in Scotland was more secure, since they already enjoyed a widespread background of popular support, while the position of the English Calvinists was potentially even stronger, despite the accession of Mary in 1553 and the resulting persecutions. The previous reign had witnessed an official reception of the Calvinist faith, the memory of which served to encourage the radical Calvinists under the Marian reaction to make their revolutionary appeal directly to the largely sympathetic body of the people. The consequence of these differences was that, while the Calvinists on the continent tended to content themselves with reiterating the more cautious theory of resistance by inferior magis-

---

[1] For this letter, see *sub* Du Hames in the bibliography of primary sources, and for Kingdon's discussion see Kingdon, 1958, p. 228.

trates, the Scots and English revolutionaries instead began to exploit the more individualist and radically populist implications of the private-law argument.

This is not to say, however, that the constitutional theory was wholly ignored by the Scots and English Calvinists. It continued to supply John Knox (1505–72) with his fundamental argument in favour of political resistance, even in his most radical tract, *The Appellation*, which he addressed 'to the nobility and estates of Scotland' in 1558 – his appeal being against the sentence of death passed on him by the Catholic bishops after his first preaching expedition in Scotland in 1556.[1] Knox begins his presentation of the case for active resistance by assuring the Scots nobility that they are 'powers of God ordained' for the 'protection and defence' of the people 'against the rage of tyrants' (p. 469). Both the governing assumptions of the constitutional theory are already implicit in this assurance. One is that the nobility no less than the monarch must be counted as 'powers ordained of God' who are 'joined with their kings' as public authorities (pp. 497, 498). The other is that when God 'by his own seal marked' the nobles 'to be magistrates', he was careful to 'assign to the powers their offices' (pp. 481, 482). This means that the monarch and the inferior magistrates have in no case been placed above the people 'to reign as tyrants without respect to their profit and commodity'. They have all been 'ordained for the profit and utility of others', their chief duty being 'to take vengeance upon evil doers, to maintain the well doers, and so to minister and rule in their office' (pp. 482, 483).

It is on the basis of emphasising that 'all lawful powers be God's ministers', and that 'there is no honour without a charge annexed' that Knox proceeds to call on the nobles as inferior magistrates to mount a Calvinist revolution in Scotland (p. 483). There is thus a good deal of truth in the assertion that his theory of resistance is not strictly speaking a *political* theory at all, since his appeal to the nobility is couched entirely in terms of their alleged religious obligations.[2] First they are told that their chief duty is 'to hear the voice of the eternal your God, and unfeignedly

---

[1] Ridley, 1968, p. 171, claims that Knox's use of the constitutional theory of resistance represents his 'special contribution to theological and political thought', and that his argument was subsequently taken over by the English Calvinists, notably Ponet and Goodman. But the theory which Ridley regards as Knox's 'special contribution' had already been developed, as we have seen, by a number of Protestant theologians as well as jurists over a generation before. It is doubtful, moreover, if a case can be made for Knox's direct influence on Ponet and Goodman. Apart from the question of whether Knox was the first of these writers to defend the justifiability of resistance (which is doubtful in itself), the theory which Ponet and Goodman present is quite different in character. They mainly rely on private-law arguments about the justifiability of violence, whereas Knox makes no mention of this doctrine at any point in his published works.

[2] For this assertion see Gray, 1939, p. 147 and cf. Janton, 1967, p. 347.

to study to follow his precepts' (p. 495). Next they are reminded that God's 'chief and principal precept' is that you should 'promote to the uttermost of your powers his true religion' and 'defend your brethren and subjects whom he has put under your charge and care' (p. 495). It is then taken to be obvious what they should do in any case where the superior power set to rule over them proves to be 'a man ignorant of God' or 'a persecutor of Christ's members' (p. 495). The answer is that 'you are bound to correct and repress whatsoever you know him to attempt expressly repugnant to God's word, honour and glory' (p. 495). Knox concedes that 'this part of their duty, I fear, do a small number of the nobility of this age rightly consider', since 'the common song of all men is, We must obey our kings, be they good or be they bad, for God has so commanded' (pp. 495–6). But he insists that this is simply to ignore the vital distinction, which he assures us St Paul intended to make in enunciating his doctrine of obedience, between the office and the person of the magistrate. We are of course obliged to obey our rulers as long as they continue to promote true religion and take proper care of their subjects, thereby discharging the office for the sake of which they have been ordained. But we are no longer obliged to obey them at all if they begin to ignore these duties, to act 'against God's glory' and 'cruelly without cause' to 'rage against their brethren' (p. 496). When this happens, it becomes the duty of the nobles as inferior magistrates to uphold the law of God even against their superiors, recognising that in these circumstances God 'has commanded no obedience' to our rulers, 'but rather has approved and greatly rewarded such as have opposed themselves to their ungodly commandments and blind rage' (p. 496).

But the main development of the constitutional theory of resistance came not from the Calvinists in Scotland and England, but rather from Calvin himself and his disciples on the continent. One of the earliest expressions of the theory by a Calvinist is contained in the defence of Calvin's conduct in the Serveto affair which Beza mounted in 1554 in his tract on *The Punishment of Heretics by the Civil Magistrate* (cf. Bainton, 1953b, pp. 207–12). The date is worth stressing, especially in view of the fact that Knox's *Appellation* has often been described as 'the first breakaway by a Calvinist' from Calvin's own doctrine of non-resistance.[1] Knox's book was not published until 1558, four years after Beza's tract, which had already commended 'the outstandingly famous and brave' people of Magdeburg, and argued that 'if princes abuse their office', and if in these circumstances 'the inferior magistrates' fail 'to ensure that pure religion is maintained', then they are failing in the principal duty for the

[1] For this claim see for example Morris, 1953, p. 155; Ridley, 1968, p. 171.

sake of which they have been ordained, and are thus 'disarming the Church of an extremely useful and necessary defence' (pp. 6, 133).

Beza may in turn have had an influence on Peter Martyr (1500–62), who enjoyed extensive contacts with Calvin and his followers in Geneva after he was forced to leave England at the accession of Mary in 1553 (Anderson, 1975, pp. 165–85). Martyr defends a version of the constitutional theory of resistance both in his *Commentaries upon the Epistle of St Paul to the Romans*, and in *A Commentary upon the Book of Judges*, which he completed in 1558 and 1561 respectively (Anderson, 1975, pp. 546–7). It is true that Martyr's theory is more generalised than the one stated, for example, by his friend Martin Bucer, since it includes no explicit reference to the civil law concepts of *merum imperium* and the power of the sword. Martyr's analysis is also far from coherent, since his later *Commentary upon the Book of Judges* appears to withdraw much of what he had earlier allowed in his commentary on Romans. There is no doubt, however, that in discussing the *locus classicus* of passive obedience theory in his commentary on Romans – the injunction in Chapter 13 that every soul must be 'subject to the higher powers' – Martyr turns sharply away from the orthodox Calvinist position, and proceeds to offer an unusually decisive statement of the constitutional theory of resistance.

Martyr begins of course by endorsing St Paul's assertion that 'the powers that be are ordained of God'. But he wishes to correct what he takes to be two prevalent misunderstandings of this claim. The first is that 'some in vain cavil that they should do no reverence to inferior magistrates'. They 'think it sufficient if they be subject to the higher powers, as to Emperors and to kings'. St Paul's assertion is not limited to the case of superior powers, however, but 'comprehends all manner of power', including the authority of 'such as have the charge of cities, or are appointed governors of provinces' (fo 429a). The other misunderstanding consists of failing to recognise that St Paul's demand for submission to our rulers is limited to the case of lawful powers. Martyr first makes the point that 'the thing itself, that is, the principal function, must be distinguished from the person', thus stressing that our rulers are ordained to discharge a particular office, and have a duty to 'take the rules of their administration out of these offices here described by St Paul' (fos 427b, 430b). He then adds the much stronger claim that although the office, 'forasmuch as it is good, cannot come from anywhere else but from God', this leaves open the possibility that the person holding it, 'forasmuch as he is a man, may abuse a good thing' to such an extent that it may no longer be appropriate to think of him as a power ordained of God (fo 427b). Once St Paul is correctly interpreted on both these points, Martyr concludes, he cannot be taken to be preaching a doctrine of absolute non-resistance. It remains forbidden of course 'for any private man to kill a tyrant' at any time (fo 430a). But it does not follow 'that superior powers cannot be put down by inferior magistrates' (fo 430b). Since all our rulers count as ordained powers, and since all of them are ordained to fulfil a particular office, it follows that even the highest powers can be lawfully 'constrained' by inferior magistrates 'if they transgress the ends and limits of the power which they have received' (fo 430b).[1]

Kingdon has plausibly suggested that Beza, in adopting the same radical political stance in his defence of Calvin in 1554, may in turn have had an influence on Calvin himself (Kingdon, 1955, p. 95). Certainly there are signs that Calvin began to modify his doctrine of passive obedience at the end of the 1550s, and started to move towards an acceptance of the constitutional theory of resistance. One piece of evidence is provided by the letter he wrote to Coligny in 1561 about the failure of the conspiracy of Amboise.[2] But the main evidence comes – albeit in conditional form – in his *Homilies on the first Book of Samuel*, which he appears to have delivered in 1562 and 1563, although they remained unpublished until 1604.[3] The twenty-ninth sermon addresses itself directly to the question of whether a tyrant can ever be lawfully resisted. Calvin begins in orthodox style by conceding that God may sometimes deliberately turn princes into tyrants if he feels that the sins of the people warrant such a punishment (p. 551). But he then makes the almost contradictory claim that our rulers are ordained by God to fulfil a special set of duties, and in particular 'to study the common good of the people' and 'to lead them with justice and equity' (p. 552). If a ruler fails to discharge this office, the people themselves are not of course allowed to take any action, since they still have a duty, as Samuel reminds us, of 'submitting patiently to the yoke'. This does not mean, however, that 'no remedies at all are allowable against such a tyrant', since God may also have ordained other 'magistrates and orders' to whom 'the care of the commonwealth is committed' no less than to the supreme magistrate (p. 552). The remedy which is thus said to be available is that if the supreme magistrate 'should happen to fail in his office', and if we have in fact been granted these inferior magistrates as a part of 'God's gift to us', then 'they are able to constrain the prince in his office and even to coerce him' in the name of upholding good and godly government (p. 552).

---

[1] As Kingdon has observed, Martyr repeated the same radical conclusions in his posthumously published book of *Commonplaces*. See Appendix III, 'The Political Thought of Pietro Martire Vermigli' in Kingdon, 1967, pp. 216–19.
[2] For this letter see Calvin, *Opera Omnia*, ed. Baum *et al.*, vol. 18, esp. p. 426.
[3] For these details see Calvin, *Opera Omnia*, ed. Baum *et al.*, vol. 29, pp. 238–9.

Finally, we may note that once the constitutional theory became accepted by the orthodox Calvinists in the 1560s, it soon began to be used by the Calvinists and their allies in the Netherlands to legitimate the movement of resistance which began in earnest after the Duke of Alba, at the head of nine thousand troops, arrived in August 1567 with the aim of putting down any further opposition to Spanish rule (Elliott, 1968, pp. 166–7). Alba immediately set up his notorious 'Council of Troubles' and proceeded to execute a number of prominent dissidents amongst the nobility, including Egmont and Horn (Elliott, 1968, pp. 167–8). By the start of the following year this prompted William of Orange – at this period in exile in Germany – to mount an invasion of the Netherlands in protest against this new and savage phase of repression by the Spanish government. It is not surprising that in these circumstances a number of pamphlets should have taken up the available version of the constitutional theory of resistance. One of the most militant of these was a tract signed 'Eusebius Montanus' which originally appeared in 1568.[1] This not only recognised that Alba's campaign demanded an equally militant response, but also that William of Orange, as a member of the official Council of State, was eminently qualified to count as an inferior magistrate with authority to resist a superior engaging in acts of idolatry and injustice. The writer thus proclaims that 'the inferior magistrates' in any well-ordered government have 'a charge and ordinance' no less than 'the superior authorities' to uphold the cause of godly rule, and so to 'oppose unjust violence, and offer legitimate and necessary resistance to tyrants' when they act beyond the bounds of their offices.

The same theory was again invoked at the next major crisis in the revolt of the Netherlands, which developed after the appointment of Alexander Farnese as governor in 1578. Farnese was able to exploit the growing divisions between the north and south, and in this way to recover the loyalty of the Walloon nobility who had remained faithful to the Catholic Church (Elliott, 1968, pp. 286–7). This in turn meant that the most radical Calvinist nobles in the north, such as Philippe de Marnix, became increasingly anxious to persuade William of Orange finally to abjure his oath of loyalty to Spain, and to assume the leadership of a full-scale war against the Catholic provinces. So we find de Marnix writing to William in March 1580 to assure him that there can be no doubt about 'the lawfulness of taking up arms against our king' (p. 277).[2] The reason he gives is that 'the principal office of rulers' is 'to uphold piety and justice', and that

[1] My paraphrase of this tract is taken from Mesnard, 1936, p. 367. He mistakenly dates it, however, to 1588. For the correct date, and a full paraphrase, see Doumergue, 1899–1927, vol. 5, p. 526.

[2] For this letter see *sub* Marnix in the bibliography of primary sources.

if they fail in this duty they may lawfully be resisted in the name of justice itself (pp. 279–80). Such acts of resistance are not of course permitted to 'individual persons', since they are 'without any vocation from God' to exercise 'the power of the sword' (p. 280). But where God has ordained any countervailing 'powers' with 'a legitimate vocation' to serve as magistrates, it is not merely lawful for them to act 'against an oppressor of the country', but is actually their duty to oppose him with force (p. 285).

There is one striking difference, however, between the original statement of the constitutional theory of resistance by the Lutherans and these restatements of the same argument by the Calvinists. The Calvinists are in general far more cautious – sometimes to the point of confusion – in their presentation of the radical case. This is especially noticeable in Beza's tract on *The Punishment of Heretics*. Although he begins by vindicating the lawfulness of opposition by inferior magistrates, he ends up by withdrawing the argument altogether.[1] After discussing the office of magistrates, he reverts at the end of the book to the question of 'what is to be done if the civil magistrate abuses his powers?' (p. 189). All he feels able to offer by way of an answer is that 'in times of great iniquity it is our task to bear ourselves with patience' (p. 189). He explicitly repudiates any suggestion that 'it is permitted to us to do more'. Whatever our rulers may do, 'the word of the Apostle stays fixed, that we ought to be subject in conscience to all the higher powers' (pp. 189–90).

The same tendency to equivocation is equally marked in the case of Peter Martyr's *Commentaries*. As we have seen, his *Commentary on Romans* includes a forceful statement of the constitutional theory of resistance. But his *Commentary on Judges*, completed only three years later, reverts to arguing that since 'the present state of things' has been 'instituted by God', it follows that it 'ought not to be altered without him' (fo 149b). This does not mean, of course, that the ungodly commands of a tyrant ought to be obeyed, for it remains true that 'we must obey God rather than men' (fo 264b). But it does appear to mean that passive disobedience rather than active resistance is all that remains open to us, for Martyr now insists that 'if it happens that tyrants or wicked princes obtain the government of things', then 'they must be suffered, as much as is by the word of God allowed' (fo 256a).

Perhaps the clearest evidence of these uncertainties is provided by the reaction of the continental Calvinists to John Knox's growing radicalism in the course of the 1550s. One of the questions about political obligation

---

[1] Kingdon, 1955, p. 93 rightly claims the tract as 'one of the first justifications' of resistance by an orthodox Calvinist, but he fails to mention that in the course of his argument Beza contrives to deny as well as to assert the lawfulness of resistance.

which Knox put to Calvin as well as Bullinger in 1554 was concerned with whether an 'idolatrous sovereign' might be lawfully resisted by the nobility or other inferior magistrates (p. 225). Calvin and Bullinger were both extremely careful to repudiate any such possibility. Calvin wrote to Bullinger to assure him that he had informed 'the Scot' that active resistance is in no circumstances justifiable (Ridley, 1968, p. 179). And Bullinger in his written reply to Knox agreed that all 'godly persons' must ensure that they avoid 'making any rash attempt' to resist, and must in particular ensure that they 'attempt nothing contrary to the laws of God' (p. 226). Five years later Calvin was still upholding the same completely unyielding attitude, as is clearly indicated by his famous altercation with Sir William Cecil about his attitude towards Knox's political works. The argument arose when Calvin, who had been revising his *Commentary on Isaiah* in 1559, sent the new edition with a congratulatory Epistle to Queen Elizabeth. His messenger 'brought him back word that his homage was not kindly received', since he had permitted Knox's inflammatory writings against female rulers to be printed at Geneva. Calvin's response, even at this late stage, was to reply to Cecil protesting that he had sufficiently shown his 'displeasure that such paradoxes should be published', and insisting that he completely dissociated himself from Knox's radical point of view.[1]

After the outbreak of the Schmalkaldic war in 1546, the Lutherans not only revived the constitutional theory of resistance, but also went on to develop the other revolutionary argument they had originally employed in the 1530s – the private-law theory of resistance which Brück and his associates had derived from the civilians and the canonists. They first of all ensured that the existing statements of the theory were again put into circulation. Luther's *Warning* went through numerous reprints both at the outbreak of the war and in several subsequent years. Melanchthon's *Epitome of Moral Philosophy* was reissued in 1546, while his *Prolegomena to Cicero's Treatise on Moral Obligation*, containing his most elaborate statement of the private-law argument, was republished in 1554. The same year saw the reprinting of Melanchthon's *Epitome*, as well as an English translation of Luther's *Warning* with an introduction by Melanchthon in which Luther's appeal to the private-law theory was enthusiastically commended.

As in the case of the constitutional theory, however, the most important restatement of the private-law theory was again contained in the *Confession* of Magdeburg in 1550. The second section of the tract includes two

[1] For this interchange see Knox, *Works*, ed. Laing, vol. 4, pp. 356–7.

statements of the argument, the earlier and more important of which takes as its point of departure the account given by Luther himself in his *Warning* (sig. A, 2a). First it is emphasised that all the powers that be are ordained in order to fulfil a particular office. Then it is claimed that since 'the magistrate is ordained by God in order that he should be an honour to good works and a terror to the bad', it follows that 'if he begins to be a terror to good works and to honour the bad', then 'he cannot any longer be counted as an ordinance of God' (sig. F, 3a). The inference is said to be that any governor who exceeds the bounds of his office in this way automatically ceases to count as a genuine magistrate. The reason given for this conclusion, however, is of a more dramatic character than in the earlier statements of the same theory of resistance. It is no longer suggested that a tyrannous ruler ceases to be a genuine magistrate because, in exceeding his authority, he automatically reduces himself to the status of a felonious private citizen. Instead it is claimed, in a less legalistic and more theological spirit, that if a ruler fails 'in his obligation to God to act according to his offce', and proceeds to inflict 'atrocious and notorious' injuries on his subjects, then the reason he no longer counts as a genuine magistrate is that he automatically ceases to count as a power ordained by God (sig. F, 1b–2a).

It is in the light of this analysis that the lawfulness of forcible resistance is then vindicated. Since any magistrate acting beyond his office automatically ceases to count as a 'power', it follows that 'anyone who resists such actions is not resisting an ordination of God', but merely a wielder of unjust force who may lawfully be repelled (sig. F, 3a). This rather brisk statement of the private-law argument is then elaborated in two further ways. The first is that the authors of the *Confession*, being orthodox Lutherans at heart, exhibit a special anxiety to avoid the implication – which their argument might otherwise seem to carry – that is is ever permissible for individual citizens, or even the whole body of the people, to defend themselves against tyrannical rulers. This difficulty is circumvented by an ingenious combination of the private-law argument with the theory of inferior magistrates. It is first emphasised that 'whoever resists, it is essential that he should resist according to his place and because of his vocation' (sig. F, 3b). It is then pointed out that 'the nearest in vocation to the supreme magistrate must be another magistrate', who may well be 'inferior to the one who is following the injurious course', but will nevertheless be 'ordained of God' as 'an honour to good works and a terror to bad' (sig. F, 3b). This allows the conclusion that it must be for these authorities, and these authorities alone, to resist any other magistrates who may be acting outside the bounds of their offices.

The other way in which the authors of the *Confession* develop the private-law argument is by including a far more extended analysis than Luther or Melanchthon had ever provided of the grades of injury which deserve to count as 'atrocious and notorious', and thus as sufficiently grave to justify resistance. The first 'grade of injury' covers the sort of situation in which 'the magistrate is careless or commits injuries in a rage'. There is said to be no justification at all in such circumstances 'for the inferior magistrates to exercise their office against their superiors with the sword' (sig. F, 2a). The second grade includes all cases 'in which one's life, or one's wife and children, are put at risk by unjust force'. These are accepted as instances of 'atrocious and notorious injury', but we are still told to 'be prepared to suffer such injuries with patience' (sig. F, 2a, 4a–b). The third grade is concerned with any situation 'in which the inferior is compelled into certain sin'. This again is atrocious, but even here it is not suggested that forcible resistance would be justifiable (sig. F, 4b). But there is no doubt about the lawfulness of resistance when we come to the fourth and final grade, where the ruler 'continually, and with deliberation, tries to destroy the good works of everyone' (sig. F, 4b). Luther himself is cited in support of the conclusion that if any ruler 'proceeds to this insanity' – which 'is already happening at the moment amongst our highest magistrates' – then it becomes the clear religious duty of the inferior magistrates to oppose such rulers in the name of upholding godliness and good government (sig. G, 1a–b).

When we turn to the Calvinists, we find once again that they tended to confront the mid-century crisis of Protestantism by taking over and reiterating this earlier Lutheran justification of resistance. As we have seen, however, they were more cautious about invoking this argument, which is seldom found in the writings of the continental leaders of Calvinism. The only important exception appears to be Calvin himself. When he published the final Latin edition of his *Institutes* in 1559, he inserted into the final chapter, for the first time, a single dramatic phrase which appears at least to contain an allusion to the private-law theory of resistance. The wording is (as ever) highly equivocal, and includes no mention of the idea that, if a ruler exceeds his legitimate authority, he automatically reduces himself to the status of a felonious private citizen. But the passage does contain the clear suggestion that a ruler who goes beyond the bounds of his office automatically ceases to count as a genuine magistrate. Calvin points to the example of Daniel, when he 'denies that he has committed any offence against the King when he has not obeyed his impious edict' (p. 1520). The reason this was justified, Calvin is now prepared to claim, is that 'the King had exceeded his limits, and had not merely been a wrongdoer against men, but, in lifting up his horns against God, had himself abrogated his power' (p. 1520).

It is true that Calvin appears to be speaking in this passage of disobedience rather than active resistance. But if we turn from the *Institutes* to the Commentaries on the Bible which he began to issue in the closing years of his life, we find him beginning to develop his allusions to the private-law argument into a theory of lawful opposition to tyrants. The earliest decisive instance occurs in his *Commentary on the Acts of the Apostles*, first published between 1552 and 1554. The crucial passage occurs in his discussion of the injunction that 'It is better to obey God rather than man' (p. 108). He argues that every ruler has a godly office to perform, and adds that 'if a king or prince or magistrate conducts himself in such a way as to diminish the honour and right of God, he becomes nothing more than an ordinary man' (*non nisi homo est*) (p. 109). He says no more at this point, but when he reverts to the theme of political obedience in commenting on Chapter 17, he makes a significant addition to his earlier argument. He now maintains that 'it is in fact possible to claim that we are not violating the authority of the king' in any case where 'our religion compels us to resist (*resistere*) tyrannical edicts which forbid us to give Christ and God the honour and worship which is their due' (p. 398).

A similar development of his earlier allusions to the private-law argument occurs in Calvin's *Readings on the Prophet Daniel*, which he first published in 1561.[1] He again turns, as in the *Institutes* two years earlier, to Daniel's denial of Darius's command, and again argues that Daniel in this case 'committed no sin', since 'in any case where our rulers rise up against God', they automatically 'abdicate their worldly power' (pp. 25–6). This has sometimes been dismissed as nothing more than 'a casual phrase'[2] but Calvin in fact discusses the same passage once more, with a clear willingness to accept its most radical implications, in the *Sermons on the last Eight Chapters of the Book of Daniel* which were posthumously published in French in 1565. Again he insists that Daniel 'committed no sin when he disobeyed the King', and again he gives as his reason the fact that 'when princes claim that God is not to be served and honoured', then 'they are no longer worthy to be counted as princes' (p. 415). This is not only taken to mean that 'we no longer need to attribute to them any further authority'; Calvin now quite clearly adds that 'when they raise themselves up against God', then 'it is necessary that they should in turn be laid low' (*mis en bas*) (p. 415).

[1] For these details see Calvin, *Opera Omnia*, ed. Baum *et al.*, vol. 40, pp. 521–2.
[2] See Allen, 1957, p. 57.

It remains true, however, that such references to the private-law theory of resistance are very rare amongst the continental leaders of Calvinism at this time. The theory is never mentioned in the 1550s by Beza or Martyr, and it is always employed with self-conscious caution by Calvin himself. He never deleted from the *Institutes* any of the contradictory passages in which he continued to uphold the duty of non-resistance, and he always continued to insist, even in the 1560s, that the exceptions he had begun to allow were in no case to be taken to include the possibility of resistance by individual citizens or the body of the people. A good example of the fierce language he continued to employ in making this point is provided by the *Three Sermons on the Story of Melchisedec*, first issued in French in 1560. He still holds that 'it is absolutely forbidden to any private individual to take up arms', since this would be 'to despoil God of his honour and right' (p. 644). And he never ceases to inculcate the harsh lesson that, since 'private individuals must absolutely abstain from all violence', they must also 'have the courage to suffer when it pleases God to cast them down' (p. 644).

When we turn, however, from the continental leaders of Calvinism to the more revolutionary protagonists of the movement in England, we find a very different situation: we find a completely unequivocal statement of the private-law argument being deployed as the main justification for the lawfulness of forcible resistance. The earliest presentation of this case occurs in *A Short Treatise of Politic Power* by John Ponet (1514–56). Ponet had been made Bishop of Winchester when his hated rival, 'the devil Gardiner', was deprived of the see in 1551 (cf. p. 85). Ponet himself was forced out only two years later, after the accession of Mary,[1] and fled into exile in Frankfurt, where his *Treatise* was written and published in the year of his death.[2] The same theory was then developed by Christopher Goodman (*c.* 1520–1603) in *How Superior Powers Ought to be Obeyed of their Subjects*, which was first published at Geneva early in 1558, where Goodman (who had been Lady Margaret Professor of Divinity at Oxford under Edward VI) had gone into exile and become pastor to the English Protestant community.[3] Finally, a few wisps of the same argument can

---

[1] Despite his deprivation, Ponet continued to use his style as a Bishop, for his *Treatise* is signed on the title-page D.I.P.B.R.W., i.e. Dr John Ponet, Bishop of Rochester and Winchester.

[2] The *Treatise* has been republished, in a facsimile of the first edition, at the end of Hudson, 1942. All my citations refer to Hudson's pagination of the book.

[3] See Garrett, 1938, pp. 163–4. It is perhaps worth noting two rather prevalent misconceptions about the intellectual relations between Ponet and Goodman and the sources of their thought. It tends to be argued that 'the basic assumptions of the two men were quite different', and that Ponet's theory bears 'little resemblance to that of Goodman' (see for example Allen, 1957, p. 118 and Walzer, 1966, p. 103 note). But the main aim of both writers was to develop

also be found in the marginal annotations added to the translation of the Old Testament which William Whittingham – with the assistance of Gilby and Goodman – produced at Geneva in 1560.[1]

Ponet and Goodman both begin with the contention – familiar by now amongst radical Protestants – that all our rulers are ordained to fulfil a particular office. This is summarised in the form of the claim that, as Ponet puts it (p. 26) 'princes are ordained to do good, not to do evil', and thus that they are ministers of God, as Goodman agrees, ordained 'to punish the evil and to defend the good' (p. 190). Ponet's argument is sometimes contrasted with Goodman's at this point, on the grounds that Ponet's concern with the duties of princes is 'more profane than holy', whereas Goodman exhibits 'virtually no social connections or sympathies', since he is wholly concerned with the obligation of all rulers to uphold the true faith (Walzer, 1966, pp. 102–3). It is doubtful, however, whether such a distinction can be sustained. Goodman as well as Ponet insists that our rulers are ordained 'for our profit', with a duty 'to obtain peace and quietness', to maintain 'the preservation of the people' and 'to see justice administered to all sorts of men' (pp. 36, 113, 118, 191). And Ponet no less than Goodman accepts that our rulers are 'but executors of God's laws' and that their enactments must never be 'contrary to God's law and the laws of nature' (pp. 22, 43). The same claims are reiterated in the annotations to the Geneva Bible, especially at the point in the Book of Samuel where the children of Israel ask God for a king. The limited character of the monarchy which God assigns to them is strongly emphasised, and we are also told to 'note that kings have this authority by their office', the duties of the office being to uphold good order and godliness (fo 124).

Both Ponet and Goodman next proceed to consider the position of a ruler who, in Ponet's words, fails to discharge the duties of his 'office and authority' and turns instead to the infliction of atrocious and notorious injuries, attempting 'to spoil and destroy the people' instead of protecting them (pp. 100, 112). There is a certain tentativeness at this point – both in Ponet's analysis and in the relevant annotations to the Geneva Bible – in making any direct appeal to the private-law theory of resistance. It is never explicitly stated that a ruler who acts tyrannically automatically reduces

a theory of lawful resistance, and both relied on the same private-law argument in the statement of their case. The other misconception is that John Knox inspired Goodman's and Ponet's theories, as well as the radical annotations to the Geneva Bible (see for example Allen, 1957, pp. 110, 116; Morris, 1953, p. 152; Ridley, 1968, pp. 171, 288). But Ponet and Goodman both rely mainly on the private-law theory of resistance, a theory which, as we have seen, makes no appearance in Knox's political works.

[1] For the production of the Geneva Bible see Berry, 1969, esp. p. 8. For Gilby's role see Danner, 1971. For the political implications of the marginal glosses see Craig, 1938.

himself to the status of a felonious private citizen. There is an apparent allusion to the doctrine, however, in at least one section of the Geneva Bible – in the passage (already cited by Calvin) where Daniel refuses to obey the unlawful commands of Darius (fo 361). And there is a much stronger allusion to the same doctrine in Ponet's central chapter on 'Whether it be lawful to depose an evil governor and kill a tyrant' (p. 98). With citations from both the civil and canon law, Ponet argues that the crimes of a ruler who exceeds the bounds of his office are in fact no different – and ought to be treated no differently – from the same crimes when committed by any ordinary citizen. 'If a prince rob and spoil his subjects, it is theft, and as a theft ought to be punished.' And 'if he kill and murder them contrary or without the laws of his country, it is murder, and as a murderer he ought to be punished' (p. 113).

By the time we come to Goodman's account, this tentativeness is entirely overcome, and the distinction between the office and the person of the magistrate is much more clearly emphasised. The issue is first raised in Chapter IX, where Goodman seeks to meet the objection that St Paul's injunction to obey all constituted authorities entails an unmitigated doctrine of non-resistance (p. 106). His answer takes the form of repeating that our rulers are not *merely* ordained, but are 'ordained to see justice administered to all sorts of men' (p. 118). This means that if they 'transgress God's laws themselves, and command others to do the like, then have they lost that honour and obedience which otherwise their subjects did owe to them, and ought no more to be taken for magistrates' (pp. 118–19). The same doctrine is then repeated in Chapter XIII, which finally vindicates the lawfulness of forcible resistance (p. 175). Here again it is insisted that, if our rulers become tyrants or murderers, 'then are they no more public persons', since they are 'condemning their public authority in using it against the laws', and are thus 'to be taken of all men as private persons', and no longer as genuine magistrates (pp. 187–8).

It is in the light of this private-law doctrine that Ponet and Goodman next proceed to defend the lawfulness of forcible resistance. Ponet also considers a number of other possible justifications, and much of his argument is based simply on citing Biblical precedents. It is the private-law theory which he finally invokes, however, in his chapter on 'Whether it is lawful to depose an evil governor', and it may be significant in this connection that – according to his own account – one of his chief 'comforters' in his exile from England after 1553 was Melanchthon, one of the earliest Protestants to employ the private-law theory of resistance (Robinson, 1846, I, p. 116). The essence of Ponet's argument is that, according to

'the laws of many Christian regions', it is permissible in certain circumstances even for 'private men' to repel the unjust force of malefactors –
'yes, though they were magistrates' (p. 111). Ponet next proceeds to outline the types of situation in which it is justifiable to engage in such acts
of resistance. The examples he gives are mainly taken – though without
acknowledgement – from the discussion in the Digest of the right to kill in
defence of one's person or property. One such situation is said to be 'when
a governor shall suddenly with his sword run upon an innocent'. Another
such situation – already mentioned by Melanchthon – is when the magistrate is 'found in bed with a man's wife, or going about to deflower and
ravish a man's daughter'. And worst of all, as Ponet concludes in his most
minatory tones, is the situation in which the ruler 'goes about to betray
and make away his country to foreigners' (p. 111). The magistrates in all
these cases are taken to be 'abusing their office' and exceeding their
authority so notoriously that one's duty is no longer to submit to their
ungodly and tyrannical acts, but rather to resist them and ensure that
they are 'deposed and removed out of their places and offices' (pp. 104,
105).

Finally, the same conclusions are also spelled out by Goodman, especially
in his chapter examining a number of supposed objections to his position
derived from the Old and New Testaments. He begins, somewhat in the
manner of Magdeburg *Confession*, by considering how grave the injuries
inflicted by a tyrannical ruler need to be before an act of resistance can be
justified. It can never be lawful to resist, even if our magistrates are 'rough
and froward', as long as their wickedness is not 'manifestly against God
and his laws' (p. 118). The situation is quite different, however, 'if without
fear they transgress God's laws', for in these circumstances they are 'no
more to be taken for magistrates', but simply as felonious private citizens
(pp. 118–19). It then becomes lawful to resist them in the same way that
it is justifiable to resist the unjust force of any other private malefactors,
treating them as 'private persons' and ensuring that they are 'punished as
private transgressors' (pp. 119, 188). The whole theory is once again summarised in Chapter X, when Goodman replies to the alleged counter-
examples found in the Old Testament (p. 123). His final word is that when
'kings and rulers are become altogether blasphemers of God, and oppressors and murderers of their subjects', then 'ought they to be accounted
no more for kings or lawful magistrates, but as private men, and to be
examined, accused, condemned and punished by the law of God, where-
unto they are and ought to be subject' (pp. 139–40).

THE DEVELOPMENT OF CALVINIST RADICALISM

While the Calvinists in the 1550s were largely content to adopt and reiterate the radical arguments which the Lutherans had already evolved a
generation earlier, it would be an exaggeration to imply that they added
nothing of their own to the development of revolutionary political ideologies at this time. One distinctive contribution they made was to confront
and resolve a dilemma which had arisen in connection with the distinction
between the office and the person of a magistrate. This distinction had
become central to both the theories of resistance we have examined, since
they both depended on the contention that our rulers are ordained to do
good but not evil, and are thus to be counted as genuine magistrates only
so long as they continue to discharge the duties of their office. The use of
this distinction, however, gave rise to some acute theoretical difficulties,
since it had the effect of placing a question mark against one of the most
fundamental assumptions of orthodox Reformation political thought. It
had always been assumed that all rulers and magistrates, regardless of
whether they discharged the duties of their office, had to be seen as powers
ordained of God. Once it began to be emphasised instead that all such
powers are in fact ordained to fulfil a particular set of duties, the new
question which arose was whether a magistrate who fails to meet these
obligations ought still to be regarded as a genuinely ordained power.

The radical Lutherans had found it impossible to answer this question
in a satisfactory way. There was no question of their abandoning the belief –
central to all Reformation political thought – that our magistrates are
assigned to us, as Calvin repeatedly insists in the *Institutes*, as a direct
outcome of 'divine providence and holy ordinance' (p. 1489). But when
they attempted to combine this belief with the suggestion that tyrants
are not in fact ordained, they were left without any means of explaining
how it comes about that legitimate but tyrannical governors are sometimes
set to rule over us. Nor could they resolve the problem by reverting to
Luther's original Augustinian contention that tyrants are sometimes
ordained by God as a just punishment for our sins. Since they wanted
above all to be able to say that tyrants may be justly opposed, they
could not possibly accept that their tyranny itself might be justly imposed. But if they were to insist that tyranny is always evil, while
agreeing that tyrants are sometimes ordained of God, they would be
committing themselves to the blasphemy of suggesting that God is sometimes the deliberate author of evil and injustice.

The solution to this dilemma adopted by most of the Lutherans was
that they tended – surely deliberately – to remain completely silent about

this aspect of their argument. This happens, for example, both in Luther's *Warning* of 1531 and in the exposition of the private-law argument which Melanchthon added to his *Prolegomena* in 1542. Both contrive to avoid any reference to the key Lutheran belief that all legitimate magistrates, however they may choose to conduct themselves, must always be seen as powers ordained of God. This enabled them to avoid altogether the awkward question of whether 'tyrants by practice' are or are not to be seen as ordained. And this in turn allowed them to avoid having to ask how one might seek to vindicate the justice of God if one answered in orthodox Lutheran style by saying that even tyrants are in fact ordained.

It is true that some of the radical Lutherans showed themselves more willing to explain the phenomenon of 'tyranny by practice', but this merely had the effect of rendering their argument incoherent rather than incomplete. The resulting confusions can be seen, for example, both in Bucer's *Explications* and in Martyr's *Commentaries*. Both begin by accepting that, as Martyr puts it in his *Commentaries on Romans*, 'in kingdoms many things are done . . . unjustly' and 'laws are perverted' so that 'many think that it cannot be that such powers should be of God' (fo 427b). The solution they both propose consists of reverting to the orthodox assumption that even when a magistrate exceeds the bounds of his office he must still be regarded as a power ordained of God, since (as Martyr remarks) God may sometimes decide 'to use wicked and ungodly princes' (fo 428a). They recognise that this appears to make God the author of evil, but they meet this objection by adding the further orthodox claim that unjust rulers are in fact given to us justly, since they are ordained as a punishment for our sins. Bucer takes the example of Saul, whom he treats as an ordained power even though he was a tyrant, and argues that 'God gave the people this king in his anger with them' (fo 54b). Similarly, Martyr concedes in his *Commentary on Judges* that God sometimes 'makes a hypocrite to reign, and in his fury gives kings' because 'he used them to punish the sins of the people' (fo 150a). And in his *Commentaries* he adds that 'it is not enough' to answer that 'God does not do these things, but only permits them', since God often 'executes his just judgment' by means of evil princes, and 'therein commits no offence', because he 'provides tyrants to afflict the people' on account of 'their grievous wicked acts'.[1]

It is obvious, however, that this attempt to resolve the dilemma merely results in the collapse of the theory of resistance which it was the original intention of these writers to articulate. Bucer and Martyr both set out with the aim of vindicating the lawfulness of resistance by inferior magistrates on the grounds that they have a duty to uphold the laws of God and

---

[1] See Martyr, *Commentary on Judges*, fo 256b and Martyr, *Commentaries on Romans*, fo 428a.

to attack all forms of tyranny and ungodliness. But they now suggest that the ungodly behaviour of tyrannical magistrates must nevertheless be seen as justly ordained. It thus appears that any act of resistance even to a wicked ruler must still be seen as an act contrary to the just ordinances of God, and must in consequence be liable after all – as the orthodox Lutherans had always affirmed – to bring damnation upon anyone daring to perform it. By spelling out the implications of their argument, they merely succeeded in destroying it.

It is only when we come to the most radical Calvinists of the 1550s – Ponet, Goodman and to a lesser extent Knox – that we find these problems being squarely faced and satisfactorily resolved. Ponet and Goodman both begin by conceding that if we think of God as ordaining wicked princes, while arguing at the same time that it is lawful to resist them, we are unquestionably treating God as the author of evil and injustice in the world. Ponet makes the point in his chapter on the need for rulers to be subject to law, arguing that it would be 'a great blasphemy' to suppose that God countenances 'the robbery of their subjects' by tyrannical magistrates (p. 43). Goodman repeats the same judgment in his chapter on the apostolic doctrine of obedience. He maintains that when St Paul says 'there is no power but of God', he 'does not here mean any other powers but such as are orderly and lawfully instituted of God'. The alternative would be to say that God must ordain and approve 'all tyranny and oppression', which is not only blasphemous but morally impossible, since God has 'never ordained any laws to approve', but only 'to reprove and punish' all 'tyrants, idolaters' and other oppressors (p. 110).

As Ponet and Goodman both clearly recognise, the only coherent answer to the dilemma thus raised is to abandon the cardinal Augustinian assumption that, even if our rulers fail to discharge the duties of their offices, they must still be regarded as powers ordained of God.[1] This is acknowledged by Ponet early in his central chapter on the lawfulness of resistance, when he states directly that 'a prince or judge is not always ordained by God' (p. 104). For a Protestant to make such a claim was of course revolutionary, and Ponet finds himself totally bereft of any suitable authorities to cite. He is obliged to fall back – with copious apologies – on one of the suggestions put forward by d'Ailly, Gerson and the other leading conciliarists at the Council of Constance: the suggestion that 'an evil prelate and unreformable seems not to be ordained by the will of God' (p. 103). After

---

[1] As we have seen, a hint of this development had already appeared in the Magdeburg *Confession*, and had been taken up, with scant regard for consistency, by Martyr in his *Commentaries*. But it remains true to say that the earliest systematic statement of the position and its implications in Protestant political thought is owed to the Calvinist revolutionaries of the 1550s, and especially to Ponet and Goodman.

citing this conciliarist argument, Ponet anxiously adds that his purpose in rehearsing 'these doings of Popes' is not in any way to endorse their 'usurped authority', but only to point out that while their cause is undoubtedly bad, their arguments are admittedly good, and are thus 'meet to be received and executed' by all 'reasonable creatures' (pp. 102–3). Goodman is – as usual – less troubled about underpinning his arguments with suitable authorities, and simply contents himself with offering, in the course of considering the Pauline doctrine of obedience, a very brisk restatement of the same conclusions. He repeats that when the Apostle says 'there is no power but of God' he only intends to refer to 'such power as is His ordinance and lawful' (p. 111). He does not mean to include 'tyranny and oppression', for these 'are to be called rightly disorders and subversions in commonwealths and not God's ordinance' at all (p. 110). The crucial conclusion is immediately repeated. When our rulers are tyrants or oppressors, 'they are not God's ordinance', so that 'in disobeying and resisting such, we do not resist God's ordinance' (p. 110).

If tyrannous magistrates are not ordained by God, how do they ever come to rule over us? Ponet and Goodman answer by way of analysing the way in which legitimate rulers come to be chosen and installed in office. They appeal in particular to the model of the Davidic kingdom in the Old Testament, arguing that all legitimate governors are instituted as the result of a choice which is originally made by God and is then ratified by the godly people. Ponet mentions the favourite cautionary tale of Saul, which he uses to illustrate the claim that a good king must always be 'chosen according to the will of God' and not merely elected 'according to the minds and desires of the sinful people' (p. 104). The same point is developed more fully by Goodman, as well as being taken up by Knox at the end of his *First Blast of the Trumpet*, first published at almost the same time as Goodman's book on *Superior Powers*. Goodman asserts that 'the first point or caution that God requires of his people is that they choose such a king as the lord appoints, and not as they fantasy' (p. 49). And Knox repeats in more menacing tones that before we can assume that the election of a ruler is 'lawful and acceptable before God', we must remember that 'God cannot approve the doing nor consent of any multitude concerning anything against his word and ordinance' (p. 415).

The suggestion that a truly godly people will always elect the magistrates whom God has chosen for them had already been advanced by Bucer, whose *Explications of the Four Gospels* also included an account of the Davidic kingdom.[1] When we come to the discussion of the same issue by Ponet, Goodman and Knox, however, we encounter two impor-

[1] Baron, 1937, includes a very valuable discussion of this point.

tant new developments. They now pay much more attention to the criteria which God is said to have laid down in order to enable the godly people to recognise and thus to accept whatever ruler He has already selected. The point is only mentioned in passing by Ponet, but it supplies Knox with his major theme in the *First Blast of the Trumpet*. His entire argument is founded on the assertion that 'nothing can be more manifest' than the fact that it is contrary to God's will that 'a woman should be exalted to reign above man' – as in the case of Mary of Guise, then Regent of Scotland, or Mary Tudor, then Queen of England (p. 378). God is said to have pronounced 'the contrary sentence' in his advice to the godly throughout the Old and New Testaments, while the same judgment is said to be corroborated by 'innumerable more testimonies of all sorts of writers' (pp. 378, 389). The same theme is also taken up by Goodman in his chapter on the necessity of obeying God rather than men – a less celebrated but more careful and comprehensive treatment of the same problem of women rulers. This too begins by assuming that the Bible supplies us with 'notes to know whether he be of God or not whom we would choose for our king' (p. 50). As in Knox's account, and earlier in Bucer, one positive criterion is immediately proposed, namely that our ruler must be 'a man that hath the fear of God before his eyes' (p. 51). A number of negative criteria are then added. The first is that 'God's will is that he should be chosen from amongst his brethren, and should be no stranger (p. 51) – an evident allusion to the unsuitability of Philip of Spain, the husband of Mary Tudor, to be received as king of England. The second is that the people must 'avoid that monster in nature and disorder amongst men which is the empire and government of a woman' (p. 52) – a clear allusion to the female (and Catholic) rulers of Scotland and England. And finally, they are told to avoid any ruler with great personal riches, who 'trusts in his own power and preparation of all things for defence of himself' (p. 57).

These accounts of how to choose and elect a ruler are then used to explain how it comes about that evil or tyrannical magistrates are sometimes set in authority over us. As we have seen, Bucer and Martyr had tended to revert at this point to saying that this must still be the result of an ordinance of God, an ordinance which He sometimes chooses to enact as a just punishment for our sins. When we come to Ponet, Goodman and Knox, however, we find a new and quite different answer – and one which achieves complete consistency, in a way that Bucer and Martyr signally failed to achieve, with the rest of their theory of resistance. Their suggestion is that if the people find themselves with an idolatrous or tyrannical ruler, this can only mean that they made a mistake in selecting him. They must have failed to read the signs and follow the criteria which God has provided in order to enable us to recognise a truly godly prince. They must instead have made their own choice, electing a ruler whom God has neither ordained nor wishes to recognise, and in this way guaranteeing themselves an unsuitable and very probably a tyrannical governor – a reflection of their own fallen natures rather than a gift of God. Ponet makes the point by citing, again with some embarrassment, the alleged parallel of a Papal election. If the Pope is 'not one that seeks God's glory', it follows that he cannot have been elected 'according to the will of God', and can only owe his position to the fact that the cardinals 'erred in choosing him' (p. 104). Goodman and Knox both reiterate the same argument, developing it at greater length and applying it more closely to the contemporary political scene. Goodman laments the 'ignorance and unspeakable ingratitude' which has caused the English people to ignore the will of God and 'to choose and procure themselves princes and kings after their own fantasy'. The miserable outcome of their folly is that they now find themselves 'shamefully oppressed' by the ungodly magistrates whom they have allowed to rule over them (pp. 48–9). And Knox's final word, in the Preface to his unwritten *Second Blast of the Trumpet*, is to the same effect.[1] He first claims that, in the electing of magistrates, 'the ordinance which God has established' must always be observed. He next intimates that this has recently been ignored, since the people have 'rashly . . . promoted' and 'ignorantly have chosen' their own magistrates. The result has been the rule of idolaters and tyrants who are 'unworthy of regiment above the people of God', and whom the people must now 'depose and punish', since they 'unadvisedly' agreed to 'nominate, appoint and elect' them out of ungodly ignorance (pp. 539–40).

The other distinctive contribution which the Calvinists made to the theory of revolution in the 1550s was that some of them showed themselves far more permissive than the Lutherans in considering the crucial question of who may lawfully resist an idolatrous or tyrannical government. As we have seen, the Lutherans had always taken great care to insist that kings and other supreme magistrates can only be opposed by other ordained 'powers', and in particular by inferior magistrates. A number of Calvinists now went on to add a further dimension to the theory of resistance by arguing that there are at least two other agencies who may lawfully take up arms against their rulers in suitable circumstances.

One such agency was said to be a special class of popularly elected magistrates, a class described by Calvin in the *Institutes* as 'magistrates of the people, appointed to restrain the wilfulness of kings' (p. 1519).

[1] See *sub* Knox, *John Knox to the Reader*, in the bibliography of primary sources.

This suggestion was not of course an invention of the Calvinists themselves. The idea was an ancient one, and Calvin would have been sure to know of Cicero's discussion of the issue in *The Laws*, in which he had insisted that 'it was not without good reason' that 'ephors were set up' in Sparta to check the power of their kings, and that tribunes were established 'in opposition to the consuls' at Rome (p. 477). There are some signs, moreover, that a similar concept of popular magistracy first entered the political consciousness of the Reformation some time before the Calvinists began to develop it. For example, we already find Melanchthon appealing to the idea in his *Commentaries on Some of the Books of Aristotle's Politics*, which he first published in 1530. It is doubtful whether Bohatec and the other authorities who have pointed to this source are correct in treating it as an important influence on Calvinist radicalism, since the only modern parallels cited by Melanchthon are 'the bishops', 'the Imperial electors' and 'certain princes in France' none of whom he could possibly have believed to be popularly elected magistrates.[1] But there is no doubt that Melanchthon already possessed the vocabulary in terms of which the concept of popular magistracy was soon to be debated by the radical Calvinists. He notes in general that 'certain nations have added guardians to their kings, who are given the power to keep them in order' in addition to the restraints imposed by the laws (p. 440). And he specifically goes on to mention the example of 'the ephors of Sparta, of whom Thucydides writes, who possessed the authority to control their kings' (p. 440).

A second and more plausible source for the Calvinist theory of popular magistracy is provided by Zwingli's account of 'ephoral' authorities (McNeill, 1949, p. 163 note). He developed the idea in a vernacular sermon, *The Pastor*, which he delivered to the clergy attending the Zurich Disputations in January 1523 and published in the following year. It is true that Zwingli is still inclined to speak of the pastors as 'given by God' to defend the people, and that the examples he mentions tend not to be cases of elected officials acting to restrain their rulers, but rather of Old Testament priests protesting on behalf of the people against the iniquities of their kings (pp. 27–33). Nevertheless, he does cite amongst his historical examples a number of magistrates 'with the power to check their rulers' who undoubtedly had elective status, including 'the ephors in Sparta and the tribunes in Rome' (p. 36). And he goes on to make the crucial suggestion that there may be a number of magistrates in existing communities who, while they may not strictly speaking be 'ephors', may still be credited with the capacity to exercise 'ephoral' powers in order to 'uphold the interests of the people' (p. 36). But in spite of these earlier

[1] See Melanchthon, p. 440 and cf. Bohatec, 1937, pp. 82–3.

hints, it would still be true to say that the main development of the idea
of 'ephoral' authority is owed to the Calvinists, and that the most important statement of the concept is supplied by Calvin himself. He presents his
account in a single highly-charged passage in the *Institutes*, a passage which
is placed strategically on the final page of the closing chapter of the book.[1]
It is true that Calvin is not completely consistent in equating 'ephoral'
authorities with popularly elected magistrates, since he adds at the end of
his discussion that they are also 'placed over us as guardians by the ordinance of God'. But it seems misleading to suggest (as Baron and Chenevière have done) that Calvin's analysis exhibits nothing more than an
'almost literal conformity' with Bucer's theory of inferior magistrates, and
that we ought not to think of Calvin's popular magistrates as representatives of the people, since 'their authority comes from God and not from
the populace'.[2] Calvin never alludes to the concept of inferior magistrates
in this (or any other) discussion about political resistance, while the
vocabulary he uses in this key passage makes it clear that, even though he
thinks of 'ephoral' magistrates as ordained of God, he also thinks of them
as elected by and responsible to the people. He opens his discussion by
referring to them not as 'inferior' but as 'popular' magistrates (*populares
magistratus*) and proceeds to emphasise that they are appointed (*constituti*)
– he does not say ordained (*ordinati*) – in order 'to moderate the power
of kings'. And when he turns to defend their right 'to oppose the ferocious
license of kings', the justification he offers is that they would be involving
themselves in 'an act of nefarious perfidy' if they failed to engage in such
opposition, since they would be conniving at 'a fraudulent betrayal of the
liberty of the people'. The impression created by this language is corroborated by the examples Calvin cites of magistrates whom he credits
with the possession of 'ephoral' powers. The three instances he mentions
from the ancient world are the Spartan ephors themselves, 'the tribunes
of the plebs amongst the Romans' and 'the demarchs amongst the
Athenians' – all of whom, as Calvin would have known, were annually
elected officials. The same point applies even more clearly to the suggestions he makes about 'ephoral' authorities in the modern world. He not
only repeats Zwingli's crucial suggestion that 'there may be magistrates
appointed at the present time to moderate the power of kings', but goes
on to suggest that, if this indeed be the case, then perhaps the most likely

[1] Since the precise vocabulary used by Calvin in this paragraph is important, and since it seems
to me to have been somewhat misleadingly translated in both the standard English versions
of the *Institutes*, I have preferred at this point to make my own translation directly from the
Latin edition of 1559. All page-references are thus to Calvin *Institutes* in *Opera Omnia*,
ed. Baum *et al.*, vol. 2, p. 1116.

[2] For these contentions see Baron, 1939, p. 39 and Chenevière, 1937, p. 335.

candidates are 'the three estates of each kingdom when they are gathered together'. Since the convening of such assemblies, as Calvin was well aware, required an election, there seems little doubt that his final suggestion – while phrased with characteristic caution – is that the power to resist tyrannical rulers may well be lawfully vested, in the kingdoms of his own day, in a number of magistrates who are elected by the people, serve as their representatives, and remain responsible to those who have elected them.

It would of course be easy to exaggerate the significance of Calvin's discussion, and it is arguable that this has happened in those commentaries which have sought to emphasise his republican and antimonarchical sympathies.[1] Calvin's whole account, which is extremely brief, is also extremely oblique and conditional in tone. He never explicitly asserts that *there are* any assemblies possessing 'ephoral' powers in any existing kingdoms of Europe. And he never straightforwardly argues that, even if such authorities exist, they do in fact have an unequivocal duty to oppose the rule of tyrannical magistrates. It must also be conceded that, doubtless in consequence of this circumspection, Calvin's discussion appears at first to have exercised singularly little influence. There is a brief allusion to ephors, tribunes and demarchs at the start of Ponet's *Short Treatise*, but even this appears more akin to Melanchthon's than to Calvin's analysis, since it emphasises that all such powers are ordained, without suggesting that they ought also to be treated as representatives of the people (pp. 11–12). This appears, moreover, to be the only occasion on which Calvin's doctrine was immediately taken up, even amongst his most radical disciples in the 1550s. There is no reference to ephors or 'ephoral' magistrates in the political writings of Beza or Martyr from the same period, nor is the idea ever mentioned even in the most revolutionary writings of Knox and Goodman at the end of the decade.

In spite of this lack of immediate impact, there are good reasons for treating Calvin's analysis as an important contribution to the stock of radical political ideas available to his followers at the time of the midcentury crisis of Protestantism. His account serves in the first place to introduce a secular and constitutionalist element into the discussion of political authority which the Lutheran theorists had all deliberately avoided. While the 'inferior magistrates' discussed by Bucer and his followers are still said to derive their authority from being powers ordained of God, the popular magistrates discussed by Calvin are clearly regarded not simply as ordained powers, but also as elected officials with a direct

---

[1] See for example Hudson, 1946, McNeill, 1949, and Biéler, 1959, who speaks (p. 65) of Calvin as 'the leader of a subversive political movement'; see Biéler's account, pp. 65–137.

responsibility to those electing them. A further reason for treating the development as one of great importance is that, in consequence of introducing this essentially historical dimension into his political thought, Calvin was eventually able to bequeath to his revolutionary Huguenot followers a crucial means of broadening the basis of their support. The source of this dimension in Calvin's thought appears to have been the training he received in the fashionable techniques of legal humanism as a law student at the University of Bourges, where he was actually taught by Andrea Alciato between 1529 and 1531 (Ganoczy, 1966, pp. 51–2). The outcome of this union between the *mos docendi Gallicus* and Protestant political thought – soon to be brilliantly cemented by François Hotman – was that Calvin in effect encouraged his followers to look for alleged examples of 'ephoral' authorities within the ancient – and, to the humanist legal scholar, the normative – constitution of France, so prompting them to sustain their revolutionary conclusions with arguments drawn from legal and historical as well as purely theological sources. This had the effect of helping to commend their ideology to a far wider spectrum of opinion than they could ever have hoped to reach with purely sectarian arguments. And this in turn proved vital to the development and influence of radical Calvinism throughout the latter half of the sixteenth century.

The other and more dramatic way in which the Calvinists tended to be more permissive than the Lutherans in discussing the question of who may lawfully resist an idolatrous or tyrannical government was that, in some of the most radical Calvinist writings of the 1550s, it finally came to be accepted that in certain circumstances it might be legitimate not merely for magistrates, but even for individual citizens, and thus for the whole body of the people, to engage lawfully in acts of political violence. One way in which this conclusion was reached was by developing the private-law theory of resistance in such a way as to highlight its most individualist and populist implications. It had always been recognised that, in vindicating the lawfulness of repelling unjust force with force, the private-law theory appeared to be granting the authority to oppose 'notorious' tyrants not merely to inferior magistrates, but also to each and every private citizen. While the Lutherans had always taken the greatest care to block off this suggestion, however, it now began to be deliberately emphasised by a number of revolutionary Calvinists.

It is true that this argument was handled with caution even by the most radical writers. Knox makes no appeal to it, and even Ponet and Goodman continue to argue that the most fitting leaders of any resistance movement must be inferior magistrates rather than the ordinary body of citizens. Ponet wants 'all things in every Christian commonwealth' to be 'done decently and according to order and charity', a commitment which makes him very unhappy with the idea 'that any private man may kill', or even that the whole body of the people may choose to resist, unless they are 'commanded or permitted by common authority' (pp. 111–12). And Goodman agrees that, whenever our superiors behave tyrannically, 'all will confess that it chiefly belongs to inferior magistrates to see a redress in such disorders', the reason being that 'it chiefly appertains to their office' to see justice executed (pp. 145, 182).

But in spite of these scruples there is no doubt that Ponet and Goodman both make a decisive break with the assumption – hitherto unquestioned by all the radical Lutherans as well as Calvinists – that a legitimate ruler, however tyrannical his actions, can only be lawfully resisted by another ordained magistrate. Ponet reverts at this point to his earlier reliance on conciliarist arguments. Just as the Pope 'may be deprived by the body of the Church', so 'by the like arguments, reasons and authority may emperors, kings, princes and other governors abusing their office be deposed and removed out of their places and offices' by 'the body of the whole congregation or commonwealth' (pp. 103, 105, 106). Goodman appeals to the same authority, while adding a fuller account of how this leads him to endorse the same populist and revolutionary conclusion. He begins by repeating that all magistrates are ordained specifically to discharge their offices, since 'God has not placed them above others to transgress his laws as they like, but to be subject unto them as well as others over whom they govern' (p. 184). He then declares that 'when the magistrates and other officers cease to do their duty', the people 'are, as it were, without officers, yea, worse than if they had none at all' (p. 185). He thus arrives at his most revolutionary political claim: since the ruler in such circumstances is nothing more than a felonious private citizen, he may be lawfully resisted by any or all of his own subjects, since God at this point 'gives the sword into the people's hand' (p. 185). He concedes that it may 'appear at the first sight a great disorder that the people should take unto them the punishment of transgression' rather than leaving it to their lawfully appointed magistrates (p. 185). But his final word at the end of the chapter consists of a resounding repetition of the same argument. If the upholding of godly rule and the extirpation of heresy are 'not done by the consent and aid of the superiors', then 'it is lawful for the people, yea it is their duty, to do it themselves', thereby ensuring that they 'cut off every rotten member' and impose the law of God 'as well upon their own rulers and magistrates as upon others of their brethren' (pp. 189–90).

There was another and distinct route by which the most radical Calvinists of the 1550s attained the same revolutionary conclusion: by emphasising the concept of the covenant. Luther and Calvin had both stressed the idea of a covenant between God and his people, but in markedly contrasting ways. Luther had focused on the New Testament, speaking of a covenant of Grace which superseded the Old Law and affected anyone who received baptism in the name of Christ. Calvin laid the basis for a quite different doctrine when he treated Christ's promises in the New Testament as a reaffirmation of the Old Law, which he in turn represented as a series of formal agreements originally made necessary by Adam's first disobedience (Niesel, 1956, pp. 92–109). This idea forms a major theme of Book II of the *Institutes*, on the consequences of the Fall, in which the religious development of mankind is measured by a sequence of *foedera*, the first of which was concluded between God and Adam, while the later agreements were ratified by Noah, Abraham and especially Moses, and finally renewed through Christ's sacrifice. Since Calvin believed, moreover, that in each case the essence of the covenant consisted of an agreement to obey the Ten Commandments, he went on to teach that it must be possible at any time for a group of godly men formally to reaffirm their contractual relationship with God. The outcome in practice was the peculiarly Calvinist concept of the covenanting community, the prototype of which was established in 1537, when all the citizens of Geneva were asked to swear an oath binding them to abide by the Ten Commandments.[1]

The idea that every godly individual can become a signatory of a covenant with God makes no appearance in Ponet's *Short Treatise*. But it supplied Goodman with a second argument in favour of popular revolution in his book on *Superior Powers*, and it enabled Knox – in spite of his basic adherence to the Lutheran theory of inferior magistrates – to supplement this essentially anti-populist argument with a violent demand for popular revolution, a demand which he first voiced at the end of his *Appellation* to the nobility, and immediately repeated in his direct appeal to the people in his *Letter Addressed to the Commonalty of Scotland*.

Goodman presents his account of the covenant in Chapter XII of *Superior Powers*, which is concerned with how far the people are 'charged' by God, and with 'what things they have promised' Him (p. 160). God's agreement with Moses is cited, and it is argued that this continues to serve as a model to 'all such as are or would be God's people', since it reveals 'what God requires of them and what they have promised to Him' (pp. 164–5). It shows that every individual citizen, as a 'signer' of the covenant, is charged above all to help promote and maintain the rule of

---

[1] For the oath see McNeill, 1954, p. 142. For a fine account of the political implications of Calvin's covenanting theology, see Wolin, 1961, pp. 168–79.

godliness, and to ensure that his commonwealth is 'ruled by no other laws and ordinances than by such as God has given them' (p. 163). Knox offers a very similar analysis, both in the *Appellation* and in the *Letter to the Commonalty*. The *Appellation* refers to 'the solemn oath and covenant' which God made with Asa, and next to the covenant with Moses which made it 'the duty of every man' to 'declare himself enemy to that which so highly provokes the wrath of God', and in this way to ensure the rule of godliness (pp. 500, 503). It is then argued, just as in Goodman's account, that all Christians of the present day are equally bound by 'the same league and covenant' that God made with 'his people Israel', with the result that they have an overriding duty to 'remove such enormities from amongst them as before God they know to be abominable' (pp. 505, 506).

It is on the basis of their account of these promises that Goodman and Knox finally arrive at their defence of popular revolution. Their argument takes the form of the familiar claim that to promise to do something is to incur an obligation to do it. Each individual citizen is taken to have promised God to uphold his laws. Each is accordingly taken to have a sacred duty to help resist and remove all idolatrous or tyrannical magistrates. Goodman states this conclusion at the start of Chapter XIII, after presenting his analysis of the covenant and before returning to the private-law argument. He begins by repeating that every individual has covenanted 'without all exceptions' to follow the commands of God (p. 181). The chief command God issues is of course to uphold His laws, 'to root out evil' and to repudiate all forms of idolatry and tyranny (p. 180). So it follows that if our magistrates 'wholly despise and betray the justice and laws of God', it becomes the sworn duty of 'every person both high and low', and thus of 'the whole multitude', to whom 'a portion of the sword of justice is committed', to 'maintain and defend these same laws' against their own magistrates, and in this way to resist and repudiate the idolatry and tyranny of their government (pp. 180–1, 182). Finally, the same revolutionary conclusion is reached by Knox at the end of his *Appellation*. He now insists that 'not only the magistrates, but also the people, are bound by that oath which they have made to God' to uphold the rule of godliness and 'revenge to the uttermost of their power' any injuries 'done against His majesty' or laws (p. 506). He thus concludes that the punishment of idolatry and tyranny is in fact a sacred duty laid by God not just upon 'kings and chief rulers', but also upon 'the whole body of the people', a duty which is equally 'required of the whole people, and of every man in his vocation' (pp. 501, 504).

Since the most radical Calvinists of the 1550s conceive of resistance to

idolatry and tyranny as a duty imposed by God upon every individual
citizen, the guise in which they finally appear before their readers, as
Walzer has observed, is that of minatory Old Testament prophets (Walzer,
1965, p. 98). This enables them finally to reverse the most fundamental
assumption of orthodox reformation political thought: they assure the
people not that they will be damned if they resist the powers that be, but
rather that they will be damned if they fail to do so, since this will be
tantamount to breaking what Knox calls the 'league and covenant' which
they have sworn with God himself (p. 505). Ponet promises that if they
continue to submit to 'idolaters and wicked livers, as the papists are', God
will send them 'famine, pestilence, seditions, wars' as a punishment for
this failure to uphold His commands (pp. 176, 178). Goodman reminds
them of the 'horrible punishments' God has 'appointed for the dis-
obedient', and calls on the people to turn aside 'the great wrath of God's
indignation' by removing all idolatrous and tyrannical rulers, thereby
fulfilling their obligations to God (pp. 11, 93). And Knox repeatedly
insists, in the fiercest tones of all, that if the nobles and people continue
to submit to the rule of tyrants and idolaters, they will all be damned
together. 'God will neither excuse nobility nor people' if they continue to
'obey and follow their kings in manifest iniquity', but 'with the same
vengeance' will punish 'the princes, people and nobility, conspiring
together against Him and His holy ordinances' (p. 498). Nor did these
warnings go unheeded, for in December of 1557 the leaders of the Scottish
nobility agreed to sign a solemn league and covenant by which they
constituted themselves 'the congregation of Christ' and bound themselves
to oppose their Catholic overlords, 'the congregation of Satan'. Having
been assured that it was their duty to resist, and that they would be
damned if they failed to do so, they duly reaffirmed their promises to
God, and went on to serve as the leaders of the first successful Calvinist
revolution (Brown, 1902, pp. 48, 57–73).

8

The context of the Huguenot revolution

The theory of popular revolution developed by the radical Calvinists in the 1550s was destined to enter the mainstream of modern constitutionalist thought. If we glance forward more than a century to John Locke's *Two Treatises of Government* – the classic text of radical Calvinist politics – we find the same set of conclusions being defended, and to a remarkable extent by the same set of arguments. When Locke asks in the final paragraphs of the *Second Treatise* 'who shall be judge' of whether a government is discharging the duties of its office, he insists that the authority to give the answer, and to resist any ruler who exceeds his lawful bounds, lies not merely with the inferior magistrates and other representatives of the people, but also with the citizens themselves, since 'the proper umpire in such a case should be the body of the people' (pp. 444–5). And when he defends this conclusion in his closing chapters on Tyranny and the Dissolution of Government, the argument he chiefly invokes is the private-law theory of resistance. His basic assumption is that anyone in authority who 'exceeds the power given to him by the law' automatically 'ceases in that to be a magistrate'. His main conclusion is thus that anyone 'acting without authority' may be lawfully opposed, even though he may be the king, in the same way that 'any other man' may be opposed 'who by force invades the right of another' (pp. 418–19). The reason, he later repeats, is that 'in whatsoever he has no authority, there he is no king, and may be resisted: for wheresoever the authority ceases, the king ceases too, and becomes like other men who have no authority' (p. 442).

Nevertheless, there is still one point at which a wide conceptual gulf continues to separate the theories of Ponet, Goodman and Knox from this classic 'liberal' theory of popular revolution. When Locke defends the lawfulness of resistance, he invariably defends it as 'a right of resisting', and specifically as 'a right to defend themselves' enjoyed by 'the body of the people' in virtue of the nature and ends of political society (p. 442). The point is most clearly brought out in the final chapter, which argues that whenever there is a 'breach of trust' on the part of our rulers, they 'forfeit the power the people had put into their hands for quite contrary ends, and it devolves to the people, who have a right to resume their original liberty, and, by the establishment of a new legislative (such as they shall think fit) provide for their own safety and security, which is the end for which they are in society'.[1]

By contrast, the radical Calvinists of the 1550s have no such concept of political resistance as a right. While they are willing to defend the revolutionary suggestion that it may be lawful for the whole body of the people to limit and depose their governors, they continue to assume that the fundamental reason for the existence of political society must be to uphold the laws of God and the exercise of the true (that is, the Calvinist) faith. They continue in consequence to think of political society as ordained of God, to treat tyranny as a form of heresy, and to construe the lawfulness of resistance as a religious duty – a duty based on a promise to uphold the laws of God – and not as a moral right at all.

To complete this survey of the foundations of modern revolutionary ideology, we accordingly need to consider two further questions. First we need to ask when the concept of a religious duty to resist became transformed amongst Protestant theorists into the modern and strictly political concept of a moral right of resistance. This can be quickly answered. The modern theory was first fully articulated by the Huguenots during the French religious wars in the second half of the sixteenth century.[2] It was then taken over by the Calvinists in the Netherlands, after which it passed into England and came to form an important part of the ideological background to the English revolution of the 1640s. We also need to ask how and why it happened that this theory first came to be developed in the course of the French religious wars. It is usual to invoke the idea of a direct set of links between the theories developed by the radical Calvinists in Scotland and England during the 1550s and the theories adopted by the Huguenots after the massacre of St Bartholomew in 1572.[3] It is of course plausible to assume that the arguments of Ponet, Goodman and Knox may have exerted a direct influence in France during the 1570s. But it is arguable that this way of thinking tends to obscure the vital fact that the position of the Huguenots at the outbreak of the religious wars was pervasively different from that of the Calvinists in Scotland and England

---

[1] For these contentions see pp. 430–1, and cf. pp. 422, 446. For this account of Locke's theory of political rights, and for the idea of Locke as essentially a radical Calvinist political philosopher, see especially Dunn, 1969, pp. 245–61, 262–4.

[2] It is obscure why the French Calvinist should have been labelled Huguenots, but the term was first applied by their contemporary enemies, and has been used ever since. For some etymological speculations see Léonard, 1965–7, II, p. 113 and note.

[3] See for example Hudson, 1942, pp. 196–8; Salmon, 1975, p. 6, etc.

a few years earlier. This led the Huguenots to develop a different political strategy, and eventually prompted them to articulate a different and in some ways a more radical theory of resistance. To understand the origins and development of their ideology, it is thus essential to begin by considering the nature of the situation in which they found themselves at the start of the civil wars in 1562. Once this context is established, it will be possible to examine and seek to explain the evolution and the special characteristics of Huguenot political thought. The present chapter will accordingly be devoted to considering the problems and opportunities confronting the Huguenots, while the next will be concerned with analysing their actual political works, seeking to indicate the ways in which they eventually tried to promote and legitimate the first full-scale revolution within a modern European state.

THE PROSPECT OF TOLERATION

During the early stages of the religious wars, the basic strategy adopted by the Huguenots was that of avoiding as far as possible any direct confrontation with the government of Catherine de Medici. They insisted on upholding the fiction that they were merely opposing the government's enemies, and continued to pin their hopes on the possibility of winning an official measure of religious toleration as a by-product of Catherine's efforts to pacify the various warring elements in the kingdom. This relatively passive strategy was partly forced on the Huguenots by their lack of any very powerful basis of popular support. Their numbers were at no point overwhelmingly large, so that there was never any question of their attempting – in the manner of Ponet, Goodman or Knox – to call on 'the whole body of the commonwealth' to rise up against the rule of anti-Christ.[1] Moreover, such support as they did succeed in winning tended to remain concentrated in the more remote corners of the land. They were effectively prevented from proselytising in Paris, and soon encountered a growing hostility to the new religion throughout the north-eastern areas of France (Kingdon, 1956, p. 55). Even though the trained missionaries sent out by the Geneva company of pastors after 1555 quickly produced a

---

[1] It appears from an account of Huguenot activity sent to Cardinal Farnese in 1558 that the Huguenots may only have amounted to one fiftieth of the total population of France on the eve of the religious wars. Romier, 1913–14, II, p. 250 cites this figure, although he thinks it much too low. It is worth noting, however, that according to the official census of the Huguenots conducted on the orders of Henry IV at the end of the religious wars, at a time when (according to Léonard's analysis) their numbers had reached their peak before the start of their long decline throughout the seventeenth century, the total number of Huguenots was only estimated at slightly over one in twenty of the whole population. For these figures see Léonard, 1948, pp. 153, 157.

large crop of converts in the cities of the central plain, most of the Huguenot strongholds were located in the outlying areas of the south-east – in
Languedoc, Provence and near the borders with Switzerland – rather than
in any of the major power-centres of the north.

While these considerations virtually forced the Huguenots to proceed at
the outset with as much circumspection as possible, it was also rational for
them to hope that they might be able to emerge from the growing factional
conflicts with a respite from persecution and a measure of official toleration
for their faith. The most obvious reason for this optimism was that
Catherine de Medici, the Queen Mother and the power behind the throne
of Charles IX, made it clear throughout the early phases of the civil wars
that she was emphatically in favour of a policy of religious compromise.
It is of course necessary, in attributing this outlook to Catherine and her
government, to make a sharp distinction between the periods before and
after 1572. The summer of 1572 saw the final collapse of Huguenot hopes,
when Catherine suddenly abandoned any further attempts at conciliation
and sanctioned the mass-murder of the Huguenot leadership in the
massacre of St Bartholomew. How far this shattering move was premeditated has been debated ever since, but it seems apparent that Catherine's original intention may only have been to dispose of the chief
Huguenot spokesman, Admiral Coligny (Sutherland, 1973, p. 340). The
traditional story that she acted out of a growing hatred for his influence
over the young king has recently been discounted, but there is no doubt
that she had begun to fear the increasing military as well as political
strength of the Huguenots, especially after they began to threaten her
perpetual efforts to preserve peace abroad as well as to contain the factional struggles at home (cf. Sutherland, 1973, pp. 147, 316). The immediate threat in the summer of 1572 arose out of Coligny's demands for a
campaign in support of the developing – and partly Calvinist – opposition
to the rule of the Spanish in the Netherlands (Sutherland, 1973, pp. 263,
276). This was the point at which Catherine evidently decided that
Coligny would have to be eliminated. But the plot miscarried, the
assassin's bullet wounding but not killing him. Catherine then appears to
have panicked, and in a mood of desperation ordered the murder of the
entire Huguenot leadership (Sutherland, 1973, pp. 338, 341). The outcome, the massacre of St Bartholomew's Eve, involved the slaughter of
some two thousand Huguenots in Paris, and perhaps as many as ten
thousand more throughout the provinces (Héritier, 1963, pp. 327–8; cf.
Erlanger, 1960, pp. 191–3).

But before this *volte face*, and throughout the decade of civil warfare
which preceded it, Catherine had made continual attempts to bring about

an agreed measure of religious toleration for the Huguenots. To explain this conciliatory approach, and thus to explain what made it rational for the Huguenots to pin their hopes on the government, we need to consider the delicate constitutional position in which Catherine had found herself ever since 1560, when her son Francis II had died within eighteen months of succeeding her husband Henry II. The accession of her younger son Charles IX, who was barely ten years old, clearly called for the appointment of a regency. The position was openly coveted by the Guises, the most powerful Catholic family in the land, who had virtually assumed control of the government during the brief reign of the young Francis II. Although Catherine succeeded in forestalling this ambition by accepting the regency herself, she still found her government under strong pressure to abide by the policies which the Guises had initiated, and in particular the increasing persecution of the Huguenots (Romier, 1924, pp. 1–11). It soon became clear, however, that Catherine would jeopardise her own authority if she allowed such a policy to be maintained. One danger, as she found to her cost both in 1560 and again after 1572, was that if the Guises succeeded in imposing their demand for religious uniformity, this would be equivalent to overcoming their rivals amongst the Huguenot nobility, and would thus be equivalent to making themselves completely dominant in the kingdom's affairs (Sutherland, 1973, pp. 7–10). But the main danger arose out of the violent retaliations which the intransigence of the Guises soon began to provoke. The first came in March 1562, after the Duc de Guise's private army massacred a congregation of Huguenots at Vassy. This immediately prompted the Prince de Condé to mobilise on behalf of the Huguenots, and so sparked off the first of the religious wars (Léonard, 1965–7, II, p. 129). The same pattern was repeated in 1567, after the Guises succeeded in curtailing the liberties of the Huguenots in the settlement which brought the first of the civil wars to an end. Again this prompted Condé to mobilise – after an abortive attempt to seize the person of the king – and the fighting then continued almost uninterruptedly, and with the greatest ferocity, throughout the next three years (Romier, 1924, pp. 320–5).

As Catherine quickly perceived, her best hope of retaining power in the midst of these recurrent crises lay in trying to give the Huguenots a measure of religious liberty, hoping in this way both to appease the violence of Condé and to avoid the domination of the Guises (Romier, 1924, pp. 110–26). This accordingly became her policy throughout the 1560s, a fact which does much to explain the cautious, almost royalist tones adopted by most of the Huguenot pamphleteers at this time. She first attempted to get both sides to iron out their differences at the Colloquy of Poissy in September 1561, at which she encouraged the Huguenots to appoint a spokesman, accepted their nomination of Theodore Beza, and insisted that he should be heard on the same terms as his Catholic adversaries (Giesendorf, 1949, pp. 129, 135–6). After the failure of this remarkably conciliatory move, she tried to avert the imminent conflict in January 1562 by promulgating an Edict of Toleration, in which she recognised the system of synods and consistories which the Huguenots had established, and guaranteed them freedom of public worship everywhere except within the cites (Lecler, 1960, II, pp. 69–70). Finally, after the vicious fighting of 1567–70, Catherine made a last effort to promote the same policy, confirming all the provisions of the Edict of 1562 and adding the right of the Huguenots to be given access to all existing schools and Universities (Lecler, 1960, II, pp. 86–7).

A second reason which helps to explain why the Huguenots hoped that they might succeed in winning an official measure of toleration in the 1560s was that, even before the outbreak of the civil wars, a large number of educated Frenchmen had already come to feel that any attempt to impose a policy of religious uniformity by force would amount to a serious political and even a moral mistake.

It has often been argued that even the most sympathetic propagandists in favour of religious liberty at this time treated the policy as nothing more than a *pis aller*. Neale remarks, for example, that 'toleration, as that age saw it, was not homage to the rights of conscience, but the recognition that one of two faiths was not strong enough to suppress the other, or that it would only succeed in doing so at the cost of wrecking the State' (Neale, 1943, p. 53). There is much truth in this claim, but it overlooks the fact that a growing number of humanists – in Europe as a whole, but especially in France – had already come to the conclusion that religious uniformity ought not to be enforced, and had gone on to defend this claim in terms which clearly implied that the rights of conscience ought to be accorded their due.

There were two distinct arguments in favour of what might be called the principled rather than merely *politique* defence of religious liberty. The first arose out of the typically humanist assumption – classically stated by Pico della Mirandola – that there must be a common, universal truth underlying all the major religions of the world (cf. Kristeller, 1956, p. 271). The most famous exposition of this argument by a French humanist was given by Guillaume Postel (1510–81) in his book on *The Concord of the World*. Postel had begun by winning a brilliant reputation as a classical scholar while still in his twenties, and in 1538 had been appointed professor of Greek at what subsequently became the Collège de France (Bouwsma, 1957, pp. 3, 8). He lost this position in 1542 as a result of his involvement in a court intrigue, and it was at this point that he turned to writing *The Concord of the World*, which appeared in 1544 (Bouwsma, 1957, p. 9). The book is in four parts, the first of which offers to prove 'that Christianity is the true religion' while the second goes on to give 'an exposition and refutation of the beliefs of the Mohammedans' (pp. 1, 136). The final section is largely devoted to furnishing practical advice about the conversion of the Mohammedans and Jews. Postel's underlying assumptions, however, are much more eirenic and ecumenical than this outline may tend to suggest. His belief in the truth of Christianity derives from seeing it essentially as a set of demonstrable moral truths, not a set of dogmatic theological claims, while his confidence in the possibility of converting the infidel is based on the linked assumption that these truths will be sure to commend themselves to all rational men as soon as they learn of them.[1] He is thus led to argue that the forcing of individual consciences can never be necessary, and for this reason alone can never be justified. As he emphasises in Part III – the most original and important section of the book – the proper task of the missionary ought rather to be that of pointing out the underlying truths of 'the religion and law held in common throughout the whole world', seeking by means of rational argument to win a widening recognition for these 'common tenets' (*communes canones*) underlying the surface varieties of religious belief (pp. 261, 290).

Postel's arguments were taken up by a number of other French humanists on the eve of the religious wars. The fullest restatement occurs in the tract entitled *Concerning Heretics: whether they are to be Persecuted*, which first appeared in 1554. This was published under the name of Martin Bellius, but was actually the work of Sebastian Castellio (1515–63). Castellio had been born near Lyons, where he received a humanist education and became converted to Protestantism, leaving in 1540 to join Calvin in exile at Strasbourg (Buisson, 1892, I, pp. 21, 102). He was appointed Principal of the College of Geneva after Calvin's return to that city, but resigned in 1544 after a quarrel with his leader, and moved to live in the more congenially humanist atmosphere of Basle, where he became University Professor of Greek in 1553 (Buisson, 1892, I, pp. 140, 237, 260). The disapproval he had evidently come to feel in the early 1540s for Calvin's religious intolerance clearly remained with him, for his book on the persecution of heretics was basically intended as an attack on his former mentor for having acceded to the execution of Miguel Serveto

---

[1] On this point see Bouwsma, 1957, p. 127 and cf. the very full account of Postel's thought given in Mesnard, 1936, esp. pp. 434–51.

(1511–53), a Spanish theologian burnt at Geneva for having questioned the doctrine of the Trinity (Bainton, 1953b, pp. 21, 207–12). (One of the chief aims of Beza's book on *The Punishment of Heretics*, published six months later, was to offer a point-by-point refutation of Castellio's arguments.) The main body of Castellio's text consists of twenty extracts from the writings of famous theologians in defence of religious toleration, but the chief importance of his book derives from the arguments he himself develops in a prefatory Dedication to the Duke of Württemberg. He begins, like Postel, with the typically humanist thesis that the essence of Christianity consists of trying 'to live in this world in a saintly, just and religious manner in the expectation of the coming of the Lord', an assumption which leads him to conclude that all doctrinal disputes are in fact irrelevant to the conduct of a genuinely Christian life (p. 122). He then proceeds to argue that, just as a gold coin is everywhere acceptable as money, 'no matter what the image' it may happen to bear, so there is a gold coin of religion which is everywhere acceptable to all rational men, underpinning all the apparent divergences of their various creeds and sects (p. 130). The implication is that since everyone is agreed on the basic currency of true religious belief, and since this coinage is incapable of being debased by any local differences, there can never be any justification for the forcing of individual consciences.

The same contentions reappear in the massive treatise entitled the *Colloquium of the Seven*, perhaps the most emancipated discussion of religious liberty produced in France in the course of the religious wars (cf. Sabine, 1931). The *Colloquium* was the last work of Jean Bodin (1530–96), the greatest French political philosopher of the age, and appears to have been completed in 1588.[1] The text may never have been intended for publication, and it only circulated in manuscript during Bodin's own lifetime. The *Colloquium* is set in Venice, and opens with the observation that this is 'the only city that offers immunity and freedom' for such discussions to take place (p. 3). The host is a liberal Catholic Venetian, Coronaeus, and the other participants in the six dialogues are evidently intended to represent the whole spectrum of serious religious opinion: we are introduced in turn to a Lutheran (Podamicus), a sceptic (Senamus),[2] an exponent of natural religion (Toralba), a Calvinist (Curtius), a Jew (Barcassius) and a convert to Islam (Fagnola). The idea that all men

---

[1] The date usually given is 1593, but the earliest known manuscript, recently rediscovered in the Bibliothèque Mazarine, bears the date 1588; see Kuntz, 1975, p. xxxvii and note. The *Colloquium* remained unpublished until 1857.

[2] Lecler, 1960, II, p. 181 calls Senamus a syncretist, but in the light of his contribution to the dialogues I tend to agree with the characterisation of 'sceptic' offered by Kuntz, 1975, p. xxxviii.

of genuine religious beliefs will be sure to agree about the fundamental tenets of their faith is the first suggestion put forward when they turn in the fourth dialogue to discuss the foundations of their rival creeds. Fagnola raises the issue when he declares that 'the Jews and Mohammedans hold in common almost everything which pertains to religion', and Toralba soon afterwards begins to develop the idea, winning a considerable measure of agreement for his characteristically humanist claim that 'if true religion is contained in the pure worship of eternal God, I believe the law of nature is sufficient for man's salvation' (pp. 213, 225). The same suggestion is taken up at the end of the last dialogue, in particular by Senamus, at the point where the dangers of religious intolerance are specifically discussed. He calls on the other participants to recognise that they have in fact agreed on the most important point, which is that 'God is the parent of all gods'. This means there is nothing to hinder them all 'from appeasing with common prayers the common Author and Parent of all nature, so that He may lead us all into a knowledge of the true religion' (pp. 465, 466). This in turn means that, as soon as this basis of agreement is properly acknowledged, there will never be any further excuse for religious persecution or intolerance. For if only 'all people could be persuaded' that 'all the prayers of all people which come from a pure heart are pleasing to God', then 'it would be possible to live everywhere in the world in the same harmony as those who live under the Emperor of the Turks or Persians' (p. 467).

As well as reiterating Postel's eirenic beliefs, Bodin and Castellio both go on to mount a far more radical argument in favour of religious liberty. This is based on the assumption not of an underlying unity but rather of an unavoidable uncertainty at the heart of our religious beliefs. This is in fact the main claim put forward by Castellio in the Dedication to his book *Concerning Heretics*. He begins by asking the meaning of heresy, and answers that all he has been able to discover 'after a careful investigation' is 'no more than this, that we regard those as heretics with whom we disagree' (p. 129). He then makes a distinction between two possible forms of religious disagreement. On the one hand, we may argue about questions of conduct. He offers the analogy of discussing the proper method of dealing with 'brigands' who refuse to 'correct their lives'. Castellio concedes that in this type of case the man concerned may be penalised with a full sense of justice, since it is 'engraved and written in the hearts of men' that the life of a brigand is morally wrong and worthy of punishment (pp. 130-1). On the other hand, we may find ourselves disagreeing about questions of religious dogma. We may find, as Christians continually do, that we are arguing about 'baptism, the lord's supper, the invocation of the saints, justification, free will and other obscure questions'. He then claims that 'if these matters were so obvious and evident as that there is but one God, all Christians would agree among themselves on these points as readily as all nations confess that God is one' (p. 132). The fact is, however, that all these issues have at all times formed the subject of violent disputes. It follows from this, he concludes, that all such discussions must in fact 'arise solely from ignorance of the truth' (p. 132).

The very radical, even sceptical conclusion which Castellio defends is thus that all religious persecutions are based in effect on a presumption of certainty about a range of questions over which no certainty can ever be attained. 'To judge of doctrine', as he puts it, 'is not so simple as to judge of conduct.' Given this assumption, his plea for toleration follows naturally. He treats the forcing of a man's conscience as a wicked act of ignorance, since 'he who lightly condemns others shows thereby that he knows nothing precisely' (p. 133). He also regards it as a sin before God, who cannot possibly want us to make a pretence of certainty where none can exist. All we can do, Castellio affirms, is to follow the word of God as best we may, but without compelling anyone else to take exactly the same path, recalling instead the words of St Paul, 'Let not him that eats despise him that eats not' (p. 132).

There is a hint of the same sceptical argument in Bodin's greatest work of political theory, *The Six Books of a Commonweal*, first published in 1576. The hint is dropped at the point where Bodin is discussing the dangers to the security of the commonwealth created by subversive ideologies. He first lays it down that unless a given belief happens to rest 'upon most plain and undoubtful demonstrations' there can never be any hope of ensuring that it 'may not by disputations and force of arguments be obscured and made doubtful'. He then makes it clear that he sees no such indubitable foundations for any religious creed. They are all based 'not so much upon demonstrations or reason, as upon the assurance of faith and belief only'. And this means that those who 'seek by demonstration and publishing of books' to insist on the acceptance of their own outlook 'are not only mad with reason, but weaken also the foundations and grounds of all sorts of religions' (p. 535).

In the *Six Books*, however, the radical implication that this degree of uncertainty ought to generate an attitude of mutual forebearance is nowhere explicitly stated. It is only in the later *Colloquium* that Bodin goes on to develop the sceptical argument which Castellio, with greater boldness, had already dared to state – and to publish – over thirty years before. It is of course the figure of Senamus whom Bodin chiefly uses to represent this point of view. When the discussion of rival religions is first mooted at the beginning of the fourth Dialogue, Senamus roundly declares that all religious leaders have at all times 'had so many conflicts among themselves that no one could decide which is true among all the religions' (p. 152). The main reason, he explains later in the same discussion, is that while we may all agree that 'the religion which has God as its author is the true religion', this still leaves us without enough information to be sure 'whether He is the author of this religion or that religion' (p. 172). The moral of such uncertainty is that 'since the priests of all religions are disagreeing among themselves so violently', the only proper outlook to embrace must be one of complete tolerance. It is our duty to recognise that it must always be 'safer to admit all religions than to choose one from many', since our ignorance is such that we may choose one which is false and exclude another 'which may be the truest of all' (pp. 152, 154).

Although this argument is mainly voiced by the figure of the sceptic, there is a sense in which the whole tendency of the *Colloquium* is to move towards the acceptance of this point of view. By the end of the Dialogues all the participants recognise that no one has been able to persuade any of the others to accept any of his own distinctive beliefs (p. 463). They appear to acknowledge that this must be due to the fact that religion is not a proper subject for discursive argument, since we are told in conclusion that 'afterwards they held no other conversation about religions, although each one defended his own religion with the supreme sanctity of his life' (p. 471). The moral the participants draw from this state of uncertainty is the same as the moral which Senamus began by pointing out. They concede that since it is clearly possible for men of unimpeachable sincerity to hold conflicting religious opinions on which they can never hope to agree, the only decent course of action to adopt must be one of complete open-mindedness. So we are told that 'everyone approved' when the Lutheran Podamicus, the least tolerant speaker in the dialogues, brought the discussion to a close by allowing that it must always be wrong 'to command religion', since it can never be right that anyone should be 'forced to believe against his will' in matters of personal faith (p. 471).

A further reason why it was rational for the Huguenots to pin their hopes on winning an official measure of toleration in the 1560s was that an influential group of moderate Catholics had by that time come to the conclusion that any attempt to impose a policy of religious uniformity by force would constitute a serious tactical even if not a moral mistake. This became the characteristic platform of the so-called party of *politiques*, who argued that uniformity was no longer worth preserving, however valuable it might be in itself, if the cost of enforcing it seemed liable to be the destruction of the commonwealth.

The persuasive force of this position came to seem so obvious after the outbreak of the religious wars in 1562 that a number of humanists, having originally presented the case for toleration as a positive moral value, began to add this *politique* contention to their own array of arguments. This happened, for example, in the case of Castellio, who published a tract of *Advice to a Desolated France* immediately after the outbreak of the first civil war in 1562. He makes no appeal to the uncertainties of religious argument as a reason for mutual forbearance. He begins instead with an impartial attack on the Catholics and Huguenots for their 'false remedies', especially their 'forcing of consciences' and their decision 'to fight and kill each other' as a way of settling their difference (pp. 19, 24, 27). He then calls on both sides to live together in amity, and 'not to do to one another that which you would not have done to you' (p. 36). This position is defended not merely as 'the commandment of God', but also – in true *politique* style – as the only means of ensuring that mutual religious enmities do not result in the ruin of the commonwealth (pp. 36, 75–6).

The *politique* case was mainly presented, however, by those who had no belief in religious liberty as a positive moral value, but merely believed in the unfortunate necessity of conceding it as the only alternative to endemic civil strife. As we have seen, this soon became the policy of the government itself, and as the crisis of 1560–2 deepened, the position was brilliantly and very influentially expounded by the new Chancellor, Michel de l'Hôpital (1507–73), in a series of speeches to the assembled Estates. L'Hôpital was appointed to the Chancellorship in May 1560, and it is clear that at this point he was still thinking about the religious divisions of the commonwealth in traditional terms (Lecler, 1960, II, pp. 42–3). His address at the opening of the States General in December 1560 centres on the time-honoured demand for 'one faith, one law, one king' (*une foi, une loi, un roi*) (p. 398). He argues that 'it is folly to hope for peace, repose and amity between peoples of different religions' and goes on to call for an end to 'the names of Lutherans, Huguenots and Papists' and a return to a unified faith (pp. 396, 402). He quickly came to realise, however, that in spite of the unquestioned value of religious agreement, the price of trying to impose it was becoming ruinous. This appears most clearly in his opening address to the representatives of the Parlements assembled at St Germain in January 1562.[1] He begins with two uncontentious claims: that religious uniformity is always desirable, but that 'those of the new

---

[1] The dating of this speech to August 1561 by Duféy, the editor of l'Hôpital's *Complete Works*, is a mistake. For the correct details, see Lecler, 1960 II p. 68 and n.

religion have become so much bolder' of late that any attempt to enforce uniformity will now be liable to constitute a grave danger to civil peace (p. 442). He then proceeds to introduce two new principles of the most far-reaching significance. He argues that while the government may be said to have a duty to defend the established religion of the commonwealth, it has an even more compelling duty 'to maintain the people in peace and tranquillity' (p. 449). Where these two duties collide, he is now prepared to contemplate separating the fate of the kingdom from that of the Catholic faith, insisting that the fundamental question at issue 'is not about the maintenance of religion but about the maintaining of the commonwealth' (p. 452). He then goes on to offer the reassurance that such a loss of unity need not have any very catastrophic effects, since religious uniformity is not in fact essential to the well-being of France. He cites with approval the claim that 'many can be citizens who will not be Christians', and insists that it must be possible for the kingdom as a whole 'to live in peace with those who have different opinions', if only because it has already been proved in the case of individual families that 'those who remain Catholic do not cease to love and live in amity with those who adopt the new faith' (pp. 452, 453). His conclusion is thus that the traditional priorities are simply inapplicable in the present circumstances. The enforcement of uniformity 'may be good in itself' but 'experience has shown it to be impossible' (p. 450). It merely leads to the jeopardising of peace in the name of religious unity, whereas the only sane policy is to abandon the quest for unity in the name of peace.

L'Hôpital's *politique* solution clearly commended itself to a majority of moderate Catholics on the eve of the religious wars. His policy was endorsed by the States General in 1561, which included in its *cahiers* the demand 'that persecution on account of religion shall cease' (Van Dyke, 1913, p. 495). The same arguments were taken up by a number of Catholic pamphleteers, one of the most persuasive being the anonymous author of the *Apology For the King's Edict*, a defence of Catherine's and l'Hôpital's policies which first appeared in 1563. But the most important *politique* tract to be published at this time was the *Exhortation to the Princes*, which first appeared as early as 1561, and seems to have influenced l'Hôpital himself in his rapid adjustment from a position of religious conservatism to a fully *politique* point of view (Lecler, 1960, II, p. 69). The authorship of the *Exhortation* has recently been much disputed, but there seems little doubt that it was written by Estienne Pasquier (1529–1615), a *habitué* of the humanist *salons* of Paris as well as one of the most learned historical and constitutional writers of the age.[1] Pasquier begins his *Exhortation* by

[1] The ascription is traditional, but both Lecler, 1960, II, pp. 49–55 and Caprariis, 1959, pp.

making it plain that he sees himself as a loyal member of the Catholic Church, who views with disapproval the continuing proliferation of new religions and sects. But he immediately adds, with conscious suddenness, that there is 'absolutely no other means' to be adopted in the current crisis than 'to permit two Churches' in the commonwealth, 'one Roman and the other Protestant' (pp. 46–7). He imagines the fury this solution is bound to provoke, but insists that there is really no alternative course to be pursued (p. 48). To banish the Protestants will scarcely banish their views, and to try to exterminate them will merely reveal that 'we cannot ruin the Protestants by now without involving our own general ruin as well' (p. 51). The only solution is thus to tolerate the Huguenots in the name of preserving the commonwealth. Pasquier is far from treating this policy as an ideal to be striven for, for he ends by emphasising once again that he is 'in no way an advocate of the Protestants', and regards the loss of religious uniformity as a national calamity (p. 85). He merely concludes that since the sole alternative seems to be civil war, the acceptance of a *politique* settlement must appear to anyone who values 'public repose' to be infinitely the lesser of the two evils currently facing the government (p. 85).

Despite their obvious good sense, these attempts to avert the coming conflict were all doomed to failure. The government completely lost the power to steer a *politique* course after the violent renewal of the fighting in 1568, at which point l'Hôpital was forced to concede defeat and withdraw from public life (Michaud, 1967, pp. 27–8). Next, the government threw away any remaining chance of a *politique* settlement after the massacre of St Bartholomew, which finally forced the Huguenots into a direct revolutionary confrontation with the Valois monarchy. By the middle of the 1570s, however, the very ferocity of these renewed conflicts began to be treated by many political writers as the clearest possible sign that a policy of toleration was in fact the only sane course of action for the government to pursue. The outcome was a revival, with a renewed sense of urgency, of the suggestion that such a policy ought immediately to be adopted as the only means of avoiding the total ruin of France.

This revival was of course partly the work of the Huguenots themselves, many of whom clearly feared, after the massacres of 1572, that unless they could somehow promote a policy of toleration once again, they might actually find themselves facing complete annihilation. One example of a prominent Huguenot pamphleteer who sought to meet this crisis by

153–8 have challenged it. A very strong case for Pasquier's authorship has however been established by Thickett, 1956a; see items 50, 51 and the discussion at p. 78. For a judicious survey of the debate, see Beame, 1966, pp. 256–60. For a discussion of Pasquier's connections with the *salons* of the French humanists, see Keating, 1941, pp. 54–9.

urging a *politique* settlement on the government was Innocent Gentillet (1535–88), who addressed a *Remonstrance* to this effect to Henry III at the time of his accession in 1574 (Lecler, 1960, II, p. 104). A further example, according to some authorities, is provided by Philippe du Plessis Mornay, whom Patry has credited with writing an anonymous *Exhortation to Peace* which appeared in 1574, pleading with the government to recognise the Huguenots as the sole alternative to continuing civil anarchy.[1]

This renewal of the *politique* programme was more than a mere reflex on the part of the Huguenots, for the same arguments were soon developed once again by a number of moderate Catholic writers, the most important being Jean Bodin, who entered a plea of this character in his *Six Books of a Commonweal* in 1576. Bodin makes no pretence of dismissing the great and enduring value of religious uniformity. He introduces the whole question of rival religions in the course of discussing, and as an example of, the dangers of 'sedition and faction', and he begins by admitting that nothing does more to 'uphold and maintain the estates and commonwealths' than religious unity, since it serves to provide 'the principal foundation of the power and strength' of the state (pp. 535, 536). Whatever Bodin may have been prepared to say and write in private, his public doctrine always took the form of claiming that there can never be any question of accepting the natural right of minority religions to be tolerated. He insists on the contrary that since all 'disputations of religion' tend more than anything else to bring about 'the ruin and destruction of commonwealths', they ought rather to be 'by most strict laws forbidden', so that any religion which is 'by common consent once received and settled, is not again to be called into question and dispute' (pp. 535, 536). These sentiments are matched, however, by a reluctant yet absolutely clear perception that, since rival religions represent such a potent source of discord, they must always be tolerated where they cannot be suppressed. Bodin cites the topical situation in which 'the consent and agreement of the nobility and people in a new religion' has become 'so puissant and strong' that 'to repress or alter the same should be a thing impossible' without incurring 'the extreme peril and danger of the whole Estate' (p. 382). Bodin has no doubt that in such a situation 'the best advised princes' must 'imitate the wise pilots, who when they cannot attain unto the port by them desired, direct their course to such port as they may' (p. 382). He immediately underscores the lesson of the simile: 'that religion or sect is to be suffered which without the hazard and destruction of the state cannot be taken away' (p. 382).

---

[1] See Patry, 1933, p. 274, cf. also Lecler, 1960, II, pp. 105–6, who inclines to accept the ascription.

Bodin's first reason for accepting this conclusion was that although the government may be said to have a duty to uphold the unity of religion, this cannot alter the fact that 'the health and welfare of the commonwealth' must remain 'the chief thing the law respects' (p. 382). Where good order is found to be in conflict with religious uniformity, the maintenance of good order must always be treated as the higher priority. The other and even more emancipated argument he advances – very much in the spirit of l'Hôpital – is that any prince ought to be capable of seeing that 'the wars made for matters of religion' – which, as he observes, have been taking place 'almost in all Europe within this fifty years' – are not in fact 'grounded upon matters directly touching his estate' (p. 535). The implication is that all religious disputes ought in the end be seen as irrelevant to the essential business of government. The duty of the prince is to ignore and avoid all such arguments as far as possible, separating the welfare of his kingdom entirely from the fate of any particular religion, and thereby ensuring that he is never driven 'to make himself a party, instead of holding the place of a sovereign judge' (p. 535).

THE GROWTH OF ABSOLUTISM

Although the Huguenots continued to hope for an official measure of toleration throughout the 1560s, they can scarcely have failed at the same time to ask themselves the question which suddenly assumed a desperate urgency in 1572: what to do if the government finally turned against them and abandoned its conciliatory policies in the name of trying to exterminate the Calvinist Church in France. The main problem this raised was whether the Huguenots might be able to mobilise a sufficiently powerful network of allies to respond with a direct revolutionary attack on the Valois monarchy. There was never any question of being able to mount a successful revolution simply by calling on the somewhat dispersed ranks of their own co-religionists. It was always evident that they would need to draw together as many enemies of the government as possible, whether Catholic or Protestant in their religious allegiances. This prospect faced the Huguenots with a novel as well as an exceptionally difficult ideological task. Since they were in a considerable minority, they could scarcely hope to invoke the available Calvinist theory of revolution, and demand in the manner of Ponet, Goodman or Knox that the whole body of the godly people should rise up against the congregation of Satan in order to establish the congregation of Christ. They needed to develop a revolutionary ideology capable of appealing not merely to the enemies of the Catholic Church, but also to the various groups of Catholic malcontents who might be prepared to join – or at least to countenance – a general movement of resistance to the most Christian king of France.

It is thus of crucial significance that the developing theory and practice of the Valois monarchy in the first half of the sixteenth century had already made it an object of hostility and disillusionment amongst important sectors of the French ruling classes. It was due to this increasingly prevalent disaffection that the Huguenots were able to evolve a constitutionalist and not merely a sectarian ideology of opposition to the government. And it was due in turn to the widespread appeal of this ideology that, after the massacres of 1572 finally precipitated them into outright rebellion, they were able to enlist enough support to lead a general attack on the whole fabric of Valois government.

The most widespread cause of resentment amongst the ruling classes was that the apparatus of government had become less open to the hereditary nobility, and more centred around the court and person of the king. One indication of this trend, especially noticeable after Henry II's reforms of the Council in 1547, was the increasing tendency to rely on a small group of professional secretaries of state, several of whom – especially de Laubespine and Villeroy – happened to be officials of the highest capacities (Sutherland, 1962, pp. 16, 157). They attended the Council, followed the Court and so linked up with the thirteen departments of local government, and by these means (as Sutherland observes) 'came to replace the great ministers and officers of state whom at first they had served' (Sutherland, 1962, p. 52). A similar and even more significant development was the atrophying of the legal and representative elements in the constitution at the same time. It is true that the framework of the medieval constitution, including the authority of the Parlements and the States General, remained theoretically intact throughout the first half of the sixteenth century.[1] There is no doubt, however, that these representative elements were beginning to be treated by the government with increasing neglect and contempt. This is most evident in the case of the States General, which had met fairly regularly in the course of the fifteenth century to sanction additional measures of taxation. Its status began to be jeopardised towards the end of that period, when the crown succeeded in establishing the *taille* as a direct tax imposed solely by the authority of the royal Council. This enabled the government to raise more and more revenue without consent, increasing the yield from one and a half million *livres* at the start of the sixteenth century to four millions by the end of Francis I's reign and six millions by the 1550s – an important cause of

[1] This point is greatly – perhaps excessively – emphasised in Major, 1960, esp. p. 141 and in Major, 1962, esp. pp. 113, 124–5. For a valuable corrective see Salmon, 1975, pp. 62–6.

resentment in itself (Doucet, 1948, II, 576–7). The consequence was that the States General ceased to be summoned altogether, holding no further meetings after 1484 until the fiscal and constitutional crisis of 1560 obliged the government to resurrect it (Wolfe, 1972, pp. 118–21). By this time the sense of grievance felt by the representatives of the Third Estate had become so acute that they not only dared to point out in their formal list of grievances in 1561 that their authority had been 'despised through illegitimate procedures', but refused to vote the crown any further funds until their own constitutional position had been clarified (Van Dyke, 1913, p. 493; Major, 1951, pp. 104, 106–8).

During the same period the government adopted a similarly high-handed attitude towards the Parlement of Paris, which nominally occupied a key constitutional role through its right to register royal edicts (*le droit d'enregistrement*) and to lodge petition against them if they were judged legally unacceptable (*le droit de remonstrance*). These rights were directly challenged at the accession of Francis I in 1515, when Antoine Duprat, the Chancellor, simply announced the King's proposed policies to the Parlement without making any pretence of seeking their judgment or even their advice (Maugis, 1913–14, I, p. 548). When Marthonie, the President, demanded in reply that their petitions should be heard, this traditional request was promptly and haughtily dismissed (Maugis, 1913–14, II, p. 549). The same challenge was renewed in 1526, when the Parlement found itself faced with a royal demand for 'a ban on introducing any limitation upon the ordinances or edicts issued by the king' (Maugis, 1913–14, II, pp. 582–3). These absolutist tendencies reached a climax after 1560 under the Chancellorship of l'Hôpital. He opened his speech to the Parlement in June 1561 by assuring the members that although the King had summoned them to offer advice 'on the greatest affairs of state', this only gave them a right 'to furnish counsel and offer advice on certain matters', while leaving the King with complete authority to issue such a summons 'only when it pleases him to request it' (p. 419). He went even further in his opening address at the next session in November 1561, beginning with the maxim that 'one person must command and all others obey' and stressing that 'a form of jurisdiction without appeal is attributed to our kings' (pp. 9, 14). The President of the court attempted on this occasion to protest against the implication that the traditional right to remonstrate against royal edicts 'constituted any disobedience' or in any way 'amounted to a rupturing of the laws' (p. 17). But this only prompted l'Hôpital to insist with greater emphasis on his absolutist interpretation of the proper relations between the king and the officers of the court. When he next came before them at the opening of the session in November 1563, his address took the form of a protest in which he remonstrated with them for their failure to recognise that 'even if kings command anything which seems unjust', it remains the duty even of their leading advisers 'to use modesty and prudence in such a situation, and not to oppose themselves directly to the will of the king' (pp. 85, 87–8). The reason, he was now prepared explicitly to insist, is that it can never be lawful 'to oppose oneself directly to the will and commandments of kings', since 'they are jealous of their powers' and we must in consequence 'expect to suffer defeat' at their hands if we make presumptuous attempts to thwart them in the exercise of their absolute authority (p. 88; cf. Shennan, 1968, pp. 209, 213).

It is of course true that while the functions of the government were becoming increasingly concentrated on the king and his professional advisers, there were still large numbers of judicial and administrative posts which remained the monopoly of the nobility, and so provided them with a continuing means of taking part in the business of central and local government. But the method of allocating these positions became a further and extremely potent cause of disaffection in the first half of the sixteenth century. During this period the government first began to follow the practice of auctioning off the full range of these offices to the highest bidder, treating them simply as additional sources of revenue and continually multiplying their numbers in order to increase the spoils.[1] The system became one of 'all-out venality' (*venalité au bout*) during the reign of Francis I (Wolfe, 1972, pp. 101–2, 129–31). In the Parlement of Toulouse, for example, the number of offices was more than tripled during this period, rising from twenty-four in 1515 to eighty-three by the middle of the century, with every appointment being put on sale (Mousnier, 1945, pp. 27–8; Romier, 1922, II, p. 16). During the next reign, moreover, the abuse was suddenly and spectacularly increased, when the system of providing a second incumbent (*l'alternatif*) was introduced in the case of virtually every fiscal position in the government (Wolfe, 1972, pp. 131–2; cf. Romier, 1922, II, p. 20).

This system was instituted at a time when the nobles felt themselves ill-equipped to meet the additional expenditure involved. Beginning in the 1520s, most of the nobility began to suffer a sharp decline in real income, and it has been estimated that by the middle of the century eight out of ten noble families had either forfeited some of their property or had fallen seriously into debt (Bitton, 1969, p. 2). A revealing account of their predicament is provided by the Huguenot noble François de la Noue (1531–91) in his *Political and Military Discourses*, which he composed in

[1] See Mousnier, 1945, pp. 20–1 and cf. Doucet, 1948, I, pp. 410–11.

prison during the early 1580s (Hauser, 1892, pp. 139–47; Sutcliffe, 1967, pp. x, xv). La Noue devotes his eighth Discourse to 'the poverty of the nobility', and treats them as a class ruined not merely by adverse economic conditions, but also by their own wasteful indulgence in 'vain expenses' (p. 195). He denounces the extravagance of their dress, their 'vehement passion' for new buildings, the profusion of their furnishings and their lavish hospitality (pp. 191–5, 198–200). And he adds that all these reckless tastes are being pursued at a dangerous time, for while he concedes that 'their fathers may not have had even a half of their revenues', he estimates that all their costs have risen four-fold in the same period (p. 201; cf. Hauser, 1892, pp. 167–70).

The fact that the nobles were finding – or at least persuading themselves[1] – that by the middle of the sixteenth century they could no longer match their sense of status with their incomes caused the government's systematic sale of offices to make it a particularly potent object of hostility. As La Noue makes clear, the nobles were of course resentful at the exorbitant increases which resulted in the cost of entering the royal service. But they were even more concerned about the threat to their position inherent in the creation of a *noblesse de robe*, a growing army of merchants and other rich commoners who were beginning to use their wealth to buy positions carrying patents of nobility, thereby elbowing out the traditional office-holders and diluting the ranks of the aristocracy with the phenomenon of the *bourgeois gentilhomme* (Romier, 1922, II, pp. 21–3; Salmon, 1975, pp. 42–3, 96–8, 109–10). By the middle of the sixteenth century, this development was being denounced with increasing vehemence by a number of influential moralists. Montaigne and Rabelais both vent their scorn on venal place-seekers, while writers such as Noël du Fail (*c.* 1520–91) and Guillaume Des Auletz (1529–81), seeing themselves as spokesmen for the traditional aristocracy, began to produce a nostalgic form of social criticism in which the aspirations of the *parvenu* seigneurs were ruthlessly satirised. Du Fail's *Rustic Subjects* of 1547 is largely a lament for 'the passing away of all good customs' with the increasing corruption of social relationships (p. 16). The same note is struck in the *Harangue to the French People against Rebellion* which was published anonymously by Des Auletz in 1560 (Young, 1961, pp. 158–9). This includes an attack on 'men of low condition who take over the honours due to men of greater nobility', and goes on to argue that none of these *arrivistes* 'have any idea of how to behave in order to uphold their repu-

[1] The possibility of self-deceit is implied by Braudel, who claims that some of the nobility's real wealth from land actually increased during this period. See Braudel, 1972–3, I, pp. 525–7. But for a local study which gives a much more pessimistic picture – more in line with contemporary perceptions – see Le Roy Ladurie, 1967, pp. 293–300.

tations' (Young, 1961, p. 169). When the representatives of the nobility presented their *cahiers de doléances* to the States General in 1560, they too took up the same complaint. The deputies from Toulouse denounced the 'infinite numbers' of corrupt officials who had sprung up in the previous reign, who 'had nothing at the start' and were now the possessors of 'great goods, seigneuries and mansions' (Mousnier, 1945, p. 55). The culmination of these criticisms was an unsuccessful attempt by the representatives of the nobility to ensure, first in 1560 and subsequently at the next meeting of the States General in 1576, that a portion of the government's patronage should be reserved for those who were already of noble birth (Mousnier, 1945, p. 58).

These feelings of hostility towards the government were exacerbated by the conduct of its numerous apologists. During the first half of the sixteenth century, an important group of 'legist' political philosophers began to argue in an increasingly aggressive style that the concentration of authority upon the king, and the atrophying of any institutional checks upon his rule, ought both to be regarded as legitimate interpretations of the fundamental constitution of France (Church, 1941, pp. 42–3). The development of this strongly royalist ideology can be traced as far back as the reign of Louis XII, when Jean Ferrault wrote and dedicated to the King his enumeration of the *Twenty Special Privileges of the most Christian King of France*, a tract which sought to claim almost unlimited powers for the French monarchy (Poujol, 1958, pp. 15–17). It is true that Ferrault's tract was somewhat unusual, in that most of the legist writers in the early part of the century were anxious to retain some elements of a more traditional and hence a more constitutionalist account of the king's authority.[1] This commitment is still reflected, for example, in the *Catalogue of the Glory of the World*, a major survey of legist arguments by Barthélemy de Chasseneuz (1480–1541) which was first published in 1529 (Franklin, 1973, p. 6). By the time we reach the final decade of Francis I's reign, however, we find a new and more absolutist style of legal and political thinking beginning to predominate over these surviving elements of constitutionalist thought (Church, 1941, p. 45). The leading example of this development is provided by the work of Charles Du Moulin (1500–66), perhaps the greatest legal philosopher of the age. His *Commentaries*

---

[1] It is thus something of an exaggeration to say that in the realm of theory 'the absolute monarchy was already constituted' by the time of Francis I's accession in 1515. For this judgment see Mesnard, 1936, p. 490, and cf. Poujol, 1958, p. 25. As Franklin has emphasised, most of the early sixteenth-century legists were still concerned to uphold a 'delicate balance between monarchist and constitutionalist ideas'. See Franklin, 1973, p. 6, and cf. Church, 1941, p. 74ff., and Kelley, 1970, p. 195.

on the Customs of Paris, which began to appear in 1539, were inspired throughout, as Church has remarked, 'by ideas of omnipotent royal authority', and are said to have exercised a direct influence in shaping the monarchy of the *ancien régime* (Church, 1941, pp. 180–1). The same trend is also evident in the more conventional legist writings of the same period, the most important being the work of Charles de Grassaille, who produced a strongly absolutist analysis of *The Regale of France* in 1538.[1] Finally, the trend towards a theory of virtually unlimited royal supremacy became even more pronounced during the reign of Henry II. This can be seen in the writings of such lesser figures as Guillaume de La Perrière, whose *Mirror of Policy* appeared in 1555, and Etienne de Bourg, who published a treatise in 1550 with the revealing title of *The Dominion of the most Christian King of France over the supreme Court of the Parlement of Paris* (Allen, 1957, p. 284; Church, 1941, pp. 340, 343). The same development is also reflected in the writing of Pierre Rebuffi, the outstanding legist of this generation. His *Commentary on the Royal Constitutions and Ordinances*, which first appeared in 1549, provides the best illustration of the extent to which, by the middle of the sixteenth century, even the most orthodox theorists of the French constitution were beginning to write in an almost unyieldingly absolutist style (Franklin, 1973, pp. 16–17).

We can best measure the stages and extent of this drift towards absolutism if we compare these treatises with *The Monarchy of France*, a famous and far more moderate account of the French constitution written in 1515 and first published four years later (Poujol, 1961, pp. 91–2). This was the work of Claude de Seyssel, who had served in the Parlement of Paris and risen to become a member of the Grand Council instituted by Louis XII (Hexter, 1973, p. 214). Seyssel does not fail, of course, to emphasise the grandeur and importance of the king of France, whom he regards as directly ordained by God and absolute within the proper sphere of his jurisdictions. But he is equally concerned to stress that any tendency towards absolutism in France is perpetually held in check by a series of 'bridles' (*freins*) upon the king's authority – the bridles being *la police*, *la religion* and *la justice* (p. 113). The most complex and constitutionally significant of these is *la police*, a concept which may be said to involve three elements (Gallet, 1944, pp. 11–16). The king is limited first of all by two fundamental laws 'which even princes are not allowed to change' (p. 119). One of these, cited at the opening of the discussion, stipulates that 'the domain and royal patrimony may not be alienated without absolute necessity' (p. 119). The other, which is separately mentioned at

[1] See Franklin, 1973, p. 7 note. For the other, lesser legist predecessors of Du Moulin, including Angleberme, Bohier, Lemair de Belges and Tiraqueau, see Kelley, 1970, esp. pp. 185, 195.

the start of Seyssel's account of the peculiarities of the French monarchy, is the requirement of the Salic law that 'the kingdom must go by male succession without falling into the female line' (p. 112). The second element of *la police* amounts in effect to a check on the power of the king by the authority of custom, and in particular by a conception of 'the good order and harmony which exists between all classes of men in the kingdom' (p. 127). A pyramidal structure of society has grown up over the centuries which serves to assign each stratum of society its proper status and its accompanying rights and obligations (pp. 121–4). The king has a duty not to oppress or alter any aspect of this established social hierarchy, and to ensure that each man is rendered his due according to the rightful place he occupies within it. Finally, the king is said to be bridled by an obligation to take counsel, the third element of *la police*. The importance of soliciting and acting upon wise advice is particularly emphasised at the beginning of Part II, where Seyssel discusses 'the things necessary for the conservation and augmentation of the French monarchy' (p. 129). Since the monarch 'must never do anything suddenly or with a disordered will', it is vital that 'in all his actions, especially concerning the commonwealth, he must follow good counsel', which is absolutely essential to the smooth running of affairs (p. 133).

If we turn from Seyssel to the later legists, we find a gradual but increasing erosion of the idea that *la police* constitutes a check upon the absolute authority of the king. This development is not of course a sudden one, nor was it by any means complete by the middle of the sixteenth century. The most absolute of the legists continued to endorse the suggestion that the king is bridled by the fundamental laws. This is true even of Du Moulin, the most systematic defender of royal supremacy. In the first part of his *Commentaries* he still acknowledges that the lands of the king of France 'are not alienable even by the prince himself' (p. 79, col. 1). And he appears to endorse Ferrault's contention that 'the law of France established at the time of Pharamond' unquestionably lays it down that 'no woman can ever succeed to the crown of France'.[1] Similarly, there was still a strong sense that the king must be bridled by the customary rights of his subjects. This is particularly evident in Chasseneuz and La Perrière, both of whom lay considerable emphasis – in a humanist as much as a legist style – on the idea of the commonwealth as a harmoniously ordered whole.[2] The same assertions recur in the most orthodox of the later

[1] See the reprinting of Ferrault's account of *The Laws and Privileges of the King of France* in the second volume of Du Moulin's *Works*, and for this quotation see vol. 2, p. 549, col. 2.
[2] The entire organisation of Chasseneuz's *Catalogue* is based on this assumption, beginning with the prince as 'head' of the body politic (Section V) and proceeding through the hierarchy of 'members', including the feudal dignitaries (VI), the legal office-holders (VII), the nobility

legists, for example in Rebuffi, who continues to insist in his discussions of the concept of law that it 'must never be enacted against the customs of the inhabitants', and must always be made 'convenient to the time and place' as well as congenial 'to the prevailing customs of the country' (p. 9).

Nevertheless, there are two crucial points at which the check of *la police* is gradually slackened by these later legist writers. They first of all move decisively towards a denial of the necessity of counsel (Church, 1941, p. 60). This trend is already apparent in Chasseneuz, whose discussion of the maxim that 'the king of France is Emperor in his own kingdom' leads him to lay a novel emphasis on the extent to which the king stands above and apart from his subjects in all respects (Section V, fo 26a; cf. fos 26b, 32b).[1] By the time we come to Rebuffi, writing twenty years later, the check of counsel has virtually disappeared. He still believes that 'laws are concluded in a more satisfactory manner' when they are 'sent to the highest court before they are promulgated' (pp. 7, 9). But he no longer thinks of the king of France as limited by any formal obligation to seek legal or political advice. He notes that while it used to happen that 'there were consultations with the highest court in France before laws were passed', this convention now appears to have lapsed. And he accepts that the king's right to promulgate laws without taking counsel is now unquestionable, since 'the ordinances of the king in this kingdom have the force of law', and the king is able 'both to abrogate the law and allow customs contrary to law' solely by virtue of his own authority (p. 34).

The other point at which the legists weakened the check of *la police* was by questioning Seyssel's fundamental assumption that the commonwealth should be regarded as a harmoniously ordered whole. Although this attitude survived, there was also a contrary and increasing tendency to focus on the person of the monarch, treating him less as the head of a feudal hierarchy and more as an absolute ruler over all his subjects. This was partly the product of applying the Roman law concept of *Imperium*, in a direct neo-Bartolist style, in order to elucidate the prerogatives of the king of France. But it was also the outcome of a new and more humanist tendency to focus on the ways in which the kings of France had built up their absolute supremacy over time by the gradual acquisition of more and more 'marks' of sovereignty (Kelley, 1970, pp. 198–9). The chief of these

(VIII), the military (IX), the learned (X) and the lower classes (XI). It is even arguable in the case of La Perrière that his writings have been misclassified (for example by Church, 1941, p. 44) in being seen as the work of a legist. While his account of monarchy is similar, it is presented wholly in a humanist rather than a legist manner, with copious citations from Patrizi, Pontano, More and even Machiavelli as well as from Plato and Aristotle. (According to Cardascia, 1943, p. 130, La Perrière's citations from Machiavelli are the earliest by any French writer.) For La Perrière on the king as head of the body politic, see Sig. G, 1a.

[1] The foliation of the *Catalogue* begins anew with each separate section.

'marks' was taken to be the right to appoint the highest magistrates, followed by the right to make war and peace, the right to hear appeals and grant pardons, and a long list of lesser *iura regalia* which extended, in Chasseneuz's heroic calculation, to no less than two hundred and eight items (Kelley, 1970, pp. 198–9).

This development received a magisterial endorsement with the publication in 1539 of the first part of Du Moulin's *Commentaries on the Customs of Paris*, which included a systematic attack on the feudal vision of French society as a stratified and harmoniously ordered whole.[1] Du Moulin's point of departure in this attempt to elevate the absolute powers of the crown was a technical one: he begins his *Commentaries* by considering and exposing 'the futile conjectures' of those who have sought to locate 'the invention and origin of fiefs in the Roman law' (p. 3, col. 1). This involves him in denouncing – not without a certain relish – the humanist jurists whom he professes most of all to admire, including Budé, Zasius and Cujas, all of whom had sought to establish that the concept of vassalage, and thus the notion that a fief carries with it an obligation of personal service, had originated in the *patronus–cliens* relationship of Imperial Rome (p. 6, col. 2). Du Moulin responds by pointing out that 'there is not a single word in the entire Code of Roman law' about the idea that 'clientage is to be equated with vassalage' (p. 3, col. 2). There is of course a great deal about the *patronus–cliens* relationship itself, but the patron 'is never called a lord' (*dominus*), nor are his clients 'ever called vassals' (*servi*) (p. 5, col. 1). Du Moulin thus concludes that the idea of a fief as the foundation of a social system is not a Roman development at all, but 'an invention of the old Frankish kingdom' in the later sixth century, 'this being the true origin of fiefs, and there being no possibility of finding any older source for them' (p. 3, col. 1; p. 5, col. 1).

This analysis provides Du Moulin with the basis for an epoch-making attack on the pyramidal structure of legal rights and obligations characteristic of feudalism. He has established, he claims, that this form of social organisation is totally foreign to Roman law. But he also assumes that Roman law provides the legal basis for the fundamental constitution of France, which he still tends to treat in a neo-Bartolist style as a direct continuation of the ancient *Imperium* of Rome (Gilmore, 1941, p. 63). It follows that the system of vassalage and seigneurial rights still prevailing in France must be a late, customary and illegal usurpation of the absolute *Imperium* originally and rightfully possessed by the French monarchy. Du Moulin thus moves directly from technical legal analysis to absolutist

---

[1] It is thus a somewhat serious mistake to classify Du Moulin (as for example Allen has done) as one of the theoretical opponents of the Valois monarchy. See Allen, 1957, pp. 385–6.

political conclusions. This implication of his argument first becomes evident in his long gloss on the concept of a fief. He insists that this must be understood to refer simply to a form of landholding, and must not be taken to include 'any rights of personal service from the vassal', the basic reason being that no legalised form of personal subjection can ever be owed to anyone except the king (p. 69, col. 1). He later confirms this interpretation in his gloss on the feudal oath, in which he claims that all seigneurial jurisdictions are technically held as delegations of the king's authority, and not as independent rights, since 'it must be emphasised that throughout every part of this kingdom the king is the source of all justice, holding all jurisdictions and enjoying full *Imperium*' (p. 128, col. 1). The same absolutist conclusions are also drawn from the account which follows of the king's relations with his subjects. Du Moulin's argument is that, since the king enjoys complete control over 'all temporal lords, whether secular or ecclesiastical', everyone must occupy the same status in relation to the crown: everyone must equally be a subject (*subditus*), since everyone must equally be in dependence on the king's absolute authority 'for the exercise of their jurisdictions and lordships' (p. 128, col. 1; cf. p. 133, col. 1; see also Church, 1941, p. 187).

Any account of the process which served to bring about and legitimate the rule of an absolutist monarchy in France needs to find an important place for the critique of feudal relationships inaugurated by Du Moulin's great work.[1] For there can be no doubt about the ideological significance of Du Moulin's pioneering attack on the 'Romanist' thesis about the origins of feudal society. It developed into a new orthodoxy within his own lifetime, being reiterated and extended by René Choppin, Louis le Caron and many other legist advocates of an absolute monarchy (Kelley, 1970, p. 193). All these writers decisively question the image of society as a stratified hierarchy, an image which had survived, as we have seen, even in the writings of the legists themselves in the first part of the century. The new structure which begins in consequence to emerge is recognisably that of an early modern absolutism: the feudal pyramid of legal rights and obligations is dismantled, the king is singled out as the holder of complete *Imperium*, and all other members of society are assigned an undifferentiated legal status as his subjects.

The development of this ideology not only served to loosen Seyssel's bridle of *la police*, but tended at the same time to call in question the other two checks he had sought to place on the powers of the French monarchy.

---

[1] It seems a weakness of the remarkable attempt which Anderson had made to trace the *Lineages of the Absolutist State* that he finds no space for analysing the role of such anti-feudal ideologies in the formation of modern absolutism (cf. Anderson, 1974, pp. 85–112).

These had both been linked in Seyssel's analysis to the basic assumption that 'the true office of the prince' – who is said to be 'deputed by divine providence to execute this great and honourable charge' – is that of acting as a judge appointed by God Himself in order to ensure that His will is duly carried out in the world (p. 150). This means that the principles of justice, and not the mere will of the king, must form the basis of the laws in any well-ordered commonwealth (p. 117). A second bridle on the absolute authority of the king is thus said to be constituted by the check of *la justice* (p. 117). This traditional image of the king as a reflection of God's justice also means that, as a way of ensuring that the royal ordinances duly embody the principles of justice, the king himself must be wholly governed by the laws of God. A final bridle on absolutism is thus said to be constituted by *la religion*, the check which Seyssel mentions first and regards as the most fundamental of all (p. 115).

According to Seyssel, these further constraints carried with them two practical implications about the proper conduct of the government of France. Since the concept of *la justice* is said to form the foundation of the commonwealth, it follows that there must be an essential place in the French constitution for the courts of justice, and especially for the Parlement of Paris, the highest court in the land. If the king fails to render justice to his subjects by means of his ordinances, he is liable to find them challenged or even repudiated by the Parlements, 'which have principally been established in order to check the absolute power which kings might otherwise seek to exercise' (p. 117). The other implication is that, since it is vital to the administration of justice that the Parlement should be able to call the king to account, it is necessary that 'the officers who are deputed to administer justice should be perpetual, so that it is beyond the power of the king himself to depose them' (p. 118). If they are appointed during the king's pleasure, they will be liable to be frustrated in their most important task, that of ensuring that the ordinances of the king remain in line with the dictates of natural justice. It is thus said to follow that, 'in order to uphold the exercise of justice with full assurance', they must be 'sovereign' within their own sphere (p. 118).

If we turn from Seyssel's analysis to that of the later legists, we again find a deliberate and increasing attempt to slacken these bridles of *la religion* and *la justice*. It is of course true, as before, that this process was neither sudden nor complete. The later legists continue to share the underlying image of the king as a judge, and in particular as the mirror of God's justice in the world. Du Moulin still insists, in analysing the concept of fealty in the first part of his *Commentaries*, that the proper way to envisage the king's majesty is to see him as 'a living law' and 'a kind of corporeal God within his kingdom', dispensing the judgments of God Himself (p. 247, col. 1). And even Rebuffi, writing ten years later,[1] begins his gloss on the concept of law by stressing the same relationship between the law and the king, citing God's own pronouncement in Proverbs that 'through me kings reign' and adding that our rulers must be seen as God's representatives, whom He has ordained 'to uphold His just laws and ordinances' in the world (p. 6).

There are two crucial points, however, at which these later legists begin to erode the checks of *la religion* and *la justice*. They first of all argue that although the Parlement of Paris undoubtedly holds the right to constrain the unjust actions of one subject against another, it has no such right to interfere with the judicial behaviour of the king (Church, 1941, p. 71). The beginnings of this shift are already apparent in Chasseneuz, who devotes Part VII of his *Catalogue* to analysing the structure and authority of the Parlement. He still gives an elevated account of its dignity, comparing it with the Senate of ancient Rome and insisting that 'the king out of his ordinary power is unable to rescind any of its acts' (Section VII, fo 6b). Since he also argues, however, very much as James I was later to argue against Sir Edward Coke, that the king's powers are 'double' – that is, they are both 'ordinary' and 'absolute' – we are left with a strong sense that, even if the king's ordinary powers may not be sufficient to challenge the Parlement, his absolute authority may always be invoked to override its judgments (Church, 1941, p. 64; Franklin, 1973, pp. 12–14). The same line of thought is carried much further by Du Moulin, who treats it as a corollary of his claim that all offices take the form of delegations of the king's supreme *Imperium*. It follows that the idea of a court capable of checking the powers of the king himself must be a legal impossibility. The argument is presented in the long gloss on the concept of a fief in the first part of the *Commentaries*. Du Moulin begins with the axiom that 'the authority to constitute magistrates must be counted amongst the king's regalian rights' (p. 79, col. 2). This means that the judges 'cannot be the independent owners of their jurisdictions', since 'they merely administer them' in the name of the king (p. 80, col. 1). The status of the Parlement of Paris is thus held to be no different from that of any other court: the officers possess *jurisdictio* but not *Imperium*; they receive their authority as a *concessio* from the king; and they thus remain 'in dependence' upon the king's authority (p. 80, col. 1; pp. 97, col. 2 to 98, col. 1). By the time we come to Rebuffi's *Commentary*, written nearly a decade later, this new relationship between the king and the Parlements is simply registered as a fact about the constitution of France. He notes that 'at one time the

---

[1] So too La Perrière, writing even later; see sig. Gg., 1b–2b.

highest courts even controlled the kings themselves', but adds that nowadays the kings 'do not obey them, and are no longer governed by their advice' (p. 21). The loss of status and independence which this has brought about is later confirmed when Rebuffi comes to discuss the role of supplications to the king (pp. 286–306). He concludes at this point that 'it is well known to everyone' by now that 'it is not lawful for the Parlements to make appeals, but only to supplicate their prince' (p. 289).

Finally, this view of the dependence of the Parlements on the king is confirmed by the repudiation of Seyssel's suggestion that the officers of the courts must be irremovable from their positions even by the king himself (Church, 1941, pp. 51–2). This further implication is pursued most extensively by Du Moulin in the first part of his *Commentaries*. He recognises that to grant such a right to officeholders would be to concede them not merely *jurisdictio* but also *Imperium* (p. 79, col. 1). But since he has already laid it down that in France the king alone is possessed of *Imperium*, while 'any rights which anyone holds in an office are merely donated and ceded to them by our supreme king', he concludes that any such grant of jurisdiction must always be capable of being revoked (p. 78, col. 1). This is subsequently confirmed in the gloss on the swearing of homage to the king (pp. 126–30). Since the ruler 'is the source of every grade and type of jurisdiction', it is always open to him to demand that the rights of any office should revert 'to the crown from which they emanated' (p. 128, col. 2). The argument is clinched by an appeal to the celebrated dispute between Azo and Lothair. Du Moulin revives the claim – which began in consequence to regain its former ascendancy – that 'in relation to the kingdom of France the opinion of Lothair is absolutely correct' in emphasising that 'all right, dominion and possession resides in the prince alone' (p. 79, col. 2). So Seyssel's ideal of a mixed constitution with an independent judiciary is completely overturned. Du Moulin's final word is that 'the king must in every case retain the right to add "So long as it pleases us" ' in making any appointment to any office what-soever in the commonwealth (p. 80, col. 1).

THE REASSERTION OF CONSTITUTIONALISM

As well as relying on the fact that the monarchy had rendered itself so unpopular in the first half of the sixteenth century, the Huguenots had a further reason for hoping that, if they found themselves forced into a revolutionary confrontation with the government, they might be able to respond by rallying a general and not merely a sectarian movement of resistance to its rule. In reaction to the theories of royal supremacy which the legists had developed to such a pitch by the end of Henry II's reign, a number of moderate Catholic political writers had already begun to demand a reversion to a more traditional and hence a less absolutist form of constitutionalism.[1] This in turn meant that they had already begun to question the absolutist pretensions of the Valois monarchy, and in this way to lay the foundations for a constitutional and not merely a religious ideology of opposition to its authority.[2] The significance of this background from the point of view of the Huguenots was that, when they were finally driven into outright rebellion in 1572, they were able to build on these existing traditions of constitutionalist thought, to amalgamate them with their own heritage of revolutionary Calvinist ideas, and in this way to develop a theory of resistance capable of appealing not merely to the ranks of their own co-religionists, but also to a much wider spectrum of opposition to the government.

The attack on the theory of royal supremacy during the 1560s partly took the form of a reversion to the older constitutionalist doctrines which Seyssel had summarised at the start of the century (Church, 1941, p. 98). This is the attitude we find, for example, in the writings of Bernard de Girard, the Seigneur Du Haillan (c. 1535–1610), particularly in his account of *The State and Success of the Affairs of France*, first published in 1570.[3] The start of Book III, which is devoted to analysing the constitutional structure of France, consists of an attack on 'a number of extremely bold writers' who 'have written that it is a crime of *lèse majesté*' to speak of any constitutional checks on the French monarchy, since they hold that 'this diminishes to nothing its authority, grandeur and power' (fo 170b). As a response to this dangerous development, Du Haillan

---

[1] The leading figures in this movement were Pasquier, Bodin and Du Haillan. The fullest recent attempt to treat them together is in Caprariis, 1959, pp. 257–371. It may appear misleading to characterise Bodin as a moderate Catholic during the 1560s. His orthodoxy was often in doubt, and he even seems to have been imprisoned in 1569–70 as a suspected Huguenot. But there is no doubt that his public stance at this time was that of a moderate *politique* member of the Catholic Church, and he duly swore the required oath of allegiance to the Catholic faith when he began to practise law in Paris in 1562. After the 1560s he became increasingly hostile to Calvinist radicalism, both in the Netherlands and in France, and subsequently became a member of the Catholic League. Although his private opinions in his later years have rightly been characterised by Kuntz as 'completely tolerationist', his public stance remained that of a moderate member of the Catholic Church. For these and other details of Bodin's religious opinions, see Kuntz, 1975, esp. pp. xx–xxv.

[2] It is arguable that by laying such a strong emphasis on the surviving elements of constitutionalism in legist thought, Franklin has underestimated the extent to which the constitutional theorists of the 1560s were deliberately attacking both the methodology and the doctrines of the legists discussed in the previous section of this chapter. I must stress, however, that in spite of this difference in emphasis, my account of both the methodology and the doctrines adopted by these writers is greatly indebted to Franklin's two brilliant books; cf. Franklin, 1963 and Franklin, 1973.

[3] For this work see *sub* Girard in the bibliography of primary sources, and for further details see Kelley, 1970, pp. 233–8.

draws the attention of his readers to 'the views of Claude de Seyssel in his *Monarchy of France*'. From Seyssel's account, he ingenuously adds, 'we have taken all our points' about the institutions of the French monarchy, and 'have followed his analysis almost word for word' (fos 170a, 174b). This is amply confirmed by the narrative history of the French constitution which occupies Books I and II of Du Haillan's work. The chief moral of the story is said to be that it illustrates 'the behaviour of our kings in relation to *la religion*, *la justice* and *la police*', and in this way serves to indicate the ways in which 'the authority of our kings is bridled (*bridée*)by the laws which they themselves have made' (fos 10b, 168b).

But the main significance of the constitutional writers of the 1560s derives from the fact that they were not content merely to turn back to Seyssel and reiterate the doctrines of medieval constitutionalism. Instead they based their attack on the legists on the newly fashionable humanist approach to the study of the law which a number of jurists had already begun to employ as a way of challenging the traditional methods of scholastic jurisprudence. The legists had mainly continued to follow the scholastic approach, treating the Roman law as an immediately applicable authority, and arguing that the absolutism of the French monarch should be seen as a direct continuation of the *Imperium* of the later Roman Empire. As we have seen, however, this approach had already been denounced by a number of *quattrocento* humanists, especially Valla, Poliziano and their disciples, and by a number of Italian jurists who had accepted their critical findings, including Pomponio, Alciato and Salamonio. Moreover, Alciato had brought these new methods to France in the 1520s, putting them to work in his teaching at Avignon and especially at Bourges. This in turn had made him the centre of a vital new school of French humanist jurisprudence, a school whose methods soon came to be known as the *mos docendi Gallicus*, the French way of teaching, as Alciato's techniques and findings were taken up and propagated by such distinguished teachers and writers as Cujas, Hotman, Baudouin, Pasquier and Le Douaren (Kelley, 1970, pp. 100–15).

The main scholarly effort of the early humanist writers on Roman law had gone into reconstructing the history and development of the civil code, a project which had led them to attack the traditional Bartolist preoccupation with applying the wisdom of the ancient law-books directly to the modern world. One outcome of the increasing popularity of the humanist approach was thus that the established methods of legal education began to be called into question. As the immediate applicability of Justinian's Code began to appear increasingly problematic, it no longer

seemed at all obvious that the essence of any proper legal training ought
to consist of glossing the contents of the Code and applying the results
directly to prevailing circumstances. This implication began to be pursued
in an increasingly polemical fashion during the 1560s, first by François
Baudouin in his *Prolegomena* of 1561, and most incisively by François
Hotman in his *Anti-Tribonian* of 1567 (Mesnard, 1955, pp. 127–33;
Franklin, 1963, pp. 36–58). Hotman introduces his polemic with an assault
on the prevailing methods of teaching law. He first stresses the complete
irrelevance of Roman law to existing legal practice. He sees the Code as an
inferior compilation, hastily thrown together in a decadent period of
Roman rule, and in any case designed for a society in no way comparable
with that of sixteenth-century France. This makes the analysis of the Code,
as he insists at the beginning of Chapter II, 'an art which is out of use and
futile' (p. 4). He then argues that the proper object of study in any relevant
form of legal training for 'the youth of France' ought not to be the Roman
law at all, since 'the differences between the existing state of France and
that of Rome are so great and enormous' that 'there cannot be any justification' for studying the laws of Rome 'with so much curiosity' as the usual
methods of instruction presuppose (pp. 9, 11). The basic aim ought rather
to be that of studying the history and development of the indigenous laws
and customs of one's own country. The polemic culminates in a satirical
contrast between the lunacy 'of spending all one's life in making a curious
study' of Roman practices, as compared with the obvious value of learning
about 'the officers of the crown and of justice in our own kingdom', 'the
rights and sovereignty of our own king', and all the details of the existing
laws and customs actually in force in France (pp. 12–13).

The leading constitutional writers of the 1560s all adopted this new
methodology: they repudiated the immediate relevance of Roman law, and
turned instead to studying the history of the ancient customs and constitutions of France. The outcome was a tendency to present their theoretical
conclusions in the form of national histories (cf. Gilmore, 1941, p. 4). The
pioneer of this approach was Estienne Pasquier, who had actually been a
pupil of Alciato's at Bourges (Kelley, 1970, p. 272). He began to publish
his massive *Researches on France* in 1560, and included a structural analysis
of the French constitution in Book II, which he first issued in 1565. The
same themes were then taken up by Du Haillan, first in his *State and
Success* of 1570, and later in his *History of France* in 1576. It seems probable that Du Haillan was the main target of the accusation of plagiarism
which Pasquier levelled at his pupils in later editions of his *Researches*,
giving this as his reason for having delayed the publication of all but his
first two volumes until the closing years of his life (cols 1–3). But the

most influential exponent of this approach to the French constitution was Bodin in his *Method for the Easy Comprehension of History*, first published in 1566. The Dedication speaks (p. 1) of 'the way in which one should cull flowers from History to gather thereof the sweetest fruits', and much of the ensuing book is concerned with showing us how to learn the most valuable lessons from the past – discussing the choice of sources, the proper order of reading them, the arrangement of materials and the evaluation of one's discoveries (cf. Brown, 1939, pp. 86–119). This is followed by a long chapter on 'The type of government in States' in which these lessons are duly put to work, the result being a comparative and historical analysis of the governments of Rome, Sparta, Germany, Italy and – finally and especially – France.

It would be an overstatement to claim that, in consequence of following this anti-Bartolist approach, the constitutional theorists of the 1560s completely repudiated the more absolutist ideology adopted by the legists in the first half of the sixteenth century. They continued in particular to endorse the legist assumption that the king must be viewed as a supreme judge, and thus as the ultimate source of law in the commonwealth. Pasquier begins his discussion of the Parlements by conceding that 'our kings have been given absolute power by God, so that any legal restrictions on the crown must be 'an invention of the kings themselves', a conclusion which he seeks to prove historically by tracing the development of the Parlements to their alleged origins in the *placita* of Charlemagne (pp. 48, 66). Bodin goes even further, arguing that the concept of mixed monarchy is inherently 'absurd' and confused (pp. 154, 178). He continues to endorse the legist assumption that the principal 'mark' of sovereignty must be that of 'creating the most important magistrates and defining the office of each one', and thus argues that in the case of a monarchy (which he takes to be the best form of government) there can be no constitutional decrees which 'have force in any way' unless 'the prince himself orders them' (pp. 172, 176; cf. pp. 271, 282). The same thesis is reiterated by Du Haillan in Book IV of the *State and Success*, which is given over to analysing the prerogatives of the French monarchy (fo 302ff.). He assures us that he is 'at no point arguing that France is a commonwealth composed of three forms of government' in the manner of Seyssel, or even that it is 'divided in its absolute power into three parts' (fo 171a). He admits on the contrary that all its 'laws and constitutions' were originally 'instituted by our kings for their own grandeur and for the good of the commonwealth' (fo 168b). And he follows Pasquier with suspicious closeness in his account of the Parlements, conceding that 'this innovation was first established by Martel', confirmed by Charlemagne and finally accepted as part of the constitution in the edicts promulgated by Philip IV at the start of the fourteenth century (fos 37a, 182a).

But in spite of these concessions, the main importance of all these writers undoubtedly lies in the fact that they revived a more traditional form of constitutionalism, established their arguments on a new set of theoretical foundations, and turned the resulting analysis against the more absolutist pretensions of the legists. This can be observed first of all in their discussions of *la police*. Their humanist methodology helped them to revive the discussion of this theme in a new and more powerful form. It led them to insist on the key assumption that if a given check on the powers of the crown can be shown to have originated in the fundamental constitution, or to have developed over a sufficiently long period of time, then it follows that there must be a right to enforce the same limitation on the powers of the present-day government (Church, 1941, p. 203). According to Church, Pasquier was the first political writer who explicitly stated that this theoretical implication could be derived from the increasing volume of research into the ancient constitution of France (Church, 1941, pp. 141–3; cf. Huppert, 1970, pp. 6–9). Soon afterwards, the same approach was taken over by Du Haillan, with no less evident self-consciousness. He claims at the start of Book III that the bridle of custom 'is so anciently established in this kingdom that any prince, however depraved he might be, would be ashamed to break it' (fo 172b). And he thinks that 'it follows from this' that 'the sovereign and monarchical power of our kings' must still be 'governed and moderated by honest and reasonable means originally introduced by these kings themselves' (fo 172b). It was in the light of this belief about the normative character of the fundamental constitution that Pasquier and Du Haillan turned to excavating the ancient and medieval history of France, and duly discovered that the powers of the monarchy throughout this period had indeed been checked by a growing network of customs and customary rights. The outcome was a renewed emphasis on the idea that the king must remain bound at all times by these customary laws, and thus a revival of the Seysellian check of *la police*. As Du Haillan puts the point, 'the splendid constitutions of France' make up '*la police* of the monarchy', and so serve to ensure that the king remains 'ruled, limited and bridled by good laws and ordinances' in such a way that 'nothing is permitted to him except what is just, reasonable and prescribed by the ordinances themselves' (fos 10b, 170a).

These writers tend to place an even greater emphasis on the bridles of *la religion* and *la justice*. And since they conceive of *la religion* (in the manner of Seyssel) as being bodied forth in the dictates of *la justice*, it is on the latter concept that they chiefly concentrate. This comes out most clearly in Bodin's discussion of 'the form of monarchy' (p. 201ff.). He argues that the king cannot properly be regarded as above the law, since he has a duty to ensure that his laws remain in line with *la justice*. This means that 'princes use sophistry against the people when they say that they themselves are released from the laws so that not only are they superior to the laws but also in no way bound by them' (p. 203). The same concern is evident in Du Haillan's narrative outline of the development of the French constitution. He begins by claiming that 'the excellence of the French kings' ever since Pepin has chiefly been revealed by the fact that they have been careful 'to establish their laws upon the foundations of *la religion* and *la justice*' (fo 4a). And he constantly stresses that all true monarchs have a duty to bridle their authority by means of *la justice*, 'to ensure that they do not have too much power, and to ensure that it may be justly exercised' (fo 6a).

There is one respect in which these writers have an even wider conception of the check of *la justice* than Seyssel himself. While emphasising the legal limitations on absolutism, Seyssel had remained relatively uninterested in the idea of representative institutions as a constraint on the monarchy, and had mentioned the States General only once – and in passing – in the whole of *The Monarchy of France*. The theorists of the 1560s, by contrast, display a growing awareness of the origins and authority of the assembly of the Three Estates. Pasquier remains cautious, confining himself to observing that 'the assembly of the Estates has a very ancient history', while stopping short of insisting on its rights under the fundamental constitution (p. 85). But Bodin roundly declares that the king of France 'cannot destroy the laws peculiar in the entire kingdom or alter any of the customs of the cities or ancient ways without the consent of the Three Estates' (p. 204). And by the time we come to Du Haillan's account, we find the idea of the States General as a customary check on the crown beginning to be treated as an essential feature of the ancient constitution. He maintains that the assembly of the Estates 'has at all times served as the sovereign medicine of kings and people' (fo 186a). And he confirms the constitutional position of the assembly by pointing out that 'after the calling of the Estates became established, our kings adopted the custom of holding them frequently, and not engaging in any great enterprise without calling them together' (fo 185a).

As with Seyssel, however, the check of *la justice* in the constitutional writings of the 1560s was chiefly seen as a matter of placing legal limitations on the powers of the crown. Bodin introduces a novel emphasis at this point by focusing on the French coronation oath, affirming that it binds the kings to 'judge with integrity and religious scruple' and to' give rightful laws and justice to all classes' (p. 204). This is taken to constitute an important limitation on the king's authority, since 'having sworn, he cannot easily violate his oath; or if he could, yet he would be unwilling to do so, for the same justice exists for him as for any private citizen, and he is held by the same laws' (p. 204; cf. Franklin, 1973, p. 37). But the main legal check on the monarchy is said to be constituted by the authority of the courts, and in particular by the Parlement of Paris, the highest court in the land. All these writers insist that the duty of the king to take counsel from the Parlement is not an optional but an essential feature of the existing constitution of France. The most fulsome account is given by Pasquier, who continually stresses – in a favourite phrase – that 'our kings by an ancient custom have always wished to reduce their wills to the civility of the law' (p. 66). This means that 'they have wished their edicts and decrees to pass through an alembic of public order' (p. 66). And this in turn means that the Parlement, as the chosen alembic for reducing the king's will to the dictates of justice, must be treated as 'the principal nerve of our monarchy' and 'the foundation stone in the conservation of our commonwealth' (pp. 85, 237). Bodin expresses the same sentiments, arguing that 'those who have been trying to overthrow the dignity of these courts seek the ruin of the State, since in these is placed the safety of civil order, of laws, of customs, and of the entire State' (p. 257). And Du Haillan goes on to repeat (and indeed to plagiarise) Pasquier's analysis, claiming that the king has a duty 'to reduce his will to the civility of the law', to achieve this result 'by causing his edicts and decrees to pass through the alembic of this public order', and to recognise in consequence that the Parlement represents an essential feature of the fundamental constitution of France (fo 182b).

These conclusions are said to be confirmed by the fact that the Parlement has the power to oppose and even to veto the will of the king if he attempts to impose an edict out of line with the dictates of natural justice. Pasquier is absolutely decisive on this point (cf. Huppert, 1970, pp. 49–51). 'Once the Parlement was set up, it was found to be right that the wills of our kings should in no case attain the status of edicts unless verified and ratified by the Parlement' (p. 64). He concedes, of course that 'edicts have sometimes been pushed through against the opinion of the court', but he maintains that this is a recent phenomenon – the Duke of Burgundy in the fifteenth century being 'one of the first' to countenance it – as well as being an illegal and 'usurping' constitutional practice (pp. 65–6). The same claims are forcefully restated by Bodin. He asserts that there is no law in France 'more sacred than that which denies to the decrees of the prince any force unless they are in keeping with equity as well as truth'. And he adds that 'from this it comes about that many are cast out by the magistrates', so that 'no help to the wicked' can ever be expected from the will of the prince (p. 254). Finally, the same conclusions are reiterated by Du Haillan, again plagiarising Pasquier's account. He repeats word for word Pasquier's assertion that 'it was found to be right' once the Parlement had been set up 'that the wills of our kings should in no case attain the status of edicts unless verified and ratified by the Parlement' (fo 182b). And he adds, more optimistically than Pasquier, that 'the authority of the judges and sovereign courts is so great' in France that 'there is no prince so mighty, nor any subject so presumptuous, that he would dare to disobey them' (fo 172a; cf. also fo 184a).

Seyssel had concluded that in order to assure the independence of the Parlements in checking the edicts of the king, it must be essential that the officers of the court should be secure from dismissal even by the king himself. Pasquier and Du Haillan have nothing to say about this final safeguard, possibly silenced by the authority of Du Moulin, who had meanwhile revived, as we have seen, the opinion of Lothair to the effect that no mere magistrate can ever be endowed with such a degree of judicial independence. But Bodin is much bolder, even though he admits that Alciato and Du Moulin have both rejected the belief that 'the opinion of Azo was the more correct' in relation to the constitution of France (p. 173). He is naturally somewhat diffident at the prospect of arguing against these peerless authorities, and begins by acknowledging that he probably 'should not dare' to venture an opinion on the issue, especially 'since it is of great importance' (p. 255). Nevertheless, he goes on to raise a number of difficulties arising out of the alleged right of a ruler to dismiss his magistrates. 'What would the magistrates dare to do contrary to the power and desire of princes if they feared that their honours would be taken from them? Who will defend the weak from servitude? Who will guard the interest of the people, if the magistrate has been driven away and they must comply with the demands of the mighty?' (p. 255). He is finally persuaded that the right answer must be to insist after all that if the magistrates are to be 'feared by the wicked' and 'reverenced by the prince', it is essential that everyone, prince and people alike, should accept that such officers 'cannot be driven from power except for crime' (p. 256).

MONTAIGNE AND STOICISM

So far we have focused on the conditions relatively favourable to the emergence of a Huguenot theory of revolution after 1572. To complete this survey of the ideological circumstances in which the Huguenot theory arose, we need finally to consider the reactions of those who remained hostile to any justifications of political activism or resistance. One important source of this hostility arose out of the resurgence in the 1570s of a sceptical and quietist form of stoic moral and political thought – an outlook which, as we have seen, had already become popular in the later phases of *quattrocento* humanism. Some elements of the same outlook can already be discerned in such works as Du Fail's *Rustic Subjects*, with its condemnation of large cities as natural centres of sedition, and its advocacy of rural living both as a sign of moral vigour and as a symbol of political innocence. But the main revival of stoic doctrines amongst French humanists occurred in the chaotic years immediately following the massacres of 1572, with the most famous statement of the position being provided in the *Essays* of Montaigne.

It is true that the role of stoic ideas in the evolution of Montaigne's *Essays* has sometimes been exaggerated. When Pierre Villey produced his pioneering analysis of Montaigne's intellectual development, based on an examination of the successive revisions in the so-called 'Bordeaux copy' of the *Essays*, he popularised the idea of distinguishing three main stages in the evolution of Montaigne's thought: the first Book of *Essays*, mainly written in 1572–4, was taken to reflect an 'impersonal' phase of stoic and especially Senecan influence; the second, mainly composed between 1578 and 1580, was said to follow from a 'pyrrhonian crisis' in 1576; and the last Book, completed between 1585 and 1588, was felt to embody Montaigne's mature 'philosophy of nature', in which both stoicism and scepticism were eventually seen as extreme positions (Villey, 1908). A number of scholars have recently criticised this account as excessively schematic, and it is certainly true that in every phase of his writing Montaigne presents us with an outlook in which the elements of stoicism are more freely criticised, as well as being more closely intertwined with sceptical and epicurean beliefs, than Villey's analysis tends to suggest.[1] Nevertheless, it would still be true to say that the moral theory of the stoics, filtered through the sensibility of the earlier Renaissance humanists, seems to have exercised a special fascination on Montaigne in the early 1570s. The change he decided to make in his own way of life at this time was very much in line with the stoic tendency to value the life of *otium* more highly than that of *negotium*. Montaigne had been serving since 1557 as a *conseiller* to the Parlement of Bordeaux, an office which his father had purchased three years before (Frame, 1965, pp. 46–62). When Montaigne

---

[1] See for example the discussions in Sayce, 1972, pp. 149–53, 161–7, 170–201, and in Naudeau, 1972, pp. 55–60, 103–5.

failed to gain promotion to the upper chamber in 1569, he immediately sold his position, retiring a year later to the château he had inherited on his father's death in 1568. There he set up at the entrance to his study an inscription commemorating his decision to withdraw from 'the servitude of the court and of public employments', and there he began almost at once to beguile his retirement with the composition of the *Essays* – a concept and an art-form which he may almost be said to have invented (Frame, 1965, pp. 114–15, 146). There is no doubt, moreover, that Montaigne's earliest *Essays* are the most conspicuously stoic both in tone and subject-matter, and that when the first two books were published in 1580, it was chiefly as a stoic moralist that he won acclaim and began to exercise his distinctive influence. When Pasquier published his letters in 1587, he included an appreciation of the *Essays* in which he hailed Montaigne as 'another Seneca in our language'.[1] When the *Essays* were reissued in 1595, the new edition contained a sonnet by Claude Expilly in which Montaigne was apostrophised as a 'magnanimous stoic' and praised for 'defying the inconstancy and tempests of the age' (Boase, 1935, pp. 9–10). And when Louis Guyon produced his collection of *Diverse Readings* in 1604, he descended to outright plagiarism, including a chapter on the need to reflect on mortality which was virtually a repetition of Montaigne's early essay in defence of the stoic contention that 'to philosophise is to learn to die'.[2]

As the religious wars continued throughout the 1570s and into the next decade, the posture of stoic endurance cultivated by Montaigne came to seem an increasingly appealing response to what he himself described as 'the public death' of 'our poor country' amidst 'the violence of our civil wars' (pp. 241, 467, 800). This helps to account for the growing popularity of stoicism both in France and in the no less war-torn Netherlands towards the end of the sixteenth century, just as it helps to explain the recrudescence of the same pattern of ideas amongst the defeated royalists in England during the 1650s (Skinner, 1972, pp. 81–2). The leading French exponent of stoicism at this period was Guillaume Du Vair (1556–1621), a studiously moderate Catholic, later Bishop of Lisieux, who became clerk to the Parlement of Paris in 1584, and was widely employed as a conciliator in the final phases of the religious wars (Radouant, 1908, pp. 76, 312). During the siege of Paris in 1590 he composed a stoic dialogue on the theme of constancy, first published in 1594 and translated into English in 1622 as *A Buckler against Adversity* (Radouant, 1908, p. 234 and n.). The most celebrated exponent of the same outlook in the Netherlands at the

---

[1] See Thickett, 1956b, p. 46 and for Pasquier's publication of his letters see ibid., p. xxviii.
[2] See Villey, 1935, pp. 130–7 and cf. *The Essays*, ed. Frame, p. 56.

end of the century was Justus Lipsius (1547–1606), a Catholic by birth who left the Low Countries in 1571 to teach at the Lutheran University of Jena, later transferring to the Calvinist University of Leyden and finally returning to the Catholic Church and the Professorship of Latin at Louvain in the early 1590s (Zanta, 1914, pp. 155–61). He wrote a stoic treatise *On Constancy* in 1584, and the publication of his letters two years later revealed him to be an early and enthusiastic reader of Montaigne, who in turn saluted him in later editions of the *Essays* as the most learned man of the age.[1] Lipsius's main statement of his neo-stoic political philosophy appeared in his *Six Books of Politics*, which was first published in Latin in 1589, translated into English five years later, and for a time enjoyed an enormous vogue. It was one of the very few modern works to be cited with approval by Montaigne, and it obviously provided Du Vair with many of the leading ideas in his *Buckler against Adversity*.[2]

The point of departure for all these writers is supplied by the concept of Fortune, which they personify in typically humanist style as an inscrutable goddess, capricious and potentially overwhelming in her power. One of the chief criticisms of Montaigne's *Essays* made by the Papal censor in 1581 was his excessive fondness for invoking this pagan deity (Frame, 1965, pp. 217–18). Montaigne does not appear to have taken the complaint to heart, for the same preoccupation – summarised in the proposition that 'Fortune, not wisdom, rules the life of man' – continues to recur throughout Book III of the *Essays*, first published seven years later (p. 753). Lipsius is similarly emphatic in his *Politics* about the irresistible powers of Fortune and destiny, though he is usually more careful to equate these forces with 'the decrees of God' (p. 190). And the same sense of man's helplessness in confronting his fate permeates Du Vair's treatise on adversity, in which the fickle attentions of Fortune are cited to account for the rise and fall of kingdoms as well as individual men (pp. 40ff., 63ff.).

The chief lesson these moralists preach is the need to remain steadfast in the face of Fortune's changeability. This is held to be particularly necessary in time of civil war, a time which is never far from their thoughts. Montaigne continually inveighs against 'this miserable age of ours', given over to 'wars which at this moment are oppressing our State' (pp. 322, 547). Du Vair's treatise on adversity begins with a similar outcry against the 'storm of worse than civil wars' which has brought about 'the ruin

---

[1] See Zanta, 1914, pp. 158–9; Boase, 1935, pp. 19–20; and cf. Montaigne, *The Essays*, ed. Frame, p. 436.
[2] The main modern study of Du Vair speaks of his tendency to be 'far too docile in his imitation of Lipsius'; see Radouant, 1908, p. 260. See also Radouant, pp. 267–8, on Montaigne's presumed influence.

and subversion of our country' (pp. 4, 5). As a way of confronting what Lipsius calls 'this very sea of calamities', the response they seek to inculcate is one of stoical forbearance (p. 187). According to Montaigne, the precepts we must cultivate are those of 'resoluteness and constancy', always 'bearing troubles patiently' and acting 'with resolution and patience' (pp. 30, 802). Our basic duty, as Du Vair adds, is to ensure that even if God's anger 'continues against us, what Fortune soever falls upon us, we must bear it patiently' (pp. 32, 89).

This outlook carried with it a distinctive set of political implications, the most important being the idea that everyone has a duty to submit himself to the existing order of things, never resisting the prevailing government but accepting and where necessary enduring it with fortitude. Two aspects of this cardinal obligation are particularly stressed. The first is the need to hold fast to the existing form of religion established in the commonwealth. Du Vair is very emphatic about this implication, and issues a warning to Henry IV that it is essential 'for the perfect union of his subjects' that he should abandon his Huguenot faith and allow himself to be received into 'the religion of the kings his predecessors' (p. 52). Lipsius is even more anxious about the preservation of religious uniformity, a requirement he stated so sharply in his *Politics* that he became involved in consequence in an angry dispute with Dirck Coornhert (1522–90), whose major work on liberty of conscience, first published in 1590, took the form of an attack on Lipsius's intolerance (Lecler, II, 1960, pp. 281–5). Lipsius remained unrepentant, even in later editions of his book, and continued to argue that princes must only allow a single form of worship within their territories, one which must always be 'according to the ancient customs' of the country concerned (p. 62). While he concedes that private dissenting may sometimes be allowed, he insists that where a new religion is publicly espoused, and where the heretics 'by commotions do enforce others to do the like', they 'ought to be punished' with great severity, there being 'no place for clemency' in dealing with the disruption of traditional observances (pp. 62, 63).

It has often been doubted whether Montaigne should be held to have accepted the same conservative implications of his stoic premises. One reason is that he was certainly far more tolerant – by comparison not merely with Lipsius, but with the most learned political writers of his age. Bodin, for example, recommends the persecution of witches without a qualm, but Montaigne has a fine passage in his essay *Of Cripples* in which he makes clear his utter distaste for such cruelties (pp. 788–91; cf. Monter, 1969, pp. 384–9). But the main reason is that Montaigne has often been portrayed as something of a sceptic in matters of religious belief. This reputation is chiefly owed to his *Apology for Raymond Sebond*, by far the longest and most pyrrhonian of his essays. Sebond was a Spanish theologian of the fifteenth century, who had sought to demonstrate in his *Natural Theology* (which Montaigne had translated in 1567–8) that all the truths of Christianity are capable of being established from the evidence of nature (Popkin, 1968, p. 45). Montaigne's defence of Sebond against his detractors takes the curious form of insisting that human reason is too weak a guide for any form of certainty ever to be possible. This was the point at which he took as his motto the question 'What do I know?' and came to the conclusion that 'reason does nothing but go astray in everything, and especially when it meddles with divine things' (pp. 386, 393). Montaigne's claim to be defending Sebond thus begins to sound ironic, making it possible to believe that his underlying intention may have been to shake the foundations of Christianity itself. This was the interpretation originally proposed by the *libertins erudits* of seventeenth-century France, and echoes of the same suspicion can still be heard in several recent commentaries.[1]

There are good grounds for arguing, however, that Montaigne's scepticism about the possibility of proof in the domain of religious belief was allied to a perfectly sincere and mainly conventional adherence to the tenets of the Catholic faith. He always maintained the outward forms of religion, and according to Pasquier's account he died in the full rites of the Catholic Church (Thickett, 1956b, pp. 48–9). His attack on rationalism may not have been orthodox, but it still constituted a recognisable theological position, comparable with the attack which Ockham and his disciples had mounted on the Thomists over two centuries before. As one recent commentator has put it, Montaigne's basic feeling about his own religious faith appears to have been that it 'remained outside the realm of doubt because it remained outside the realm of reason' (Brown, 1963, p. 43). There can be no question, moreover, that Montaigne believed very strongly in the necessity of upholding religious uniformity and traditional religious observances – in spite of the fact that he remained opposed to all forms of persecution, never denouncing the Huguenots for their actual beliefs, but only for the social consequences of their attempts to impose them on other people. The best evidence of his continuing commitment to the time-honoured ideal of 'one faith, one law, one king' is provided by Dreano in his study of Montaigne's religious thought (Dreano, 1969, pp. 89–91). When Catherine de Medici's Edict of Tol-

---

[1] Popkin, for example, speaks of Montaigne's evident 'indifference' to Christianity, and claims that 'at best' he can only have been a 'mildly religious' man, 'without any serious religious experience or involvement' (Popkin, 1968, pp. 55–6).

eration was promulgated in January 1562, the Parlement of Paris demanded as an act of defiance that a renewed oath of loyalty should be sworn to the Catholic Church. Montaigne was in Paris at the time, and appears not only to have opposed the Edict (like his friend La Boetie), but also 'to have accepted with joy', as Dreano puts it, his obligation to take the new oath (Dreano, 1969, p. 90). This attitude is wholly consistent with the conservative outlook voiced by Montaigne throughout the *Essays* on the need for religious uniformity and on the rights of the Church authorities. He affirms that he will 'hold it as execrable' if his writings are found to contain anything 'against the holy prescriptions of the Catholic, apostolic and Roman Church, in which I die and in which I was born' (p. 229). He emphasises that his own attitude towards the controversies with the Huguenots 'on whose account France is at present agitated by civil wars' is that 'the best and soundest side is undoubtedly that which maintains the old religion and the old government of the country' (p. 506). And he exhorts his fellow Catholics not to give in to the Huguenots by making even a 'partial surrender of their beliefs', arguing that the best course of action must be to 'submit completely to the authority of our ecclesiastical government' (p. 134).

The other aspect of this cardinal duty of submission which the stoic moralists emphasise is the need to remain obedient at all times to the powers that be, however imperfectly they may happen to discharge their offices. Lipsius adopts his most Biblical tones in exhorting every subject to 'take thy shield to thee, rather than thy sword, yea, I say, thy shield of sufferance', since the idea of offering violence even to a tyrant 'is a heavy thing, yea and for the most part a thing unfortunate' (p. 200). Du Vair agrees that 'the subject is inexcusable that foresakes the party of the laws and public welfare', since he 'ought indeed to have for his end the public welfare and the justice whereon it depends', and ought in consequence 'never to dissemble in the beginning of commotions, nor consent to anything unjust or against the laws' (pp. 123, 133–4, 135). But the gravest warnings against the dangers of 'novelties' are issued by Montaigne, especially in the famous essay *Of Custom, and not easily changing an accepted law* which he wrote at the time of the major Huguenot insurrections of 1572–4. He insists that everyone must 'wholly follow the accepted fashion and forms', since 'it is the rule of rules, and the universal law of laws, that each man should observe those of the place he is in', and regard it as 'a fine thing to obey your country's laws' (p. 86). La Boetie is praised for having 'sovereignly imprinted in his soul' the injunction 'to obey and submit most religiously to the laws under which he was born', while Plato is cited with approval for wanting to prevent any citizen from

enquiring 'even into the reason of the civil laws, which are to be respected
as divine ordinances' (pp. 144, 233). We are continually reminded that
although 'we may wish for different magistrates', we 'must nevertheless
obey those that are here', and we are assured that the greatest of all the
marks of 'justice and utility' in the Christian religion lies in its 'precise
recommendation of obedience to the magistrates and maintenance of the
government' (pp. 87–8, 760).

Given these assumptions, it is hardly surprising to find that Montaigne
and the other stoic moralists were vehemently opposed to any attempt to
vindicate the lawfulness of political resistance. They were especially
hostile to the religious revolutionaries in France and the Netherlands, who
were daring to lead an insurrection in the name of the new faith, and
daring to couple this 'novelty' with the almost equally impious demand
for wholesale constitutional change. All of them accordingly focus on what
Montaigne calls the most solemn question of all, the question of 'whether
it is lawful for a subject to rebel and take arms against his prince in defence
of religion' (p. 323). Montaigne's own answer reveals an utter detestation
for the Huguenots. He leaves us in no conceivable doubt as to his loathing
for their 'feverish factions', their 'excesses and injustice' and 'their violent
and ambitious enterprises' (pp. 323, 775). He never mentions the adherents of 'the so-called reformed religion' without sarcasm, and he
repeatedly insists that their faith is only a pretext for their treason, since
their boasted zealousness is nothing more than a 'propensity to malignity
and violence' (p. 602; cf. pp. 323, 467). Even if their sincerity were
unimpeachable, he concludes, their actions would still be no less evil,
since they are 'seeking to disturb and change the state of our government
without worrying whether they will improve it' (p. 144). The same hatred
of religious revolutionaries and suspicion of their motives are no less
strongly voiced in the writings of Lipsius and Du Vair. Lipsius is convinced that 'civil war cannot be honestly enterprised', and that 'for the most
part the end of taking arms is wicked', since the leaders of such disturbances 'under a pretext of the public profit do each of them strive for their
private authority' (p. 202). And Du Vair's main reason for hoping that
Henry IV will soon become converted to Catholicism is that this alone
will enable him to overcome 'the obstinacy of those who seek their greatness in public ruins' (p. 53) – an evident allusion to Henry's factious
Huguenot followers, and to the other 'ambitious and wicked men' who
are trying to 'turn upside-down all order, laws and politic government'
(p. 122).

These attacks on religious radicalism are based on the more general
claim that all the revolutionary movements of the age are equally and

unforgivably destructive, so that the very idea of political resistance, on whatever grounds, deserves to be completely repudiated. The main reason given for this conclusion is simply a general sense of horror at the cruelties and disorders of civil war (McGowan, 1974, pp. 104–8). Montaigne cries out against the 'monstrous war' which is 'tearing France to pieces and dividing us into factions', and sees in the prevalence of party divisions a 'true school of treachery, inhumanity and brigandage' (pp. 502, 760, 796). Lipsius thinks it better to 'endure any kind of punishment' at the hands of tyrants rather than abet 'so great a cruelty', adding that 'nothing is more miserable, nothing more dishonourable' than to allow a civil war to take place (pp. 187, 203). And Du Vair strengthens the argument by threatening those who have dabbled in 'this venom of sedition' and 'prostituted their wits to serve other men's passions' with the certainty that they will eventually find themselves 'inexcusable before God', just as they are already inexcusable before their fellow-countrymen (pp. 123, 126).

As well as emphasising his belief in the need for submission, Montaigne adds a final warning of his own about the danger of 'novelties', a warning which is based on his general scepticism about the powers of reason, and gives rise to an almost Burkean form of conservatism. He thinks the Huguenots exhibit an appalling 'self-love and presumption' in having such a high regard for their own opinions that, in order to be sure of imposing them, they are prepared to 'overthrow the public peace and introduce so many inevitable evils, and such a horrible corruption of morals, as civil wars and political changes bring with them' (p. 87). The reason he thinks this so wickedly presumptuous is based on his sense that 'it is very doubtful whether there can be such evident profit in changing an accepted law, of whatever sort it be, as there is harm in disturbing it' (p. 86). This insight causes him to be 'disgusted with innovation, in whatever guise', and leads him to feel that 'the worst thing I find in our state is instability, and the fact that out laws cannot, any more than our clothes, take any settled form' (pp. 86, 498). He is convinced that programmatic political change can never be made to work, since 'the difficulty of improving our condition and the danger of everything crumbling into bits' is so great that 'in public affairs there is no course so bad, provided it is old and stable, that it is not better than change and commotion' (p. 497). He even thinks that the Huguenots secretly know this themselves, for he can hardly believe that 'a single one has been found of so feeble an understanding as to have been genuinely persuaded' that 'by overthrowing the government, the authorities and the laws' he can hope to 'bring help to the sacrosanct sweetness and justice of the divine word' (p. 798). Montaigne's final word thus amounts to a plea that we should leave our laws and government exactly as we find them. Since 'we can hardly twist them out of their accustomed bent without breaking up everything', the most basic moral to be grasped is that 'the oldest and best-known evil is always more bearable than an evil that is new and untried' (pp. 730, 732).

BODIN AND ABSOLUTISM

As well as becoming an object of hatred to all men of conservative temperament, the Huguenot party found itself under increasing attack after 1572 from a number of political writers who had hitherto been content to adopt a moderate or even a radically constitutionalist stance. By far the most important theorist to change his mind in this way was Jean Bodin, who issued his *Six Books of a Commonweal* at the height of the Huguenot revolution in 1576. Abandoning the constitutionalist position he had adopted in his *Method for the Easy Comprehension of History*, Bodin reveals himself in the *Six Books* as a virtually unyielding defender of absolutism, demanding the outlawing of all theories of resistance and the acceptance of a strong monarchy as the only means of restoring political unity and peace.

Bodin's point of departure has much in common with that of the stoic humanists we have just considered, with Machiavelli's *Discourses* providing an obvious common source for some of their more pessimistic beliefs. One of the basic presuppositions of Bodin's thought is his sense of the extreme difficulty as well as the absolute necessity of establishing a fitting order and harmony in every commonwealth.[1] The climax of Book III – which is concerned with political institutions – accordingly takes the form of a celebration of the need 'in all things' to 'seek after a convenient and decent order, and deem nothing to be more ugly or foul to look upon than confusion and broil' (p. 386). This is immediately followed at the start of Book IV – which discusses the rise and fall of commonwealths – with an account of the problem of establishing such a system of justice, and the corresponding fragility of any political order we may manage to achieve. Bodin may have felt that he had learned about the ever-present threat of anarchy from his own experience, for he had been a witness to the massacre of St Bartholomew, in which he had narrowly escaped with his life (Chauviré, 1914, p. 35). He may also have learned the same lesson from Machiavelli, whose emphasis on the inexorable tendency of all kingdoms and republics to fall into corruption and collapse is echoed throughout the *Six Books*. Whatever the cause of his fears, the outcome was a conviction that 'the flourishing estate' of any commonwealth can never hope to be

[1] For a strong emphasis on this point see Greenleaf, 1973, p. 25 and Villey, 1973, p. 69.

'of any long continuance', due to the continual 'changes of worldly things, which are so mutable and uncertain' (p. 406).

Given this vision of the frailty of 'order' and the paramount need to maintain it, Bodin clearly saw his major ideological task in the *Six Books* as that of attacking and repudiating the Huguenot theory of resistance, which he had come to regard as the greatest single threat to the possibility of re-establishing a well-ordered monarchy in France.[1] This sense of his fundamental purpose comes out most clearly in the programmatic Prefaces attached to successive editions of his great work. He expresses the utmost horror at the fact that subjects are 'arming themselves against their princes', that seditious writings are 'being brought out openly, like firebrands to set commonwealths ablaze', and that people are claiming that 'princes sent by providence to the human race must be thrust out of their kingdoms under a pretence of tyranny' (p. A71). He repeatedly indicates that his main intention in writing is to answer these 'dangerous men' who are attempting under a pretext of popular liberty to 'induce the subjects to rebel against their natural princes, opening the door to a licentious anarchy, which is worse than the harshest tyranny in the world' (p. A70).

Bodin's response to the Huguenot revolutionaries is direct and uncompromising: he insists that no public act of resistance by a subject against a legitimate sovereign can ever be justified. The point is mainly brought out in the course of discussing different types of government at the start of Book II. After distinguishing (p. 200) three forms of monarchy – the 'royal', 'lordly' and 'tyrannical' – Bodin proceeds in Chapter V to ask 'whether it be lawful to lay violent hands upon a tyrant' (p. 218). He notes, in a direct allusion to the revolutionary writings of the Huguenots, that a number of books have recently been 'publicly imprinted' which claim that 'subjects may take up arms against their prince' in any case of alleged tyranny, and may lawfully 'take him out of the way' in the name of the public good (p. 224). These he denounces with the greatest ferocity, arguing that it can never be lawful 'for any one of the subjects in particular, or all of them in general, to attempt anything either by way of fact or justice against the honour, life or dignity of the sovereign, albeit he had committed all the wickedness, impiety and cruelty that could be spoken' (p. 222). He adds that 'if any man shall so much as conceit a thought for the violating' of his sovereign prince, then he is 'worthy of death', even though he may have 'attempted nothing' (p. 222). And he ends by citing

[1] The idea that the *Six Books* 'cannot be fully understood except as an ideological reaction to the seeming menace of the new constitutionalism' of the Huguenots after 1572 has recently been convincingly argued in Salmon, 1973, pp. 361, 364 and in Franklin, 1973, in which the above quotation appears at p. vii. See also pp. 50, 93. My own analysis is greatly indebted to both these valuable accounts.

with full approval Cicero's remark to the effect that no cause can ever be 'just or sufficient for us to take up arms against our country' (p. 225).

Once this basic doctrine is hammered home, Bodin can afford to be liberal at the fringes of his theory, and proceeds to allow two qualifications. Since he is only discussing legitimate government, he concedes that a ruler who is a tyrant *ex defectu tituli* – in the sense of being a usurper – can always 'be lawfully slain' by 'all the people or any of them' (p. 219). His other and less conventional qualification is that since he is only discussing the relationship between a subject and his sovereign, he is prepared to allow that a legitimate ruler who falls into tyranny may be lawfully resisted by the intervention of a foreign prince. He not only thinks it 'lawful for any stranger to kill a tyrant', but even admirable – as Grotius was later to agree – for 'a valiant and worthy prince' to invade the lands of such a ruler in order 'to defend the honour, goods and lives of such as are unjustly oppressed by the power of the more mighty' (pp. 220–1).

Bodin is absolutely insistent, however, that none of these exceptions should be taken to cast the least shadow across his basic argument. When the radical Calvinists sought to exploit his suggestion about the role of liberating princes (an argument which recurs in several revolutionary tracts of the 1570s) Bodin published an *Apology* in which he reiterated his most absolutist conclusions, indignantly repudiating any suggestion that he might have intended to countenance a foreign invasion of France (Franklin, 1973, p. 95 and n.). He continued to confront the Huguenots with the claim 'that it is not lawful for a man not only to kill his sovereign prince, but even to rebel against him, without an especial and undoubted commandment from God' (p. 224). And he added, perhaps somewhat disingenuously, that all the Protestants ought to regard themselves as bound to accept the same doctrine, since it had been enunciated by Luther and Calvin themselves. He insists – quite mistakenly – that when the German princes enquired of Luther whether it was lawful for them to resist the Emperor, he 'frankly told them that it was not lawful, whatsoever tyranny or impiety were pretended' (p. 225). And he dismisses the apparent right of resistance allowed by Calvin to 'ephoral' authorities, pointing out that he only says they may 'possibly' resist, and adding that he never intended even this to be 'lawful in a right monarchy' (p. 225).

Bodin's attack on the theory and practice of the Huguenot revolution brings us to the heart of the positive doctrines enunciated in the *Six Books*, since it brings us to the discussion of sovereignty, which he treats as 'the principal and most necessary point for the understanding of the nature of a commonwealth'. Bodin admits that if a ruler 'be no absolute sovereign', there is 'no doubt but that it is lawful' for his subjects to resist him and 'to proceed against a tyrant by way of justice' (p. 221). He lays it down, however, that since the fundamental aim of government must be to secure 'order' rather than liberty, any act of resistance by a subject against his ruler must be altogether outlawed in the name of trying to preserve the fragile structure of the commonwealth. He is thus drawn by the logic of his own ideological commitment into arguing that in any political society there must be a sovereign who is absolute in the sense that he commands but is never commanded, and so can never be lawfully opposed by any of his subjects. The conclusion is fully stated in Book I, Chapter 8, which is entitled *Of sovereignty*.[1] Bodin begins by defining sovereignty as 'the most high, absolute and perpetual power over the citizens and subjects in a commonwealth' (p. 84). He then makes it clear that in characterising the sovereign as 'absolute', what he has in mind is that, even if his commands are never 'just and honest', it is still 'not lawful for the subject to break the laws of his prince' or in any other way to oppose him 'under the colour of honesty or justice' (p. 105). The sovereign is in short immune by definition from lawful resistance, for the person 'in whom the sovereignty rests' is required 'to give account to none but to the immortal God alone' (p. 86). Already the foundations are fully laid for Hobbes's later construction of 'that great Leviathan' as a 'mortal God' to whom 'we owe under the immortal God our peace and defence' (p. 227).

There is much in Bodin's argument in this key chapter which is reminiscent of the legist political writers we have already discussed. It would by no means be a misleading characterisation of the *Six Books* to say that they represent a continuation and development of the absolutist claims advanced by such theorists as Chasseneuz and especially Du Moulin, both of whom are cited with approval in the preface to the *Method*, while Du Moulin is hailed in the *Six Books* as one of the 'princes of legal science'and the 'ornament of all lawyers'.[2] While Bodin is clearly influenced by these neo–Bartolists, however, there are two points at which he may be said to have shifted the basis as well as strengthened the structure of their arguments, thereby supplying a novel as well as far more powerful legitimation of the emergent absolutist state.

The first is that he not only treats the doctrine of non–resistance as an analytical implication of sovereignty, but goes on to treat the idea of absolute sovereignty as an analytical implication of the concept of the state.[3] This constitutes a crucial transition in the development of

---

[1] p. 84. As Salmon has emphasised, there is thus a sense in which Bodin's theory of sovereignty is a *thèse de circonstance*; cf. Salmon, 1973, pp. 3–8.

[2] See Bodin, *Method*, p. 5, and *Six Books*, pp. A71, 108.

[3] For this way of putting the point, see Church, 1941, p. 226 and Franklin, 1973, pp. 23, 93.

absolutist political thought. As we have seen, the legist analysis of supreme authority had proceeded by itemising a series of 'marks' of sovereignty which, taken together, might perhaps be said to yield the idea of absolutism. It is true that Bodin still includes in the *Six Books* a fairly conventional chapter in which he runs through a similar account of nine 'true marks of sovereignty' – the power to legislate, to make war and peace, appoint higher magistrates, hear final appeals, grant pardons, receive homage, coin money, regulate weights and measures and impose taxes (pp. 159–77). But the governing assumption in the chapter on sovereignty is that the idea of supremacy in the state can never be adequately elucidated simply by examining the way in which this mosaic of rights may have arisen in the course of historical development. Bodin begins by insisting that the proper approach must instead consist of seeking to *define* 'what majesty or sovereignty is' by reflecting on the concepts of the state and of political supremacy in themselves (p. 84). He boasts that hitherto no 'lawyer nor political philosopher' has ever managed to supply such a definition, but that he himself has now succeeded in the task (p. 84). He has already established, he claims, that the state must be defined as 'the lawful government of many families' by means of a 'high and perpetual power' (p. 1; cf. p. 84). He has now laid it down that the concept of sovereignty must be taken to denote just such a 'high, absolute and perpetual power over the citizens'. So it follows, he concludes, that the absolute and non-accountable form of authority which he has annexed to the idea of sovereignty must by definition be exercised by some determinate individual or group within any association which is properly to be classified as a state (p. 84).

This new approach in turn leads Bodin to reject the traditional typology of forms of rule which the legists had continued to endorse. The point is taken up at the start of Book II, in the chapter entitled *Sorts of commonwealths* (p. 183). Polybius is cited as the populariser of the suggestion that there must be seven different types of commonwealth: three 'commendable' forms (monarchy, aristocracy and democracy), three 'faulty' versions of these, and 'the seventh compounded of the mixture of the three first' (p. 184). Bodin notes that a number of modern authorities, including Machiavelli and Sir Thomas More, have confirmed this analysis, in particular by assuming that the 'mixed state' is the most commendable form of all (p. 184). He then insists that, in accepting this conclusion, all these authorities 'have erred and been deceived' (p. 184). He has already laid it down that the 'high and perpetual' power of sovereignty must by definition be held by some determinate individual or group within the commonwealth. This implies that the only way of classifying forms of rule must be in terms of the number of persons who may be said to hold sovereignty. This in turn means that only 'three estates or sorts of commonwealth' are possible – namely, monarchy, aristocracy or democracy, depending on whether the sovereignty is held by one or a few or all the citizens (p. 184). The 'mixed state' is thus taken to be 'a thing impossible', and Bodin ends by showing that all purported examples are in fact reducible either to monarchies, aristocracies or democracies (pp. 184–5).

The second novel feature of Bodin's analysis is his claim that sovereignty must be fundamentally legislative in character. This again represents a decisive break with the earlier arguments of the legists, who had tended to treat the ruler essentially as a judge, with his leading 'mark' of sovereignty being taken to be his right to appoint all other magistrates. As we have seen, this was still Bodin's own attitude when he published the *Method* in 1566. By the time he completed the *Six Books* a decade later, however, he had reached the distinctively modern legal-positivist conclusion that the highest (and in some sense the sole) 'mark' of sovereignty must be that of 'giving laws to the subjects in general without their consent' (p. 98). The point is elaborated in the chapter entitled *The true marks of sovereignty* (p. 153). Bodin begins by claiming, in an evident allusion to the legists, that even those who 'have written best' about the idea of the state have never correctly 'manifested this point' (p. 153). He then goes on to repeat that 'the first and chief mark of a sovereign prince' – the one which may be said to contain all others as aspects or implications – must be the power 'to give laws to all his subjects' without seeking the consent 'of any other greater, equal or lesser than himself' (p. 159).

This contention carries with it a rejection of the orthodox belief, still largely endorsed by the legists, that since the ruler is essentially a judge, his primary function must be that of upholding the sense of justice already embodied in the laws and customs of the commonwealth. Bodin argues instead that the concept of positive law must be defined 'without any other addition' as 'the command of a sovereign concerning all his subjects'. He thus insists, with an epoch-making lack of equivocation, that 'the laws of a sovereign prince, although they be grounded on good and lively reasons, depend nevertheless upon nothing but his mere and frank good will' (pp. 92, 156). Finally, he stresses that this in turn means that any sovereign must by definition be *legibus solutus* – totally 'acquitted' from any obligation to obey the positive laws of the state (p. 91). He must certainly be 'exempted from the laws of his predecessors', since his sovereignty would otherwise be infringed (p. 91). And he can never 'be subject to his own laws', since 'there can be no obligation which takes its state from the mere will of him that promises the same' (p. 92).

It remains to ask how Bodin seeks to justify his conclusion that an absolute and irresistible form of legislative sovereignty must by definition be located at some determinate point in every genuine state. The answer lies in examining his application of humanist techniques to the study of public law. He begins by taking over the humanist critique of Bartolist legal science which had already been adopted by the constitutional theorists of the 1560s. The traditional story that Bodin opposed these developments and sided with the forces of Bartolist reaction while teaching law at Toulouse in 1554 has been shown to be 'beyond doubt a legend' (Mesnard, 1950, p. 44). By the time he began his legal training in the late 1540s, the exponents of the *mos docendi Gallicus* had already triumphed at Toulouse, and it is manifest from Bodin's own writings that he accepted their conclusions. He assumes, that is, that Roman law is not *ratio scripta*, but is simply the legal code of one particular ancient society, standing in need of explication according to the distinctive philological and historical techniques of the humanists. As the preface to the *Method* makes clear, he has nothing but scorn for the Bartolist attempt 'to establish principles of universal jurisprudence from the Roman decrees', and he regards any attempt to found a science of jurisprudence on 'the legislation of one particular state' as nothing more than an 'absurdity' (p. 2).

During the 1560s, however, when Bodin left the academic study of law to practise as an advocate in Paris, he came to feel (as he tells us in the preface to the *Method*) that the humanist jurists were tending to become far too cloistered a sect, and were failing in consequence to go far enough in the reformation of legal science. By concentrating on the correction of anachronisms in the Bartolist understanding of Roman law, they had allowed themselves to become sidetracked into an obsession with purely historical and philological niceties (Kelley, 1973b, p. 133). The worst offender is said to be Cujas, who is implicitly attacked in the Preface to the *Method* as the leader of those 'who prefer to be regarded as grammarians rather than jurisconsults', and is later denounced by name in the 1578 Preface to the *Six Books* for occupying himself with 'disputes in schoolboy fashion over words and trivial matters'.[1] According to Bodin, these preoccupations with 'the quantities of syllables' have caused the humanists to neglect two further tasks which are both central to the construction of a genuine legal and political science.[2] One is that the techniques of the humanists need to be applied not merely to the study of ancient Rome, but to every other known system of law, the idea being to 'bring together

[1] See Bodin, *Method*, p. 7 and *Six Books*, p. A71.
[2] For the discussion of these features of Bodin's methodology and their relations to his political thought I am deeply indebted to Kelley, 1973b and especially Franklin, 1973.

and compare the legal frameworks of all states'. The other essential task is to engage in a far more wide-ranging study of 'the custom of the peoples' in all the most famous kingdoms and republics, the aim in this case being nothing less than a comparative analysis of 'the beginnings, growth, conditions, changes and decline of all states'.[1]

The execution of this further and vastly ambitious enterprise required, according to Bodin, the immediate undertaking of a two-part programme of work. It was obviously essential in the first place to collect all the relevant data. Bodin speaks in the Preface to the *Method* of the need to learn about the laws and social structures of ancient Persia, Greece, Egypt, Rome and the commonwealth of the Hebrews, as well as modern Spain, England, Italy, Germany, Turkey and France (p. 3). By the time he came to publish the *Six Books* a decade later, it is evident that he had largely completed this heroic course of reading. The second vital exercise – which, Bodin complains, has hardly ever been attempted – is that of 'arranging things in correct order and polished form', beginning with 'the main types and divisions' of law, proceeding to establish 'postulates on which the entire system rests', and concluding with a set of definitions and rules (pp. 1–3). Again, it is clear that by the time he came to plan the organisation of the *Six Books*, this further task had also been carried out, at least to his own satisfaction. It is true that Bodin has often been assailed for presenting his argument in complete 'chaos' and 'disorder'.[2] But it is arguable that such judgments are based on a failure to grasp the principles of classification which are actually employed in the *Six Books*. If we approach the work with the anti-Aristotelian canons of Ramist logic in mind, beginning as Ramus advises with a definition of the area to be considered and moving on to bifurcate each topic into successively smaller sub-divisions, we discover that the first half of the *Six Books* is entirely organised around these characteristically Ramist categories of 'invention' followed by 'disposition' or judgment (Duhamel, 1948–9, pp. 163–71; McRae, 1955, p. 319). The first Book singles out the issue to be considered – that of systems of command – and subdivides the topic into private systems (the family) and public (the state). The second Book goes on to subdivide the idea of the state into all its possible forms, and the third to subdivide its internal organisation into all its constituent parts. We end with 'the ordering of citizens', who are taken to constitute the ultimate units into which it is possible to analyse the subject-matter of political science.

---

[1] For these contentions see Bodin's Preface to the *Method*, pp. 2, 8.
[2] This is especially true of the older commentaries. For the claims cited above, see Chauviré, 1914, p. 487 and Allen, 1957, p. 404.

This programme of data-collection and logical arrangement is controlled by two distinct 'scientific' purposes, the execution of which amounted – according to Bodin himself – to the construction of a genuine science of politics. The first is the attempt to supply an inductively grounded account of all the variables which, although beyond human control, can be shown to affect the destiny of commonwealths, and are thus 'of great weight and importance for the best appraisal of legislation'.[1] What Bodin manages in effect to provide is an analysis of the humanist concept of Fortune: he considers all the natural and occult causes of the rise, flourishing and decline of states, with the aim of making each legislator sensitive to the special constraints under which he is obliged to act, thereby enabling him to produce the most suitable laws for his own particular commonwealth. The outcome, set forth in Books IV and V, is a survey of *naturels* which seeks to explain the influence of the stars and of certain mystic numbers of the fortunes of states, and culminates in a study of climate as a cause of the varying customs, religions and social structures to be found in the three distinct climatic zones of the civilised world. It is sometimes claimed that the earliest systematic study of the influence of such natural causes was the achievement of Montesquieu, and even that 'the whole study of historical jurisprudence dates from '*L'Esprit des Lois*' (Martin, 1962, p. 152). But this overlooks the extent to which Montesquieu was in fact drawing on an existing tradition of analysis – a tradition which was already well-established at the time when Bodin was writing, and which Bodin went on to develop to a point of sophistication and completeness scarcely exceeded even by Montesquieu himself.

Bodin's other 'scientific' purpose stands in complete contrast with this essay in moral relativism. He aims to disclose – somewhat in the manner of Pareto – the residues underlying the surface variety of legal and political arrangements, a bedrock which he assumes it is possible to uncover by a proper comparative and historical survey of every known commonwealth. Since he believes, as he stresses in the Preface to the *Method*, that 'in history the best part of the universal law lies hidden', he thinks it must be possible to establish inductively what laws any commonwealth *needs* to possess by examining what laws all successful commonwealths have at all times possessed. His ultimate intention in seeking 'to bring together and compare the legal frameworks of all states' is thus to establish 'scientifically' the contents of 'the common law of all nations', thereby revealing what features any satisfactory legal system must *ex hypothesi* include (p. 2).

These assumptions together serve to indicate why Bodin believes he

---

[1] See Bodin's Preface to the *Method*, p. 8.

has managed to furnish a proof of his key contention in the *Six Books* to the effect that an absolute and irresistible sovereign power must by definition exist in any viable state. According to his sociological and historical investigations, the existence of such an authority is in fact a central feature, as he tells us, of the legal systems 'of France, of Spain, of England, Scotland, Turkey, Muscovy, Tartary, Persia, Ethiopia, India, and of almost all the kingdoms of Africa and Asia' (p. 222). And according to the methodology governing his researches, to establish such a claim with such a degree of empirical density is in effect to establish that the embodiment of precisely this kind of authority in any political society must be a necessary condition of its counting as a genuine state.

As well as constituting the central feature of his political system, Bodin's concept of sovereignty has come to be the centre of a considerable controversy amongst interpreters of the *Six Books*. The problem is to determine how far he intended that the powers of the sovereign should be taken to be absolutely unlimited. The consensus amongst the older commentaries was that, as Gierke expresses it, Bodin 'totally extinguished the idea of a constitutional state'.[1] It is arguable, however, that if we approach Bodin's analysis with the traditional checks of *la police*, *la religion* and *la justice* in mind, we find that a number of significant elements of these constraints on absolutism still appear to be consciously retained.[2]

As in the writings of the earlier legists, there is one aspect of the check of *la police* which unquestionably survives in the *Six Books*. This is the constraint of the *Leges Imperii*, the two fundamental laws of France 'which concern the state of the realm and the establishing thereof' in such a way that 'the prince cannot derogate from them' (p. 95). The first is the Salic law guaranteeing a male succession, which Bodin defends in Book VI with the Knoxian claim that 'the rule and government of women is directly against the law of nature' (p. 746; cf. pp. 753–4). The other prescribes that even in an absolute monarchy the ruler enjoys 'the use only' and never the true ownership of the royal domain (p. 653). This in turn means that 'all monarchs and states have held it for a general and undoubted law'

---

[1] See Gierke, 1939, p. 158 and for similar judgments cf. Hearnshaw, 1924, pp. 124–5, and the numerous authorities cited in Lewis, 1968, p. 214.

[2] The trend amongst more recent commentators has been to argue that the extent to which Bodin's doctrine was intended as an affirmation of absolutely unlimited sovereignty has traditionally been overestimated. See for example Shepard, 1930, pp. 585, 588–9 and more recently the discussions in Giesey, 1973, p. 180, Salmon, 1973 and Franklin, 1973. These accounts, however, have tended to concentrate on internal evidence for and against the constitutionalist interpretation of Bodin's thought, rather than employing the approach I have attempted to follow here, namely that of recalling the traditional limitations on the idea of absolute sovereignty, and using these as a benchmark against which Bodin's doctrine can in effect be measured off.

that the lands granted to the sovereign in order to enable him to 'live of his own' cannot lawfully be mortgaged, alienated or sold, since they represent a part of 'the public revenues' and as such must be 'holy, sacred and inalienable' (p. 651).

It is sometimes complained that this treatment of the law about the alienation of the fisc represents a confusion in Bodin's theory of sovereignty (e.g. Sabine, 1963, p. 408). But Bodin is careful to emphasise that the prohibition on its alienation is intended as part of his definition of sovereignty. He accepts that the sovereign must be granted the material means to rule. He then argues that these will need to be assigned to him in the form of a special grant, since he cannot be assumed to possess them himself. Given these assumptions, there is no confusion in concluding that even an absolute sovereign cannot alienate any property given to him in this way. Since the domain is annexed to the sovereignty rather than the sovereign, it retains the status of public revenue, never becoming the private property of the sovereign himself. And since this entails that the true owner of the domain must at all times be the commonwealth rather than its ruler, there is no inconsistency in concluding that even the most absolute sovereign has no more right to alienate it than he has to dispose of any other piece of property owned by his subjects (cf. Burns, 1959, p. 176).

As well as retaining this aspect of *la police*, Bodin continues to insist on one crucial feature of the linked checks of *la religion* and *la justice*. He argues that although the *form* of the positive laws may be nothing more than the declared will of the sovereign, their *contents* must remain at all times in line with the dictates of natural justice (cf. Lewis, 1968, p. 215). It follows that the sovereign must be checked by a genuine law in all his public acts, since he is bound to regard the laws of nature and of God as his main guides to upholding a system of natural justice.[1] This crucial limitation on the will of the sovereign is enunciated with great emphasis in the chapter entitled *Of Sovereignty*. To say that an absolute ruler is 'free from all laws' is to say nothing about 'the laws of God and nature', since 'all princes and peoples in the world' must be subject to these ordinances, and it can never be 'in their power to impugn them' without being 'guilty of high treason to the divine majesty' (p. 92). This means in effect that all princes are more strictly bound than their subjects to obey the laws of nature and of God, for 'they cannot be from the same exempted, either by the senate or the people, but that they must be enforced to make their

[1] As Giesey has remarked, the resulting category of laws which are 'seemingly civil, actually natural' constitutes 'by far the most important element in whatever case can be made for Bodin the constitutionalist'. See Giesey, 1973, p. 180.

appearance before the tribunal seat of almighty God' (p. 104). So to argue 'that princes are not subject to laws' without making it clear that this never applies to the laws of nature and of God is to 'do great wrong both to God and nature' (p. 104).

This doctrine carries with it a number of implications which Bodin is clearly anxious to underline. One is that every subject must have a duty – arising from his prior obligation to obey the laws of God – to disobey any command from his sovereign which is contrary to these laws or to the laws of nature based on them. The point is taken up in Book III, in the chapter on the obedience of magistrates (pp. 309–25). Bodin continues to maintain that even if the commands of the sovereign run counter to the laws of nature as well as his own positive laws, there can never be any question of lawful resistance on the part of any of his subjects. He even insists that if 'the commandment of the prince be not contrary to the laws of God and nature', but merely contrary to the civil laws of the state, then the magistrate has no right even of passive disobedience, since 'it belongs not to the magistrate to examine or censure the doings of his prince, or to cross his proceedings concerning a man's law, from which the prince may as he sees cause derogate' (p. 313). He concedes, however, that this doctrine applies only to 'civil justice and utility', and not 'if such commands be contrary to the laws of nature' (p. 313). If the prince issues a command which is contrary to these higher laws, it remains the duty not merely of the magistrates but of all the people to disobey, since 'the honour of God' and the need to respect the laws of nature 'ought to be to all subjects greater and more precious than the wealth, the life, the honour of all the princes of the world' (p. 324).

The obligation of the sovereign to follow the dictates of natural law also serves to place a number of constraints upon his own behaviour, two of which Bodin goes on to emphasise. Despite the fact that he is *legibus solutus*, he remains obliged to honour his contracts, even those he makes with his own subjects (p. 106). The reason is that the obligation to keep one's promises is a stipulation of the law of nature. Now Bodin has already laid it down that 'the prince has nothing above the subject' in respect of his duty to uphold this higher law (p. 93). So he is very emphatic that 'we must not then confound the laws and the contracts of sovereign princes'. While the law depends upon 'the will and pleasure of him that has the sovereignty', any contract 'between the prince and his subjects is mutual, which reciprocally binds both parties, so that the one party may not start therefrom to the prejudice or without the consent of the other' (p. 93).

Bodin also stresses the sovereign's obligation to respect the holding of private property by his subjects as an inalienable right. This constraint upon *Imperium* by *dominium* follows from his belief that the family unit constitutes both the origin and the essence of the commonwealth. To imagine a commonwealth without families, he declares, is like imagining 'a city without houses' (p. 8). But if we cannot conceive of a common-wealth without families, then we cannot conceive of a commonwealth without private property, since 'a community of all things' would be 'incompatible with the right of families', which need to retain their property in order to maintain their material existence (p. 11). The objec-tion – so often canvassed at this point by scholastic writers – that the laws of nature seem to specify an original community of goods is rather briskly dismissed with an appeal to the fact that the law of the Decalogue 'expressly forbids us to steal' (p. 11). This is taken to show that the holding of private property is in fact presupposed by the law of nature, and thus that Plato's ideal of 'a community of all things' must be founded on a mistake. The dictates of the Decalogue are taken to reveal, on the contrary, that all states must have been 'appointed by God' to render in common that which is genuinely common, while reserving 'unto every man in private that which unto him in private belongs' (p. 11).

The implication of these assumptions for the relationship between *Imperium* and *Dominium* is spelled out in the key chapter *Of Sovereignty*. Bodin first repeats that nothing is 'more religiously by God's laws for-bidden than to rob and spoil other men of their goods' (p. 109). He then reminds us that even 'a sovereign prince may not remove the bonds' established by 'the everlasting laws of nature' (p. 109). So he concludes that those who say 'a sovereign prince has power by violence to take away another man's goods' are preaching a doctrine directly contrary to the laws of God (p. 109). Even the most absolute sovereign can never have the right to 'take nor give another man's goods without the consent of the owner' (p. 110). Anyone who cites the maxim ' "All to be the prince's" ' must therefore be understood to be speaking simply of 'power and sovereignty', for even in the most absolute monarchy 'the property and possession of every man's things' must still be 'reserved to himself' (p. 110).

As Bodin is obliged to recognise, this defence of private property carries with it a somewhat awkward practical consequence for his theory of absol-ute sovereignty. If it is contrary to the laws of God for a sovereign to remove his subjects' goods, it seems that the imposition of taxes must be equivalent to an act of confiscation, incapable of being justified unless the subjects happen for some reason to approve of it. Bodin makes no attempt to evade this implication of his argument: he consistently maintains that all taxation requires explicit consent, and that new taxes ought so far as possible to be avoided. This was the position he put forward publicly when he was elected a member of the States General in 1576 – an honour which he mentions several times in the *Six Books* with somewhat comical vanity. The meetings of the assembly were dominated by Henry III's attempts to raise funds, and Bodin appears to have forfeited his rising favour at court by insisting in a number of speeches that the deputies ought to refuse any increase in taxation (Ulph, 1947, p. 292; cf. p. 289). His grounds for adopting this stance are made clear in the course of the long chapter entitled *Of Treasure* at the end of the *Six Books* (pp. 649–86). He begins by conceding that when a commonwealth is 'suddenly oppressed either by the enemy or by some other unexpected accident', the charges 'which are then imposed upon the citizens' are 'religious and godly', as the commonwealth might otherwise be 'quite ruined' (p. 663). But he goes on to warn the kings of France that, since the holding of property is a right under the law of nature, even the most absolute princes have no authority 'to lay any imposition' on their subjects 'nor to prescribe that right without their consents' (p. 665). And he adds the reminder that 'nothing does sooner cause changes, seditions and ruins of states than excessive charges and imposts' – a fact which he thinks is well illustrated by the current revolt in the Netherlands.[1]

It seems clear, then, that if we focus on Bodin's handling of the traditional checks of *la police*, *la religion* and *la justice*, we find that a number of constitutionalist elements continue to survive even within the apparently monolithic structure of the *Six Books*. It is no less clear, however, that between the publication of the *Method* in 1566 and the *Six Books* a decade later, Bodin decisively changed his mind about the rights of subjects.[2] In the *Six Books* he deliberately withdraws all the specific

---

[1] Bodin has frequently been accused of contradicting himself here, since his argument scarcely seems compatible with his original account of sovereignty as a power of 'giving laws to the subjects in general without their consent' (p. 98). Allen professes to find the whole discussion of taxation 'bewildering', and Franklin insists that 'Bodin was inconsistent' at this point. (See Allen, 1957, p. 410; Franklin, 1973, p. 87.) Wolfe has recently sought to explain how the inconsistency may have arisen. Bodin's argument, he suggests, needs to be appraised in relation to his fundamental commitment to defending the authority of the French monarchy. Since Bodin saw taxation as the main cause of unrest, and since he thought that the main policy of the crown ought to be that of seeking peace at all costs, he wished the power of taxation to be made as difficult as possible to exercise, taking this to be a means of defending the monarchy. (See Wolfe, 1968, pp. 277–84.) The explanation is ingenious, but it is arguable that there is no very deep inconsistency to be explained away. For it might be supposed that what Bodin's discussion of taxation reveals is not so much a fault in the construction of his theory of sovereignty as a further illustration of its intended character, and in particular a confirmation of his claim that the rights of absolute sovereignty must always be tempered by the laws of nature.

[2] It is true that this is not a wholly uncontentious claim to make. The older authorities – such as Chauviré – tended to speak of the 'essentially profound continuity' between the arguments

constitutional safeguards which the *Method* had sought to impose, and retreats with obvious alarm into a far more uncompromising defence of royal absolutism.[1]

Apart from defending the *Leges Imperii*, Bodin completely obliterates the check of *la police* throughout the *Six Books*. As we have seen, the essence of this constraint had been the suggestion that the king must be limited by the customary laws – to such an extent that France had been classified by Seyssel as an example of a mixed state. Bodin now maintains that those who describe the French monarchy as 'mixed and composed of the three kinds of commonwealth' are voicing 'an opinion not only absurd but also capital', since 'it is high treason to make a subject equal to the king' (p. 191). His own view is that law and custom must be distinguished so completely that the idea of a check of custom on the right to legislate is automatically ruled out. He concedes that many people tend to assume that 'customs have almost the force of laws', although they 'depend not of the judgment or power of the sovereign prince' (p. 160). But he promptly dismisses both the arguments implicit in this belief (p. 160). The power of custom is not at all like that of law, for 'custom has no force but by sufferance, and so long as it pleases the sovereign prince', who in turn possesses the sole authority to convert a custom into law 'by putting thereunto his own confirmation'. Furthermore, the power of custom is unquestionably dependent on the prince, for 'all the force of law and custom lies in the power of him that has the sovereignty in a commonwealth' (p. 161).

As well as removing the check of *la police*, Bodin goes on to withdraw all the specific restraints which the constitutional theorists of the 1560s had revived in opposition to the legists, and had gone on to discuss under the rubrics of *la religion* and *la justice*. Bodin himself had argued in the *Method* that a ruler always needs the consent of the Three Estates to alter

of the *Method* and the *Six Books*, and this interpretation has recently been revived by King in his survey of Bodin's political thought (see Chauviré, 1914, p. 271 and cf. King, 1974, pp. 300–10). King specifically asks whether Bodin's commitment to absolutism is 'more marked' in the *Six Books* than in the *Method*, and answers that 'the point cannot be made' (p. 303). As I seek to argue, however, such a refusal to discriminate between the two books seems to overlook the specific changes which Bodin introduced when considering the key constitutional question of whether the powers of the French monarchy can be legally and institutionally checked.

[1] For this interpretation see Reynolds, 1931, p. 182, a view which has been developed in Salmon, 1973, pp. 365–71 and in Franklin, 1973, pp. 54–69. In what follows I largely accept these valuable accounts, although I believe that Salmon (e.g. p. 378) perhaps over-emphasises the extent to which the changes in Bodin's outlook can all be explained in terms of his desire to respond to the revolutionary Huguenots of the 1570s. It is arguable that a further motive may have been his desire to repudiate his own former self, and to attack the whole trend towards constitutionalism which had developed amongst French political writers in the course of the 1560s.

any well-established custom or ancient form of procedure. He now maintains that although the laws of France have not usually been changed
except 'after general assembly of the Three Estates', it is never 'necessary
for the king to rest on their advice', and it is always open to him to 'do the
contrary to that they demand, if natural reason and justice so require'
(p. 95). Apart from the power to withhold their consent to taxation, the
Estates have no authority 'in any thing to command or determine or to
give voice, but that which it pleases the king to like or dislike' (p. 95). So
when the king of France – or Spain or England – issues a summons to the
Three Estates, he is merely acknowledging that 'it is a courteous part' of
the business of legislating 'to do it by the good liking of the senate'. There
is never any implication 'that the sovereign prince is bound to any such
approbation, or cannot of himself make a law without the authority and
consent of the Estates or the people' (p. 103).

Finally, Bodin had laid a special emphasis in the *Method* on the legal
(as opposed to the representative) limitations on the powers of the French
crown. Three distinct checks had been cited, all of which he now deliberately withdraws. He had argued in the first place that the king is bound by
his coronation oath. By the time he came to write the *Six Books*, however,
he was evidently alarmed by the elective implications of this doctrine,
which had been exploited in the meantime by the Calvinist revolutionaries. Beza and Hotman had both alighted on the oath of the Aragonese,
which they took to be claiming that the people have a duty to obey their
rulers only so long as they keep their promises – and 'if not, not' (Giesey,
1968, pp. 20–4). Bodin refers to the oath in the *Six Books*, and argues that
those who have invoked it in order to 'make a confusion of laws and of a
prince's contract' have been dangerously mistaken (p. 92). The only way
in which the conduct of a genuine sovereign can be limited is through his
obligation to act in such a way 'as right and justice require' (p. 94). This
in turn means that any 'sovereign prince' must always be free, without any
accusation of perjury, to 'frustrate and disanull' any oaths or promises he
may have made, wherever he finds that 'the reason and equity of them' has
ceased (p. 94). To remove this discretionary power and insist that 'princes
should be bound by oaths to keep the laws and customs of the country' is
simply to 'overthrow all the rights of sovereign majesty' (p. 101).

Bodin had also argued in the *Method* that the Parlement of Paris had a
right to veto any proposed act of legislation, so that any unjust edicts of
the king will always be liable to be 'cast out' by the court (p. 254). By the
time he published the *Six Books* he had come to regard this as a 'false
opinion' and a pernicious one (p. 323). In the meantime he had come to
see that one of the main arguments available to those who wished 'to take

up arms against their prince' was the suggestion that the judges have a right to refuse 'to verify and put into execution the edicts and commands of their prince' (p. 323). He is now prepared to insist that such a doctrine is not merely 'contrary to right and law', but involves a total misunderstanding of the constitutional history of France. He finds the origins of the true relationship between the crown and Parlement in the reign of Philip the Fair, who 'made it an ordinary court' in order 'to take from it the dealing with the affairs of state' (p. 266). The next decisive step was taken when the king 'advised the court to meddle only with the deciding of controversies and the equal administration of justice', and warned its officers 'not to become his tutors or protectors of the realm' (p. 266). The same relationship was finally confirmed under Francis I, when he issued a decree 'whereby the Parlement of Paris was forbidden' in any way 'to call in question the laws or decrees proceeding from the king concerning matters of state' (p. 267).

The third and final legal check which Bodin had emphasised in the *Method* was the independence of the judges and the impropriety of removing them from their posts except for serious crimes. In the *Six Books* he still maintains that all magistrates ought to have security of tenure, but he now thinks of their powers as entirely dependent on those of the sovereign prince. The issue is discussed at length in Book III, in the chapter on *The power and authority of a magistrate*, in which the argument between Azo and Lothair is once again reviewed (pp. 325–42). Whereas Bodin had cautiously inclined in the *Method* to Azo's side, he is now quite clear that the right way 'to decide the general question' between them is to recognise that all 'magistrates and commissioners' are 'mere executors and ministers of the laws and of the princes', and never the holders of any independent authority or 'any power in this point or respect in themselves' (p. 333). The whole issue is finally summarised at the start of the key chapter on the concept of sovereignty. While a sovereign may always elect to delegate his authority, it must always be open to him to 'take to himself the examination and deciding of such things as he has committed to his magistrates or officers', and at any time 'take the power given them by virtue of their commission or institution, or suffer them to hold it so long as shall please him' (p. 85).

This plea for a personal and absolute legislative sovereignty was destined to have an immediate and extremely powerful influence. As early as the 1580s Gabriel Harvey observed that 'you cannot step into a scholar's study' without the chances, as he put it, being ten to one that you will find him reading either Le Roy on Aristotle or Bodin's *Six Books*.[1] During the

---

[1] See Salmon, 1959, p. 24 and cf. Mosse, 1948.

same period Bodin's distinctive analysis of sovereignty was taken over by a large number of political theorists in France, including Jean Duret, François Grimaudet and Pierre Gregoire, and a little later Pierre de Belloy, Jacques Hurault, François Le Jay and Louis Servin (Church, 1941, pp. 245–6). To this list we should add the names of two Gallicised Scotsmen, Adam Blackwood and William Barclay. Both went on to turn these arguments specifically against the writers whom Barclay dubbed the 'monarchomachs' or king-killers, and in particular against their own fellow-countryman George Buchanan, the most radical of all the Calvinist revolutionaries. As a result of this onslaught Barclay was later singled out by Locke at the end of the *Second Treatise* as one of the greatest 'assertors' of 'the power and sacredness of kings', a description to which all the other French writers on absolutism at this time are equally entitled (p. 437). They all begin by taking over Bodin's claim that an absolute form of legislative sovereignty needs by definition to be located at some determinate point in every state. To this they add the originally Protestant belief that all such powers are directly ordained of God, so that to offer any resistance to the king is strictly equivalent to resisting the will of God (cf. Church, 1941, pp. 244–5). With the union of these two arguments, the distinctive concept of the 'divine right' of kings is finally articulated, and the outlook later made famous by Bossuet in France and Sir Robert Filmer in England may be said to be fully formed. By the end of the religious wars, the foundations had thus been firmly laid for the ideology which was subsequently used to legitimate the mature absolutism of *le grand siècle*.

9

The right to resist

At the outbreak of the religious wars in 1562, the Prince de Condé, as leader of the Huguenots, issued a *Declaration* justifying his decision to resort to arms (Caprariis, 1959, p. 100, n.). He argued that by entering Paris at the head of an army, the Guises had 'placed the will of the Queen in captivity', and had thus usurped the lawful government, 'their sole aim being to dispose of the kingdom at their own pleasure' (pp. 229, 231). His own aim in mobilising, he maintained, was simply 'to seek for all legitimate means' to 'put the persons of the King and Queen at full liberty', and in this way to 'uphold the observation of the edicts and ordinances of the king's majesty' (p. 232). The *Declaration* culminates in the claim that since the Guises are attempting 'to intimidate the King's council with menaces and force', it is the duty of all 'good and loyal subjects' to take up arms, since in doing so they will be 'sustaining the authority of the King and Queen' against the attempts of 'seditious rebels' to 'ruin the entire commonwealth' (pp. 229, 232, 233–5).

Given the constraints under which the Huguenots were acting, Condé's strictly limited and carefully constitutional justification of resistance can readily be understood. A minority group, committed to looking for allies, anxious to appease the Catholic moderates, the Huguenots needed to be able to repudiate as explicitly as possible the existing heritage of revolutionary Calvinism, especially the suggestion that it might be lawful – as Ponet, Goodman and Knox had all argued – for the whole body of the godly people to rise up in spontaneous rebellion against an idolatrous government. So we find Hotman writing to Calvin in December 1558 to assure him that 'everyone was pleased with your letters in which you openly indicated that you were outraged' by the inflammatory writings of Goodman and Knox.[1] Similarly, we find Calvin completely dissociating himself from the various conspiracies being hatched by his more irresponsible followers in France. When the Genevan Council found evidence

[1] For this letter see Calvin, *Opera Omnia*, ed. Baum *et al.*, vol. 17, pp. 396–7.

early in 1558 of a plot being planned in Bordeaux, they forestalled it by informing the French authorities (Kingdon, 1956, p. 68). And when a number of refugees from the failed conspiracy of Amboise claimed in 1560 that the Genevan leadership had approved of La Renaudie's attempted *coup* against the French government, both Calvin and Beza responded by lodging suits for slander, so preventing any further discussion of their alleged complicity (Kingdon, 1956, pp. 69, 71).

The best evidence of this anxiety on the part of the Huguenot leadership to repudiate any idea of popular revolution is provided by their reaction to the one tract published during the 1560s which called for a general uprising of all godly people against the impiousness of the French government. This was produced in Lyons in 1563 at the heady moment when Condé had taken the city on behalf of the Huguenots, Pierre Viret had arrived as pastor, and a Huguenot governor, Soubise, had been installed in defiance of the royal authorities (Doucet, 1939, pp. 417–20). The title of the tract, which appeared anonymously in French, was *The Civil and Military Defence of the Innocents and the Church of Christ* (Caprariis, 1959, p. 113). As Kingdon remarks, its arguments appear to have been 'more radical than almost all other early Protestant pleas for resistance', since it vested the right of resistance in the populace as a whole rather than in any constituted authorities (Kingdon, 1967, p. 153). The response to its publication by the Huguenots who had seized control of the city was one of complete horror. Viret issued a public denunciation of the book, while Soubise proclaimed the death-penalty for anyone found selling it and demanded that all copies should be recalled and burnt (Kingdon, 1967, pp. 154–5). His orders appear to have been faithfully carried out, for no copy seems to have survived, and the contents of the work are known only from a reply which Charles Du Moulin felt constrained to publish after the fantastic suggestion had been made by one of his numerous enemies that he had actually written it (Caprariis, 1959, p. 113, note).

In the course of the 1560s, however, the Huguenots found it increasingly difficult to sustain the fiction that they were merely defending the lawful government against the usurpations of the Guises. Catherine's military preparations in 1567 panicked Condé into open hostility, and he responded by trying to seize the person of the King and mount a blockade of Paris (Salmon, 1975, pp. 169–70). After the failure of this adventure, Catherine and the Huguenots began to view each other with a greatly increased sense of suspicion (Mercier, 1934, pp. 236–7). Condé proceeded to issue a new and far more threatening manifesto, in which he invoked the arguments already being developed by the radical constitutionalist writers, claiming that the fundamental constitution of France was being perverted by the behaviour of the government (Salmon, 1975, p. 170). The same arguments recur in a large number of anonymous tracts published in 1567–8, including a *Protestation* bewailing the loss of French liberties and a *Discourse* arguing that the true government of France, now being usurped, was originally and rightfully mixed in character.[1] Finally, it is clear from internal evidence that Hotman's *Francogallia* – the greatest and most radical Huguenot treatise on the fundamental constitution of France – was also drafted at this time, although it remained unpublished until 1573.[2]

Any attempt to reconcile active resistance with defending the monarchy was finally abandoned after the massacres throughout the country at the end of August 1572. The Huguenot stronghold of La Rochelle immediately repudiated its loyalty to the crown, and was followed in this act of defiance by a number of cities in the south (Léonard, 1965–7, II, pp. 145–6). Within a year Languedoc had virtually become a separate Huguenot enclave within the kingdom, operating its own federal system of government and demanding to be recognised and tolerated (Neale, 1943, pp. 83–4). During the same period the need to legitimate this direct attack on the Valois monarchy began to call forth the classic texts of revolutionary Huguenot political thought. The first to appear was Hotman's *Francogallia*. Hotman had fled to Geneva at the start of October 1572 – never again to return to France – after a narrow escape from the massacre of the Huguenots at Bourges (Kelley, 1973a, pp. 218–19). He at once began to rework his existing draft of *Francogallia*, and by July 1573 he had gained permission from the Genevan authorities to publish it (Giesey and Salmon, 1972, p. 50). While revising his manuscript he was evidently consulted by Theodore Beza, who started to write his somewhat similar account of *The Right of Magistrates* at the same time, publishing it in French early in 1574 and in Latin in 1576.[3] Later in 1574, three further tracts of major importance appeared, all in French and all by writers whose identities have remained unknown. The first was a dialogue entitled *The Politician*. The second – also in dialogue form – was called *The Awakener*,[4]

[1] On this point see Mercier, 1934, p. 237n., and Giesey and Salmon, 1972, pp. 39–40.
[2] See Giesey, 1967, p. 590 and cf. Giesey and Salmon, 1972, pp. 7, 38–9.
[3] For Beza's consultations with Hotman and his 'manifest borrowings' from *Francogallia*, see Giesey, 1967, p. 582 and note. For the printing history of *The Right of Magistrates*, and the relationship between its French and Latin versions, see Schelven, 1954, pp. 62–5.
[4] This is my translation of the title *Le Reveille Matin*. Unfortunately Salmon has already translated it as *The Alarm Bell* (cf. Salmon, 1975, p. 189). I have preferred, however, to reserve the title *The Alarm Bell* as my translation for the tract of 1577 entitled *Le Tocsin*. The authorship of *The Awakener* has never been definitively settled. Barrère and Schelven both suggest that it may have been written by Hotman. (See Barrère, 1914, pp. 383–6 and Schelven, 1954, p. 75n.) But this hypothesis has been convincingly dismissed by Giesey, 1967, p. 589 and note. Both Kelley and Giesey and Salmon instead suggest that the author may have been Hugues Doneau. (See Kelley, 1970b, p. 551 and n., and Giesey and Salmon, 1972, p. 74n.)

while the third, *Political Discourses*, was the most revolutionary of all, presenting a more anarchic theory of resistance than any other work of Huguenot political thought.[1] Two years after this, Simon Goulart (1543–1628), later Beza's successor at Geneva, published a three-volume series of *Memoirs of the State of France under Charles IX*,[2] in which a large number of revolutionary tracts were reprinted and given a wider circulation, including *The Right of Magistrates*, *The Politician* and *Political Discourses*, as well as a French translation of *Francogallia* based on the second and much expanded Latin edition which Hotman had issued earlier in 1576 (Giesey and Salmon, 1972, p. 82). The following year saw the publication of *The Alarm Bell*, an anonymous account of St Bartholomew's Day which seems to have exercised a potent influence in shaping later Protestant views about the meaning and causes of the massacres (Sutherland, 1973, pp. 318, 325). Finally, two years after this there appeared perhaps the greatest and undoubtedly the most famous contribution to the Huguenot theory of revolution, the *Defence of Liberty against Tyrants* by Philippe Du Plessis Mornay (1549–1623), which gives the fullest summary of all the major arguments developed by the Huguenot 'monarchomachs' in the course of the 1570s.[3]

Although the main aim of these tracts was undoubtedly to justify a direct attack on the Valois monarchy, it is important to add that even after the massacres of 1572 the Huguenots were still anxious to repudiate as far as possible any populist or insurrectionary elements in the heritage of Calvinist political thought. While their chief concern was to call their own party to arms, they also needed to broaden the basis of their non-sectarian support and to minimise as far as possible the growing hostility of the Catholic moderates, whose sympathies were becoming increasingly alienated – as we have seen in the case of such observers as Montaigne – as a

---

The Awakener consists of two dialogues: the first, issued separately in 1573, outlines the story of the massacres of 1572, while the second, which was published together with the first in 1574, discusses the general principles of political resistance. Figgis can only be thinking of the first when he says that *The Awakener* is 'merely a narrative of the facts, and says nothing of general principles' (cf. Figgis, 1960, p. 174).

[1] Giesey and Salmon, 1972, p. 74 speak of *The Awakener* as 'perhaps the most radical of the responses to the massacre of 1572', but it seems to me that the prize must go to the *Political Discourses*.

[2] The first edition appeared between 1576 and 1577. A second edition ('revised, corrected and augmented' according to its own title-page) appeared in 1578, and was reissued in a different format in 1578–9. I have used the 1578 edition throughout. Both editions were published in Geneva, not in Middelburg as their title-pages assert. For the ascription to Goulart and details of the printing-history, see Jones, 1917, pp. 14, 560–3.

[3] Here I cut through an apparently endless debate about whether Mornay or Languet or both or neither wrote the *Defence*. The best modern scholars, ranging in time from Figgis to Franklin, have always been inclined to accept Mornay's authorship. See Figgis, 1960, p. 175 and Franklin, 1969, pp. 138–40. For a bibliography on the issue, see the references given in Franklin, 1969, p. 139n. and p. 208n.

result of the continuing drift towards anarchy. The outcome of these conflicting pressures was that, even though the leading Huguenots began to
urge the right of active resistance on their followers, they continued at the
same time to lay as much emphasis as possible on the limited, constitutional and essentially defensive character of their call to arms.

They were careful in the first place to exclude any idea of resistance by
individuals or even by the whole body of the people. It is true that at one
point some impatience is expressed at the rigorous exclusion of tyrannicide
which this involved. The author of the *Political Discourses* mounts a
scornful attack on the 'so-called theologians and preachers' who assume
that no one may ever lawfully kill a tyrant 'without a special revelation
from God'. He goes on to claim that 'in their total prohibition of this
means' of freeing a people from oppression he can find 'nothing solid at
all in any of their arguments' (fo 293a). This is highly exceptional, however, for even in Mornay's *Defence*,[1] the most consistently militant of the
major revolutionary tracts, the lawfulness of tyrannicide is only mentioned as a remote possibility and is handled with the utmost cautiousness.
Mornay concedes of course that 'by means of his divine justice' God may
sometimes 'send us a Jehu' in order to 'overturn and deliver us from
tyrants' (S., p. 214). But he repeatedly stresses that 'where God has not
spoken' in this way, any man who feels 'called' to exercise such a grave
responsibility 'must be extremely circumspect and sober', since he runs
the terrible risk that he may 'confuse himself with God', and may thus
be led to 'conceive vanities and beget lies' instead of serving as a genuine
instrument of justice (F., p. 156).

All the other Huguenot theorists approach the problem of tyrannicide
with even greater care, basing their arguments on the traditional distinction between tyrants by usurpation and tyrants by practice. As Beza
warns us in *The Right of Magistrates* – a representative treatment of the
whole question – there is 'a very considerable difference between these
two cases' of oppressive government (p. 109).[2] A tyrant by usurpation is

---

[1] There is no full and reliable English translation of Mornay's *Defence*. The translation edited
by Harold J. Laski as *A Defence of Liberty against Tyrants* (London, 1924) was originally
made in 1648, and is naturally full of archaisms, as well as being misleadingly free throughout
and straightforwardly mistaken in many places. The translation made by Julian Franklin in
Constitutionalism and Resistance (New York, 1969) is accurate and admirable, but only repro-
duces a truncated version of the original Latin text. When quoting from the *Defence* I have
thus felt obliged to follow two different policies. When citing a passage included in Franklin's
edition, I have used his translation. When citing a passage not included in his edition, I have
made my own translation from the original edition of 1579. Thus when I put an 'F' in
brackets with a page number after a quotation, the reference is to Franklin's translation in
Constitutionalism and Resistance (New York, 1969) is accurate and admirable, but only repro-
number, the reference is to my own translation from the first edition ('Edinburgh', 1579).
[2] All page references to *The Right of Magistrates* refer to the translation in Franklin, 1969,
pp. 101–35.

someone who 'by force or fraud' has 'usurped a power that does not belong to them by law' and in consequence has no legal right to rule (p. 105). This makes it lawful for 'each private citizen' to 'exert all his strength to defend the legitimate institutions of his country', and so to resist any tyrant 'whose authority is not legitimate' (p. 107). But the situation is far more complicated in the case of a tyrant who, as Beza expresses it, is a genuine 'sovereign magistrate' who is 'otherwise legitimate' (p. 108). It is essential in this case to be able to claim a clear 'vocation' to resist, such as might possibly be asserted on behalf of the magistrates or the people's representatives (pp. 102, 129). But this is a claim which no 'private person' can ever rightfully advance, since the people are never 'authorised' to take the law into their own hands (p. 129). It follows that individual citizens, and even the body of the people as a whole, 'have no other remedy' against a tyrant by practice than 'penitence and patience joined with prayers'. Any other attempted cure will be bound to incur 'the danger of God's curse' (p. 129).

A further way in which the Huguenots sought to insist even after 1572 on the purely defensive character of their resistance was by stressing as much as possible that the withdrawal of their allegiance was a move forced on them by the utter vileness of Catherine de Medici's government. They started the rumour – spread by Marlowe in *The Massacre at Paris* – that the massacre of St Bartholomew had been a carefully planned conspiracy, executed with the deliberate intention of exterminating the Protestants in France (Sutherland, 1973, p. 314). One of the earliest instances of this charge occurs in *The Awakener*, which adds the wild allegation that over a hundred thousand Huguenots were murdered in the summer of 1572 (pp. 45–71, 78). The same contentions are embroidered by Goulart in his *Memoirs*, especially in the discussion entitled *The Preparations for the Massacres*. This treats it as certain that the 'terrible designs' against the Huguenots were plotted as far back as the peace of Saint-Germain in 1570, and were subsequently approved at three separate Council meetings held by the King and Catherine de Medici in the early months of 1572 (fos 265–9). More generally, the Huguenots claimed that the massacres merely represented the culmination of an impious and Machiavellian set of policies already being practised by Catherine and her government (cf. Kelley, 1970b). Catherine was of course the daughter of the man to whom Machiavelli had dedicated *The Prince*. This made it irresistible for her enemies to allege that the entire government of France was now being conducted, as La Noue proclaimed in his sixth *Discourse*, under the influence of Machiavelli's 'wretched and dishonourable ways' (p. 160). The historical section of *The Awakener* continually denounces 'the opinions of Machiavelli' as 'a pernicious heresy in matters of state,' maintaining that 'the King was actually persuaded by the doctrines of Machiavelli' to attempt the extermination of the Huguenots (pp. 21, 37). The same charge is pressed by the author of *The Alarm Bell*, who introduces the argument with a long and typically humanist disquisition on the form of education necessary for instilling in a good prince the habits of prudence and virtue (fo 21a ff.). This is then contrasted with the education which Catherine de Medici is said to have prescribed for her children, who 'have learnt their lessons', it is claimed, 'above all from the treatises of the atheist Machiavelli', whose book on *The Prince* is said to be 'the guide of the Queen Mother's actions' and the chief means by which the young King has come to be instructed 'in the precepts most suitable for a tyrant' (fo 33a).

These denunciations soon broadened out into a special *genre* of anti-Machiavellian rhetoric, which in turn succeeded in burying Machiavelli's serious reputation as a political scientist – which Bodin was still prepared to concede without hesitation – under a mountain of crude invective and abuse. One of the earliest examples of the trend is provided by the *Marvellous Discourse* on the 'Machiavellian' attributes of Catherine de Medici, an anonymous tract attributed to Henri Estienne[1] which first appeared in 1575 and was later reprinted in Goulart's *Memoirs*. This begins by stressing that 'amongst all nations Italy takes the prize for finesse and trickery', and proceeds to show how this 'science of cheating', originally perfected in Machiavelli's Florence, has now been imported by Catherine and her advisers into France, with the result that she has become 'an exemplar of tyranny in all her public acts' (fos 423a, 424a). But the major example of the *genre* is of course the *Anti-Machiavel* of Innocent Gentillet (*c.* 1535–*c.* 1595), first published in French in 1576, four years after Gentillet had fled to Geneva as a refugee from the massacre of St Bartholomew (Rathé, 1965, pp. 186–91). This long and furious tirade seems to have played a significant role in creating for Machiavelli the vulgar reputation he has never entirely lost – that of a purely satanic writer of textbooks on how to lead the life of a tyrant (cf. Meinecke, 1957, pp. 54–6; Raab, 1964, pp. 56–9). Although Gentillet is partly concerned to reaffirm the traditional ideals of *la police*, *la religion* and *la justice*, his main aim, as we have already seen, is to denounce the wicked 'maxims' which he claims – often highly tendentiously – to have culled from *The Prince* and the *Discourses*. Having established to his own satisfaction that 'Machia-

---

[1] See *sub* Estienne, Henri, in the bibliography of primary sources. This ascription is accepted by Salmon, 1975, p. 189. But as early as 1892 Weill was complaining that the ascription has always been made 'without serious reason'; see Weill, 1892, p. 94n.

velli's main intention is to instruct the prince in how to become a complete tyrant', Gentillet goes on to insist that the massacres of Vassy and St Bartholomew were both the direct outcome of Machiavelli's influence over Catherine de Medici and her government (pp. 269, 444–5, 473). The accusation is mainly pressed home in the Preface to Book I, which bitterly laments 'the abolition of the good old laws of the realm' and their replacement by 'the doctrines of Machiavelli' as practised by 'the current Italian rulers of France' (pp. 38–9). The same claim is repeated in the opening epistle, which justifies the whole book by arguing that the examination of Machiavelli's doctrines will also serve as 'an indication of the source' of 'the infamous vices which are now taking root' in the government of France.

Given this emphasis on the tyranny of the government, the Huguenots were able to present their decision to resist as nothing more than a necessary and hence a legitimate act of self-defence. A number of tracts published immediately after the massacre of 1572 concentrate almost exclusively on this theme. This is the first point taken up in *Whether it is Lawful for Subjects to Defend Themselves*, a brief pamphlet published anonymously in 1573 and reprinted in the *Memoirs* of Goulart. This insists on behalf of the Huguenots that 'we have at no point been the aggressors in any of the four civil wars conducted for the sake of religion'. The entire blame for the conflict is laid on 'our adversaries', who are said to have 'violated every right' in 'the conduct of their rule' and in this way brought on themselves a policy of retaliation (fo 239b). The same allegation forms the theme of an anonymous *Declaration* – also reprinted by Goulart – which first appeared in 1574. The resistance at La Rochelle is justified on the grounds that the Huguenot population had been placed in 'an insupportable situation' and merely took up arms in self-defence 'against the designs of those who wished to ruin them' (fos 39a–b). Again the government is presented as the aggressor, since the Huguenots are said to have had good reason 'to feel menaced' by the possibility of 'another general massacre' (fo 43a). And again this prompts a defence of the Huguenots on the grounds that 'they had no other recourse than to take to arms', since they had no other means of securing their 'common conservation' against the threat of total annihilation by the tyrants and idolaters ruling over them (fo 43a).

THE APPEAL TO POSITIVE LAW

The next and more positive move the Huguenots made was to try to develop the heritage of revolutionary Calvinism in such a way as to meet what we have already seen to be their two most pressing ideological needs. On the one hand, it was essential for them to construct an ideology capable of defending the lawfulness of resisting on grounds of conscience, since they needed to be able to reassure their followers about the legitimacy of engaging in a direct revolutionary confrontation with the established government. On the other hand, it was no less essential to produce a more constitutionalist and less purely sectarian ideology of opposition, since they obviously needed to broaden the basis of their support if they were to stand any chance of winning what amounted to a pitched battle with the Valois monarchy.

The first attempt they made to meet these two contrasting needs took the form of a theory which sought to build on the constitutionalism of the 1560s and to remodel it in a more revolutionary style. The earliest major work to employ this approach was Hotman's *Francogallia*. As a teacher of law, Hotman had become one of the leading exponents of the *mos docendi Gallicus* in the course of the 1560s. By this time he had already become a convert to Protestantism, having started to move towards an acceptance of the Genevan faith as early as 1547 (Kelley, 1973, pp. 40–4). His special contribution as a theorist of the Huguenot revolution consisted of fusing these two roles. He showed, that is, how a humanist investigation of the French ancient constitution could be turned into a revolutionary ideology in the service of the Huguenot cause.

Hotman's methodology in *Francogallia* is adopted from the other radical constitutionalists of the 1560s. His basic assumption is that the ancient constitution of France is normative for the present, so that an investigation of 'the wisdom of our ancestors in constituting our commonwealth' will serve at the same time to reveal how it ought to be organised (pp. 143, 147). As he was later to insist, *Francogallia* was simply 'an historical book, the history of a fact' (Giesey, 1967, p. 585). His treatise thus takes the form of a narrative of the constitution, and it seems that his original intention, when he first drafted it in the late 1560s, may simply have been to extend the historical foundations of the anti-Bartolist case which he had already begun to argue in his *Anti-Tribonian* (Giesey, 1967, pp. 591, 595–6, 610). By the time he published the book in 1573, however, he had come to recognise with complete self-consciousness – and with more than a touch of tendentious scholarship – that if one could show that the constitution was originally populist in character, one might be able to insist that the same mechanisms of popular control ought to be maintained in operation at all times. With the presentation of this case, it may be said that the use of historical evidence as a form of political argument – already adumbrated in contrasting ways by such theorists as

Pasquier and Du Moulin – suddenly came of age. Thereafter it began to exercise a wide-ranging influence in Holland and England as well as in France, and later came to play a central role in helping to legitimate the attack mounted by the common lawyers on the English monarchy at the start of the following century (Pocock, 1957, pp. 30–55; Skinner, 1965).

Hotman's thesis is in part presented in the same style as that of the other constitutionalist writers of the 1560s. First of all, he stresses that the crown must at all times be controlled by the 'check' of *la police*. Here he partly has in mind the *Leges Imperii*, which he cites in every edition of *Francogallia*, but especially in the final version of 1586, in which he devotes a whole chapter to these 'laws established to restrict kings' (p. 459). But he also has in mind the idea (originally emphasised by Seyssel) that the king is further controlled by the customs and established feudal structures of France. This too is mentioned in every edition, and in particular in 1586, when Hotman quotes at length from Seyssel's own account of 'the institutions and practices of the kingdom which have been sanctioned throughout many ages and confirmed by long-standing custom' (p. 473). As with other constitutionalists, however, the most important checks on the powers of the crown are said to be furnished by *la religion* and *la justice*, although Hotman's account is somewhat unusual in its total devaluation of judicial at the expense of legislative constraints. This is not to say that he completely ignores the suggestion that the courts may impose legal limitations on the crown, for he adds a special chapter to the 1586 edition in which he defends the right of the Parlement of Paris to ensure that 'neither the king's laws nor his edicts' are ever accepted 'unless they have been examined' and 'approved by the opinion of its judges' (p. 459).[1] But his general attitude towards the *noblesse de robe* is one of scornful hostility – a biographical fact of some interest, as his father had been a highly successful member of the class, a *conseiller* in the Parlement of Paris from 1544 until his death in 1555 (Kelley, 1973, pp. 12–13). Hotman prefers to lay all his emphasis on the power of the States General to ensure that the legislative actions of the government remain in line with the dictates of *la religion* and *la justice*. He dismisses the Parlements as nothing more than a late and usurping invention of the Capetian kings, who are said to have made certain that the members of this 'spurious senate' could always be 'depended upon to be accommodating' to the crown's most absolutist pretensions (p. 505). And he compares the powers of the courts invidiously with the far greater and more ancient authority lodged with the Estates – an argument which had already been hinted at in Bodin's *Method* and in the

---

[1] The special reasons for the insertion of this extra chapter in 1586 are excellently discussed in Franklin, 1969, pp. 28–9.

second volume of Pasquier's *Researches*. According to Hotman, even the term 'Parlementum' has been usurped, since it originally referred to the assembly of the Three Estates, which he pictures as 'a solemn and public council' convened at least once a year under the ancient constitution and endowed with such extensive powers 'to deliberate on the general welfare' that it came to be 'held as something sacrosanct' by our ancestors 'over a vast tract of time' (pp. 323, 397; cf. pp. 499–501).

While Hotman is clearly appealing to existing accounts of the right to check the monarchy, the special significance of *Francogallia* lies in the fact that he goes on to pursue the intimations of this available tradition in an altogether more revolutionary way. His chief innovation consists of extending the argument already presented in Bodin's *Method* about the binding force of coronation oaths. This forms the background to the first theoretical claim Hotman derives from his history of the French constitution: the claim that originally the monarchy was entirely elective in character. The phraseology of the first edition appears to imply that this power of election was initially lodged with the whole body of the people. When Hotman reissued the book in 1576, however, he was careful to emphasise that in speaking of 'the authoritative decision and desire of the people', what he actually had in mind was the decision of 'the orders, or as we are now accustomed to say, of the Estates' (pp. 231–3; cf. p. 287). The central contention he makes about the French monarchy is thus that the ancient Frankish habit of 'the placing of the designated king upon a shield and his elevation upon the shoulders of those present' must be taken to indicate that the crown of France was originally bestowed entirely by the will of the people's representatives, with each successive king being 'constituted by the authoritative decision' of the Estates rather than 'by any hereditary right' (pp. 231, 233; cf. pp. 155, 221, 287).

Hotman corroborates this claim by adopting a far more populist view of the supremacy of the Estates – and the correspondingly limited powers of the crown – than we find in any of the constitutionalist writers of the 1560s. His next general claim is that the right of election must by no means be treated as a single act of sovereignty which the people relinquish as soon as it is exercised. He makes it clear on the contrary that the people's representatives must be acknowledged to retain a right of constant surveillance, for he repeatedly insists that 'in as much as it was the right and power of the Estates and the people to constitute and maintain kings', it was always accepted as a corollary under the ancient constitution that 'the supreme power not only of transferring but also of taking away the kingdom lay within the competence of the assembly of the people and the public council of the nation' (pp. 235, 247; cf. p. 287). Finally, he adds the further general claim that since the Estates must at all times be recognised as possessing the power to set kings down as well as to set them up, it follows that the status of the king of France can never be higher than that of a 'magistrate of the whole people', a mere official appointed to serve as a presiding officer at the meetings of the Estates (pp. 295, 323–5). Under the ancient constitution, the nature of the relationship between the king and Estates is thus said to be that 'the authority of the council was greater than that of the king', who was never assigned 'all power' in 'the manner in which the Roman people gave it to the Emperors', but was always 'restrained by those pacts and conditions through which he was entrusted with the loyalty and authority appropriate to a king' (pp. 417, 419; cf. p. 205).

The outcome of Hotman's historical analysis is thus a theory of popular sovereignty in which 'the highest administrative authority in the kingdom' is said to be vested at all times in 'the assembly of the Three Estates' (p. 291; cf. pp. 303, 343). It is evident, moreover, that this was intended as a theory of absolute popular control, not a mere theory about the possibility of restraining a king *in extremis*. This is obvious from the various 'marks' of sovereignty which Hotman assigns to the Estates in the course of discussing 'the sacred authority of the public council' in Chapter XI of his book (p. 333). Apart from the omission of three marks which might be said to have a particularly personal character (hearing appeals, granting pardons and receiving homage) Hotman's list is actually identical with the nine marks of sovereignty which Bodin was later to single out in the *Six Books* as the criteria for recognising the presence of an absolute sovereign in the state.

Hotman presented this historical 'discovery' about the elective character of the French monarchy in such a way as to provide an attractive solution to both the major problems confronting the Huguenots in their attempts to develop a revolutionary ideology. His argument was well calculated to persuade a wide spectrum of opinion that the Valois government was acting unconstitutionally, and was thus calculated to win a broadly-based and not merely a sectarian measure of support for the Huguenot revolution. One sign that this was evidently in Hotman's mind was the care he took to relate his arguments to those of earlier constitutionalist writers, and to set out his theory in terms of their familiar vocabulary of 'checks' and 'bridles' on the king's authority. A second and deeper sign was that even though his defence of popular sovereignty reached a far more revolutionary conclusion than any of these earlier theorists would have been prepared to endorse, he nevertheless sought to retain his links with their outlook as far as possible by implying that his own theory amounted to little more than a restatement of the traditional Seyssellian idea of a mixed monarchy. When he describes the founding of the elective kingship with 'the general advice of all the Estates', he somewhat disingenuously equates this process with the establishment of a 'mixed and tempered commonwealth embodying the three kinds of government' (p. 297; cf. p. 323). And when he attempts in later editions to support this contention with an appeal to suitable authorities, the main and most reassuring source he is anxious to cite is the account of 'the harmony of all the orders' offered by Seyssel in *The Monarchy of France* (p. 293).

But Hotman's argument is no less carefully calculated to appeal specifically to the Huguenots, and to reassure them in the most unimpeachable terms about the lawfulness of political resistance. Hotman performs this further task by cunningly phrasing his key contention about the right of deposing as well as electing kings in such a way as to make it appear to be nothing more than an application of one of Calvin's own arguments in the *Institutes*. As we have seen, Calvin had concluded his chapter on Civil Government by suggesting that it might be appropriate to think of modern representative assemblies as the bearers of 'ephoral' powers, and that it might in consequence be right to think of them as possessing the authority to resist tyrannical kings. What Hotman does is to clarify the studied vagueness of these claims, arguing that they can in fact be justified as an interpretation of the fundamental constitution of France. This is first suggested in the chapter on the nature of the constitution, where Hotman discusses the 'right of holding assemblies' as a device for ensuring that the people 'reserve the highest authority' in the commonwealth for themselves. He immediately goes on to add that exactly the same purpose was served by 'that celebrated law of the Spartans associating the ephors with the kings', which ensured that the ephors 'acted as restraints (*freni*) on the kings' while 'the latter governed the commonwealth by their advice and authority' (pp. 301, 305). Hotman later repeats the same illustration in the chapter on the distinction 'between the king and the kingdom', a distinction which is said to be marked with particular clarity in the case of the 'solemn oath' which 'the king of the Spartans and the ephors' acting as 'the king's guardians and overseers' swore to each other every month (p. 403). The implication of the allusions is clear: it is correct to think, as Calvin did, of ephors as 'overseers' of kings; and it is also correct to think of the assembly of the Estates in France as an 'ephoral' authority. The obvious importance of the argument is that it enables Hotman to offer as orthodox Calvinist teaching his own conclusion that it is indeed within the power of the Estates to 'restrain the ferocious licence of kings' as Calvin had originally implied.

The care Hotman took to present his most subversive conclusions in

terms of the existing concepts of Calvinist and constitutionalist theory
had an immediate influence.[1] The other Huguenot revolutionaries first of
all took over his analysis of representative 'checks', presenting their
arguments in the same reassuring style as a version of Calvin's theory of
'ephoral' authorities. When the author of *The Awakener* – who refers us
to the authority of 'the great Hotman in his *Francogallia*' – discusses the
power of representative assemblies 'to set up and set down kings', he
offers as an exact analogy 'the rein and bridle' constituted by the ephors of
ancient Sparta, 'to whom it was lawful to condemn and chastise their kings
when they abused their office' (pp. 86, 88, 116). Beza invokes the same
analogy with kings 'elected with definite conditions' by the Spartans
together with 'ephors to keep them in check' in *The Right of Magistrates*
(p. 115). And Mornay's *Defence* reiterates the underlying idea that the
power of representative assemblies is in fact 'ephoral' in character, as well
as adding the purely historical but politically suggestive fact that in a sense
the Spartan ephors were 'more powerful' than the Spartan kings (S.,
p. 102).

These writers also emphasise – more decisively than Hotman – the idea
of legal as opposed to representative checks, again attempting to state the
argument in a vocabulary designed to appeal to Protestant susceptibilities.
They begin by referring to the originally Lutheran idea of resistance by
'inferior magistrates', a concept specifically invoked in *The Awakener*,
employed throughout *The Right of Magistrates*, and later adopted both by
the author of *The Politician* and by Mornay in his *Defence*.[2] They then
proceed to bring this Lutheran terminology into line with the characteristically Calvinist concept of 'ephoral' authorities. They do not speak
of the inferior magistrates as directly ordained by God, as the Lutherans
had always done. They instead think of them as constituted by the people,
and thus endowed, no less than the Estates, with the same 'ephoral'
powers to check and bridle kings. This argument is implicit both in *The
Awakener* and *The Right of Magistrates*, and is later stated with the greatest
clarity in *The Politician* and in Mornay's *Defence*. According to *The
Politician*, the best example of the right of 'inferior powers' to exercise a
form of 'sovereign authority' is provided by 'the ephors of Sparta' who

---

[1] It is often said that after 1572 the Huguenots adopted a 'new creed' and an entirely changed
political stance. (See for example Stankiewicz, 1960, p. 34.) This is of course true in a sense,
but such an emphasis could perhaps be misleading, since the Huguenots also tried to hold
fast as far as possible to existing theories of radical constitutionalism, seeking as Hotman had
done to revise and develop them in such a way as to meet their own ideological needs. For
Hotman's influence on Beza's and Mornay's development of the case for active resistance,
see Giesey, 1970.

[2] For the discussion in *The Awakener*, see p. 85; in *The Politician*, see fo 81a. For citations of
'inferior magistrates' in the *Defence*, see the original edition at pp. 47, 89, etc.

were elected by the people to serve 'as bridles on the king' (fo 81a). The same analogy is repeatedly cited by Mornay, who describes the monthly oaths which 'the kings of Sparta and the ephors' swore to each other, and adds that 'the officers of the kingdom' in France are instances of 'ephoral' authorities, to whom 'the people give the administration' of the kingdom no less than to the king and the Estates (F., pp. 181, 194). If the king 'breaks his oath' or 'wrecks the commonwealth', these inferior magistrates are said to have 'an even greater obligation' to protect the kingdom against the king, 'since, like the ephors, they were established primarily for this purpose' (F., p. 194).

These writers also share Hotman's ambition to speak not merely to their own party, but also to the *politiques*, the moderate Catholics, the uncommitted and even to the nation as a whole. This intention is reflected in their continual references to the familiar constitutionalist terminology of 'checks' and 'bridles' on the king, and on at least one occasion it is explicitly avowed. This happens at the end of *The Awakener*, when the author steps forward to assure us that he is writing 'not as a Huguenot at all', since he finds his co-religionists 'far too gentle and servile' in the face of oppression. He instead presents himself 'entirely as a true and natural Frenchman', hoping to appeal equally to all his fellow-countrymen to recognise and put an end to their miseries (p. 181).

The chief means these writers employ in trying to fulfil this more general ideological commitment is to reiterate and add to Hotman's already extensive use of feudal concepts and arguments. They lay a similar emphasis on the significance of reciprocal engagements and promises, and agree that the coronation oaths sworn by the kings of France reveal the monarchy to be essentially elective in character. Beza's discussion of the French constitution – which appears to rely almost entirely on Hotman – begins by referring to the election of the first Merovingian rulers, and goes on to quote 'the oath taken in those days by the kings of France'. This opens with the king conceding that 'you have elected me to rule' and acknowledging that the continued enjoyment of his kingly dignity must at all times remain contingent on his willingness to render each citizen 'his privilege, right and justice, in both ecclesiastical and secular affairs' (p. 120; cf. also p. 123). The same appeal to the familiar feudal image of a reciprocal relationship based on the swearing of an oath is repeated by Mornay in his *Defence*. He first argues, at the start of his account of the 'constituting' of kings, that although 'in certain regions the right of free elections almost seems no longer to exist', yet 'in all properly constituted kingdoms the practice still remains inviolate', so that 'even those who seem today to come to the throne by succession must first be inaugurated by the people' (F., pp. 160, 161). Later he seeks to prove that France is no exception to this rule. Although 'it is commonly thought that pure succession obtains', the truth is that 'when a king of France is inaugurated' the bishops 'ask all the people present whether it is their will and pleasure to have the designee as king', so that there is in fact 'a statement in the coronation formula itself that the people have elected him' (F., p. 183).

Hotman's references to these existing constitutionalist ideas are also carried a stage further by the later Huguenot theorists. They frequently allude to the venerable dispute between Azo and Lothair, reviving the Bartolist suggestion that magistrates may be capable of exercising *Imperium* in the way that Azo had affirmed. This is implicit in the title of Beza's tract, and is clearly brought out in his section on 'lesser magistrates' when he denies 'that the sovereign is the author and source of their rights' (p. 111). The same contention is more elaborately developed by the author of *The Politician*. He concedes that it may appear that 'no one other than the sovereign' may exercise 'the power of the sword', but he insists that 'sovereign magistrates under the prince' may sometimes 'have sovereign power communicated to them' and may thus be able rightfully to stand out against tyrannical princes (Goulart, III, fos 80b, 94a). Mornay makes a similar allusion to the traditional debate about the wielding of the *ius gladii* at the start of his analysis of the relationship between the people and the king. He begins by distinguishing 'the officers of the kingdom' from 'the officers of the king'. He then argues that while the latter are merely 'domestics of the king established only to obey him', the former are 'associates in the royal power' amongst whom the king is merely a 'president', while 'all of them are bound, just like the king, to look after the welfare of the commonwealth' (F., pp. 161–2).

Finally, these writers also revert to stressing the legal right of the Parlements to act as a check on the king – another traditional feature of French constitutionalist thought, but one which Hotman had oddly tended to denigrate. The fullest account again appears in Mornay's *Defence*, in the section on the people's relations with the king. He sees the Parlement of Paris as a 'judge between the king and the people, and especially between the king and particular individuals'. If the king 'should seek to act' against an individual 'in contravention of the law', the Parlement has a duty as well as a right to see that justice is done. If the king 'passes any edict or decision in his private council, or if a war is to be declared or peace is to be made', the authorisation of the Parlement must in every case be sought. The Parlement, in short, is once again assigned a central place in the constitution of France, signalled by the fact that 'everything relating to the commonwealth has to be entered in the record of its acts', with nothing being 'considered ratified' until its approval has been formally expressed (F., p. 165).

THE APPEAL TO NATURAL LAW

Although Hotman's *Francogallia* undoubtedly made a vital contribution to the ideology of the Huguenot revolution, its purely historical arguments soon proved vulnerable and hence inadequate as a basis on which to justify active political resistance. One important weakness, as a number of royalist writers quickly pointed out, was that Hotman's use of historical evidence was frequently tendentious and inaccurate. This failing was damagingly criticised by Antoine Matharel (1537–86), the *procureur général* to Catherine de Medici, who published a chapter-by-chapter *Reply to François Hotman's Francogallia* in 1575 (Ronzy, 1924, p. 172 and note). When Hotman issued a vituperative counterblast, Matharel's claims were upheld in a Latin *Response* by the humanist historian Papire Masson (1544–1611), who was employed at this time as an official historiographer to Catherine de Medici, and seems to have collaborated with Matharel in the production of his earlier *Reply* (Ronzy, 1924, pp. 153–4, 163–212). Hotman is convincingly accused in both these works of deliberately suppressing inconvenient evidence. Matharel notes, for example, that in his description of the fundamental constitution of France Hotman fails to mention that 'three hundred years elapsed' between the earliest king and the coming of the Merovingians, and that 'throughout these three centuries the kingdom of France was never bestowed by election, but always by the right of hereditary succession' (p. 34). Both accounts go on to accuse Hotman of deliberately falsifying the evidence he actually cites. This charge also had some substance, the most glaring instance being the crucial alteration Hotman introduced when quoting from Sigebert's chronicle on the coronation of the early Frankish kings. Sigebert speaks of the custom by which the people *erigunt* their new king – raised him up on their shields – but Hotman deftly changes this to read *eligunt* – so asserting that they elected him (p. 230 and note).

These detailed criticisms broaden out into a general attack on Hotman's understanding of the French constitution – the origins of the later debate between Dubos, Boulainvilliers and Montesquieu about the 'Germanist' *versus* the 'Romanist' origins of the monarchy.[1] Both Matharel and Masson – soon to be followed by Louis Le Roy – argue that it must be

---

[1] For Boulainvilliers' 'Germanism', see Buranelli, 1957. For Dubos's 'Romanism' and Montesquieu's 'Germanism', see Ford, 1953. For a hint of how Hotman's subversive type of

'fundamentally and absolutely false', as Matharel puts it, to suppose that the French monarchy was at any time elective and hence limited in character (p. 58; cf. Gundersheimer, 1966, pp. 81–3). They all cite copiously from early chronicles in order to insist on two quite contradictory points. First they allege that, as Masson declares, the customary laws of France have at all times allowed 'the right of hereditary succession, which has never been denied' (p. 8). It is then said to follow that the king of France must have an undivided *Imperium*, not in any way shared with the Estates, whose status they take to be purely consultative. Matharel concludes his rival analysis by discussing the formula 'it is our pleasure', which has always been used, he claims, in the promulgation of royal edicts, and which proves that they are legally binding as they stand, whether or not they happen to have been endorsed by the Estates (pp. 86–7).

As well as proving vulnerable to this type of counterattack, Hotman's analysis also contained one critical weakness from the point of view of the Huguenots themselves. What they needed was a form of political argument capable of justifying a direct revolutionary challenge to the alleged tyranny of the existing government. What Hotman provided was little more than a history (and a highly debatable history) of the fundamental constitution of France. It is of course true that his way of telling the story, for those who could accept it, conveyed a strong implicit criticism of the entire Valois regime. But this was far from being adequate to sustain the sort of revolutionary conclusions which the Huguenots were now committed to support. What they needed, and what Hotman had failed to supply, was an absolutely explicit attack on the behaviour of the government, carrying with it an equally explicit demand for the people to take to arms.

The reception of *Francogallia* may thus be said to have left the Huguenots in a dilemma. On the one hand they needed to construct a more radical as well as less vulnerable form of argument than Hotman had managed to provide. But on the other hand there was nothing in the existing traditions of radical Protestant thought to which they could hope to appeal in making this further move. Hitherto, as we have seen, the Protestants had sought to defend the lawfulness of resistance by one of three main arguments: the Lutheran theory of inferior magistrates; the Calvinist theory of 'ephoral' authorities; and the private-law theory of individual resistance in cases of self-defence. The first two of these claims, however, the Huguenots had already exploited to the full, while

'Germanist' thesis survived and developed in the intervening period, see Rothkrug, 1965, esp. pp. 343–51.

the third they had special reasons for wishing to avoid, especially after its anarchic implications had been so alarmingly spelled out by Ponet, Goodman and the author of the *Civil and Military Defence.*

The solution adopted by Beza, Mornay and the other leading Huguenots in the face of this dilemma was an obvious but nonetheless a paradoxical one: they turned to the scholastic and Roman law traditions of radical constitutionalism. They rejected the characteristically Protestant tendency to suppose that God places all men in a condition of political subjection as a remedy for their sins. Instead they began to argue that the original and fundamental condition of the people must be one of natural liberty. This in turn enabled them to abandon the orthodox Pauline contention that all the powers that be must be seen as directly ordained by God. Instead they inferred that any legitimate political society must originate in an act of free consent on the part of the whole populace.

It is of course true that there were some precedents for this attempt to steal the ideological clothing originally manufactured by their Catholic enemies. It may be highly significant in this connection that Calvin himself was originally a pupil of John Mair's, under whom he studied theology at the Collège de Montaign before becoming a law student under Alciato at Bourges (Ganoczy, 1966, pp. 39–41). Calvin was undoubtedly far more sympathetic to the scholastic as well as the legal-humanist approach to politics than any of the earlier reformers, and these influences can be observed even more clearly in a number of his most radical followers. Beza had already suggested, for example, at the start of his tract on *The Punishment of Heretics* in 1554 that we need to think of our magistrates as 'constituted by the consent of the people' in order to act as 'guardians of the laws' which the people originally decided to establish over themselves (p. 22). Ponet had argued in his *Short Treatise* two years later that all rulers originally 'have their authority of the people' who appoint them 'upon trust' and for this reason retain the authority 'upon just occasion' to 'take away what they gave' (p. 107). And two years after this Goodman in his book on *Superior Powers* had even appealed to the language of natural rights, declaring that men 'may lawfully claim' their liberty 'as their own possessions', and concluding that 'if they suffer this right to be taken from them' they are letting themselves be robbed no less than if they let their rulers remove any of their other goods.[1]

With the earliest Calvinist revolutionaries, however, such allusions to natural-law arguments had been little more than marginal asides, which

---

[1] See Goodman, *Superior Powers*, pp. 149, 160, and for further appeals to the 'subjective' concept of rights see pp. 154, 180, 188, 214. The idea of a right to property recurs in the Geneva Bible's translation of the story of Naboth's vineyard. See esp. fo 163a.

remained unrelated to – and rather obviously inconsistent with – their basic appeal to the idea that all the powers that be are directly ordained by God. During the 1570s, by contrast, the Huguenots began to make a systematic use of radical scholastic and Roman-law theories of *Imperium*. One reflection of this development can be seen in the suggestive fact that Salamonio's dialogues on *The Sovereignty of the Roman Patriciate* were reissued in Paris in 1578 (d'Addio, 1954, p. 16). A further indication is that several Huguenot theorists, including Beza and Mornay, began to compose their tracts in a self-consciously scholastic style. Abandoning the tones of the preacher favoured by such writers as Goodman and Knox, they turned instead to copying the formal patterns of argument characteristic of scholastic legal and political treatises, beginning with the *Quaestio* to be analysed, moving on to consider various *objectiones* and concluding with a *responsio* and a summary of their case. Finally, the clearest evidence of growing scholastic influence is provided by the range of authorities a writer like Mornay feels it appropriate to cite. When he turns to the question of tyranny in the *Defence*, he explicitly refers us to Aquinas, Bartolus, Baldus and the codifiers of the Roman law.[1] And when he considers the central question of the right to resist, he reveals a close dependence on the radical background of conciliarist political thought. He quotes several decisions made at Constance and Basle, refers us on two occasions specifically to the 'Sorbonnists', and employs the theories of Gerson, Almain and Mair in order to defend the idea of an exact analogy between the thesis of conciliarism in the Church and of popular sovereignty in the commonwealth.[2]

The paradox needs little emphasis: although it has become usual in recent discussions of reformation political theory to speak of 'the Calvinist theory of revolution', it will now be evident that there are virtually no elements in the theory which are specifically Calvinist at all. The arguments used by the first Calvinist revolutionaries in the 1550s were largely Lutheran; the new arguments added in the 1570s were largely scholastic; and since the arguments taken by the Calvinists from the Lutherans had originally been taken by the Lutherans from the civil and canon law, we may say with very little exaggeration that the main foundations of the Calvinist theory of revolution were in fact constructed entirely by their Catholic adversaries.

---

[1] The significance of these citations has perhaps been obscured by the fact that none of Mornay's marginal glosses have been reproduced in any of the modern editions of the *Defence*. For the above references see the original edition at p. 195 for Aquinas; pp. 50, 130, 181, 194–5 for Bartolus; p. 204 for Baldus; and pp. 31, 50, etc. for references to the *Digest*.

[2] For references to Basle and Constance, see the original edition at pp. 48, 203–4, etc. For the 'Sorbonnists', see pp. 61–2.

The paradox is of course easily resolved: we only have to recall the aims of the Huguenots and their propagandists after the massacres of 1572. They not only needed to stage a revolution, but also to legitimate it to their own followers and as far as possible to the Catholic majority. Their first attempt to meet these needs – by developing Hotman's positive-law theory of the constitution – proved unduly vulnerable to counterattack. Their ensuing appeal to natural law arguments supplied them, as they clearly recognised, with a far more effective means of attaining the same ideological ends. It enabled them to base their theory of popular sovereignty on the logical and not merely the chronological origins of the commonwealth, thereby circumventing the weaknesses inherent in Hotman's purely prescriptivist arguments. They were able in consequence to derive the right of resistance from a general theory of *Imperium* rather than simply from a somewhat dubious defence of the right of deposition as an alleged feature of the fundamental constitution of France. And this in turn enabled them to present their demand for resistance as a purely political and non-sectarian argument, so performing the vital ideological task of appealing not merely to their own followers, but to the broadest possible spectrum of Catholic moderates and malcontents.

It is perhaps worth emphasising that this appears to be the correct resolution of the paradox, if only because this account is at odds with the sort of Weberian analysis of Calvinism as a revolutionary ideology which has recently come to be so widely accepted. The Weberian approach is characterised by insisting on a sharp distinction between the social and political theories of the Catholics and the Calvinists in the course of the sixteenth century. Hans Baron, for example, adopts this perspective when he maintains that throughout the sixteenth century the scholastic analysis of 'the sovereignty of the people' remained 'without vital importance', while the new and 'vigorous anti-monarchic spirit' of Calvinism began to exercise its distinctive influence. This leads him to claim that 'Calvinist political thought' – in contrast with the conservatism of neo-scholastic ideas – succeeded 'more than any other tendency of the time' in preventing 'a full victory of absolutism' (Baron, 1939, pp. 40–2). The modern radical is thus viewed as the heir of a specifically Calvinist set of political beliefs, which are taken to have radiated downwards 'to the political thought of modern times', carrying with them a distinctive set of 'modernising' political tendencies (Baron, 1939, pp. 31, 41).

This contrast between scholastic and Calvinist political theory has been developed in a number of recent studies of the Protestant Reformation and its ideological influence.[1] One of the most remarkable examples has been

[1] See for example Pinette, 1959, p. 223, a view reiterated in a number of current textbook

Michael Walzer's *Revolution of the Saints*. This treats the theory of political resistance espoused by the Catholics in the course of the sixteenth century as little more than a reiteration of Thomist beliefs. Suárez is taken as the paradigm of the Catholic attitude, and his view of resistance is said to be that it constitutes 'a temporarily necessary form of legal violence', ending as soon as order is restored (Walzer, 1966, p. 111 and n.). This backward-looking theory is then contrasted with the 'new' politics of Calvinism, a politics which is said to centre on the far more radical attempt to 'set legality and order aside' in order to accommodate the theory and practice of 'permanent warfare' (Walzer, 1966, pp. 111–12). The outcome, as in Baron's analysis, is to make 'the origins of radical politics' dependent on a specifically Calvinist set of political beliefs. 'The novelty of Calvinist politics' is said to be that it helped to show 'previously passive men' how to claim 'the right of participation in that ongoing system of political action that is the modern state' (Walzer, 1966, pp. 4, 18).

But there seems to be a vitiating confusion underlying this approach to analysing the role of Calvinism as a revolutionary ideology in early modern Europe. It is of course true that the men who argued in favour of revolution during this period tended to be Calvinists. But it is not true that in general they made use of specifically Calvinist arguments. The suggestion that the theories lying behind the rise of modern radical politics were distinctively Calvinist in character only remains plausible so long as we ignore the radical elements in civil and canon law, as well as the whole tradition of radical conciliarist thought stemming from d'Ailly and Gerson at the start of the fifteenth century. It is true that if, like Walzer, we restrict ourselves to comparing the Calvinists with such a theorist as Suárez, the supposed contrast between the radical Huguenots and the more backward-looking Catholics can be made to look convincing. But if we instead compare the Huguenots with Bartolus or Salamonio amongst the jurists, or with Ockham, Gerson, Almain and Mair amongst the theologians, we find the picture reversed. So far from breaking away from the constraints of scholasticism to found a 'new politics', we find the Huguenots largely adopting and consolidating a position which the more radical jurists and theologians had already espoused.

Although the main revolutionary argument which the Huguenots developed in the 1570s was undoubtedly scholastic in provenance, it

accounts. It must be stressed, however, that my critique of this approach does not apply to the older authorities, who saw much more clearly than many recent commentators the role played by scholastic ideas in the Calvinist revolution. See for example Lagarde, 1926, pp. 265–8 and Allen, 1957, p. 313.

would be an overstatement to imply that all the Huguenot theorists abandoned the more providentialist approach characteristic of earlier Protestant political thought. A number of lesser pamphleteers continued to
avoid all reference to scholastic ideas about the origins and character of
legitimate political societies, and fell back instead on the more cautious
theory of resistance which the Lutherans had originally developed in the
1530s out of the feudal interpretation of the Imperial constitution. They
began by insisting on the Pauline assumption that all the powers that be
must be ordained by God. Then they proceeded to add two further
arguments – in the manner originally proposed by Bucer and his followers – in such a way as to produce a defence of political resistance
compatible with this providentialist starting point. The first – as formulated for example in the anonymous tract entitled *Whether it is Lawful
for Subjects to Defend Themselves* – was that all the powers that be must
equally be ordained by God – not merely princes, but also 'inferior powers'
(*puissances inférieures*) whom God has called to serve as magistrates
(fo 243b). The second was that all these powers must be intended by God
to perform a specific function, that of 'doing good works' and upholding
'the exercise of religion' in a truly Christian way (fos 243b, 245b). The
outcome was a restatement of the providentialist version of the theory
that inferior magistrates have a positive duty to oppose tyrannical governments. As the tract on lawful defence concludes, whenever the chief
magistrate fails 'to oppose the devil and anti-Christ as his office requires',
it becomes the duty of 'the inferior powers' to 'offer a valid and legitimate
opposition to the supreme power', their aim being to ensure that the
people are able 'to defend themselves against anti-Christ', that the triumph
of the true Church is assured, and thus that the purpose for the sake of
which they have been ordained is duly fulfilled (fos 243b, 244b, 246a).

This theory stands in sharp contrast to the views about inferior magistrates developed by Hotman, Beza and Mornay at the same time. As we
have seen, they treated these 'inferior powers' as instances of 'ephoral'
authorities, and thus saw them not merely as ordained by God for
religious purposes but also as constituted by the people to guarantee their
own welfare. Their premises were thus incompatible with, and not merely
more radical than, those of the more conservative pamphleteers. This was
not enough, however, to deter both Beza and Mornay from adding the
providentialist version of the theory of inferior magistrates to their own
battery of arguments. The effect on Beza's theory of resistance is relatively slight, merely prompting him to stress that, as well as having an
obligation to guard the welfare of the people who have created them, all
inferior magistrates have a higher duty 'to employ all the means God has

given' them in order to ensure that He is 'recognised and served as king of kings' (p. 133). But the effect on Mornay's theory is much more marked, for it leads him to enunciate two quite different views about the nature of the covenant which he thinks of as underlying any legitimate political society, and two correspondingly different – and barely compatible – views about the grounds of legitimate resistance.

One of the covenants Mornay discusses is the typically scholastic idea of a contract between the king and the representatives of the people. This is analysed in the third *Quaestio*, which examines the purely political question of whether a prince 'who oppresses or devastates a common-wealth' may be lawfully opposed (F., p. 158). But the other covenant he describes is the specifically Protestant idea of a contract in two parts between the king, the inferior magistrates and God. The first part of this agreement, which is considered in the opening *Quaestio*, is said to be 'between God and the king' (F., p. 143). We are assured that 'all kings are ministers ordained by God to govern justly and rule on His behalf' (S., p. 7). We are then told that this ordination takes the form of a covenant 'regularly concluded between the king and God' by which the king promises to ensure that his commands 'are not in conflict with God's law' (F., pp. 142, 143). The other part of the agreement, which is taken up in the second *Quaestio*, is described as 'a covenant between God and the people' (F., p. 146). Mornay begins by reverting to Bucer's contention that God regards it as 'dangerous to entrust' the supreme duty of main-taining his Church 'to a single, all-too-human individual', and has accordingly decided to ordain not merely kings to rule but also 'magistrates below the king' to ensure that the king's duties are properly fulfilled (F., pp. 147, 149). Mornay then argues that the king, together with these magistrates acting on behalf of the people, may be said to have covenanted with God as joint 'promissory parties', both being 'conjointly obligated' to ensure that the commonwealth remains founded on the laws of God, and that the fundamental duty 'of maintaining his Temple and his Church among them' is faithfully discharged (F., p. 147).

The outcome of this twofold system of contracts is that Mornay arrives at two distinct justifications of resistance. One arises out of the scholastic idea that because the people create their rulers on set terms, they must always retain a right of resistance if these terms are not hon-oured. But the other arises out of a different and incompatible view about the origins and purpose of the commonwealth. Both the king and the inferior magistrates are said to have promised to uphold the true Church and the law of God. This is taken to mean that if the king fails in this duty and instead 'commands unholy actions or prohibits holy ones', it not only falls to the inferior magistrates to resist him, but actually becomes a religious duty on the part of these lesser powers to 'drive out idolatry from their walls' by ensuring that the king is forcibly removed (F., p. 154). If they fail to use force when the king 'overturns the law and the Church of God', they will be failing in their promise to God and will thus be 'guilty of the same crime' and 'subject to the same penalty' as their ungodly king (F., p. 149). Mornay's appeal to the inferior magistrates is as much a threat as a reminder of their powers, and culminates in a warning that if they refuse to 'use force against a king who corrupts God's law' they will 'very gravely sin against the covenant with God' (F., p. 157).

It was unusual, however, for a leading Huguenot theorist after 1572 to place such a strong emphasis on purely providentialist arguments. By this time, as we have seen, the central problem facing the Huguenots had become that of developing a more secular as well as a more radical means of justifying active resistance. The main question they faced, as Beza puts it in *The Right of Magistrates*, was how to advance 'arguments from reason' in order to show that the remedy for tyranny 'is to be found in human institutions' (pp. 103, 124). The main answer they gave involved them in turning away from providentialist assumptions in order to develop an essentially scholastic theory about the origins and character of legitimate political societies.

Like their scholastic predecessors, they begin by opposing the thesis of patriarchalism, arguing that man's fundamental condition must be one of natural liberty. They generally defend this proposition by insisting that its denial involves an absurdity. As Beza declares, it involves assuming that peoples are 'created for their rulers', whereas it is 'self-evident' that 'peoples do not come from rulers', but are, so to speak, 'older than these rulers', whom they originally decide to constitute simply in order to achieve a better regulation of their affairs (p. 104). The same argument is immediately taken up by the authors of *The Awakener*, *The Politician*, and *Political Discourses*, at several points being repeated word for word. To say that anyone is naturally in a state of subjection, *The Awakener* maintains, is to forget that 'assemblies and groups of men existed everywhere before the creation of kings', and that 'even today it is possible to find a people without a magistrate but never a magistrate without a people'. To argue against the fundamental liberty of mankind is thus said to involve the bizarre mistake of supposing that 'the people must have been created by their magistrates' when it is obvious that 'magistrates are always created by the people'.[1] Mornay later reiterates the same argument in the third

---

[1] See *The Awakener*, pp. 80–1; cf. *The Politician*, fo 73a and *Political Discourses*, fos 218b 222b, 238b.

Quaestio of his *Defence*. The absurdity of believing in a state of original subjection is first of all underlined. Since 'no one is born a king, and no one is a king by nature', and since 'a king cannot rule without a people, while a people can rule itself without a king', it is 'clear beyond all doubt' that the people must originally have lived without kings or positive laws, and only decided at some later date to submit themselves to their rule (F., p. 160). The underlying assumption that the condition in which men are placed in the world by God must be one of natural liberty is then spelled out. We are all 'free by nature, born to hate servitude, and desirous of commanding rather than yielding obedience'. And we are all said to possess this freedom as one of our natural rights, as 'a privilege of nature' which can never be rightfully withdrawn (S., p. 107).

If no one is naturally in a state of subjection, how and why are political societies ever brought into existence? In answering this question the Huguenots produce an analysis which parallels that of the radical scholastic theologians at every point. They begin by discussing – to use their own scholastic jargon – the final cause of establishing a commonwealth. They all agree that, as *The Awakener* puts it, 'if we ask about the cause and occasion of the creation of magistrates', it is impossible to conceive of any other reason than 'the safety, the welfare and the conservation of the people' (p. 83). Mornay endorses the same argument in his *Defence*. If the people agree to set up a commonwealth, thus putting an end to their state of natural liberty, this can only be due to the fact that 'they expect some very considerable profit to arise out of agreeing in this way to submit themselves to the commands of others' (S., p. 107). And he adds that it behoves all kings to remember that 'it is due to the people, and for the sake of the people's welfare, that they exercise their power', so that 'they must not say, as they often do, that they hold their sword by the ordination of God unless they also say that it was the people who first placed it in their hands' (S., p. 79).

The idea that the people must be pictured as establishing political societies in order to improve their natural lot is sometimes expressed – notably in Mornay's *Defence* – as a claim not about the maintenance of general welfare, but rather about the preservation of individual rights. And in discussing the concept of a right Mornay follows precisely the analysis we have already encountered in the writings of Gerson and his followers, and particularly in Mair's *Questions* on Lombard's *Sentences*. Mair had explicated the concept of 'having a right over something' in terms of having the freedom to dispose of it within the bounds of the law of nature. He had thus treated the right to hold and dispose of one's property – one's clothes or one's books – as the paradigm case of a right, treating it as evident that the things over which I can most readily be said to have an absolute freedom of disposal must be my own possessions. It is clearly this analysis of a right which Mornay has in mind in the third *Quaestio* of his *Defence*. When he equates the welfare of the people with the need to ensure that their 'rights and privileges' are never 'given up' to 'the unbridled liberty of their king', he mainly concentrates on their right to retain those possessions which they must originally have held before the establishment of the commonwealth, insisting that these above all must be protected once the commonwealth has been set up (F., p. 162; cf. S., pp. 139, 158). He endorses the scholastic assumption – later made famous by Locke – that the point at which the people must originally have found it necessary to establish political societies must have been 'when the concepts of *meum* and *tuum* first entered the world, and differences began to arise within the body of the people over the question of the ownership of material goods' (S., p. 109). And he adds that the main motive the people must have possessed for setting up a commonwealth must have been that of ensuring a greater security for their property and 'the prevention of any devastation of their territories or any other such material calamities' (S., p. 109).

It would be a misrepresentation, however, to suppose that when the Huguenots state this equation between the welfare of the people and the preservation of their rights to property, they intend no more than to point to the ruler's obligation to maintain his subjects in the enjoyment of their material goods. Like Locke a century later, the Huguenots assume that amongst the things we may be said to have the freedom and thus the right to dispose of within the bounds of the laws of nature are those properties – as we still punningly call them – which are intrinsic to our personalities, and in particular our lives and liberties. So when the Huguenots treat the people's welfare as the final cause of the commonwealth, and proceed to equate this with their right to enjoy their properties, they often make it clear that what they have in mind is the duty of the ruler to uphold the inalienable and natural rights of the people to their lives and liberties – these being the fundamental and natural properties which everyone may be said to possess in a pre-political state. This is clearly the train of thought underlying the allegation by the author of the *Declaration* that the massacres of 1572 brought the French people to the limits of political obligation. The reason he gives is that such a deliberate deprivation by the government of the lives of so many of its citizens must be held to constitute an action 'contrary to the inviolable right of men' (*le droit de gens qui est inviolable*) and in this way contrary to the ends for the sake of which the government was originally instituted (fo 38b). The corresponding assumption that the fundamental justification of government lies in its capacity to preserve the natural rights of its citizens, in particular their untrammelled enjoyment of their lives, liberties and estates, is clearly adumbrated in *The Politician*, developed with characteristic incisiveness in the *Political Discourses* and summarised most fully by Mornay in the third *Quaestio* of his *Defence*. *The Politician* actually opens by raising the question of 'whether it is lawful in a case of extreme oppression for subjects to take up arms to defend their life and liberty' (fo 61a). The author of the *Discourses* provides a decisive answer in connection with his claim that a right of resistance must always exist against any government which attempts 'to make the people slaves'. When the people refuse to allow themselves to be enslaved, they are merely defending 'their possession of liberty' (*le bien de liberté*). And when they defend their liberty, they are merely 'procuring that which is their natural right' (*droit naturel*) (fos 293a–b). Finally, the same assumptions are even more clearly spelled out by Mornay, who concludes his discussion of prescription and 'the right of the people' by insisting that no action by any lawful government 'must ever detract in any way from the right of the people's liberty'. The main reason he gives is that the chief concern of any government 'must always be to act as the guardians of the liberty and security of the people' (F., p. 168; S., p. 106).

If the final cause of setting up a commonwealth is the people's welfare, and especially the preservation of their rights, then according to the Huguenots the only possible efficient cause must be the general consent, freely expressed, of all the citizens involved. Beza states this claim so strongly in his *Right of Magistrates* that he is even prepared to argue that 'if a people knowingly, and in complete freedom, has consented to something that is in itself manifestly irreligious and contrary to the law of nature, the obligation is invalid' (p. 124). The same assumption that, as he earlier puts it, an act of 'free and lawful consent' is always needed for the creation of any 'legitimate rulers' is then reiterated by all the other leading Huguenot theorists (p. 107). 'The first magistrates', as *The Awakener* agrees, were not only 'created by common consent', but 'no Empire or government can ever be considered just or legitimate' unless it is inaugurated with the consent of the people (pp. 81, 84). The same assumptions underlie the more elaborate account of how 'kings are created by the people' which Mornay offers at the start of the third *Quaestio* of his *Defence* (F., p. 158). He lays more emphasis on the role of the magistrates who actually choose the king, stressing that it is 'those who represent the people's majesty' who assign the king his office 'together with the sceptre and the crown' (F., p. 160). But he still insists that one of the necessary conditions for the legitimacy of any ruler is that he should be established in power by the free consent of at least a majority of the people. This is made clear from the detailed description he gives of the installation of Saul as King of Israel. Even in this case it was not enough that the king had already been 'selected' by God. He still needed to be 'established' by the general consent of the people, which they duly expressed first by 'acclamation' and subsequently by a formal vote which revealed a majority in favour of accepting him (F., p. 159).

Although the people's consent is said to be essential before any ruler can be installed, the Huguenots recognise that this requirement, especially in such a large and populous country as France, poses certain practical difficulties. The solution they propose is that we must think of the people as having delegated their authority to choose and subsequently to control their supreme magistrate to a body of lesser magistrates who are specially selected for this purpose. As Mornay explains, it is obvious that 'good government depends on a degree of order that cannot be maintained' if a 'large multitude' is allowed to take part directly, and it is equally obvious that there are many 'affairs of state' that 'cannot be communicated publicly' to the whole body of the people 'without danger to the common interest'. This makes it desirable that the sovereign rights and privileges originally held by the people as a whole should be exercised by their elected 'officers of the kingdom' on their behalf and in their own best interests (F., p. 150).

The accounts Beza and Mornay provide of this process of delegation appear to reflect an anxiety to ensure that their natural-law arguments remain compatible with their earlier appeals to French constitutional history. The 'officers of the kingdom' are said to be of two kinds. There are the local and seigneurial magistrates, 'among whom may be numbered', according to Beza, 'dukes, marquises, counts, viscounts, barons and chatelains' as well as 'the elected officers of towns' (p. 110). Mornay lays a special emphasis on the last-named group, claiming that 'each of the towns that form part of the kingdom' must be taken to have 'individually and expressly sworn' to act on behalf of the people as a whole (F., p. 152). Then there are the magistrates elected to sit as representatives of the people in the assembly of the Three Estates. Beza gives a long account of their powers (evidently lifted directly from Hotman's *Francogallia*) which culminates in the claim that 'the Estates of the country' hold a right of 'sovereign governance' which has been assigned to them directly by the whole body of the people (p. 123). Mornay agrees that the same powers are held 'in every properly constituted kingdom' by 'the Parliament, Diet and other such assemblies', and that this assigns them the highest duty of ensuring that 'no harm is suffered either by the commonwealth or by the Church' (F., p. 150).

This account of the procedure by which legitimate rulers are said to be selected and controlled is taken to have two important implications. The first is that when Beza and Mornay speak of 'the people' as a collectivity, they are not in fact referring to the whole body of the citizens, but only – as Mornay explains – to 'those who receive authority from the people, that is, the magistrates below the king who have been elected by the people' (F., p. 149; cf. S., p. 120). The other implication is that while the people never forfeit their ultimate sovereignty, they do give up their right to exercise it directly. As Mornay adds, this follows from the fact that the covenant with the king, setting out the terms of his rule, is never sworn by the whole body of the people, but only by their selected representatives. So the corresponding right to hold the king to his promises can never be a property of the people as a whole, but only a property of 'the authorities that have the power of the people in them' (F., p. 154).

The final point the Huguenot theorists make about the process of setting up a legitimate commonwealth may be said to follow from these claims about welfare and consent: if the commonwealth has to be inaugurated with the consent of the people, and if the reason for setting it up is to improve their welfare and secure their rights, then it seems that the actual mechanism which brings it into being must take the form of a contract or *Lex Regia* agreed between the representatives of the people and their prospective ruler, a contract which stipulates that the king will in fact pursue the welfare and uphold the rights of the people who have agreed to his ruling over them for this express purpose.

This contract (*pactum*) is wholly separate from the idea of the religious covenant (*foedus*) which the Huguenot theorists also invoke. In discussing the *foedus* they were concerned with the duty of both the magistrate and the people to uphold the laws of God. But in discussing the *pactum* they are simply concerned to establish that, as Beza declares, 'wherever law and equity [have] prevailed', no nation has ever 'created nor accepted kings except upon definite conditions' (p. 114). It is this contention which leads them to speak of a second and purely political contract, one which takes the form, in Beza's words, of 'a mutual oath between the king and the people' (p. 118). The character of this agreement is stated in general terms by all the leading Huguenot writers. *The Awakener*, for instance, speaks of the 'mutual and reciprocal obligation between the magistrate and his subjects' (p. 80). Similarly, *The Politician* cites 'the reciprocal arrangements between prince and subject' which 'cannot be violated without injustice by either of the parties' (fo 85a). But the fullest account of these reciprocal obligations is given by Mornay in the third *Quaestio* of his *Defence*, which includes a special section on 'The covenant, or compact, between the king and the people' (F., p. 180). Mornay's main concern is to stress that whereas the people's representatives swear a 'conditional' obligation to the king, the king swears an 'absolute' obligation to these representatives (F., p. 181). When 'the people made the king' at the point when they first decided to establish the commonwealth, they caused him to swear an absolute oath to 'preserve the people's welfare'. The representatives of the people then made the conditional promise in return that 'they would faithfully obey, as long as his commands were just' (F., pp. 180–1). The outcome is said to be the creation of 'a mutual obligation' between the king on the one hand and the magistrates on the other, an agreement which 'cannot be superseded by any other compact, or violated in the name of any other right'. Mornay concludes the section by insisting that the force of this contract is so great 'that a king who breaks it wilfully may properly be called a "tyrant", while a people that breaks it may properly be called "seditious" ' (F., p. 185).

The Huguenots are also in complete agreement with the most radical of their scholastic predecessors about the character of the commonwealth which follows from depicting men in a pre-political condition consenting and so contracting to set it up. The main conclusion they state is a theory of popular sovereignty. This forms the core of their constitutionalism, with their most celebrated argument – their defence of resistance – merely being an implication of it (Franklin, 1967, pp. 117, 123). The conclusion itself is most clearly presented by Mornay in his *Defence*, using a series of feudal analogies. He insists that since the people are originally free of government, and only consent to establish it for their own purposes, they must at all times be regarded as 'the true proprietor' of the commonwealth, exercising 'supreme dominion' over it in the same way that the owner of a fief remains in ultimate control, even though he may choose to delegate its actual administration to someone else (F., pp. 162, 191). Mornay is careful to use the precise vocabulary of the most radical scholastics at this point, not the more conservative language favoured by the Thomists. The Thomists generally argued that, although the people are originally sovereign, the act of instituting a ruler involves them in what Suárez was to describe as 'a sort of alienation' of their powers, such that the ruler they install is 'above and greater than' the whole body of the people. Mornay argues on the contrary that the people at all times 'remain in the position of the owner' of their original sovereignty, which they merely delegate to their ruler 'in order that he may exercise it for the public good' (S., p. 86). There is thus no question of the king being 'above the people'. It is evident on the contrary that 'the whole people is greater than the king and is above him' (F., p. 190). As Mornay roundly concludes, once we realise that the people never alienate their sovereignty, but merely delegate the right to exercise it to their king, 'it can hardly be thought strange if we insist that the people must be more powerful (*potior*) than the king' (S., p. 88).

This central contention carries with it two further implications about the character of the lawful commonwealth which the Huguenot theorists finally spell out. The first concerns the status of magistrates. They are said to be the servants of the kingdom, not of the king, since their responsibility is to the people who create them, not to the king whom they create. Beza and Mornay are both extremely emphatic on this point. As Beza expresses it, they hold their offices 'properly speaking, not of the sovereign but of the sovereignty', so that 'when the sovereign magistrate dies, they nonetheless remain in office, just as the sovereignty itself remains intact' (p. 111). The same point is confirmed by Mornay, who speaks of the magistrates as servants 'not of the king but of the kingdom', since they 'receive their authority from the people in public council, and cannot be removed unless that body consents' (F., pp. 161, 162). Finally, the other implication they emphasise concerns the status of the king. Here again they are careful to invoke the terminology of the most radical scholastics, not the more conservative language of the Thomists. The Thomists had insisted that even though the king is installed in his office by the people, he must thereafter be regarded as *legibus solutus* – a genuine sovereign free from any obligation to obey his own positive laws. Both Beza and Mornay maintain on the contrary that a lawful king cannot in this sense be regarded as a sovereign at all, since he is merely, as Mornay puts it, 'a kind of minister to the commonwealth' (F., p. 161). His status is merely that of an 'agent' of the people, 'while the people is the true proprietor' of the commonwealth (F., p. 191). Mornay repeatedly makes it clear in his descriptions of the office of kingship that he sees the status of a lawful king as more like that of a salaried official than a sovereign magistrate. The ruler is described as a servant of the commonwealth (*servus reipublicae*), as a guardian (*custos*) and especially as an administrator (*minister*), and he is said to be 'merely the supervisor and executor of the laws' (e.g., S., pp. 86, 114, 125). This in turn means there can be no question of his being *legibus solutus*. For as Beza insists, 'there is not a single law to which the ruler is not bound in the conduct of his government, since he has sworn to be the protector and preserver of them all'. The saying that the ruler 'is not subject to the laws' is thus dismissed as 'the false maxim of detestable flatterers, not of a subject loyal to his prince' (p. 113). The same conclusion is strongly supported by Mornay, who thinks it 'completely ridiculous for kings to regard it as a disgrace to be subject to the law', since this ignores the fundamental fact that 'kings receive their laws from the people', who remain the 'owners' of the commonwealth (S., pp. 86, 115, 119).

This essentially scholastic analysis of the origins and character of legitimate political societies supplied the Huguenots with a complete answer to the ideological problems they needed to resolve. They were able in the first place to minimise any remaining fears about the anarchic or insurrectionary nature of their political thought, and in particular to insist that it was no part of their argument to suggest that individual citizens possess the right to kill or even to resist their magistrates. This limitation was said to follow from the fact that the act of consent which brings a legitimate commonwealth into existence is an act performed by the whole body of the people considered as a collectivity. This means, as Mornay explains, that although the ruler is *minor universis*, since 'the entire people is above the king when taken as a body', he is nevertheless *maior singulis*, since all individual citizens and even magistrates remain 'below the king as individuals' (F., p. 162). It follows that no private individual can possibly be said to have a right of resistance against a lawfully constituted king. Since the people 'create the prince not as individuals but all together', their rights against him are the rights of a corporation, not the rights of 'any single individual' who may happen to be a member of it (F., pp. 154, 195). Any private individuals who 'draw the sword' against their king are thus 'seditious, no matter how just the cause may be', since no commonwealth is ever derived from or founded upon purely individual interests (F., p. 195).

The appeal to scholastic arguments also enabled the Huguenots to insist that their theory of resistance was legal and constitutional in character, and not a mere call to the many-headed multitude to rise up in rebellion against their lawful overlords. This further limitation was said to follow from their insistence that, although the people as a whole retain the ultimate sovereignty, they must be understood to have delegated the right to exercise it to their specially chosen magistrates. As Mornay stresses, this implies that 'when we speak of the people collectively, we mean those who receive authority from the people, that is, the magistrates below the king' and 'the assembly of the Estates' (F., p. 149). When the king promises to rule in the name of the people's welfare, he signs this contract not with the people themselves, but only with the magistrates to whom the people 'have given their sword' (F., p. 196). It follows that even the whole body of the people can never be said to have a direct right of resistance against a lawfully constituted king. When a king governs tyrannically, he is not breaking any promises made to the body of the people, but only the promise he has made to what Mornay characterises as an 'epitome' of duly constituted magistrates and representatives. So the authority to resist a tyrant can never be lodged with the body of the people, but only with the magistrates 'to whom they have transferred their authority and power' (F., p. 195). It is only to these 'officers of the kingdom' that the king has given his promise to act justly; it is only they who may in consequence be said to possess the corresponding right to hold the king to the performance of his duties, and to 'defend the commonwealth as a whole from oppression' if he fails to keep to the terms of his contract (F., p. 195).

A further ideological difficulty which the Huguenots needed to be able to resolve arose out of their need to produce a justification of resistance with a wider and less purely sectarian appeal than the theories developed by the earlier generation of Calvinist revolutionaries. This too they were now able to achieve by way of appealing to the same set of scholastic arguments. They were able, that is, to make the epoch-making move from a purely religious theory of resistance, depending on the idea of a covenant to uphold the laws of God, to a genuinely political theory of revolution, based on the idea of a contract which gives rise to a moral right (and not merely a religious duty) to resist any ruler who fails in his corresponding obligation to pursue the welfare of the people in all his public acts.

It is true that, even at the moment of making this fundamental conceptual shift, the Huguenots still tend to organise their arguments in such a way as to place their main emphasis on the idea of a duty rather than a right to resist. As Beza declares, the position of the magistrates as representatives of the people is such that they have 'a sworn duty to preserve the law' (p. 112). They 'have promised', Mornay agrees, to 'use every means at their disposal' to provide for the 'protection and defence' of the people, and in consequence 'have a duty to demand of their agent an account of his administration' (F., p. 193; S., pp. 195–6). The implication is that if their ruler degenerates into a tyrant, they have a duty to resist him with force, a duty which arises (in Mornay's phrase) out of having 'promised their strength and energy to the kingdom' (F., p. 195). This is the form in which the justification of resistance is finally asserted both in Beza's and in Mornay's accounts. The lesser magistrates, as Beza maintains, 'are obliged' to 'offer resistance to flagrant tyranny' and to do so 'by force of arms' in order 'to safeguard those within their care'. To act in this way 'is not to be seditious or disloyal towards one's sovereign', but 'to keep one's faith towards those from whom one's office was received, against him who has broken his oath and oppressed the kingdom he ought to have protected' (p. 112). Mornay endorses the same conclusion with no less force. 'The officers of the kingdom' are said to be 'not only permitted but obliged, as part of the duty of their office' to ensure that if a tyrant 'cannot be expelled without resort to force', they must 'call the people to arms, recruit an army, and use force, strategy and all the engines of war against him who is the declared enemy of the country and the commonwealth' (F., p. 191; cf. pp. 195, 196).

But in spite of this way of putting the point, it will by now be evident that the essence of the Huguenot case rests on the general contention that the act of promising analytically implies the acceptance of a moral obligation on the part of the agent who makes the promise, and a corresponding moral right on the part of the other signatory to demand that the terms of the promise should be kept. As the author of *The Awakener* puts it, 'the rights of the people' (*les droits du peuple*) must include the right to demand that their magistrates and elected representatives should at all times follow 'the good customs of the realm', since these 'officers of the kingdom' enjoy their special status in virtue of having promised to uphold the laws and the people's welfare. Furthermore, these officers in turn have a right to insist that their king should rule in such a way that he does indeed uphold the people's welfare, since he has been given the dignity of kingship in return for promising to perform this precise task (pp. 88–9). It follows that if the king neglects this promise and becomes a tyrant, 'he can by right (*par droit*) be resisted' by the people's representatives (p. 90). Beza reaches the same crucial conclusion in his *Right of Magistrates*. If the king violates the terms of the contract by which he has been installed in office, then the lesser magistrates – and even more clearly the representatives of the people – 'have the right to correct the person they have elevated to dominion', since 'those who have power to give' authority to kings 'have no less power to deprive them of it' (pp. 114, 118). And Mornay repeats the same argument at the end of the third *Quaestio* of his *Defence*. Any king 'who violates the compact wilfully and persistently' is 'a tyrant by conduct', and in such a case 'the officers of the kingdom' are 'empowered by their own right to drive him out'.[1]

The essence of the Huguenot case is thus that the magistrates and representatives of the people have the moral right to resist tyrannical government by force, a right which is founded on the prior and natural right of the sovereign people to treat the commonwealth as a means for

---

[1] Franklin, 1969, pp. 196–7. I have given my own translation of the last clause.

securing and improving their own welfare (cf. Mesnard, 1936, pp. 345–6). If we ask why they should have chosen to state this final and revolutionary conclusion in the language of duties as much as of rights, the answer is of course in part a tactical one. After 1572 the main task of the Huguenot revolutionaries was to call the natural leaders of the people to arms. To argue in these circumstances that they had a right to resist would merely have been to make the point that morally speaking they need not fear to fight. To put the same claim in the form of saying that they had a duty to resist was to make the much stronger claim that they must not fail to fight. It made resistance not just morally possible but mandatory, enabling them to exhort the 'officers of the kingdom' in the strongest possible terms to recognise, as Mornay assures them, that 'it is absolutely clear' that they can and ought to 'take up arms and fight against tyranny', and 'not merely for the sake of religion, but also in the name of our hearths and homes' (S., p. 208).

The theory developed by Beza, Mornay and the other leading Huguenots after 1572 soon began to exercise a potent influence, in particular in the Netherlands, where a similar revolutionary situation arose in 1580 (cf. Griffiths, 1959). After Farnese was appointed governor in 1578, the Spanish began to campaign with growing success against the rebels, soon regaining the allegiance of the Catholic nobility in the southern provinces. Philip II insisted on following up these victories in June 1580 by proscribing William the Silent and putting a price on his head (Elliott, 1968, p. 289). This in turn drove William into a direct confrontation with his sovereign and a final abjuration of his allegiance. As a result, William and his followers found themselves turning to the arguments already developed by the Huguenots as a way of legitimating their own revolutionary stand against the authority of the Imperial government. A good example of this influence is provided by the anonymous pamphlet entitled *A True Warning* which appeared in Antwerp in 1581. The writer begins by appealing to the scholastic idea of the natural and fundamental liberty of mankind, arguing that 'God has created men free' and that they 'cannot be made slaves by people who have no power over them save that which they themselves have granted' (pp. 228, 230). This is used to sustain the claim that all legitimate rulers must be 'chosen and installed' by those who represent the whole body of the community (p. 229). These magistrates are said to 'bind the king or lord whom they install' in such a way that he has an absolute duty to ensure that 'righteousness and justice' are upheld in the commonwealth (pp. 228, 229). This in turn means that if the king is found to be 'breaking the conditions' on which the people's representatives 'accepted him as their lord and prince', this gives them a right, in view of his broken promise, to resist him and 'resume their original rights' (p. 229). The same crucial conclusion is endorsed by William himself both in the extensive *Apology* which he presented to the States General in December 1580 – the text of which was almost certainly drafted by Languet and Mornay – and in the official *Edict of the States General* of July 1581 which declared 'that the king of Spain has forfeited his sovereignty' (p. 216). As the latter document insists, the provinces of the United Netherlands have finally been forced, 'in conformity with the law of nature', to invoke their undoubted right to resist tyrannical government and 'to pursue such means' as seem likely to secure their 'rights, privileges and liberties' (p. 225).

THE DEFENCE OF POPULAR REVOLUTION

With the publication of the major Huguenot treatises of the 1570s, Protestant political theory passes across a crucial conceptual divide.[1] Hitherto even the most radical Calvinists had vindicated the lawfulness of resistance in terms of the paramount duty of the powers that be to uphold the true (that is, the Protestant) faith. But with Beza, Mornay and their followers, the idea that the preservation of religious uniformity constitutes the sole possible grounds for legitimate resistance is finally abandoned. The result is a fully *political* theory of revolution, founded on a recognisably modern, secularised thesis about the natural rights and original sovereignty of the people.

If we pause once more, however, to compare this argument with the one presented by John Locke in the *Two Treatises of Government*, we find that, in spite of these developments, the thesis advanced by the Huguenots still differs at two important points from the classic version of early-modern constitutionalism. Locke not only vindicates the lawfulness of resistance entirely in the language of rights and natural rights, but goes on to locate the authority to resist with 'the body of the people' and even with 'any single man' if 'deprived of their right'.[2] By contrast, Beza, Mornay and their followers continue to think in terms of the religious duty as well as the moral right of resistance, and to limit the exercise of this right to lesser magistrates and other elected representatives, deliber-

---

[1] This is to imply that the very similar treatises which began to appear in the Netherlands in the latter part of the sixteenth century were basically derived from French sources. This appears largely to have been the case, but the possibility of mutual influence ought not to be ruled out. A great deal more research in the Dutch sources will be needed, however, before it will be possible to pronounce with confidence on this point.

[2] Locke, *Two Treatises*, pp. 397, 437. For the shift in the course of the English revolution from the theory of resistance by lesser magistrates to Locke's (and, earlier, Lawson's) far more populist position, see Franklin, 1978.

ately excluding individual citizens and even the whole body of the people from taking any direct political initiative. It remains finally to ask, therefore, at what point the revolutionary Calvinists first succeeded in sweeping away these remaining features of a more conservative and religious constitutionalism, and managed to articulate a fully populist as well as a completely secularised theory of the right to resist.

As one might expect, the answer is that this move was first made in Scotland in the period after the first-ever successful Calvinist revolution in the late 1550s. By this time Scotland had become a vociferously Calvinist country, so that the idea of calling on the whole body of the people to resist their Catholic overlords became a realistic option in a way that it never became for the Huguenots. Furthermore, the theories of Goodman and Knox had already served to legitimate the suggestion that it might be lawful for all the godly people, and even for individual saints, to oppose the rule of an idolatrous tyrant. It only remained to restate their theory in the language of rights rather than religious duties in order to attain a fully secularised as well as a populist ideology of revolution. What prompted this final move was that, although Scotland officially embraced the Calvinist faith after the meetings of the Reformation Parliament in 1560, the government remained under the control of an unshakeably Catholic Queen. This anomaly was removed with the deposition of Mary Queen of Scots in 1567, an action which called forth an extensive discussion of whether the people could properly be said to have the right to repudiate a legitimate prince. By far the most important theorist to answer in the affirmative was George Buchanan (1506–82) in his Latin dialogues on *The Right of the Kingdom in Scotland*.[1] Buchanan seems to have begun to draft this remarkable work in 1567, although he only published it in 1579, in the wake of the treaties of Beza and Mornay. Meanwhile, however, some elements of his argument appear to have been incorporated in the speeches delivered in the course of the Regent Moray's embassy to York in 1568, as well as in the discussions between the Scottish government and Queen Elizabeth's commissioners in London three years later.[2]

---

[1] Two modern translations of Buchanan's *Right of the Kingdom* are available, one by Charles F. Arrowood (Austin, Texas, 1949), the other by Duncan H. MacNeill (Glasgow, 1964). But J. H. Burns has argued that both are seriously defective; see his remarks in the *Scottish Historical Review* 30 (1951), pp. 67–8 on Arrowood, and *loc. cit.*, 48 (1969), pp. 190–1 on MacNeill. I have accordingly preferred to make my own translation directly from the original edition, though I have frequently referred to Arrowood's version, the existence of which has greatly eased my task.

[2] This reconstruction of the evolution of Buchanan's revolutionary theory is based on Trevor-Roper, 1966, esp. pp. 19–21. But Trevor-Roper's wish to insist that the 'memorial' presented to the commissioners in 1571 should be ascribed to Buchanan serves to introduce an inconsistency into his argument. First he suggests that *The Right of the Kingdom* was partly drafted as early as the summer of 1567. But later he describes the 'memorial' of 1571 as 'the earliest

Finally, Buchanan himself supplied the theory with its fullest empirical grounding in his *History of Scotland*, a work on which he had been continuously engaged throughout these years, and which he eventually published in 1582.

Buchanan is of course best known as a humanist, a Gallicised Scot who taught Latin at the Collège de Guyenne in Bordeaux, and whose Latin verses prompted Montaigne to describe him in his essay on the education of children as 'that great Scottish poet' (p. 129). But he also received a scholastic training at the University of St Andrews between 1524 and 1526, where one of his teachers was the redoubtable John Mair (Burns, 1954, pp. 85, 92–3). Moreover, he seems to have been an early convert to Calvinism, becoming a friend and correspondent of Beza's and Mornay's while in France, and serving as a member of the General Assembly of the Church of Scotland on his return from exile after the successful Calvinist revolution of 1560. By intellectual training as well as ideological commitment, therefore, Buchanan was peculiarly well-suited to develop the heritage of radical scholastic thought in such a way as to place it at the service of the Calvinist revolution.

Buchanan begins his *Right of the Kingdom* by endorsing the familiar scholastic – and Huguenot – assumption that, in order to deduce the character of a legitimate political society, we need to begin by considering the condition in which men must originally have lived before they arrived at the decision to set up a commonwealth. However, the account which he goes on to give of this condition is very different from that of the Huguenots. The Huguenots had tended to accept the Thomist contention that, although the natural condition of mankind cannot have been political, it must undoubtedly have been social in character. As the author of the *Political Discourses* had expressed it, the reason we can be sure of this is that 'God almighty has not thought it good that men should live alone' (fo 238b). But when the interlocutors in Buchanan's dialogues – Buchanan himself and the easily bullied figure of Maitland – address themselves to the same question, Buchanan describes man's pre-political life in a manner which contrasts sharply with these orthodox – and fundamentally Aristotelian – accounts. As befits a prominent humanist, Buchanan seems to derive his analysis from stoic rather than scholastic sources, and in particular from the view of man's natural condition which Cicero had enunciated at the beginning of his treatise *On Invention*. 'There was a time', Cicero had claimed, 'when men wandered at large in the fields like

extant formulation of Buchanan's political theory'. For a discussion of this and other difficulties in Trevor-Roper's analysis, see G. W. S. Barrow in *Annali della Fondazione italiana per la storia amministrativa* 4 (1967), pp. 653–5.

animals'; when 'they did nothing by the guidance of reason, but relied chiefly on physical strength'; when there was 'no ordered system of religious worship nor of social duties'; and when men were 'hidden in sylvan retreats' before becoming transformed 'from wild savages' into social and political animals (pp. 5–7). As we have seen, some elements of this anti-Aristotelian picture had already been sketched by a number of Ockhamist writers, in particular by Jacques Almain and Buchanan's own teacher John Mair. Buchanan reiterates essentially the same analysis at the start of his dialogues. There must have been a time, he assures Maitland, 'when men lived in huts and even in caves'; when they followed 'a wandering and solitary life'; and when 'they moved about like so many aliens, having neither laws nor even any fixed abode' (pp. 8–9).

As with the Huguenots and their scholastic predecessors, Buchanan's reason for beginning with this portrayal of man's natural condition is to insist that political societies are not directly ordained by God, but arise naturally out of a series of decisions made by men themselves. In describing the process by which legitimate commonwealths come into existence, however, Buchanan differs from the Huguenots at two crucial points. Beza and Mornay had spoken of two separate contracts which the people may be said to sign at the inauguration of a commonwealth: the religious covenant or *foedus* by which they promise God to act as a godly people; and the political covenant, embodied in the *Lex Regia*, by which they agree to transfer their *Imperium* to an elected ruler on certain mutually acceptable terms. By contrast, Buchanan makes no mention of the religious covenant at all – an eloquent silence which was also to be maintained by Johannes Althusius (1557–1638) in his massive treatise of 1603 entitled *Politics Methodically Set Forth*, the most systematic statement of revolutionary Calvinist political thought. As Buchanan and Althusius both make clear in the titles of their works, they now see themselves as talking exclusively about politics, not theology, and about the concept of rights, not religious duties.[1] Moreover, while Buchanan is content simply to ignore the religious *foedus*, Althusius underlines this deliberate omission, emphasising in his Preface that all the jurists – including even Bodin – have been guilty of confusing the science of politics with that of law,

[1] This explicit concern to emancipate the theory of politics from any religious premises prompted Gierke in his classic study of Althusius to treat him as the pivotal figure in the evolution of modern constitutionalism, and to describe him as the first political philosopher who shook off 'the whole theocratic conception of the State'; see Gierke, 1939, p. 71. It is true that this is something of an exaggeration of Althusius's significance – if only because the same approach had been adopted by Buchanan a generation before. But there is no doubt that Gierke is right to emphasise the degree of self-consciousness which Althusius exhibits in his efforts to 'deduce his system in a rational way from a purely secular conception of society', and so to arrive at a recognisably 'modern' conception of 'politics' as a sphere of enquiry with its own distinctive subject-matter; see Gierke, 1939, pp. 16, 70, 75.

while all the theologians have been equally at fault in continuing to sprinkle their political writings with 'teachings on Christian piety and charity', failing to recognise that such considerations are almost equally 'improper and alien to political doctrine' (pp. 1–2). More self-consciously even than Buchanan, Althusius has the ambition to emancipate the study of 'politics' from the confines of theology and jurisprudence, and to return 'all merely theological, juridical and philosophical elements to their proper places' in the name of concentrating exclusively on the independent subject-matter of political science (p. 8).

The other vital difference between Buchanan and the Huguenot revolutionaries arises out of his account of the contract which leads to the formation of a legitimate commonwealth. The Huguenots had evolved a theory of representative rather than direct popular sovereignty, arguing that the people sign away their authority to choose and control their rulers to an 'epitome' of magistrates. Again, Buchanan is eloquently silent on this additional contract, insisting that 'the whole body of the people' must be pictured as 'coming together' to elect 'someone to deliberate and concern themselves with the affairs of each member of the community' (pp. 9, 12). There is no suggestion that the citizens delegate their authority to create a ruler in the way that Beza and Mornay had supposed. On the contrary, Buchanan makes it clear that when the people institute a ruler, they do so by means of a straightforward contract, without intermediaries, in which one signatory is the prospective ruler and the other 'the whole body of the people' (pp. 9, 12).

Buchanan next points out that this account of the formation of political society implies a radical thesis of popular sovereignty. When the people consent and subsequently contract to establish a ruler over themselves, they are by no means alienating their original sovereignty in the manner assumed by Aquinas and his followers. Buchanan agrees with the more radical scholastics – especially Almain and Mair – that the people merely delegate their authority to a ruler whose status is not that of a sovereign who is *maior universis* and *legibus solutus*, but is rather that of a *minister* who remains *minor universis* and in consequence bound by the positive laws of the commonwealth. As Buchanan rather crushingly affirms, the people not only 'have the power to grant *Imperium* to their king', but must not be imagined to make any 'transmission' of their original sovereignty, since they simply 'prescribe to their king the form of his *Imperium*' with the aim of ensuring that 'he acts like a guardian of the public accounts' (pp. 32–3, 58, 62).

This radical scholastic analysis of the legal character of any legitimate commonwealth had of course been taken up already by Beza, Mornay and their disciples. But Buchanan is far more revolutionary in the account he goes on to give of the right to resist a ruler if he fails to keep to the terms of the *Lex Regia* enacted at the inauguration of his rule. He bases his argument on the essentially stoic description he gives of the condition in which men may be said to make the decision to set up a commonwealth. As Suárez was shortly to point out in *The Laws and God the Lawgiver*, an appallingly anarchic view of political obligation seems to be implied if one concedes that 'the power of a whole community of individuals assembled together must be derived from men as individuals' (I, pp. 165–6). For this suggests that the reason for setting up a commonwealth must be to protect individual rights rather than the common good, thus leaving open the alarming possibility that the whole body of the people, and even individual citizens, may be said to have the authority to resist and kill a legitimate ruler in defence of their rights. For Suárez, as for Beza and Mornay, this implication was enough to make it seem obvious that an individualist account of the condition in which men consent to the formation of political society must be a complete mistake. For Buchanan, by contrast, one of the reasons for insisting on a stoic rather than an Aristotelian account of man's pre-political condition may well have been the fact that it helped him to legitimate a highly individualist and even anarchic view of the right of political resistance. He first of all stresses that, since the whole body of the people agree together to set up a lawful government, it follows that the entire populace, and not merely their elected representatives, must retain a corresponding right to resist. As we have seen, a hint of this argument had already been dropped by a number of Gerson's followers, most notably by Mair in his *History*. But Buchanan is the first constitutional theorist to state it in a completely unequivocal and consistent form.[1] Since the people as a body create their ruler, it is said to be possible at any time 'for the people to shake off whatever *Imperium*' they may have imposed on themselves, the reason being that 'anything which is done by a given power can be undone by a like power' (p. 62; cf. p. 52). Furthermore, Buchanan adds that, since each individual must be pictured as agreeing to the formation of the commonwealth for his own greater security and benefit, it follows that the right to kill or remove a tyrant must be lodged at all times 'not only with the whole body of the people' (*universo populo*) but 'even with every individual citizen' (*singulis etiam*)

---

[1] This seems to me to make Buchanan by far the most radical of all the Calvinist revolutionaries, which perhaps suggests an element of doubt about the claim which has often been made that – as Franklin for example expresses it – 'the boldest and most systematic' theories of popular sovereignty to be articulated in early modern Europe all originated in France; cf. Franklin, 1967, p. 122.

(p. 97). So he willingly endorses the almost anarchic conclusion that even when, as frequently happens, someone 'from amongst the lowest and meanest of men' decides 'to revenge the pride and insolence of a tyrant' by simply taking upon himself the right to kill him, such actions are often 'judged to have been done quite rightly', and such men are commonly left unmolested, with 'no question ever being made against the killers' (pp. 61, 79, 81; cf. Burns, 1951, pp. 65, 66–7).

At this critical moment Buchanan considers the obvious objection – which Maitland duly if rather feebly raises – that these conclusions in favour of rebellion and tyrannicide run counter to the Pauline doctrine of ordination and non-resistance. The answer Buchanan rather testily gives is that this is 'to fall into the usual error' of allowing a single sentence in the Bible to outweigh all the evidence of law and philosophy – a typically humanist impatience with the orthodox political philosophy of the evangelical Reformation (pp. 69, 71–2). Speaking *in propria persona* as a humanist interpreter of texts, Buchanan proceeds to offer an ingenious exegesis of the Pauline injunctions in which he seeks to establish that the Apostle was merely speaking for his own time and place rather than attempting to enunciate any universal maxims of political prudence (pp. 71–2, 76–7). Reverting to his more scholastic mood, Buchanan then goes on to reiterate once again that a right of resistance and deposition must at all times be lodged with the whole body of the people. This is first defended – very much in the manner of d'Ailly, Gerson and the later conciliarists – by reference to the fact that an heretical or incapable pope can always be rightfully deposed by a General Council of the Church (pp. 77, 84 ff.). But Buchanan then treats the same conclusion as a straightforward corollary of his theory of popular sovereignty. Since the people create their rulers, and remain 'more powerful' than any rulers they may create, it follows that they can remove them at will, for 'whatever rights the populace may have granted to anyone, they can with equal justice rescind' (p. 80). Buchanan makes it clear, moreover, that in speaking of this power of deposition he is thinking in terms of the people's 'subjective' right to dispose of their kings, for he adds that any right (*ius*) they may grant to a king 'may properly be said to belong' (*proprie pertinet*) to the whole body of the people, taking the form of a possession over which they may be said to retain an ultimate control even though they may choose to delegate the use of it (pp. 81–2). Finally, the fortunes of four kings of Scotland are cited – in a highly tendentious fashion – to corroborate the central claim that in the case of rulers 'who have governed cruelly and scandalously' the people have not only possessed but have not hesitated to exercise the right 'to have called them to account, and even to have placed some in perpetual imprisonment, and to have exiled or put others to death' (pp. 61, 81–2; cf. Burns, 1951, p. 66).

In the course of the 1580s, as the result of a sudden shift of fortune in the French religious wars, a number of Catholic theologians began to adopt a very similar and no less radical justification of political resistance. To explain this development, we need to recall that, at the death of the Duke of Anjou in 1584, the direct heir to the French throne became Henry of Navarre, an avowed Huguenot (Green, 1964, pp. 261–2). The Guises responded to this threat by reviving the Catholic League and increasing their pressure on Henry III, while their leading pamphleteers – well aware that the vast majority of the population remained faithful to the Catholic Church – proceeded to put a demand for a general insurrection against the Valois monarchy directly to the whole body of the people. The most important writers to adopt this stance were Jean Boucher (1548–1644), who published a defence of tyrannicide in 1589 entitled *The Just Renunciation of Henry III*, and Guillaume Rose (*c.* 1542–1611) who proclaimed the same theme even more stridently in the title of his enormous treatise of 1590 on *The Just Authority of a Christian Commonwealth over Impious and Heretical Kings* (Labitte, 1866, pp. 165–73). But the most notorious of the Catholic defences of rebellion and tyrannicide to appear during this period was contained in Mariana's account of *The King and the Education of the King*. The second and third sections of Mariana's book consist of relatively conventional humanist discussions about the type of education and the range of virtues needed to produce a successful prince (Book II), and about the qualities needed by magistrates, bishops and other councillors in order to govern a kingdom successfully in war and peace (Book III). Mariana's controversial reputation chiefly rests on Book I, which includes a complete restatement of the most radical theory of *Imperium* put forward by such jurists as Salamonio and such theologians as Almain and Mair. Moreover, Mariana expresses his views with exceptional clarity and assurance, as well as illustrating them – in the manner of Mair and Buchanan – by reference to a number of lessons and principles already enunciated in the massive *History of Spain* which he had published in 1592.[1]

Mariana's opening chapter is headed 'Man is by nature a social animal'.[2] But his account of the origins of political society is far from being

---

[1] For Mariana's use of history to corroborate his political claims, see Lewy, 1960, p. 45.

[2] Since the precise wording of this aspect of Mariana's theory is important, I have preferred at this point to make my own translation directly from the original edition (Toledo, 1599) rather than – as previously – making use of George A. Moore's translation (Washington, D.C., 1948).

presented 'in the traditional Aristotelian way' as some commentators have maintained (Hamilton, 1963, p. 31). The chapter begins with the essentially stoic contention – already advanced by Buchanan and soon to be repeated almost word for word by Althusius – that 'men at first were solitary wanderers' (*solivagi*) who 'moved about in the manner of wild animals' and 'had no settled abode'. Their sole concern was 'to preserve their lives and to procreate and bring up their children', and in these pursuits 'they were restrained by no laws, neither were they held together by the *Imperium* of any ruler' (p. 16). This condition is said to have continued for some time, with each family living a peaceful and self-sufficient life 'without fraud, lies or the exercise of power' and 'with no warlike sounds to make the lives of men anxious' (p. 17). After a further period, however, the depredations of wild animals, and of lawless men 'who began to terrorise the rest', rendered it unsafe to go on living this 'life of natural instincts and impulses' (pp. 16, 20). The outcome was that 'those who felt exploited drew together' and 'felt constrained to make a pact with each other to form a society', after which 'men went on to establish towns and principalities' (p. 20). As in Buchanan, there is no reference to the making of any religious covenants: the establishment of political society is seen in wholly naturalistic terms as a product of man's attempts to improve his natural lot (cf. Lewy, 1960, p. 48).

After discussing various forms of government and the problem of succession, Mariana boldly turns in Chapter VI to ask 'Whether it may be permissible to oppose a tyrant?' (p. 65). He replies that since the people have established their commonwealths themselves, 'there can be no doubt that they are able to call a king to account' (p. 72). He first of all concedes that, if we ask what authority is needed to remove a tyrannical ruler, the answer is that normally we need a properly constituted Assembly, or at least a public meeting of all the people (pp. 75–6). But he then goes on to argue, in a passage that became notorious, that 'if you ask what can be done if the power of the public meeting is laid aside', the answer is that 'anyone who is inclined to heed the prayers of the people may attempt to destroy' a tyrant, and 'can hardly be said to have acted wrongly' in making such an attempt to serve as an instrument of justice (pp. 76–7). There is thus said to be an ultimate right of tyrannicide 'which can be exercised by any private person whatsoever (*cuicumque privato*) who may wish to come to the aid of the commonwealth' (p. 76).

Finally, Mariana concludes his discussion – in Chapters VIII and IX – by spelling out the radical theory of *Imperium* on which his argument is based. He admits that 'many erudite men' (including almost all his fellow Jesuits) maintain that 'the commonwealth gives up (*deferre*) the supreme

THE RIGHT TO RESIST

power to its ruler without any exception', thereby creating a *princeps* who is *legibus solutus* and 'above' the entire *regnum* as well as its individual citizens (pp. 93, 99). He points out, however, that since 'the power of the king, if it is legitimate, has its source in the citizens', it must be 'by their concession (*iis concedentibus*) that all kings are at first placed in authority in every commonwealth' (p. 88). This leads him to insist that the orthodox Thomist suggestion 'that the citizens as a whole give up their power without any exception' must be 'exceedingly improbable' (p. 90). He accordingly rejects any suggestion that 'a *princeps* can ever be *legibus solutus*', or even that he is capable of wielding 'a power greater than that of the community' (*maiorem universis*) (p. 90). On the contrary, Mariana affirms that a ruler must be seen not as the owner (*dominus*) but simply as the helmsman and guide (*gubernator*, *rector*) of his kingdom (pp. 59, 100). His status can never be higher than that of an elected official who is paid a salary (*merces*) by the citizens in order to look after their interests (p. 59). Should he fail to do so, Mariana takes it to be obvious that any one of the citizens, or all of them together, must retain the right to remove and even kill him.

The Jesuit Mariana may thus be said to link hands with the Protestant Buchanan in stating a theory of popular sovereignty which, while scholastic in its origins and Calvinist in its later development, was in essence independent of either religious creed, and was thus available to be used by all parties in the coming constitutional struggles of the seventeenth century. The articulation of these purely secular and wholly populist doctrines may thus be said to have laid the foundations for the later challenge to the two main traditions of absolutist political philosophy which, as we have seen, had also become established by the close of the sixteenth century. One of these was the providentialist tradition, later associated in particular with Filmer in England and Bossuet in France. The other was the more rationalist tradition stemming from Bodin and the neo-Thomists, and reaching its climax in the natural-law systems of Grotius and Pufendorf. John Locke in the *Two Treatises of Government* may be said to have mounted the definitive attack on both these traditions, modifying Pufendorf's absolutist theory of the social contract as well as repudiating Filmer's patriarchalism (Laslett, 1967, pp. 67–78). It is a mistake, however, to think of the development of this modern 'liberal' theory of constitutionalism essentially as an achievement of the seventeenth century.[1] As will by now be clear, the concepts in terms of which

---

[1] This seems to be the assumption governing the remarkable but historically somewhat misleading account which Macpherson has given of the rise of 'possessive individualism'; cf. Macpherson, 1962, esp. pp. 1–4, 263–71.

Locke and his successors developed their views on popular sovereignty and the right of revolution had already been largely articulated and refined over a century earlier in the legal writings of such radical jurists as Salamonio, in the theological treatises of such Ockhamists as Almain and Mair, as well as in the more famous but derivative writings of the Calvinist revolutionaries. Nor did the radical Saints of the seventeenth century hesitate to make use of the dialectical weapons which had thus been fashioned for them by their papist enemies. A generation before Locke produced his classic defence of the people's right to resist and remove a tyrannical government, Oliver Cromwell had already found it quite sufficient (according to Burnet's report) to reassure himself about the lawfulness of executing Charles I by engaging in 'a long discourse' about 'the nature of the regal power, according to the principles of Mariana and Buchanan' (Burnet, I, p. 76).

Conclusion

By the beginning of the seventeenth century, the concept of the State – its nature, its powers, its right to command obedience – had come to be regarded as the most important object of analysis in European political thought. Hobbes reflects this development when he declares in the Preface to his *Philosophical Rudiments*, first published as *De Cive* in 1642, that the aim of 'civil science' is 'to make a more curious search into the rights of states and duties of subjects' (pp. x, xiv). How had this development come about? One of the main aims of this book has been to suggest an answer. The aim of these concluding remarks will be to summarise the argument by recapitulating what I take to be the most important preconditions for the acquisition of the modern concept of the State.

One precondition is clearly that the sphere of politics should be envisaged as a distinct branch of moral philosophy, a branch concerned with the art of government. This was of course an ancient assumption, classically embodied in Aristotle's *Politics*. The idea was lost to view, however, with Augustine's immensely influential insistence in *The City of God* that the true Christian ought not to concern himself with the problems of 'this temporal life', but ought to keep his gaze entirely fixed on 'the everlasting blessings that are promised for the future, using like one in a strange land any earthly and temporal things, not letting them entrap him or divert him from the path that leads to God' (pp. 193–5). As I have sought to argue, this in turn suggests that any attempt to excavate the foundations of modern political thought needs to begin with the recovery and translation of Aristotle's *Politics*, and the consequent re-emergence of the idea that political philosophy constitutes an independent discipline worthy of study in its own right. When William of Moerbeke issued the first complete Latin translation of the *Politics* in the early 1250s, he described 'the highest community' which Aristotle discusses at the beginning of Book I as the *communicatio politica*, the political community, and in this way helped to put the concept of 'politics' (*politica*) into currency for the first time.[1] Soon after this we encounter the earliest references to 'political science' as a distinct form of practical philosophy concerned with the principles of government. Perhaps the first writer to think of himself with complete self-consciousness as a political scientist was Brunetto Latini, Dante's revered teacher, whose *Books of Treasure*, completed in the 1260s, made a pioneering contribution to the *genre* which, we have seen, may be said to culminate in Machiavelli's *Prince*.[2] At the start of his book Latini promises that his discussion will conclude with a study of 'the means by which rulers ought to govern those who are set under them' – an aspect of 'practical philosophy' which he describes as 'politics' (p. 17). And when he turns to fulfil his promise in the closing chapter on 'The Government of Cities', he not only speaks of 'politics' as 'the science concerned with government', but goes on to proclaim that, in devoting himself to the study of politics, he is investigating 'the noblest and greatest of all the sciences', as 'Aristotle has proved in his book' (p. 391).

It is sometimes suggested that, even when we turn to Latini's ultimate heirs, the humanists of the sixteenth century, we must still concede that they were not 'in our modern sense of the term "political theorists" ', and that it must still be anachronistic to place their thought 'under this essentially more modern category' (Dickens, 1974, p. 70). It is arguable, however, that such a degree of caution itself leads to anachronism. By the beginning of the sixteenth century Guillaume Budé was already insisting that 'political science' (*science politique*) constitutes a distinct form of enquiry, and in his *Education of the Prince* he repeatedly proclaims that his main concern is to elucidate 'the elements of the political sciences' (pp. 19, 88, 93, 118). By the second half of the century, this sense the humanists had of themselves as students of 'politics' began to be reflected in the titles of their works: in 1556 Ponet published his *Short Treatise of Politic Power*; in the 1580s La Noue completed his *Political and Military Discourses*; in 1589 Lipsius issued his *Six Books of Politics*; and in 1603 Althusius outlined the principles of a new, secularised political science in his treatise entitled *Politics Methodically Set Forth*. By this time, the foundations of the modern idea of 'politics' as the study of statecraft had been firmly laid.

[1] For the date of Moerbeke's translation, see Knowles, 1962, p. 192. For Moerbeke's rendering of Aristotle's references to 'the highest community', see Susemihl's edition of Moerbeke's translation, p. 1 and *passim*. For this edition, see *sub* Aristotle in the bibliography of primary sources. For the fact that the term *politica* (in the nominative plural) begins to be current only after this period, see Latham, 1965, p. 357, noting that the earliest occurrences of the term in English sources date from the 1320s.

[2] For the claim that Latini's writings represent 'the *point de départ* for the history of the word ["politics"] in modern Europe', see Whitfield, 1969, p. 163.

A second precondition for coming to think of the State as the main subject-matter of political philosophy is that the independence of each *regnum* or *civitas* from any external and superior power should be vindicated and assured. The acceptance of this idea was scarcely possible so long as it was agreed that the *princeps* of Justinian's Code should be equated with the Holy Roman Emperor, who thus came to be treated as the sole genuine bearer of *Imperium* in medieval Europe. One of the most important steps towards the formation of the modern concept of the State was thus taken when Bartolus and his pupils insisted that the *civitates* of the *Regnum Italicum* were not merely in a position of *de facto* independence from the Empire, but ought to be legally acknowledged as *universitates superiorem non recognoscentes*, as 'independent associations not recognising any superior' in the conduct of their political affairs. It has even been argued by one recent authority that Bartolus and Baldus together constructed the entire 'legal foundations' on which 'the modern theory of the State rests'.[1]

A further precondition for arriving at the modern concept of the State is that the supreme authority within each independent *regnum* should be recognised as having no rivals within its own territories as a law-making power and an object of allegiance. Any such unitary image of political sovereignty was precluded in medieval Europe by the legal assumptions underpinning the feudal organisation of society, and by the Church's claims to act as a law-making power coeval with rather than subordinate to the secular authorities. A further conceptual change of far-reaching significance was thus engineered when the concepts of seigneurial and ecclesiastical jurisdiction began to be challenged. As we have seen, the earliest full-scale attack on the Church's status as a *regnum* was launched in the first half of the fourteenth century, when Marsiglio of Padua argued in *The Defender of Peace* that all coercive power is secular by definition, and that the highest authority possessed by any priest 'with respect to his office' can only be 'to teach and practice', without exercising any 'coercive authority or worldly rule' (pp. 114, 155). This dismissal of the legal and jurisdictional powers of the Church was taken over with equal enthusiasm in the course of the sixteenth century by the legist supporters of absolutism, especially in France, and by the Lutheran exponents of the theory that the true Church consists of nothing more than a *congregatio fidelium*. By this time, moreover, such legists as Charles Du Moulin – whom Bodin was to hail as 'the ornament of all lawyers' – had

[1] See Wahl, 1977, p. 80. But as Wahl emphasises, Baldus was much more disposed than Bartolus to continue to accept the ultimate legal supremacy of the Holy Roman Emperor. Cf. Wahl, 1977, pp. 85–6.

also begun to challenge the structure of seigneurial rights, arguing that the powers of the crown should not be envisaged as the apex of a feudal pyramid, but rather as a unified and absolute authority under which all citizens should be ranged in a legally undifferentiated fashion as a *subditi* or subjects (Church, 1941, pp. 239, 242). By the end of the sixteenth century, the foundations had thus been fully laid for the idea of the State as the sole bearer of *Imperium* within its own territories, all other corporations and organisations being allowed to exist only with its permission.

Finally, the acceptance of the modern idea of the State presupposes that political society is held to exist solely for political purposes. The endorsement of this secularised viewpoint remained impossible as long as it was assumed that all temporal rulers had a duty to uphold godly as well as peaceable government. The sixteenth-century reformers were entirely at one with their Catholic adversaries on this point: they all insisted that one of the main aims of government must be to maintain 'true religion' and the Church of Christ. As we have seen, this in turn means that the religious upheavals of the Reformation made a paradoxical yet vital contribution to the crystallising of the modern, secularised concept of the State. For as soon as the protagonists of the rival religious creeds showed that they were willing to fight each other to the death, it began to seem obvious to a number of *politique* theorists that, if there were to be any prospect of achieving civic peace, the powers of the State would have to be divorced from the duty to uphold any particular faith. With Bodin's insistence in his *Six Books* that it ought to be obvious to any prince that 'wars made for matters of religion' are not in fact 'grounded upon matters directly touching his estate', we hear for the first time the authentic tones of the modern theorist of the State (p. 535; cf. McRae, 1962, p. A14).

The surest sign that a society has entered into the secure possession of a new concept is that a new vocabulary will be developed, in terms of which the concept can then be publicly articulated and discussed. So I treat it as a decisive confirmation of the argument I have now sketched that, by the end of the period with which I have been concerned, the term 'State' began to be freely used for the first time in a recognisably modern sense.

The Latin term *status* had of course been employed by legal and scholastic writers throughout the later Middle Ages in a variety of political contexts. But even if we feel justified in assuming that *status* should be translated in these cases as 'State' – an assumption which perhaps tends to be made rather readily by some medieval historians[1] – it is clear that

---

[1] See for example Post, 1964, pp. 241–6 and *passim*.

what is at issue is very different from the modern idea of the State. Before the sixteenth century, the term *status* was only used by political writers to refer to one of two things: either the state or condition in which a ruler finds himself (the *status principis*); or else the general 'state of the nation' or condition of the realm as a whole (the *status regni*).[1] What was lacking in these usages was the distinctively modern idea of the State as a form of public power separate from both the ruler and the ruled, and constituting the supreme political authority within a certain defined territory.[2] It has plausibly been argued that this modern and more abstract meaning may have arisen directly out of earlier discussions about the prince's need 'to maintain his state' in the sense of maintaining his established range of powers (Dowdall, 1923, p. 102). But as Post has emphasised, it is usually clear in pre-sixteenth-century discussions that, when 'the state of the prince' is being discussed, the intention is not to distinguish the ruler's powers from those of the State, but rather to assert that they ought to be identified, the aim being to insist that the prince himself should be taken to constitute 'the final authority and therefore the real government' of the realm (Post, 1964, p. 334; cf. Hexter, 1957, p. 118).

By the end of the *quattrocento*, however, especially in those humanist writers whose main concern was to discuss the *status principis* or *lo stato del principe*, we begin to see some signs of the crucial transition from the idea of the ruler 'maintaining his state' to the more abstract idea that there is an independent political apparatus, that of the State, which the ruler may be said to have a duty to maintain. One example occurs at the beginning of Patrizi's treatise on *The Kingdom and the Education of the King*. He not only seems to make a distinction between the powers of magistrates and the powers inherent in different types of regime, but employs the term *status* in going on to speak of these regimes as 'types of state'.[3] But the work which contains the strongest hints of this transition is of course Machiavelli's *The Prince*. One of Machiavelli's most suggestive passages occurs at the end of Chapter IX, where he declares that the populace ought to recognise that they owe an obligation in times of adversity to their prince and his government for having maintained them in times of peace – a contention which he expresses by pointing out that in such circumstances 'the state has need of its citizens' (*lo stato ha bisogne*

---

[1] On this point see Hexter, 1957, p. 118; Post, 1964; and Tierney, 1966, esp. pp. 13–14.

[2] Dowdall impressively claims that he has been unable to find 'any single instance from Cicero to Grotius in which the word *status*, standing alone, is used' for 'a state' in the modern sense; cf. Dowdall, 1923, p. 101.

[3] See Patrizi, *The Kingdom*, p. 11. For other references to 'the state' in Florentine political thought before Machiavelli, cf. Rubinstein, 1971.

de' cittadini).[1] But perhaps the most suggestive usage occurs in Chapter XIX, where Machiavelli assures the prince that the ability to defend himself against conspirators is easier to acquire than he may suppose, since it is always open to him to overawe his enemies by calling on the support of 'the majesty of the state' (*la maestà dello stato*) (p. 74).[2]

Even in *The Prince*, however, it is generally clear that, when Machiavelli speaks of his desire to advise 'a prince wishing to maintain his state' (*uno principe volendo mantenere lo stato*), what he usually has in mind is the traditional idea of the prince maintaining his existing position and range of powers.[3] To find the term 'State' being freely used for the first time in a more abstract and recognisably modern sense, we need to turn to the heirs of the Italian humanists, especially in sixteenth-century France and England, and above all to those whose chief interests lay in the field of legal humanism.

As one might expect, this transition first appears to have been accomplished in France. Far more than in Italy, the material preconditions for such a development were all present: a relatively unified central authority, an increasing apparatus of bureaucratic control, and a clearly defined set of national boundaries.[4] So too – earlier than in England or Spain – were the intellectual preconditions: the reception of Italian humanist advice-books concerned with the problems of 'maintaining one's state', together with the development of legal-humanist views about the origins and character of *Imperium*, the supreme law-making power within the temporal commonwealth. So we find that, in the writings of such pioneers of legal humanism as Guillaume Budé – especially in his

---

[1] Since Machiavelli's exact phraseology is important to my argument at this point, I am translating from, and referring to, the Italian edition of *The Prince* (ed. Bertelli, 1960–5), both in this and in the next citation from the text.

[2] Hexter, 1957, pp. 127–8 cites this passage as an apparent counter-example to his general argument about Machiavelli's use of *lo stato* in *The Prince*, but argues that Machiavelli merely has in mind 'the capacity of the prince's power of command to inspire awe' (p. 128).

[3] For Machiavelli's use of this phrase, see *The Prince*, ed. Bertelli, p. 80 and *passim*. It has often been assumed that, when Machiavelli speaks of *lo stato*, we can translate this as 'the State' in its modern sense. See for example Cassirer, 1946, pp. 133–4, 140–1, 154–5. This assumption has been convincingly challenged by Hexter as the result of a painstaking analysis of virtually all the occurrences of the term *lo stato* in *The Prince*. See Hexter, 1957, esp. pp. 115–17 and 135–7 for his attack on Chiappelli for assuming that *lo stato* already has its modern meaning in *The Prince*. See also Gilbert, 1965, p. 177. It is possible, however, that a similar linguistic analysis of *The Discourses* might reveal a stronger inclination on Machiavelli's part to speak of *lo stato* in a more abstract way. Sternberger has recently emphasised, as the outcome of a comparative analysis of the vocabulary of *The Prince* and the *Discourses*, that the latter can be meaningfully described as a more abstractly 'political' work. See Sternberger, 1975. For some passages in which it might be argued that Machiavelli is discussing 'the state' in the *Discourses* in a relatively abstract way, see *The Discourses*, ed. Crick, pp. 340, 349, 365, etc.

[4] Cf. Anderson, 1974, pp. 88–91, 93–7. For the importance of the evolution of relatively impersonal bureaucratic systems in 'the Renaissance State' cf. Chabod, 1964, esp. pp. 33–6 and 40.

treatise on *The Education of the Prince* – the transition to a more abstract concept of the State begins to be recognisably made.

It is true that Budé continues to address his prince in the traditional manner on the need 'to maintain your state' (*maintenir votre estat*) (e.g., p. 134). But there are several occasions on which he appears to hover between this well-established usage and a more abstract meaning of the term, especially in his analysis of 'the types of politic state' (*les espèces d'estat politique*) (p. 149). Furthermore, there are one or two points at which he seems quite consciously to embrace the idea of the State as a locus of political power distinct from the powers of the prince. In Chapter XXVII, for example, he speaks of the prince's duty to give 'a proper foundation to the public state' (*l'estat publique*) (p. 110). And in the next chapter, discussing the example of ancient Sparta, he equates 'the public state' with the apparatus of government, explaining that the Spartan state was governed by – but apparently remained separate from – 'the name and authority of their kings' (p. 115).

Within a generation, Budé's terminology began to be adopted with increasing confidence by a number of other French humanist writers on legal and political thought. In his address to the States General in 1562, l'Hôpital spoke to the assembled deputies about the role of law 'in maintaining and conserving all States and Republics' (*Estatz et Republiques*) (I, pp. 449–50). In his history of *The State and Success of the Affairs of France*, first published in 1570, Du Haillan began by discussing the foundations of 'the state (*l'estat*) of France', and promised to describe 'the progress, accidents and fortunes of this state' (p. 1). And in his *Six Books of a Commonweal* in 1576, Bodin indicated most clearly of all that he was willing to think of the State as a locus of power distinct from either the ruler or the body of the people.

It is of course true that Bodin continues to speak of *la République* rather than *l'État*, and that Richard Knolles, in translating the *Six Books* into English in 1606, generally preferred to render Bodin's key term as 'commonwealth' rather than as 'State'. Nevertheless, it is clear from Bodin's analysis of the concept that he thinks of the State as a distinct apparatus of power, and it is instructive that he not only speaks of it on numerous occasions as *l'État*, but that Knolles generally felt able to translate this term as 'State', and to employ the term with some consistency in a recognisably modern sense.[1]

It is clear in the first place that Bodin distinguishes the State from its citizens, for he claims that we may sometimes find that 'the people' are

---

[1] See for example p. 3 and *passim* on 'the State'; p. 547 on 'matters of State'; p. 561 on 'men of State'; p. 700 on the comparison between 'every kind of State', etc.

'into divers places dispersed, or else be utterly destroyed', even though 'the city or state' may remain 'standing whole' (p. 10). Similarly, he distinguishes the powers of the State from those of its rulers, for he speaks of 'magistrates and officers' as having a duty 'to command, judge and provide for the government of the state', and points with dismay to the difficulties which tend to arise when the conduct of affairs falls into the hands of 'such princes as have no experience of governing of the state' (pp. 382, 561). He thus arrives at a conceptualisation of the State as a locus of power which can be institutionalised in a variety of ways, and which remains distinct from and superior to both its citizens and their magistrates. As he expresses the point in discussing the concept of a 'Popular Estate' in Book III, 'albeit that the government of a commonweal may be more or less popular, aristocratic or royal', yet 'the state in itself receives no comparisons of more or less', since its powers are always 'indivisible and incommunicable', and are not to be identified with the powers of those who may happen to have charge of the government (p. 250).

The next country in which the same fundamental conceptual shift took place appears to have been England. By the end of the Cromwellian regime of the 1530s, a similar set of material as well as intellectual pre-conditions for this development had been achieved: an increasingly bureaucratic style of central government, together with a growing interest amongst English humanists in the problems of 'politics' and public law.[1] Perhaps the earliest instance of the term 'State' being used in a corres-pondingly impersonal sense can be found in Starkey's *Dialogue between Pole and Lupset*, completed in 1535.[2] It is true that, like Budé, Starkey continues to use the term in the traditional sense, speaking of the need for the prince to maintain 'the most perfect and excellent state of policy and rule', and for the legal system to uphold 'every man's state according to

[1] On the development of a relatively impersonal and bureaucratic form of state apparatus in the 1530s, see Elton, 1953, esp. pp. 415–27. Since it appears to have been in France and England that the corresponding shift to a relatively impersonal concept of 'the State' first took place, and since my main concern is with the original formulation of the concept, I have not attempted to pursue the history of the term in Spain, the other major nation-state of sixteenth-century Europe. But it is perhaps worth adding that, by the end of the sixteenth century, a number of Spanish political philosophers began to use the term *status* in order to refer to 'the State' in what sometimes seems to be a distinctly modern sense. See for example Suárez, *The Laws and God the Lawgiver*, I, p. 197 on the *status publicus*.

[2] This is the earliest use of 'the State' in the required sense recorded in the *Oxford English Dictionary*. Dowdall, 1923, p. 120 cites the Dictionary entry, but adds that it appears to be an 'extraordinarily early and, I believe, isolated instance'. However, Starkey in fact uses the term 'state' in the same way at several other points in his *Dialogue*, a usage which was soon repeated by several other humanist writers on 'politic' power. Nor can they simply have copied the usage from Starkey, for the *Dialogue* remained unpublished until the nineteenth century. I conclude that the term 'State' in an abstract and recognisably modern sense was in fact current in humanist circles in England, as in France, by the middle of the sixteenth century.

his degree'.[1] But he also begins to hover between this and a more abstract sense, as in his discussion of 'whether the state of the commonalty' should 'be governed by a prince, or certain wise men, or by the whole multitude', and in the emphasis he places on the duty of 'heads and rulers' to 'maintain the state established in the country' in which they are magistrates (pp. 61, 64). And finally, he sometimes seems to speak with full self-consciousness of the State as a distinct constitutional structure. He thinks of princes as 'rulers of the state'; he insists that those who 'have authority and rule of the state' must 'look not to their own singular profit'; and in discussing the role of Parliament in the constitution, he argues that its fundamental purpose is to 'represent the whole state' (pp. 57, 61, 167).

As in France, so in England, we find this terminology being used with increasing confidence in the next generation by several humanist writers on moral and political thought. John Ponet in his *Short Treatise of Politic Power* in 1556 defends the key contention that the authority 'to redress and correct the vices' of governors and magistrates lies with 'the whole body of every state' (pp. 105–6). And Lawrence Humphrey in his book on *The Nobles* in 1563 offers a clear account of the relations – and the distinctions – between the prince, the nobility and the State. When he discusses the need for the prince to set a good example to his subjects, he explains that if a ruler lives a life of vice, the effect may be to 'spread the same into the whole state' (sig. Q, 8b). When he defends the role of the nobles in society, he insists that a lack of 'degree' will tend to 'unjoin the state, and rend it in wretched sort', and that the maintenance of 'degree' is accordingly essential 'in a well-ordered and Christian-like governed state' (sig. B, 6b; sig. C, 3b). And when he concludes by declaring that nothing is 'at this day more lamentable than the ignorance of magistrates and nobles', the main reason he gives for voicing this concern is that such ignorance is always the 'head cause of all evils both in the state and religion' (sig. X, 2b). Finally, by the time we come to such a 'politic' humanist as Sir Walter Raleigh, writing at the turn of the century, we find him boldly entitling one of his tracts *Maxims of State* and discussing the concept of the State in a thoroughly familiar style. He begins by laying it down that 'State' refers to 'the frame or set order of a commonwealth' (p. 1). Next he considers the act of 'founding a state', the different 'parts of the state', and the various 'rules of preserving the state' (pp. 5–6, 9). And in the course of this analysis he explicitly insists that the State's powers must be distinguished from those of particular rulers or magistrates. He defines 'a monarchy or kingdom' as 'the government of a state by one head or chief', and he points out that in some monarchies the ruler may be assigned 'the

---

[1] For these quotations, see pp. 47, 100, and for similar instances see pp. 63, 70, 72, 75, etc.

whole power of ordering all state matters', but that in others he may have 'no full power in all the points or matters of state' (pp. 1–2).

It would of course be easy to exaggerate the confidence with which these writers employ this new concept of the State. It was only discussed in the final decades of the period we have attempted to survey; it was only invoked by the most secular-minded and sophisticated political theorists; and it left them in considerable confusion, especially in their attempts to analyse the relationship between the powers of the State and those of the ruler, and in their efforts to explain what it might mean to be the citizen of a State as well as the subject of a prince. Nevertheless, the acquisition of the concept of the State may be said to be the precipitate of the historical process which this book has attempted to trace. By the end of the sixteenth century, in a work such as Bodin's *Six Books*, we not only find the term 'State' being employed in a recognisably modern sense, but also find the rights and powers of the State beginning to be analysed in a distinctively modern style. It is evident in the first place that Bodin thinks of the State as the holder of supreme political power within its own territories. For in discussing the 'letters of command' which sovereign princes use to announce their will, he speaks of these as 'rescripts of state' and as 'letters of command or state', indicating that the authority by which they are issued is that of the State (p. 312). It is also evident that he thinks of the State as the institution to which all citizens owe their political allegiances. For he treats the crime of sedition as an offence not against the ruler but the State, describing the slave revolts of ancient Rome as risings 'against the state', and speaking of 'seditious people' as those who attempt to 'take upon them the government' by 'invading the state' (pp. 38, 791). Finally, he clearly thinks of the State as a purely civil authority which is assigned its powers for purely civil ends. As Knolles remarks in the Preface to his translation of the *Six Books*, Bodin's main assumption is that the aim of the political philosopher, in studying 'matters of state', is simply to elucidate the conditions which best serve to promote 'the quiet common good' (pp. iv, v). With this analysis of the state as an omnipotent yet impersonal power, we may be said to enter the modern world: the modern theory of the State remains to be constructed, but its foundations are now complete.

Further Reading

(1) *Calvin*. There is a great deal of biographical material in Doumergue, 1899–1927, and a much more concise and up-to-date biography by Parker, 1975. Niesel, 1956, provides a valuable survey of Calvin's theology, and McNeill, 1954 discusses the evolution of the Calvinist Church. For general introductions to Calvin's political thought see Allen, 1957, Chapter 4 and Wolin, 1961, Chapter 6. For an excellent full-scale account see Chenevière, 1937, and for Calvin's social and economic ideas see Biéler, 1959. On the question of Calvin's political radicalism see Baron, 1939, McNeill, 1949 and Walzer, 1966.

(2) *Bodin*. Chauviré, 1914, is still the best biographical account, though it needs to be supplemented by Mesnard, 1950. For the context of Bodin's thought see Church, 1941. On Bodin's methodology see Franklin, 1963 and Kelley, 1970. On his Ramist assumptions see McRae, 1955. Bodin's *Method* is discussed by Reynolds, 1931 and by Brown, 1939, and his transition to a more absolutist political theory is analysed and explained by Franklin, 1973 and Salmon, 1973, both very valuable accounts. For further details about the composition of the *Six Books*, see McRae, 1962. Some important articles on special topics: on Bodin's view of constitutional law, see Burns, 1959; on his view of taxation, see Wolfe, 1968; on his theory of sovereignty, see Lewis, 1968 and Giesey, 1973.

(3) *The Huguenot 'Monarchomachs'*. For the ideological background to the French religious wars, see Kingdon, 1956 and 1967. For the political background, see Salmon, 1975, and for a fuller narrative see Romier, 1913–14 and 1922. Figgis, 1960, provides a classic introduction to the 'monarchomachs', and there are excellent and more up-to-date introductions in Franklin, 1967 and 1969, and in Giesey, 1970. Walzer, 1966, includes a more general account of radical Huguenot thought. Caprariis, 1959, gives a full survey of Huguenot political literature up to 1572, but there is no comparable analysis for the crucial years after the massacre of St Bartholomew. The only 'monarchomach' of this period who has so far received detailed attention has been Hotman. Mesnard, 1955 and Kelley, 1970 discuss his legal theories, Giesey and Salmon, 1972, furnish a comprehensive analysis of *Francogallia*, and Kelley, 1973 provides an excellent outline of his career and thought.

Bibliography of primary sources

d'Ailly, Pierre, *A Tract on the Authority of the Church* [*Tractatus de Ecclesiae . . . Auctoritate*] in Jean Gerson, *Opera Omnia*, ed. Louis du Pin, 5 vols (Antwerp, 1706), vol. 2, cols 925–60.

Almain, Jacques, *A Brief Account of the Power of the Church* [*Libellus de auctoritate Ecclesiae*] in Jean Gerson, *Opera Omnia*, ed. Louis Ellies du Pin, 5 vols (Antwerp, 1706), vol. 2, cols 976–1012.

An Exposition of the Views of William of Ockham concerning the Power of the Pope [*Expositio, circa Decisiones Magistri Guillielmi Occam, super potestate summi pontifici*] reprinted as *Concerning Ecclesiastical and Lay Power* [*De Potestate Ecclesiastica et Laica*] in Gerson, *Opera Omnia*, ed. Du Pin, vol. 2, cols 1013–1120.

A Reconsideration of the Question of Natural, Civil and Ecclesiastical Power [*Quaestio Resumptiva, De Dominio Naturali, Civili et Ecclesiastico*] in Gerson, *Opera Omnia*, ed. Du Pin, vol. 2, cols 961–76.

Althusius, Johannes, *Politics Methodically Set Forth*, trans. and ed. Frederick S. Carney as *The Politics of Johannes Althusius* (London, 1965).

[Amsdorf, Nicolas von], *The Confession and Apology of the Pastors and Other Ministers of the Church at Magdeburg* [*Confessio et Apologia Pastorum et Reliquorum Ministrorum Ecclesiae Magdeburgensis*] (Magdeburg, 1550).

[Anonymous], *The Alarm Bell against the Massacrers and Authors of the Confusions in France* [*Le Tocsin, contre les massacreurs et auteurs des confusions en France*] (Rheims, 1577).

[Anonymous], *The Awakener of the French and their Neighbours* [*Le Reveille-matin des François et de leur voisins*] (Edinburgh [Basle?], 1574).

[Anonymous], *A Declaration of the Causes which have led those of the* [*Reformed*] *Religion to take up arms for their Conservation* [*Déclaration des causes qui ont meu ceux de la religion à reprendre les armes pour leur conservation*] in [Simon Goulart], *Mémoires de l'état de France sous Charles neufième*, 2nd edn, 3 vols (Middelburg [Geneva], 1578), vol. 3, fos 38a–42b.

[Anonymous], *Political Discourses on the various forms of power established by God in the World* [*Discours politiques des diverses puissances établies de Dieu au monde*] in [Goulart], *Mémoires*, vol. 3, fos 203b–296a.

[Anonymous], *The Politician: A Dialogue concerning the Power, Authority and Duty of Princes* [*La politique: dialogue traitant de la puissance, autorité et du devoir des princes*] in [Goulart], *Mémoires*, vol. 3, fos 66a–116b.

[Anonymous], *The Preparations for the Massacres* [*Preparatifs . . . pour les massacres*] in [Goulart], *Mémoires*, vol. 1, fos 265a–8b.

[Anonymous], *Question: to know whether it is lawful for subjects to defend themselves against the magistrate in order to maintain the true Christian religion* [*Question: à savoir s'il est loisible au sujets de se défendre contre le magistrat pour maintenir la religion vraiment chrétienne* in [Goulart], *Mémoires*, vol. 2, fos 239a–46a.

[Anonymous], *A True Warning to all Worthy Men of Antwerp* in *Texts concerning the Revolt of the Netherlands*, ed. E. H. Kossmann and A. F. Mellink (Cambridge, 1974), pp. 228–31.

Aquinas, St Thomas, *The Summary of Theology* [*Summa Theologiae*] vol. 28, *Law and Political Theory*, ed. Thomas Gilby (London, 1966).

The Summary of Theology [*Summa Theologiae*] vol. 38, *Injustice*, ed. Marcus Lefébure (London, 1975).

Aristotle, *The Politics* [*Politicorum Libri Octo*] trans. William of Moerbeke and ed. F. Susemihl (Leipzig, 1872).

Augustine, St, *The City of God against the Pagans*, trans. George E. McCracken, William M. Green, *et al.*, 7 vols (London, 1957–72).

Bale, John, *The Acts of English Votaries* (Wesel [?London], 1546).

A Brief Chronicle Concerning the Examination and Death of the Blessed Martyr of Christ, Sir John Oldcastle, the Lord Cobham, in *Select Works*, ed. Henry Christmas (Cambridge, 1849), pp. 5–59.

A Comedy Concerning Three Laws, of Nature, Moses and Christ in *The Dramatic Writings of John Bale*, ed. John S. Farmer (London, 1907), pp. 1–82.

The Image of Both Churches in *Select Works*, ed. Henry Christmas, pp. 249–640.

A Tragedy of John, King of England in *The Dramatic Writings of John Bale*, ed. Farmer, pp. 171–294.

Barnes, Robert, *A Supplication . . . unto . . . King Henry VIII* (London, 1534).

That Men's Constitutions, which are not grounded in Scripture, bind not the conscience of Man, in N. S. Tjernagel, *The Reformation Essays of Dr Robert Barnes* (London, 1963), pp. 81–93.

What the Church is and Who be Thereof, in Tjernagel, *Essays*, pp. 37–52.

Bartolus of Saxoferrato, *Commentaries on the Second Part of the New Digest* [*In II Partem Digesti Novi Commentaria*] in *Opera Omnia*, 12 vols (Basle, 1588), vol. VI.

Bekinsau, John, *The Supreme and Absolute Power of the King* [*De Supremo et Absoluto Regis Imperio*] (London, 1546).

Bellarmine, Robert, *Concerning Councils* [*De Conciliis*] in *Opera Omnia*, ed. Justin Fèvre, 12 vols (Paris, 1870–4), vol. 2, pp. 187–407.

Concerning Justification [*De Justificatione*] in *Opera Omnia*, ed. Fèvre, vol. 6, pp. 149–386.

The Members of the Church [*De Membris Ecclesiae*] in *Opera Omnia*, ed. Fèvre, vol. 2, pp. 409–633 and vol. 3, pp. 5–48.

The Supreme Pontiff [*De Summo Pontifice*] in *Opera Omnia*, ed. Fèvre, vol. 1, pp. 449–615 and vol. 2, pp. 5–167.

The Word of God [*De Verbo Dei*] in *Opera Omnia*, ed. Fèvre, vol. 1, pp. 65–231.

Beza, Theodore, *The Punishment of Heretics by the Civil Magistrate* [*De Haereticis a civili Magistratu Puniendis*] (Geneva, 1554).

The Right of Magistrates over their Subjects, in Julian H. Franklin, *Constitutionalism and Resistance in the Sixteenth Century* (New York, 1969), pp. 101–35.

Biel, Gabriel, *The Circumcision of the Lord*, trans. Paul L. Nyhus in Heiko A. Oberman, *Forerunners of the Reformation* (New York, 1966), pp. 165–74.

Bodin, Jean, *Colloquium of the Seven about Secrets of the Sublime*, trans. Marion L. D. Kuntz (Princeton, N.J., 1975).

Method for the Easy Comprehension of History, trans. Beatrice Reynolds (New York, 1945).

The Six Books of a Commonweal, trans. Richard Knolles and ed. Kenneth D. McRae (Cambridge, Mass., 1962).

Bossuet, Jacques-Bénigne, *Politics taken from the Words of Holy Writ* [*Politique tirée des propres paroles de l'Ecriture sainte*] ed. Jacques Le Brun (Geneva, 1967).

[Boucher, Jean], *The Just Renunciation of Henry III by the Kingdom of France* [*De Iusta Henricii Tertii Abdicatione e Francorum Regno*] (Paris, 1589).

Brant, Sebastian, *The Ship of Fools*, trans. Alexander Barclay in *The English Experience*, No. 229 (Amsterdam, 1970).

Brück, Gregory, *Whether it is lawful to resist a judge who is proceeding unlawfully* [*Iudici procedenti iniuste an licitum sit resistere*] in Heinz Scheible, *Das Widerstandsrecht als Problem der deutschen Protestanten, 1523–1546* (Gütersloh, 1969), pp. 63–6.

Bucer, Martin, *Commentaries on the Book of Judges* [*Commentarii in Librum Judicum*] (Geneva, 1554).

Explications of the Four Gospels [*In Sacra Quattuor Evangelica Enarrationes Perpetuae*] (Geneva, 1553).

Buchanan, George, *The Right of the Kingdom in Scotland* [*De Iure Regni apud Scotos*] (Edinburgh, 1579), in *The English Experience*, No. 80 (Amsterdam, 1969).

Budé, Guillaume, *The Education of the Prince* [*De l'institution du prince*] (Paris, 1547, reprinted Farnborough, 1966).

Bugenhagen, Johann, *Brief* [To the Elector John of Saxony, September, 1529] in Heinz Scheible, *Das Widerstandsrecht als Problem der deutschen Protestanten, 1523–1546* (Gütersloh, 1969), pp. 25–9.

Burnet, Gilbert, *The History of My Own Times*, 6 vols (Oxford, 1833).

Calvin, Jean, *A Commentary on the Acts of the Apostles* [*Commentarius in Acta Apostolorum*] in *Opera Omnia*, ed. Wilhelm Baum *et al.*, 59 vols, Brunswick, 1863–1900), vol. 48, pp. 1–574.

Homilies on the First Book of Samuel [*Homiliae in Primum Librum Samuelis*] in *Opera Omnia*, ed. Baum *et al.*, vol. 29, pp. 232–738 and vol. 30, pp. 1–734.

Institutes of the Christian Religion [*Institutio Christianae Religionis*] (1559 edition) in *Opera Omnia*, ed. Baum *et al.*, vol. 2, pp. 1–1118.

Institutes of the Christian Religion, trans. Ford L. Battles and ed. John T. McNeill, 2 vols (London, 1960).

Letter to Coligny [Epistola 3374: *Calvin à Coligny*, April, 1561] in *Opera Omnia*, ed. Baum *et al.*, vol. 18, pp. 425–31.

Readings on the Prophet Daniel [*Praelectiones in Danielem Prophetam*] in

Opera Omnia, ed. Baum *et al.*, vol. 40, pp. 517–722 and vol. 41, pp. 1–304.

Sermons on the Last Eight Chapters of the Book of Daniel [*Sermons sur les huit derniers chapitres du Livre de Daniel*] in *Opera Omnia*, ed. Baum *et al.*, vol. 41, pp. 305–688 and vol. 42, pp. 1–176.

Three Sermons on the Story of Melchisedec [*Trois sermons sur l'histoire de Melchisedec*] in *Opera Omnia*, ed. Baum *et al.*, vol. 23, pp. 641–82.

Castellio, Sebastian, *Advice to a Desolated France* [*Conseil à la France désolée*] ed. Marius F. Valkhoff (Geneva, 1967).

Concerning Heretics: Whether they are to be Persecuted, trans. Roland H. Bainton (New York, 1935).

Chasseneuz, Barthélemy de, *A Catalogue of the Glory of the World* [*Catalogus Gloriae Mundi*] (Lyons, 1529).

Cicero, Marcus Tullius, *The Laws*, trans. Clinton Walker Keyes (London, 1928).

On Invention, trans. H. M. Hubbell (London, 1949).

The Civil Law, trans. and ed. S. P. Scott, 17 vols (Cincinnati, 1932).

Condé, Louis I de Bourbon, Prince de, *A Declaration issued by the Prince de Condé* [*Déclaration faite par Monsieur le prince de Condé*] in *Mémoires de Condé*, 6 vols (London–La Haye, 1743), vol. 3, pp. 222–35.

Decree Concerning the Canonical Scriptures in *Canons and Decrees of the Council of Trent*, trans. H. J. Schroeder (London, 1941), pp. 17–18.

Decree Concerning the Edition and Use of the Sacred Books in *Canons and Decrees*, trans. Schroeder, pp. 18–20.

Decree Concerning Justification in *Canons and Decrees*, trans. Schroeder, pp. 29–46.

Dudley, Edmund, *The Tree of Commonwealth*, ed. D. M. Brodie (Cambridge, 1948).

Du Fail, Noël, *Rustic Subjects* [*Propos Rustiques*], ed. Louis-Raymond Lefèvre (Paris, 1928).

Du Hames, N., *Letter to Count Louis of Nassau* [February, 1566] in *Archives ou correspondence inédite de la maison d'Orange-Nassau*, ed. G. Groen von Prinsterer, Series I, 8 vols (Leiden, 1835–47), vol. 2, pp. 34–8.

Du Moulin, Charles, *The First Part of the Commentaries on the Customs of Paris* [*Prima Pars Commentariorum in Consuetudines Parisienses*] in *Opera Omnia*, 5 vols (Paris, 1681), vol. 1, pp. 1–665.

The Laws and Privileges of the King of France [*De Legibus et Privilegiis Regni Franciae*] in *Opera Omnia*, vol. 11, pp. 539–50.

Du Vair, Guillaume, *A Buckler against Adversity*, trans. Andrew Court (London, 1622).

Edict of the States General of the United Netherlands [26th July, 1581] in *Texts concerning the Revolt of the Netherlands*, ed. E. H. Kossmann and A. F. Mellink (Cambridge, 1974), pp. 216–28.

Erasmus, Desiderius, *On the Freedom of the Will*, trans. E. Gordon Rupp and A. N. Marlow in *Luther and Erasmus: Free Will and Salvation*, ed. E. Gordon Rupp *et al.* (Philadelphia, 1969), pp. 35–97.

The Praise of Folly, trans. and ed. Hoyt H. Hudson (Princeton, N.J., 1941).

[Estienne, Henri], *A Marvellous Discourse on the Life, Actions and Bearing of*

Catherine de Medici, the Queen Mother [*Discours merveilleux de la vie, actions et déportements de Catherine de Medici, reine mère*] in [Simon Goulart], *Mémoires de l'état de France sous Charles neufième*, 2nd edn, 3 vols (Middelburg [Geneva], 1578). vol. 3, fos 422b–485a.

Filmer, Sir Robert, *Patriarcha*, ed. Peter Laslett (Oxford, 1949).

Fish, Simon, *A Supplication for the Beggars*, ed. Frederick J. Furnivall (London, 1871).

Fortescue, Sir John, *The Praise of the Laws of England* [*De Laudibus Legum Anglie*] trans. and ed. S. B. Chrimes (Cambridge, 1942).

Foxe, Edward, *The True Difference between the Regal Power and the Ecclesiastical Power*, trans. Henry, Lord Stafford (London, 1548).

Foxe, John, *The Acts and Monuments*, ed. Stephen R. Cattley, 8 vols (London, 1837–47).

Gansfort, Johann Wessel, *Letter in Reply to Hoeck*, trans. [in part] Paul L. Nyhus in Heiko A. Oberman, *Forerunners of the Reformation* (New York, 1966), pp. 99–120.

Gardiner, Stephen, *The Oration of True Obedience* in *Obedience in Church and State*, ed. Pierre Janelle (Cambridge, 1930), pp. 67–171.

Geneva Bible: A facsimile of the 1560 Edition, introd. by Lloyd E. Berry (Madison, Wisc., 1969).

Gentillet, Innocent, *Anti-Machiavel*, ed. C. Edward Rathé (Geneva, 1968).

Gerson, Jean, *On Ecclesiastical Power* [*De Potestate Ecclesiastica*] in *Oeuvres Complètes*, vol. 6: *L'Oeuvre ecclésiologique*, ed. P. Glorieux (Paris, 1965), pp. 210–50.

On the Unity of the Church, trans. and ed. James K. Cameron in *Advocates of Reform: From Wyclif to Erasmus*, ed. Matthew Spinka (London, 1953), pp. 140–8.

Ten Highly Useful Considerations for Princes and Governors [*X Considerationes Principibus et Dominis Utilissimae*] in *Opera Omnia*, ed. Louis Ellies du Pin, 5 vols (Antwerp, 1706), vol. 4, cols 622–5.

Towards a Reformation of Simony [*Ad Reformationem Contra Simoniam*] in *Oeuvres Complètes*, ed. Glorieux, vol. 6, pp. 179–81.

A Tract on Simony [*Tractatus de Simonia*] in *Oeuvres Complètes*, ed. Glorieux, vol. 6, pp. 167–74.

Girard, Bernard de, seigneur du Haillan, *The State and Success of the Affairs of France* [*De l'état et succès des affaires de France*] (Paris, 1611).

The Golden Bull of the Emperor Charles IV in *Select Historical Documents of the Middle Ages*, trans. and ed. Ernest F. Henderson (London, 1905), pp. 220–61.

Goodman, Christopher, *How Superior Powers ought to be Obeyed of their Subjects, and wherein they may lawfully by God's Word be Disobeyed and Resisted* (Geneva, 1558).

[Goulart, Simon], *Memoirs of the State of France under Charles IX* [*Mémoires de l'état de France sous Charles neufième*], 2nd edn, 3 vols (Middelburg [Geneva], 1578).

Grebel, Conrad, *Letters to Thomas Müntzer* in *Spiritual and Anabaptist Writers*, ed. George H. Williams (Philadelphia, 1957), pp. 73–85.

Grievances and Demands of the Craft Guilds of Cologne (1513) in Gerald Strauss,

Manifestations of Discontent in Germany on the Eve of the Reformation (Bloomington, Ind., 1971), pp. 138–43.

Gringore, Pierre, *The Folly of the Prince of Fools* [*La Sottie du prince des Sots*]. ed. P. A. Jannini (Milan, 1957).

Hobbes, Thomas, *Leviathan*, ed. C. B. Macpherson (Harmondsworth, 1968).

Philosophical Rudiments Concerning Government and Society in *The English Works*, ed. Sir William Molesworth, 11 vols (London, 1839–45), vol. 2.

Hooker, Richard, *Of the Laws of Ecclesiastical Polity* in *The Works*, ed. John Keble, 7th edn, revised by R. W. Church and F. Paget, 3 vols (Oxford, 1888).

Hotman, François, *Anti-Tribonian* [*L'Antitribonian*] in *Opuscules Françoises* (Paris, 1616), pp. 1–112.

Francogallia, trans. J. H. M. Salmon and ed. Ralph E. Giesey (Cambridge, 1972).

Huguccio, *Unless Detected in Heresy* [*Nisi Deprehendatur a fide Devius*] [Gloss on Decretal] in Brian Tierney, *Foundations of the Conciliar Theory* (Cambridge, 1955), pp. 248–50.

Humphrey, Lawrence, *The Nobles, or Of Nobility* (London, 1563) in *The English Experience*, No. 534 (Amsterdam, 1973).

Hutten, Ulrich von, *A Dialogue on the Roman Triad* [*Trias Romana Dialogus*] in *Opera Omnia*, ed. Ernest Münch, 3 vols (Berlin-Leipzig, 1821–3), vol. 3, pp. 425–506.

Letters of Obscure Men, trans. Francis G. Stokes in *On the Eve of the Reformation* (New York, 1964).

Knox, John, *The Appellation from the Sentence Pronounced by the Bishops and Clergy* in *The Works*, ed. David Laing, 6 vols (Edinburgh, 1846–55), vol. 4 pp. 461–520.

Certain Questions Concerning obedience to lawful Magistrates in *The Works*, ed. Laing, vol. 3, pp. 217–26.

The First Blast of the Trumpet Against the Monstrous Regiment of Women in *The Works*, ed. Laing, vol. 4, pp. 349–420.

The History of the Reformation in Scotland, ed. William Croft Dickinson, 2 vols (London, 1949).

John Knox to the Reader in *The Works*, ed. Laing, vol. 4, pp. 539–40.

A Letter Addressed to the Commonalty of Scotland in *The Works*, ed. Laing, vol. 4, pp. 521–38.

La Noue, François de, *Political and Military Discourses* [*Discours politiques et militaires*] ed. F. E. Sutcliffe (Geneva, 1967).

La Perrière, Guillaume de, *The Mirror of Policy* (London, 1598).

Las Casas, Bartolomé, *In Defense of the Indians*, trans. and ed. Stafford Poole (DeKalb, Ill., 1974).

Latini, Brunetto, *The Books of Treasure* [*Li Livres dou Tresor*], ed. Francis J. Carmody (Berkeley, Calif., 1948).

l'Hôpital, Michel de, *A Speech made at the opening of the session of the States General assembled at Orleans* [13 December, 1560] [*Harangue . . .*] in *Oeuvres complètes de Michel l'Hôpital*, ed. P. J. S. Duféy, 3 vols (Paris, 1824–25), vol. 1, pp. 375–411.

A Speech made to the Parlement of Paris on the Edicts concerning religion [28

June, 1561] [*Harangue* . . .] in *Oeuvres complètes*, ed. Duféy, vol. 1, pp. 418–434.

The Speech of the Chancellor l'Hôpital at the opening of the Parlement [12th November, 1561] [*Harangue* . . .] in *Oeuvres complètes*, ed. Duféy, vol. 2, pp. 9–19.

The Speech of Michel l'Hôpital, Chancellor of France, to the assembly of the States General at St Germain-en-Laye [January, 1562] [*Harangue* . . .] in *Oeuvres complètes*, ed. Duféy, vol. 1, pp. 441–58.

The Speech of the Chancellor l'Hôpital at the opening of the Parlement [12th November, 1563] [*Harangue* . . .] in *Oeuvres complètes*, ed. Duféy, vol. 2, pp. 85–97.

Lipsius, Justus, *Six Books of Politics or Civil Doctrine*, trans. William Jones (London, 1594) in *The English Experience*, No. 287 (Amsterdam, 1970).

Locke, John, *Two Treatises of Government*, a critical edition with an Introduction by Peter Laslett, second edn (Cambridge, 1967).

Luther, Martin, *Admonition to Peace*, trans. Charles M. Jacobs in *Luther's Works*, vol. 46, ed. Robert C. Schultz (Philadelphia, 1967), pp. 3–43.

Against the Robbing and Murdering Hordes of Peasants, trans. Charles M. Jacobs in *Luther's Works*, vol. 46, ed. Robert C. Schultz (Philadelphia, 1967), pp. 45–55.

The Appeal of Martin Luther to a Council [*Appellatio F. Martini Luther ad Concilium*] in Martin Luther, *Werke*, vol. 7 (Weimar, 1897), pp. 75–82.

The Bondage of the Will, trans. Philip S. Watson and Benjamin Drewery in *Luther's Works*, vol. 33, ed. Philip S. Watson (Philadelphia, 1972), pp. 3–295.

Colloquies, Meditations and Consolations [*Colloquia, Meditationes, Consolationes* . . .], ed. H. E. Bindseil, 3 vols (Halle, 1863–6).

Concerning the Answer of the Goat in Leipzig in *Luther's Works*, vol. 39, ed. Eric. W. Gritsch (Philadelphia, 1970), pp. 117–35.

Dr Martin Luther's Warning to his Dear German People, trans. Martin H. Bertram in *Luther's Works*, vol. 47, ed. Franklin Sherman (Philadelphia, 1971), pp. 11–55.

The Freedom of a Christian, trans. W. A. Lambert in *Luther's Works*, vol. 31, ed. Harold J. Grimm (Philadelphia, 1957), pp. 327–77.

The Judgment of Martin Luther on Monastic Vows trans. James Atkinson in *Luther's Works*, vol. 44, ed. James Atkinson (Philadelphia, 1966), pp. 243–400.

Letter . . . *in Opposition to the Fanatic Spirit*, trans. Conrad Bergendoff in *Luther's Works*, vol. 40, ed. Conrad Bergendoff (Philadelphia, 1958), pp. 61–71.

Letters, trans and ed. Gottfried G. Krodel in *Luther's Works*, vols 48–50 (Philadelphia, 1963–75).

Ninety-Five Theses, trans. C. M. Jacobs in *Luther's Works*, vol. 31, ed. Harold J. Grimm (Philadelphia, 1957), pp. 17–33.

On the Councils and the Church, trans. Charles M. Jacobs in *Luther's Works*, vol. 41, ed. Eric W. Gritsch (Philadelphia, 1966), pp. 3–178.

Preface to the Complete Edition of a German Theology, trans. Harold J. Grimm in *Luther's Works*, vol. 31, ed. Harold J. Grimm (Philadelphia, 1957), pp. 71–6.

Preface to the Complete Edition of Luther's Latin Writings, trans. Lewis W. Spitz in *Luther's Works*, vol. 34, ed. Lewis W. Spitz (Philadelphia, 1960), pp. 323–38.

A Sincere Admonition . . . to All Christians to Guard against Insurrection and Rebellion, trans. W. A. Lambert in *Luther's Works*, vol. 45, ed. Walther I. Brandt (Philadelphia, 1962), pp. 51–74.

Table Talk [Collected by Conrad Cordatus], trans. Theodore G. Tappert in *Luther's Works*, vol. 54, ed. Theodore G. Tappert (Philadelphia, 1967), pp. 171–200.

Temporal Authority: to what Extent it Should be Obeyed, trans. J. J. Schindel in *Luther's Works*, vol. 45, ed. Walther I. Brandt (Philadelphia, 1962), pp. 75–129.

To the Christian Nobility of the German Nation, trans. Charles M. Jacobs in *Luther's Works*, vol. 44, ed. James Atkinson (Philadelphia, 1966), pp. 115–217.

To the Pious Reader [*Martinus Luther Lectori Pio*] in Martin Luther, *Werke*, vol. 26 (Weimar, 1909), pp. 123–4.

Two Kinds of Righteousness, trans. Lowell J. Satre in *Luther's Works*, vol. 31, ed. Harold J. Grimm (Philadelphia, 1957), pp. 293–306.

Whether Soldiers, Too, Can be Saved, trans. Charles M. Jacobs in *Luther's Works*, vol. 46, ed. Robert C. Schultz (Philadelphia, 1967), pp. 87–137.

Machiavelli, Niccolo, *The Discourses*, trans. Leslie J. Walker, S.J., and ed. Bernard Crick (Harmondsworth, 1970).

The Prince [*Il Principe*] in *Opere*, ed. Sergio Bertelli *et al.*, in *Biblioteca di classici italiani*, 8 vols (Milan, 1960–65), vol. 1, pp. 13–105.

Mair, John, *Clear Expositions of the Four Gospels* [*Expositiones Lucentes in Quattuor Evangelica*] (Paris, 1529).

A Disputation on the Authority of a Council, trans. J. K. Cameron in *Advocates of Reform: From Wyclif to Erasmus*, ed. Matthew Spinka (London, 1953), pp. 175–84.

An Exposition of St Matthew's Gospel [*In Mattheu ad Literam Expositio*] (Paris, 1518).

A History of Greater Britain, as well England as Scotland, trans. and ed. Archibald Constable (Edinburgh, 1892).

The Most Useful Questions on the Fourth Book of Lombard's Sentences [*In Quartum Sententiarum Quaestiones Utilissimae*] (Paris, 1519).

The Power of the Pope in Temporal Affairs [*De Potestate Papae in Temporalibus*] in Gerson, *Opera Omnia*, ed. Du Pin, vol. 2, cols 1145–1164.

The Status and Power of the Church [*De Statu et Potestate Ecclesiae*] in Gerson, *Opera Omnia*, ed. Du Pin, vol. 2, cols 1121–1130.

Mariana, Juan de, *The King and the Education of the King* [*De Rege et Regis Institutione*] (Toledo, 1599).

The King and the Education of the King, trans. George Albert Moore (Washington, D.C., 1948).

Marnix, Philippe de, *Letter to William of Orange* [March, 1580], in *Archives*, ed. Prinsterer, Series I, vol. 7, pp. 276–86.

Marshall, William, 'Preface' to Marsiglio of Padua, *The Defence of Peace*, trans. William Marshall (London, 1535).

Marsiglio of Padua, *The Defender of Peace*, trans. Alan Gewirth (New York, 1956).

Martyr, Peter, *Commentaries . . . upon the Epistle of St Paul to the Romans*, trans. H. B. (London, 1568).

A Commentary upon the Book of Judges, trans. John Day (London, 1564).

Masson, Papire, *The Response of Papire Masson to Hotman's Maledictions [Papirii Massoni Responsio ad Maledicta Hotomani]* (Paris, 1575).

Matharel, Antoine, *A Reply to François Hotman's Francogallia [Ad Franc. Hotomani Franco-Galliam . . . Responsio]* (Lyons, 1575).

Maxwell, John, *Sacro-Sancta Regum Maiestas, or the Sacred and Royal Prerogative of Christian Kings* (Oxford, 1644).

Melanchthon, Philipp, *Commentaries on Some of the Books of Aristotle's Politics [Commentarii in Aliquot Politicos Libros Aristotelis]* in *Opera Omnia*, ed. C. G. Bretschneider, 28 vols (Halle-Brunswick, 1834–60), vol. 16, pp. 416–452.

Commentaries on the Epistle of St Paul to the Romans [Commentarii in Epistolam Pauli ad Romanos] in *Opera Omnia*, ed. Bretschneider, vol. 15, pp. 497–796.

Common Topics in Theology [Loci Communes] in *Melanchthon on Christian Doctrine*, trans. and ed. Clyde L. Manschreck (New York, 1965).

The Epitome of Moral Philosophy [Philosophiae Moralis Epitome] in *Opera Omnia*, ed. Bretschneider, vol. 16, pp. 20–163.

Prolegomena to Cicero's Treatise on Moral Obligation [Prolegomena in Officia Ciceronis] in *Opera Omnia*, ed. Bretschneider, vol. 16, pp. 533–680.

Milton, John, *Of Reformation* in *The Complete Prose Works of John Milton*, vol. 1, ed. Don M. Wolfe (New Haven, Conn., 1953), pp. 517–617.

The Tenure of Kings and Magistrates, in *The Complete Prose Works of John Milton*, vol. 3, ed. Meritt Y. Hughes (New Haven, Conn., 1962), pp. 189–258.

Molina, Luis de, *Six Books on Justice and Law [De Iustitia et Iure Libri Sex]*, 2 vols (Mainz, 1659).

Montaigne, Michel de, *Essays* in *The Complete Works of Montaigne*, trans. Donald M. Frame (London, 1957), pp. 1–857.

More, Sir Thomas, *The Dialogue Concerning Tyndale*, ed. W. E. Campbell (London, 1927).

Morison, Richard, *A Lamentation, showing what ruin and Destruction comes of Seditious Rebellion* (London, 1536).

An Exhortation to stir all Englishmen to the Defence of their Country (London, 1539).

An Invective against the Great and Detestable Vice, Treason (London, 1539).

Apomaxis Calumniarum (London, 1537).

A Remedy for Sedition (London, 1536).

[Mornay, Philippe du Plessis] *A Defence of Liberty against Tyrants [Vindiciae contra Tyrannos]* (Edinburgh [Basle], 1579).

Müntzer, Thomas, *Sermon Before the Princes* in *Spiritual and Anabaptist Writers*, ed. George H. Williams (Philadelphia, 1957), pp. 49–70.

Nicolaus of Cusa, *On Universal Harmony* [*De Concordantia Catholica*] in *Opera Omnia*, vol. 16, ed. Gerhard Kallen (Hamburg, 1963).

Osiander, Andreas, *Brief* in F. Hortleder, *Der Römischen Kaiser und Königlichen Maierstaten* . . ., 12 vols (Gotha, 1645), vol. 2, pp. 83–5.

[Pasquier, Estienne], *An Exhortation to the Princes and Seigneurs of the King's Privy Council* [*Exhortation aux princes et seigneurs du conseil privé du roi*] in *Écrits Politiques* ed. D. Thickett (Geneva, 1966), pp. 33–90.

Pasquier, Estienne, *Researches on France* [*Les Recherches de la France*] in *Les Oeuvres*, 2 vols (Amsterdam, 1723), vol. 1, pp. 1–1015.

Patrizi, Francesco, *The Kingdom and the Education of the King* [*De Regno et Regis Institutione*] (Prato, 1531).

Pole, Reginald, *A Defence of Ecclesiastical Unity* [*Pro Ecclesiasticae Unitatis Defensione*] trans. as *Défence de l'unité de l'Église*, ed. Noëlle-Marie Égretier (Paris, 1967).

Ponet, John, *A Short Treatise of Politic Power*, reprinted in Winthrop S. Hudson, *John Ponet* (1516?–1556), *Advocate of Limited Monarchy* (Chicago, 1942), after p. 246.

Possevino, Antonio, *A Judgment on the Writings of Jean Bodin, Philippe Mornay and Niccolo Machiavelli* [*Iudicium . . . Joannis Bodini, Philippi Mornaei et Nicolai Machiavelli quibusdam scriptis*] (Lyons, 1594).

Postel, Guillaume, *The Concord of the World* [*De Orbis Terrae Concordia Libri Quattuor*] (Basle, 1544).

Raleigh, Sir Walter, *Maxims of State* in *The Works*, 8 vols (Oxford, 1829), vol. 8, pp. 1–34.

Rebuffi, Pierre, *A Commentary on the Royal Constitutions and Ordinances* [*Commentaria in Constitutiones seu Ordinationes Regias*] (Lyons, 1613).

Ribadeneyra, Pedro, *Religion and the Virtues of the Christian Prince against Machiavelli*, trans. and ed. George Albert Moore (Maryland, 1949).

[Rose, Guillaume], *The Just Authority of a Christian Commonwealth over Impious and Heretical Kings* [*De Iusta Reipublicae Christianae in reges Impios et Haereticos authoritate*] (Antwerp, 1592).

Rousseau, Jean-Jacques, *The Social Contract* [*Du Contrat Social*] in *Oeuvres Complètes*, ed. Bernard Gagnebin and Marcel Raymond, vol. 3 (Paris, 1964), pp. 347–470.

St German, Christopher, *A Dialogue in English betwixt a Doctor of Divinity and a Student of the Laws of England* (London, 1530).

An Answer to a Letter (London [1535]).

A Little Treatise Called the New Additions (London, 1531).

A Treatise concerning the Division between the Spirituality and the Temporality in *The Apology of Sir Thomas More, Knight*, ed. Arthur I. Taft (London, 1930), Appendix, pp. 201–53.

Salamonio, Mario, *The Sovereignty of the Roman Patriciate* [*Patritii Romani de Principatu*] (Rome, 1544).

Sampson, Richard, *An Oration Teaching Obedience* [*Oratio qua docet . . . ut obediant*] (London, 1534).

The Schleitheim Confession of Faith in *The Protestant Reformation*, ed. Hans J. Hillerbrand (London, 1968), pp. 129–36.

Seller, Abednego, *The History of Passive Obedience since the Reformation* (Amsterdam, 1689).

Seyssel, Claude de, *The Monarchy of France* [*La Monarchie de France*], ed. Jacques Poujol (Paris, 1961).

Skelton, John, *The Complete Poems*, ed. Philip Henderson (London, 1931).

Sleiden, Johann, *The State of Religion and Commonwealth during the reign of the Emperor Charles the Fifth*, trans. John Daus (London, 1560).

Soto, Domingo de, *Ten Books on Justice and Law* [*Libri Decem de Iustitia et Iure*] (Lyons, 1569).

Starkey, Thomas, *A Dialogue between Reginald Pole and Thomas Lupset*, ed. Kathleen M. Burton (London, 1948).

An Exhortation to the People, Instructing them to Unity and Obedience (London, 1536).

Statement of Grievances presented to the Diet of Worms (1521) in Gerald Strauss, *Manifestations of Discontent in Germany on the Eve of the Reformation* (Bloomington, Ind., 1971), pp. 52–63.

Staupitz, Johann von, *Eternal Predestination and its Execution in Time*, trans. Paul L. Nyhus in Heiko A. Oberman, *Forerunners of the Reformation* (New York, 1966), pp. 175–203.

Suárez, Francisco, *A Defence of the Catholic and Apostolic Faith against the Errors of the Anglican Sect* [*Defensio Fidei Catholicae et Apostolicae adversus Anglicanae Sectae Errores*], 2 vols (Naples, 1872).

A Treatise on the Laws and God the Lawgiver [*Tractatus de Legibus ac Deo Legislatore*], 2 vols (Naples, 1872).

Tudeschis, Nicolaus de [Panormitanus], *A Commentary on the Second Part of the First Book of the Decretals* [*Commentaria secundae partis in Primum Decretalium Librum*] (Venice, 1591).

Tyndale, William, *An Answer to Sir Thomas More's Dialogue*, ed. Henry Walter (Cambridge, 1850).

The Obedience of a Christian Man in *Doctrinal Treatises*, ed. Henry Walter (Cambridge, 1848), pp. 127–344.

Vitoria, Francisco de, *Civil Power* [*De Potestate Civili*] in *Relecciones Teológicas del Maestro Fray Francisco de Vitoria*, ed. Luis G. Alonso Getino, 3 vols (Madrid, 1933–36), vol. 2, pp. 169–210.

The Power of the Church [*De Potestate Ecclesiae*] in *Relecciones*, ed. Getino, vol. 2, pp. 1–168.

The Power of the Pope and the Council [*De Potestate Papae et Concilii*] in *Relecciones*, ed. Getino, vol. 2, pp. 211–80.

The Recently Discovered Indies [*De Indis Recenter Inventis*] in *Relecciones*, ed. Getino, vol. 2, pp. 281–438.

William of Ockham, *A Brief Account of the Power of the Pope* [*Breviloquium de Potestate Papae*], ed. L. Baudry (Paris, 1937).

Eight Questions on the Power of the Pope [*Octo Quaestiones de Potestate Papae*] in *Opera Politica*, vol. 1, ed. J. G. Sikes (Manchester, 1940), pp. 1–221.

Philosophical Writings, trans. and ed. Philotheus Boehner (London, 1957).

The Dialogue [*Dialogus*], trans. [extracts] in Ewart Lewis, *Medieval Political Ideas*, 2 vols (London, 1954), vol. II, pp. 398–402.

The Power of Emperors and Popes [*De Imperatorum et Pontificum Potestate*,] ed. C. Kenneth Brampton (Oxford, 1927).

William of Orange, *The Apology*, ed. H. Wansink (Leiden, 1969).

Wyclif, John, *The Church and her Members* in *Select English Works of John Wyclif*, ed. Thomas Arnold, 3 vols (Oxford, 1869–71), vol. 3, pp. 338–65.

Zasius, Ulrich, *An Epitome of the Custom of Fiefs* [*Usus Feudorum Epitome*] in *Opera Omnia*, 7 vols (Darmstadt, 1964–66), vol. 4, cols 243–342.

Judgments, or Legal Opinions [*Consilia, sive Iuris Responsa*] in *Opera Omnia*, vol. 6, cols 9–576.

Zwingli, Huldreich, *The Pastor* [*Der Hirt*] in *Sämtliche Werke*, ed. E. Egli *et al.*, 13 vols (Berlin–Leipzig, 1905–63), vol. 3, pp. 1–68.

Bibliography of secondary sources

d'Addio, Mario (1954), *L'Idea del contratto sociale dai sofisti alla riforma e il 'De Principatu' di Mario Salamonio* (Milan, 1954).

Allen, J. W. (1957), *A History of Political Thought in the Sixteenth Century* (revised edn, London, 1957).

Allen, P. S. (1906–58), *Opus Epistolarum Des. Erasmi Roterodami*, 12 vols (Oxford, 1906–1958).

Althaus, Paul (1966), *The Theology of Martin Luther* (Philadelphia, 1966).

Anderson, Marvin W. (1975), *Peter Martyr, A Reformer in Exile (1542–1562)* (Nieuwkoop, 1975).

Anderson, Perry (1974), *Lineages of the Absolutist State* (London, 1974).

Aston, Margaret (1964), 'Lollardy and the Reformation: Survival or Revival?' *History* 49 (1964), pp. 149–70.

Backer, Augustin and Alois (1853–61), *Bibliothèque des Écrivains de la compagnie de Jésus*, 7 vols (Liége, 1853–61).

Bainton, R. H. (1953a), *The Reformation of the Sixteenth Century* (London, 1953).

(1953b), *Hunted Heretic: The Life and Death of Michael Servetus, 1511–1553* (Boston, 1953).

Barcia Trelles, Camilo (1933), 'Francisco Suárez (1548–1617)', *Académie de droit international: recueil des cours* 43 (1933), pp. 385–553.

Baron, Hans (1937), 'Religion and Politics in the German Imperial Cities during the Reformation', *The English Historical Review* 52 (1937), pp. 405–427 and 614–33.

(1939), 'Calvinist Republicanism and its Historical Roots', *Church History*, 8 (1939), pp. 30–42.

Barrère, Joseph (1914), 'Observations sur quelques ouvrages politiques anonymes du XVIe siècle', *Revue d'histoire litteraire de la France* 21 (1914), pp. 375–86.

Bataillon, Marcel (1937), *Érasme et l'Espagne: Recherches sur l'histoire spirituelle du XVIe siècle* (Paris, 1937).

(1954), 'Pour l' "epistolario" de las Casas: une lettre et un brouillon', *Bulletin Hispanique* 56 (1954), pp. 366–87.

Baudry, L. (1937), 'Préface' to William of Ockham, *Breviloquium de Potestate Papae* (Paris, 1937), pp. v–xx.

(1950), *La Querelle des futurs contingents* (Louvain, 1465–75) (Paris, 1950).

Baumel, Jean (1936), *Les Problèmes de la colonisation et de la guerre dans l'oeuvre de Francisco de Vitoria* (Montpellier, 1936).

Baumer, Franklin Le van (1937), 'Christopher St German: the Political Philosophy of a Tudor Lawyer', *The American Historical Review* 42 (1937), pp. 631–51.

——— (1940), *The Early Tudor Theory of Kingship* (New Haven, Conn., 1940).

Bayley, C. C. (1949), 'Pivotal Concepts in the political philosophy of William of Ockham', *The Journal of the History of Ideas* 10 (1949), pp. 199–218.

Beame, E. M. (1966), 'The Limits of Toleration in Sixteenth Century France', *Studies in the Renaissance* 13 (1966), pp. 250–65.

Bell, Susan G. (1967), 'Johann Eberlin von Günzburg's *Wolfaria*: the first Protestant Utopia', *Church History* 36 (1967), pp. 122–39.

Bender, Harold S. (1953), 'The Zwickau Prophets, Thomas Müntzer, and the Anabaptists', *The Mennonite Quarterly Review* 27 (1953), pp. 3–16.

Benert, Richard R. (1967), *Inferior Magistrates in Sixteenth-Century Political and Legal Thought* (Ph.D. Dissertation, University of Minnesota, 1967).

——— (1973), 'Lutheran Resistance Theory and the Imperial Constitution', *Il Pensiero Politico* 6 (1973), pp. 17–36.

Bergendoff, Conrad (1928), *Olaus Petri and the Ecclesiastical Transformation in Sweden* (New York, 1928).

Berry, Lloyd E. (1969), 'Introduction' to *The Geneva Bible: A Facsimile of the 1560 Edition* (Madison, Wisc., 1969).

Biéler, André (1959), *La pensée économique et sociale de Calvin* (Geneva, 1959).

Bitton, Davis (1969), *The French Nobility in Crisis, 1560–1640* (Stanford, Calif., 1969).

Black, Antony (1970), *Monarchy and Community: Political Ideas in the Later Conciliar Controversy 1430–1450* (Cambridge, 1970).

Blanke, Fritz (1961), *Brothers in Christ*, trans. Joseph Nordenhang (Scotdale, Pennsylvania, 1961).

Bleznick, Donald W. (1958), 'Spanish Reaction to Machiavelli in the Sixteenth and Seventeenth Centuries', *The Journal of the History of Ideas* 19 (1958), pp. 542–50.

Boase, Alan M. (1935), *The Fortunes of Montaigne: A History of the Essays in France, 1580–1669* (London, 1935).

Boehmer, Heinrich (1946), *The Road to Reformation*, trans. J. W. Doberstein and T. G. Tappert (Philadelphia, 1946).

Bohatec, Josef (1937), *Calvins Lehre von Staat und Kirche* (Breslau, 1937).

Boisset, Jean (1962), *Erasme et Luther: Libre ou serf arbitre?* (Paris, 1962).

Bonini, Cissie R. (1973), 'Lutheran Influences in the early English Reformation: Richard Morison Re-Examined', *Archiv für Reformationsgeschichte* 64 (1973), pp. 206–24.

Bornkamm, Heinrich (1958), *Luther's World of Thought*, trans. Martin H. Bertram (St Louis, Mo., 1958).

——— (1961–2), 'Zur Frage der Iustitia Dei beim jungen Luther', *Archiv für Reformationsgeschichte*, 52 and 53 (1961–2), pp. 16–29 and 1–60.

Bouwsma, William J. (1957), *Concordia Mundi: The Career and Thought of Guillaume Postel (1510–1581)* (Cambridge, Mass., 1957).

Brampton, C. Kenneth (1927), 'Introduction' to *The De Imperatorum et*

Pontificum Potestate of William of Ockham (Oxford, 1927), pp. ix–xxxviii.

Brandi, Karl (1939), *The Emperor Charles V*, trans. C. V. Wedgwood (London, 1939).

Braudel, Fernand (1972–3), *The Mediterranean and the Mediterranean World in the Age of Philip II*, trans. Siân Reynold, 2 vols (London, 1972–3).

Brodie, D. M. (1948), 'Introduction' to Edmund Dudley, *The Tree of Commonwealth* (Cambridge, 1948), pp. 1–17.

Brodrick, James (1928), *The Life and Work of Blessed Robert Francis Cardinal Bellarmine, S.J., 1542–1621*, 2 vols (London, 1928).

Brown, Frieda S. (1963), *Religious and Political Conservatism in the Essais of Montaigne* (Geneva, 1963).

Brown, John L. (1939), *The Methodus ad Facilem Historiarum Cognitionem of Jean Bodin: a Critical Study* (Washington, D.C., 1939).

Brown, P. Hume (1902), *History of Scotland*, vol. II: *From the Accession of Mary Stewart to the Revolution of 1689* (Cambridge, 1902).

Bruce, F. F. (1970), *The English Bible: A History of Translations*, rev. edn (London, 1970).

Buisson, Ferdinand (1892), *Sébastien Castellion: sa vie et son œuvre (1515–1563)*, 2 vols (Paris, 1892).

Buranelli, Vincent (1957), 'The Historical and Political Thought of Boulainvilliers', *The Journal of the History of Ideas* 18 (1957), pp. 475–94.

Burns, J. H. (1951), 'The Political Ideas of George Buchanan', *The Scottish Historical Review* 30 (1951), pp. 60–8.

(1954), 'New Light on John Major', *The Innes Review* 5 (1954), pp. 83–100.

(1955), 'Knox and Bullinger', *The Scottish Historical Review* 34 (1955), pp. 90–91.

(1959), 'Sovereignty and Constitutional Law in Bodin', *Political Studies* 7 (1959), pp. 174–7.

Caprariis, Vittorio de (1959), *Propaganda e pensiero politico in Francia durante le guerre di religione*, vol. I (1559–1572) (Naples, 1959).

Cardascia, Guillaume (1943), 'Machiavel et Jean Bodin', *Bibliothèque d'humanisme et renaissance* 3 (1943), pp. 129–67.

Cargill Thompson, W. D. J. (1969), 'The "Two Kingdoms" and the "Two Regiments": Some Problems of Luther's *Zwei-Reiche-Lehre*', *The Journal of Theological Studies* 20 (1969), pp. 164–85.

Carlson, Edgar (1946), 'Luther's Conception of Government', *Church History* 15 (1946), pp. 257–70.

Carlyle, R. W. and A. J. (1936), *A History of Medieval Political Theory in the West*: vol. VI: *Political Theory from 1300 to 1600* (London, 1936).

Carsten, F. L. (1959), *Princes and Parliaments in Germany* (Oxford, 1959).

Cassirer, Ernst (1946), *The Myth of the State* (New Haven, Conn., 1946).

Chabod, Federico (1946), 'Was there a Renaissance State?', in *The Development of the Modern State*, ed. Heinz Lubasz (New York, 1964), pp. 26–42.

Chambers, R. W. (1935), *Thomas More* (London, 1935).

Chauviré, Roger (1914), *Jean Bodin, auteur de la 'République'* (Paris, 1914).

Chenevière, Marc-Edouard (1937), *La Pensée politique de Calvin* (Paris, 1937).

Chester, Allan G. (1954), *Hugh Latimer: Apostle to the English* (Philadelphia, 1954).

Chrimes, S. B. (1936), *English Constitutional Ideas in the Fifteenth Century* (Cambridge, 1936).

(1972), *Henry VII* (London, 1972).

Chrisman, Miriam U. (1967), *Strasbourg and the Reform* (New Haven, Conn., 1967).

Church, William F. (1941), *Constitutional Thought in Sixteenth Century France* (Cambridge, Mass., 1941).

Clasen, Claus-Peter (1972), *Anabaptism: A Social History, 1525–1618* (New York, 1972).

Clebsch, William A. (1964), *England's Earliest Protestants, 1520–1535* (New Haven, Conn., 1964).

Connolly, James L. (1928), *John Gerson, Reformer and Mystic* (Louvain, 1928).

Copleston, Frederick (1953), *A History of Philosophy*, vol. III: *Ockham to Suárez* (London, 1953).

Costello, Frank B. (1974), *The Political Philosophy of Luis de Molina, S.J. (1535–1600)* (Rome, 1974).

Craig, Hardin (1938), 'The Geneva Bible as a Political Document', *The Pacific Historical Review* 7 (1938), pp. 40–9.

Cranz, F. Edward (1959), *An Essay on the Development of Luther's Thought on Justice, Law and Society* (Cambridge, Mass., 1959).

Cronin, Timothy J. (1966), *Objective Being in Descartes and in Suárez* (Rome, 1966).

Daniel-Rops, H. (1961), *The Protestant Reformation*, trans. Audrey Butler (London, 1961).

(1962), *The Catholic Reformation*, trans. John Warrington (London, 1962).

Danner, D. G. (1971), 'Anthony Gilby: Puritan in Exile: a Biographical Approach', *Church History* 40 (1971), pp. 412–22.

Dickens, A. G. (1959a), *Lollards and Protestants in the Diocese of York, 1509–1558* (London, 1959).

(1959b), *Thomas Cromwell and the English Reformation* (London, 1959).

(1964), *The English Reformation* (London, 1964).

(1966a), 'The Reformation in England', in *The Reformation Crisis*, ed. Joel Hurstfield (London, 1966), pp. 44–57.

(1966b), *Reformation and Society in Sixteenth Century Europe* (London, 1966).

(1968), *The Counter Reformation* (London, 1968).

(1974), *The German Nation and Martin Luther* (London, 1974).

Donaldson, Gordon (1960), *The Scottish Reformation* (Cambridge, 1960).

Doucet, R., *et al.* (1939), *Histoire de Lyon*: I: *Des origines à 1595* (Lyon, 1939).

(1948), *Les Institutions de la France au XVIe siècle*, 2 vols (Paris, 1948).

Doumergue, E. (1899–1927), *Jean Calvin: les hommes et les choses de son temps*, 7 vols (Lausanne, 1899–1927).

Dowdall, H. C. (1923), 'The Word "State" ', *The Law Quarterly Review* 39 (1923), pp. 98–125.

Dreano, M. (1969), *La Religion de Montaigne*, 2nd edn (Paris, 1969).

Duhamel, Pierre A. (1948–9), 'The Logic and Rhetoric of Peter Ramus', *Modern Philology* 46 (1948–9), pp. 163–71.

Duke, John A. (1937), *History of the Church of Scotland to the Reformation* (Edinburgh, 1937).

Dunkley, E. H. (1948), *The Reformation in Denmark* (London, 1948).

Dunn, John (1967), 'Consent in the Political Theory of John Locke', *The Historical Journal* 10 (1967), pp. 153–82.

(1969), *The Political Thought of John Locke* (Cambridge, 1969).

Edwards, Mark U. (1975), *Luther and the False Brethren* (Stanford, Calif., 1975).

Eells, Hastings (1931), *Martin Bucer* (New Haven, Conn., 1931).

Elliott, J. H. (1963), *Imperial Spain, 1469–1716* (London, 1963).

(1968), *Europe Divided, 1559–1598* (London, 1968).

Elton, G. R. (1949), 'The Evolution of a Reformation Statute', *The English Historical Review* 64 (1949), pp. 174–97.

(1951), 'The Commons' Supplication of 1532: Parliamentary Manoeuvres in the reign of Henry VIII', *The English Historical Review* 66 (1951), pp. 507–34.

(1953), *The Tudor Revolution in Government* (Cambridge, 1953).

(1955), *England under the Tudors* (London, 1955).

(1956), 'The Political Creed of Thomas Cromwell', *Transactions of the Royal Historical Society* 6 (1956), pp. 69–92.

(1960), *The Tudor Constitution: Documents and Commentary* (Cambridge, 1960).

(1963), *Reformation Europe* (London, 1963).

(1972), *Policy and Police: the Enforcement of the Reformation in the Age of Thomas Cromwell* (Cambridge, 1972).

(1973), *Reform and Renewal: Thomas Cromwell and the Commonweal* (Cambridge, 1973).

Erikson, Erik H. (1958), *Young Man Luther: A Study in Psychoanalysis and History* (London, 1958).

Erlanger, Philippe, *St Bartholomew's Night: The Massacre of St Bartholomew*, trans. Patrick O'Brian (London, 1960).

Fairfield, Leslie P. (1976), *John Bale, Mythmaker for the English Reformation* (West Lafayette, Indiana, 1976).

Fenlon, Dermot (1972), *Heresy and Obedience in Tridentine Italy: Cardinal Pole and the Counter Reformation* (Cambridge, 1972).

Fernández de la Mora, Gonzalo (1949), 'Maquiavelo, visto por los tratadistas politicos Espagñoles de la contrarreforma', *Arbor* 13 (1949), pp. 417–49.

Fernández-Santamaria, J. A. (1977), *The State, War and Peace: Spanish Political Thought in the Renaissance, 1516–1559* (Cambridge, 1977).

Fichter, J. H. (1940), *Man of Spain: Francis Suárez* (New York, 1940).

Fife, Robert H. (1957), *The Revolt of Martin Luther* (New York, 1957).

Figgis, J. N. (1914), *The Divine Right of Kings*, 2nd edn (Cambridge, 1914).

(1960), *Political Thought from Gerson to Grotius, 1414–1625*, with an Introduction by Garrett Mattingly (New York, 1960).

Flick, Alexander C. (1930), *The Decline of the Medieval Church*, 2 vols (London, 1930).

Ford, Franklin (1953), *Robe and Sword: the Regrouping of the French Aristocracy after Louis XIV* (Cambridge, Mass., 1953).

Frame, Donald M. (1965), *Montaigne: A Biography* (London, 1965).

Franklin, Julian H. (1963), *Jean Bodin and the Sixteenth-Century Revolution in the Methodology of Law and History* (New York, 1963).

(1967), 'Constitutionalism in the Sixteenth Century: the Protestant Monarchomachs', in *Political Theory and Social Change*, ed. David Spitz (New York, 1967), pp. 117–32.

(1969), *Constitutionalism and Resistance in the Sixteenth Century* (New York, 1969).

(1973), *Jean Bodin and the Rise of Absolutist Theory* (Cambridge, 1973).

(1978), *John Locke and the Theory of Sovereignty* (Cambridge, 1978).

Friedenthal, Richard (1970), *Luther: His Life and Times*, trans. John Nowell (New York, 1970).

Gallet, Léon (1944), 'La Monarchie française d'après Claude de Seyssel', *Revue historique de droit français et étranger* 23 (1944), pp. 1–34.

Ganoczy, Alexandre (1966), *Le Jeune Calvin: genèse et évolution de sa vocation réformatrice* (Wiesbaden, 1966).

(1968), 'Jean Major, exégète gallican', *Récherches de science réligieuse* 56 (1968), pp. 457–95.

Garrett, Christina (1938), *The Marian Exiles* (Cambridge, 1938).

Gerrish, B. A. (1962), *Grace and Reason: a Study in the Theology of Luther* (Oxford, 1962).

Getino, Luis G. Alonso (1930), *El Maestro Fr. Francisco de Vitoria* (Madrid, 1930).

Gierke, Otto von (1900), *Political Theories of the Middle Ages*, trans. F. M. Maitland (Cambridge, 1900).

(1934), *Natural Law and the Theory of Society, 1500–1800*, trans. Ernest Barker, 2 vols (Cambridge, 1934).

(1939), *The Development of Political Theory*, trans. Bernard Freyd (London, 1939).

Giesendorf, P.-F. (1949), *Théodore de Bèze* (Paris, 1949).

Giesey, Ralph E. (1967), 'When and Why Hotman wrote the *Francogallia*', *Bibliothèque d'humanisme et renaissance* 29 (1967), pp. 581–611.

(1968), *If Not, Not: the Oath of the Aragonese and the Legendary Laws of Sobrarbe* (Princeton, N.J., 1968).

(1970), 'The Monarchomach Triumvirs: Hotman, Beza and Mornay', *Bibliothèque d'humanisme et renaissance* 32 (1970), pp. 41–56.

(1973), 'Medieval Jurisprudence in Bodin's Concept of Sovereignty', in *Jean Bodin: Proceedings of the International Conference on Bodin in Munich*, ed. Horst Denzer (Munich, 1973), pp. 167–86.

Giesey, Ralph E., and Salmon, J. H. M. (1972), 'Editors' Introduction' to François Hotman, *Francogallia* (Cambridge, 1972), pp. 1–134.

Gilbert, Felix (1965), *Machiavelli and Guicciardini: Politics and History in Sixteenth Century Florence* (Princeton, N.J., 1965).

Gilmore, Myron P. (1941), *Argument from Roman Law in Political Thought, 1200–1600* (Cambridge, Mass., 1941).

Gough, J. W. (1957), *The Social Contract: a Critical Study of its Development*, 2nd edn (Oxford, 1957).

Gray, John R. (1939), 'The Political Theory of John Knox', *Church History* 8 (1939), pp. 132–47.

Green, V. H. H. (1964), *Renaissance and Reformation*, 2nd edn (London, 1964).

Greenleaf, W. H. (1973), 'Bodin and the Idea of Order', in *Bodin*, ed. H

Denzer (Munich, 1973), pp. 23–38.

Griffiths, Gordon (1959), 'Democratic Ideas in the Revolt of the Netherlands', in *Archiv für Reformationsgeschichte* 50 (1959), pp. 50–63.

Grimm, Harold J. (1948), 'Luther's Conception of Territorial and National Loyalty', *Church History* 17 (1948), pp. 79–94.

(1954), *The Reformation Era, 1500–1650* (New York, 1954).

Gundersheimer, Werner L. (1966), *The Life and Works of Louis Le Roy* (Geneva, 1966).

Haller, William (1963), *Foxe's Book of Martyrs and the Elect Nation* (London, 1963).

Hamilton, Bernice (1963), *Political Thought in Sixteenth-Century Spain* (Oxford, 1963).

Hamon, Auguste (1901), *Jean Bouchet, 1476–1557?* (Paris, 1901).

Hanke, Lewis (1949), *The Spanish Struggle for Justice in the Conquest of America* (Philadelphia, 1949).

(1959), *Aristotle and the American Indians: a Study in Race Prejudice in the Modern World* (Chicago, 1959).

(1974), *All Mankind is One* (DeKalb, Ill., 1974).

Harris, G. L. (1963), 'A Revolution in Tudor History? Medieval Government and Statecraft', *Past and Present* 25 (1963), pp. 8–39.

Harris, Jesse W. (1940), *John Bale: a Study in the Minor Literature of the Reformation* (Urbana, Ill., 1940).

Hauser, Henri (1892), *François de la Noue (1531–1591)* (Paris, 1892).

Hearnshaw, F. J. C. (1924), 'Bodin and the Genesis of the Doctrine of Sovereignty', in *Tudor Studies*, ed. R. W. Seton-Watson (London, 1924), pp. 109–32.

Heiserman, A. R. (1961), *Skelton and Satire* (Chicago, 1961).

Héritier, Jean (1963), *Catherine de Medici*, trans. Charlotte Haldane (London, 1963).

Hexter, J. H. (1957), '*Il principe* and *lo stato*', *Studies in the Renaissance* 4 (1957), pp. 113–38.

(1973), *The Vision of Politics on the Eve of the Reformation: More, Machiavelli and Seyssel* (New York, 1973).

Heymann, Frederick G. (1955), *John Žižka and the Hussite Revolution* (Princeton, N.J., 1955).

(1959), 'John Rokycana: Church Reformer Between Hus and Luther', *Church History* 28 (1959), pp. 240–80.

(1970), 'The Hussite Revolution and the German Peasants' War', *Medievalia et Humanistica*, New Series 1 (1970), pp. 141–59.

Hildebrandt, Franz (1946), *Melanchthon: Alien or Ally?* (Cambridge, 1946).

Hillerbrand, Hans J. (1958), 'The Anabaptist View of the State', *The Mennonite Quarterly Review* 32 (1958), pp. 83–110.

Hogrefe, Pearl (1937), 'The Life of Christopher St German', *The Review of English Studies* 13 (1937), pp. 398–404.

Holborn, Hajo (1937), *Ulrich von Hutten and the German Reformation*, trans. Roland H. Bainton (New Haven, Conn., 1937).

Hortleder, F. (1645), *Der Römischen Kaiser und Königlichen Maierstaten . . .*, 12 vols (Gotha, 1645).

Hudson, Winthrop S. (1942), *John Ponet (1516?–1556): Advocate of Limited Monarchy* (Chicago, 1942).

(1946), 'Democratic Freedom and Religious Faith in the Reformed Tradition', *Church History* 15 (1946), pp. 177–94.

Hughes, Philip (1950–4), *The Reformation in England*, 3 vols (London, 1950–4).

(1965), *The Theology of the Reformers* (London, 1965).

Huppert, George (1970), *The Idea of Perfect History: Historical Erudition and Historical Philosophy in Renaissance France* (Urbana, Ill., 1970).

Hyma, Albert (1965), *The Christian Renaissance: a History of the 'Devotio Moderna'*, 2nd edn (Hamden, Conn., 1965).

Iserloh, Erwin (1968). *The Theses Were not Posted: Luther between Reform and Reformation* (London, 1968).

Janelle, Pierre (1930), *Obedience in Church and State* (Cambridge, 1930).

Janton, Pierre (1967), *John Knox (ca. 1513–1572): l'homme et l'œuvre* (Paris, 1967).

Jarlot, Georges (1949), 'Les idées politiques de Suárez et le pouvoir absolu', *Archives de Philosophie* 18 (1949), pp. 64–107.

Jarrett, Bede (1935), *The Emperor Charles IV* (London, 1935).

Jedin, Hubert (1957–61), *A History of the Council of Trent*, trans. Ernest Graf, 2 vols (London, 1957–61).

Jones, Leonard C. (1917), *Simon Goulart, 1543–1628* (Paris, 1917).

Jordan, W. K. (1968), *Edward VI*, vol. 1, *The Young King* (London, 1968).

Keating, L. Clark (1941), *Studies in the Literary Salon in France, 1550–1615* (Cambridge, Mass., 1941).

Kelley, Donald R. (1970), *Foundations of Modern Historical Scholarship* (New York, 1970).

(1970b), 'Murd'rous Machiavel in France: a Post-Mortem', *The Political Science Quarterly* 85 (1970), pp. 545–59.

(1973), *François Hotman: a Revolutionary's Ordeal* (Princeton, N.J., 1973).

(1973b), 'The Development and Context of Bodin's Method' in *Bodin*, ed. H. Denzer (Munich, 1973), pp. 123–50.

(1976), 'Vera Philosophia: the Philosophical Significance of Renaissance Jurisprudence', *The Journal of the History of Philosophy* 14 (1976), pp. 267–79.

Kelly, Michael (1965), 'The Submission of the Clergy', *Transactions of the Royal Historical Society* 15 (1965), pp. 97–119.

Kidd, B. J. (1933), *The Counter-Reformation* (London, 1933).

King, Preston (1974), *The Ideology of Order: a Comparative Analysis of Jean Bodin and Thomas Hobbes* (London, 1974).

Kingdon, Robert M. (1955), 'The First Expression of Theodore Beza's Political Ideas', *Archiv für Reformationsgeschichte* 46 (1955), pp. 88–100.

(1956), *Geneva and the Coming of the Wars of Religion in France, 1555–1563* (Geneva, 1956).

(1958), 'The Political Resistance of the Calvinists in France and the Low Countries', *Church History* 27 (1958), pp. 220–33.

(1967), *Geneva and the Consolidation of the French Protestant Movement, 1564–1572* (Geneva, 1967).

Knowles, David (1962), *The Evolution of Medieval Thought* (London, 1962).

Kreider, Robert (1955), 'The Anabaptists and the Civil Authorities of Strasbourg, 1525–1555', *Church History* 24 (1955), pp. 99–118.

Kristeller, P. O. (1956), *Studies in Renaissance Thought and Letters* (Rome, 1956).

Kuntz, Marion L. D. (1975), 'Introduction' to Jean Bodin, *Colloquium of the Seven about Secrets of the Sublime* (Princeton, N.J., 1975), pp. xiii–lxxxi.

Labitte, Charles (1866), *De la démocratie chez les prédicateurs de la ligue*, 2nd edn (Paris, 1866).

La Brosse, Olivier de (1965), *Le Pape et le concile* (Paris, 1965).

Lagarde, Georges de (1926), *Recherches sur l'esprit politique de la réforme* (Paris, 1926).

(1963), *La Naissance de l'esprit laïque au déclin du moyen âge*, vol. v, *Guillaume d'Ockham: Critique des structures ecclésiales*, new edn (Paris, 1963).

Landeen, William M. (1951), 'Gabriel Biel and the Brethren of the Common Life in Germany', *Church History* 20 (1951), pp. 23–36.

Laski, Harold J. (1936), 'Political Theory in the Later Middle Ages', *The Cambridge Medieval History*, ed. J. R. Tanner *et al.*, 8 vols (Cambridge, 1911–36), vol. 8, pp. 620–45.

Laslett, Peter (1967), 'Introduction' to John Locke, *Two Treatises of Government*, 2nd edn (Cambridge, 1967), pp. 1–145.

Latham, R. E. (1965), *Revised Medieval Latin Word-List* (London, 1965).

Launoy, Jean de (1682), *Academia Parisiensis Illustrata* (Paris, 1682).

Lecler, Joseph (1960), *Toleration and the Reformation*, trans. T. L. Westow, 2 vols (London, 1960).

Lehmberg, Stanford E. (1970), *The Reformation Parliament, 1529–1536* (Cambridge, 1970).

Lemonnier, Henri (1903), *Les guerres d'Italie, La France sous Charles VIII, Louis XII et François Ier (1492–1547)* in *Histoire de France*, ed. Ernest Lavisse, vol. v, Part I (Paris, 1903).

Léonard, E.-G. (1948), 'Le Protestantisme français au XVIIe siècle', *Revue historique* 72 (1948), pp. 153–79.

(1965–7), *A History of Protestantism*, trans. Joyce M. H. Reid and R. M. Bethell, 2 vols (London, 1965–7).

Le Roy Ladurie, Emmanuel (1967), 'Difficulté d'être et douceur de vivre: Le XVIe siècle' in *Histoire de Languedoc*, ed. Philippe Wolff (Toulouse, 1967), pp. 265–311.

Levy, Fritz J. (1967), *Tudor Historical Thought* (San Marino, 1967).

Lewis, J. U. (1968), 'Jean Bodin's "Logic of Sovereignty"', *Political Studies* 16 (1968), pp. 206–22.

Lewy, Guenter (1960), *Constitutionalism and Statecraft during the Golden Age of Spain: a Study of the Political Philosophy of Juan de Mariana, S.J.* (Geneva, 1960).

Linder, Robert D. (1964), *The Political Ideas of Pierre Viret* (Geneva, 1964).

Loades, D. M. (1970), *The Oxford Martyrs* (London, 1970).

Lortz, Joseph (1968), *The Reformation in Germany*, trans. Ronald Walls, 2 vols (London, 1968).

Losada, Angel (1970), *Fray Bartolome de Las Casas* (Madrid, 1970).

Lunt, William E. (1962), *Financial Relations of the Papacy with England, 1327–1534* (Cambridge, Mass., 1962).

McConica, James K. (1965), *English Humanists and Reformation Politics under Henry VIII and Edward VI* (Oxford, 1965).

McDonough, Thomas M. (1963), *The Law and the Gospel in Luther* (Oxford, 1963).

McFarlane, K. B. (1972), *Wycliffe and English Nonconformity* (Harmondsworth, 1972).

McGowan, Margaret M. (1974), *Montaigne's Deceits: the Art of Persuasion in the 'Essais'* (London, 1974).

McGrade, Arthur S. (1974), *The Political Thought of William of Ockham* (Cambridge, 1974).

MacIntyre, Alasdair (1966), *A Short History of Ethics* (New York, 1966).

Mackay, Aeneas J. G. (1892), 'The Life of the Author', in John Mair, *A History of Greater Britain*, trans. and ed. Archibald Constable (Edinburgh, 1892).

Mackensen, Heinz F. (1964), 'Historical Interpretation and Luther's Role in the Peasant Revolt', *Concordia Theological Monthly* 35 (1964), pp. 197–209.

Mackinnon, James (1925–30), *Luther and the Reformation*, 4 vols (London, 1925–30).

McNeill, John T. (1941), 'Natural Law in the Thought of Luther', *Church History* 10 (1941), pp. 211–27.

(1949), 'The Democratic Element in Calvin's Thought', *Church History* 18 (1949), pp. 153–71.

(1954), *The History and Character of Calvinism* (New York, 1954).

Macpherson, C. B. (1962), *The Political Theory of Possessive Individualism: Hobbes to Locke* (Oxford, 1962).

McRae, Kenneth D. (1955), 'Ramist Tendencies in the Thought of Jean Bodin', *The Journal of the History of Ideas* 16 (1955), pp. 306–23.

(1962), 'Introduction' to Jean Bodin, *The Six Books of a Commonweal* (Cambridge, 1962), pp. A3–A67.

Major, J. Russell (1951), *The Estates of 1560* (Princeton, N.J., 1951).

(1960), *Representative Institutions in Renaissance France, 1421–1559* (Madison, Wisc., 1960).

(1962), 'The French Monarchy as seen through the Estates General', *Studies in the Renaissance* 9 (1962), pp. 113–25.

Manschreck, Clyde L. (1957), 'The Role of Melanchthon in the Adiaphora Controversy', *Archiv für Reformationsgeschichte* 48 (1957), pp. 165–82.

(1958), *Melanchthon, the Quiet Reformer* (New York, 1958).

(1965), 'Preface' to *Melanchthon on Christian Doctrine* (New York, 1965), pp. vii–xxiv.

Martin, Jules (1906), *Gustave Vasa et la réforme en Suède* (Paris, 1906).

Martin, Kingsley (1962), *French Liberal Thought in the Eighteenth Century*, ed. J. P. Mayer (London, 1962).

Massaut, Jean-Pierre (1968), *Josse Clichtove: l'humanisme et la réforme du clergé*, 2 vols (Paris, 1968).

Maugis, Édouard (1913–14), *Histoire du Parlement de Paris: de l'avènement des rois Valois à la mort d'Henri IV*, 2 vols (Paris, 1913–14).

Meier, Ludger (1955), 'Contribution à l'histoire de la théologie à l'Université d'Erfurt', *Revue d' histoire ecclésiastique* 50 (1955), pp. 454–79 and 839–66.

Meinecke, Friedrich (1957), *Machiavellism*, trans. Douglas Scott(London, 1957).

Mercier, Charles (1934), 'Les théories politiques des calvinistes en France au cours des guerres de religion', in *Bulletin de la société de l'histoire du protestantisme français* 83 (1934), pp. 225–60.

Mesnard, Pierre (1936), *L'Essor de la philosophie politique au XVIe siècle* (Paris, 1936).

(1950), 'Jean Bodin à Toulouse', *Bibliothèque d'humanisme et renaissance* 12 (1950), pp. 31–59.

(1955), 'François Hotman (1524–1590) et le complexe de Tribonien' *Bulletin de la société de l'histoire du Protestantisme français* 101 (1955), pp. 117–37.

Michaud, Hélène (1967), *La Grande Chancellerie et les écritures royales au seizième siècle (1515–1589)* (Paris, 1967).

Miller, Edward W. (1917), *Wessel Gansfort: life and writings* 2 vols (NewYork, 1917).

Moeller, Bernd (1972), *Imperial Cities and the Reformation: Three Essays*, trans. and ed. H. C. E. Midelfort and Mark U. Edwards Jr (Philadelphia, 1972).

Monter, E. William (1969), 'Inflation and Witchcraft: the Case of Jean Bodin', in *Action and Conviction in Early Modern Europe*, ed. Theodore K. Rabb and Jerrold E. Seigel (Princeton, N.J., 1969), pp. 371–89.

Morrall, John B. (1960), *Gerson and the Great Schism* (Manchester, 1960).

Morris, Christopher (1953), *Political Thought in England: Tyndale to Hooker* (London, 1953).

Mosse, G. L. (1948), 'The Influence of Jean Bodin's *République* on English Political Thought', *Medievalia et Humanistica* 5 (1948), pp. 73–83.

Mousnier, Roland (1945), *La Vénalité des Offices sous Henri IV et Louis XIII* (Rouen, 1945).

Mozley, J. F. (1937), *William Tyndale* (London, 1937).

(1953), *Coverdale and his Bibles* (London, 1953).

Muller, James A. (1926), *Stephen Gardiner and the Tudor Reaction* (New York, 1926).

Naudeau, Olivier (1972), *La Pensée de Montaigne et la composition des Essais* (Geneva, 1972).

Neale, J. E. (1943), *The Age of Catherine de Medici* (London, 1943).

Niesel, Wilhelm (1956), *The Theology of Calvin*, trans. Harold Knight (Philadelphia, 1956).

Oakley, Francis (1962), 'On the Road from Constance to 1688: the Political Thought of John Major and George Buchanan', *The Journal of British Studies* 2 (1962), pp. 1–31.

(1964), *The Political Thought of Pierre d'Ailly: the Voluntarist Tradition* (New Haven, Conn., 1964).

(1965), 'Almain and Major: conciliar Theory on the Eve of the Reformation', *The American Historical Review* 70 (1964–5), pp. 673–90.

(1969), 'Figgis, Constance and the Divines of Paris', *The American Historical Review* 75 (1969–70), pp. 368–86.

Oberman, Heiko A. (1963), *The Harvest of Medieval Theology* (Cambridge, Mass., 1963).

(1966), *Forerunners of the Reformation* (New York, 1966).

Ogle, Arthur (1949), *The Tragedy in the Lollards' Tower* (Oxford, 1949).

Oyer, John S. (1964), *Lutheran Reformers against Anabaptists* (The Hague, 1964).

Parker, T. H. L. (1975), *John Calvin: a biography* (Philadelphia, 1975).

Parry, J. H. (1940), *The Spanish Theory of Empire in the Sixteenth Century* (Cambridge, 1940).

Pas, P. (1954), 'La Doctrine de la double justice au Concile de Trente', *Ephemerides Theologicae Lovanienses* 30 (1954), pp. 5–53.

Patry, Raoul (1933), *Philippe du Plessis-Mornay: un huguenot homme d'état* (Paris, 1933).

Pelikan, Jaroslav (1968), *Spirit versus Structure: Luther and the Institutions of the Church* (London, 1968).

Petit-Dutaillis, Charles (1902), *Charles VII, Louis XII et les premières années de Charles VIII (1422–1492)*, in *Histoire de France*, ed. Ernest Lavisse, vol. IV, Part II (Paris, 1902).

Philips, G. (1971), 'La Justification Luthérienne et le Concile de Trente', *Ephemerides Theologicae Lovanienses* 47 (1971), pp. 340–58.

Pickthorn, Kenneth (1934), *Early Tudor Government: Henry VIII* (Cambridge, 1934).

Pineas, Rainer (1962a), 'William Tyndale's Use of History as a Weapon of Religious Controversy', *Harvard Theological Review* 55 (1962), pp. 121–41.

(1962b), 'John Bale's Nondramatic Works of Religious Controversy', *Studies in ihe Renaissance* 9 (1962), pp. 218–33.

(1964), 'Robert Barnes's Polemical Use of History', *Bibliothèque d'humanisme et renaissance* 26 (1964), pp. 55–69.

(1968), *Thomas More and Tudor Polemics* (Bloomington, Ind., 1968).

Pinette, G. L. (1959), 'Freedom in Huguenot Doctrine', *Archiv für Reformationsgeschichte* 50 (1959), pp. 200–34.

Pocock, J. G. A. (1957), *The Ancient Constitution and the Feudal Law* (Cambridge, 1957).

Popkin, Richard H. (1968), *The History of Scepticism from Erasmus to Descartes*, 2nd edn. (New York, 1968).

Porter, H. C. (1958), *Reformation and Reaction in Tudor Cambridge* (Cambridge, 1958).

Post, Gaines (1964), *Studies in Medieval Legal Thought* (Princeton, N.J., 1964).

Post, R. R. (1968), *The Modern Devotion: Confrontation of Reformation and Humanism* (Leiden, 1968).

Poujol, Jacques (1958), 'Jean Ferrault on the King's Privileges', *Studies in the Renaissance* 5 (1958), pp. 15–26.

(1961), 'Introduction' to Claude de Seyssel, *La Monarchie de France*, ed. Jacques Poujol (Paris, 1961).

Putnam, George H. (1906–7), *The Censorship of the Church of Rome*, 2 vols (New York, 1906–7).

Quirk, Robert E. (1954), 'Some Notes on a Controversial Controversy: Juan Ginés de Sepúlveda and natural Servitude', *Hispanic American Historical Review* 34 (1954), pp. 357–64.

Raab, Felix (1964), *The English Face of Machiavelli* (London, 1964).

Radouant, René (1908), *Guillaume du Vair: L'homme et l'orateur jusqu'à la fin des troubles de la Ligue (1556–1596)* (Paris, 1908).

Rager, John Clement (1926), *Political Philosophy of Blessed Cardinal Bellarmine* (Washington, D.C., 1926).

Rathé, C. Edward (1965), 'Innocent Gentillet and the First "Anti-Machiavel" ', *Bibliothèque d'humanisme et renaissance* 27 (1965), pp. 186–225.

Read, Conyers (1953), *Social and Political Forces in the English Reformation* (Houston, Texas, 1953).

Renaudet, Augustin (1953), *Préréforme et humanisme à Paris pendant les premières guerres d'Italie (1494–1517)*, 2nd edn (Paris, 1953).

Reu, M. (1930), *The Augsburg Confession: a Collection of Sources with an Historical Introduction* (Chicago, 1930).

Reynolds, Beatrice (1931), *Proponents of Limited Monarchy in Sixteenth Century France: Francis Hotman and Jean Bodin* (New York, 1931).

Reynolds, E. E. (1955), *Saint John Fisher* (London, 1955).

Rice, Eugene F. (1962), 'The Humanist Idea of a Christian Antiquity: Lefèvre d'Étaples and his Circle', *Studies in the Renaissance* 9 (1962), pp. 126–60.

Ridley, Jasper (1968), *John Knox* (Oxford, 1968).

Ritter, Gerhard (1971), 'Romantic and Revolutionary Elements in German Theology on the Eve of the Reformation', in *The Reformation in Medieval Perspective*, ed. Steven E. Ozment (Chicago, 1971), pp. 15–49.

Roberts, Agnes E. (1935), 'Pierre d'Ailly and the Council of Constance: a study in "Ockhamite" Theory and Practice', *Transactions of the Royal Historical Society* 18 (1935), pp. 123–42.

Roberts, Michael (1968), *The Early Vasas: a History of Sweden, 1523–1611* (Cambridge, 1968).

Robinson, H. (1846), *Original Letters Relative to the English Reformation*, 2 vols (Cambridge, 1846).

Romeyer, B. (1949), 'La Théorie Suarézienne d'un état de nature pure', *Archives de Philosophie* 18 (1949), pp. 37–63.

Romier, Lucien (1913–14), *Les Origines politiques des guerres de religion*, 2 vols (Paris, 1913–14).

(1922), *Le Royaume de Catherine de Médicis: La France à la veille des guerres de religion*, 2 vols (Paris, 1922).

(1924), *Catholiques et Huguenots à la cour de Charles IX* (Paris, 1924).

Ronzy, Pierre (1924), *Un humaniste italianisant: Papire Masson (1544–1611)* (Paris, 1924).

Rothkrug, Lionel (1965), *Opposition to Louis XIV* (Princeton, N.J., 1965).

Rubinstein, Nicolai (1971), 'Notes on the word *stato* in Florence before Machiavelli', in *Florilegium Historiale*, ed. J. G. Rowe and W. H. Stockdale (Toronto, 1971), pp. 313–26.

Rupp, E. Gordon (1949), *Studies in the Making of the English Protestant Tradition* (London, 1949).

(1951), *Luther's Progress to the Diet of Worms, 1521* (London, 1951).

(1953), *The Righteousness of God* (London, 1953).

Saarnivaara, Uuras (1951), *Luther Discovers the Gospel* (St Louis, Mo., 1951).

Sabine, George H. (1931), 'The *Colloquium Heptaplomeres* of Jean Bodin', in

Persecution and Liberty: Essays in Honor of George Lincoln Burr (New York, 1931), pp. 271–309.

Sabine, George H. (1963), *A History of Political Theory*, 3rd edn (London, 1963).

Salmon, J. H. M. (1959), *The French Religious Wars in English Political Thought* (Oxford, 1959).

(1973), 'Bodin and the Monarchomachs', in *Bodin*, ed. H. Denzer (Munich, 1973), pp. 359–78.

(1975), *Society in Crisis: France in the Sixteenth Century* (London, 1975).

Sawada, P. A. (1961), 'Two Anonymous Tudor Treatises on the General Council', *The Journal of Ecclesiastical History* 12 (1961), pp. 197–214.

Sayce, R. A. (1972), *The Essays of Montaigne: a Critical Exploration* (London, 1972).

Scarisbrick, J. J. (1968), *Henry VIII* (London, 1968).

Scheible, Heinz (1969), *Das Widerstandsrecht als Problem der deutschen Protestanten, 1523–1546* (Gütersloh, 1969).

Schelven, A. A. van (1954), 'Beza's De Iure Magistratuum in Subditos', *Archiv für Reformationsgeschichte* 45 (1954), pp. 62–83.

Schenk, W. (1950), *Reginald Pole, Cardinal of England* (London, 1950).

Schmidt, Charles (1879), *Histoire Littéraire de l'Alsace à la fin du XVe et au commencement du XVIe siècle*, 2 vols (Paris, 1879).

Schubert, Hans von (1909), 'Beiträge zur Geschichte der Evangelischen Bekenntnis und Bündnisbildung 1529/30', *Zeitschrift für Kirchengeschichte* 30 (1909), pp. 271–351.

Scott, James Brown (1934), *The Spanish Origin of International Law* Part I, *Francisco de Vitoria and his Law of Nations* (Oxford, 1934).

Shennan, J. H. (1968), *The Parlement of Paris* (London, 1968).

Shepard, M. A. (1930), 'Sovereignty at the Crossroads: a Study of Bodin', *Political Science Quarterly* 45 (1930), pp. 580–603.

Shoenberger, Cynthia G. (1972), *The Confession of Magdeburg and the Lutheran Doctrine of Resistance* (Ph.D. Dissertation, Columbia University, New York, 1972).

Sider, Ronald J. (1974), *Andreas Bodenstein von Karlstadt: the Development of his Thought* (Leiden, 1974).

Siggins, Ian D. Kingston (1970), *Martin Luther's Doctrine of Christ* (New Haven, Conn., 1970).

Sigmund, Paul E. (1963), *Nicholas of Cusa and Medieval Political Thought* (Cambridge, Mass., 1963).

Skinner, Quentin (1965), 'History and Ideology in the English Revolution', *The Historical Journal* 8 (1965), pp. 151–78.

(1972), 'Conquest and Consent: Thomas Hobbes and the Engagement Controversy', in *The Interregnum: the Quest for Settlement*, ed. G. E. Aylmer (London, 1972), pp. 79–98.

Smith, Lacey Baldwin (1953), *Tudor Prelates and Politics, 1536–1558* (Princeton, N.J., 1953).

Smith, Preserved (1911), *The Life and Letters of Martin Luther* (London, 1911).

Spinka, Matthew (1941), *John Hus and the Czech Reform* (Chicago, 1941).

Spitz, Lewis W. (1953), 'Luther's Ecclesiology and his Concept of the Prince as *Notbischof'*, *Church History* 22 (1953), pp. 113–41.

(1963), *The Religious Renaissance of the German Humanists* (Cambridge, Mass., 1963).

Stankiewicz, W. J. (1960), *Politics and Religion in Seventeenth Century France* (Berkeley, Calif., 1960).

Stayer, James M. (1972), *Anabaptists and the Sword* (Lawrence, Kansas, 1972).

Steinmetz, David C. (1968), *Misericordia Dei: the Theology of Johannes von Staupitz in its Late Medieval Setting* (Leiden, 1968).

Sternberger, D. (1975), *Machiavellis 'Principe' und der Begriff des Politischen* (Wiesbaden, 1975).

Stout, Harry S. (1974), 'Marsilius of Padua and the Henrician Reformation', *Church History* 43 (1974), pp. 308–18.

Strauss, Gerald (1966), *Nuremberg in the Sixteenth Century* (New York, 1966).

(1971), *Manifestations of Discontent in Germany on the Eve of the Reformation* (Bloomington, Ind., 1971).

Strohl, H. (1930), 'Le droit à la résistance d'après les conceptions protestantes', *Revue d'histoire et de philosophie religieuses* 10 (1930), pp. 126–44.

Strype, John (1821), *The Life of the Learned Sir John Cheke* (Oxford, 1821).

Surtz, Edward (1967), *The Works and Days of John Fisher* (Cambridge, Mass., 1967).

Sutcliffe, F. E. (1967), 'Introduction' to François de la Noue, *Discours politiques et militaires* (Geneva, 1967), pp. vii–xxxv.

Sutherland, N. M. (1962), *The French Secretaries of State in the Age of Catherine de Medici* (London, 1962).

(1973), *The Massacre of St Bartholomew and the European Conflict, 1559–1572* (London, 1973).

Sykes, Norman (1934), *Church and State in England in the XVIIIth Century* (Cambridge, 1934).

Thickett, D. (1956a), *Bibliographie des œuvres d'Estienne Pasquier* (Geneva, 1956).

(1956b), *Estienne Pasquier: choix de lettres sur la littérature, la langue et la traduction* (Geneva, 1956).

Thomson, John A. F. (1965), *The Later Lollards, 1414–1520* (Oxford, 1965).

Thomson, S. Harrison (1953), 'Luther and Bohemia', *Archiv für Reformationsgeschichte* 44 (1953), pp. 160–80.

Tierney, Brian (1954), 'Ockham, the conciliar theory and the Canonists', *The Journal of the History of Ideas* 15 (1954), pp. 40–70.

(1955), *Foundations of the Conciliar Theory* (Cambridge, 1955).

(1966), 'Medieval Canon Law and Western Constitutionalism', *The Catholic Historical Review* 52 (1966), pp. 1–17.

(1975), ' "Divided Sovereignty" at Constance: a Problem of Medieval and Early Modern Political Theory', *Annuarium Historiae Conciliorum* 7 (1975), pp. 238–56.

Tjernagel, N. S. (1963), *The Reformation Essays of Dr Robert Barnes* (London, 1963).

(1965), *Henry VIII and the Lutherans: a Study in Anglo-Lutheran Relations from 1521 to 1547* (St Louis, Mo., 1965).

Trevor-Roper, H. R. (1966), *George Buchanan and the Ancient Scottish Constitution* (*The English Historical Review*, Supplement 3) (London, 1966).

Troeltsch, Ernst (1931), *The Social Teaching of the Christian Churches*, trans. Olive Wyon, 2 vols (London, 1931).

Tuck, Richard (1977), *Natural Rights Theories before Locke* (Ph.D. dissertation, University of Cambridge, 1977).

Tully, James H. (1977), *John Locke's Writings on Property in their seventeenth-century Intellectual Context* (Ph.D. dissertation, University of Cambridge, 1977).

Tyacke, Nicholas (1973), 'Puritanism, Arminianism and Counter-Revolution', in *The Origins of the English Civil War*, ed. Conrad Russell (London, 1973), pp. 119–43.

Ullmann, K. (1855), *Reformers Before the Reformation*, trans. Robert Menzies, 2 vols (Edinburgh, 1855).

Ullmann, Walter (1948), *The Origins of the Great Schism* (London, 1948).

Ulph, Owen (1947), 'Jean Bodin and the Estates-General of 1576', *The Journal of Modern History* 19 (1947), pp. 289–96.

Van Dyke, Paul (1913), 'The Estates of Pontoise', *The English Historical Review* 28 (1913), pp. 472–95.

Viard, Paul Émile (1926), *André Alciat, 1492–1550* (Paris, 1926).

Vignaux, Paul (1934), *Justification et prédestination au XIVe siècle* (Paris, 1934).

(1971), 'On Luther and Ockham', in *The Reformation in Medieval Perspective*, ed. Steven E. Ozment (Chicago, 1971), pp. 107–18.

Villey, M. (1964), 'La genèse du droit subjectif chez Guillaume d'Occam', *Archives de philosophie du droit* 9 (1964), pp. 97–127.

(1973), 'La Justice harmonique selon Bodin', in *Bodin*, ed. H. Denzer (Munich, 1973), pp. 69–86.

Villey, Pierre (1908), *Les sources et l'évolution des Essais de Montaigne*, 2 vols (Paris, 1908).

(1935), *Montaigne devant la postérité* (Paris, 1935).

Wahl, J. A. (1977), 'Baldus de Ubaldis and the Foundations of the Nation-State', *Manuscripta* 21 (1977), pp. 80–96.

Walzer, Michael (1966), *The Revolution of the Saints* (London, 1966).

Waring, Luther H. (1910), *The Political Theories of Martin Luther* (New York, 1910).

Watanabe, Morimichi (1963), *The Political Ideas of Nicholas of Cusa: with special reference to his 'De Concordia Catholica'* (Geneva, 1963).

Watson, Philip S. (1947), *Let God be God! An Interpretation of the Theology of Martin Luther* (London, 1947).

Weill, Georges (1892), *Les Théories sur le pouvoir royale en France pendant les guerres de religion* (Paris, 1892).

Werner, Julius (1905), *Johann Eberlin von Günzburg* (Heidelberg, 1905).

Whitfield, J. H. (1969), *Discourses on Machiavelli* (Cambridge, 1969).

Wilenius, Reijo (1963), *The Social and Political Theory of Francisco Suárez* (Helsinki, 1963).

Williams, George H. (1962), *The Radical Reformation* (Philadelphia, 1962).

Wolfe, Martin (1968), 'Jean Bodin on Taxes: the Sovereignty–Taxes Paradox', *The Political Science Quarterly* 83 (1968), pp. 268–84.

(1972), *The Fiscal System of Renaissance France* (New Haven, Conn., 1972).

Wolin, Sheldon S. (1961), *Politics and Vision: Continuity and Innovation in*

Western Political Thought (London, 1961).

Wright, H. F. (1932), *Vitoria and the State* (Washington, D.C., 1932).

Yost, John K. (1970), 'German Protestant Humanism and the Early English Reformation: Richard Taverner and Official Translation', *Bibliothèque d'humanisme et renaissance* 32 (1970), pp. 613–25.

Young, Margaret L. M. (1961), *Guillaume des Auletz: a Study of his Life and Works* (Geneva, 1961).

Zanta, Léontine (1914), *La Renaissance du stoicisme au XVIe siècle* (Paris, 1914).

Zeeveld, W. Gordon (1948), *Foundations of Tudor Policy* (Cambridge, Mass., 1948).

Zeydel, Edwin H. (1967), *Sebastian Brant* (New York, 1967).

Index